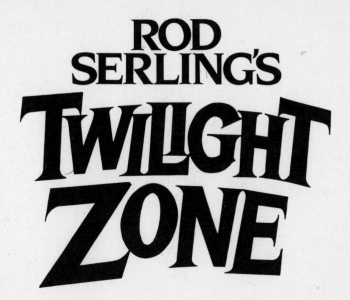

ROD SERLING was the creator, chief writer and host of "The Twilight Zone." In his scripts, Serling combined a unique blend of horror and wit, often wavering between fantasy and reality. There were 151 original episodes, written for television broadcast, and although Serling did not write scripts for every show, he acted as the executive producer throughout the program's five-year span, from 1959 to 1964. In 1959, Serling was honored with an Emmy Award by the National Academy of Television Arts & Sciences for bringing "The Twilight Zone" to the viewing audience. His success with this popular show followed almost a decade of writing for radio, television and film.

Serling began writing for "The Twilight Zone" following conflicts with network censors concerning his controversial drama scripts. At that time he said, "You always have to compromise lest somebody—a sponsor, or pressure group, a network censor—gets upset. Result is that you settle for second best. It's a crime, but scripts with social significance can't get done on TV."

Rod Serling was born on December 25, 1924, in Syracuse, New York. As an undergraduate at Antioch College, he wrote and directed radio dramas. In 1951, he made his first breakthrough in television. He sold his early scripts to such shows as Kraft Television Theatre, Studio One, Hallmark Hall of Fame and Lux Video Theatre.

It was the success of his script entitled "Patterns" for Kraft Television Theatre that brought him both critical and public acclaim. On February 9, 1955, less than one month after it was first aired, it was again performed live by popular demand. A request for a second performance had been unprecedented in the history of television. This video play, soon to be made into a major motion picture, won Serling his first Emmy Award. Two years later, in 1957, Serling won his second Emmy for his dramatic script "Requiem for a Heavyweight," which was written for "Playhouse 90."

After "The Twilight Zone" went off network TV in 1964, Serling continued to make major contributions to both the television and motion picture media. He won his fifth Emmy Award for "It's Mental Work" in 1964. The following year he created a new television series, "The Loner," but it was cancelled before the end of the season.

Rod Serling's screenplay credits include *"The Strike"* (1955); *"Seven Days in May"* (1964); *"Planet of the Apes"* (1968); *"The President's Plane is Missing"* (1969); and *"The Man"* (1971). In 1970, "Rod Serling's Night Gallery" debuted. Again, as in "Twilight Zone," Serling wrote many of the scripts and acted as both host and narrator of the show, (which was cancelled after its second season).

During the latter years of his life, Serling—by then a well-known media celebrity, writer and narrator—spent a good deal of time lecturing at various universities. He died on June 28, 1975, in Rochester, New York.

ROD SERLING'S TWILIGHT ZONE

Originally published in two separate volumes entitled
Rod Serling's Twilight Zone and *Rod Serling's
Twilight Zone Revisited.*

Adapted by
Walter B. Gibson

BONANZA BOOKS
New York

This 1983 edition is published by Bonanza Books, distributed by
Outlet Book Company, Inc., a Random House Company, 225 Park
Avenue South, New York, New York 10003, by arrangement with
Grosset & Dunlap, Inc., a division of the Putnam Publishing Group.

This book was previously published as two separate works entitled
Rod Serling's The Twilight Zone
Rod Serling's Twilight Zone Revisited

Printed and bound in the United States of America

Library of Congress Cataloging-in-Publication Data

Gibson, Walter Brown, 1897–
    Rod Serling's Twilight zone.
    Adapted from scripts written by Rod Serling for
The twilight zone.
    Contents: Rod Serling's The twilight zone—Twilight
zone revisited.
    1. Fantastic fiction, American. 2. Supernatural—
Fiction. I. Serling, Rod, 1924–   . II. Gibson,
Walter Brown, 1897–   . Twilight zone revisited.
1983. III. Title.
PS3513.I2823R6   1983   813'.54   83-3834

ISBN 0-517-41318-3

15 14 13 12 11 10 9 8

Contents

Foreword

Here is a parade of strange, uncanny stories, all original in treatment. To give them authenticity, they have been based in varying degree upon well-recorded incidents or experiences in which many persons have sincerely and implicitly believed; particularly those who participate in weird events. As a result, these tales combine the elements of actuality and fantasy, putting them in that bourne where they so rightfully belong—The Twilight Zone.

A few classic cases have been told with stress on their original details, but with due effort to capture the moods of the individuals involved and to add the dramatic quality needed for their full appreciation. Mere narrative is often insufficient to portray the emotional reactions of those who are confronted by the unknown, or who find themselves boxed in that borderland of existence where it becomes impossible to distinguish the real from the unreal. Only by living those experiences with them—as you most certainly will in these pages—can it become possible to recognize what they really underwent.

Other traditions of ghostland have been developed in these stories with special emphasis on modern settings where they could very well occur. Incidents of similar nature have been incorporated to give them stronger impact; and every story has been carried to a plausible culmination, which is a far cry from the legendary tales that often disintegrated more rapidly and thoroughly than the evanescent phantoms who formed their principal characters. In short, the recognized factors found in cases of the uncanny have been treated as they could—or even might!—occur in everyday life, assuming that ghostly conditions do exist.

There is a singular fascination in these stories of the grotesque and unexplainable that combine the true with the incredible. This interest began in ancient times, as witness a famous story, by the Roman author Pliny, which involved the ghost of an old man complete with clanking chains. It became a dominant factor in the life of the Middle Ages, when warlocks and witches presumably roamed at will. It has reached a new peak through the efforts of modern psychic investigators to gain new insight on such subjects. All indications are that this field will expand in times to come.

This may seem surprising in that it forms a link between the superstition of the past and the scientific progress of the future. But what is our modern learning other than a series of forays into the unknown, which grows to vaster and unbelievable proportions the farther we advance into that uncharted realm!

The ancient alchemists talked of transmuting lead to gold, only to be ridiculed by the chemists of a later day. Yet those first students of natural philosophy, as science was then called, would have derided any prophet who might have correctly predicted the wonders of nuclear physics that lay only a few hundred years ahead.

As for ghosts, there were skeptics a hundred years ago who laughed at stories of haunted rooms in the castles and manor houses of a century before. But if those same scoffers could have been projected to the present, they would have had their wits scared out of them if they had walked into a modern living room and seen a television set in full operation.

There is, of course, the question: where can we find solid ground for all this ghost stuff? The answer, already indicated, is: in the authenticity of the original accounts themselves. It does not matter whether a reported occurrence was magnified or distorted. That goes on in our newspapers every day, yet we still accept the things we read as facts. Day after day, people who swear in courtrooms that they will "tell the whole truth and nothing but the truth," come up with statements so conflicting that only one can be right while the other must be wrong. Yet each person's testimony, if honestly given, is to some degree acceptable in the eyes of the law.

So it goes with psychic phenomena. All we need to know is whether a person who saw a ghost or heard ghostly sounds was sincere in his report. Then we know that, right or wrong, it was a phase of human experience. What it proves or disproves is not the immediate point. Something happened; that at least is established. Other persons believed—or disbelieved—what they heard; and out of that came some final conclusion, whether true or false. Still something happened, like the time an apple dropped from a tree and hit Sir Isaac Newton on the head. After wondering why the apple fell down instead of up, Sir Isaac propounded the Law of Gravitation. If instead, he had laid down a line of fine logic proving that neither he, the apple, nor the tree had ever existed, historians still would agree on one thing: somebody was hit on the head by something.

So it is with persons who claim they have seen ghosts. Somebody was hit by something; not on the head but *in* the head. Such is the impact of a full-fledged ghostly experience, the sort of "shocker" that turns a doubter into a believer. While such adventures may not be too happy in real—or unreal—life, one thing is certain. It is fun to read about them, as you will find out when you delve into the pages that follow.

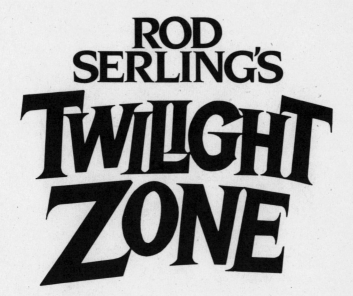

The Ghost of Ticonderoga

Donald Campbell, Laird of Inverawe, halted his horse on the steep hillside as he studied the scene below. At the bottom of the rugged roadway lay the green slope of a glen, where a silvery stream cascaded from thick woods to join the muddy river that wound its way through the well-tilled valley. Beyond the glen rose another hillside. Like the one on which Inverawe paused, it was studded with huge, odd-shaped stones and patched with clumps of purple heather.

Through the gap above the glen, Inverawe could see mountains rising like gigantic steps to the twin peaks of Ben Cruachan, which towered like mighty sentinels against the cloudy sky. Off in the distance, the struggling afternoon sunlight caught the blue glint of a deep-set loch, a narrow lake of the Scottish Highlands.

All that was beyond Inverawe's domain. He was master only of this winding valley, with its glen and skirting hillsides; and at that, his rights were scarcely more than a landowner's. But his heart lay far beyond, off amid those misty, ever-beckoning Highlands, where past and future blended in a timeless present and the wild freedom of Scotland ever seemed to dwell.

How often Inverawe would view that scene again was a question. For this was the summer of 1755, and war with France threatened the United Kingdom of England and Scotland. Already, reports of wilderness fighting in the outposts of America were causing war clouds to thicken over Europe; and Inverawe, as an officer of the Royal Highlanders, probably would be called for active duty. So it was with a pang of regret that he wrenched his gaze from the distant mountains, whose clouds seemed somehow ominous, and resumed his ride down to the glen. Then, as he raised his eyes in a parting glance, he caught sight of movement much closer by.

A ragged, furtive figure was dodging down the hillside, stopping at one rock, then another, as though to hide himself from something above, for he was continually looking back up toward the ridge. As Inverawe reined in his horse to watch, the man continued his frantic tactics, never realizing that he was being observed from below, until he was almost at the road. Then the fugitive stopped in sheer fright at sight of the horseman blocking his path. He seemed about to dive for futile shelter in the heather; then desperation evidently gave him sudden decision. Stumbling forward, he raised his quivering hands in frantic appeal.

"Help me!" the man gasped. "Save me, before they overtake me! My life is at stake!"

"Who are you?" Inverawe parried. "An escaped prisoner? Or an outlaw?"

"Neither. It all grew from an argument in a tavern. There was a brawl and I killed a man. But it was in fair fray. I swear it, on my honor as a MacNiven!"

"A fair fight, you say?" rejoined Inverawe. "Then why not give yourself up to the law?"

"Because blood avengers are on my track," MacNiven insisted hoarsely. "They would kill me on sight! That I do not doubt."

Nor did Inverawe doubt it.

He could tell that MacNiven had been in a fight. The fellow's face was bruised and his clothes were blood-stained from wounds more severe than scratches from the brambles that had torn them. Tavern brawls were frequent in the surrounding villages, and the participants became vengeful if any of their friends were hurt. For nearly ten years, all Scotland had been seething with hotheads and malcontents, following the final effort of Charles Edward, the Stuart Pretender, to regain the British throne then occupied by George II.

Inverawe himself had been engaged in that struggle, but on the side of King George. He had fought at Culloden against some of the Highland clans whose names he respected. And afterward, he had secretly sheltered and protected some of those very rebels, rather than have them fall prey to the vengeful English. So for the moment, MacNiven's pleas were reaching sympathetic ears.

"You must save me!" MacNiven pleaded. "I'm giving myself up to you. You can't let them kill me like a dog."

Inverawe weighed the plea; then agreed:

"I can hide you for a few days, long enough to make sure that you will be given a fair trial."

"But there can be no fair trial hereabouts—"

"In that case, I shall send you safely on your way."

"You will swear to that?"

"Aye, on the word of an Inverawe, which never yet has been known to fail friend or foe."

Inverawe's promise braced MacNiven, who realized that he had met the laird of this locality. Inverawe, close to middle age and a man of commanding appearance, was the sort whose word would stand. But now, MacNiven's fearful glances up the hillside told that he expected pursuers to appear upon the brow at any moment. Again, he pleaded:

"You must hide me quickly, Inverawe. But where?"

"Down in yon glen," returned Inverawe. "Hurry there, while I watch for pursuers and divert them if need be."

"But they will scour the glen and find me there—"

"Not where I intend to hide you. Get down there and wait."

MacNiven bounded full speed down the road. Inverawe waited until he had almost reached the glen. Then, since no pursuers had appeared, the laird rode down and joined the fugitive. Inverawe tethered his horse and guided MacNiven on foot up the slope beside the tumbling stream. A great hush lay beneath the overhanging fir boughs, which cut off the sunlight and produced a weird gloom that added to MacNiven's terror, but Inverawe was too occupied to notice it. Near a high rock, he indicated a tiny rivulet that came down a steep embankment and ordered:

"Follow me up beside this burn; and stay close."

MacNiven clambered close behind his guide and it was well he did, for above the bank, Inverawe turned sharply and was swallowed by a thicket of evergreens. MacNiven pressed through and found Inverawe waiting beside a low, overhanging ledge.

"Under there," the laird said, "you will find a safe hiding place. By dusk, I shall be back with food for you. So in you go."

MacNiven stooped to look beneath the ledge.

"Why, it's no larger than a fox hole!" he exclaimed. "How can a body hide in there?"

"Two bodies did," returned Inverawe. "One was William Wallace and the other Robert Bruce. That was four hundred years ago, and the secret of this hiding place has been handed down from one Laird of Inverawe to the next, ever since. So until now, I alone knew of its existence."

"But if others should find it, they would turn this fox hole into a fox trap," protested MacNiven. "I am no Wallace — nor a Bruce —"

"That I know," interposed Inverawe, a ring of sarcasm in his tone. "They were brave Scots; perhaps there are no longer any like them. But my ancestors gave refuge to those who needed it, and they, in their turn, kept the secret. I offer you safety, on those same terms."

As MacNiven still hesitated, Inverawe stooped beneath the ledge and slid feet first into a narrow hole that slanted down between the rocks. He was swallowed bodily from view. until his voice came hollowly from the depths:

"Follow me down here!"

Encouraged, MacNiven followed and found Inverawe in a high-roofed cave that arched beneath the steep slope of the glen. From there, Inverawe led MacNiven to an inner cavern, where a pool of clear water trickled down into the rocks.

"All the spring water you need," the laird told the fugitive. "I shall bring food later, as I promised."

Inverawe squeezed his stocky bulk up out through the fox hole and started down to the path. As he looked back, he saw MacNiven's wan, nervous face peering from beneath the ledge; but he darted quickly from sight as both men heard distant shouts and the muffled barking of dogs, indicating that pursuers were approaching the glen. They had gone by, however, when Inverawe reached his horse, which was patiently waiting for him. So he mounted and rode on around the next hill to his mansion, which stood surrounded by outlying farm buildings.

There, Inverawe found a villager named Drummond awaiting him.

Twitching his cap between his hands, Drummond announced: "We're tracking down a murderer, Laird, so while the rest went on ahead, I waited here to tell you. Your cousin, Ian Campbell—well, Laird, you see it was like this—"

Inverawe smiled knowingly. His cousin Ian was several years younger than he, but the two were as close as brothers. Ian, bold, dashing, quick to accept any challenge, was just the sort who would be leading the hunt for a murderer. Inverawe could understand why the villagers were so close on MacNiven's trail, if Ian had roused them.

"You mean you have a message for me from my cousin Ian?"

"Aye, in a way, yet not exactly so." Drummond halted, twisting his cap worriedly. "My message is *about* your cousin. It was Ian who was murdered, and in cold blood, sir! Since the slayer headed this way, we thought you should be on the watch for him —"

Drummond broke off. The color had left Inverawe's face and his body swayed as from a sudden shock. Drummond, knowing nothing of Inverawe's meeting with MacNiven, attributed the laird's stunned silence solely to the news of Ian's death. Excusing himself, the villager hastened off to rejoin the search party, leaving Inverawe alone outside his front door.

Long minutes passed; then Inverawe, like a man in a trance, entered the house and made his way numbly to the kitchen. The servants, like the members of the family, who had already heard the news, discreetly stayed away, feeling that the laird would want to be alone with his grief. So Inverawe did, but he had a duty first. In the kitchen, he cut slabs of cold mutton and thick slices of cheese, which he wrapped with flat, round buns called scones. That done, Inverawe stabled his horse and taking a lantern along with the bundle of food, walked back through the gathering dusk to the already darkened glen.

There, he lighted the lantern and made his way to the cave, where he called to MacNiven. The fugitive recognized the laird's voice and came to the mouth of the cave to receive the bundle of food. The darkness of the cave was not sitting well with MacNiven, whose voice came in almost a whimper:

"You can't leave me alone here — it's fearful —"

"As it should be," Inverawe replied coldly, "for a man with blood on his hands. I promised you shelter — nothing more."

"But how will I know when the way is clear?"

"Tomorrow I shall bring more food and tell you if the search has ended. Then you would do well to go your way before I regret my promise."

Grimly, Inverawe made his way from the glen, extinguishing the lantern as he emerged into the moonlight. From behind him, the whisper of the wind-swept firs, the ripple of the burn, sounded like strange, taunting voices. On the way back to the mansion, he had a feeling that he was being followed; and at intervals, he swung quickly about, wondering if MacNiven, the murderer, had become suspicious and bold enough to stalk him from the cave.

But only the weaving trees, the hulking contours of the hills, eerie shapes in themselves, were visible in the moonlight. Soon the white walls of the farm buildings loomed like welcoming specters; then the stone mansion itself, with darkened windows. Inverawe entered and went straight to his own room; there, propped in bed, he tried to sleep, but the events of the afternoon disturbed him.

The meeting with MacNiven, the oath that Inverawe had so unwittingly taken, the fact that his own cousin, Ian, was the slayer's victim, all carried a touch of fate that stirred his Highland imagination. Half aloud, Inverawe muttered, "I wonder if the like of this has happened before!" Then, to put the question to the test, he lighted a pair of candles on the table beside him and chose a book from the shelf above. The volume contained the prophecies of Coinneach Odhar, a famous Highland seer of the century before, many of whose predictions had been fulfilled during the years between.

As Inverawe delved through the musty pages, an odd thing first annoyed him, then puzzled him. It was the repeated wavering of the candle flames. It couldn't be due to a draft from the hallway, for the door was tightly shut. The window was open, but not a breath of air was stirring outside, as Inverawe could tell from the tree leaves, which were as motionless as if frozen by the silvery moonlight. Yet the flickering continued, and with it, Inverawe felt a weird, chilling sensation that caught the tempo of his heartbeats. Then, as he tried to shake off the feeling and return to his book, a shadow slowly stretched across the page.

Inverawe looked up, and the icy throbs faded as his heart warmed with sudden joy. Beside the bed stood his cousin, Ian Campbell, studying him with a fixed, solemn gaze. Ian, here — and still alive! Welcoming words sprang from Inverawe's lips, only to fade as quickly. In the flickery light, Ian's face was as waxen as the candles themselves, except for streaks of blood that came from his clotted blond hair, down his cheeks and chin to the open neck of his torn jacket. There, Inverawe saw great knife gashes across Ian's throat and chest. Any one of them would have been sufficient to have caused his death, for his jacket, too, was all gory.

Ian's lips barely moved as he spoke in a hollow tone:

"Shield not the murderer, Inverawe! Blood must be shed for blood!"

As Inverawe blinked in disbelief, Ian's image faded. This could be no dream, for Inverawe was wide awake. And now all he saw were the white walls of the room, the closed door, and the open window with the trees beyond; everything exactly as it had been before. Strained, shaken, he snuffed out the candles and tried to go to sleep.

With morning, Inverawe was morose. His family said nothing about Ian's death; and he, in turn, kept silence. The hunt was on again for MacNiven, who had last been seen heading over the hill and was thought to be boxed in this area. Inverawe rode out on his horse and ran into Drummond with a group of uniformed fencibles from a neighboring village.

"Take care if you meet up with MacNiven, Laird! With blood already on his hands, he will not stop at another murder. He is a desperate man — and dangerous!" Drummond warned.

Desperate, MacNiven might be, but more fearful than dangerous. Cannily, Inverawe inquired:

"This tavern fight between Ian and MacNiven. Was it a fair one?"

"Aye, it might be said so," Drummond admitted grudgingly. "But only because Ian was quick to turn about before MacNiven could dirk him in the back, as he would have, gladly. MacNiven won because he had the longer knife, though he fought fair when Ian forced him to it. But we'll not hold that in MacNiven's favor, once we find him. He'll die like the dog he is!"

They were closing in upon the glen, to scour it as MacNiven had feared and as Inverawe had anticipated. Later in the day, Inverawe joined the searchers there, carrying a knapsack with him. He knew that they would never find the secret cave, and when they had finally gone, Inverawe climbed to the cave and quietly called MacNiven, who came cautiously from the fox hole.

"Here's food again," announced Inverawe, "But I can shield you no longer. They have searched the glen, so you now are free to escape as best you can."

"But what if they are still close by?"

"That will be your concern. I shall come here again tomorrow. If you are gone by then, good riddance. If not, you will have overstayed your time and you must take the consequences."

Inverawe left the glen and returned home, satisfied that he had done his duty both toward his unwelcome guest, MacNiven, and the uninvited ghost of his cousin Ian. At dinner, the laird was more his usual self. His family — which included a son not quite of age — was relieved by the way he had taken Ian's death. But as the evening went by, Inverawe began to brood anew.

Had he done right to grant further refuge to MacNiven? Or should he have obeyed the order of Ian's ghost? Torn between his oath and his duty, Inverawe decided that tomorrow might hold the answer. He went to bed, but before snuffing out the candles, he reached for the book of prophecies again, wondering how much it had influenced him. As he glanced through the pages, the candles flickered as before, and a shadow crept across the opened volume.

Inverawe looked up slowly. Again, he saw the figure of his cousin Ian, and from those slow-moving lips came the same accusation:

"Shield not the murderer, Inverawe! Blood must be shed for blood!"

"But I have talked with MacNiven today," Inverawe whispered. "He is no longer under my protection. Yet you still demand that blood must be shed for blood!"

Inverawe's own words echoed from the surrounding walls, as though Ian had repeated, *"Blood must be shed for blood!"* But that could not be, for again the ghost was gone and Inverawe was blinking in the candlelight, the book between his tight-clenched hands.

In the morning, Inverawe had breakfast with his family. Then, quietly, determinedly, he set out for the glen. Today, he carried no slices of mutton, no slabs of cheese, no scones. Beneath his tunic, he took a dirk, the longest in his collection of trophies from the battlefields where he had fought. Oath or no oath, if he found MacNiven there still, he intended to bury that weapon in the cringing murderer's flesh, the vengeance Ian wanted.

But the cave was empty. The slayer had gone — and so had Inverawe's troubles. Back home again, the laird listened quietly while his family spoke of Ian's funeral, to be held in the kirk beyond the hills on the following day. That night, Inverawe was ready for sleep. He felt that with MacNiven gone, Ian's ghost surely must be satisfied. Then, to satisfy his own whim, Inverawe decided to finish reading a passage from the prophecies of Coinneach Odhar, the Highland seer. He turned to a page and read:

"On one occasion, the seer was passing Millburn, where he noticed the old mill, a very primitive building, thatched with divots. Speaking to the mill, he said: "The day will come when thy wheel shall be turned for three successive days by water red with human blood, for on the banks of thy pond, a fierce battle shall be fought at which much blood shall be spilt.' This prophecy is waiting to be fulfilled."

Inverawe paused in his reading and exclaimed aloud:

"But it has been fulfilled since this book was written! I know that mill, for it is close by Culloden, where the Duke of Cumberland scattered the Pretender's army. Aye, much blood was spilt there — much blood —"

Inverawe's words trailed as the candles flickered and a shadow fell across the page. Inverawe looked up to see the ghost of Ian Campbell, its face as pale, its body as gory as before. From the ghostly lips came a croak:

"*Aye, much blood shall be spilt! Now, there can be no other way. I told you, Inverawe, shield not the murderer. Blood must flow for blood.*"

"But I am not shielding him," protested Inverawe. "He has gone his way, at my order."

"*With blood still on his hands,*" came the stern answer. "*Blood that must someday be avenged. I warned you twice, but you did not heed me. Now, it is with your own blood that you must pay. Once more we shall meet, Inverawe: then you shall pay.*"

"But where —"

"*We shall meet again at Ticonderoga. Remember, Inverawe. Ticonderoga. . . .*"

The word trailed away even as the figure vanished, and Inverawe, not knowing whether to be dismayed or relieved, found himself repeating the strange name uttered by his cousin's ghost:

"Ticonderoga — Ticonderoga."

With morning, Inverawe and his family journeyed to the village where the body of Ian Campbell lay in state, a tragic victim to the murderer Mac-Niven, who somehow had escaped from the very midst of the avenging clans. Inverawe, though steeled to the sight of death, felt misgivings when he viewed his cousin's body. Ian's face, though recognizable, was chalk white; his hair was still matted from his head wounds, while his cheeks showed faint blood streaks. Even the gashes from the murderer's dirk were visible above the victim's collar line. Surely, then, it *must* have been the ghost of Ian Campbell who had three times appeared in Inverawe's bedroom, to utter an ominous prophecy that could be summed in a single word: Ticonderoga.

After the funeral, Inverawe found time to ask Drummond and others who had witnessed the fatal fray if they had ever heard Ian speak that name. They shook their heads. Once back home, the laird kept repeating "Ticonderoga" in frequent undertones, until he noticed that his family and friends were studying him with worried glances. Then, one day, in a sudden fervor, he told his story to those he trusted most: his wife, his oldest son, one faithful servant whom he had known since boyhood; and a neighboring laird who had known Ian Campbell well.

All agreed that Inverawe had acted according to his proper lights. As for Ian's ghost, they hinted that it might have been the product of Inverawe's shock at hearing of his cousin's death, plus his own strained imagination. But they did not hint too strongly, for like Inverawe, they had the Highland tradition in their blood. A ghost—real or unreal—could not appear thrice without a definite mission. Gradually, though, they discounted the ghostly message because no one had ever heard of a place called Ticonderoga and probably no one ever would. They said as much, hoping Inverawe would brood no longer.

But Inverawe brooded all the more. During the autumn, he rose among the hills, stopping to view the distant mountain mists above the fir-speared glen that now seemed so ominous. During the long winter nights, he sat silently before the crackling fire. With the approach of springtime, those who knew his secret wondered what would happen when he roamed the old familiar terrain and reawakened those tragic memories of the year before.

Then came good fortune, at least for Inverawe. The war with France flamed into actuality. Inverawe's regiment, the Forty-second, was called to the colors. The Laird of Inverawe left his native heath and, as Major Donald Campbell, embarked for America with his troops, landing in New York in June. From there, the regiment was sent to Albany, New York, where British forces were being assembled for the proposed invasion of French Canada.

Frustration followed, for all except Inverawe. While the French and Indians were attacking settlements, faint-hearted British commanders kept calling for reinforcements, fearing they were too few to fight back, though they actually outnumbered the foe. Two years passed, with homesick Highlanders yearning either for action or return to their homeland.

Inverawe wanted action, but even without it, he preferred America to Scotland. He knew that a return to the Highlands would strike him with remorse as deadly as the dirk MacNiven had used to murder Ian. Beneath the laird's grim exterior was a deep-felt sentiment toward the cousin whose death he had failed to avenge. Still through his mind throbbed those ghostly words: "Inverawe, we shall meet at Ticonderoga. Blood must be shed for blood."

Reports of Indian massacres, treachery on the part of both French and British, the terrors and sufferings of helpless American settlers, all left Inverawe cold. He was ready to face any hardship or torture, rather than be reminded of an oath that had bound his hands when they should have delivered the vengeance that blood-ties demanded.

One man alone understood. That was Inverawe's son, who had joined the regiment in America as a junior officer. Often, when they chatted with officers in Albany and tales of massacres were related, Inverawe would come out of his reverie and listen intently to the names of the places that they mentioned. There was Oswego, which meant "the pouring out of waters" and Oneonta, "the stony place." There were others like Nowadaga, "where mud turtles dwelt" or Canajoharie, "the bowl that washes itself," which referred to a pothole in a river gorge.

All those names and many more had the lilt of the name which was constantly in Inverawe's mind, but which he never heard: Ticonderoga. Nor did he mention it, though often his face turned grim when he lapsed into a reflective mood.

At last, in the summer of 1758, the expedition was ready for the invasion of Canada. An army of twenty thousand, the largest in the history of America, was assembling under General Abercrombie. The Highlanders were ordered to Fort Edward, near the upper end of Lake George. The officers held a dinner at the Tontine Coffee House in Albany; and along with talk of Scotland, there was mention of Indian names.

That combination roused Inverawe's memories to the bursting point. "Have any of you heard of a place called Ticonderoga?" he asked suddenly.

The name was new to all the Scottish officers. All shook their heads.

"For two years now," declared Inverawe, "I have been expecting to reach Ticonderoga, but no one seems to know anything about it. So I concluded that it might be on our route to Canada."

"You'll find no Ticonderoga that way, Major," Colonel Grant, the commanding officer of the regiment, told him. "We start from Fort Edward; thence to Lake George, so named in honor of our king, God save him. From there, boats will take us thirty miles northward to the foot of the lake. There, the French have fortified the stream leading from Lake George into Lake Champlain."

"Do you know the name of the French fort, Colonel?"

"It is called Fort Carillon," returned Grant. "They have named it that, according to our scouts, because it is close by a waterfall and the sound is like a chime."

"And beyond Fort Carillon?" inquired Inverawe. "What then?"

"Beyond that, we shall reach Lake Champlain itself, a long but straight route to the Richelieu River, which we shall follow into the heart of Canada."

"And still no Ticonderoga."

Inverawe's vague, faraway tone brought a narrowed gaze from Colonel Grant. The other officers sensed something strange and listened intently when Grant demanded:

"Where did you hear that name, Ticonderoga, Major? And from whom?"

Inverawe, studying the faces at the tables about him, felt an overwhelming urge to tell them all.

"I heard it in Scotland, from the ghost of a man who had never left the Highlands!" he announced.

The flickering candles on the walls, the rough-hewn beams and darkened panels added to the drama as Inverawe launched into the tale that explained his moodiness of the past two years. He told how he had met MacNiven, the vow that he had given the murderer, the accusation uttered by his cousin's ghost, and the prophecy of a future meeting at Ticonderoga.

The older officers sat silent when Inverawe finished. The younger ones were half amused, expecting the story to turn into a joke; but when they glanced at Inverawe's son, he gave them a warning gesture. Colonel Grant caught the sign and eased the situation. With due solemnity, he raised his glass.

"A toast to Ticonderoga," he proposed, "if there is such a place. If not, let us drink to ourselves and success to our cause."

The next day, the Highlanders marched to Fort Edward. From there, they continued to Lake George and joined the army that was embarking in hundreds of large, flat-bottomed rowboats, some with supply rafts in tow. The army included red-coated English grenadiers, Colonial militia in varied uniforms, and green-clad rangers, who formed the advance guard and scouted the paths and landing places along the lake's thirty-mile shore.

While the Highlanders were being assigned to their boats, Colonel Grant was called to a meeting of General Abercrombie's staff. With him, the colonel took a young lieutenant to make any necessary notes. The orders concerned the disposition of the various troops when they reached the lower end of Lake George, but since that depended upon the positions held by the French, detailed descriptions were given of the terrain toward Lake Champlain.

Among the reporting scouts was an Indian of the friendly Mohawk tribe, who delivered a harangue that was translated, sentence for sentence, by a ranger who served as interpreter.

"The enemy has moved out from their fort," the ranger interpreted, "which is close to the place where the waters meet. They are expecting more men from Canada, so unless we attack them soon we can never drive them from their place between the lakes."

During the Indian's speech, Colonel Grant twice caught a word that was familiar. As the interpreter was leaving, Grant asked him:

"Can you repeat exactly what the Indian told you?"

"Why, yes. He said that the enemy has moved out—"

"No, no. I mean can you repeat it in the Indian's own tongue?"

The ranger reflected; then went into the language that the Indian had used. As he finished, Grant commented:

"Twice you used the word, Ticonderoga. What does it mean?"

"Either 'where the waters meet' or 'between the lakes,' which is about the same thing," explained the ranger. "That's what the Indians call the place where the French built Fort Carillon. Ticonderoga."

Colonel Grant turned to the young lieutenant beside him.

"Say naught of this to Major Campbell," the colonel warned. "Nor, for that matter, to anyone. After the story that the major told in Albany, it might shake their confidence. Even the boldest men become superstitious on the eve of battle."

That afternoon, the Highland regiment embarked as part of the vast flotilla that stretched half the length of the thirty-mile lake. Inverawe, looking from the bow of a whaleboat, was fascinated by the scene ahead. The long, narrow surface of Lake George had the glint of a Scottish loch, nestled amid woods and mountains. It impressed the other Scots the same way, but only Inverawe suffered pangs of regret when his thoughts harkened back to his native Highlands.

Others, watching Inverawe, guessed what was in his mind, but none made mention of it, least of all Colonel Grant. When the regiment encamped that night on a point that jutted from the west shore, Inverawe sat alone, still wrapped in thought, while the others chatted or sang songs of their homeland. Cannily, Colonel Grant did not even approach Inverawe, feeling that a chance remark or even a glance might bring up the name, Ticonderoga. If so, the colonel was sure that his own face might give some inkling of what he had learned.

With morning, a mist lay over the lake. It lifted gradually as the boats plied the smooth blue water, and new scenes of magnificence were revealed. In the distance, Inverawe saw rising mountains, some with craggy heights reminding him of the twin peaks of Ben Cruachan, a grim reminder of the very view that he had hoped to escape. Sad memories of his cousin Ian loomed stronger than ever, until, as the boat neared the end of the lake, the sound of gunfire turned his mind to action.

Upon landing, the Scots learned that the British advance force had driven back the French in a spirited skirmish, though not without serious losses of their own. That night, outposts were placed in the woods, and the next day the British advanced in greater numbers, forcing the French back to their earthworks on the slope leading up to Fort Carillon.

On the third day, General Abercrombie decided to drive the French from those defenses, so that he could besiege Fort Carillon and prevent Montcalm, the French commander, from receiving reinforcements. So instead of waiting to bring up cannon from rafts on Lake George, Abercrombie ordered a direct assault by the English Grenadiers and the Royal Americans, with Grant's Highlanders being held in reserve.

This did not please the Scottish regiment. Some of these dark-kilted veterans had belonged to the Forty-second when it had been known as the Black Watch and famed for its fighting qualities. So Colonel Grant conferred with various officers, advising them how to control their men if they became impatient. But he did not summon Major Campbell to any of these meetings. Of all the officers, Inverawe had been closest to his military duties, making such advice unnecessary.

The assault on the French earthworks resulted in disaster. The English regulars and Colonial militia encountered barricades of felled trees with sharp-pointed branches just short of the French trenches. While struggling with those obstacles, they were mowed down by French cannon and musket fire. Sight of such carnage would have restrained any reserves other than the Highlanders. Instead, it goaded them to action.

Without waiting for orders, they surged forward and their officers were unable to restrain them, for a very good reason. In the first wave that started up the slope was the commanding figure of Inverawe, going along with his men. Too late did Colonel Grant realize that discretion was not the greater part of the valor that inspired Major Campbell.

The barricades meant nothing to the charging Highlanders. As they reached the spiked abatis, they flung away their guns and hacked their way with claymores, huge two-edged swords with double-handed hilts. Some reached the French trenches, but they were too few to capture them, because by then, most of their companions had fallen under a hail of devastating fire.

Among those was Inverawe. His officer's uniform had made him the chief target of Montcalm's marksmen. Close to the barricade, the brave major sprawled, with bullets in his legs and body. Despite his agony, he rolled to the shelter of a tiny hummock, where he looked ahead and saw the wave of Highlanders reach its crest and then subside under the pall of bluish smoke from the merciless French guns.

Inverawe gestured back to the rest, telling them to take to shelter, as he had. They obeyed, almost to a man, waiting to join the next wave of their fellow-attackers, not realizing that Inverawe himself would never arise for the assault. But Inverawe was thinking of his men alone; and when his eyes scanned the slope about him, he was amazed to see one figure standing close by, gazing down impassively, his whole form, with folded arms, half-veiled by the curling gunsmoke.

Propped on one elbow, Inverawe slapped his other hand against the turf as he gasped:

"Drop down, man — or you'll be a dead one —"

Then he broke off—for the man standing there was already dead. Though Inverawe's eyes were smarting from smoke and his gaze had dimmed from loss of blood, he knew that face. Chalk white, even to its lips, it was the ghostly face of Ian Campbell.

"We meet again, Inverawe." There was no accusation in those words, though their tone was as solemn as a knell. *"We meet, as I promised — at Ticonderoga."*

From Inverawe's parched lips came the gasp: "Ticonderoga!"

"Aye," the ghost responded. *"You have paid the price for shielding a murderer. Blood has been shed for blood."*

A sound interrupted. It was the drone of bagpipes, followed by shrill notes spurring the main body of the regiment to its next charge. Inverawe looked down the slope and saw the kilted figures of the Black Watch driving upward, the pipers among them, with men rising all along the way to join the new assault upon the impregnable French positions!

The shrill of the pipes was drowned by the roar of guns, accompanied by spurts of flame along the entire rim of the French defenses. Inverawe looked up into the thickening smoke that now was billowing down the slope and saw Ian's figure still standing there, dimming as in a mist. As bullets sang through the phantom form, hidden lips issued the parting words:

"Farewell, Inverawe!"

Next, Highlanders were charging up through that swirl, spreading the smoke where Ian's form had been, showing only vacancy there. Bullets now were taking toll, for Inverawe could see the attackers falling, two or more at a time, as they met the close-range fire from the French earthworks.

Further charges followed, all with disastrous results. In between were lulls, while the French reloaded and conserved their ammunition for coming assaults. During these respites, men crawled up the slope, gathered in their wounded comrades and carried them back to safety below. Then those same rescuers joined the next wave of attackers, only to be mowed down. There were four hours of this, until General Abercrombie finally ordered a retreat; but he was less stubborn than the attacking Highlanders. The command had to be issued three times, before they finally withdrew from the slope where slaughter reigned.

Among those carried to the boats was Inverawe. There Colonel Grant found him, suffering from mortal wounds. Before Grant could speak, Inverawe understood what lay behind the colonel's saddened gaze. A glint showed in Inverawe's eyes, as he declared:

"*This* is Ticonderoga. You must have learned it somehow, Colonel. That is why you were avoiding me."

"It is," Colonel Grant admitted. "But how did you find out?"

"Because I saw him once again, the ghost of my murdered cousin Ian. He told me we would meet at Ticonderoga — and we did."

More than three hundred members of the Highland regiment were slain in that battle, Inverawe's own son among them. Several days later, Inverawe himself died of his wounds, fulfilling the ghostly prediction. On the very verge of death, he was heard to mutter: "Blood shall be shed for blood."

Such was the story of the prophetic ghost, seen thrice in Scotland; then, for the last time, three years later, at Ticonderoga. So it has come down through the years, as attested by Inverawe's family and friends. At the time he described the ghostly visitations that occurred at his home in Scotland, and mentioned that odd word, Ticonderoga, the French had not even begun to build Fort Carillon at the place which only the Indians knew by its native name.

As for Inverawe's final meeting with the ghost on the battlefield itself, that account was recorded by James Grant, lieutenant-colonel commanding the Forty-second Highland Regiment, who had heard it from the dying man's own lips.

But that was not all.

On the very day that the battle was fought at Ticonderoga in the backwoods of America, a distinguished Danish physician, Sir William Hart, was strolling with an English friend around the Castle of Inveraray, in Scotland. Against a sullen, clouded sky, they saw a strange mirage of fighting men in Highland uniforms, engaged in a fierce battle. The doctor and his friend called to a Scottish servant, who stared in wonder at the gigantic images in the sky, many of whose faces he identified and called by name, groaning as he saw them fall.

That same amazing vision was reported by a young Scottish lady and her sister, who were crossing the new bridge over the Aray River on their way to Inveraray, when they chanced to look up at the sky. They, too, recognized many friends among the Highlanders, including Inverawe and his son, both whom fell as the astonished women watched the fantastic scene unroll itself.

Other persons also reported that strange sight in the sky. Added up, the accounts included a surprisingly large number of identified dead. Weeks later, bulletins arrived from America, confirming the tragedy of Ticonderoga almost to the final detail.

Perhaps the massed minds of the dying victims projected their agonized message to their Scottish homeland to prepare their kinfolk for the shock that was to come. Whatever the answer, if you have your doubts, don't mention them in the Scottish Highlands. There are people there who still believe in the ghost of Ticonderoga and the vision over Inveraray. What is more, they are likely to convince *you*.

Back There

The heavy April shower turned into a torrential downpour as the cab pulled up beside a red brick house on a quiet Washington side street. The driver studied the white double doorway with the dull bronze plaque beside it.

"Guess this is it, mister," said the cabby. "I can see the sign, even though I can't read it. You'll get soaked, though, if you try to make it in this rain."

Peter Corrigan thrust the fare into the cabby's hand.

"I'll chance it," Corrigan said. "Just wait until I make sure it's the right place. If it isn't, I'll hop back into the cab and we can try again."

Hatless, Corrigan pulled his coat up over his head and grabbed his suitcase as he left the cab. He dashed across the sidewalk and up the step to the shelter of the tiny portico above the double door. Wiping the rain from his eyes, he read the bronze plaque. It said:

POTOMAC CLUB
Founded
1858

Corrigan gave the cab a wave of dismissal and pounded the big brass knocker. No one answered; and now the cab was gone, while the terrific rain kept pelting in at a sharp angle, soaking Corrigan. Then, just as he was looking about for better shelter, the door was opened by a solemn, stoop-shouldered attendant in a faded blue uniform jacket with a dull, gold-braided collar.

"I'm sorry, but I didn't hear your knock, sir," the attendant apologized. "I was busy elsewhere. You must be Mr. Corrigan."

Then, as Corrigan nodded, the man added:

"I had no idea it had begun to rain so hard. Why, you're drenched, sir! Let me provide you with some other clothes while I have yours dried and pressed."

Crablike, he ushered Corrigan up a short flight of marble steps. They crossed a tiled foyer and as Corrigan looked back, he noted that the front door was out of sight below the curving stairs, so it was not surprising that the attendant had been unaware that it was raining.

Corrigan felt as though he had stepped into another world, here in the silence of the huge, high-ceilinged foyer of the Potomac Club, where even footfalls were hushed. Or rather, it could be a forgotten world, for Corrigan felt engulfed in a timeless atmosphere. Everything was old, from the antique light brackets that cast a dull glow on the carved, oak-paneled walls to the gilt-framed portraits that adorned them.

Even the pictured faces belonged to the past, as was evident from their stern expressions and their old-fashioned costumes. Yet they were like a gallery of living men as the attendant conducted Corrigan past them, each surveying the dripping newcomer with an air of disapproval. As Corrigan was ushered through a cloakroom, he looked back and had the uncanny feeling that he caught parting glances from the last portraits in the line.

The young man shuddered off a sudden chill. Whether it was induced by those painted eyes, or the dampness of his rain-soaked clothes, he wasn't sure. Then he was in a little dressing room where the solemn attendant opened a large wardrobe cabinet stocked with old-fashioned suits.

"I'm sure you will find your size, sir," the attendant told Corrigan, "if you don't mind wearing one of these old costumes. We keep them for official receptions, honoring the founders of the club. So you won't feel out of place—"

A voice interrupted, calling through from the cloakroom:

"William, you're needed in the lounge!"

Bowing, the attendant told Corrigan, "I'll be right back, sir."

Corrigan tried on a light blue suit with long-tailed coat and broad lapels. He rather liked the ruffled shirt front and shoestring necktie that formed part of the costume. As he combed his hair and studied the result in a full-length mirror, Corrigan grinned. This was certainly an excellent way of acclimating himself to these old-time surroundings.

A brilliant young astrophysicist, Corrigan recently had been accepted for membership in the Potomac Club, which especially welcomed men of scientific achievement. His sponsors were here, awaiting his arrival from New York on this first visit to the club. Corrigan was still chuckling at their probable reaction to his present getup, when William returned.

In the soft light of the dressing room, the attendant's face seemed suddenly youthful. Momentarily, his shoulders were erect and his uniform lost its faded look. Somehow, Corrigan remembered his face from somewhere, as though he had been an old friend. Then he decided that it must have been the sincerity of William's welcome; the nod of approval that the attendant now gave. For as William picked up Corrigan's suit with his left hand and draped it over his right arm, the attendant slumped back into his stoop-shouldered, wrinkle-faced self.

William conducted Corrigan out through the foyer, where the portraits now seemed less austere. From their expressions, they approved Corrigan in his present garb, and he still could not shake off the uncanny sensation that those were living eyes surveying him from the surrounding walls. At least, he was beginning to feel that he belonged to the Potomac Club, though the grip was uncomfortably tight.

William's voice broke Corrigan's reverie. With a sweep of his left hand, the attendant gestured Corrigan through a doorway, saying:

"Your friends are waiting for you in the Monument Room, sir."

Three men looked up from their table as Corrigan arrived. They were Roy Millard, noted researcher in the field of parapsychology; Louis Whittaker, the famous biochemist; and Zachary Jackson, dean of American historians. Millard and Whittaker were middle-aged professors, who took their work seriously and showed it. They stared at Corrigan in slight annoyance, until Dr. Jackson, elderly and with twinkling eyes, chuckled from deep in his gray-white beard and commented:

"We wondered when you would get here, Mr. Corrigan. From the theories Millard here has been expounding, we expected you to come whirring in from the future in a time machine. Instead, you have stepped from out of the past." He gestured to an old portrait that hung above the great stone fireplace. "Why, you look just like Bushrod Chichester, who founded the Potomac Club."

Smilingly, Corrigan explained that his cab had encountered a cloudburst coming in from the Washington airport and that William had supplied him with this temporary wardrobe to replace his own. That seemed to satisfy Professor Millard, who promptly returned to his pet theme.

"In your work, Mr. Corrigan," declared Millard, "you talk about breaking the sound barrier. I am trying to break the time barrier. It can only be done through a study of momentary relativity."

"And what," put in Whittaker, "is momentary relativity?"

"You should know," returned Millard. "You once took some time exposures so that a plant appeared to grow visibly, though it actually required a few months. You also made slow-motion shots of falling rose petals that barely seemed to drift downward. What if you put both on one synchronized film?"

"It would look as though the plant bloomed while the petals fell," replied Whittaker, "or the other way about, if you prefer."

"Let's consider people instead of plants," suggested Jackson. "According to your theory, Millard, our moments of comprehension contract and expand, so that sometimes things move so fast that they cause a mental blur, while at other times, they are painfully slow, as in a dream state."

"Exactly," nodded Millard. "That is momentary relativity."

"And you believe," persisted Jackson, "that people can project themselves into another time era, physically as well as mentally?"

"I do. When they reach a state of complete physical and mental inertia, induced perhaps by surrounding conditions, they break the time barrier, precipitating themselves into another sphere from which they may—or may not—return."

This was striking home to Corrigan, who already felt himself a misfit. From the moment he walked into the Potomac Club, he had seemed to be playing a part in an old-time drama that grew stronger as it progressed. Right now, he was engaged in a scientific discussion with an ultra-modern group, yet feeling as well as looking as though he belonged back in some earlier time. With something of a mental wrench, Corrigan snapped himself into the present.

"Suppose you went back in time to the day before the stock market's greatest crash, October 28, 1929," he said to Millard. "With your knowledge of what was due to happen, couldn't you have sold out before the prices fell?"

"Of course I could have," returned Millard, "and a lot of people did. That was probably the very thing that caused the crash."

"Do you mean to tell me that they acted on the advice of someone who had come from the future and therefore could tip them off?"

"They might have. I have checked that very case. There is documentary evidence to show that a large number of investors took the advice of an astrologer whose yearly horoscopes, printed in January, 1929, predicted the Wall Street crash almost to the exact date, saying that it would be caused by unfavorable planetary conditions, and advising people to sell before that time."

"So the stock market crashed because of a faker who pretended to know the future."

"Not one who pretended to know. One who really did know."

"And you think that the astrologer gained his information from a person who was projected back in time and told him?"

"How else could he have learned it? I don't believe in astrology, Mr. Corrigan, any more than you do. No one can predict the future. So the only way to find out about it is from someone who has actually experienced it."

"But the past is fixed," Corrigan argued. "The mere act of projecting a person into it would change it, and it can't be changed because it *is* fixed. That spikes your theory, Professor Millard. All logic is against it."

"We are beyond the bounds of logic," retorted Millard. "Take your own case, Mr. Corrigan. As an astrophysicist, you are planning to project human beings to the moon and other planets. That was once regarded as impossible and therefore illogical."

Millard swung next to Whittaker.

"As a biochemist," continued Millard, "you are constantly confronted by the illogical, such as forms of plant life, chemical elements, or even animals that have developed unaccountably. And in your studies, Jackson"— Millard turned to the elderly historian—"you must know of many cases where persons disappeared so strangely that they might have been swallowed by time, rather than space."

"There have been such cases," acknowledged Jackson, "so I can accept your theory, dependent upon more tangible proof or evidence."

"But tell me, Dr. Jackson," persisted Corrigan. "Wouldn't this projection of the individual change history as we know it?"

"Not necessarily," returned Jackson. "A projected person could become part of the historic incident in question. He might thereby help to shape it, but he certainly could not change it. I have my own theories on that score."

Jackson glanced over the top of his glasses at Millard and Whittaker, who were beginning a private debate. Jackson took Corrigan by the arm and suggested:

"Come, let me show you around the club as a new member, while I express some of my own opinions."

They stopped first by the fireplace, where the low crackle of burning logs and the wavering gray smoke seemed to blend with the elderly historian's reminiscent tone.

"That portrait of our founder, Bushrod Chichester, was placed here the day the club opened in 1858," Dr. Jackson began. "So were these other paintings"—he indicated two framed canvases on opposite walls, each representing a sylvan scene from ancient Greece—"and this crystal chandelier."

Jackson pointed toward the ceiling fixture, which glittered in the reflection of electric bulbs that had replaced its old-time gas jets.

"They came from Pendleton's gambling establishment on Pennsylvania Avenue," explained Jackson. "He died the year this club was founded. Many of the tables and chairs were bought at auction from Pendleton's Palace of Fortune. I often fancy that I can hear the click of the roulette wheel, or the call of the faro dealers."

Corrigan almost heard them himself, only to identify the click as the snap of a burning log and the calls as the voices of Millard and Whittaker.

Next, Jackson took Corrigan into the lounge, where the elderly historian pointed out antiques from old Washington residences, exquisite objects of Oriental art that Commodore Perry had brought back from Japan, and souvenirs President Buchanan had collected just before the Civil War. As Dr. Jackson summed it:

"Everything in the Potomac Club is exactly as it was a century or more ago. It grips you with that spirit and sometimes, when I leave, I feel about to step out into the past. That is why I go along, to some extent, with Millard's theory."

"I should go along with it, too," Corrigan chuckled, glancing down at his attire, "considering I am dressed for the part."

As they reached the foyer, Dr. Jackson indicated the portrait gallery.

"These men were our founders," he declared. "See how their eyes grip you with the spirit of their time! Those eyes viewed stirring scenes of the Civil War. They were eyes that saw Lincoln; some even witnessed his assassination. They draw you back, wanting to tell you more. If we could only meet those men and ask them—"

"Excuse me, sir," interposed Corrigan. "There goes William. I must ask him if my suit is ready."

"Do that." Dr. Jackson nodded. "I will be back with the others."

William was near the marble steps when Corrigan overtook him. The tiled floor of the foyer was damp, but Corrigan didn't notice it. That mental slip resulted in a physical slip as well. Corrigan's feet shot out from under him, carrying him down the steps. He caught at the wooden rail, twisted himself half about, and luckily broke his fall; but it wasn't enough to avoid a stunning thump as the back of his head hit the post at the bottom of the stair.

Corrigan caught a fleeting glimpse of William's wrinkled face looking down at him in horror. That sight was obliterated by a galaxy of shooting stars that instantly blacked out. Then, gradually, Corrigan came back to consciousness once more and opened his eyes to see William again.

"You had a bad spill, sir," said William, as Corrigan rubbed the back of his head. "I couldn't catch you. How do you feel now?"

Corrigan wasn't entirely sure. For one thing, William looked younger at this close range. His face was smooth; his uniform and its gold braid were brighter. He was stronger, too, for with his left arm, he brought Corrigan to his feet and steadied him there.

"I guess I'm all right," decided Corrigan, as he tried to review past events. "I wonder—is it still raining?"

"Raining?" repeated William. "No, sir, it isn't raining."

"It's probably stopped by now," agreed Corrigan. "I think I'll take a little walk. Some fresh air will help me."

Corrigan went slowly down the steps, guided by William's supporting arm. The attendant moved ahead to open the door inward with his left hand, half-obscuring his figure as he did. Corrigan nodded a thank-you and stepped out into the sultry April afternoon.

William was right. The rain had stopped. An open carriage was standing at the curb. From the box, a uniformed coachman tipped his high hat. Still feeling unsteady, Corrigan decided to ride instead of walk. He climbed into the rear seat and settled back.

"So you have these hacks in Washington now, just like Central Park," he remarked.

"Central Park?" queried the coachman. "Where is that?"

"In New York."

"Oh." The driver nodded. "Well, whatever you have in New York, we have here in Washington."

"Everything except subways."

"Subways?" Puzzled, the coachman shook his head; then queried: "Where would you like to go, sir? To Willard's?"

The name struck a familiar note with Corrigan.

"Yes. Make it Willard's."

The coachman clucked to his horse and leaned back as the carriage started. In a confidential tone, he stated:

"You know how bad these side streets are, sir. Wouldn't it be better if I took the Avenue, even though it is a little longer?"

"The Avenue will be all right."

Eyes half-closed, Corrigan thought back, wondering if all this was part of his initiation as a new member of the Potomac Club. Perhaps William had been instructed to give him the old-fashioned costume. That talk about time travel, Jackson's remarks on the ancient atmosphere of the club rooms, this antique carriage waiting out front, all seemed too pat. Corrigan decided to draw out the coachman.

"Tell me," asked Corrigan. "When did the rain stop?"

"The rain? We haven't had any today, sir. It's been muggy, as you can see"—the coachman flicked his whip toward the dull, leaden sky—"but nary a drop of rain."

Corrigan looked at the narrow, red-brick sidewalk and saw that it was entirely dry. So, for that matter, was the unpaved street along which they bumped. To his amazement, Corrigan saw some pigs crossing in front of the carriage, grunting moodily because they could find no mud in which to wallow. Even more surprising, the coachman pulled up the horse to let a flock of honking geese waddle by in search of water.

"You can see how dry it is," observed the coachman. "We had a little rain early in the week, but it didn't last."

"And when did the cherry blossoms come out this spring?"

"Cherry blossoms?" The coachman was really puzzled. "I never heard of them blooming here in Washington."

That, Corrigan thought, was carrying it too far, though he had been almost ready to believe he had really stepped into the past when he left the Potomac Club. Then, as the carriage swung into Pennsylvania Avenue, he was suddenly and totally convinced.

This was unquestionably Washington, but completely different from the city as Corrigan had last seen it. The Capitol building loomed a few blocks to the southeast, but its dome was very new and glittery, while the immediate surroundings were strangely barren of other buildings. Yet here, where Pennsylvania Avenue should have been practically an open park, there were rows of buildings on both sides, with carriages and wagons hitched in front of them.

Not an automobile nor even a trolley car was in sight; only horse-drawn vehicles, like a scene from an old photograph. As Corrigan's carriage turned into traffic and rattled along the cobbles away from the Capitol, Corrigan studied the building fronts. He saw tall, striped barber poles, some red and white, others more patriotic, in red, white, and blue. A huge wooden watch face hung above a jewelry store; an even larger wooden musket represented a gunsmith; while life-sized wooden Indians peered from the doorways of tobacco shops.

On opposite corners at the right stood two large but squatty hotels. One bore the sign: THE NATIONAL. The other, THE METROPOLITAN, was smaller, but impressive because of its marble front. But when the carriage had joggled a few blocks farther, Corrigan was shocked by the contrast on the left. There a dilapidated row of buildings gave way to a conglomeration of clumsy wooden sheds flanked by tumbledown shacks with hog pens in the offing.

"The Center Market," the coachman said. "A busy spot, all during the war. We call it the Marsh Market because of the marsh around it."

The man evidently referred to the marshy ground that ran clear back to a muddy ditch that looked like an old canal. Then the scene changed for the better. Set back from the Avenue, in a neatly landscaped area, stood a group of reddish stone buildings with odd-shaped towers that Corrigan recognized as the Smithsonian Institution, which he had often visited while engaged in his scientific research.

But it was different from the Smithsonian that Corrigan remembered— not from the past, but from the future. Different, too, was the scene straight up the Avenue, where Corrigan saw a bulky structure of red brick. Puzzled, he asked:

"Isn't that where the White House should be?"

"It's there," the coachman assured him. "But it's around the corner of the Treasury Building. You're looking at the red barn that Old Buck built on the grounds while he was still President."

Corrigan's gaze drifted to the left; his eyes narrowed as he viewed a square-shaped ruin that stood more than a hundred feet high.

"And what is that? An old abandoned chimneystack?"

"Why, that's the Washington Monument, sir," the coachman proclaimed proudly. "They've been fifteen years and more, getting it that high. So it should take them that much longer to finish it."

Now Corrigan's mind was in focus. The incredible had happened, but it was beginning to make sense. This must be Washington during the last days of the Civil War, for as Corrigan studied the passers-by, he saw many soldiers in bright blue uniforms, but among them, others in ragged, faded gray. Those were Confederates who had either deserted their cause or had surrendered and had been given their parole. That was why they were so friendly with the blue-clad Union troops.

Corrigan was beginning to enjoy his ride when the carriage wheeled in front of another large, rambling hotel and the coachman announced:

"Here we are at Willard's, sir."

For the first time, Corrigan thought of money. He thrust his hand into the pocket of his borrowed coat and, to his surprise, brought out a wad of paper currency. He found an odd-looking bill that at least bore the familiar figure "5," so he peeled it off and handed it to the coachman. More confident now, Corrigan stalked into what he thought would be the familiar surroundings of the Willard Hotel, which he knew as well as the Smithsonian Institution or the Capitol itself.

Only he didn't know this Willard Hotel. The famous old hostelry of the Civil War period was an absolute contrast to its modern counterpart of a century later.

The thickly carpeted lobby spread out everywhere, terminating at one end in a vast dining room already thronged with patrons who were ordering huge dinners, though it was scarcely more than late afternoon. Gentlemen in clothes like Corrigan's—he looked to make sure he was still wearing them —were bowing to hoop-skirted ladies as they descended the sweeping staircase. High-ranking Union officers were strolling by in stately style, and Corrigan stepped aside to watch the grand parade.

Corrigan's elbow nudged a stack of thin newspapers that were resting on a newsstand. He saw the title *Washington Evening Star* and purchased it with some large copper coins that he found in his pocket. About to scan the headlines, Corrigan paused first to note the paper's date:

FRIDAY, APRIL 14, 1865.

Corrigan stood stunned. This day was destined to be the saddest in the annals of America, for on the evening of this fateful Friday, the assassination of President Lincoln was to shock the nation and the world. If ever there was a chance to change the course of history, that chance was Corrigan's right now!

Frantically, Corrigan thumbed through the *Star* to find the theatrical news. He came across the announcement that President and Mrs. Lincoln and General Grant had taken a box at Ford's Theater to witness the final appearance of Miss Laura Keene in *Our American Cousin,* that night.

That was enough for Corrigan. He started out into the gathering dusk with just one thought, to get to the theater and do all he could to prevent the coming crime. A hack was standing handy, and Corrigan told the driver to take him to Ford's Theater at once. There was no need to give the address: Tenth Street between E and F. The hack driver knew it.

Arriving at the theater, Corrigan sprang across the planking that bridged the deep gutter between street and sidewalk. He rushed into the lobby and found the box-office closed. After he had rapped repeatedly at its shuttered window, the blind finally slid up and a dull-faced youth peered through the grating.

"Take your time," the youth said. "We're just opening up, and the rush hasn't even started. What price seat do you want?"

"I want to see the manager."

"He won't be here until after dinner. All I can do is sell you a ticket. They run twenty-five, fifty, and seventy-five cents."

In his pocket, Corrigan found some paper scrip, small fractional currency of less than a dollar, which was used extensively during the Civil War. He made up the right amount and pushed it through the window:

"Here is seventy-five cents."

Corrigan received his ticket and thrust it in the breast pocket of his coat. Then, sharply, he insisted:

"I still want to see the manager."

"Maybe you'll find him in the refreshment bar next door," the young man suggested. "If not, go around backstage and ask for Mr. Ford."

In the establishment next door, Corrigan asked for Mr. Ford, to meet with the return query: "Which Mr. Ford?" When Corrigan retorted, "Any Mr. Ford," he was told that no Fords were about. A few patrons of the place showed undue interest in Corrigan's inquiry, so rather than become involved with them, he left abruptly. Around the block, he found a dingy alley and walked through it past a stable, where a brownish horse lifted its nose and whinnied a greeting. At the stage door, Corrigan pounded emphatically until a stocky man in overalls appeared and demanded to know what he wanted.

"I want to see Mr. Ford, the manager."

"About what?"

"About the President coming here to the theater tonight. He is in danger. Someone wants to kill him and he must be warned."

"You won't find the manager around here."

"Suppose I see for myself."

As Corrigan pushed by, the stocky man made a hard, wide swing with his fist. Expecting it, Corrigan parried and countered with a short, telling jab. Staggered, the stocky man howled for help, and immediately three other men came running in response. While Corrigan tangled with them, the stocky man deserted his pals and ran from the alley. He returned with two men in blue frock coats and round straw hats, who grabbed Corrigan from each side, clamped handcuffs on him, and dragged him to a waiting wagon.

There, Corrigan learned that he was in the coils of the Metropolitan Police. All the way to their headquarters, Corrigan kept berating them: "Let me go, you fools! Don't you know that the President is in danger? That's what I was trying to tell them at the theater!"

"Then tell it to the sergeant," one of the officers retorted. "He'll listen."

The sergeant did listen.

"While you idiots are holding me," argued Corrigan as he faced the desk at headquarters, "President Lincoln will be shot tonight during the performance by a man named Booth."

"Isn't there a play actor named Wilkes Booth?" quizzed the sergeant.

"That's the one," rejoined Corrigan. "John Wilkes Booth."

The sergeant picked up a playbill that was lying on the desk and smiled indulgently.

"Ford's Theater was handing these out today," he said. "But there's nothing here about Booth. He isn't even in the show."

"But he'll be hanging around the theater, waiting his chance!" Corrigan insisted.

The sergeant turned to the two patrolmen.

"Did you see anyone hanging around Ford's Theater?"

"Only this fellow." One patrolman indicated Corrigan. "We were called in to get rid of him by a stagehand named Ned Spangler."

"Spangler!" The name rang a bell to Corrigan. "He's one of them!"

"One of whom?" demanded the sergeant.

"The plotters who are out to kill the President!"

The sergeant gestured to the cell room and ordered:

"Put this man away. He's either drunk or crazy."

Behind the bars, Corrigan waxed even more indignant, shouting loud enough for the sergeant to hear him:

"Drunk or crazy, you say! You'll find out differently! I tell you, I know, I *know* that tonight Wilkes Booth plans to assassinate President Lincoln. Don't ask me why or how I know. I just *know* — and I intend to prevent it, even if I have to break down these bars!"

From the desk, the sergeant glowered in the direction of Corrigan's cell. Then, glancing about at his men, he demanded:

"One of you find a way to calm that fool down!"

A young patrolman responded: "I know a way, Sergeant."

"And what would that be, Frescott?"

"To listen to him. Maybe he is talking sense."

"Have you gone daft, too, Frescott?"

"Hardly, Sergeant. I just know that he sounds positive about what he says. A man who talks that way may know something."

Corrigan quieted as he heard that, thus adding weight to Frescott's words. But the sergeant was still unconvinced.

"What would you have me do?" he demanded. "Send all the reserve patrolmen to Ford's Theater on the word of some demented fool?"

"It wouldn't hurt," rejoined Patrolman Frescott, "to put a guard on the President's box."

"But the President already has a guard, a regular man assigned from this department. If he wants more, he can call for them. Who are we to tell the President what to do? Besides, he has the whole army at his disposal, if he needs it. Don't forget, General Grant will be at the theater with him."

The sergeant let those words sink in; then added:

"I'm telling you, Frescott, unless you use more judgment in sizing up these situations, you won't go far in this department!"

That might have settled it but for Corrigan, who renewed the clatter from his cell door, hoping to stir Frescott to further action. A frown on his roundish face, Frescott began a new protest, only to be interrupted by a well-dressed man who strode into the patrol room, glanced toward Corrigan's cell, and turned to the desk.

"Sergeant," the newcomer asked, "is that the man who created the disturbance at Ford's?"

"Yes. He says his name is Corrigan. What about him?"

"I want you to release him in my custody."

"And who might you be?"

The visitor drew a calling card from his pocket and handed it to the sergeant, who read slowly:

" 'Bartram J. Wellington, M.D.' So you're a doctor —"

"A specialist in mental ailments. The government has assigned me to cases like this. We've picked up dozens of persons who have been talking about assassinations and other plots. It has reached the proportions of an epidemic."

"That wouldn't surprise me. What do you do with these cases?"

"We examine them, to find the cause of their dementia, if we can. Sympathetic treatment, proper rest, a full consideration of their stories will often bring about a cure. There's nothing criminal in their actions."

"There is when they assault someone, Dr. Wellington. Like the way this Corrigan was pitching into Spangler."

"Spangler? Who is he, Sergeant?"

"Ned Spangler, a stagehand up at Ford's," the sergeant explained. "He was the one who made the complaint."

"I'm told they all pitched into Corrigan. That's why the case was reported to our department." Wellington strolled over to Corrigan's cell, and studied him with a friendly smile. Then, swinging about, he added: "I think I can handle him, Sergeant, if he's willing to come with me."

"How about it, Corrigan?"

From his cell, Corrigan agreed. "I'm willing."

As a turnkey was unlocking Corrigan's cell, a patrolman arrived and handed a note to the sergeant. Corrigan approached the desk and said:

"Let me tell you one thing, Sergeant. The President is in more danger than you suppose. General Grant will *not* be there with him tonight—"

The sergeant gave Corrigan a quick, sharp stare.

"What makes you say that?"

"I happen to know — well, that is — I just guessed—"

"And you guessed right. This message says that General Grant is leaving by train for Philadelphia and won't be at the theater tonight."

Real suspicion was gleaming in the sergeant's eyes now, which was exactly the opposite of what Corrigan wanted. It would be best to go along with Dr. Wellington, an intelligent man who seemed ready to listen. It was Wellington himself who swayed the balance. A sympathetic smile upon his broad, handsome face, he remarked quietly:

"You see how quickly a man in this condition grasps for every straw? Believe me, Sergeant, it is the business of our medical department to find out where such people come from and how they learn the things they do. We always manage to sift the facts. I'll have Corrigan's story soon enough."

Corrigan was willing to bet that Wellington wouldn't, but he did not say so. It was better to play along with this keen-mannered physician. The sergeant waved dismissal, and Corrigan walked out with his new friend. From behind him, Corrigan heard the earnest voice of Patrolman Frescott:

"I still think there is something to that plot, Sergeant."

"You'd better get back on duty, Frescott, or quit your job for keeps."

"And what if I should quit right now?"

"Before you've finished making tonight's rounds, when we're as short-handed as we are? It will be the Blue Jug for you, if you try that trick!"

The voices dwindled as Corrigan and Wellington reached the outside air. It was still muggy, with a slight touch of chill. But Wellington disregarded it.

"It's only a short walk to the National Hotel," he said. "That's where I'm stopping, and we'll find it easier to talk there."

"But President Lincoln is in grave danger—"

Corrigan caught himself rather than start an excited tirade that would cause Wellington, too, to class him as demented. Quietly, Corrigan asked:

"What time is it, doctor?"

Wellington consulted a large gold watch.

"Just half-past six."

"Then the play won't start for another two hours," declared Corrigan, much relieved. "That allows us plenty of time."

To Wellington's apparent surprise, Corrigan dropped the subject entirely and took an interest in the passing throng as they continued on to the National Hotel. Once there, Wellington conducted Corrigan through a lobby almost as lavish as the Willard's and up the stairs to a distant room on the second floor. There, they sat down together, and the physician made out a simple report, listing Corrigan's full name, age, residence, and occupation. On the verge of saying "astrophysicist," Corrigan quickly changed it to "scientist."

"A scientist," repeated Wellington. "Are you acquainted over at the Smithsonian?"

"Not with any of the present personnel," Corrigan answered quickly.

"What gave you the idea that the President would be assassinated?" Dr. Wellington asked next.

"I just happen to know," began Corrigan. "Well, call it a premonition. After all, you should understand such things. You are a psychiatrist—"

"A what?"

Corrigan was quick to correct himself, realizing that he had used a term not yet known to the English language. "I meant to say," he declared, "that you, too, are a scientist. Perhaps it wasn't a premonition. Maybe I just heard too much talk."

"Then why didn't you say that before?" Wellington eyed Corrigan closely. "What started you off on this? Did you have an accident?"

"Well, no. Not exactly."

Instinctively, Corrigan pressed his hand to the back of his head. Wellington promptly stepped over, turned up the gaslight, and took a close look. He pressed the bruised spot gently, and Corrigan winced.

"A bad contusion," declared Wellington professionally. "When did this happen — and how?"

"About an hour ago," replied Corrigan. "I slipped on some steps and hit the back of my head."

"That could account for your delusions." Wellington stepped over and closed the window, to cut off the blaring music of a parading band. "You need rest and quiet. First, let me attend to that bruise."

From a drawer, Wellington brought out a large handkerchief and soaked it with a liquid that smelled like witch hazel. He bandaged Corrigan's head with the handkerchief; then produced a wine bottle and a glass.

"A little sherry will help you," said Wellington. "That blow may have given you a slight concussion, enough to cause a mental lapse."

"But I don't ordinarily drink wine—"

"Call it a doctor's prescription then. Perhaps it will enable you to relax and remember some point you have forgotten."

Corrigan liked that suggestion. As he sipped the wine, he began thinking of ways to win Wellington's full cooperation.

"If you could reach someone close to the President," suggested Corrigan, "I'm sure I could recall more details of the plot, enough to forestall it completely. But there is no time to lose."

"That I understand," agreed Wellington, "so lie back and rest, while I send a messenger direct to the surgeon general's office. That should gain us an immediate hearing."

Corrigan closed his eyes. He heard the slight thump of the closing door; then a prolonged, scratching sound, as of a key turning slowly in the lock. He opened his eyes and tried to rise, but his arms and legs seemed chained. He finally managed to start forward, only to slump as he reached the door, which was locked from the outside as he had feared. His mind was alert, but his body was paralyzed. Thinking it might be due to the stuff on the handkerchief, he managed to pull away the bandage.

It was dark now, but in the glow of city lights from the window, Corrigan noted the initials J.W.B. on the corner of the handkerchief. Even his vocal cords seemed paralyzed as he gasped:

"Bartram J. Wellington. . . . B—J—W. . . . B—J—" Corrigan's breath came with a hard gasp. "J—W" Another gasp — "J—W—B. . . . J—W—B." His mind, still alert, turned those initials into a name: "John Wilkes Booth!"

Horror riveted Corrigan as he realized how he had been duped by the arch-fiend of the conspiracy. Booth must have been among the group in the bar on Tenth Street. From Spangler, Booth had learned how Corrigan had tried to barge in through the stage door. Actor that he was, Booth had played the part of a physician in order to remove Corrigan — the man who knew too much — from the police cell where his shouts might eventually have brought him an intelligent hearing.

With that realization, Corrigan's head swam. He collapsed into unconsciousness which persisted until a dull, slow pounding gradually aroused him. It came from the door, where a voice was calling, "Is anybody in there?" Corrigan found his own voice and responded, "Yes." A key rattled, the door opened, and a man entered, almost stumbling over Corrigan. The man found the gas jet and turned it up. In the glow, Corrigan stared at the blue-coated, straw-hatted figure of Patrolman Frescott.

The glitter of Corrigan's eyes, white and wide with dilated pupils, told Frescott more than Corrigan himself realized.

"Knockout drops!" exclaimed the patrolman. "That's what Booth gave you. I should have suspected it."

Pulled to his feet, Corrigan mumbled: "What time is it?"

"Ten o'clock," Frescott replied. "Nobody would listen to me, Corrigan. I had to find you to learn what you know."

"I know this. We must get to Ford's Theater right away!"

Corrigan still moved numbly as Frescott rushed him down to the lobby and out to the street. Among the waiting carriages, Corrigan saw the one that had brought him from the Potomac Club. He managed to wave, and the carriage wheeled over. Frescott pushed Corrigan into the seat and told the coachman:

"Ford's Theater — and hurry!"

As they sped post-haste along the Avenue, Frescott told Corrigan all that had happened during those intervening hours.

"While I made my rounds," stated Frescott, "I had a friend check things for me. He brought me word that there is no Dr. Wellington and no mental department. But he also said that my description of the man fitted the actor, John Wilkes Booth. When I learned that Booth was staying at the National Hotel, I finally quit my rounds and went there. I made the manager give me a key to Booth's room, and there I found you. So what can we do right now?"

"A lot," rejoined Corrigan, moving his arms and legs to find out if they were working again. "At the theater, we must go right to the President's box and backtrack from there. Even if we cause a commotion, it will spoil Booth's game. He will panic, because he was really afraid of going to Ford's until he heard at headquarters that General Grant would not be there."

"But where did you learn so much about this plot, Corrigan?"

"I'll explain that later. Even if nobody is willing to believe me, I won't care. If only we can get to that theater in time!"

Along Pennsylvania Avenue, soldiers and other passers-by were rushing out to stop the dashing horse and rattling carriage, thinking it was a runaway. While the coachman slapped the reins and lashed his whip, Frescott kept lifting himself up from his seat, showing his blue police uniform and waving people back with his straw hat, letting them know that this was an emergency. Corrigan clung tightly to the carriage rail, as they rounded the final corner.

Arriving at the theater, Frescott sprang out, and Corrigan managed to follow. But they never reached the lobby. As they were crossing the planking, frantic people came surging from the theater shrieking:

"They've shot the President! They've shot the President!"

"It was Wilkes Booth who did it!" shouted Corrigan, fighting to get through the crowd. "By now, he's on his horse, heading down through Maryland."

A man grabbed the lapels of Corrigan's coat, shoved him back toward the carriage, and snarled:

"Yes, it was Booth who did it. But how would you know that? You were out here, not in the theater."

"And if you knew that Booth would ride for Maryland," another man demanded, "why didn't you go and head him off?"

"I'll tell you why he didn't," the first man asserted. "He's in cahoots with Booth, that's why! He wants to put us on a false trail."

"String him up," came another shout, "for the traitor that he is!"

Lynch law was taking over. A growing mob began to drag Corrigan to the nearest lamppost. Aleady weak, he was beaten into submission, his protests were being smothered, when Patrolman Frescott charged the throng, breaking it up with his nightstick. Frescott thrust Corrigan bodily into the carriage, and shouted to the driver:

"Get him away from here and keep going!"

Then the horse was springing forward, with Frescott beating off a couple of men who tried to board the carriage. Dazed, Corrigan sprawled back in the seat and heard the howls of the mob dwindle in the distance. Then there was only the rapid clop-clop of the horse's hoofs as they swung around a corner into a secluded, dimly lighted street.

"Here we are, sir."

The coachman had brought Corrigan back, not to the National Hotel, but to their first starting point, the Potomac Club. In the flicker of a gaslit street lamp, Corrigan made out the white doors and the portico above. He eased to the curb, pulled all the bills from his pocket and gratefully thrust them into the coachman's appreciative hand.

The horse and carriage had clopped from sight by the time the door opened to Corrigan's knock. It was William who bowed him in, and the attendant's face was wrinkled in a puzzled frown.

"I wondered where you had gone, Mr. Corrigan," said William. "Your suit is ready, and they are waiting for you to join them at dinner in the grill."

"Dinner? At this hour?"

"I know it's only six o'clock, sir, but they said you might be planning to go out on an evening plane, so they decided to have dinner early."

It was Corrigan's turn to be puzzled. As he changed back to his own clothes, he realized that he had experienced an entire evening's adventure during his journey into the past; yet he had arrived back in the present within an hour or so of his original starting time!

Definitely, Corrigan was now willing to go along with Millard's theory of breaking the time barrier. With a pang of regret, he also agreed with Jackson. If you were projected into the past, you might help shape history, but you couldn't change it.

As he approached the dinner table in the grill room, Corrigan wondered whether to tell of his experience. His fellow club members probably wouldn't believe his story; even worse, they might think that he was making up a yarn to ridicule them. Indeed, Corrigan was beginning to doubt the whole thing himself. So he decided to keep silent.

Professor Whittaker had left, and another man was with the group, talking earnestly to Millard. Dr. Jackson waved Corrigan to a chair, then gestured toward the newcomer.

"Let me introduce another of our members, Mr. Corrigan. This is Mr. Ray Frescott."

Blankly, Corrigan found himself shaking hands with a man whose face was the image of the Washington patrolman who had shoved Corrigan into a carriage a century ago. It was obvious, however, that this twentieth century Frescott did not recognize Corrigan.

"Mr. Frescott was starting to tell an unusual story," declared Dr. Jackson. "I know that you will want to hear it, Mr. Corrigan."

"It's about my great-grandfather," related Frescott. "He was a patrolman with the Washington police the evening President Lincoln was assassinated. Somehow, he sensed that it might happen, and he tried to warn people, but nobody would listen, not even the police superintendent, who was in the theater audience at the time.

"Finally, he found some crackpot who seemed to know about Booth's plot, and brought him to the theater to prove his point. But they got there just too late. Afterward, some sergeant wanted to fire my great-grandfather because he had gone off his beat. But by then, he was the biggest hero on the force. He later became a police chief, a councilman, and finally a building constructor. He joined the Potomac Club, and some of our family have been members ever since."

"And what happened to the other man?" queried Corrigan. "The crackpot whom your great-grandfather brought to the theater with him?"

"The crowd tried to mob him, thinking he was in the plot with Booth," rejoined Frescott, "but my great-grandfather sent him off in a carriage, and nobody ever heard from him again."

The waiter arrived with the dinner menu, and the talk turned to the subject of a bridge game that was to follow. Corrigan said nothing about time travel. He was wondering if that bump on the head had jarred his mind into a discordance of past, present, and future. As the evening progressed, and his head no longer throbbed, he began to feel sure that this had been the case.

William was still at the door when Corrigan left for the airport. While Corrigan waited for a cab which the doorman had summoned, he remarked:

"By the way, William, you didn't have a great-grandfather who worked here at the Potomac Club — or did you?"

"No, sir. Not a great-grandfather," responded William. "A great-grand-uncle. His name was William, too, and he fought in the Union Army. He was badly wounded in the right arm at Gettysburg, so he took a job as doorman here. Several people have asked me if there was another William working here long ago. I don't just know why, except—" the doorman looked up and gave one of his wrinkled smiles — "well, when you get to know this club, sir, you will realize how it grips you. Some people might say that it's filled with ghosts, but I don't think so. To me, it is just a place where time stands still."

The cab was arriving on the well-lighted street where Corrigan now was looking in vain for the gaslit lamppost that had been the coachman's beacon when the carriage arrived back from the theater. William flagged the cab, and as Corrigan was getting in, the doorman handed him a bit of cardboard.

"This was in the pocket of that old-time suit you were wearing," said William. "So I suppose it must be yours. Good night, Mr. Corrigan."

Soon the cab was speeding along a smooth street into the blaze of lights that represented downtown Washington. They passed the now completed Washington Monument, which was illuminated to its full height; and off beyond, Corrigan saw the stately pillars of the magnificent Lincoln Memorial. Then, as the cab reached the bridge leading to the airport, Corrigan studied the printed cardboard strip that William had handed him.

Deliberately, he tore the strip in half; then again, again, and again. Near the middle of the bridge, Corrigan tossed the pieces from the cab window. Caught by the night breeze, they fluttered over the rail and down to the broad bosom of the Potomac River.

Those scattered scraps were all that remained of a unique collector's item — the only unused ticket to Ford's Theater on its closing night of April 14, 1865.

The Ghost-Town Ghost

Topaz City, Nevada, was practically a ghost town when Jim Gilbert arrived there around the time of the big gold strike down Death Valley way. The rush had begun to fabulous new towns like Goldfield and Rhyolite, where fortunes were being made overnight and millions of dollars were squandered every day. Even the railroads were racing each other to lay tracks into that bonanza land and build ornate stations to receive them.

Hence Topaz City, a carry-over from the big bust that had followed the silver boom some thirty to forty years before, was becoming more and more deserted. Some of the old silver mines were still being worked in a small way, so there were enough jobs in town to keep a few stores open, but otherwise things were more than quiet. They were all but dead.

That was why Jim Gilbert liked it. A man in his early thirties, he was something Topaz City had never seen before. He was an artist and a rather good one. Complete with brushes, palette, canvases, easel, and smock, he rented one of the many empty, weather-beaten stores on the town's main and only street, turned it into a studio and went right to work. The only thing Jim lacked was the artist's trademark of the early 1900's, a beard. That was superfluous in Topaz City, where beards were a common thing, though they were of the bushy type, not the artistic Van Dyke cut. So Jim decided to remain clean-shaven, a novelty around these parts.

As an artist, Jim fortunately did not have to depend upon the local trade. His paintings, which really captured the spirit of the West, had a ready-made market in New York. He had problems, though, in finding models in Topaz City, as well as a variety of scenery, without going too far afield. The man who finally solved those problems was Bert Tolliver, a local character who was termed "a card" in the parlance of the period. That, at least, was the opinion of Bert's fellow townsmen. In the opinion of Jim Gilbert. Bert Tolliver was the most unappreciated man he had ever met.

Though Bert was less than ten years older than Jim, he looked double the artist's age. The reason was that Bert Tolliver had grown up with Topaz City, starting from early boyhood, becoming as rugged as the lusty town itself during its palmy days and eventually as weather-beaten, though by no means as decadent. For Bert Tolliver still had the sparkling spirit and the twinkle in the eye that all the rest of Topaz City lacked, yet badly needed.

Now only about forty, Bert was practically an old man bcause he had never known any youth. From a messenger boy at the age of six, he had become a printer's devil at ten and a blacksmith's apprentice at fourteen. He had driven twenty-mule teams across the desert, dealt faro in a gambling house, served as turnkey in the county jail, played the piano in the town's only saloon, and ridden shotgun on a stagecoach. He had even become the driver of the mail itself; but that was one week before it quit.

Such was the tragedy of Bert Tolliver. He had always been dependent upon circumstances, with no hope of any escape. He had given far more than he should have for payments received, but had never gained an added reward. Sober, honest, and reliable, he had been taken at face value, nothing more. He was like the silver on which the town depended for its very existence, yet belittled because it was not gold.

Between jobs, Bert had gone on trips with prospectors, but never with a chance of sharing in their discovery. Always, he had been hired as a guide, a cook, or a mule driver. Often, he had gone on the promise of wages that were never paid. Yet Bert had held no grudges; instead, he had been proud of his adventures, even when they had proven misadventures, and he had kept up his spirits by reciting them in detail. As a result, his fellow townsmen had classed him as a blowhard.

During the decline of Topaz City, Bert Tolliver had become broke, and worse. His services were often demanded by canny creditors who knew that he was so honest that he would work cheap to pay off his debts. So when Jim Gilbert paid him cash for whatever he did, Bert simply outdid himself. He introduced Jim to ranchers and mine owners who let the artist paint pictures on their property, and he talked cowhands and miners into acting as models in those settings.

They made a striking contrast, these two men: Jim Gilbert, the slender, youthful artist from the East, with his thin, clean-shaven face, always serious in expression; and Bert Tolliver, heavy of build, yet light of step, whose beard, though the bushiest and darkest in town, was still not heavy enough to hide the ruddiness and broad grin of his ever-smiling features.

Perhaps it was due to those very extremes that they got along so well; at any rate, Jim Gilbert recognized it and put up a proposition that to Bert Tolliver was the opportunity of a lifetime.

"How would you like it, Bert," said Jim, "if I grubstaked the two of us and we went partners in an all-out hunt for gold?"

"You mean head down toward Death Valley and join the gold rush?" exclaimed Bert. "Why, you're taking the words right out of my mouth!"

"Not a chance on that," rejoined Jim. "That boom may go bust any day, and when it does, everybody will twenty-three skidoo right out of there. I was up in the Klondike painting pictures of the gold rush in Ninety-eight, so I've seen all of that I want. No, I have something a whole lot better."

"Like what?"

"Like this."

Jim made sure that the studio door was locked. Then, from a portfolio, he brought out a map and spread it on a large table that it completely covered. Bert studied the details of the map, which included contours, elevations, tiny streams, and other features.

"Say!" exclaimed Bert. "Those are the Skeleton Mountains that lie way south of here; and this is the best map of them I've ever seen."

"Better than that," Jim added, "those special marks show portions of the range that have already been prospected for gold or searched for treasure, at the time this map was made."

"Fine! That should cut three years' work down to one."

"You mean that the Skeleton range is that big?"

"It is big, Jim, and rough. Say, how did you get this map?"

"It was made up from some old maps that my uncle pieced together and enlarged. That was Uncle Ben, my mother's brother, the man who brought me up to be an artist, and sent me to Paris to study. My dad, whose name was Harvey Gilbert, made a lot of money during the silver boom up in Virginia City. He brought my mother and myself back to New York. Then my mother died there. So Dad left me with Uncle Ben and went West again to manage his silver mines. He sent back money at intervals, but finally he sold out his shares, and we didn't hear from him after that. I went to the Klondike, hoping I would run into Dad up there, but no luck. Then later, Uncle Ben heard from someone that Dad had died, but he didn't learn just when or where."

Bert Tolliver nodded sympathetically. He had heard many such stories before. Without them, there would be no West. People came there to find fortune, to forget sorrow, to regain losses, or to seek adventure. Some were born to it, as Bert himself was, and the tough part was that you could get trapped right here in places like Topaz City and never manage to take advantage of the wonderful opportunities all around you.

All that went through Bert's mind as he shrewdly told Jim:

"We've got to play this smart, pardner. You've picked the greatest time ever to go prowling around the Skeleton Mountains. Most everybody else has headed for Goldfield and Rhyolite, so we won't have any competition, provided we keep our traps shut."

"You mean we won't tell anybody where we are going?"

"Absolutely not. Mum is strictly the word. Why, if any of these stay-at-home galoots even guessed where we were bound, they'd flock down to the Skeleton Mountains like a plague of seven-year locusts!"

"Then there is gold in the Skeleton Range?"

"For certain. First, the Spaniards started mining there, three or four times, maybe. Then the Mexicans did the same, but always the Indians closed them out and never left any survivors. Some made markers along the trail, and later some of the old mines were rediscovered. But whenever anyone went back and tried to find them, they never could."

"And why not?"

Bert hesitated. Finally he put a cautious query of his own:

"Do you believe in ghosts, Jim?"

"Well," Jim replied, "I've never seen one."

"And if you did see one, would you be afeared of it?"

"Not necessarily. Are you trying to tell me that those mountains are full of Spanish and Mexican — or even Indian ghosts?"

"Worse than that. It was later that the ghosts began to haunt those canyons. A couple of prospectors would stumble upon an old mine and start to work it. Then others would see them doing it and would murder them then and there. Next, the killers would turn on each other until only one was left. He'd be scared to trust anybody with his secret and even worse scared to go back to the mountains alone. Then he'd finally die, leaving a map that was about half wrong. Somebody would pick it up and go down to the Skeleton Mountains and then the killing would begin all over."

"And which are the ghosts, the original victims or the killers who got theirs later?"

"The ghosts," declared Bert seriously, "would be mostly those of persons who had a rightful claim. Like prospectors who found the old mine workings entirely on their own, not just by having somebody show them the way there, or by working from a map. When a man makes a gold strike, it grips him, like it was a thing of life or death. He'd give his life to keep his secret, and he'd come back from death to stop anyone from stealing it."

This was one of those rare instances when Jim Gilbert really wanted to smile, but he managed to keep his habitual straight face as he asked:

"You know of actual cases like that, Bert?"

"Sure," Bert returned. "The Deacon's mine, for one. They figured the Deacon was working it, because other prospectors kept seeing him down around the Skeleton Range. Besides, he was always showing up in different towns, bringing gold with him. Never enough to cause too much stir in any one place, but it must have added up considerable."

"And did they try to track this Deacon?"

"They really dogged him, but he shook them off. He was a loner from the start, so whatever he found was his, with nobody to tell about it. He made friends with oldtimers around Topaz City and other places; and they cashed some of his gold for him, but he never told them where it came from."

"Has the Deacon's ghost been seen down in the Skeletons?"

"Some folks say, yes. But it could only be within the past ten or fifteen years, 'cause before that, the Deacon was still around hisself."

"Did you ever see his ghost, Bert?"

"No, never. But I'd know it if I did, for I saw the Deacon up here in Topaz City, when he was still alive. Solemn-looking bloke, kind of along in years, though you couldn't be sure of that. Maybe he just looked old on account of the black trousers and black shirt he always wore. He had big black boots, too, and a black Stetson, one of those real wide kind, so you could never get a look under the brim to see if he had gray hair. Those eyes of his would bore at you, like they were asking why you were messing in his business. It wasn't smart to bother the Deacon then, any more than it would be smart to pick a quarrel with his ghost right now."

"So you really think his ghost is around the mine he found?"

"His ghost might be around anywhere. I never heard of a ghost being pinned down to one spot, 'cept when it had gotten into some sort of trouble there and maybe had a grudge to settle. The Deacon never was in any trouble that I heard about. But if you don't believe in ghosts, I'm not trying to convince you. Why should I scare you away from the Skeleton Mountains, considering that map you've got?"

"You haven't scared me, Bert, but you have convinced me."

"Convinced you of what, Jim?"

"That the Deacon's mine is real and that we can't let anybody know we are going to look for it. We must make them think we're heading some place else."

"Like to Goldfield or Rhyolite, to join the gold rush?"

"That's our ticket, Bert. Let's shake on it."

They shook on it and began planning their campaign then and there. Within a few days, Jim Gilbert was casually telling people how he had gone to the Klondike and made paintings of the gold rush there, even doing a little prospecting on the side. Now, he was getting the urge to head down Death Valley way and do the same. He had thought the rush would soon be over, but now he felt it was just beginning, so it would be wise to get in on it.

Bert Tolliver was spreading a totally different yarn. For once, he was purposely living up to his reputation as the town braggart. He was telling the Topaz City folks how he had talked Jim Gilbert into a big deal. They were going to join the gold rush and Jim would paint while Bert panned. That way, they were bound to make some money, and anyway, Bert could not lose, because Jim was putting up the grubstake.

From then on, they put on an act that was ludicrous and therefore all the more real. Jim, the perfect example of an Eastern tenderfoot, began buying any and all supplies that his partner suggested. Bert, the town show-off, couldn't resist swaggering around Topaz City and flashing his limitless bank-roll in the stores where his credit had been nil, a week before.

Storekeepers and clerks hopped from shelf to shelf, saying, "What else, Mr. Tolliver?" and "Yes, we have it, Bert, old boy." Paying cash was such a novelty for Bert that it was easy indeed for local merchants to load him with supplies, particularly when Jim, the money man, put the O.K. on every purchase.

Bert, however, was doubly smart as he played the big shot in his own home town. While paying full price for goods with Jim's money, he suggested that the local merchants should forget what he already owed them. So they began tearing up Bert's old tabs, hoping to get further patronage from him, with the result that he was actually buying goods at wholesale.

Privately, Bert made full accounting to Jim, the partner that everybody thought he was taking for a sucker. The two of them had many laughs behind the closed shutters of the artist's studio that they were turning into a supply center. They had bought many times as much as they would need for their trip to gold rush territory, where they could buy more as needed; but Jim argued that the prices would be higher than in Topaz City, so the more they bought the better.

Under cover of all that, they were really stocking up for a three-months stay or longer in Skeleton Valley, their secret destination. Meanwhile, everyone was wondering how the would-be prospectors hoped to carry all their surplus goods. Jim and Bert solved that problem by buying four of the strongest horses available, along with a wagon that was the biggest Topaz City had seen since the almost forgotten days of the famous prairie schooners.

All the town assembled to see the two partners off and have a laugh at their expense. Judge Gomez and Doc Hinckley, both regarded as keen wits, were there to exchange pleasantries. The judge gazed askance at the big wagon and fired the opening remark:

"Why, Bert, old boy, you'll never get to Goldfield with that rig. You'll be driving through so much alkali dust, you'll need a twenty-mule team. So if you'd like to make a trade, say one horse for two mules, with a little cash thrown in —"

"Sorry, Judge," interposed Bert, "but I've thought all that out. I used to drive a mail coach, so I know the roads right good. Instead of going straight to Goldfield, I'm going to take the Southern Trail almost to the border, then go southwest over the Apache cutoff and come northwest by the old Silver Trail. That ought to do it."

"It sure ought," the judge agreed seriously. "But since you'll be a little out of your way, why don't you go right around by the northwest to start. There's a nice trail called the Oregon Trail —"

The rest was drowned in the guffaws of the crowd, which enjoyed Bert's pained expression. If there was anything they liked in Topaz City, it was to see Bert Tolliver "tooken," as they phrased it. The laughter finally subsided so that the townfolk could listen to Doc Hinckley bait Jim Gilbert, who was loading some fancy saddles into the back of the wagon.

"Lookee, young fellow," drawled Doc, "you won't be needing saddles with those drayhorses of yours. Your problem is that your wagon is likely to break down. If you'd like to swap those saddles for a couple of extra wagon wheels, I can accommodate you. The wheels are odd sizes, but that won't matter, since you'll be driving in a circle anyway."

Again there was a roar of laughter, but Jim played it seriously.

He beckoned to Bert, and they went back into the studio, then came out rolling a pair of wagon wheels which they hoisted into the wagon.

"Sorry, Doc," commented Bert. "We'd already bought a couple of spares. Both of them the same size, too."

That turned the laugh on Doc, but he came right back:

"And where do you expect to use those saddles — and why?"

"Where?" Jim replied. "All along the trail. And why? Because I'll be painting Western scenes, every time we stop. I'll need Bert to pose in a saddle as a cowboy, along with anybody else we meet up with on the way."

"There used to be Indians in these parts," reminded Doc. "Don't you intend to include them in your paintings?"

"I sure do." Jim gestured to Bert, who opened the last box that he was loading on the wagon. From it, they took out some Indian costumes and displayed them. "That's why," added Jim, "we decided to take these along."

Again the laugh was on Doc, and Bert added a dry comment:

"If you'd like to come along, Doc, we'll let you play Indian. All you will have to do is set still on a horse and pretend you're Sitting Bull."

With that, the partners clambered aboard the wagon. Bert Tolliver cracked his whip, and they rolled out of town with all the flare of the old days, when Bert had driven the mail coach along that very same Southern Trail.

"Nice going, Jim," complimented Bert, as they clattered along, "the way you kidded Doc when he mentioned the saddles. He's the only person who might suspect that we have been planning to hide this wagon somewhere and take to the saddle instead."

"Won't he still think that, even after what I told him?"

"He will think about it, sure. But he won't be likely to talk to anybody about it. That's all that counts where we are concerned."

Jim began to worry as they rolled along. He wondered, too, how far they would get, since they had started late in the day. But Bert had included everything in his calculations. After they had driven a couple of hours, he turned off on a narrow road to the east, which followed a muddy stream that he identified as the Copper River. When the road doubled back toward the main trail, Bert swung the wagon into a grove of cottonwood trees.

"I'll unhitch the horses and let them drink," declared Bert. "You set up your easel and start to paint. But keep your eye on the trail we just left. If anybody comes along, either way, we'll go back on the trail and continue south, so we will be accounted for, later. But if nobody shows up, we'll keep on down this river road."

Nobody did show up. Bert built a small fire and cooked dinner along toward dusk, then came over to Jim with a cup of coffee.

"You've painted enough now," declared Bert. "Here's mud in your eye, fresh from the Copper River. It adds something to the coffee."

After dinner, they harnessed up and drove all night along the river trail, under a clear, moonlit sky. Toward dawn, they stopped in another grove of trees, waited there all day and drove again by night. They continued that policy night after night, their wagon gliding like a phantom under the silvery moon, along level back roads that Bert had followed often during his somewhat checkered career.

During their trek, they veered from east to southeast, south and finally southwest, following a route that reminded Jim Gilbert of an Indian's drawn bow and causing him to wonder if Bert Tolliver really knew where he was bound. But one fine dawn, as the horses labored up a smooth but steady rise, they came to the top of a hump where Bert pointed ahead with his whip and announced:

"There, partner, is where we're bound. Those are the Skeleton Mountains."

They were well named. White, gaunt, with great crags furrowed by centuries of wind and rain, the entire range had the appearance of a long, sprawled skeleton; not of some human giant, but of an antediluvian monster that might have been stranded on the bed of a vast receding sea. To Jim, the sight was weird even in daylight, but to Bert, it was like coming home. He clucked the horses over the open ground, picking a course between mesquite trees and giant saguaro cactus plants. Even though the horses were tired, Jim thought they would reach the mountains within an hour; but it took more than half the day, for distance was deceptive in this arid atmosphere. As they approached, the contours of the mountains changed at intervals, due to new angles of view. Bert pointed out some of the more familiar peaks that Jim recognized from the map: Gray Dome, a mighty mass of granite; Crystal Point, glittering with quartz; Black Beauty, a rounded summit composed of basalt; and other formations that showed the reddish tinge of rhyolite and the green stripes of serpentine.

As the wagon reached the base of the range, the mountains loomed more formidably than ever. They became a frowning wall, towering to inaccessible heights, with no apparent way to pierce the mighty barrier.

"If there is gold anywhere," declared Jim, in an awed tone, "these mountains should have it. But how do we get in to get at it?"

"Getting in is easy," Bert assured, "for anybody that has been here as often as I have. But getting at the gold is another matter. You've got to find it first, and nobody has done that since the Deacon was around here."

Jim decided that the subject of the old Deacon could wait. Right now, he was more interested in how they were to penetrate these mountain fastnesses. Bert soon showed him how. He drove along beside the mountains for another mile, and finally an opening showed in the towering rocks.

"This is Skull Portal," stated Bert, pointing through to a low dome shaped roughly like a death's head. "It's where the Indians used to trap the miners, before they found other ways of coming in or out. But since there's no Indians around any more, we'll use this way. It's easiest."

It was easy indeed. The ground was like a broad, level roadway as it wound in through the mountain furrows. It narrowed, though, as they turned the horses into a side canyon, where great crags seemed almost to meet, a thousand feet above, and the side walls were streaked like bony fingers reaching down to clutch the intruders.

"The Giant's Cleft," Bert said. "Kind of gets you, the first time in; but you'll soon forget it. There's so much else that's worse."

From the cleft, the road widened and took them into a side passage that curved into a dead end.

"We'll leave the wagon here," stated Bert, "where nobody is apt to find it, though it won't matter if they do. From here, we go by pack horse up to Hidden Valley and make our headquarters there."

The route proved a tricky one from the start. They loaded the four horses and led them up a rough incline that Jim thought was another dead end. But Bert knew differently. They reached a low, arched opening in the form of a natural tunnel and went through to another valley. More turns brought them to a hidden cleft between two weather-hewn pillars that Bert termed The Twins. Always, their course was upward, until they found an opening that brought them into a natural bowl, surrounded by a low rim of rock. There, Jim gaped in utter astonishment.

The bowl formed a small, fertile valley, with plenty of grass for grazing, as well as grapevines, berry bushes, and even fruit trees. Near a low but steep cliff was an old hut with a crude fence extending from its corner to the rocky wall, where water oozed down in tiny rivulets that joined into a small stream.

"We can corral the horses over beside the cabin," declared Bert, "and then get busy and patch it up. We can even plant some vegetables. I brought seeds along, figuring we'd be here long enough."

"But how can this valley be so fertile," queried Jim, "when the mountains themselves are practically a desert?"

"Only they aren't a desert," returned Bert. "There's enough rain, hereabouts, but it comes all at once. The mountains have been gullied, so it sweeps right through them, except in a few places like this valley, where the water gets impounded. Lots of prospectors worked out of here."

"You mean like the Deacon?"

"No, the Deacon was a loner, like I told you. He kept watching everybody else. I guess nobody will ever know where he made his base."

In the weeks that followed, Jim Gilbert came to know the Skeleton Mountains well, and he was impressed by their more fearful aspects. Bert Tolliver insisted that eyes were always watching in these parts, and Jim was inclined to believe it despite himself. Both were to learn why and how the Skeleton Mountains had taken so much human toll, regardless of outright murder or avenging ghosts, though it seemed almost as though the latter were to blame. Soon, however, they began to wonder if some protective power also functioned.

While hunting for lost mines, they frequently crossed the markings of so-called treasure trails. These included crude drawings of arrows, snakes, and horses, all indicating the direction in which mines or treasure would be found. Other symbols meant to go back or follow a bend or look for special landmarks. But Bert sniffed at all such signs.

"If you owned a mine," Bert said to Jim, "or had treasure hid somewhere, would you go putting up markers telling everybody where to look?"

"No, I wouldn't," conceded Jim, "but why do you take so much interest in them, if they don't lead you anywhere?"

"Because maybe they were put there to lead you the wrong way," returned Bert cannily, "or maybe lead you into trouble. There's one that you are supposed to follow" — he indicated a pointed knife blade painted on a rock — "and maybe when you get where it takes you, it will cut your heart out."

"Let's follow it," suggested Jim with a grin, "and find out."

They were on horseback for this particular trip, and they soon came to a domed rock that bulged a few hundred feet above. High on the rock was a painted circle with lines extended from it like the rays of a rising sun.

"That means there should be a mine shaft straight down below," declared Bert in a scoffing tone. "Why don't you climb up and look down?"

"No, thanks," rejoined Jim, "but I think I'll do a painting of it."

Jim unlimbered easel and canvas from beside his saddle, set them up, and went to work. Bert, having nothing else to do, decided he would scale the rock, if only to prove that the sun symbol was wrong. When Bert finally reached a jutting rock just below the crag, Jim called up to him:

"Stay there, and I'll include you in the picture."

Jim sketched Bert's figure; then waved that he was finished. But as Bert started to resume his climb, Jim saw a slight motion in the rock above. He sprang to his feet, shouting:

"Bert! Look out — it's a rock slide!"

Quick as a cat, Bert reversed his course and squirmed beneath the jutting rock just as a mass of cracking stone tumbled down over it, raising a huge pile of dust as it swept down the face of the cliff.

The avalanche carried the jutting rock with it, and Jim expected to see Bert's broken body at the base of the cliff when the dust cleared.

Instead, a call caused Jim to look up, and there was Bert perched in a crevice where he had wedged himself, letting the slide ride out beyond him. Soon, Bert made his way down to the base and declared:

"See what I mean, Jim? It was a booby trap, fixed so some fool like myself would go up and jar it loose. Thanks, Jim, for warning me." Bert looked at Jim's painting and added: "Say, that's great! You had actually put me in it, when the thing happened!"

Bert stopped, then shifted his gaze from canvas to cliff and back again. "Funny thing," he said. "The top of the cliff looks like a face in your painting, but the cliff itself doesn't. Kind of like the old Deacon, with the dome as his hat."

"I did get a face into it," admitted Jim, stepping back and scanning the canvas with half-closed eyes, "but it was accidental. I've noticed this in my paintings, though; if something odd shows up in them, it is generally traceable in the original scene."

"Then why doesn't the Deacon's face show on the cliff now?"

"Because it isn't the same as it was." Jim was studying the cliff as he spoke. "The face was formed by the loose rock that broke away and nearly took you with it. Maybe the Deacon was looking out for you, Bert."

"Or for you more than me, Jim. You were smart enough not to go up there at all. I only hope he wasn't looking out for his mine, too."

"What do you mean by that, Bert?"

"Well, if it's at the foot of the cliff, it's covered so deep with loose rock that we would need a hundred men to clear it by the end of summer. But I don't think the mine is down there. Like I said, some of those signs are put there to trap you; and that goes in this case."

"Only the Deacon helped us out of it. Let's hope he stays on our side, next time we're in trouble."

Jim Gilbert made other paintings of key scenes while he and Bert Tolliver continued their exploration of the Skeleton Mountains, concentrating on the unmarked portions of Jim's map. Whether they went on horseback or on foot depended upon the distance to be covered, as well as the type of terrain.

They were already into their second month when Bert suggested a hike over the brow of Hidden Valley to explore the vicinity of Crystal Point, which was an open area on the map. Jim took along brushes and canvas; and while Bert was probing the bed of a dry stream for traces of gold, Jim did a painting of Crystal Peak with low, blackish clouds gathering off beyond. He had finished when Bert came lumbering up from the stream, shaking his head and muttering that he'd had no luck. Then, glancing at Jim's canvas, Bert exclaimed: "I'm doggoned if you haven't done it again!"

"Done what, Bert?"

"Put the old Deacon into a picture. There he is, black hat and all, sort of a profile, as you call it, made out of the edges of those clouds. I wonder if they really look like that."

Jim noted the resemblance that he had inadvertently worked into the cloudscape, but he shook his head. "They can't be the same now," he said, "because the clouds have kept on gathering since I finished the picture."

"I'll say they have!" exclaimed Bert, looking at the sky. "Those are storm clouds, and we'd better skedaddle back to the valley by the quickest way." He took a look at the map and traced it with his finger. "That would be through Ledge Canyon. Let's go!"

As they jogged toward the canyon, Bert had more to say.

"Believe me, Jim," he insisted, "this is another warning from the Deacon. He's on our side — or his ghost is — because when a storm hits these mountains, you're really in for it. But in the canyon, we'll be protected from the wind and rain."

Bert was right. The steep walls and narrow gap at the canyon top provided shelter when the storm broke. They paused there, on a slight slope well down the canyon, and Bert pointed up to a streak of rock that showed white in the thickening darkness.

"That's the ledge they named this canyon after. Looks kind of ghostly up there, don't it? For my money, this is the spookiest place in these mountains —"

Bert was interrupted by a distant moan that grew suddenly into an echoing howl. With it, the chill of a ghostly breeze swept through the canyon. Bert shoved Jim up the rough face of the cliff and shouted above the fearful echoes:

"Keep climbing, and don't stop until you reach the ledge!"

They were some twenty feet up from the canyon floor, when a whitish shape appeared at the upper end and swelled to a fantastic size as it approached with a deafening roar. Momentarily, Jim thought that he was viewing a gigantic ghost until he recognized it as the crest of a mighty flood tide. The heavens had opened with a deluge, and all the water from the cloudburst was funneling down this canyon in an increasing wave!

By the time the flood arrived in full, Bert had climbed another twenty feet to the ledge and was leaning down with extended hand. He grabbed the canvas that Jim still carried even though it had impeded him. Then Bert hauled Jim himself up to the safety of the narrow projection. By now, loose chunks of rock were dropping from the canyon walls into the torrent that would have battered Jim and Bert into eternity, had they let it catch up with them. Now the rain was coming through the canyon in a devastating sheet, with wind strong enough to whip them from their precarious perch.

But Bert, by then, had found a gap at the inner wall of the ledge. He dragged Jim into its shelter, and they were both amazed to find that it opened into a snug cave. Bert used a flashlight to study the walls.

"This cave has been hand hewn!" exclaimed Bert. "*This* is where the Deacon must have ducked whenever he was seen around Ledge Canyon. Everybody thought he'd skinned out the other end ahead of them; but all the while, he was living up here behind a ledge that nobody ever climbed to take a look at."

"We wouldn't have either," agreed Jim, "if you hadn't heard those flood waters coming and known what they were."

"Yeah, and we wouldn't have even come this way if the Deacon's ghost hadn't warned us by cramming itself into another of your pictures."

"You really believe that, Bert?"

"I sure do, considering that we've wound up high and dry in the Deacon's own hideaway. Why, we wouldn't have even made it if we hadn't stumbled onto footholds that he must have hacked in the rock, so neat like that I'd never noticed them before. That's why our climb was so easy."

Jim couldn't dispute that argument, so he didn't try. Soon the roaring waters had run their course, so Jim and Bert came from the cave and made their way down from the ledge, finding that the footholds were the very sort that Bert claimed. An hour later, they were back in Hidden Valley, which had escaped much of the storm, and they found the horses unharmed.

They had brought supplies for a good three months, which was fortunate, as they still were searching for the Deacon's mine when that period was nearly ended. Bert had planted corn and other vegetables, much to Jim's amusement. But now they had been harvested and were proving a welcome change from a canned and dried food diet.

Bert finally suggested an expedition beyond Gray Dome and into the southern portion of the range. They took all four horses, riding two and using the other pair as pack horses; but at times, the going became so rough that they divided the packs among the horses and led them all.

Their gold-hunting technique was simple, but tedious. They worked their way down what Bert termed a likely-looking mountain stream, panning for gold all the way. As more streams joined the original one, the task became bigger and when they reached the valley two thousand feet below, they were dealing with a small river. But Bert insisted that they keep at it and finally, when they were working in a shoal of sand, their pans came up with a few gold flakes. Jim became enthusiastic, only to be curbed by Bert.

"Not enough," declared Bert. "Now we've got to work upriver and find out which stream these flakes washed down from."

In working back up, they gave special care to little pools and rocky pockets where small streams joined the large one. They were well up to the headwaters and running out of supplies as well as patience, when their pans showed better results and Bert was sure they had found the real gold-bearing tributary. His confidence increased as they continued up it.

"I'll keep panning," Bert told Jim, "while you start painting. Most galoots that make a gold strike never can describe the place just right or even remember what it looks like when they go to find it again. They get kind of overexcited, I reckon. So while I'm getting warm, you keep cool and get that picture done. Then we'll know where we are, for sure."

Oddly, Jim himself was nervous. He stalked about, unable to find the right spot. He had the feeling that eyes were watching him from the rocks above. As a result, he kept glancing over his shoulder every time he was about to paint. He finally settled for a view that showed a high rock at the right and a lesser slope at the left, with Bert working upstream in between. When he finished the painting, Jim called to Bert, who couldn't hear him above the rushing water. So Jim took the canvas down to show it to Bert, who let out a "Yippee!" just as Jim arrived.

"We've got it, Jim!" shouted Bert. "It's panning out like I hoped. There's gold close by and plenty of it. Now, if we only knew which way to look —"

Bert stopped, more interested in Jim's painting than in the gleaming find that he himself had made. "The Deacon!" he said in an awed tone. "You've got him in the picture again. See how his face shows on that big rock, looking down across the gulch?"

Jim saw it, too, and was pleased, for this was one picture that they could check by the original scene. They did so and found that Jim's brush had captured an actual rock formation that resembled a staring face. The hollows that represented eyes were fixed on the slope opposite, so Bert decided to explore that sector first.

"If it's good enough for the Deacon," he declared, "it's sure good enough for me."

Directly up the slope, Bert found traces of a dry gully down which the gold could have washed. He followed the gully up to some chunky rocks which looked as though they had been cemented in place. Bert started hacking away with a pickaxe and told Jim to get another; but before Jim could get one, there was a crash and Bert disappeared in the dust of flying rock and the splintering of wooden timbers beneath. Jim rushed to the mouth of the shaft and heard Bert's voice come up from a dozen feet below:

"Don't bother about that pickaxe. Bring a lantern instead!"

Soon, Jim joined Bert in the shaft and found him brushing himself off, with no serious hurts. Here, the shaft began a gradual descent beneath the slope. They followed to the end, where the lantern's glow showed chunks of yellow-streaked quartz projecting from the wall. Bert hammered off some pieces and studied them closely.

"Gold, all right," he declared. "This must be the Deacon's diggings, but it goes back to the Spanish days. If we don't find other shafts or tunnels around here, we can sink some ourselves. We've struck it rich, Jim."

By daylight, the samples impressed Bert even more. That night, the partners sat around their campfire happily discussing the future. Jim went to sleep soon after they turned in, but he awoke at fitful intervals and always, he saw Bert moving about, sometimes tending the horses; at others, stalking to or from the mine shaft to make sure it was still there.

At breakfast, Bert looked haggard and worried, scarcely listening to Jim's suggestion that they should go back to Hidden Valley and bring down all their remaining supplies to make this their new and permanent base. Then, suddenly, Bert halted Jim's discourse with an abrupt objection:

"Listen, Jim. We've got to go our separate ways, right now, today. We're still pardners, you understand, but I want you to go and put in our claim while I stay here and work the mine. When you come back, bring a crew with you. Then we'll really be in business, understand?"

"Sure, Bert, sure. But why can't we work together?"

"Because we've got too big a secret for just the pair of us. You know what's happened in these mountains. Pardners turn on one another, and that's the end of it. Each wants what the other has got. He wants all for hisself, the whole kit and caboodle. That's the way it goes."

"But that couldn't happen with us. Look how we've gotten along."

"Sure, it's all for fun, pard, as long as you're just hoping for a strike. But when you've hit it — or even think you're going to hit it — you begin playing for keeps. That's human nature."

"You might just call it inhuman nature, Bert."

"Why not? It's all one and the same. You get a crazy idea and you stick to it, like a mule that won't budge, or a bronco that wants to buck. Critters show it and give theirselves away; but humans nurse it like a grudge."

"There couldn't be a grudge between us, Bert!"

"Couldn't there? Hah!" Bert brought a wad of tobacco from his pocket and bit off a chaw. "I've had grudges against everybody in Topaz City — and with good reason, the way they've treated me. Now that I'm rich, I'd like to take it out on those galoots.

"So last night, I began saying to myself, 'How is this Jim Gilbert any different from those mavericks?' and then I answered, 'Bert, you varmint, he grubstaked you and took you as a pardner.' Then, I said, 'Sure, he took me 'cause he couldn't get nobody else he could trust. That's how everybody else has always treated Bert Tolliver.' And do you know what that made me think?"

"No," snapped Jim, a bit angrily, "but I'd like to know."

"It made me think that here was the first chance I ever had to cross up a guy before he could turn around and do me dirt. Believe me, you and I are real pals, Jim, because if we weren't, I would have done you in last night. I was tempted that much. Maybe if it grows on me, I won't be able to hold off."

"And from the way you're talking, Bert, that might go for me. You're beginning to get my dander up. So what's our next move?"

"Just this. You saddle up one of the hosses — the strongest one is Lubec, so take him — and go down to the foot of the mountain. Ride due west across the desert, and straight ahead, you'll see the lower end of another range, the Ragged Mountains, they are called. Keep going, and you'll come to the town of Monad. That's the county seat, where you register our claim."

"How far is it across the desert, Bert?"

"Three days' ride at most, with water holes along the way. Just keep straight for the lower end of the mountains, and you can't miss. But whatever you do, don't turn northward."

"Why not?" Jim asked.

"Because that's where you will see mirages. Nice blue lakes and green woods. Sometimes even towns. The mountains look so far away, while the mirages look so close, they fool you. But it's twice as far up the desert as it is across. People who head north are never heard from again."

Jim saddled Lubec, packed a bag of sample ore from the mine, hung his canvases on his saddle, and filled his canteen.

"I'll take three days' supply of food," Jim told Bert. "That will leave you enough to stay here and work the mine until I get back."

A few hours later, Jim Gilbert was riding across the desert, finding it easy going with a good horse like Lubec, though rather monotonous. Giant saguaros dominated the scene, with occasional traces of a roadway among them. The water holes, however, proved dry at this season. When Jim finally made camp at one, he found barely enough water for Lubec to drink his fill.

The second day proved worse, but Jim kept steadily on his course and felt sure that he and his sturdy horse could stave off the ravages of thirst long enough to complete their crossing of the desert. At noon, they reached another water hole, but found it totally dry. Jim dismounted and took the horse along by the bridle, while they both studied the situation. Then, patting Lubec, Jim said, "We'll have to try the next place, old fellow."

With that, Jim gripped the pommel of the saddle and raised one foot to a stirrup. It was then that Lubec gave a whinny and began to rear. At the same instant, Jim heard a warning rattle from the ground. He wheeled about, drew his revolver, and blazed away at a snake that was starting to strike at the horse. The shots made short work of the rattler; but when Jim turned to mount his horse, Lubec was gone.

Utterly terrified by the rattlesnake, the horse had galloped off into the desert, leaving only a trail of dust among the saguaros and the other cactus clumps. Worse, he had carried Jim's saddle, pack, and water canteen with him. Left with only his gun, Jim stared hopelessly for a few moments; then started on the run, hoping to overtake the horse.

The course led northward, and as Jim kept up his pace, the dust cloud dwindled. But there was no sign of the horse beyond it. Instead of slackening speed, Lubec had kept on outdistancing Jim to such a degree that now the desert had swallowed the horse without a trace. Jim paused, mopped his sweating forehead, and then began calling for Lubec. But his voice choked in his dry throat.

Desperately, Jim plodded onward, managing to call at intervals, but finding the cause increasingly hopeless. Finally, when ready to drop in his tracks, he looked up at the sun and judged that he had wasted at least three hours in his hopeless quest. No sign of his horse; and now there was no turning back, for even if he found the faint trail again, it would bring him only to a dry water hole at the halfway point of a journey he knew he could never make on foot.

In that moment of utter despair, Jim Gilbert had one grim solace, his revolver. It still had bullets in it and when the time came that he could trek no farther, nor stand the anguish of his already tormenting thirst, he could at least cut the agony short. A bullet through his brain would do it, and Jim had heard it recommended as the only procedure for a plight like this.

He tried to struggle on, only to settle hopelessly in the sand that seemed thicker, hotter than ever, its clutch that of a living monster. Then, as he swallowed hard and tried to call again for Lubec, a quiet voice interposed:

"Well, it looks like you've gone and lost yourself out here."

Jim turned and blinked up at the speaker, wondering where he could have come from. He saw a solemn, weather-dried face beneath a wide hat brim and decided that the man must be an old-time prospector. He certainly knew his way about the desert, for like Jim, the stranger was on foot, yet showed no signs of physical exhaustion.

"Yes, I've lost myself," gulped Jim, "and I've lost my horse, too. I don't know which way to go — on ahead, or back to the trail."

"Go on ahead, until you find a water hole."

"But I may not find one — and if I do, it may be dry — and anyway, I'll be lost that much worse — and still without my horse —"

"No, no. You'll find your horse waiting for you, son."

Jim blinked. He could still see the man's face, floating there, but the rest of his figure seemed all blacked out, due to the effect of the sun on Jim's eyes. The man's expression, like his tone, was sympathetic, but Jim could not quite make sense from what he said.

"You mean — if I find a water hole — I'll find —"

"You'll find your horse. You're new to the desert, son, or you would know that a horse will go for a water hole whenever he needs it. Some of them are right smart at finding water, too."

"They've got horse sense." Jim managed to grin despite his predicament. Then, glumly, he added: "Only I don't have it. I wouldn't be here if I did. So without my horse to guide me I can't find the water hole where you say my horse is."

"I know this desert pretty well," the solemn man rejoined. "Maybe I can steer you there. Come along, son."

He reached out a hand as if to help Jim to his feet, but by then, Jim was up and struggling forward. He managed to keep side by side with his older companion, who maintained a slow but even pace, pointing with his hand whenever he wanted Jim to turn in another direction. To Jim, it seemed that they were zigzagging all over the desert, but the sun was lower now and Jim's brain at least was clearer. He could see the oldtimer's full figure now, a black outline against the desert's white.

And then, as Jim was meeting the stranger's steadying gaze and noting the fixed but sympathetic smile upon his lips, the man spoke in his same even tone:

"Look straight ahead of you, son."

A horse's neigh greeted Jim as he obeyed. There was Lubec, at what looked like a water hole. As Jim urged himself on, the horse pawed at the ground, dipped its head, and took a drink. Arriving there, Jim found a muddy ooze that had satisfied Lubec and that the horse seemed willing to share. But Jim settled for a drink out of his canteen, which was still hanging from the saddle.

Then, remembering the stranger who had guided him here, Jim turned. "Sorry, friend," he said apologetically. "I should have offered you a swig first. How about one now?"

Jim proffered the canteen, but the man shook his head.

"I'll be heading along," he said. "I haven't far to go. Tomorrow, you head that way — to the north."

Jim looked in the direction indicated, and the prospect was indeed inviting. In the midst of the desert, he could see the sheen of blue water, glistening from far away. He studied it for several minutes, telling himself that it could only be a mirage. Then, suddenly it faded. Jim turned again to the stranger, only to find him gone. Momentarily, Jim wondered if he had been a mirage, too. Then Jim laughed at his own folly.

While he had been gawking toward the north, his benefactor had left, as he had been about to do. In the deepening shadows now thrown by the surrounding cactus plants, it would be as hard to trace a walking person as Jim had found it to track his running horse, a few hours earlier.

That night, Jim tethered Lubec, then rolled himself into a blanket, for the desert night was growing cold. After an hour of looking up at the clear stars, he drifted into a comfortable sleep. When he awakened after what seemed several hours, he found himself staring into the starlight again; but his view was partially obscured and when Jim saw why, a chill gripped him.

Looming above him was a figure, swaying slightly as though ready to deliver a downward gunshot or a knife thrust. The shape seemed ghostly at first; then Jim's mind jumped back to the stranger who had guided him here. He could almost picture those eyes boring down at him, with a smile, no longer sympathetic, but cryptic. No wonder the stranger hadn't far to go; he had simply eased from sight among the saguaros and bided his time for murder until now.

But why? As Jim lay there, the perfect victim, keeping motionless only to prolong these last few moments, he suddenly had the answer. He felt a light touch on his neck that could have been a ghostly breeze emanating from a phantom figure; but reason told him that it must be the probing glide of human fingertips. Bare hands were locating Jim's throat, so as to strangle him and leave him here, apparently a victim of thirst beside a dried-out water hole. No bullets, no knife wounds, just the inevitable death that came to those who strayed from the trail and headed north.

Now the indefinable touch was gone, and through Jim's frantic mind ran another thought: Bert Tolliver! All that talk of breaking up, of the need for one to establish the claim, while the other worked the mine, was simply a clever means to an evil end. Questions galore flocked through Jim's harassed brain:

Had Bert sent him out into the desert where the smiling stranger waited? Were the two in cahoots, hoping to get rid of Jim? Had Bert warned against heading north, figuring that Jim would go against his advice? Had Bert started an argument, with that very scheme in mind? Could this killer, whose strangling hands were ready now, be Bert himself? Could Bert have come along and overtaken Jim on the trail? If so, how did the stranger figure?

One bigger question shouted down all the others. Jim seemed to scream it to himself aloud: "What am I doing lying here? What am I doing —"

He should be doing anything but lying there, a helpless victim. Unfortunately, Jim's gun was in his saddlebag with his holster, but he still had hands of his own, and they could strangle, too. That thought brought action. With a sideward roll away from the figure who crouched above him, Jim struggled to get free of the blanket and attack on his own.

It was like getting out of a strait-jacket. Before Jim managed to work free of that troublesome blanket, he could have been shot or knifed a dozen times. But all that while, the threatening figure remained immobile, a few yards away. By the time Jim managed to get to his feet, he saw that it was neither ghost nor human. It was a horse, his horse.

Lubec had slipped his noose during the night and had wanted company. He had strolled over and gone to sleep standing up with his nose dipped almost to Jim's chest. Viewed upward from below, the horse's head and neck had looked exactly like a human form in the starlight. The touch that Jim had mistaken for a ghostly breeze or the approach of strangling fingers had merely been Lubec's friendly nuzzles.

Relieved, Jim patted the horse, tethered him again and went back to sleep. Soon, dawn was streaking the sky and Jim arose and made ready for an early start. He saddled Lubec and laughingly told the horse:

"Did you hear what the oldtimer said? Go north! He was a mirage himself, the way he tried to lure me on. I'm going to go by what Bert told me, because Bert is okay. So today, we will go back to that trail and follow it, the way Bert told us —"

Jim was turning the horse southward while he spoke; but now, he paused as he noticed something odd in Lubec's gait. Jim sprang from the saddle and studied the horse's hoofs. Jim's sudden fear was right; Lubec had lamed one forefoot, either during his mad gallop or while pawing at the water hole. It didn't matter which. What did matter was that the horse could not go on, at least not any faster than Jim himself.

The oldtimer's parting words rang through Jim's brain like the clear chime of a bell:

"Tomorrow, you head that way — to the north."

That was the only way. Already, Jim had figured that it would be suicide to return alone and on foot to the waterless cross-trail. With Lubec badly lamed, the result would be the same. Having come this far north already, the only hope was to go on, trusting in the stranger's advice. Jim took the bridle and clucked:

"Come on, Lubec."

They went on, northward, all that day, under the burning sun, plodding through sand that was growing deeper, taxing Jim more than it had the day before. Jim gave Lubec his head, hoping that the horse might find another water hole, but with no result. Lubec preferred to let Jim lead him.

By dusk, they were both exhausted. How many miles they had come, Jim didn't know, except they were too few. But as Jim stood there, ready to make camp in the gathering desert twilight, a voice spoke from beside him:

"Tomorrow, son, keep heading north."

It was the same stranger, with the same smile. Jim saw him plainly, clearly now; the long face beneath the wide-brimmed black Stetson; below, black shirt, black trousers, black boots, all silhouetted against the dimming sky. Then darkness deepened; again, the figure was gone.

Another dawn; another trek. Jim, leading his patient horse along, kept staring dead ahead, as in a dream. He saw a blue lake, green woods, vistas of towering cities beyond. Jim kept asking the plodding horse, "Do you see them, too, Lubec?" and the answer kept coming, "Yes — yes — yes —" in the form of steady nods, the result of the horse's slow, painful gait.

But always, each alluring scene was gone when Jim blinked and looked again. At last, there was only one thing that he could see, floating there ahead of him — the face of the smiling stranger. Then the man's full figure formed itself again, all in black, gesturing forward as he said:

"Keep heading to the north!"

"Tomorrow," panted Jim. "We head north, Lubec and I, tomorrow —"

"Today, son. Right now. Head north now."

Jim was sagging to the sand, with Lubec ready to settle beside him. But he came to his feet now, tugging at the bridle, repeating, "Head north — now," as they wobbled on together, horse and man. Then Jim's disjoined thoughts began to express themselves in panted phrases:

"Look ahead, Lubec — mirages, that's all — all we will see. Lakes — woods — cities — you never get to them. They all — go away — and all you see is the horizon. A thin black line, Lubec — and you never get to it either. One long line — straight across — no, two lines, now —"

Laughing crazily, Jim tugged at the bridle, steadying himself, thanks to the horse. Then, stumbling on, he kept saying:

"Two lines now — a high one and a low one. You take the high line — I'll take the low line. They're spreading more now; one higher, one lower. We'll get to one horizon — the low one, the near one — even if we never reach the high one, the far one —"

It seemed a crazy, meaningless struggle, but Jim kept it up, for he and Lubec were no longer alone. Beside them was the stranger from the desert, back again, his words a monotone tuned to the ringing in Jim's ears:

"Keep — on — go-ing . . . Keep — on — go-ing . . . Keep — on, son. Keep — on —"

The ringing drowned the words, and when Jim looked toward the man, he saw only a black blur beside him. But when he stared ahead, he could still see that close horizon, a broad black streak now, straight across the desert and right in front of him. It glistened in the sunlight, so it would have to be a mirage; but it was close, so close that Jim was sure that he could reach it. Then he was actually there, gasping gratefully as he sank to the ground, closing his eyes against the blinding sun and still clutching Lubec's bridle as the horse stood patiently with lowered head.

A weird wail came from the distance, shrilling lounder, closer, each time it was repeated. With it, Jim was conscious of a roaring sound. He opened his eyes and looked along the line that he had mistaken for a horizon. Now he saw what it was, a railroad track, its steel rails stretching straight across the desert. The shriek was from the whistle of a locomotive that was thundering in Jim's direction, its black smoke clouding the desert sky.

As Jim came to his feet and waved his arms, the engine chugged to a halt. The crew of the work train jumped to the ground and helped Jim into the caboose. They gave Lubec a pail of water and led the horse up an improvised planking into an open box car. The locomotive started, and the train was under way again.

While they were rolling toward the town of Monad, Jim learned the surprising facts behind his lucky rescue. He had stumbled upon a new branch line that had been pushed across the desert to reach the thriving gold fields. The work had been done within the past few months, while Jim and Bert had been exploring the Skeleton Mountains. Hence Bert's advice against heading northward had been sound, so far as he had known.

Now Jim's concern was for the solemn stranger who had guided him to safety in the very middle of the desert, where other persons previously had perished from thirst and exhaustion. But none of the train crew had seen anyone answering to the description that Bert gave. From their smiles, it was plain that they doubted such a man existed.

After a few days' rest in Monad, Jim hired a crew of mine workers. They crossed the desert on a train, unloaded horses, mules, and equipment; then trekked down to the claim that Jim had registered. There, Bert had uncovered another old mine shaft, and soon they were bringing out loads of pay ore.

When the mine was on an organized basis, the partners put a superintendent in charge and made a trip to Topaz City to close out their business there. Stacks of mail had accumulated, and while Jim was going through the letters, Bert entered the studio and stared at a canvas resting on an easel. Bert's tone carried a note of awe as he asked:

"When did you paint that, Jim?"

"Over in Monad," replied Jim, "while I was taking a rest. I didn't finish it there, but I've been adding bits from memory every now and then. From the way you're looking at it, I'd say it reminded you of someone."

"It sure does. Why, it's the old Deacon, to the dot!"

The full-length portrait showed a solemn man with a faint smile on his weather-beaten face. His hair was completely hidden by the broad brim of his black Stetson. Black trousers, black boots, black shirt open at the top, completed his attire, forming a sharp outline against the desert background, which Jim had also painted. Understanding dawned in Bert's gaze as he queried:

"You mean this was the oldtimer — the stranger you told me about — the man who met you out there and told you to keep heading north?"

"That's right, Bert."

"I should have known it. You must have had the Deacon on your mind, the way his face showed in those mountain scenes you painted. You were sure to see him some day and you did, when you needed him most out there on the desert. Seems to me he must have been with you all along, Jim, looking out for you."

"I know he was," declared Jim solemnly. "He wanted us to find that mine, and he wanted me to live so I could keep my share."

Jim picked up a letter from the table. "This came from my Aunt Ethel," he said. "She enclosed a picture from a lot of family photographs. The only one she could find of my father, and she is sure it was taken not long before he died. Here it is."

Jim handed the photo to Bert, who studied it in amazement. It was the face of the painting, the face of the man Bert had known as the Deacon, the same man Jim had met on the desert. "I should have known it then," Jim said softly. "He said, 'Keep heading north — son.' And when he said 'son' there was something in his voice that made me think he meant it. And now" — there was a choke in Jim's own voice — "now I know he really did!"

Judgement Night

Silent, stealthy, sinister, the sea fog wrapped its all-pervading swirls about the slowly moving ship, blanketing it in an utter hush. At moments, those misty coils opened into rifts, allowing glimpses of the gliding vessel, had there been eyes to see it. Then the creeping ship was blanketed again, as if feeling its way through eternity.

For the grip of the fog was not only nebulous; it was timeless. Rather than a solid motorship of steel and substance, the craft could have been a figment of the fog itself. True, this was wartime, when caution often forced a skipper to adopt a ghostly style of navigation in dangerous waters. But for all that, this still could be a ship that never was and never would be, considering how the reluctant fog allowed so little to be seen of it.

A lone ship, going on and on to nowhere.

So it seemed to the tall, light-complexioned man who stood by the mist-dampened rail, running his long fingers through his blond hair, as he muttered low, slow words. Just as the ship was groping its way through the interminable, so was this man trying to draw some recollection from the past that would orient him to the present and enable him to gauge the future.

Although only in his thirties, he had a worried air that was accentuated by the lines in his face and forehead. Though he looked like a seafaring man, he was definitely unfamiliar with everything around him. His colorless eyes were puzzled as they studied the open deck beyond a short row of cabins. He had trouble reading the name on the lifeboat hanging from its davits. Only the subdued throb of the ship's diesels struck a responsive chord in this man's nature; and that, too, was vague.

He was repeating a name, now, timing it to those pulsating motor beats: "Curtis Lanser — Curtis Lanser — Curtis Lanser —" The name was his; he knew it must be, for it was one thought that had come through to his groping mind. But it was only half right, like the peculiar *thrum-thrum* of the motor, which he recognized because it reminded him of a more familiar sound that he was unable to place.

"Curtis Lanser —"

The name would do, because it would have to do. He could read that

other name, now, the one on the lifeboat. So he was Curtis Lanser, on board
the *Queen of Glasgow,* a plodding freighter working its way through the fog.
A ship of about five thousand tons, one day out of Liverpool, bound for
New York. All that sprang to Lanser's mind in a sudden, automatic way;
and with it, a short laugh came from his set lips.

Lanser was alone, very much alone, in one sense, here on a strange ship,
groping for a glimmer of something that he knew must lie ahead. But he
wasn't so badly off; certainly no worse off than the *Queen of Glasgow.* She
was alone, too, and in a really serious plight, for she was separated from her
convoy. Lanser recognized that from the ship's reduced speed; the total lack
of warning whistles from the enshrouding fog or from the *Queen of Glasgow*
herself.

Lanser's first laugh had been guttural in tone and nervous. Now, he
laughed more lightly and with self-assurance. He was finding his bearings well
enough to chart a course; better, perhaps, than this ship could. She had fog
to deal with; he had only people. So far, Lanser had been avoiding his fellow
passengers, rather than have them find out something about him. That much
he recognized; now, he reasoned that if he did not know his own secret, he
certainly could not betray it.

Perhaps, on the contrary, he might learn something from those people
that would enable him to grope his way back to the self that he had somehow lost. Those other people would be Lanser's convoy; by meeting them,
he might return to sanity, just as the *City of Glasgow* was striving to find the
other ships that she had lost and thereby regain her safety.

"I am Curtis Lanser." The words came crisply to Lanser's lips. "I am
a passenger on the *Queen of Glasgow,* bound for New York. My cabin is" —
he fumbled in the pocket of his jacket, brought out a key and looked at it —
"Number Twenty-eight. If there are any questions that you would like to
ask —"

Lanser paused abruptly as a door opened, throwing a shaft of light onto
the deck. A uniformed steward emerged and closed the door quickly to con-
form to blackout regulations. The steward turned, saw Lanser looking at
him, and made a slight bow.

"They will be finished serving dinner soon," the steward said. "You had
best go in, sir, if you want to eat."

The steward continued along the deck, and Lanser went inside. He had
scored a triumph without speaking a single word. Previously, he would have
turned quickly to the rail to avoid a meeting with the steward or anyone else;
vaguely, he could recall having done that up to this stage of the voyage. Now
he had regained the nerve he had somehow lost. But he still was puzzled as to
who he really was, why he was here on this ship, and most of all, what was
the ominous thing that lay ahead, the secret that gnawed at his mind as re-
lentlessly as the ship's steady throb.

The ship's bell rang the time, and the sound had a familiar note that
added to Lanser's new confidence. He recognized the companionway and
went through to the ship's modest dining salon, a small room with a makeshift
bar at one end and half a dozen tables at the other. There were passengers
sitting at the tables, talking in low, strained tones. Most of them had finished

dinner, and perhaps it was the smoke from their cigars and cigarettes that gave the room a hazy appearance that reminded Lanser of the fog.

Like a figure from a dream, a man arose and shuffled across Lanser's path. From an indistinct blur, the man's face became a long, slightly drooping countenance with high-bridged nose and somewhat baldish forehead. He was probably in his late forties and his manner was friendly as he asked:

"You are Curtis Lanser, aren't you?"

"Yes." In the crisp tone that he had used on deck, Lanser added, "I am Curtis Lanser."

"I'm Jerry Potter," returned the baldish man. "We looked for you at dinner. We saw your name on the purser's list, you know, and we were wondering what you looked like."

He was ushering Lanser over to a table where some other passengers were seated, and Lanser accepted the chair that Potter offered. Introductions were in order, so Potter made them. There was Potter's wife, an attractive woman for her age, but with a forced, coy smile that marked her as a former show girl, still trying to play the part. Next, there was Major Devereux, broad and beefy of face, with his back and shoulders set at ramrod stiffness in the jacket of his British uniform. Brusquely, the major introduced Mrs. Devereux, a gaunt, tired, gray-haired woman who did not smile at all.

Finally, there was Barbara Stanley, a girl just out of her teens, who was doing her best to hide a nervousness that the others masked in more accomplished smiles. Like her hair, Barbara's eyes were a deep brown, and they showed a hopeful sparkle when she met Lanser's gaze. The girl seemed on the point of asking some question; then she repressed her anxiety with a quick, almost apologetic smile.

A steward was at Lanser's elbow, asking politely, "Will you have dinner, sir?" Lanser's response, "No thank you," brought another query: "Would you like dessert then?" To that, Lanser's tone became a bit petulant: "No, no, I've told you I don't want any dessert —"

Lanser stopped abruptly and eyed the steward in a puzzled manner. Somehow the man and the situation, were very familiar.

"We've been through all this before," declared Lanser, pursing his lips in a level smile. "It is your turn now, so ask me, will I have some coffee? Then I can say, 'Yes,' meaning that I would like some coffee."

"I was just going to ask you that," said the steward hastily. "Your coffee will be coming right away, sir."

To Lanser, all this was like an echo from the past. The other persons at the table failed to realize how serious Lasser was, so they smiled politely at what they thought was his idea of a joke. That broke the ice and gave Barbara the chance to ask: "Are you heading home, Mr. Lanser—or away from home?"

That was the very question that Lanser had been asking himself, out there in the fog. All this vague uncertainty, the blending of the familiar with the strange, could only end when he learned where he was really going, and why. Home! The word jarred Lanser into a mental whirl, but he sensed that the girl was studying him, wondering why he didn't answer. That meant that the others must be wondering, too. In his dilemma, Lanser heard his own lips mechanically voice what he suddenly knew was the truth.

"I am going away from home."

Barbara's eyes were studying Lanser closely. Could she be guessing at the secret which Lanser was still hoping to uncover? Did she know who he was and his reason for being here? Or was that pure sympathy that Lanser saw in those dark, meditative eyes?

While Lanser pondered such questions, tuning them to the *thrum* of the ship's motors, his problem was shelved when Mrs. Devereux commented:

"We are going away from home, too. The major is heading up a military mission in Washington."

"That's where I'm bound for," Potter told Lanser. "Washington. I'm with the War Production Board. Mrs. Potter is going on to Chicago; that's home for her. We've all become pretty well acquainted so far" — Potter included the other passengers with a gesture — "except for you, Mr. Lanser. So, naturally, we've been wondering about you."

Lanser responded with a stiff bow.

"I suppose I should feel complimented."

"Yes, you should," rejoined Potter. "I'm good at sizing people up when I see them — that's part of my work, you know — and I would say that you are a language professor, say from Oxford or some other English university?"

Potter's shot in the dark was helpful. It stirred some of Lanser's recollections back to happier times before World War II, in which he felt that he must somehow be involved, yet in a puzzling way that he could not fathom.

"Yes, I did teach languages," he answered slowly, "but not at Oxford."

"Then where," asked Potter, "did you teach?"

"In Frankfurt, Germany."

"Frankfurt, Germany!" echoed Mrs. Potter, her tone tinged with horror. "But — but what languages did you teach there?"

"English, for one."

"Oh!" Mrs. Potter's sigh expressed the relief that Lanser was sure the others shared. "You were an exchange professor there?"

"Yes, it could have been called that."

The steward was returning with the coffee; and Lanser's thoughts, eased by his faint recollection of the past, became troubled again, in terms of the inescapable present. The steward's face, developing from a hazy outline, became so solidly fixed in Lanser's mind that it crowded his memory as well.

"I've seen you before," declared Lanser. "But where?"

"I wouldn't know, sir," rejoined the steward, "unless you have traveled on this line before. Only we don't get the same passengers often."

From the shabby, neglected condition of the so-called dining saloon, it was a wonder that the *Queen of Glasgow* ever carried passengers at all. But this was wartime, and people had to take what accommodations they could get in order to reach an appointed destination. Not only did Lanser recognize that fact; he knew that it applied in his case as much as with the others.

Besides, the steward's statement belied itself. His face was not the only one that Lanser found familiar. Those of the persons seated at this table came into that same category. Lanser was sure that he had seen them all before; not just once, but often. And where else could he have seen them all, except on this plodding freighter lost in the Atlantic fog?

Eyes half shut, Lanser heard a buzz of voices:

"Here comes Captain Willoughby —"

An image sprang to Lanser's mind. When he opened his eyes, he saw the living replica. A grizzled sea dog in his sixties, with narrowed, coal-black eyes beneath bushy gray brows, a loose-fitting uniform that billowed appreciably as he eased his broad bulk into the chair at the head of the table; all that was Captain Willoughby, exactly as Lanser knew he would be. His rumbling voice was also part of Lanser's preconceived impression.

"Sorry I couldn't make it for dinner," the captain said. "We have a miserable fog out there, so I had sandwiches sent up to the bridge." He turned to the steward. "I have time for coffee now."

It was Major Devereux who queried in a casual tone:

"Any chance of sighting the rest of the convoy, Captain?"

"Not in this fog. In fact, there is no use to try. I've decided that we should go it on our own."

Lanser, listening with slightly tilted head, half closed his eyes as he commented: "Yes, I would say that you are doing exactly that."

Willoughby gave Lanser a sharp look, then turned to the others. "I don't believe that I have met this gentleman," he said.

"Allow me," put in Potter, "to introduce our hitherto missing passenger, Curtis Lanser. Or perhaps I should say, Professor Curtis Lanser."

Willoughby acknowledged the introduction with a bow.

"A keen ear you have, Mr. Lanser, to notice the gradual speed-up of the motors. You have had nautical experience?"

"Yes, particularly where motors are concerned."

Again, Lanser was reverting to an earlier time, which was coming more clearly now; but he was unable to bridge the void between those days and the present. A few more inklings and perhaps he would have it. Each statement that sprang to his lips so spontaneously was in itself a vital clue.

Now the other passengers were noticing the increased throbbing of the motors. Mrs. Devereux tried to cover her nervousness with a quick query:

"Wouldn't it be better to be with the convoy, Captain? What if a whole wolf pack should converge on us while we were all alone?"

Captain Willoughby tried to brush off the question, but Lanser answered it.

"No wolf packs would converge on a single ship, Mrs. Devereux." Lanser's tone was precise. "The principle of the submarine pack is based on the convoy attack."

The rest stared at Lanser, and Captain Willoughby's narrowed eyes were sharpest of all. Then he stated calmly:

"This gentleman is quite correct. Our chief danger would lie in the possibility of a single submarine picking up our trail."

"That is good to know," said Major Devereux. "We certainly should stand a better chance against just one submarine than against twenty."

"Still, it only takes one torpedo," argued Potter. "It's like a stab in the back, being attacked by a submarine. I'd rather have them come after us with a pocket battleship. At least that's something you can see!"

"You will see the submarine," Lanser assured him, "because it will surface. They won't waste torpedoes on a freighter like this when they can shell us and sink us from a range of a thousand meters."

If ever a face turned suddenly grim, it was Captain Willoughby's. The old sea dog gave Lanser a steady look and said bluntly:

"You talk like a U-boat commander, Mr. Lanser."

Lanser set down his cup so forcibly that he broke it, saucer and all, spilling the little coffee that was left. The steward instantly gathered the broken pieces and spread a napkin on the tablecloth. The talkative Mr. Potter promptly rallied to Lanser's cause.

"Mr. Lanser knows Germany and its people," Potter explained to Captain Willoughby. "He is an Oxford professor who taught at Heidelberg —"

"No, no!" interrupted Mrs. Potter. "He didn't say Heidelberg. He said —"

"I heard what Mr. Lanser said," snapped Potter, "and I knew him for an Oxford professor the moment that I saw him. The important thing is that he taught *English*, wherever he was in Germany."

Lanser ran his fingers through his hair again, his eyes taking on a distant stare. Perhaps he did look like a professor, but somehow he knew he wasn't. He was still groping for his real identity, just as the ship was laboring along its course, searching for safety.

The faces about him; Lanser could recall seeing them so many times before. He had heard the same worried voices; he could even repeat their words before they were uttered. The steward was bringing a fresh cup of coffee, as he had so often done before. The motors were running at top speed, and soon they would reach the breaking point. With those throbs came a distant echo like something from another world — Lanser's world.

Now Lanser had left the captain's table and was with Potter, who was introducing him to other passengers, all of whom seemed familiar. But oddly enough, he could still hear the conversation of the persons he had just left, like a dream within a dream.

"This Lanser," Major Devereux was saying, "I had him pegged for a Hun the moment he walked in. An Englishman teaching German! My word, he's more like a German trying to talk English."

"Then why," asked Mrs. Devereux, "should he be traveling on this ship?"

"I know why!" exclaimed Mrs. Potter. "He is a spy!"

Laughter followed, and Potter turned around to see what it was all about. He decided that it was unimportant, as everyone seemed to be congratulating Mrs. Potter for some bright saying. Then Captain Willoughby closed the subject.

"I doubt that we could have a spy on board, Mrs. Potter," he told her. "All our passengers have been well screened. However, I shall talk to Mr. Lanser later."

That brought an inward smile from Lanser. So the captain would talk to him later. Word for word, Lanser knew exactly what would be said, for somehow, he had experienced all this before. With that thought, his elation faded. Then, as from a distance, he heard the soft voice that he had awaited. It came from the captain's table, saying:

"I am sure we do not have a spy among us, Captain Willoughby. Good night, all."

It was the voice of Barbara Stanley. It struck the first chord of human sympathy that Lanser had so far felt, here on this ship where all were against him, yet where he knew that he must stay and fulfill some mission that he couldn't comprehend.

Lanser turned away from Potter, who now was talking to a bartender whose face Lanser felt he had seen a thousand times before. He passed tables where he saw passengers whose names, faces, even their gestures, were more familiar to him than his own. He went through the familiar companionway and the door to the deck. He was out there again, at his place beside the rail. Beyond was the fog, through which the *Queen of Glasgow* no longer glided, but literally lurched under the full speed of its overtaxed motors. The ship was seeking an opening in that impenetrable curtain to the world without; and Lanser, in his turn, was seeking a rift that would enable him to glimpse the world within.

It came with the opening of that same door. Time and again, Lanser had seen a steward come through that door, close it quickly and then go by, announcing that dinner was still being served. It was like a cue for Lanser to go through the same routine all over. But now, instead of the steward, it was Barbara Stanley who came out. As she drew her jacket tightly about her, Lanser called softly: "Miss Stanley!"

The girl turned as she heard his voice. She must have recognized Lanser despite the darkness by the rail, for she came directly there and rested her arm alongside his. Then, with a slight shudder, she exclaimed:

"I feel a chill — like a ghostly chill! It must be the fog, it's so — so weird. A fog carries a chill, doesn't it?"

"It does," replied Lanser. "Let me ask you one question, Miss Stanley. We have met before, haven't we?"

"Why, no. We couldn't have met; not until we came on board."

"You will forgive me then, but I seemed to remember you so well. Like all the others," he added.

"The others?"

"Yes. Everyone down in the dining saloon. I've seen them over and over" — Lanser thrust his fingers through his hair, pressing his head hard — "because always, I am back with them, going over the same things as before."

"I know that feeling," said Barbara sympathetically. "It grips me every now and then, but only momentarily. Does it seem that way right now?"

"No, not right now." Lanser's voice rose to an excited pitch. "This is different. This" — he paused, lacking words, as the fog suddenly cleared from about them — "this is like the rift in the mist, the moments you see clearly, only to have it close in again. You understand, don't you?"

"I think so. Tell me all you remember, from the very beginning, when you first came on board this ship."

"That's the odd part. I can't remember when or how I came on board. It was as if I suddenly woke up and found myself here on deck, standing by this rail. The door opened, a steward came out, and I went down to the dining saloon —"

"Yes, we saw you come to the table tonight."

"But I mean night after night. It happens over and over — and over. Always the same way — leaving me wondering, groping to find out about myself."

"At least you know your name. You are Curtis Lanser, once a professor in Frankfurt, Germany, where you taught English."

"Not quite. I was just Kurt Lanser, then. A schoolteacher, who taught English along with other subjects. You see, I was born in Frankfurt, and I was educated there. I did well in school, so I became a teacher."

"But you said something about being an exchange professor."

"That was Mr. Potter's idea, and I just went along with it. In a way, I was exchanged. From Frankfurt, I was sent to Hamburg, where I taught English to members of the German Navy. When war threatened, I became a —"

Lanser paused, his eyes closing, his face clouding. Barbara spoke softly, but earnestly:

"Don't try to remember everything right now. Perhaps if you could get some sleep —"

"Sleep won't help me." Lanser's voice was strained, and his words echoed the chill of the fog. "I feel as if this were a nightmare. I can tell that there is disaster out there" — he swept his hand into the thinning fog — "disaster and doom. We are being stalked. There is a U-boat out there. I know it — I *know* it!"

As he spoke, Lanser sensed that Barbara's hand had rested on his arm, the only human touch he had felt since the start of this odd but too familiar episode. Now that touch, like the girl's voice, was gone. Lanser swung about to face, not Barbara, but a ship's officer.

"The captain's compliments," the officer said. "He would like you to come with me to his quarters. Just for a short talk."

Lanser went along without argument, again aware of exactly what would happen. When they reached the captain's cabin, they found Captain Willoughby awaiting them there. He gestured Lanser to a chair and motioned for the officer to stay.

"This is Mr. Danbury, my First Officer," Captain Willoughby introduced him. "Would you mind answering a few questions, Mr. Lanser?"

"Anything you may ask, Captain."

"First of all, would you please show us your passport?"

Lanser's hand was already on its way to his inside pocket, where he went through the act of fumbling for what he knew would not be there. Then, as though he had rehearsed the words, Lanser replied:

"I am afraid I don't have my wallet. It must be down in my cabin."

"We can check on that later," Willoughby decided. "Meanwhile, isn't there something you would like to tell us?"

"I can't tell you much," Lanser confessed, "because I don't remember much. I can't recall how I came on board this ship. I only remember odd, disjointed things, as though they have happened many times before."

"At the table. Mr. Lanser, you seemed to have a good working knowledge of German submarines. Does that stir your memory?"

"I wish it could," rejoined Lanser, sincerity in his tone, "but it just doesn't. I must have been repeating things I heard somewhere."

"Just now, on deck," Danbury put in, "I heard you say that we were being stalked, that there was a U-boat out there in the fog."

"Did I say that?" Lanser's surprise was genuine. "Yes, I may have said it. After all, there are likely to be subs in these waters."

"We mentioned them at the table," Captain Willoughby told Danbury. "It may have worried Mr. Lanser, as it did the other passengers. Perhaps we had better postpone our talk, Mr. Lanser. You probably need some sleep. Mr. Danbury will see you to your cabin. Good night, sir."

This time, Lanser did not dispute the question of sleep. He went along with Danbury and when they reached the cabin, Lanser began to rummage in his luggage, muttering about his passport. Again, he knew somehow that the passport wouldn't, couldn't be there. In the midst of it, he pulled out a cap and deliberately tossed it on the bunk, where Danbury promptly picked it up and looked at it.

"Why, this is a German naval officer's cap!" explained Danbury. He turned it in his hands, studying the insignia. "A U-boat commander's cap, in fact! Where — how did you happen to pick up this?"

"Pick it up," said Lanser slowly. "I guess that's what I did. I must have just happened to pick it up."

"You mean, as sort of a war souvenir?"

"Why, yes. There's really no other way I could have gotten it."

It didn't occur to Danbury that Lanser was fighting down his own doubts, striving to ward off some stark, pitiless truth that was clutching him with unseen tentacles, more potent than the grip of the fog outside. But Danbury was beginning to feel genuinely sorry for Lanser now. He classed Lanser as a man who had been through some terrible ordeal, for Danbury had seen many such cases among the survivors of torpedoed ships. He knew how even the hint of some new danger could jar their minds into fanciful channels.

"I'll have a look at your passport tomorrow, Mr. Lanser," said Danbury. "Just a matter of routine, you know, since we don't have it listed. As for this" — he tossed the German navy cap on the bunk — "let's hope we pick up a lot more souvenirs like it, floating somewhere on the briny."

Danbury bowed out and when the door had closed behind him, Lanser picked up the discarded cap. He turned back the inner band and read the words he saw there, inked clearly against the leather:

Kurt Lanser — *Kapitan Leutnant* — *Kriegsmarino*.

Now, a hideous discordance swept through Lanser's brain. The cap dropped from his nerveless fingers. He stepped from the cabin and walked mechanically along passages and through companionways, his footsteps timed to the *thrumm-thrumm* of the motors. Even the ship's bells seemed off key as Lanser heard them chime the time. He reached the dining saloon, which he found deserted now except for the bartender, who voiced a greeting and pushed across the bottle that Lanser indicated.

Lanser poured himself a drink and asked:

"Where are all the other passengers?"

"They've turned in," replied the bartender. "It's after midnight, but I'm keeping open late. If — well, maybe people won't be able to sleep tonight. They might want to come in, you know — as you did, sir."

Lanser wasn't listening. He was studying the clock above the bar, noting the time as ten minutes after twelve. Slowly, he muttered:

"Until one fifteen. Just one hour and five minutes to go."

The bartender stared, puzzled. Lanser finished his drink and helped himself to another. He was thinking back to the cabin, trying to focus his mind on the cap that he had found there and what it really meant. Again, he spoke in a low mutter:

"Kurt Lanser — *Kapitan* —"

Another glance at the clock. How many, how often, Lanser did not notice. Time itself was all that mattered, and it was moving rapidly. It was later that Lanser stated:

"Ten minutes to one. Less than half an hour to go. Those motors, there is something wrong with them. They sound labored."

"They always sound like that," returned the bartender. "They always sound that way on this tub."

Lanser kept listening as time ticked by. First Officer Danbury paused at the bar and called through the door to the galley:

"A pot of coffee for the bridge! I'll wait for it here."

"Five minutes past one," Lanser muttered. "Only ten minutes —" He stopped abruptly, swung about to Danbury.

"Those motors are stopping!" Lanser stormed. "Why?"

"Just a routine checkup," returned Danbury. "We thought —"

"You didn't think! It would be *unthinkable* to stop them now, leaving the ship adrift in sub-infested waters, where we are absolutely defenseless. Those motors have broken down!"

"They will be repaired," Danbury said soothingly. "The fog is lifting, and we will be under way again very soon."

"The fog is lifting!" echoed Lanser. "That makes it worse! We won't be getting under way — ever. We'll drift until one fifteen —"

"That's what he's been saying all along," the barkeeper confided to Danbury. "One fifteen, like something is due to happen then."

"Yes, at one fifteen." Lanser was proclaiming it to Danbury now. "Don't you know that a U-boat has been stalking us for hours and gaining on us ever since our motors slackened speed? Don't you know that the commander of that sub can tell what those sounds mean, just as I did?"

"Calm yourself, Mr. Lanser," chided Danbury. "Practically all our passengers are imagining such things. You're suffering from nerves."

"I'm suffering from knowledge. I know that the U-boat is already surfacing off our port bow. We will be attacked, and we won't be able to run away unless you get those motors started and give them full speed ahead."

"That would be impossible at this moment, Mr. Lanser."

"Then you must warn the passengers. Get them to the lifeboats."

"Suppose we just wait ten minutes," suggested Danbury. "Once your deadline is past, you will realize how foolish your fears were."

Those minutes were ticking rapidly. Lanser wanted to act, but seemed glued to his chair. Everything about him seemed unreal; but as for what was due to happen, Lanser had never been more sure of anything in all his life.

In all his life!

Could this be his life, this strange existence in which he could not act on his own? Why did he have to depend on Danbury and others to act for him? Why did he have to listen to their parrot phrases, when he already knew the stupid things that they would say? While Lanser was debating those questions, the time for action came. The clock showed one fifteen.

Like a justification of Lanser's warning, there came an approaching screech, growing louder, louder, louder and ending with a huge explosion. The whole ship shuddered under the impact. An enemy gunner had scored a direct shell-hit on the drifting *Queen of Glasgow!*

Momentarily, Danbury was frozen with disbelief. Then he was racing to the deck, followed by the steward from behind the bar and the chef from the galley. Lanser's own limbs were now unleashed, and he was dashing along with them. As they reached the outside air, another shell came whining through the thinning fog, shivering the freighter with another crashing blast.

Passengers were surging frantically from their cabins, and Lanser recognized the faces that he had come to know so well. There was Devereux, caught in a daze of grim uncertainty; Potter, so excited that he was momentarily paralyzed; their wives, both utterly terrified. Other passengers formed a frantic throng, while the deck was bathed in the glare of a searchlight from the U-boat, a gray bulk barely distinguishable in the mist.

A stab of flame from the distant deck gun told that another devastating missile was on its way from the thousand-yard range that Lanser had predicted. The shell hit below the water line, and the *Queen of Glasgow* reeled like a stricken creature. The confused passengers were flocking back to their cabins, thinking to find safety there, while Lanser raised his voice to a bellow:

"Get to the lifeboats! It is your only chance. Don't go back into those cabins!"

Nobody heeded the shout. Lanser himself felt powerless to act, yet at the same time immune to the further danger of which he was so oddly aware. Hardly had the group scurried for their ill-chosen refuge, before a whining shell smashed the freighter's superstructure into a shapeless mass.

Not all the victims were trapped or slain in those cabins. Miraculously, a few came stumbling from the twisted ruins. Among them, Lanser saw Barbara Stanley, and he rushed forward, shouting, pointing her toward a lifeboat, the very one he had first noticed when he found himself on board the *Queen of Glasgow*.

Barbara did not see Lanser, and his warning was drowned by the burst of another shell that found the bridge and shattered it, showering chunks of metal all around. But the girl escaped unscathed, for hands were already drawing her into the partly lowered boat, which was dipping beneath the rail as the steel shower rained above.

Lanser could see the U-boat plainly now, for he had reached the bow of the sinking freighter and was shaking his fist defiantly in the glare of the searchlight. Another shell hit the *Queen of Glasgow,* again below decks. The commander of the sub had enjoyed his brutal fun and now was making short work of the freighter. Hurriedly, Lanser dashed back along the rail and waved frantically to the boat in which Barbara had gone, warning it to get away before the merciless U-boat captain shelled it, too.

Fortunately, the fog was closing in again, and the lifeboat was enveloped in its timely curtain. So was the U-boat, but Lanser was still defiant. On an odd impulse, he threaded his way through debris-strewn passages and into his own cabin, Number 28, which he found intact. On the bunk, where he had dropped it, was the cap belonging to the German naval officer, whose name, by some queer quirk, was so like with Lanser's own.

As Lanser picked up the cap, a final, jarring crash shook the old *Queen of Glasgow*. The ship literally seemed to fall apart, for the whole side of the cabin opened and a wall of water closed in on Lanser like a green sea monster. Next he was tasting, swallowing the salt water that choked him, filled his lungs, and completely engulfed him. He lashed out with his arms, trying to break free as a drumming sound beat through his brain, dulling all his recent recollections.

Then the whole watery nightmare faded, and the cabin returned to normal. The drumming sound was simply someone knocking at the door, and Lanser stepped over to answer it. He pulled on the German navy cap, ready to face Danbury or anybody else. The cabin, oddly, had shrunk to a smaller size, but Lanser did not notice that until he opened the door.

Instead of Danbury, he saw a sailor in a German naval uniform, who saluted and addressed Lanser as *"Herr Kapitan."* The man followed with a rapid report in German:

"Word from Lieutenant Mueller, sir. We have closed in on the enemy freighter and are ready to surface as you ordered."

Lanser glanced at his wrist watch. He blinked as he saw gold braid on the sleeve and realized that he was wearing an officer's uniform instead of a plain jacket. The time, too, was puzzling. It was only one o'clock, yet Lanser was positive that not so long ago he had seen a clock — a highly accurate one, as he recalled — that registered one fifteen.

In a musing tone, Lanser muttered:

"One o'clock. Fifteen minutes to go."

That cleared Lanser's mind of the crazy, confused dream that had disturbed the brief doze he was having when Mueller's message arrived. As Captain Lanser, he joined Lieutenant Mueller, a broad-faced, quiet man who was older than Lanser but lacked the decisive manner that had raised Lanser to commander of the U-boat. Together, they ascended the conning tower as the submarine surfaced.

There, Mueller indicated the outline of an old freighter drifting beneath the moonlight, its rusty hull silver-tinted by the reflected swirls of the surrounding, fading fog.

"The Queen of Glasgow, five thousand tons," recited Mueller. "She is the ship we tracked after she lost her convoy. You were right, Captain, she was overtaxing those motors and had to lay to, as you said she would. We are at the range you specified, one thousand meters."

Lanser looked toward the deck gun and saw that its crew was ready He checked his watch; saw its second hand sweeping through the final minute before one fifteen. Lanser raised his hand, ready to point to the men who were handling the searchlight. Then Lanser said to Mueller:

"A few well-placed shells and all will be over for that ship."

"Why not fire a warning shell first, Captain?" suggested Mueller. "And then wait for a brief interval?"

"A warning shell? Why? And wait — for what?"

"There are passengers on that ship, with women among them."

"Passengers have no right on board; women least of all."

"But they are human beings, like ourselves. So are the crew —"

"And therefore they must take their chances, as we do."

"Not when there is no necessity for it," pleaded Mueller. "We could still give them time to take to their boats."

"While their radio man sends out their position and gives ours with it, as well? Sentiment has begun to soften your brain, Mueller."

Lanser's glare had turned his colorless eyes as cold and hard as ice. He glanced at his wrist watch, saw the last few seconds sweep away. At precisely one fifteen, Lanser pointed his finger, and the searchlight's beam cut a swath through the night, focused squarely on the drifting *Queen of Glasgow.* At Lanser's order: "Fire!" The deck gun boomed and the first shell was on its way to a direct hit.

From then on, the freighter received an efficient, perfectly timed bombardment that rapidly sent her down by the bow. Little figures ran helter-skelter about the doomed ship's deck, disappearing amid the collapsing superstructure — except for one man who paused briefly near the sinking bow, shook his fist into the searchlight's glare, then ran for shelter. As the freighter finally slid down into the sea, Lanser ordered the searchlight to sweep the surface, and he called for the gun crew to be ready.

"They were launching a lifeboat on the starboard side," Lanser told Mueller. "If we sight it, we can spare a shell to sink it."

"You mean that you intend to add more murder?"

"I mean that I intend to complete our mission."

Lanser followed the roving searchlight through his binoculars, but the fog banks were rolling in again, even covering the spot where the *City of Glasgow* had gone down. Lanser spoke to Mueller:

"Come below. We must submerge and continue on our way."

In the ward room of the U-boat, Lanser jotted down the details of the kill and listened happily to the steady rhythm of the submerged sub's motors. He signed his report and turned to Mueller with a harsh laugh.

"Too bad I have no more space on my report, Lieutenant," Lanser said. "I could have added that you are an old woman."

"Because I didn't think it right to murder people without warning?"

"That, Lieutenant, is a question of international law."

"Perhaps it is governed by a higher law, Captain. There could be a special kind of hell waiting for us. Maybe we will have to suffer the same agony that those trapped and drowning victims did, before they finally died."

"I agree. That can happen to any of us — once."

"I don't mean just once. I mean over and over, throughout eternity."

"You talk like a foolish mystic, Lieutenant."

"We might go on trying to warn them forever, yet never be able to save them."

Lanser laughed. "I will take my chances. Go get some sleep, Mueller. I think you need it."

Lanser rose, giving Mueller a whack between the shoulders. At that moment, the whole wardroom quivered, and a muffled blast, reminiscent of the shellfire, came to their ears. Angrily, Lanser snarled:

"A depth bomb! Destroyers from the convoy. That radio man must have given our position, despite us. You see, now, Mueller, why our business is murder, as you call it, and not mercy! Where is that higher law now?"

There were more jarring bursts. The depth bombs were hitting closer. Lanser submerged the U-boat deeper, using every trick he knew to escape the impending doom, but to no avail. One violent explosion made the sub's plates quiver, extinguishing her lights and disabling her motors. Another blast, still closer, and the hull of the U-boat gave way. In upon Lanser poured that same green deluge that had inundated the cabin on the *Queen of Glasgow*. Lanser was choking, drowning as he had before, dying that same hopeless, overwhelming death.

And then:

Green water thinned to soupy fog. Instead of total saturation, Lanser felt only dampness on the ship's rail from which he raised his hand and ran his long fingers through his blond hair. He was trying to orient himself to this timeless, oft-repeated scene, as he spoke the name that was only half-familar, but best suited for these new surroundings. Curtis Lanser — the name of a passenger on the *Queen of Glasgow,* for that was the name Lanser saw on a lifeboat that was hanging from its davits. A door opened and a steward appeared. He spoke to Lanser:

"They will be finished serving dinner soon —"

Yes, Lanser had gone through this so often before; but he was still groping, wondering how he fitted into it. Somehow, it seemed endless, part of a mental treadmill so hideously unreal that it might be the only reality that he had ever known or ever would know, perhaps forever and forever.

Yet time was moving on. Time, in terms of mortal reckoning — Minutes, hours, years. Some twenty of those years had passed, and a giant liner was cleaving its way through fog-bound waters, throating a deep, warning whistle to other shipping in the area. It was the same portion of the Atlantic Ocean where a freighter called the *Queen of Glasgow* had wandered from its convoy during wartime, to be trailed to its doom by a lurking U-boat.

No need for convoys now. How different, the swift glide of this mighty ship, blaring its path through the misty shroud, compared to the throbbing, hopeless flight of the wayward freighter! That was so apparent to the woman who stood by the rail near the liner's bow, looking off into the swirling fog.

Time had been kind to Barbara Stanley. The strained, taut expression on her face was not the mark of age. It was due to her recollection of a fearful night in these same waters, when from the safety of a lifeboat, she had watched a sinking freighter carry her dead and dying friends to the ocean's depths. Tonight, almost against her will, she had come from her cabin to the deck of the liner, lured by her remembrance of that other fog-locked night.

Now, as Barbara gazed, the misty curtain parted. Off in the swirl, she saw the dreaded sight that had etched itself in her memory. There, as real as on that fatal night, was the battered hulk of the *Queen of Glasgow*, her bow nosing beneath the ocean's surface for the last long dive. And on the phantom freighter's deck, his hands waving a frantic gesture for the lifeboat to get away, was the man whose name Barbara now whispered:

"Curtis Lanser."

The liner's lookout did not see that ghost ship from the past, even though it belonged to the present — and to the future. But Barbara's glimpse through the misty curtain of time was promptly verified. As she turned from the liner's rail, she saw a muffled man standing there beside her, his eyes fixed on the closing fog. In a hushed tone, Barbara asked:

"You saw — that ship — out there?"

"Yes," came the solemn reply. "She was the *Queen of Glasgow*."

"And you saw the man who waved that warning from the rail?"

"Yes. Kurt Lanser, the commander of the U-boat that shelled her."

In all those intervening years, Barbara Stanley had half-believed that there must be such an answer. Incredible though it might seem, it was the only way to account for Lanser's presence on the freighter and all the facts that he had known. Now, as Barbara studied the broad face of the solemn man beside her, she was suddenly inspired to ask:

"But how do you know all this — about Kurt Lanser?"

"Because I was his second in command. My name is Hans Mueller, and as we watched from the conning tower, I somehow knew what Lanser's fate would be. Within an hour, our U-boat was sunk by depth bombs from a British destroyer. Kurt Lanser believed that he would perish like his victims, only once. But time and again, I have stood at the rail of a ship like this and watched him go down with the *Queen of Glasgow*."

"The ghost of an unhappy man," Barbara spoke in a sad whisper, "trapped forever on the ghost of an unfortunate ship." She was staring hard into the thickening fog, picturing the strange sight that had been unveiled there. "Yes, Kurt Lanser was alone that night, as he was tonight."

The fog had closed in again, but Barbara was still gazing into its impenetrable folds, as she spoke again to the man beside her:

"But tell me, Mr. Mueller, if your submarine was depth-bombed, how could there have been any survivors? How do you happen to be here?"

There was no reply. Barbara turned and stared with wide, amazed eyes. No one was standing there beside her. She was alone, under the fog-blurred lights that showed the broad, open stretch of the liner's sweeping deck.

As in a dream, Barbara Stanley went back to her cabin.

The Curse of Seven Towers

Against the late afternoon sky, the frowning battlements and tall turrets of Seven Towers presented a strange, fanciful picture of a giant's castle wrested from its storybook setting and transplanted to modern times. High above the ancient stronghold jet planes were leaving long, snakish trails behind them, catching the gold and crimson rays of the sunset, like streaks from a master painter's brush. Through the deer park in the darkening foreground, past the shadowy outlines of boxed hedges and stately yew trees, the lights of approaching cars were following the curved driveways leading to the massive greystone pile.

Surrounding these mighty bastions was a water-filled moat, which gave the impression that the castle was floating on the surface of a dark, sylvan pool. At the very center of the huge, sprawling structure was a mammoth gateway. From it extended a drawbridge, like a giant's tongue thrust from a yawning mouth. Above, the great iron grating of a raised portcullis resembled tremendous teeth, ready to champ down upon unwelcome visitors who tried to enter the inner court beyond.

But this evening, all visitors were welcome. In contrast to forgotten men-at-arms who had once ridden their warhorses through the fortified castle, the present arrivals drove their cars — convertibles, compacts, station wagons into the gaping maw of the great stone castle. There, they parked in the very spaces where steeds carrying bound and helpless prisoners had formerly been tethered. Like those medieval captives, some of the newcomers were a bit bewildered as they unlimbered themselves from their cars.

To find themselves suddenly planted half a dozen centuries back was something of a shock to those who first experienced it. But to others, those who had visited Seven Towers before, this was just the beginning of the fun. They, too, had been dumfounded on their first trip here; now they relished seeing others in a like plight.

Paul Corley, regarded as a prankster by his London cronies, was one of the regular visitors, who liked to prod newcomers with pointed quips. His roundish moonface totally solemn, Corley approached a rugged, square-jawed Australian named Gordon Woodrow and announced seriously:

"You were lucky, Woodrow, that you didn't hit a deer coming through the park. In the old days, they cut your ears off and branded you twice over for a trifling offense like that."

Helene Loland, a striking, vivacious blonde, overheard Corley's remark as she was alighting from her chauffeured limousine.

"Don't believe anything Paul tells you, Mr. Woodrow," said Helene. "We are all lucky to be invited to Seven Towers for these old-time revels."

"And you are the luckiest of all, Helene," retorted Corley. "If the old original Sieur Dubois hadn't built his gateway wide enough for his horsemen to ride two abreast, that hired hack of yours would have lost all four fenders coming through the gate."

Gordon Woodrow, his lips firmed in restrained impatience, waited until Corley had finished. Then Woodrow put a quick query;

"You say revels, Miss Loland. I thought we were invited here to engage in a ghost hunt, or am I misinformed?"

Both Helene and Corley gave quick, hushing gestures. "Never use that term," Corley said in an undertone. "You don't hunt ghosts in Seven Towers. They hunt you. In fact, don't mention ghosts until the subject is duly introduced. Somebody might hear you up there!"

From Corley's sepulchral tone, Woodrow thought he meant the towering heights above and some spectral beings that might dwell therein, particularly as Corley made an upward gesture as he spoke. Then, as Woodrow scanned the central tower, his gaze came downward and he saw what Corley meant.

On an iron-railed balcony just above the courtyard, a slender man with a gaunt, pale face was studying the arrivals. There, the earlier lords of the castle had taken their stance in olden days, to appraise the booty that their raiding henchmen had brought home. This was the modern version of that line of feudal barons, the Honorable James Boyce, present master of Seven Towers and the direct descendant of the original Sieur Dubois.

Instead of wearing an expression of malevolent contempt, as suited his ancestral bearing, Boyce was greeting everyone with a truly disarming smile that marked him as the hunted type, rather than a hunter. The lips that showed disdain were Gordon Woodrow's, as the burly Australian contrasted the massive bulk of Seven Towers with the insignificant build of its owner.

"He reminds me of a dried walnut kernel," commented Woodrow, "rattling about in an oversized shell."

"That's our Jimmy Boy," Corley chuckled. "I couldn't have pegged him better myself."

The last of the two dozen guests had arrived; now a few of the cars were leaving, among them Helene's hired limousine, which was going back to London.

Servants clad in faded, ancient livery carried the luggage past a guardroom, where a watchman pressed the switch of an electric motor that lowered the portcullis by modern cable, cutting off the outside world.

"Our cars are parked safely for the night," said Corley, in his same sepulchral tone. "Just as we will be later, let us hope."

James Boyce had come down from the outside balcony to welcome his guests as they entered the great hall. After that formality, they were conducted to their assigned apartments, with servants as guides. They passed through chambers hung with heavy ancient tapestries, along a hallway flanked by suits of burnished armor, up grand stairways and spiral staircases to corridors that turned and angled through the labryinthic floors above.

Though it was still daylight, the slanted rays of the setting sun were dimmed by narrow windows and stained glass panes, bringing early gloom to the interior of the castle. Despite her familiarity with these scenes, Helene was gripped anew by their weird spell. That was due partly to the effect of the surroundings on Helene's companion, Cynthia Gifford, a dark-eyed brunette, who had come along on the trip from London. Cynthia, who was playing lead roles in television productions of early English dramas, had been very eager to visit Seven Towers; but so far, the effect upon her had been more than overwhelming. It was chilling.

"I actually froze when I passed those suits of armor," Cynthia confided. "They seemed so icy. I was sure that monsters were crouching inside them."

"Except," corrected Helene, "you can't crouch inside a suit of armor."

"Perhaps I can't," returned Cynthia, "but that doesn't mean a monster couldn't." Cynthia broke off with a sharp gasp and pointed wildly at the servant who accompanied them, as he went into a crouch of his own. But he was only stooping to unlock a door. Promptly, he opened it and bowed Helene into a high-ceilinged room with massive furniture dominated by a large four-poster bed, all vaguely visible by the fading light from a deep-set window in the wall beyond.

"This is my regular room," announced Helene, "and I like it. I come here for a rest cure, in case you don't know. It is quieting, comforting, and far away from the city. I sleep better here than anywhere else."

The liveried servant was turning on electric lamps, and although they were too few to illuminate the room brightly, they gave it a cozy effect.

"That's why I brought you here, Cynthia," continued Helene in her volatile but emphatic way. "I felt it would soothe your jangled nerves. Your room is around the corner in the next corridor. You will like it."

Helene waved to the servant, who conducted Cynthia out into the corridor and around the corner. Helene called a last reminder:

"Leave the light on in your room, Cynthia. I always do, so I can find my way back. These corridors become really, really dark later."

Soon Cynthia found herself in a room that was very similar to Helene's, but a little smaller, which meant that it was better lighted. This pleased Cynthia all the more. She changed to a dinner gown, left the room, and closed the door behind her. She reached the corner of the corridor, then guided herself by the dim light from Helene's door, which was open. Helene was also dressed for dinner, and they went downstairs together.

All the other guests were gathered there, and they were ushered into the great banquet hall, which occupied the entire ground floor space beneath the Tudor tower. Some fifty feet square, the banquet hall was more than two stories in height, allowing for a balcony where minstrels and musicians put on a continuous show, paced by a jester in medieval cap and bells.

The dinner itself was lavish, but quite modern, except for a few special delicacies and rare wines that were served in the Dubois tradition. The party sat at a T-shaped table with James Boyce at the head, facing the musicians' balcony. On Boyce's right was an elderly but keen-faced man, whose manner was remarkably alert. He was Cyril Morcroft, former Cambridge professor and a noted historian, whose works had gained acclaim in literary circles.

Seated on Boyce's left was Gordon Woodrow, who also rated as a special guest of honor. Apparently, the Australian had formed a better opinion of his host, for the two conversed quite amiably, a fact that Corley noted and mentioned — in due undertone — to Helene, who was next to him at the long table. There was something else, however, that impressed them more. Seen side by side, there was a certain resemblance between Boyce and Woodrow; but like their general physique, it was largely in the Australian's favor.

Of the two, Boyce was unquestionably the younger, but he looked older than Woodrow. Boyce, though handsome, was too jaded for a man in his early thirties. Perhaps his years as a confirmed bachelor and an incorrigible playboy had taken their toll. His face was becoming paunchy, his hair thin and balding. His eyes were dull and reflective, brightening only when something of special interest snapped him from his moodiness.

In contrast to Boyce's flabby features and sickly pallor, Woodrow had a firm, sharp-chiseled profile and tawny complexion that marked him as a rugged outdoor man. Only the strong furrows of his high forehead and the gray streaks in his dark hair placed him in his mid-forties, for he still showed all the vigor of youth. As the dinner progressed, Woodrow became all the more dynamic, while Boyce, by contrast, seemed to droop.

After the final course, the guests were served coffee from antique pots, and cordials from musty bottles. While they sat and sipped, the servants and entertainers all departed. The time was ripe for after-dinner speeches, and, rather painfully, James Boyce rose to the occasion.

"Many of you," Boyce began slowly "may wonder how I can afford to keep up Seven Towers in such lavish style. The truth of the matter is, I can't. Except for a few workers who keep the grounds in shape and a few old retainers who refuse to leave, all the rest, minstrels as well as servants, were either hired or volunteered for this occasion.

"Then why do I stay here? Why don't I let the castle go to rack and ruin? Because" — Boyce's tone went hollow — "as the last lineal descendant of the original Sieur Dubois, I am under a curse, which might follow me wherever I go, or might even draw me back to Seven Towers."

As Boyce paused, lighted torches set in wall brackets began to flicker, casting grotesque shadows across the banquet table. The torches had been lighted to provide an old-time atmosphere, as well as to supplement the inadequate electric illumination. Now, running short of oil, they had begun to waver. Only the guests, however, were perturbed. Boyce gave no notice.

"Seven Towers is said to be haunted," Boyce continued, "like many other baronial mansions. Perhaps the ghosts exist only in the imagination of those who think they see them; certainly, they have never been known to harm anyone directly. But they do carry a baleful influence. When they appear in full force, it is a prediction of disaster indeed, immediate doom for the Master of Seven Towers, who right now happens to be myself.

"For this reason I have arranged to turn Seven Towers over to the

League for Preservation of Historic Sites. In the future, if the ghosts do stalk someone to his doom, it will not be myself, but the Director of the L.P.H.S., who happens to be my old and esteemed friend on my right, Professor Cyril Morcroft."

The elderly historian acknowledged the favor with a dry smile, while a buzz of interest throbbed through the guests. Boyce then turned to introduce Gordon Woodrow.

"All this will be of particular interest to the honored guest on my left," Boyce said. "He came especially from Australia to visit English castles and steep himself in their traditions. When he learned that I gave occasional house parties here at Seven Towers, he arranged for an invitation through the Midlands Estate and Home Financiers, Limited.

"Since they happen to hold the mortgage on Seven Towers, I was induced, so to speak, to hold another party, which, I must frankly acknowledge, is being given at their expense. This is, therefore, a farewell event; but as always, I would like everyone to report tomorrow anything unusual that they may notice tonight."

As Boyce sat down, Morcroft put in a dry comment:

"What Mr. Boyce means is that all of you are guinea pigs. Guests new to the scene here may prove more responsive to unknown influences than those already acclimated to these surroundings. Anything you may note may prove significant to those who have delved into the traditions of this castle."

"Speaking strictly as a guinea pig," asserted Woodrow, in a strong, challenging tone, "I am Australian bred, and I have a kick like a full-sized kangaroo. Bring along your ghosts, and I'll plant them right back in their proper haunts."

Woodrow's expressed contempt for ghosts gave bravado to the other guests. As they left the banquet hall, several of them peppered Boyce with questions, which he brushed away in a defensive manner.

"I can't go into details," Boyce insisted. "I might influence your minds. Talk to Professor Morcroft in the library. He knows more about Seven Towers than I do. Now, if you will excuse me, I would like to turn in early. This has been a very trying day."

Most of the guests followed Cyril Morcroft into the library, a room with nooks and alcoves that were literally walled with rare volumes pertaining to British heraldry, lineage, and family tradition. There, the professor gave a scholarly dissertation on Seven Towers, telling how it was originally a Saxon fortress that was taken over by the Normans. They, in turn, had added on a huge corner tower which they styled the Keep. At least two more towers were added within the century that followed.

The Tudor Tower, Morcroft believed, had been the seventh and last; but long before that, the original Saxon Tower had been rebuilt. Two other towers had figured in the Wars of the Roses, when much of the castle had been demolished. Since the building of the Tudor Tower, the castle had been greatly expanded, and many windows had replaced the narrow wall-slits once used by archers. But Morcroft continually smiled off all references to the castle ghosts.

"Tomorrow," he promised, "we can talk about them. Ghosts are much better discussed in the daylight. Seven Towers is steeped in tradition, and tradition breeds legends. That is all that I can say right now."

"And all I can say right now," Helene told Cynthia, "is that I'm tired."

"You mean tired of all this ghost talk."

"Just plain tired. I'm going up to my room and get some sleep."

"A good idea," agreed Cynthia. "I'll come along."

Cynthia didn't add that she wanted to avoid that long trip alone. Some of the other guests evidently felt the same way, for they started upstairs in a group.

The tapestried chambers were dim now; and their walls seemed peopled with lurking figures. In the sparse electric lighting of the long hall, suits of armor seemed to sway like living forms as they reflected the shadows of the passing guests. Life-sized portraits, gazing down from their frames, became real faces in the uncertain light. As they parted from the others at a stairway, Cynthia whispered to Helene:

"I'm scared to look back. Wait a moment. Listen!"

From behind them, came the repeated whisper: "Listen."

"Just an echo," said Helene with a smile. "But you are right, Cynthia. In this place, it is not good to look back. That's the trouble with Jimmy Boy. His mind is so lost in the past that he is afraid of the future."

By then, they were at Helene's room, where the open door still threw a welcoming shaft of light into the corridor.

"I'll light you on to the corner," said Helene. "Remember, don't look back. You'll be all right when you reach your own room."

After Cynthia turned the corner, Helene closed her door. Now Cynthia was in a dilemma that she hadn't anticipated. She had left the lights on in her own room, but she had neglected to leave the door open, as Helene had. Cynthia was groping along a totally darkened passage, feeling as though solid, pressing blackness had closed in behind her. Frantically she tried to find her door, but couldn't. Almost hysterical, she wanted to scream for help, but a sudden recollection froze her lips.

That whispered word: *"Listen!"* Perhaps it had been a mocking reality, not just her own echo. Should she cry out now, she might raise answering shrieks from some eldritch denizen of these unhallowed halls!

Chilled to a standstill, Cynthia could almost feel the clutch of invisible hands. She was ready to dash headlong down the passage into deeper blackness, if only to escape the smothering pall that seemed to choke her.

Then, as Cynthia swayed under the overwhelming spell of her self-induced terror, she saw something that made her give one faint gasp of hope.

As from afar, a spot of light appeared at the deep end of the passage. Gradually, it spread into a luminous orb that assumed an oval shape, the upper edges growing hazier as it enlarged. By then, Cynthia realized that it was coming closer and taking on a human form, for the glow revealed the head and shoulders of an elderly man, his flowing hair and large white beard producing the surrounding haze.

The venerable figure was slow and stately in its approach, and Cynthia saw that the bearded man was wearing an ancient tunic with an embroidered coat-of-arms. It resembled the uniforms worn by the servants in the banquet hall, but it was more elegant. That, coupled with the bearded man's dignified poise, made Cynthia decide that he must be the castle caretaker.

In the radiance that now suffused the passage, she saw the door of her room right beside her. As she found the knob and pressed it, she turned to speak to the bearded man, who at that moment was passing by.

"Thank you for bringing the light," began Cynthia. "I never could have found my room without it."

Cynthia cut herself short. Viewing the man's face at close range in the upward spreading light, she saw that, far from being kindly, his features were cold and cruel. His eyes, staring straight ahead, formed deep hollows below his shaggy hair; while his profile, etched sharply through the glowing beard, was as firmly fixed as his gaze. It struck Cynthia that he was so intent upon some purpose that he had failed utterly to notice her and that even now, he did not hear her words of gratitude.

As she watched the figure continue along the passage, Cynthia was numbly concious of a chilling gust that followed in his wake.

She had opened the door of her room, and she glanced in that direction, thinking that the breeze might have come from there. When she looked along the passage again, the bearded man had gone, though how he had reached the turn so quickly, Cynthia could not understand. Nor did she try; instead, she stepped into her room, closed the door and bolted it, hoping to block out those imaginary terrors that had swept her.

The room with its massive furniture and solid walls was a fortress against fear, a miniature stronghold within the great castle itself. Cynthia stepped to the deep-set window and took a long breath of fresh air. She wondered, though, how a breeze could have come from there, for the night was very still. Too tired to wonder long, she dismissed the matter, turned out the lights, and went to bed.

Whatever the mission or the station of the bearded man who had passed by Cynthia's room, he was making extended rounds tonight. Two other guests, Janice Petersham and Della Weldon, were coming to a stair top, when they sensed a passing breeze. Janice suddenly exclaimed: "Look there!"

Della looked, in time to see a bearded figure turning into what appeared to be a lighted passage. He was gone a moment later, and when they reached the turn, there was no sign of him. What puzzled Janice and Della still more, the light had gone out, too. But since their rooms were on the next floor, they didn't bother to look farther. Instead, they continued up the stairs .

Downstairs, most of the guests had dispersed, leaving only Cyril Morcroft and Gordon Woodrow in the alcoved library. There, the Cambridge professor was spreading old records and ancient diagrams over a large table. All these pertained to Seven Towers and other Midland castles, a subject that the visiting Australian found intensely interesting.

"You can't always trust these old documents," warned Morcroft. "Descriptions of one castle sometimes refer to another. Plans of barbicans or sally ports may never have been carried to completion. Often, they were even falsified, to mislead neighboring barons in the feudal days."

"From what you say," observed Woodrow, "I take it that the lords of Seven Towers were as bad a lot as any of them."

"They were worse," returned Morcroft. "They were like savages."

"That sounds a bit exaggerated," said Woodrow, "considering some of the savages I have met, such as the head hunters in North Borneo."

"Some of the early Saxons were as brutal as any head hunters."

"But the Dubois family were Normans, weren't they?"

"Originally, yes, but they married Saxons, blending a strain of refined cruelty with utterly barbaric natures. They thought nothing of exterminating a rival faction, even by sheer treachery. That is why grim legends have grown about Seven Towers. Let me show you an example."

Morcroft went to a shelf and began looking through some vellum-bound volumes. The stillness was deep, when Woodrow asked suddenly:

"What was that?"

Morcroft raised his head from a book, but heard nothing.

"It sounds like the clank of armor," declared Woodrow. "The slow tramp of men-at-arms. Come over this way and perhaps you can hear it."

Morcroft joined Woodrow near the library door. Both remained completely silent for a few moments. Then Morcroft nodded.

"I hear it now," he said. "Let's look into this."

Stealthily, the two men moved into the great hall, only to have the sound fade. Half a dozen doorways led from the hall, so the clanking could have gone in almost any direction. Woodrow, as alert as though tracking prey in the wilds of Borneo, beckoned Morcroft into a little anteroom.

"This should make a good sound box," whispered Woodrow. "If we hear it again, we can probably locate it."

They did hear it and they located it, a slow *clink-clank* from a passageway that led past the banquet hall. The sound was ominous enough to frighten off most persons, but not this pair of ghost hunters. They hurried to the passage, followed it to the end, and stopped short. Here it ran into a cross passage; and Woodrow, listening intently, heard a faint *click-click* coming from a closed door on the right.

"In there, Morcroft."

Together, they flung open the door and burst into a lighted room as two other men swung about to meet them. This pair was armed, but not with swords. Their improvised weapons were billiard cues. This happened to be the billiard room, and the invaders had interrupted Paul Corley in the midst of a game with a friend named Jeff Aubrey.

"What is this, Corley?" demanded Morcroft. "Another of your jokes?"

"It strikes me that *you* are the joker," retorted Corley, "smashing in on us in such an unseemly fashion."

Woodrow softened the situation by telling how he and Morcroft had been trailing the clanking sound only to be misled by the clicks of the billiard balls. Morcroft still thought that Corley had been spoofing them, even though Jeff Aubrey vouched for the fact that he and Corley had been playing billiards and nothing more. Then Corley himself came up with an idea.

"If you chaps have really picked up a ghostly trail," he declared, "why waste time here? Let's all of us get on with the hunt!"

A few minutes later, they were fanning out from the great hall, listening for·the elusive *clanks*. Woodrow heard the sound again and called to the others. They converged, of all places, in the armory hall. There, Corley walked along the flanking rows, lifting the visor of each helmet, to make sure there was no one inside.

The suits of armor were empty; but Corley established one fact. The clang of each helmet, as he closed it, was exactly like the sound of the phantom marchers. That was proven, when the ghostly footbeats came again from a more distant passage. This time, they all heard it; and the four men took up the chase, hoping to block off the unseen procession.

Somewhere they miscalculated, for when they met again, outside the guardroom, they heard the clang from the direction of the banquet hall. They doubled back, and Aubrey reached a tapestried chamber just in time to hear the footfalls dwindling down the passage beyond. He called to the others, and Corley hurried around by another route, coming beneath a stairway just as the tramp of clanging marchers ascended the steps above his head.

Corley shouted the news to Woodrow, who relayed the word to Morcroft. The professor took a short cut to a spiral staircase leading up through the servants' wing and came back to meet the approaching footfalls. But before he reached them, he heard them change direction in the darkness. From their passage, the spectral troop ascended another stairway, and their muffled clangor faded somewhere on the floor above.

When the four men arrived breathless back in the library, the full nature of the chase dawned on Corley and his friend Aubrey. They began to wonder what they would have done if they had run head on into the phantom marchers. Morcroft put their minds at ease on that score. He explained that no one had ever seen the marching ghosts, though many people, over the years, had heard their rhythmic tramp.

To prove that, Morcroft produced a floor plan of the castle, studded with colored dots that gave the exact places and dates of such reports. Woodrow, in particular, was keenly interested in the chart; but after studying it briefly, he gave a disappointed shrug and said: "Most of the places where we heard the sounds tonight are already marked on the chart."

"But not in their correct order," Morcroft reminded him. "Until now, they have been reported singly, hit-or-miss. By checking back on our own movements tonight, we can trace the entire course of the mysterious march."

"In that case," decided Corley, "we've done our stint. What say we call it a night, Jeff, and let these chaps·carry on?"

The two left the library, but Morcroft and Woodrow continued their survey for the next hour or more. Finally the library lights blinked off, and soon after, Seven Towers became totally dark, something like a crouching monster, beneath the sable canopy of the starlit sky.

All was silent during the succeeding hours until the soft light of dawn pervaded the scene. The song of the lark came from the meadow, tuned to the call of the thrush from the woods. Stately swans settled on the wide portion of the moat beneath the Norman Keep and glided serenely along the water's glassy surface. Even the deer nosed from the sheltering forest to nibble the tender grass of the lawn.

Viewed at that hour, the castle was at its best. The sunlight was not strong enough to reveal the tumbledown segments of the battlements, nor the rusted chains of the drawbridge which itself was in need of repair. Nor did the modern additions to Seven Towers show their lack of paint. Indeed, it was difficult to tell the old from the new, except for the deep-set windows, one of which marked the room in which Helene Loland slept.

There, the quiet that lay over Seven Towers seemed to pervade the room itself. Ordinarily, Helene could sleep until noon in such hushed surroundings; but today she was awakened suddenly by an odd clatter that developed into sharp hammering and heavy pounding. As Helene started to spring from her bed, she was momentarily startled by threatening figures in the half-light. Then she gave a laugh of relief.

Those looming shapes receded into their proper perspective as Helene blinked and rubbed her eyes. They were simply the ornate chairs, tables, and other bulky furnishings that gave all these old rooms a somewhat haunted look. But that didn't explain the racket that had awakened Helene and was now continuing outside her door.

Obviously, a crew of carpenters was at work, for Helene could hear the clatter of dropped boards, the rasp of saws cutting lengths of wood, with hammers keeping up a noisy obbligato as the boards were nailed in place. At each pause in sawing or when a sharp stroke of a hammer told that a final nail had been driven home, voices rose in raucous laughter.

"There's another for Old Beardie!" came a rough, thick tone. "Make haste, now — we need five more of these!"

A saw sped its pace to a swift whine. A splintering sound told that another board had been cut. In confirmation, a voice announced:

"Aye, and here is another. That makes number nine."

Hammers and saws were both at work now, rapidly finishing their task which, from the sounds, indicated that they were constructing a crude flight of steps.

"There's ten — and eleven — and twelve —"

Hands pressed to her throbbing temples, Helene wondered whether it was the late party, the early awakening, or just this incessant sawing and hammering that was giving her a splitting headache. Then, as voices broke into loud, jeering laughter, with the chorus, "There's thirteen for Old Beardie!" Helene could stand it no longer. She sprang from the old-fashioned bed, found her dressing gown, and wrapped it about her as she picked a zigzag course among the furniture until she reached the door. There, she drew back the ancient chain-bolt and looked into the hallway, ready to voice her indignation at the disturbance.

To Helene's astonishment, the carpenters were gone, and had taken their tools and work with them. Where Helene had expected to see some sort of a ladder standing thirteen steps high, there was only the dim, empty passageway, without a sign of anyone in either direction. The floor, at least, should have shown traces of sawdust; but there was none there.

Still puzzled, Helene went back to bed, but her sleep was fitful. In brief dreams, she seemed to hear echoes of that same sawing, hammering, and shouting, until she finally awoke and saw that it was broad daylight. The twitter of birds had become incessant from the high branches of the trees, and Helene's wrist watch showed the time as half past ten.

She dressed and went downstairs. She passed through the great banquet hall, which was singularly subdued in contrast to last night, and came into the cozy yet roomy breakfast room. Beneath a Gothic window with stained glass shields of the Boyce forebears, a dozen guests were helping themselves to kippers, kidneys, eggs, and muffins from a buffet table.

Cynthia was in the group, and she exchanged smiles with Helene as they passed. Armed with a breakfast tray, Helene sat down at a circular table set in a large curved window. There, James Boyce was chatting with Cyril Morcroft and Gordon Woodrow as they looked out across the moat to the rolling lawns and distant trees.

Boyce had shaken off his morbid mood of the night before. In the sunlight, his face showed a ruddy gleam, and his smile was genuine. Perhaps his relief over the coming disposal of Seven Towers was making him forget the past. Boyce seemed ready for a joke when Paul Corley joined the group.

"Well, shall we all start lying now about things that happened to us last night?" he asked. "Or shall we wait until the rest of the crowd come shrieking down from upstairs, with ghosts snapping at their heels?"

"Let's tell our own adventures first," suggested Helene, "so we will be conditioned for something really gruesome. Then we can go rouse the others and find out how many are dead in their beds."

"There's nothing really weird about Seven Towers," Boyce said, as though anxious to convince himself. "My ancestors thought they saw ghosts because they spent long winter evenings beside the flickering firelight, with nothing better than a feeble candle flame to hunt for imaginary creatures in the shadows."

"But what about people hearing things?" demanded Helene. "How do you explain that?"

"All the more easily," returned Boyce, with a broadening smile. "In the dark, all sorts of trifling sounds are magnified."

"I don't mean in the dark. I mean in the daylight, early this morning."

"When you were half asleep and probably dreaming."

"When I was as wide awake as I am now." Helene was emphatic. "I've always had the same room here at Seven Towers, and the first time, it gave me a bit of the creeps, but I soon got over that. Today, however —" Helene stopped and turned to Corley. "You weren't staging one of your hoaxes, were you, Paul?"

Corley shook his head, and Helene went on:

"No, it couldn't have been a hoax, nor a ghost." She faced Boyce again and added: "It was your carpenters I heard. But *why* so early in the morning?"

Despite the glow of the sunlight, Boyce's face was draining white. His voice shook: "What carpenters?"

"Why, don't you have carpenters regularly repair the castle?"

"I haven't had one here for the past two weeks."

"Then they must have come on their own," claimed Helene. "They were sawing and hammering outside my door, building steps, of all things. I even heard them counting them; there were thirteen in all" — Helene gave a nod of recollection — "and they were making them for someone called Old Beardie!"

Boyce's face was sheet-white now, the sunlight accentuating its utter pallor. His coffee cup rattled in its saucer as he lowered both to the table. Helene saw the effect that the name "Old Beardie" had produced, and she wished she hadn't uttered it. What made it worse, Cynthia arrived at that unfortunate moment and happened to overhear her friend's words.

"Old Beardie!" echoed Cynthia. "What a quaint name! Why, it sounds like the caretaker, or whoever he was I met outside my room last night. He had a white beard and long hair —"

Boyce's hollow tone came in sudden interruption:

"This bearded man came from the far end of the passage?"

"That's right," Cynthia agreed, "and I saw him very clearly. I even noticed his odd old uniform, there in the light."

"But there is no light in that passage."

Boyce's slow words carried a note of utter despair, like the toll of a death knell. Cynthia's recollections became a stark horror.

"But I saw him so clearly — he must have been carrying a light — but no, he wasn't — the glow just moved along with *him!*" Cynthia choked, panicky, then blurted: "I must have been seeing a ghost!"

"A ghost!" The double echo came from Janice Petersham and Della Weldon, who were just now joining the group. Then Della exclaimed, "Why, we saw that bearded man, too!"

Without a word, the master of Seven Towers turned and stalked quickly through the banquet hall. The rest sat in stunned silence, until they heard the slam of a door. Then Morcroft exclaimed: "We must stop him!"

Some of the group hurried after Boyce, while others found a way out through an old sally port leading to a rustic bridge that crossed a corner of the moat. But before they could overtake Boyce, his red convertible roared out beneath the raised portcullis and across the old drawbridge. Crouched like a racing driver, Boyce sped the car shrieking around the turns, until its red streak was swallowed by the green mass of the deer park.

On the lawn, the guests congregated about Cyril Morcroft, asking if he knew where Boyce had gone and why he had left so hurriedly.

"He has probably gone to Yarwick," stated Morcroft, "to see his solicitor and make sure that the castle deed has been transferred."

"From the way he was driving," observed Corley, "he'll be lucky to get that far. You'd have thought the devil was after him."

"Perhaps he was," returned Morcroft dryly. "In the lore of Seven Towers, there is not much choice between the devil and Old Beardie."

That brought startled looks from Cynthia and the others who had seen the glowing, bearded figure of the night before. Morcroft suggested that they adjourn to the castle library, where he would explain the situation fully. So, a quarter of an hour later, all were assembled in the alcoved room.

"Until now," asserted Morcroft, "I was not free to discuss the curse of Seven Towers. My purpose here was to track down old superstitions and debunk them. But now that the ghosts have actually walked, and certain portents have been manifested, explanations are in order.

"The curse dates back to the fifteenth century, toward the end of the

Wars of the Roses. Sir Reginald Dubois, who had been rebuilding Seven Towers, openly favored the House of York but secretly sided with the House of Lancaster. Among the Lancastrians who knew this was Sir Cedric Shapley, who had once been engaged in a bitter feud with Sir Reginald Dubois.

"After a battle that went against the Lancaster forces, it was said that Sir Cedric and the remnants of his bodyguard fled for refuge to Seven Towers, trusting that Sir Reginald would hide them if the Yorkists searched the castle. Later, Sir Reginald claimed they had never arrived there and that they must have been ambushed on the way. The fact that stands is that Sir Cedric and his followers never were seen again."

"And what," put in Woodrow, "did Sir Cedric's friends do about it?"

"They did nothing, because they could prove nothing. But as time went by, suspicion centered on Sir Reginald, due to reports of armored feet tramping through the halls of Seven Towers, presumably the ghosts of Shapley's men!"

"Did Sir Reginald Dubois ever hear those footsteps himself?"

"Definitely, yes." Morcroft thumbed the pages of a heavy-bound volume, "and so did his descendants, in the years that followed, along with other persons, like ourselves last night. But Sir Reginald may well have had a guilty conscience, for he was driven mad by those phantom footbeats. His enemies had sworn that they would capture and hang 'Old Beardie,' as they contemptuously called Sir Reginald. They never did, but when he was on his deathbed, new sounds were heard about the castle. Those of carpenters preparing the thirteen steps of a gallows for Old Beardie."

Helene Loland stared aghast at the professor.

"According to tradition," continued Morcroft, "Sir Reginald, dying, passed on a guilty secret to the heir who succeeded him. Since then, the grim secret has been handed down to each new master of the castle. Whenever one is about to die, the ghost of Old Beardie himself stalks these halls; and the sound of carpenters building his gallows is heard as a threat of doom."

"And what has been done," asked Woodrow, "to end this family curse?"

"Some persons have given up their inheritance to escape it," declared Morcroft. "One branch of the family changed its name to Boyce, as we know, but that was little help. The first Boyce who claimed Seven Towers as his rightful property was given the secret, and found that he had inherited the curse as well. Since then, it has been passed along in the customary way."

"What if something happened to the owner of the castle before he had a chance to pass along the secret?" Paul Corley asked.

"The curse itself has taken care of that," explained Morcroft. "Whoever owns Seven Towers has one advantage — or should I say disadvantage? He knows in advance when his time is up, so he can plan accordingly. The ghost of Old Beardie and the phantom carpenters who build their invisible scaffold see that he receives due notice."

"And Jimmy Boy received his notice this morning!" observed Corley. "From the way he was driving, he's likely to miss that sharp turn at the Yarwick River bridge. If he does, he will never pass the secret along."

"He wants it to die with him," declared Morcroft calmly. "So far as records show, he is the last of the Boyce line. That is why he planned to nationalize the castle and avoid the curse. But it has overtaken him."

Gordon Woodrow gave a disdainful grunt that showed how little he believed in superstition or tradition. In a gruff tone, he demanded:

"Just what is tangible about this curse? How is the castle itself supposed to figure in the strange riddle?"

"There is supposed to be a secret chamber," explained Morcroft, "which holds the full answer. But I have studied all the records of the castle's reconstruction and additions over a period of five hundred years, and I can find no clue nor reference to its existence, other than hearsay."

"But if it does exist, Jim Boyce must know about it."

"Yes, but he would be sworn not to tell anyone except a proper heir."

"Have people ever tried to find the hidden room?"

"Yes. About a century ago, a group of guests went through the castle while the master was away. They hung a towel from each window they came to, intending to check them later, from outside. Any window without a towel might have represented the secret room."

"But they didn't find it?"

"No. The owner of the castle came back while they were still hanging out towels, and ordered them all to leave."

Slowly, Woodrow drew his hand along his rugged chin and gave a knowing nod to the other guests.

"Do you know," he said, with a slight laugh, "that is not a bad idea. If Jimmy Boy, as you call him, is so afraid of the family curse, why not relieve him of his worry? We can work the towel trick ourselves, before he gets back from Yarwick. Maybe we'll find the secret chamber."

The plan swept the group like wildfire. By now, all the rest of the guests had come downstairs, so there were two dozen willing workers. Woodrow formed them into squads, which he assigned to different sections of the castle. In the empty guardroom, Corley found keys with tags bearing the names of the doors they unlocked. These were sorted and distributed among the proper squads. Some of the keys unlocked linen closets, where sheets and pillow slips were available along with towels.

This was truly an all-out effort to crack the riddle of the Seven Towers, but it proved to be a formidable task indeed. There were actually a few hundred rooms in the vast expanses of the castle, counting all the side nooks and dead-end hallways. These, in turn, had from one to a dozen windows each, depending on their size. So the squads had a long way to go.

Woodrow decided to go to the top of the Norman Keep himself, hanging towels from the archers' slits along the way. Helene brought along a reserve supply, and when they emerged through a trap door to the open roof and its surrounding parapet, Woodrow decided to take some pictures with a camera he carried. While he was thus engaged, Morcroft joined them, smiling as though the climb meant nothing. The professor was surprisingly agile.

The parapet around the tower was topped by stone posts, or merlons, with narrow intervening spaces called crenelles, through which ancient archers had shot arrows from their cross-bows. As Woodrow leaned against one of the merlons to focus his camera on the distant landscape, part of the stone post gave way. Helene cried out a warning as the rangy Australian caught himself. Then, daringly, Woodrow leaned across the widened embrasure to watch the falling chunk splash into the moat, far below.

"It must be deep, that moat," remarked Woodrow casually. "Muddy, too, with quite a current."

"It comes from the river," explained Morcroft. "The old records tell how they cut a special channel to supply it."

"Yes, I can see its course, now —"

Woodrow was leaning against another merlon to look down. Morcroft tugged him back and just in time, as another loose stone went plunging to the muddy depths.

"Thanks," said Woodrow, as though having his life saved was a regular occurrence. "I must say, there is a fine view from here."

"Since this is the highest tower," returned Morcroft, "it should give us a fine view. You might find it still finer, looking up from the moat."

"A good touch, Professor," chuckled Woodrow, "but don't worry about me. I've walked ledges a thousand feet up, and I'm as sure-footed as a cat. Well, I can't waste time taking pictures now. I must go down and see how the search is getting along." He paused and then suggested: "Why don't you two stay up here and watch for that red car of Boyce's?"

Morcroft and Helene decided that would be a good idea. To Helene, the next hour proved fascinating indeed, for Morcroft was steeped in the history of this region. The professor pointed out the remnants of forests where outlaws had roamed; he traced the course of a river through a distant battlefield and indicated a hill where ancient Druids had held their pagan rituals. So engrossed was Helene that neither she nor Morcroft noted the approach of Boyce's car until they saw it tearing in through the entrance to the deer park.

Frantically, Helene raced down the tower stairs, Morcroft following. As she flew through the gloomy corridors of the floors below, she forgot that these were ghostly haunts, as she shouted for everyone to hang out the last towels in a hurry, as Boyce was coming back. Helene reached the front lawn before Boyce's car arrived, and looking up, she saw an intriguing sight.

Towels, sheets, and curtains were dangling from every window, not only from the castle front, but from the side walls as well, as far as Helene could see. Wherever battlements rose above the inner court, the telltale markers showed there, too. Woodrow's squads had done a thorough job, and even now, some of the guests were surging from the castle gates to take an admiring look at their handiwork.

One person who did not admire the sight was James Boyce. His car came streaking through from the deer park and shrieked to a halt before it reached the drawbridge. Boyce sprang out, his face red with rage. To him, those cloths were hostile banners that flouted his authority.

Boyce waved to a few gardeners who so far had paid no attention to the goings on within the castle. He shouted for them to get upstairs and snatch the telltale markers from the windows. Next, he summoned the few servants who were in their quarters and ordered them to do the same. While the flaunting banners gradually disappeared, Boyce came storming from his castle to berate the somewhat sheepish guests now clustered on the lawn.

Helene noted that Woodrow was not among them. It wouldn't have mattered, because Boyce promptly singled out Corley as the ringleader.

"This is one joke of yours that has gone too far!" Boyce fairly screamed. "I never should have invited you here. Now, you can get out — and stay out — and take this whole motley mob of ingrates with you!"

"Righto, Jimmy Boy," returned Corley blandly. He turned to the silent guests. "We'd better all get out, before the high constable shows up and tags our cars for parking in the castle courtyard."

As one car after another left, Boyce stood with folded arms and watched them go. The only man who remained was Cyril Morcroft, who gestured for both Helene Loland and her friend Cynthia Gifford to stay.

"Too bad this had to happen," Morcroft said soberly. "But when James Boyce gets over his anger, he will be looking for someone who can help settle the ghost question — which you two can. You, for one" — he spoke directly to Cynthia — "saw Old Beardie. And you" — he turned to Helene — "heard the phantom carpenters."

"And I," a man's voice said from close beside them, "helped track the tramping ghosts. Don't you think I should be welcome, too?"

It was Gordon Woodrow, more poised than ever. His smile was broad and hard, showing that he was ready to challenge anyone who might object. Now that Corley had taken the blame for flaunting the towels from the castle windows, Boyce had no reason to suspect Woodrow had been the instigator. After glancing up at the castle, where by now at least half the improvised banners had been withdrawn from the windows, Boyce returned to the few persons who remained.

"Now," he said, "I am at least with people I can trust. Let's go inside and talk this over."

They went into the library, where the whole mad caper had begun, and Helene felt hypocritical indeed. She was beginning to wonder just who could be trusted. In that mood, she told Boyce:

"Look, Jimmy, since the rest have left, Cynthia and I are going, too, as soon as we can order a car to take us up to London."

"I have to call my solicitor's office in Yarwick," declared Boyce, "so I'll have him order a car from there."

Boyce went to telephone. While he was gone, Helene turned to Woodrow with an accusing glare and demanded:

"Where were you while everyone was being ordered to get out?"

"Making the rounds," responded Woodrow calmly, "taking pictures of the castle from every angle." He brought some rolls of film from his pocket and handed them to Morcroft. "Have these developed," continued Woodrow, "and add them to the archives of Seven Towers. They will definitely prove what I am sure I saw while I was taking the pictures."

"And what did you see?" asked Morcroft eagerly.

"A towel hanging from *every* window. I studied each section of the castle carefully as I took the pictures. None of the windows can possibly belong to a secret chamber."

"Good," Morcroft nodded. "That should help soothe Boyce's worries.

But I wouldn't talk to him about the curse until he is in a calmer mood."

Helene decided to go along with Morcroft's policy, since he seemed sincerely interested in Boyce's welfare. As the afternoon progressed, Boyce became impatient, wondering why his solicitor had not come from Yarwick, bringing the final papers from the finance corporation. Helene, too, was piqued because the hired car did not arrive. Woodrow, as composed and self-assured as ever, talked Boyce into a game of billiards. Helene and Cynthia sat by and watched the match until Boyce's petulance reached the breaking point.

"I'm going to talk to the servants," he decided, "and have them prepare dinner. We can't wait all night for my solicitor to show up, but until he does, we won't know when your car will get here, either."

After Boyce left, Woodrow put his cue in the rack and suggested:

"How about the three of us going up to the top of the Norman Keep to see the sunset? I can take some good color photos with the camera—"

"Not me," interposed Cynthia, with a shudder. "It's beginning to grow dark, and I don't want to run into Old Beardie again."

"Let's go into the library and talk to Professor Morcroft," said Helene.

Woodrow hooked the camera strap over his shoulder and started off alone in the direction of the great tower. The route he followed was the very one the girls had taken to their rooms, the night before. Woodrow passed Helene's door, where she had heard the phantom carpenters building their invisible scaffold. He came to the spot where Cynthia had seen Old Beardie walk by, and continued on to the far end of the passage, where the glowing ghost had first appeared. There, in the gathering dimness, Woodrow took the stairs to the higher floor where Morcroft had tracked the tramping footbeats of the unseen men-at-arms.

Then, instead of continuing on to the Norman Keep, Woodrow paused beneath an arched opening that connected two sections of the castle. All about was solid masonry of closely fitted stones. Woodrow inserted a flash bulb in his camera and shot a closeup of the archway. He followed that with another from a different angle. Next, he began tapping the wall and running his fingers among the crevices as though hoping to discover something.

As Woodrow crouched in the thickening gloom, his keen ear, trained to detect stealthy sounds in the jungle, caught a slight stir from the passage alongside him. He whipped about and saw a white face in the shadows, its lips spread in a grim, challenging grin. Woodrow laughed gruffly.

"Hello," he said. "I rather expected you to show up here."

This was no ghost. It was James Boyce. His sickly smile was forced, but he managed to back it with a show of indignation.

"*You* put them up to that window trick," he said accusingly. "It wasn't like Paul Corley to take the blame without an argument, so I finally figured he was covering for somebody. Except for Morcroft, you were the only man who stayed around and tried to bluff me. You, with that cool way of yours and that camera you carry. Now, tell me — what are you trying to find?"

"The secret chamber," returned Woodrow bluntly. "It hasn't any window, so it must be deep in the castle walls themselves. All the ghostly manifestations stemmed from here, so this must be the place."

Boyce's short laugh sounded hollow beneath the archway.

"Suppose I told you that the castle has no secret chamber?"

"I wouldn't believe you, Boyce," Woodrow replied calmly. "I would start to take this castle apart, stone by stone, beginning with this archway."

"A good idea, Woodrow," Boyce remarked sarcastically. "Why not talk with the Midland finance group before they turn the castle over to the Preservation League?"

"I did. And they have turned over the castle to me instead. That's why your solicitor has failed to show up with the final papers."

Boyce's eyes narrowed to slits as he groped for words.

"You can't — no, they can't allow it. No one has a right to betray a secret belonging only to the descendants of Sieur Dubois—"

"No one will betray it," rejoined Woodrow coolly. "I simply used part of the millions I made from Borneo rubber plantations to buy out the Midlands Estate and Home Financiers, and reclaim my family inheritance."

"*Your* family inheritance?"

"Yes. The Boyces aren't the only descendants of Sieur Dubois who changed their name, you know. One branch adopted the name of Wood, the literal translation of the French word *bois*. One member of that group married into a family named Rowe and the name became Wood-Rowe. When a later generation migrated to Australia, where hyphenated names are not as popular as here in England, it was simplified to Woodrow."

"Then you are actually my distant cousin — a claimant to Seven Towers."

"More than that, *Cousin* Jim," interposed Woodrow sharply. "I have records to prove that a generation back, this castle should have gone to a member of the Woodrow family; not to the Boyce who later left it to you. *I* am the real master of Seven Towers."

His eyes still narrowed and his forced smile tense, Boyce realized that Woodrow could be telling him the truth.

"So you see," sneered Woodrow, "it is I who should be giving you the answer to the riddle of Seven Towers and the true story of the family curse; not the other way about. But rather than have you thrown out as a usurper, I am willing to let you fulfill the pledge you must have made when you were told the castle's secret; namely, to pass it along to the rightful descendant of Sieur Dubois."

Boyce's whitened lips went tight, as though in absolute refusal.

"It's either now or later, Cousin Jim," Woodrow said. "If you don't tell me the secret, I won't be sworn to keep it when I do uncover it."

"All right, Cousin Gordon," Boyce retorted suddenly. "You win. But you're asking for it, you know — something that will really shock you —"

"I'm used to shockers, Cousin Jim. I've met up with head hunters, remember? And I've given them rough punishment in return."

"Don't forget there is a curse that goes with this family secret."

"And that curse will become mine instead of yours," chuckled Woodrow. "I'm helping you get out from under, Cousin Jim."

"Very well, then," said Boyce. "Do you have a flashlight?"

Woodrow produced one and turned it on. Boyce gestured for him to focus it on the side wall of the arch. Then, in the glow, Boyce probed the crevices with his fingertips, finding the spaces between two special stones. They were linked by some hidden mechanism that required double pressure, for a muffled click came from within the masonry. Boyce paused, brought out a flashlight, and said:

"Now, you try it, Woodrow — I mean Cousin Gordon."

Woodrow copied Boyce's probe and was rewarded by the same click. Boyce told him tensely: "Now press steadily, against the stonework itself."

Woodrow pressed. An upright segment of the solid wall swung downward, inward, showing jagged edges where the stonework had fitted to exactitude. Five feet in height and three in width, it formed a thick slab hinged at the bottom and governed by a hidden counterweight below. It finally reached the horizontal, held there by the pressure of Woodrow's outstretched hand. The end of the slab settled upon a broad stone step that marked the bottom of a steep stairway hewn in the castle wall itself.

"I was sure this would be it," affirmed Woodrow, in a satisfied tone. "This is where the old Saxon Tower meets the Norman Keep. The walls here must be doubly thick."

He stooped to go through the opening, where the lowered slab was like a drawbridge to the steps beyond. Then he drew back, smiling.

"After you, Cousin Jim," Woodrow invited.

In the glare of the flashlight, Boyce's return smile was bitter, as though recognizing Woodrow's mistrust. Obligingly, Boyce crossed the five-foot bridge, stamping it to assure Woodrow that it was solid and secure. Woodrow followed and squeezed himself alongside of Boyce.

"Go up one step," urged Boyce, "and watch over my shoulder. You will see how simply it operates from this side."

Woodrow moved upward, and Boyce followed far enough to relieve the hinged slab of his weight. Slowly, the stone barrier rose of its own accord, far enough for Boyce to bring his hands beneath it and push it at arm's length into its original upright position in the wall. There was a click as it jammed there, but there was a wide space at the upper edge, here on the inside of the wall.

"You simply work your fingers in there," stated Boyce, in a subdued tone, "and pull down. That lowers it again. It can't go wrong."

Woodrow nodded and gave an upward wave of his flashlight. "All right. Now, let's go —"

He stopped short. His words, spoken in a normal tone, sounded like a shout in these stony confines. He reduced his voice to a mere whisper, the way Boyce had. "Let's go on up. I want to see that secret chamber."

Boyce turned his own flashlight upward and pressed on past Woodrow, who followed closely. The stairway came to an abrupt end beneath a stone ceiling that represented another slab. This one was different from the one below. Instead of being hinged, it simply slid horizontally, like a sliding drawer. Its mechanism was smooth, however, for it glided noiselessly into the wall, revealing a blackened gap above.

"This slab works only from beneath," stated Boyce in his strained whisper. "When closed, its ends are directly below the upright walls, so there is no way to open it from above. Prepare yourself for the worst."

There was a quiver in Boyce's whisper that Woodrow realized was inspired by sheer, stark dread. Boyce continued up the steps, beckoning Woodrow along. Then, the two cousins were standing side by side, playing their flashlights upon a grisly scene.

Sprawled about a squarish, stone-walled room were whitened figures partly clad in armor, like yeomen who had been making ready for a last assault upon a foe. Scattered about were helmets and gauntlets which they had not yet put on; hence the heads and hands of the fighting men were fully in view, nearly a dozen in all.

Those heads were grinning skulls. The hands were bony skeleton fingers, some dangling in the hilts of rusted swords that lay blunted and broken on the stone floor beside their hapless owners. One figure alone was clad in complete armor, but the visor of its helmet was partly lifted and hollow eye-sockets glared like blackened orbs from the whitened skull within. It was to that figure that Boyce gestured first.

"Sir Cedric Shapley." Boyce's whisper was full of horror. "And his loyal men-at-arms. Our mutual ancestor, Sir Reginald Dubois, hid them here so they would not be found if their enemies searched the castle. He slid the stone slab shut from beneath; then conveniently forgot to return and open it."

Coldly, Woodrow studied the sprawled figures. Their broken, blunted swords indicated that they had tried to pry open the thick slab that imprisoned them, before death overtook them. Probably they had already been weakened from starvation when lack of air had resulted in their suffocation, for they had died while rallying to their leader's call in a last effort to mount guard.

"The ghosts of these men," continued Boyce in a hushed tone, "are the marchers who have tramped through the castle ever since. They must have made a last vow to avenge themselves in death after they had failed in life, for they drove Sir Reginald to madness and doom. He could imprison their bodies, but not their spirits."

Woodrow gave a side glance and saw that Boyce's eyes were nearly shut, his face whiter than ever. Calmly, Woodrow focused his camera on the gruesome death scene of centuries ago and took a flash picture. Then he asked:

"How often have you come up here, Cousin Jim?"

"Only once before," returned Boyce, "when the secret was revealed to me. Once was enough, but I promised to pass it along when the appointed time arrived. That I have done just now."

"But you would have preferred to have the secret die with you?"

"Absolutely, and it would have, if you hadn't insisted on my revealing it to you. Remember, the portent of doom has declared itself again. Old Beardie walked last night; the invisible carpenters built their gallows this morning."

"And you actually believe in all that nonsense?"

"Yes. What else can explain the strange things that happen?"

"Imagination. It is easy for people to think they hear and see things in an old castle. As for these" — Woodrow gestured to the armed skeletons — "Sir Reginald Dubois was smart to get rid of his enemies in a quiet, inexpensive way that nobody would guess. He just happened to go crazy and tell his secret later. So ever since, his gullible heirs have taken it seriously.

"Now that I'm taking over," he went on, "I'll have this rubbish cleared out, and I'll turn Seven Towers into a real showplace, with its haunted chamber as a top attraction. So come along, Cousin Jim, or I may get absentminded and slide the slab shut, leaving you up here with Sir Cedric and his merry, merry men."

Woodrow was already starting down the stone stairs. In a panic, Boyce scrambled after him, only to have Woodrow snap a flash picture squarely in his face, recording all the terror that was etched there. While Boyce blinked and rubbed his eyes, Woodrow jeered:

"Slide the slab shut yourself, then, if you don't trust me."

Boyce obeyed, then hurried down to join Woodrow, who was already reaching for the finger space at the top of the hinged block at the bottom of the steps. He found it below shoulder level so he went down one step and was about to go another, when Boyce called in a hoarse whisper:

"Woodrow! Don't go another step!"

"What do you mean?" snapped Woodrow. "Are you threatening me?"

"I'm warning you! Don't take another step."

"*I* own this castle now," Woodrow said angrily. "And I'll —"

Suddenly Woodrow was clawing wildly in mid-air, seeking a finger hold in the crevice opposite. But his fingertips could not sustain the weight of his burly body which one step more had plunged downward into a sheer void.

From the depths of the sixty-foot shaft came back a trailing cry that was broken once, then again, and finally silenced as Woodrow's falling, thrashing form hit projecting stones along the way. A spinning streak of light accompanied him; his flashlight. Then — a distant splash from the bottom of the pit and the glow was swallowed with it.

From one step above the brink, Boyce pointed his own light downward. He saw the swirl of an ugly, murky current where the channel from the river flowed beneath the castle and on out to the moat. When no head bobbed above the surface, Boyce knew that those eddies had swept the victim along. Even worse than the fearful drop were the jutting rocks that Sir Reginald Dubois or one of his unkindly forebears had left there for the discomfort of any meddler who sought the secret chamber and blundered down the open shaft instead. They studded the route like the pins of a giant board game, making it impossible to miss.

Boyce had intended to show the death-shaft to Woodrow on their way out, but the new owner of Seven Towers had not waited long enough to learn that added secret of the castle. Now, Boyce numbly opened the stone block across from the steps and emerged into the archway, where he closed the tight-fitting wall behind him. When he reached the ground floor of the castle, he found it deserted, so he went outdoors. There, the solicitor had arrived from Yarwick and so had the car that was to take Helene and Cynthia back to London. But the two girls were still there, looking up at the high tower of the Norman Keep which was sharply etched against the fading sunset.

They were calling good-bye to Gordon Woodrow, but they were receiving no answer. That brought a worried head-shake from Cyril Morcroft, who was standing by. Morcroft turned and spoke to Boyce as he approached:

"Woodrow told the girls that he was going to the tower," explained

Morcroft, "to take some pictures of the sunset. But when he was up there earlier, he insisted upon leaning against those loose, wobbly merlons. If he tried that foolhardy stunt again, chances are we shall find him in the moat. And I think we should start looking right now."

Boyce gave immediate agreement. "I'll summon the servants," he said.

They found Woodrow's body a few hours later, under the glare of automobile headlights and powerful electric lanterns. It was near the outlet of the moat, where the strong current had carried it. From the bruises on his head and the twisted condition of his limbs, it was assumed that he had struck some of the outer bastions of the huge tower during his long fall.

At the coroner's inquest held in Yarwick, the verdict was death by misadventure. Testimony given by Helene, Cynthia, and Morcroft was substantiated by the recovery of Woodrow's camera with his body. Examination of the film showed that four pictures had been taken. The water had ruined the negatives so they were no more than a blur, but it seemed obvious that Woodrow had been taking photos of the sunset, when he must have leaned too heavily on a merlon.

Nobody asked James Boyce where he had been while Woodrow was up on the tower. For Boyce was a big loser by Woodrow's death. It turned out that Woodrow had bought Seven Towers at a higher price than the League for Preservation of Historic Sites had offered. Because of Woodrow's death, the sale was nullified and the League acquired the castle at the original figure.

Visitors to Seven Towers now will find that it is a national museum, with Cyril Morcroft as its resident curator. He knows everything about the castle's history and can trace the genealogy of its owners from the original Sieur Dubois on down. Morcroft is convinced that James Boyce escaped the curse of Seven Towers, because he was never the true master of the castle. That title belonged to Gordon Woodrow, both by right of heritage and purchase, at the time when Old Beardie last walked and the phantom carpenters built their invisible scaffold. So it was Woodrow's death that those weird happenings had presaged.

Now that Seven Towers has passed from its hereditary line, the curse must have been lifted, for Old Beardie has made no new appearance nor have the unseen carpenters rendered another audition. But on occasional nights, whn all is very quiet, the tramp of phantom men-at-arms can still be heard. Always, Morcroft listens, for — as he likes to relate — he once tracked those ghostly marchers back to their starting point, hoping he might discover a secret chamber.

But now, Morcroft has given up that quest. Among his prized possessions is a set of photographs taken by Woodrow only a few hours before he met his doom. Those pictures show every window of Seven Towers flaunting towel, pillowcase, or some equivalent emblem, accounting for every room in the castle.

So, whatever doubts may surround the legends of Seven Towers, Cyril Morcroft is definitely positive on two points: One, that Gordon Woodrow fell to his death from the parapet of the Norman Keep; the other, that the castle has no secret chamber.

The Tiger God

This is the story of the Tiger God as Harold Graylock told it. The story must be true, for Graylock not only witnessed many of the things he told about; he was in at the kill and could produce sworn affidavits. As for the other portions of the strange tale, they fitted the pattern like the missing pieces of a jigsaw puzzle.

It began at the great British Empire Exhibition held at Wembley in London, in 1924. There Graylock saw some fine displays of historic diamonds from India, and he also watched a clever show put on by a troupe of Hindu magicians. So he went to India to see if he could buy rare diamonds for the American market and also to look for even better magicians, figuring that they would be a sensation throughout the United States.

In big cities of India, Graylock met with double disappointment. He saw little that was worth while in diamonds and was told that he would have to deal with native princes who had hoards of such gems. As for the street corner magicians, or *jadoo wallahs* as they were called, they were far inferior to the troupe that had gone to Wembley.

Graylock heard talk of remarkable *yogis* who lived in Himalayan caves and floated in mid-air when the mood seized them, but they were hard to find. He also learned of an in-between group called *fakirs,* more clever than the jadoo wallahs and more worldly than the yogis. But they worked only for the privileged classes, not for the street corner trade. They were pampered in the palaces of the princes, where gates were hard to crash.

Then Graylock learned of the Rajah of Bildapore, the kindly ruler of a tiny domain that occupied only about a dozen square miles. Most of it, however, was an actual diamond mine, so the rajah had an abundance of such gems. His palace also was always open to mendicants and holy men who made pilgrimages to Benares and other sacred places, while troops of fakirs often stopped there.

So Graylock took a train for Bildapore, which was no more than a flag-stop on a branch line. Dressed in tropical white suit and pith helmet, he arrived at the palace and was ushered into the presence of the Rajah of Bildapore, a handsome, bearded man of middle age, whose vigor belied his years. A hunter and sportsman, he rated as the best rifle shot in that part of India, though he had to travel outside his limited domain to get at wild game.

Even when receiving visitors, the rajah wore a simple native costume, with only one diamond in his turban and another on a chain around his neck. With him was his daughter, the Princess Halina, whose large, dark eyes smiled a welcome though the lips of her perfect oval face formed an expressionless straight line. Halina wore diamond earrings, but the stones, though perfectly matched, were small, while her bracelets were plain gold bands.

The rajah's secretary, Shalbar, was a man in his early thirties, who wore a conservative English business suit like some underclerk in an obscure government office. However, his military haircut and short-clipped mustache gave him an air of authority and his keen eyes sized up people in one quick glance. Shalbar applied that process to Graylock.

A big, bluff, friendly man of thirty-five, Graylock had a know-it-all manner that could ruffle people. But he was quick to soft-pedal that boisterous mood, showing courtesy and appreciation that won people over because they had misjudged him. To the Rajah of Bildapore, Graylock delivered a speech so well rehearsed that it sounded natural.

"All over the world," Graylock declared, "I have seen diamonds stolen from one set of crown jewels and placed in another. I have seen fine stones cut into smaller ones to satisfy some whim. I have seen diamonds with curses, their brilliance wasted because of the greed that had tarnished them. So I came to Bildapore because here alone, there are diamonds which have been mined, kept and cherished by their rightful owners and their descendants. All that are a real part of your family heritage should stay here. But if you can spare any for true diamond lovers in other countries, I should like to place them as your agent."

"Mr. Graylock," returned the rajah, in a heartfelt tone, "many people have wanted to exploit my diamonds for cold, base profit. To meet someone like yourself — a man who feels as I do — is welcome indeed. This will take thinking, before I can give an answer. If I could make it worth your while to stay here for an extended visit, I should be overjoyed."

"Your Highness," Graylock replied smoothly, "I have been searching for higher things in the field of Oriental magic. I have heard that there are fakirs whose skill far exceeds the disappointing tricks of the jadoo wallahs I have been told that such fakirs often come here, as do other mystics."

The rajah stroked his beard, then turned to Shalbar:

"Send for Kalma, the fakir who performs real jadoo. He said he would undergo *samadhi* whenever we asked. Now we can put him to that test." Then to Graylock, the rajah explained: "Samadhi is a form of suspended animation. Through such power, a fakir like Kalma can remain buried alive for a month or more."

It took several days to locate Kalma. Meanwhile, Graylock saw other mystics at work, if it could be called such. One was Bardu, a thin, scrawny, bearded man who wore only a loin cloth and sat cross-legged in a low alcove at the end of the palace courtyard. Bardu's eyes had a faraway stare, and his lips were always moving very slightly.

"Bardu is an adept," stated the rajah, "who seldom leaves this niche. He subsists on very little food or water and he remains in *padmasana,* the lotus posture in which you now see him. He recites *mantras* or verses. Through mantra yoga,·he can attain samadhi, the sublime state that frees the mind from the body."

Graylock felt that Bardu might already have attained samadhi, for the adept paid no attention to the introduction. But Graylock maintained a discreet silence, while the rajah pointed out other mystics who were practicing *hatha yoga,* as he termed it. One was combining the lotus posture with a headstand; another was gripping his ankles with his hands and rocking on his stomach. The rajah had names for such poses and gave the lesser yogis his approval, though Bardu was the only one who rated as an adept in the rajah's estimate.

Graylock also saw *sadhus* and other ascetics who lay on beds of spikes or hung head down over smoldering fires. Some were crawling like inchworms, simply stopping off at the rajah's palace, during their creeping pilgrimage. The Rajah of Bildapore pitied such sadhus more than he approved them.

"Self-torture is not the true path to the light," he declared, "but it does show subjugation of worldly desire, which is the first step to something higher. To their minds, each moment of torture is a precious gem."

That made Graylock think of diamonds, though he carefully avoided mentioning them. One day, however, the rajah brought up the subject himself.

"I am saving my wealth for my people," he said. "The diamonds that I have inherited belong equally to the descendants of the men who minded them and to my other loyal subjects. I am keeping them in a secret repository to which two men alone have access: Myself and my faithful secretary, Shalbar."

That explained why Shalbar had been suspicious of Graylock at the start. But by now, Graylock and Shalbar had become great friends. They had found that both had served in France during World War I, Graylock with the American army and Shalbar with the British. Also, they were both fond of pets, and Graylock became chums with a mongoose named Juju which spent much of its time on Shalbar's shoulder, except when it was chasing cobras and killing them. Juju soon began jumping on Graylock's shoulder, too.

Then came the big day when Kalma the Fakir arrived at the palace with a troupe of assistants. Though attired in simple robe and plain turban, Kalma was tall and imposing, with hypnotic eyes and a gleaming smile. Graylock was disappointed, though, when Kalma began his show with the Basket Trick, in which he pushed a boy down into an oval basket; then squatted in the basket himself, and finally thrust a sword through it to prove that the boy was gone.

"I've seen that before," Graylock told Shalbar. "The boy coils inside the basket, and the fakir takes care not to stab him. It's a very old trick."

"You think so?" queried Shalbar. "Watch what Kalma does next."

The fakir was peering into the basket as though wondering where the boy could have gone. Suddenly, he lifted the basket with one hand, so he could look beneath it and sweep the solid tiling of the courtyard with his other hand. He then slammed down the basket, spread a cloth over it, whipped away the covering — and there was the boy, standing in the basket.

"But how could he pick up the basket?" sputtered Graylock. "With the boy in it, Kalma couldn't possibly have lifted that weight with one hand!"

By then, Kalma was beginning another trick. In a corner of the courtyard where the earth was deep, he set up a little tent formed by three sticks and a cloth. Beneath, he planted a mango seed, which first grew to a sprout, then to a small bush.

"I know that one," said Graylock. "I saw it in Bombay. He poked in a sprout, then a mango branch, from those cloths that are lying all about—"

Graylock stopped abruptly. By now Kalma's assistants were raising longer poles and using all the cloths to cover them. Green branches sprouted from the top of the huge tent, and the cloths scattered like a bursting cocoon, revealing a twelve-foot mango tree. The rajah turned to Graylock and told him:

"You will find that the roots are firmly planted as with all Kalma's trees. But now you will see something still more wonderful — the fabled Rope Trick!"

Kalma took the end of a coil of rope and flung it some thirty feet in air where it remained mysteriously suspended. He shouted for the boy, who came running into the courtyard and climbed the rope like a monkey to the level of the palace roof, which Graylock noted was three stories high. Kalma gave a loud cry and a handclap. The boy vanished instantly, and the rope plopped down to the courtyard, while Graylock stared up at the cloudless blue sky and the brilliant sunlight that showed the weaving leaves of palm trees, nothing more!

That evening, the Rajah of Bildapore insisted that Kalma's mysteries depended upon a subtle force called the *kundalini,* which awakened the *chakras* or psychic centers of the body, and developed hidden powers. These included *laghima,* the ability to reduce weight to nothing; that was how Kalma lifted the basket. Another was *ishita,* the creation by thought alone, which accounted for the mango tree. The Rope Trick, the rajah said, was due either to *prapti,* the power of instantaneous travel, or to *prakamya,* a form of instant realization of whatever a person wanted.

Juju, the mongoose, interrupted the rajah's dissertation by a sudden chatter from Shalbar's shoulder. Everyone looked toward the door and there stood Kalma himself. The fakir bowed to the rajah; then stated in an even tone:

"Tonight, while I was in deep contemplation, I had visions of the very near future. I have come here to reveal them. First I saw a long table — with several men — some in uniform. Beyond were windows — through them I saw a wall — a gate. I heard a voice — calling for the Rajah of Bildapore —"

"The council chamber at Delhi!" exclaimed the rajah. "They must want me there. I shall get ready to leave as soon as official word arrives."

"You cannot go to Delhi," declared Kalma firmly. "Something more important demands your presence here."

"But what could be more important than the council?"

"In my second vision" — Kalma resumed his slow tone — "I saw people running from huts. I heard them cry, 'Bagh Zalum!' And I saw a watchman — lying dead, a pool of blood beside him. I saw the headman of a village, saying, 'Bagh Zalum!' — and again the people shouted in terror, 'Bagh Zalum — the Tiger God — save us from him!' Then the vision faded and I saw no more."

For long moments, the Rajah of Bildapore sat grimly silent. Then he declared:

"I have heard of Bagh Zalum, a tyrant among tigers, so bold, so deadly that there is said to be a secret cult that worships him as a Tiger God. This vision of Kalma's can only mean that Bagh Zalum now threatens my domain. Whether he is a killer tiger or an evil spirit, it is my duty to protect my people from him." The rajah turned to Shalbar and told the solemn-faced secretary: "When the summons comes from Delhi, I shall send you in my stead, while I stay here and prepare to deal with Bagh Zalum, the Tiger God."

Graylock was astonished at the way the rajah accepted Kalma's vision as established fact; but when he thought back to the wonders that he himself had seen the fakir perform, he decided that Kalma might be capable of anything. Later, Graylock broached that point to Shalbar, who agreed without the slightest reservation.

"All that the rajah said about Kalma's power is true," asserted Shalbar, "and more besides. His visions never fail, as you will learn."

The next morning, Graylock saw Kalma perform more wonders. The fakir breathed on a stone and it became a live baby chicken. He made more stones come alive, until he had a flock of chicks running about the courtyard. He placed them in a small basket, inverted it — and instead of the chicks, out came a horde of young, hissing snakes, that made for cracks in the tiling before Juju could spring from Shalbar's shoulder and catch them.

The Rajah of Bildapore attributed that to the power of *vashita*, through which inanimate objects could be imbued with life and changed from one form to another. Also, through such power, objects could be moved without touching them.

Kalma proved that by waving his hands toward a huge water jar that immediately wobbled and then jounced itself all about the courtyard. As the great jar rocked past Bardu, who was seated in his niche, Graylock saw the old adept's stare turn into a glare of disapproval. After the jar finally stopped over by the mango tree and Kalma had departed with a bow, Graylock asked the rajah:

"What about an adept like Bardu? Why does he just sit and watch? Why can't he perform miracles far beyond Kalma's?"

"He can," rejoined the rajah. "Through laghima, Bardu could float in mid-air, retaining his lotus posture. That is a common practice among the *mahatmas* in the Himalayas, who also utilize vashita to drive wild animals away from their caves. But a true mahatma reserves these forces for his development or for self-protection; never as a public show. Instead of diverging from the main path by following such branches, the true adept like Bardu continues his upward progress to samadhi, the highest bough of the mystical tree called yoga."

"Then Kalma is one who preferred to develop his lesser forces?"

"Exactly, but he has gone far because he has worked for good instead of gain. Kalma became a fakir to convince skeptics, like you, that powers of yoga do exist. If he worked for gain, the good would be turned to evil, as wine is turned to vinegar." The rajah gave a convulsive shudder. Then: "But do not worry, Kalma would never debase his art by accepting even a rupee for a performance."

That wilted Graylock's hope of taking Kalma back to America and having him perform the genuine Indian Rope Trick in big outdoor stadiums. Instead, Graylock decided to concentrate on the diamond business. That same afternoon, he was amazed when an official telegram arrived from Delhi, fulfilling Kalma's first prophecy. It stated that the Rajah of Bildapore or a "fully accredited representative" was needed at an important conference. That special phrase meant that Shalbar could go instead of the rajah, as Kalma had recommended.

Orders were given to flag the one daily train that passed through Bildapore, and the rajah sent Shalbar to the station in the royal car, a shiny new Model-T Ford touring car, which was also the only automobile in Bildapore. Shalbar, about to leave, shook hands with Graylock, and remarked:

"If you aren't going on that tiger hunt, why don't you take charge of Juju? The little beggar is moping in my room and needs a friend like you. He will perch on your shoulder by day and sleep on your bed by night, so you won't be bothered by cobras. They stay far away from a mongoose."

The royal car drove away, and Graylock went to find the moping mongoose. Juju followed Graylock immediately, and slept on his bed that night. Next morning, they had a late breakfast together, with Juju nibbling biscuits that Graylock offered him. Meanwhile, a loud shouting began in the courtyard, so Graylock went to the window and saw a group of excited natives, bowing, kneeling and appealing to the rajah, while Princess Halina stood silently by. Graylock asked the *chokra,* or houseboy, to interpret what was being said.

"They are from an outlying village," informed the chokra, "near the great game preserve where His Highness often hunts. Last night, they had a tiger scare and they found a watchman dead at the crossroads."

Graylock heard the repeated cry, "Bagh Zalum! Bagh Zalum!" proving that the villagers had already identified the killer as the much-feared Tiger God. Kalma's second vision had thus been fulfilled; and Graylock noticed that the fakir had arrived in the courtyard and was standing beside the rajah, as if eager to take credit for his prophetic skill. Then a group of men came through an archway, all carrying rifles. The villagers changed their cry to "Nayudu! Nayudu!" Graylock turned to the houseboy and asked:

"What is Nayudu? Another killer tiger?"

"No, Sahib Graylock. Nayudu is a tiger killer."

"What sort of double talk is this? A killer tiger — a tiger killer — I see! You mean that Nayudu kills tigers. That makes him a hunter."

"Yes, sahib." The chokra pointed to a big man who was talking to the rajah. "That is Nayudu, the chief *shikari,* or hunter. The villagers love him."

Nayudu soon made arrangements, which the chokra translated:

"The villagers will work as bearers. They will carry supplies far into the jungle and build *machans,* or high platforms in trees from which the shikaris can shoot. They will serve as beaters to drive tigers from the jungle. If elephants are used in the hunt, the villagers will act as *satmans,* men with spears who follow on foot. They are all eager to get rid of Bagh Zalum."

Later, the rajah summoned Graylock and introduced him to a heavy, broad-faced Hindu named Chopra, who was an important *zamindar,* or land owner.

"Chopra will take charge of the palace until Shalbar returns," declared the rajah, "but I would like you to supervise Kalma's living burial, or samadhi, and keep a complete record of every detail while I am away."

Graylock agreed with a bow, and he received an appreciative smile not only from the rajah, but from the Princess Halina, who was thus freed of responsibility during her father's absence.

Now Kalma approached the rajah and placed a token in his hand, a flat disk of metal, with a yellowish gem set in its center.

"This is a *kavacha* talisman," the fakir told the rajah. "Its metal is simply iron, because that has long been recognized as the great protector against wild beasts. The stone in the center is,topaz, the color of a tiger's eyes. Keep it with you constantly during the hunt, and no tiger can possibly harm you, not even Bagh Zalum."

Soon the rajah was off to the hunt with Nayudu and the shikaris, who included most of the palace guards. For the next few days, all was quiet about the palace itself. Kalma was preparing for his living burial by means of special breathing exercises which were helpful to suspended animation. Messages were received from the rajah, stating that the hunting party had gone well beyond the village where tigers had been reported, but so far had seen no sign of Bagh Zalum. Then, one morning, Shalbar came in by train from Delhi.

Upon learning from Princess Halina that the rajah had left, Shalbar held an immediate conference with Graylock and Chopra. Juju enlivened the proceedings by jumping back and forth from Shalbar to Graylock as though uncertain which master to choose.

"Juju reminds me of the council up in Delhi," observed Shalbar, with a tired smile. "They're jumping every which way at nearly everybody's beck and call. It's getting pretty sticky, though, for tight little states like Bildapore. No matter how nicely they are run, this Nationalism movement is going to squeeze them out. They talk as though it might happen in thirty days, but my bet is, it will take thirty years."

"Take it easy, old man," rejoined Graylock. "Look at me. Here I am in a place I never heard of a month ago, with a mongoose on my shoulder and a fakir waiting to be buried alive while I supervise the job — unless you can stay long enough to take over."

"Sorry, but I can't," declared Shalbar. "I must join the rajah and have him go to Delhi to see the council himself. It is that important."

The chauffeur of the royal Model-T knew the way to the rajah's hunting camp and was sure that they could make it before nightfall. But before the car pulled away, Kalma approached Shalbar and said:

"Since you will not have your mongoose with you" — the fakir gestured to Juju, still on Graylock's shoulder — "I shall provide you with a kavacha talisman as a protection against cobras."

Kalma handed Shalbar a token similar to the rajah's, but with a ruby instead of a topaz as its central gem. The fakir explained that the yellow gem represented a tiger's eyes; a red gem, a cobra's, thus accounting for the special immunity that each type of talisman provided.

Shalbar left, and by nightfall, Princess Halina began to worry about her father. Kalma, who showed up in that silent way of his, again had an answer to the problem.

"I, too, have felt that the kavacha talismans were not enough protection for your father and his secretary," Kalma told Princess Halina. "So I have prepared these."

From his robe, he brought out a clay statuette, beautifully molded and painted to represent a striped tiger. Next, he produced another statuette, this one in the form of a coiled cobra, covered with gilt.

"The tiger image is for the rajah," declared Kalma, "and the cobra image is for Shalbar. But to retain their potency, they must be kept in the safest of all places. That would be the vault where the famed diamonds of Bildapore are stored. You, my princess, are the only one here who knows where it is located."

The princess hesitated. She was about to speak, when Graylock interrupted, but in a courteous manner that brought a grateful look from Halina.

"But the princess does not know," asserted Graylock suavely. "His Highness the rajah told me that only two persons know where the diamonds are kept: the rajah himself and his secretary, Shalbar."

Kalma studied Graylock with sharp, boring eyes, the sort that could ferret out the truth, and Graylock met that gaze with the confidence of a man who has told it. There was momentary annoyance in Kalma's tone as he spoke again to the princess:

"But you do have a place where you can keep the statues safely?"

"Most certainly," replied Halina. "In my own jewel cabinet."

"That should be satisfactory," Kalma decided. "But first, let me add the incantation that will make the charm itself long-lasting."

He brought out a small box, opened it, and took a pinch of powder, which he sprinkled over the tiger image. He plucked a candle from the table, held it so the melted wax dripped to the statuette. The powder ignited with a flare in which the striped figure seemed to writhe as if alive. Then, with another pinch of powder and the same candle flame, Kalma applied the magical treatment to the cobra image, producing a strange effect of twisting coils before the flame died away.

"Let them cool," Kalma told Halina, "then put them away." With a parting bow, he added, "Wherever they are, they will be safe together."

That last statement could have referred to the rajah and his secretary as well as to the images of the tiger and the cobra. As a matter of fact, the Rajah of Bildapore and Shalbar were together at that very moment, in a tent in a jungle clearing, where the hunting party had halted for the night. In the glare from a kerosene lantern, the rajah was going over a sheaf of questionnaires that Shalbar had brought back from Delhi.

"The same old story," said the rajah wearily. "They want reports on how I treat my subjects. Do they have enough food, enough clothing, enough schools? Naturally, they don't have enough of anything, except tigers. Of those they have too many and particularly one too many, a tiger called Bagh Zalum. You should have brought the council down here to help us hunt him."

"They wouldn't have believed there was a Tiger God if I had told them," returned Shalbar. "No, Your Highness. There is only one answer; we must both go to Delhi. The car will be waiting for us at the end of the short jungle trail, if we leave right now. But a few minutes more will be too late as I told the driver he could go at dark. He fears Bagh Zalum."

"Very well." The rajah scrawled a brief note and laid it beside the lantern. "This is for Nayudu, telling him that we have gone to Delhi. I won't need this" — he clanked a metal disk on the table — "Kalma's talisman that protects me against tigers. We won't find them where we are going."

"Nor will I need this." Shalbar tossed his token on the table. "Kalma says it is a talisman to ward off cobras. I won't need it in Delhi —"

Shalbar broke off as the rajah pressed his hands to his chest and straightened upward in a sudden spasm. Anxiously, Shalbar asked:

"What is it, Your Highness? Are you ill?"

"I — I seem to be burning — right here." The rajah writhed slightly as he gasped, "but it is over now." He slumped a little, drew a slow, easy breath and let his hands slide downward. "We must leave now, Shalbar. As you say, we must leave" — his tone became a smooth, persuasive purr — "and go down the jungle path together."

The rajah's eyes had narrowed to straight slits that showed a strange, amber glint in the light. Shalbar's own eyes were wide open in amazement as he saw the rajah's lips spread in a ferocious leer. Then the rajah spoke again, this time in a snarling tone:

"Let us start, Shalbar." The rajah gestured with one hand. "As you say, there is no time to lose. " The rajah stared at his hand as he raised it, closing and opening his fingers in a clawlike manner. Then he looked at his other hand, which he was clenching in the same way. His face showed utter disbelief, becoming sullen, ugly, as he huddled forward in a low crouch, as if to avoid the light. "There is no time —"

Understanding dawned on Shalbar. He knew the truth, fantastic though it was. He sprang forward and boldly pushed the rajah to his hands and knees. Then Shalbar spoke in a sharp, tense whisper:

"Stay here, Your Highness. You can't let anyone see you like this. You understand why, don't you?" Then, as the rajah nodded, Shalbar added in that same tense whisper: "I'll call to you when the way is safe." The secretary gave a low, forced whistle. "When you hear that signal, come from the tent, but not until then. You understand?"

The rajah nodded and looked up helplessly. Shalbar stepped out of the tent and into the gathering dusk. He looked cautiously from right to left; then suddenly straightened and clamped his hands to his chest, exactly as the rajah had. He felt a brief but violent burning sensation. Then he suddenly writhed to the ground and squirmed there, unable to move his hands and arms, which seemed to be bound to his sides.

Shalbar was able to lash about in the grass which now completely covered him, so he did. Not only that, he managed to rear up and look to see if Nayudu or any of the other shikaris were about. Not seeing anyone, Shalbar gave his signal. It was more than a half-whistled whisper. It was a sharp, fierce hiss.

For answer, the rajah gave a low snarl from within the tent. Just then, Shalbar reared higher and saw Nayudu going by. Shalbar hissed again, this

time as a warning, but the rajah took it as a signal to come along, so he did.
But he paused momentarily to growl at the light, which bothered him. He
reached up and gave it a hard, impatient whack with his tightly closed fist,
knocking it clear to the corner of the tent.

Fortunately, as the lantern hit the ground, its flame was extinguished. Still
crouched, the rajah came from the tent, but instead of being visible — as he
would have been against the lighted tent — his low, huddled form was obscured against the darkened backdrop of the jungle. He heard another hissed
signal and he followed it, softly, calmly, giving a purred response.

They moved down the jungle path together; Shalbar gliding ahead,
the rajah softly creeping behind him. Somewhere between the camp and the
waiting car, they slipped into the jungle. Then came a shriek followed by a
loud roar, sounds that would have frightened most jungle creatures. The
screech was the self-starter of the Model T, the roar, its motor. The driver
felt he had waited long enough.

Two glaring orbs burned along the jungle road, the headlights of the
jouncing car. Their gleam was reflected by two pairs of eyes — one pair yellow,
the other pair red — that were staring boldly from the jungle brush. But the
frantic driver was too excited even to notice them. He kept driving straight on
back to Bildapore. When he arrived at the palace late that night, the driver
of the royal car told how he had taken Shalbar to the rajah's camp.

So everyone was satisfied and pleased that both were safe. In the morning,
Kalma, informed of the driver's report, declared simply:

"My talismans and charms are protecting them. Now I can proceed with
my samadhi. I shall go into my trance and be buried alive."

At noon, on the brow of a slope a quarter mile from the palace, Kalma
was placed in a wooden casket, where he closed his eyes and slackened his
breath. Gradually, his body stiffened, and he did not seem to breathe at all.
His pulse had ceased to throb when Graylock tested it. The lid was sealed on
the casket, which was lowered into a deep pit that Kalma's followers had dug.
Those same men filled the pit with loose earth, tramped it down and then
pitched their tents on the slope just below the grave to protect Kalma from
the unforeseen.

Graylock, remembering what the rajah had told him about adepts fighting off wild animals in Himalayan caves, could well appreciate Kalma's situation. Once the fakir was in samadhi, the complete disunion of flesh and spirit,
his body was at the mercy of the elements or any prowling thing, man or beast,
that might dig him up. So his followers were keeping constant vigil.

Kalma, who was allowing himself to be buried alive for the next thirty
days, impressed Graylock as a greater wonder worker than Bardu, who called
himself an adept, but simply squatted in a comfortable alcove, sheltered from
rain, wind, and sun in the safety of the palace courtyard. Bardu could call for
help or unlimber from his lotus position at any time. Probably the reason he
sat so passively and refrained from using mystic powers was because he actually had none.

All Graylock had to do from now on was visit the hillock daily and receive a routine report from Kalma's followers. In case of dire necessity, such as a torrential rain or signs of burrowing insects, Graylock would order the coffin dug up at once. Otherwise, the living exhumation would take place on the appointed date with Graylock and the other witnesses present.

Meanwhile, a messenger arrived from the jungle camp, with a note signed by the rajah saying that he and Shalbar had gone to Delhi. Nayudu assumed that they had taken a train from a nearby junction; and he sent along the jeweled disks, which he had found on the table in the rajah's tent. Halina put them in her cabinet with the tiger and cobra images, which were so much more important. The rajah and his secretary would be protected by those effigies no matter where they went. Kalma had said so; hence, it must be so.

New reports from the tiger country told that neighboring rajahs, as well as British sportsmen, had rushed to join the great hunt. Since the shoot had been instituted by the Rajah of Bildapore, they gave him precedence. In his absence, they accepted Nayudu, his chief shikari, as the leader. Soon, a cordon of beaters and hunters closed in on a quick, soft-moving tiger that answered the description of Bagh Zalum.

One day, they trapped the Tiger God in a jungle valley surrounded by machans high in the trees, each manned by a shikari, with beaters in between. The only way for Bagh Zalum to slip out was by climbing a tree and surprising a hunter on his thatched platform. That was exactly what the cunning tiger did. He moved in on the shikari, who felt so safe in his high roost, and stunned him with a blow from a heavy, padded paw. The tiger came down and continued on his way, while the shikari was found in his machan, still dazed, an hour or so later.

At another point, some shikaris fired at Bagh Zalum while he was scrambling for the jungle. They heard the crackle of underbrush and small trees; then silence. Either the tiger was lying wounded, perhaps dead, in the brush; or he had gone through to cleared land beyond. Dozens of beaters and shikaris scoured the brush. Suddenly a very live and unhurt tiger sprang up in their midst. The striped terror bounded straight into the bed of a dry watercourse and sped away beneath the shelter of its high embankments. Nobody was on guard there, and Bagh Zalum was gone like a striped cyclone before anyone could get a shot at him.

Next, a new hunting party moved in with a herd of trained elephants, each with a *mahout* sitting in a *howdah,* as a canopied shooting platform. The mahouts were skilled shikaris, all craving a shot at the Tiger God. The satmans, or spearmen, who followed them, were an equally tough lot.

Then one mahout was frozen in astonishment when a tiger sprang from the high branches of a tree, squarely into the howdah! Again, a tree-climbing tiger, who batted the man to the ground, the rifle firing upward as he went. That wild shot made the elephant still wilder; with a scream, the great beast went plowing through the jungle. Everyone let him go, knowing that the tiger would be even more frightened and would jump right in among the satmans.

But this tiger didn't. He crouched low in the howdah and rode along on the charging elephant with all the importance of a royal dignitary, right on through the surrounding horde. The other mahouts caught up with the exhausted elephant a few hours later, but by then, the tiger had abandoned his canopied perch and had gone his way.

Once the Tiger God — for by now, all the hunters knew that he must be such — came face to face with Nayudu, the master shikari himself. Like a flash, Nayudu aimed point blank at Bagh Zalum, who was crouched snarling on an embankment only thirty feet away. Nayudu's moment of hesitation was only to make sure of the kill with his first shot, for he knew that a wounded tiger would only attack more savagely.

But in that fleeting instant, there was a stir in the brush almost at Nayudu's feet, and up rose a hooded cobra, ready to strike at the aiming hunter. Instinctively, Nayudu spun around and aimed at the snake instead, only to hear a mighty roar, as the tiger, profiting from the split-second diversion, came springing from its embankment.

Nayudu dropped low, and his shot at the cobra went wide. Rolling about, he fired from a prone position at the quarter-ton mass of flying stripes that had hurtled only a few feet above his head. But the crackle of the brush sounded ahead of Nayudu's rifle flash, and he knew that he had missed. When he came to his feet, the hooded snake had also slithered off into the jungle. It was as if tiger and cobra had gone their way together, though that, of course, was utterly impossible.

During the next two weeks, these stories and more came into Bildapore, causing great consternation there, for the hunt, after carrying far off into the great game preserve, had reversed itself and was now coming closer to the tiny native state. Chopra, the landowner who was acting in the rajah's absence, sent out reserves to meet the Tiger God's advance, but most of them scattered in terror and took refuge with other hunting parties. Chopra returned to the palace and held a grim consultation with Princess Halina and Graylock.

"You know how these townsfolk are," complained Chopra. "If you talk about a tiger, they see grass waving and leaves rustling everywhere. They get stripes before their eyes, every time they blink."

Princess Halina gave a relieved sigh and added:

"Then you don't think that Bagh Zalum is really close by?"

"On the contrary, he is very close," returned Chopra. "During the past few nights, the tiger has stolen up on guards outside the palace. He has knocked away their guns and they have had to run for their lives. They have claw marks to prove it, and that is why the guards have been deserting one by one. But when the villagers look for the tiger he has vanished as completely as in the jungle."

"Do you mean to say," said Graylock, "that Bagh Zalum goes back to the jungle by day and returns here at night, slipping through cordons each time?"

"I mean exactly that," declared Chopra, "but I have word from Nayudu that he is bringing hunting parties closer in, so that by tomorrow night, he should be able to waylay Bagh Zalum while the Tiger God is going one way or the other."

That same day, Graylock made his usual trip to Kalma's grave and talked to the fakir's followers. They, too, were aware of the tiger scare and were keeping close to their tents, which were well concealed among the trees and bushes beyond the brow of the hill. They agreed with Graylock that it was best to leave Kalma buried as he was, while they sat tight with loaded guns, ready to ambush Bagh Zalum if he prowled past their post.

All that night, one lone recruit patrolled outside the main gateway of the palace, where other guards had been attacked and had fled. Toward dawn, Graylock was awakened by a wild, piercing cry. He grabbed his revolver and dashed out through the courtyard, where Chopra, coming from another wing of the palace, joined him, carrying a rifle. Outside the gateway, they found the new guard lying in a pool of blood; and farther off, Graylock saw a striped shape diving past the corner of an abandoned hut.

Graylock took after it, blazing away with his revolver and Chopra followed but had no chance to use his rifle. In the uncertain light, it was impossible to trace the fugitive tiger through the brush beyond the hut. The killer was gone; for this time, a killer he was. When Graylock and Chopra returned to the guard, he was delivering his dying gasp: "Bagh Zalum!"

The guard's gun lay a dozen feet away, where he had lost it, while trying to ward off the attack. That the killer was a tiger was evident from claw marks that covered the victim's face and body, tearing deep into his throat. That the tiger must be Bagh Zalum seemed equally evident, for a strictly man-eating tiger would have carried away his human prey. This beast was simply a man-hater; and Graylock could now understand why many natives styled him the Evil One and some had sought to appease Bagh Zalum by forming a secret tiger cult and worshipping him as a living Tiger God.

All this while, Bardu the adept had remained complacently seated in his favorite niche, from which not even the threat of Bagh Zalum could stir him. Unfortunately, Bardu had not witnessed the slaying of the guard, because, like the earlier attacks, it had taken place beyond the outside corner of the gateway. The lesser yogis and assorted sadhus all were gone. They had quickly decided to resume their pilgrimages when they first heard talk of the Tiger God.

On the hillock, Graylock talked with the grave watchers and found they had been alarmed by the gunfire, but had seen no sign of the tiger, which must have gone another way. When Graylock returned to the palace, he found that the last few servants, frightened by the guard's death, were packing and leaving. Princess Halina refused to stop them, saying that it was their privilege. So that afternoon, Chopra drove off in the royal Model-T, hoping to find Nayudu and bring back any hunters that he could spare as palace guards.

By evening, the only living persons in the palace were Graylock himself, Bardu the adept, and the Princess Halina. There were no gates. They had been removed by the peace-loving rajah years before. So Graylock helped himself to a big hunting rifle from the rack in the rajah's gunroom and took up a lone patrol, with Juju on his shoulder, in the moonlight of the big courtyard.

Suddenly, a door opened and Princess Halina beckoned excitedly:

"There's somebody — or something — trying to come over the wall into the little back courtyard, just behind my apartment!"

Graylock started through a passage toward a door to the back court, but Halina led him up a short flight of steps to the right, into her lighted dressing room. There she pointed through a rear window down into the back court with its low outer wall. Graylock heard scratchy, scaly sounds from the gloom. Then Juju, on his shoulder, began a quick chatter. Graylock looked up and saw a huge, mobile mass come bulking over the low wall and spring lightly down into the little court. Quickly, he told Halina:

"Bagh Zalum is with us. We must get away from here — and fast!"

"I must bring my jewels," pleaded Halina. From a cabinet, she brought a dazzling array of diamonds, a trifling part of the Bildapore hoard, and folded them in a large scarf. "But I have other things still more precious. These!"

From the cabinet, she took the striped tiger figurine and that of the coiled cobra, placing one on each side of the table lamp.

"Now for something to put them in —"

Halina choked. She was looking toward the door. There, at the top of the steps, was the great head and shoulders of a huge tiger that could only be Bagh Zalum. Somehow, the beast had unlatched the door from the rear court and now had them cornered. But the tiger's fierce, yellow-eyed glare was not for Princess Halina. It was directed toward Graylock, who quickly brought the rifle to aim while Juju sprang from his other shoulder and darted to a corner, realizing that he, a mongoose, was no match for a tiger.

Nor was Graylock. Before he could fire, the big beast sprang and batted the rifle barrel aside with one huge paw. Graylock, trained in the trench warfare of World War I, reversed the gun and drove the butt end toward the tiger's snarling teeth, but the blow was only a glancing one. The tiger swung its paw at Graylock's head, to bat him away; and as he dodged, the beast tried to knock over the lamp with the same stroke; but it came short of that, too. Instead, the massive paw thudded squarely on the little clay tiger image, crunching it to powder.

Halina screamed as she saw the effigy crumble. Then the tiger's paw came up and caught Graylock beneath the chin, but it felt more like a hard stroke from a fist that jarred his teeth as his head jolted back. Next, Graylock, really dazed, found himself struggling, not with a monstrous beast, but a human antagonist who kept telling him coolly:

"Easy there, Graylock — easy, now. It's all right —"

And it was all right. As Graylock relaxed, he found himself looking into the face of the Rajah of Bildapore. Beyond him stood Halina. Her face very pale, she gave an odd, sad smile as her father turned and asked:

"That tiger image that I just crushed; who gave it to you?"

"Kalma," replied Halina. "He said it would protect you from tigers."

"I see." The rajah picked up the cobra image. "And this?"

"It was for Shalbar, to protect him against cobras."

The word "cobras" suddenly stirred Juju. The mongoose came chattering from its corner and darted down the steps, while the rajah shouted:

"Stop him, Graylock! Quickly!"

Graylock was too late. At the bottom of the steps, the mongoose shot through the now open back door into the little walled court. Juju, too, had heard the scaly, scraping sound that Graylock had noted earlier. Now Juju was springing for the weaving, whitish hood of a giant cobra. Forced to a corner, the snake was trying to rear higher, but the mongoose sprang to its neck, clutched tightly with its claws and was about to give the snake a fatal bite, when the rajah arrived, still carrying the cobra image.

The rajah flung the coiled effigy against the wall, where it smashed to bits. At that instant, the cobra seemed to rear higher, flinging the mongoose upward. Then the weird, white hood was gone, and Juju's chatter suddenly began again — this time in happy recognition as Shalbar stepped from the gloomy corner, fondling the mongoose on his shoulder. Shalbar rubbed his neck and spoke to the rajah:

"Just a few scratches, but no bites. Many thanks, Your Highness, for your timely assistance. At last we can be ourselves again."

"We still have work to do," rejoined the rajah. "Let's hope we are not too late. Better get that rifle, Graylock. We may need it."

The fantastic truth dawned on Graylock as he brought the rifle from the very room where he had struggled with a tiger that he had thought was Bagh Zalum. There was bewitchment in those clay figurines. They had turned the rajah into a tiger and Shalbar into a cobra. Either that, or they had made them appear as such creatures to all other eyes. Yet Kalma, ever artful, had not lied when he said the statuettes gave protection. The rajah, as a tiger, could hold his own against other tigers; Shalbar, as a cobra, could cope with cobras.

The rajah met Graylock at the bottom of the steps and gestured him toward the doorway to the big main courtyard, with the comment:

"Lead the way, Graylock. The princess has told me of your loyalty, and I am highly gratified that you stayed after so many others left. So you are still in charge."

"Our worries should be over," rejoined Graylock, "now that you are back, Your Highness. Chopra is due shortly with a crew of shikaris to handle the real Bagh Zalum if he shows up again —"

Graylock broke off and motioned the others back. Stalking silently across the main courtyard was a tiger, its exact size indefinable in the uncertain moonlight, but its intent very plain. It was moving straight for Bardu, the motionless adept, who was still seated with crossed legs and outspread palms in his familiar padmasana posture. Graylock handed the rifle to the rajah.

"Take this, Your Highness," he whispered. "You are a better tiger hunter than I can ever hope to be."

Graylock drew his revolver as an emergency weapon, but the rajah smiled while raising the rifle to his own shoulder.

"Weapons are unneeded," he said quietly. "I have told you that Bardu has the power of vashita and can stop wild beasts in their tracks. Watch now, and you will see a true mahatma demonstrate his mind power."

The tiger stalked steadily toward Bardu's niche, unaware that other eyes were watching, for it was meeting only the adept's unflinching gaze. Then, with a savage spring, the striped form launched itself squarely upon the seated, defenseless figure of Bardu, intent upon the kill. The power that stopped the ferocious attack was not the adept's skill at controlling wild beasts; it was the power packed in the cartridge of the rajah's rifle. A gun shot clipped the killer in the middle of his spring, rolling him over in the courtyard.

Graylock and Shalbar reached the motionless form ahead of the rajah. They didn't have to worry about whether it was still alive, for this tiger had literally come apart in two portions. This dead killer was no tiger at all. The rajah had shot and killed a man who had been wearing a tiger skin. He was lying face down, and in his outstretched hand was a murderous weapon that he had used to strike down and slash human victims, sometimes fatally, as with the guard last night.

The rajah arrived, realized the truth, and used the rifle butt to roll the dead killer face up in the moonlight. The witnesses stared at one another in new amazement when they saw the features of Kalma, the fakir who was supposedly undergoing a living burial in a state of samadhi, on the hilltop! They were still standing there, dumbfounded, when the royal car rolled in with Chopra at the wheel and a dozen shikaris brimming from its sides.

The rajah ordered Graylock and Shalmar to head the expedition that went into immediate action. Their target was the encampment on the hillside, and they moved in so fast and quietly with the shikaris that they captured and disarmed Kalma's few followers in a matter of minutes. Beneath a bush just behind a tent, Graylock found a small tunnel leading straight into the fakir's empty grave.

Once buried, Kalma had pushed open a loose side of the coffin and had wormed through a foot or so of earth into the secret outlet, which had enabled him to reach the tent and enter the back unseen. He had spent his long days in the comfort of the tent, not in the confines of the coffin, where he intended to return only when the time came for the casket to be dug up.

Aside from faking a living burial and getting credit for a real one, Kalma had been able to rove at night, masquerading as the killer tiger Bagh Zalum, using a pronged hook to deliver wounds that looked as though they had come from tiger claws, while he frightened away the surrounding villagers, as well as the guards and servants from the rajah's palace. Kalma had been the fiendish leader of the secret cult that worshipped *him* as the Tiger God!

As to Kalma's main purpose, the Rajah of Bildapore could easily explain that, in the light of all that had happened. Back at the palace, the rajah analyzed the fakir's methods as well as his motives. Graylock, Chopra, and the Princess Halina listened. Shalbar stood by to confirm the data.

"Kalma must have learned that a summons was due from Delhi," stated the rajah, "so he went out and created a tiger scare, thus making two predictions come true. Once Shalbar and I were off in the jungle, he transformed us with the aid of those images, probably through the affinity of the talismans that we already carried.

"It was a case of actual bewitchment, the sort that has often been reported through the years, but which has been difficult to prove. Now we know that such things can really happen."

"And in this case," put in Halina, "it must have happened when Kalma set fire to the powder on those images."

"Exactly," agreed the rajah, "because I felt a burning here —" He paused, pressing his hands to his chest, while Shalbar promptly added:

"And I saw His Highness change to a tiger. His face began to glare, with yellow eyes and snarling mouth. Then his hands changed to paws, his fingers to claws. That's when I knew I would have to get him into the jungle. So I started from the tent, only to get a burning sensation myself."

"And next," chuckled the rajah, "Shalbar was a cobra, hissing for me to follow him into the jungle. From then on, we beat our way back here together. It was more difficult for me, with all those shikaris thinking I was Bagh Zalum and trying to trap me. Fortunately, I was one tiger who knew as much as any hunter, so I did the things that tigers never do. Shalbar also helped me in his nice cobra fashion."

"Like the time I struck at Nayudu," recalled Shalbar. "You made up for that, Your Highness, when you saved me from my own pet mongoose, Juju."

"I was lucky enough to smash that tiger image," affirmed the rajah. "Then, of course, I realized what the cobra statue meant. While they were intact, we could not regain our human forms. That was why Kalma wanted them preserved."

"So you were still working in from the jungle," declared Graylock, "and being mistaken for Bagh Zalum, while Kalma was acting like a real killer here in Bildapore. No wonder no one could tell how the tiger managed to get back and forth between here and the jungle. But why did Kalma want to drive everyone away from the palace?"

"So he could find the secret hiding place," returned the rajah, "the treasure vault that contains all the fabled Bildapore diamonds that you yourself have said you would like to see."

"Kalma didn't find out that I knew where it was," put in Halina, "because Mr. Graylock told him that only two persons knew where they were kept. He said you, father, were one person and Shalbar was the other."

"And that," Graylock said to the rajah, "was what you told me, Your Highness."

"I told you that only two men knew where they were," corrected the rajah. "I purposely refrained from mentioning Princess Halina. I am glad now that I did. With no one to ask, Kalma had to frighten everyone away from the palace until he found only one spot still guarded. He knew that was where the vault would be; but it forced him to show his hand."

The rajah gestured his own hand across the courtyard to where Bardu the adept was still seated in what seemed an eternal pose.

"That alcove is the entrance to the diamond vault," explained the rajah. "So Shalbar and I decided to let Bardu take up his long, contemplative vigil there. Bardu himself does not know that he is guarding all the wealth of Bildapore."

The rajah walked over and spoke to the old adept, who unlimbered from his lotus posture and stepped from the niche, the first time that Graylock had ever seen him do so. Shalbar stepped forward, stooped and lifted a perfectly fitted slab that was set in the alcove. Below was a stairway, leading down beneath the palace.

"If Kalma had slain Bardu," declared the rajah, "he would have found and robbed this secret vault. Fortunately, we ended his career as Bagh Zalum, the Tiger God. Now I am willing to sell my diamonds to the world."

They went down into the vault, and while Graylock walked about, dazzled at the magnificence of the wonderful diamonds the rajah showed him, His Highness explained the reason for his sudden decision.

"From the way things are in Delhi," declared the rajah, "India will some day be nationalized. They want people to spin cotton, not to hunt tigers. So I intend to share my wealth with my subjects here in Bildapore. They can have the best of spinning wheels, diamond-studded if they want, with enough money to buy a few rifles for tiger hunting, too."

Then, with a final smile, the rajah added: "And you, Mr. Graylock, will be my sole world-wide agent for the disposal of all these diamonds."

Today, you won't find Bildapore on any map of India, for it was one of the earliest native states to be absorbed and forgotten. But you may find Graylock in his little jeweler's shop on New York's East Side. He is a kindly old man, who will gladly show you some matchless diamonds from a place called Bildapore. Also, if you ask him, he will tell you this story, exactly as you have read it here.

The Avenging Ghost

All that could be seen of Pleasant Farm was a bleak, black ruin as Hank Dawson swung his ancient car along the road that skirted Bald Eagle Mountain. A fine old farmhouse it had been, overly large, perhaps, and rather spraddled out, as Hank remembered it; but well built in good northern New England tradition, with granite foundations and solid stone chimneys. Those were all that now remained.

It was just about four months ago that the fire had occurred, on one of those stormy spring nights when the lightning flashed above the mountain peaks and the thunder came rolling in with the wild winds that swept down through the notches. Then, in the wake of all that fury, a mammoth beacon had flared against the midnight sky, rousing the quiet town of Hilldale and sending its antique fire equipment to a scene where it arrived too late to do any good.

For Pleasant Farm, situated on a fertile shelf part way up the mountain slope, was a difficult place to reach and the water supply had been inadequate to cope with such a holocaust. Fanned by the heavy wind, the flames had carried to the huge barn, so that, too was gone, except for its old foundation.

Both farmhouse and barn had been empty at the time. Pete Ryerly, who owned the place, had been raising cattle with a partner from Boston, Lloyd Proctor, but they had sold out their livestock some time before and were turning the farm into an antique shop. That, too, had gone up in smoke, but Pete Ryerly was still trying to collect insurance, which should please Lloyd Proctor, who had put up all the money. Hank Dawson, as deputy sheriff, heard of all such things.

Today, Hank had also heard from Janet Ryerly, Pete's wife, who was now living in the Stony Brook Cottage down the slope from the burned farm. Her note had said that she wanted to talk to Hank right soon, so toward sundown, he had decided to mosey out Bald Eagle way. Now, the wind was rising as the darkness settled, so instead of driving around in back of the cottage. Hank stopped on the road and walked up a path that formed a shortcut.

There were dim lights in the squatty cottage, making it all the more grotesque against the somber sky. Hank could scarcely see the outline of a storage shed behind it, because of shrouding evergreens that loomed from the hillside. Those trees were weaving in the rising wind, each with a motion of its own, turning them into a row of ghostly dancers, black against the sky.

Hank paused and shouted above the wind: "Hi, there — Janet!"

The answer was the deep, savage barking of a dog. That would be Duke, the Great Dane Lloyd Proctor had kept at Pleasant Farm until he went on a trip to buy antiques. Then he had put Duke in a kennel over in New Windsor. A good idea, Janet bringing the big dog back here as a protection.

Hank called again. The door opened, and he saw Janet waving with one hand and gripping Duke's collar with the other. As Hank entered, Duke delivered a few growls which Janet punctuated with the order, "Quiet now!" and the big dog subsided. Janet, a woman in her late twenties, was small, but by no means frail, as her handling of Duke proved. Her face showed the healthy glow of outdoor life and the big brown eyes above her cute stub-nose were quite as expressive as her well-formed lips. These lips were smiling when she said:

"You must be psychic, Hank."

"Psychic?" Hank frowned, puzzled. "What's that?"

"It means you can read thoughts at a distance. Telepathy, they call it. I wanted to ask you to come up here and stay a few hours on the first windy night, but I didn't put that in my note. Then, an hour ago, the wind started up, and who arrives but good old Hank Dawson, the man I wanted to see."

"Come to think of it, I'd just begun to see the wind stir kind of heavy when I decided to swing over here. Tell me, what's the trouble?"

"Since you are psychic, Hank, have you ever seen a ghost?"

"Not for sure, but I don't disallow that some folks may have."

"You may be seeing one tonight. Wait while I make some coffee. If Duke acts up, you'll know the ghost is around. Duke always hears it first."

While the coffee perked, Hank put a log on the fire and began to note a variety of sounds. He heard the wind roar down the chimney; he noted a low moan from a corner, but Janet laughed at that, saying it was just a tree bough scraping the roof. Then Hank brought up a subject that was worrying him.

"Tell me about Lloyd Proctor. How did he become Pete's partner?"

"It's the old story," returned Janet wearily. "Pete tells people his big ideas and finds someone to back them. Things go fine until the money runs out. Then Pete blames them and they blame him. You know how Pete brags and fools people. He promised me a wonderful home if I married him. Now look at it!"

"You mean Pleasant Farm?"

"What else? We couldn't keep it going, until somebody put up money to help. Then it burned out, and we're down to this little cottage."

Janet mused briefly; then felt less critical regarding Pete.

"Maybe Pete's ideas weren't too good," Janet went on. "But his backers weren't so good, either. They all pulled out, except Lloyd Proctor."

"You mean that Proctor was better than the rest?"

"For a while. Lloyd put up all the money to improve the farm and buy the livestock. He gave Pete cash in advance to pay the hired help and meet bills as fast as they came in."

"Then why didn't things work out?"

"Because they went at it too big. Lloyd kept taking long trips out West, buying cattle faster than Pete could sell those we were raising here. So Pete had to take on more men to run the place and buy more equipment. That made the expenses climb still bigger than the returns. So they closed out."

"I see. Now, what about the antique business?"

"They planned that as an in-between business; a stopgap, Pete called it. Lloyd went around buying antiques and shipping them into the farmhouse, until the barn could be made into a shop. Then the fire killed that."

"And where was Pete at that time?"

"Around the farm, planning the change-over, until Lloyd wanted him to go to Florida and take options on a lot of land down there. So Pete was away, too, and I was visiting friends in New York, that stormy night."

"And where are they both right now?"

"Pete is down in Florida, clinching the land deal, while Lloyd is out lining up salesmen in different territories. Lloyd mails in checks, enough to cover expenses here, so I'm just marking time until Pete gets back."

Janet had poured the coffee, and they were sipping it when the wind rose in a wild outburst, rattling the windows until the cottage itself seemed to shake. Then the fierce howl dwindled to a strange, plaintive wail that brought an echoing whine from Duke. As the wind rose again, so did the dog's tone, as though Duke wanted to howl in accompaniment.

From far off in the night came a long, sobbing note. It was more than the wind alone, for Hank Dawson, though well acquainted with the storms of this region, had never heard such a sound before. It was a call so distant that it might have come from another world; a chilling, eldritch wail that left spine-tingling shivers in its wake.

Duke was not only pricking up his ears; his hairs were bristling, his back arching, and he was tense in every muscle. His whimper showed a mingling of fear and challenge. With it, he must have recognized the call, for he came to his feet and stalked toward the door as though drawn there against his will. Then, under some frantic urge, the dog began to paw the door.

Hank Dawson had laid aside his coffee cup and was gripping both arms of his chair. Hank's eyes were as fixed as Duke's, and he strained his ears, hoping to catch a repetition of the distant call. Janet stepped over to the door, took hold of Duke's collar, and turned to Hank.

"That's the sound I spoke about," she said. "I told you that Duke would be the first to hear it. So come along" — there was a grim ring to the girl's tone — "and Duke and I will show you what happens next."

They emerged into the night, where the wind had already reached a half-gale fury, a frequent occurrence during these sudden mountain storms. There was moonlight now, but it was flickery, because of the scudding clouds. Hank could no longer hear the odd sob in the beat and tumult of the wind, but the cry must have reached a supersonic pitch that was still audible to Duke, for the dog tried to tug free and dash around the corner of the cottage.

Janet gave Duke that much leeway, then managed to restrain him a short way past the corner. The dog could still hear the strange call, however, for he was more eager to go than ever. With her free hand, Janet pointed to the white outline of the closed storage shed.

"That's where the call comes from," she shouted, above the tumult of the storm. "That's where Duke always tries to go."

"So why don't you let him?" returned Hank.

"Not yet! You'll see why if you watch the shed door."

They were moving slowly toward the shed, due to Duke's incessant tugs. Then, as though actuated by their approach, the door of the shed swung wide open. Duke reared and his tone became half yelp, half growl, the latter for Janet's benefit, since she alone was holding him back. The dog was frantic now to reach the door where that ghostly manifestation was in progress.

Ghostly it was, in more than one way. Hardly had the door opened, before it started to close again; then hesitated and wavered at the halfway mark. The wind lulled and Hank muttered loud enough for Janet to hear:

"Tricky, the way the wind is acting."

"It isn't just the wind." Janet's tone, though hoarse, was filled with awe. "It always acts the same, Hank, as if it was beckoning you on. And there is something that moves in from the night, something that you can't quite see, yet you can almost feel —"

Hank was sensing it now, very sharply. He was sure that he saw a vaguely human form take shape at the edge of the crazily swaying door, as though to hold it at the halfway mark. Then Hank realized that the outline could have been caused by the shadow of the waving tree boughs that filtered the uncertain moonlight just above the shed. Suddenly, grotesquely, the form became a tall, upright oblong, which Hank took to be simply the open doorway, as represented by the black interior of the shed.

By now, Hank had his flashlight out and was focusing it on the doorway, hoping to spot someone there. But at more than a fifty-foot range, the beam gave only a glimpse of the shed's interior; and before Hank could get closer, the door shut with an emphatic slam, as though someone inside was trying to avoid the light.

Right then, Duke took over. He was literally loping for the shed, and although Janet was hanging on and hobbling his gait, the dog was dragging her with him, as she gasped excitedly to Hank:

"Duke always does this when the door slams — he must see something go inside — because, just now I saw it — myself — like an arm —"

Hank had seen it, too, a shoulder, arm, and hand slicking in through the closing crack of the door, ahead of its sudden slam. That, too, could be an illusion, for the windswept clouds were thickening, changing the moonlight into kaleidoscopic patches of black and gray. But Hank wasn't for holding Duke back; quite the contrary. The deputy sheriff dashed forward, pulling his revolver from his holster as he shouted:

"Let the dog go!"

Janet released Duke, and he launched himself like a canine thunderbolt, reaching the shed in gigantic leaps, passing Hank on the way. Janet, coming up behind them, shouted:

"Watch the door — Hank — watch the door —"

Timed to the words, the door flipped open as of its own accord, and Duke bolted through, only to have the door slam again as though some ghostly hand had pulled it shut. Hank, arriving there, grabbed the handle and yanked hard, only to find that the latch was stuck. A few quick tries and the door came flying open, almost sprawling Hank ahead of it. Hank found his footing and surged angrily into the shed, with Janet now right behind him. With a wave of his gun and a sweep of his flashlight, Hank bawled:

"Whoever you are, stay where you are! Put up your hands and keep them up — in the name of the law!"

That order was wasted. Hank's flashlight, covering the interior of the shed, showed only a storage room a dozen feet square and about eight in height, containing a variety of implements such as a lawn mower, wheelbarrow, garden hose and stacks of boxes filled with household goods, plus an array of old bottles.

There wasn't a space in which even a midget could have hidden; but to the right, Hank saw a wooden partition, with another door in its center. There, Duke was on his hind legs, clawing, whining, half-barking as he tried to get through.

As Hank started in that direction, the door suddenly swung open, coming almost at him. Hank thought momentarily that Duke had pawed it open, for the dog was bounding through and the door was swinging shut behind him. But the outside wind still howled and Hank could feel its draft behind him, so he took it that suction had caused the door's action. At any rate, it didn't slam tight shut. Instead, it jounced partly open and Hank grabbed it on the rebound, wresting it wide, so that he could shoulder through.

Hank stood there with his gun and flashlight, in a narrow, low-roofed extension of the storage room, which was nothing more than a small workshop with a simple bench. Duke was in there with him, and the dog was barking heavily now, apparently as frustrated as Hank at finding no one there. Not only was the workshop as empty as the storage room, it was scarcely large enough to accommodate Hank and Duke together, the way they barged about it.

At the far end, however, there was another door which apparently opened outdoors. Hank tried to open it while Duke barked encouragement, but the door wouldn't budge. By then, Janet arrived, took hold of Duke's collar and quieted him, while Hank was finding out that the door was bolted on the inside.

"You can't open that," Janet told Hank. "The door doesn't even give when you try it, so I think it's nailed shut as well as bolted."

Hank agreed, but Duke reverted to his plaintive whine and kept scratching at the door, finally trying the hinged side and giving some appealing barks.

"No use, Duke," said Hank, inspecting the hinges with his flashlight. "They are fixed to stay." Then, to Janet, Hank added: "Listen to the way that wind rattles the loose boards in this shed."

"But it isn't the wind, Hank!" exclaimed Janet. "It's Duke!"

Janet was right. Duke's probing paw had rattled a loose board beside the door. Hank tried to pry it free with his fingers, then used an old chisel from the workbench. The board snapped inward, bringing three more that formed a door in the wall. But it revealed only a shallow space in the wall.

"I thought you'd found a secret door leading outside," declared Janet. "That would account for the crazy goings on around here. But it's only a tool closet."

The closet's contents consisted of a heavy-headed hammer streaked with rust, a garden spade, a pair of new work-shoes caked with long-dried mud, and a pair of dirt-stained coveralls hanging from a nail. Duke sniffed, gave a few sharp barks, then resumed his whines at the bolted door. Hank asked:

"Whom do these belong to?"

"Probably to one of the men working up at the farm," replied Janet, "or else to Lloyd Proctor. He superintended the fixing up of the cottage."

Hank left the articles in the wall closet and jammed it tightly shut. He led the way out through the front door of the shed, with Janet bringing Duke along. They circled the building and Hank tested the back door from outside, finding it solidly nailed and bolted. Duke tried to help by scratching at the door.

"Now Duke wants to get in," observed Hank. "He's still interested in that tool closet. Judging by this long grass, the back door hasn't been opened in months."

They completed the circuit of the shed, and Hank studied the latch on the front door. He found that it joggled slightly when in place, but not enough to open of itself. Hank asked:

"How did you happen to leave this loose tonight?"

"I didn't," replied Janet. "Every day, I check it before dark. I suppose somebody could sneak up and loosen it, but it has never happened except on windy nights."

"So you think the wind loosened it?"

"I wouldn't know." The wind was rising again as Janet spoke, so strongly that it almost swept them from the shelter of the shed. "What do you want to do?" she added. "Stand around and watch to see what happens?"

"No," Hank bawled back. "Let's go in the house."

Soon they were in front of the fireplace again, where Duke nestled down, nose between paws, and quietly went to sleep while Janet was heating up the coffee.

"You see?" she queried. "Duke knows it won't happen again tonight, even though the wind is getting stronger. He only hears that odd sound a short while after dark, and it always leads him to the shed and on into that little workshop."

Hank stroked his long chin. "How often has it happened?"

"Three times, I think." Janet counted back. "That's right, tonight makes four. The first time, it had me kind of scared, for I'd have sworn there was someone prowling out there. So I took an awfully long time finding out there was nobody around.

"Then, naturally, I laid it to the wind. So the second time, I wasn't scared at all. I was cautious and kept hanging on to Duke; but that was chiefly because I didn't want him to go wild and run away somewhere. So I practically laughed it off, figuring it just had to be the wind, even the opening latch and the suction that opened the inner door.

"But the third time" — Janet shivered and the coffee cup rattled as she filled it — "well, I was just petrified. It was like seeing a movie over again, or having the same bad dream. The way the door kept opening and closing, kind of inviting me in, made me want to run. If it hadn't been for Duke pulling me along. I would have run. That's why I sent that note to you, Hank. I just couldn't stay here alone another windy night."

"So each time," mused Hank, "it was just the same as tonight?"

"Almost exactly," replied Janet, "except for you being in on it and finding that tool closet.'

Hank finished his coffee, then remarked:

"Well, since you're so sure that nothing more will happen, I'll mosey along. But I'll stop by tomorrow and have a look at that shed by daylight."

During the night, the wind abated. Toward noon the next day, Hank Dawson drove up to the Stony Brook Cottage and swung in by the rutted logging road that came around the back shed. Hank was driving a newer car than his own, and with him was a polite, gray-haired man whom he introduced to Janet Ryerly, when she met them outside the cottage.

"This is John Hilliar," stated Hank, "the claim agent for the Interstate Fire Insurance Company. He wants to make an adjustment on the farmhouse insurance. I thought he ought to see some of the furnishings here in the cottage, to get an idea of what the rest was like."

"Very well," agreed Janet. She turned to the claim agent. "You see, Mr. Hilliar, we furnished the cottage from the farmhouse, to make room for the the antiques. You can look over what's in the cottage, as well as the boxes in the shed; but the real value was in the antiques."

"So I understand," said Hilliar. "What can you tell me about the antiques?"

"Very little. Most of them were still crated, just as they came in. Pete didn't want to open them until his partner Lloyd showed up, so they could go over them together. But they were both away when the fire hit."

Hilliar decided that he would have a look in the cottage, anyway. He had two other men in the car, both insurance investigators, and he told them to take pictures of the crates in the storage shed and then go up to Pleasant Farm and shoot a completely new set of photos, showing the ruins as they now stood. Meanwhile, Hilliar and Hank went into the cottage with Janet.

While Hilliar listed the furniture he saw there, Janet recalled and described similar articles that had still been in the farmhouse when it burned. Hank was helpful, too, for he had visited the farmhouse in the old days and was able to attest to some of Janet's descriptions. Then they all went out to the shed and checked the boxes there, which included lamps, pictures, household appliances, winter clothes, and some sets of dishes which Janet greatly prized.

"We planned to live in the cottage," explained Janet, "and turn the farmhouse over to antiques by degrees. But there were so many rooms up there, I would think that we lost three times as much as what we saved by bringing it down here. Wouldn't you, Hank?"

"No," amended Hank. "I would say from four to five times as much."

"We'll call it five," declared Hilliar, in a satisfied tone. "I'm quite sure, Mrs. Ryerly, that we could settle your husband's claim without question, so far as the value of the farmhouse and its furnishings are concerned. But he wants double the amount, because of the antiques."

"And so he should," asserted Janet emphatically. "Pete often told me that he carried much more insurance than he needed, just to allow for improvements and valuables. When the antiques began coming in, he was glad he was so well insured, but he began to worry because he didn't have still more."

"I understand," said Hilliar sympathetically. "We have settled claims like this before. But without an inventory, we at least need some proof."

"Lloyd Proctor is the man to ask for that. He's Pete's partner —"

"I know. That is all properly covered by the insurance policy, which allows for losses regardless of individual ownership. But since the policy is in the name of Peter Ryerly, we must look for proof of loss. How he settles with Lloyd Proctor is his business; not ours."

"Then what should I tell Pete when I hear from him?"

"Tell him to get all the data that he can from Proctor, who most certainly should have kept some list of items that he purchased, as well as the places where he bought them. Then we can check back and make a fair settlement, perhaps even a full one."

Hilliar went back into the cottage to make out his report and Janet accompanied him there, while Hank looked around the storage shed, inside and out, hoping to find some clue to the ghostly visitant of the previous evening. Hilliar had just finished his report when the honk of a horn told that the investigators had returned from their inspection of the farmhouse ruins. So Janet saw all four men off in their car. In parting, Hilliar said politely:

"Thank you for giving us so much of your time, Mrs. Ryerly. I only hope it will prove as profitable as it should. But remember" — the claim agent added this quite pointedly — "we still need that proof!"

Janet nodded as she stood there with Duke, who had behaved quite amiably today, even welcoming the strangers in the manner of an official greeter. Hank noted the dog and chuckled as he reached down beside the wheel and passed a strong leather leash out through the car window.

"Here's a present for Duke," said Hank. "It will help you to control him better at night. But if he hears noises around the shed, give him his head. Let him get there fast. He might even scare up a ghost."

The weather was mild the next few days except for a touch of frost that brought the first tints of color to the northern woodlands. Each day, Janet walked down to the rural delivery box with Duke on his new leash. There wasn't even a postcard from Pete, down in Florida, but one afternoon Janet found an envelope with the postmark of a New England town named Andalusia. In it, she found a check for a hundred dollars, signed by Lloyd Proctor, with a note saying:

"Here's more to cover expenses on the place. Hope it will be enough until business gets better." L.P.

About dusk, Janet was carrying dishes from the shed into the cottage, when she noted that the top branches of the yellowing trees were swaying. Off above the mountain, storm clouds threatened, but Janet decided they were moving the other way. After dark, a few gusts brought anticipative whines from Duke, but the wind had eased when the big dog began to bristle and growl.

"What is it?" asked Janet. "Hank again, coming up the path?"

But there was no shout from Hank; nor did Janet hear the eerie, distant cry that had perturbed Duke on past occasions. But since the big dog heard something, Janet bravely snapped on Duke's new leash and took him out. Instantly, Duke bounded for the corner of the house, then on toward the storage shed. Now he neither whined nor whimpered. He became a snarling fury.

It struck Janet that this was the chance to solve the mysterious doings centered in the shed. But she did not want to blunder into trouble, nor to give Duke his head except at her own command. The new leash worked to perfection as Janet dug both heels into the turf. Duke reared up like a reined horse. His snarl was fierce, his fangs gleaming in the cloud-filtered moonlight. As before, the shed door was swinging open; but tonight, a figure was plainly crouched before it. Duke's snarl became a raucous bark; the figure darted through the doorway, grabbing the door as it went by. Janet released the leash.

"Go!" Janet ordered. "Go, Duke, go!"

The door slammed as Duke sprang; then it bounced open, and Duke shot through with Janet close behind. The door to the little workshop also slammed shut, but Duke pawed it open instantly and went snarling through to the workshop. Janet, arriving with her flashlight, heard a man's frantic shout:

"Get him off me — get him off me — quick!"

Duke's great paws were planted on a man's shoulders, bending him down on the workbench, trying to get at his throat. Janet screamed:

"Down, Duke! Down!"

Somehow, Janet grabbed the flying leash, twisted about with a tremendous wrench and brought Duke with her. She yanked the dog into the outer room, looped the end of the leash to a hook on the wall, and turned to the workshop.

There, slumped by the bench, his coat dangling from his shoulders, was Janet's husband, Pete Ryerly. His face, ordinarily handsome, had grown haggard in the weeks since Janet had last seen him. It was sallow rather than tanned by Florida sunshine. His attempted smile became a nervous grimace.

"Why, Pete!" exclaimed Janet. "You know Duke won't hurt you —"

Interrupting snarls told that Duke didn't agree. Janet ordered, "Quiet, Duke!" and as the dog snarled a last protest, Pete came to his feet.

"Is there anyone else in the cottage, Janet?"

"No. Hank Dawson might be coming up" — Janet noted that the rising wind had died down — "but it's too late for him to be coming now."

"I'll follow you to the cottage then. But keep that beast away from me. He got so vicious that only Lloyd Proctor could handle him. That's why Lloyd had to send him to the kennel before going away."

In the cottage, Janet shut Duke in a bedroom and brought out one of Pete's other suits to replace the clothes that the dog had ripped.

"If you'd come in the front way," Janet told Pete, "you'd have been all right. When Duke heard you out back, he probably mistook you for a prowler."

"You mean there have been prowlers around here?"

"Not really," returned Janet, noting the anxiety in her husband's tone. Then, thinking that mention of ghosts might really shake him, she added: "Hank thought it was just the wind banging the shed door. Anyway, it frightened Duke."

"Frightening that monster would be something," snapped Pete. Then, eyes worried, he queried: "So you've let people go into the shed?"

"Only the insurance men. They've been very considerate. They say they can settle the claim in full, if you furnish satisfactory proof of loss."

"If only Lloyd would send a list of the antiques he bought!" exclaimed Pete. "When did you last hear from him, Janet?"

"Why, just today. He sent a check and a nice note. Here, read it."

Pete read the note; then studied the postmarked envelope.

"I've got it, Janet!" exclaimed Pete. "Tomorrow, mail Lloyd Proctor a registered letter, care of General Delivery in Andalusia. Tell him to mail that list, and tell him why it's needed. I can't write him because I'm supposed to be in Florida. Besides, if I mention the insurance, he will think I'm having trouble collecting it. Coming from you, it will sound like a routine matter."

Pete changed to his other suit; then told Janet:

"I'd like to stay overnight, but I can't let anyone know I'm here. The insurance people would want to talk to me, and I owe some bills around town. If you can clear up this insurance, Janet, everything will be smooth. I have my car out back, so keep Duke inside until I blow the horn, meaning I'm on my way."

It was fully ten minutes before the horn honked, and Janet wondered why he had taken so long to reach his car. But Duke was quiet when Janet released him, so the excitement was over for tonight.

The next day, Janet went to Hilldale by bus and mailed the registered letter to Lloyd Proctor in Andalusia. As she left the post office, she met Hank Dawson and his older daughter, Cynthia. Half-jokingly, Hank asked:

"Any ghosts prowling around the mountain last night?"

"No, just the wind," replied Janet, "and it wasn't strong enough to matter. By the way, I've written Lloyd Proctor for that list."

"Good enough," said Hank. "Let's hope you get it."

Janet did get it. Five days later, a bulky envelope arrived containing typewritten sheets with handwritten notations and the signature of Lloyd Proctor at the bottom. It described dozens of items, with the dates and places of purchase, as well as the prices paid.

Duke began barking while Janet was still studying the list. A minute later, she recognized the rumble of Hank's old car coming in by the

back road. She rushed out to meet Hank, waving the list as she shouted:
"Here it is, Hank! Just what the insurance company ordered!"

Hank's long face showed a glum expression that dampened Janet's joy.

"I just heard from Mr. Hilliar," Hank stated. "They've been trying to
trace Lloyd Proctor through insurance agencies around the country, and now
they've gotten a report on him; and a bad one. He's been gypping real estate
men with a phony land scheme. Proctor gets them to put up five hundred to
a thousand dollars for a franchise to sell Florida land; then he promises them
a list of prospects to go with it. But he just goes his way and never delivers."

"You mean that Lloyd has been doing this with the land he wanted Pete
to buy for him?"

"That's right. But Proctor hasn't bought any land. Don't worry about
Pete, though. He's in the clear. I think it would be a good idea to go down to
Boston and talk with Hilliar about this, particularly now that you have that
list. Cynthia is driving me down in her new car, so you can come along with
us and stay with her."

"That would be nice," said Janet, "but what about Duke?"

"We'll be going through New Windsor, so we can leave him at the kennel and pick him up on the way back. There's something else you ought to
know about, Janet. It has to do with this mental message stuff."

"You mean telepathy?"

"That's it. It seems that Mr. Hilliar got in touch with Proctor's parents
outside of Boston. Mrs. Proctor, that's Lloyd's mother, has been having
dreams about her son. He keeps coming back and telling her that he's drowning, or something. She's got to be told the truth; that her son Lloyd is still
alive. So you are one person who ought to talk to her."

They drove down to Boston the next day and Janet delivered the list
to Mr. Hilliar at the insurance office. The claim agent complimented Janet
on having obtained the list so promptly, and he found that the signature of
Lloyd Proctor tallied with samples that the office already had on file. But he
made it painfully plain that a complete checkup would have to be made with
all the antique dealers named in the lists. Those recent real estate swindles in
which Lloyd Proctor was involved, had placed his name definitely on the
black list.

That evening, they visited the Proctor home outside of Boston, where
they met Lloyd's father, Hubert Proctor, a kindly, gray-haired gentleman who
listened attentively to all that Janet had to say about his son. Janet was glad
indeed that she could tell how Lloyd had met his business obligations
promptly and to the full. She emphasized that Lloyd had kept on sending
checks, even after his partnership with Pete had resulted in failure. All that
gladdened Hubert Proctor, but only briefly; for when Janet had finished, he
remarked in a worried tone:

"The fact remains that you have not seen my son in the past four
months. Indeed, nobody who really knew Lloyd has seen him in all that
time. That was when his mother began having these recurrent dreams, in
which she sees him drowning and hears his calls for help. My wife has been
resting all day, so I think you should meet her now and hear what she has
to say."

Mrs. Proctor proved to be a quiet, sad-faced woman, who smiled feebly when her husband told her the nice things Janet had said about Lloyd. Hank Dawson and his daughter Cynthia were also the sort who showed real sympathy, so it took very little coaxing for Mrs. Proctor to tell about her dreams. Her eyes took on a faraway gaze as she related:

"Night after night, I have seen my son, and heard his voice. Always, it begins with a call from the dark. The words, 'Mother — mother —' keep stabbing me here." She pressed her hands to her heart, but her eyes retained that distant gaze. "Then I see his face — Lloyd's face — floating in blackness, looking up toward me, his hands raised, seeking help."

As in a trance, the woman looked upward and raised her hands in the appeal that she had just described. Silence was complete and tense in the little living room where Mr. Proctor and the visitors watched and listened. Then Mrs. Proctor lowered her hands and her head; but her eyes were unchanged as she continued:

"Then, gradually, the blackness becomes a rippling pool. I see Lloyd looking up from it, from the midst of those darkened waters. I hear him saying, 'Mother — mother — there is water all about me —' and I watch his dear face go beneath that blackness. Always, for a moment his hands remain; then they, too, dip beneath the surface, leaving only white ripples that die — die — die — until all is black again."

Mrs. Proctor's voice trailed into a drowning gurgle. Suddenly, she came bolt upright in her chair with an anguished shriek: " Lloyd — Lloyd!" Instantly, Hubert Proctor was at his wife's side, calming her, saying, "Wake up — wake up, my darling — it's all a dream —" and a moment later, Mrs. Proctor was blinking at the people whom she had just met, wondering not only who they were, but if they were actually real.

"That is how it always happens," declared Mr. Proctor solemnly. "All these months, my wife has been living and reliving this experience, hearing our son's voice cry not only for help, but for vengeance. For I truly believe that she can only be reflecting our son's real anguish, when he met with some violent death."

During the hush that followed, Janet heard her own voice asking:

"Did Mrs. Proctor have such dreams before?"

"I had other dreams, beginning years ago." Mrs. Proctor was speaking for herself, and her eyes with dimmed with tears. "Always dreams of my son Lloyd at times when he was away from home. Sometimes he was hurt, and I could hear his cry of pain. Other times, he was happy, shouting in sheer joy. And always" — her voice choked — "always —"

"Always, we heard from Lloyd soon after," put in Mr. Proctor. "Once, he wrote that he had met with an injury; again, that he had won a prize in college. Invariably, his mother's dream was in concert with Lloyd's actual experience. This happened so often through the years that when this dream came, we knew it was significant and its repetition certified that fact.

"Now you can understand why I believe our son is dead. You say that you have heard from him, young lady" — Mr. Proctor was speaking directly to Janet now — "but still, you have not seen him. I wondered why he should cry for vengeance, for Lloyd's nature was never vindicative. But since these reports have come in, slurring his integrity, I believe that in death, he has tried to clear his name as he would in life."

Next day, driving northward, Hank Dawson stopped at New Windsor and picked up Duke. As they drove on through Horseshoe Notch, Hank cast a weather eye at clouds beyond Bald Eagle Summit.

"I'll drop Cynthia at home," decided Hank, "and take you up to your cottage, Janet. If the storm hits, I'll stay until it's over."

Janet was glad to have human company. The darkened cottage was huddled like a lurking creature, while the storage shed was white and ghost-like, beneath the swaying trees that resembled hovering monsters. Hank made sure that the shed door was latched, then led the way to the cottage. Soon they had the lights on, a fire burning, and the coffee perking. Then Hank said solemnly:

"Now all we have to do is wait for the ghost."

"You believe it really is a ghost?" gasped Janet. "An avenging ghost — probably the ghost of Lloyd Proctor?"

"You have heard of crimes being reenacted," declared Hank. "Well, you saw it happen last night, through the reenactment of a dream."

"But if Lloyd was murdered four months ago, how could he have sent checks and notes and the list of antiques? And what about those reports from people who say Lloyd swindled them only recently?"

"Signatures and handwriting can be forged. And it's easy to impersonate a man if you don't try to fool people who know him well. A good guy doesn't turn swindler overnight, but somebody could make it look as if he had. Look, Janet, you went out to that shed three times before I did. Each time you saw something, but you didn't find anybody. Neither did the two of us. But if somebody had been hiding in that shed, wouldn't big Duke have found him?"

"I'm sure Duke would have; and now I can tell you why."

Janet's mind was flashing back to the night when Duke *had* found someone in the shed — Janet's own husband, Pete. That alone seemed proof that something unseen and intangible — a ghost to all intents — had figured on the other occasions. So far, Janet had held back any mention of Pete's visit because she knew he hadn't wanted it to be known. Now, in the light of things that she had learned, Janet was willing to blurt out the truth. But Hank didn't give her time.

"You don't need to tell me why you're so sure," said Hank. "I know. After what we heard last night, I'm wondering where this trail will lead. But I know where it will begin. Out there in that shed — tonight!"

The wailing wind echoed Hank's sentiment, and Duke's whimper came in turn. Already, Duke was bristling as he had before; his ear was attuned to the high pitch that no human being could hear. The big dog arose and moved slowly toward the door, throating new recognition of that distant, sobbing call.

Hank came to his feet: "Let's go."

They went. Tonight, their approach to the shed was steadier, faster than before, as they watched for the latched door to open of its own accord. They were nearly there when it made its first waver, as though extending an invitation from an invisible occupant. Duke gave his mingled yelp and growl, as he began a forward lope. This time, Hank did not hesitate. Above the furious wind, he shouted, "Let him go!" and as Janet did, Hank added: "Now, come on!"

As they started, the door swung wide. There, plain in the blackened oblong, was a whitish figure, its shape visibly human, but only for a fleeting moment. Then, it was gone, with Duke unleashed and bounding after it. Hank and Janet followed so closely in Duke's wake that they were in time to see the inner door swing wide; and again, they glimpsed that phantom form. Then Duke was following it to the back corner of the tool room, where he raised his big paws shoulder high and planted them against the bolted door.

There, in the full beam of Hank's flashlight, Janet saw the huge hound cornering his prey, as he had the other night. But Duke wasn't barking in fury; he was whining in happy recognition. The man he had cornered was stroking him, petting the dog's head and forelegs; and now, Duke was licking the face that Janet could see so clearly that she shrieked despite herself:

"Lloyd Proctor!"

Then to Janet's amazement, as she watched Lloyd's stroking hand, she could see Duke's big head through it! A moment later the hand had vanished and Lloyd's figure, though still vaguely visible, was dissolving too. Last to vanish was Lloyd's face, a kindly, somewhat handsome face that Janet clearly recognized, despite its deathly pallor. Then that vision, too, had vanished, and Duke was there alone, clawing only the bolted back door and whimpering mournfully as though longing for the touch of a hand that was gone.

Hank, too, had seen enough to be convinced. He stood by while Janet patted Duke, who nestled his head in her arms as though he had lost one friend and found another. Then Hank tried the back door and found it bolted. Janet spoke in a hushed tone:

"I saw him, Hank. As plainly as I see you now. It was Lloyd Proctor — or his ghost."

"I saw it, too," declared Hank, "and I heard you call his name. But I would have known him anyway, after seeing his father the other night. Lloyd was a dead ringer for him." Hank paused; then added grimly; "A *dead* ringer."

There was a lull. The wind was dying as though it had done its work. Then Hank spoke emphatically:

"Lloyd Proctor was murdered, right here, at this very spot. Do you know why I know? I'll show you why." He picked up a handy chisel and pried open the tool closet in the wall beside the door. "Look here!"

A moment later. Hank was staring at an empty space, almost as startled as if he had seen Lloyd's ghost again.

"Where are the things that were in here?" he demanded. "Who took them?"

"I don't know for sure," rejoined Janet in a hollow tone, "but do you want me to guess?"

"Yes. It is very important."

"Pete was here," said Janet, her voice taking on a cold, impersonal tone. "Pete Ryerly — my husband. Duke cornered him here in the shed. That's how I know a human being could be trapped here, but not a ghost. Pete was after something, because when he left the cottage, it was ten minutes at least before

I heard his car leave. I wondered then what he was after; now I'm sure it must have been those tools and clothes we found here. I should have told you all this sooner, Hank."

"And there's something I should have told you, Janet. Remember the day I brought Hilliar up here and he sent those two men to the farmhouse to take pictures there? They weren't insurance investigators, Janet; they were state police detectives. While we were in the cottage, they took those things from the tool closet; and instead of going to the farm, they drove back to Hilldale. There they bought duplicate tools and clothes, which they roughened up to match the originals. They brought the duplicates back and put them in that closet."

"And what did they do with the originals?"

"They sent them to the crime laboratory. I'd sort of figured they might be some kind of evidence; but I was thinking in terms of the fire up at the farmhouse. I suspected arson; not murder. But the lab tests showed that what looked like rust on the hammer was really blood. There were bloodstains on the coveralls, too. There was a peculiar sort of clay on both the spade and the shoes, showing that somebody had been digging somewhere."

"So whoever took those duplicate tools and things wanted to cover up," said Janet. Her voice was sad. "It must have been Pete, for he told me where to write to Lloyd and he seemed so sure I would get a reply. Pete must have picked up my letter, using Lloyd's name; then he answered it himself and sent the list."

"Let's lock up the cottage," suggested Hank. "We'll take Duke down to my house in Hilldale, and you can stay there with Cynthia and me until we've solved this case."

During the ride to Hilldale, they lined up more facts.

"Either Lloyd was staying at the cottage," declared Hank, "or Pete decoyed him there. Anyway, Lloyd must have found Pete in the workshop out in the shed. Pete hit him with that hammer, then took the body somewhere and buried it."

"Somewhere," Janet whispered, "where there is deep black water —"

"When Lloyd was slugged," Hank went on, "he must have called for Duke. Maybe it was Pete who shipped Duke to the kennel, so Lloyd could have thought Duke was still around. Anyway, Duke has been hearing that dying call ever since."

"And always on a windy night —"

"Like the night when it happened. It was windy, last spring, the night the farmhouse burned. Pete wanted it to look as if the flames carried to the barn, so he could collect insurance on that, too."

Hank was silent, thinking, until they pulled up at his home in Hilldale. Then he summarized briefly:

"In my work, I play hunches, then find proof. There's two ways to do it in this case. One is to have those insurance people check Pete's past rather than Lloyd's. The other is to get a good dowser working on that water clue, because Pete couldn't have lugged the body very far. In fact, Lloyd may still have been alive at the time. That would fit with his mother's dreams of drowning."

That same night Hank talked to Hilliar by long distance and told him of the new developments. Within the next week, Hilliar gained the anticipated results. Calls to the antique dealers established that they had made sales on the specified dates to a man purporting to be Lloyd Proctor; but their detailed descriptions fitted Peter Ryerly instead. The same applied to the more recent real estate swindle. Dupes who had named Lloyd as the perpetrator, switched promptly to Pete when shown photos of the two men.

It was plain that Pete had begun to cheat Lloyd early in the game, running up fake expenses on the farm, then buying antiques in his partner's name, selling them secretly and shipping dummy crates to Pleasant Farm. Apparently he had murdered Lloyd to prevent him from finding out too much; then, by posing as the dead man, whose signature he had learned to forge to perfection, Pete had continued to profit while laying a false trail that blackened the name of his unfortunate victim.

Meanwhile, Hank Dawson had found a dowser in New Windsor. The dowser was a man who worked at "water witching" as some people styled it, by using a large forked twig, preferably from a willow tree, to find a source of underground water. He gripped the ends of the forked twig, one in each upturned fist, so that the stem extended straight outward. Then he started from the ruined farmhouse to cover the extensive acreage of Pleasant Farm, which was heavily covered over with long grass and thick weeds.

"I never did take much stock in dowsing," Hank told Janet, as they followed along. "These fellows claim they've got an extra sense that makes the willow stick work for them. But I guess it takes something psychic, as you call it, to see a ghost, too. So who are you and I to talk?"

At times, the water witcher would pause while the stem end of the forked twig wavered downward, indicating water. But always, the symptoms were brief or inadequate, until late in the afternoon when he had reached a level spot a quarter mile from the ruined farmhouse and directly in back of Stony Brook Cottage.

There, the willow really behaved in an uncanny style. Despite the dowser's efforts to control it, the stem dipped steadily, forcibly downward pulling the man's brawny hands and muscular forearms with it. Even the skeptics in the gallery of watchers were impressed, for the dowser's face was contorted from the resistance he put up. But whether he was fighting some unseen force or merely struggling with his own subconscious, the divining rod won out. After it pointed straight downward, the dowser relaxed and panted:

"Dig there — and dig deep."

They dug until dusk settled, and in the course of digging, they struck a clayish soil that corresponded to the caked mud on the shoes and spade found in the tool closet of the shed. So Hank ordered searchlights, and in their glare, the digging was continued. Finally, the ground began to cave in funnel fashion; and loose stones, slipping down through, sent back echoing splashes. Hank told the diggers to work more carefully, and soon they uncovered the mouth of a deep well that had probably gone dry many years before and had been forgotten.

Whatever the case, it was filled with water now, and Hank remarked that it probably would show on the survey map of the farm. That map had been in the farmhouse when it burned; and Janet could understand why. If Pete had dumped Lloyd's body here and then covered up the opening, he wouldn't have wanted the well to be located ever. During the summer, grass and weeds had grown over it, leaving no trace whatever.

But the dowser's willow stick had found it; and more. As the searchers probed deep in the blackened water, they came upon the body that they sought. Janet was too sick at heart to wait while they tried to identify the waterlogged remains of Lloyd Proctor, which they soon did, by a monogrammed ring that they found on one finger.

Like the strange cry that had come with the night wind, the oft-repeated dream of a dying face in blackened waters now had become the proven positive token of an avenging ghost.

Vengeance soon caught up with Peter Ryerly. Once he was branded a wanted murderer, law enforcement officers began closing in on him. Unable to tap the bank account of a victim whose signature he could so cleverly forge, Ryerly was cut off from immediate funds and was forced to resort to petty thefts and stupid robberies to keep ahead of the law.

One night he was spotted driving a stolen car. In the chase that followed, Ryerly took to a side road, hoping to shake off a pursuing police car; but it stayed close on the trail. When Ryerly came to a dead-end sign, he didn't stop. Instead, he crashed the barrier and plunged to his death on the jagged rocks of a deep ravine.

Perhaps he mistook the white warning sign for a pale, unturned face floating in a blackened pool; possibly he thought the wail of the police siren was an eerie call carried by the night wind. Whatever his impressions, Peter Ryerly was most certainly driven to his doom by the avenging ghost of his victim, Lloyd Proctor.

Return from Oblivion

They were a great crew, as Bob Embry remembered them from that last night they spent together. Like Embry himself, each was an integral part of their ship, *King Nine*, a B-25 medium bomber that belonged to the 12th Air Force, USAAF., based in Tunisia. Tomorrow, they were going on a milk run to bomb the southern tip of Italy, as they had done before, during this intensive campaign in the year 1943.

As captain, Embry was giving his crew a pep talk, along the usual lines that always brought a responsive note.

"It's like going fishing, fellows," he declared. "Off Long Island, when the mackerel are running, or maybe the bluefish. Boy, would I like to catch up with a school of blues tomorrow! But you've got to be ready for them. You can lose a lot if your tackle is too light."

Bill Kline, who wore the chevrons of a technical sergeant, spoke up:

"Chief, you make it sound like fishing was real hot stuff."

"It is," assured Embry. "The boats go out, as we do. All there is ahead of you is sea and sky, until you reach your objective."

"You mean like Target Bluefish?"

"Like Target Bluefish. Then over go the lines, just the way we drop bombs from *King Nine*. When your mission is accomplished, you head back."

"But there's a difference, Chief. Those boats are sure to get back."

"Not always. Storms can scatter a fishing fleet, and I've been on boats that were lucky to haul into port. But I've always been lucky, fishing, so I'll be lucky tomorrow. Some day, I'll be taking all of you out on a boat to some of those fishing spots, like The Farms or Seventeen Fathoms —"

Embry's voice trailed; he put his hand to his head. The crew knew that their captain was having one of his recurrent fever turns. Kline, hoping to snap him out of it, supplied a quip:

"And to think, Chief, I lived all my life in the Bronx, but until you told us, I never even heard of anybody fishing off Long Island."

"You never even heard of Long Island," put in Jerry Blake, the copilot. "Okay, Bronx cowboy. You and your buddies scram, while I go over flight details with the chief here."

As soon as the rest were gone, Blake proffered some advice:

"You'd better see the medic, Bob, and get some more of those pills that helped before. The boys are all with you. That's why they are so anxious for you to be with them tomorrow."

"Right, Jerry." Embry rose unsteadily. "I'll go see the medic. And some day, Jerry, we'll go fishing together, like I said. There's nothing like fishing to make you forget whatever worries you."

Not that Robert Embry was the sort to worry. He had shown a cool head when he took his pre-flight training at Amarillo. He'd taken multiple engine at Randolph. Then he had gone to England and next to Africa. Now, at the age of twenty-four, he was flying his thirty-eighth mission. But when *King Nine* took off, it would just be another fishing trip for Captain Embry and his crew.

It was a hot, still, North African morning when the bombers started on their mission. Their progress was registered in an R. A. F. operations room, where keen eyes watched careful hands push different-colored markers back and forth across a table that resembled a gigantic chess board. A jargon of reports was coming in, guiding the moves in the grim game. One British officer answered a jangling phone, spoke briefly, and then announced:

"Yanks have an aircraft reporting heavy flak damage over Bari. Last heard from over Romadi and headed for the desert. We have a Mosquito group flying there. Have them keep their eyes open."

"What kind of a ship?" asked a man at the table.

"A B-25 Mitchell," replied the officer. "Designated as *King Nine*." He watched the board man move the appropriate marker. Then, over the phone, he stated: "We'll put out the call in case we hear anything, sir. Of course, if they're heading inland over the desert, the poor devils don't stand much chance."

One man who could have gone along with that opinion was Bob Embry. The captain of the *King Nine* had flown over desert wastes before and had often pictured the devastating heat of those endless sands below. Now Embry was experiencing it as an actuality, a heat so fearful that he thought at first it was his fever rising, only to realize that never, in his most delirious moments, had he been swept by a burning sensation such as this.

Face down, Embry felt that the very sand was stifling him. It wasn't soft, it was coarse and it seemed to grind into his face and hands, even penetrating the cloth of his uniform. Slowly, as in a dream, he arose, feeling the heat of the sand still clinging to his sweaty clothes. As he ran his hand across his face and forehead, he felt more sweat, with the slick of oil. He opened his eyes and saw sheer white sand, nothing more, until a stretch of blackness on a nearby dune offered a welcome relief.

As Embry approached, shading his eyes, the blackness stirred and sighed, ending with a metallic twang. Startled, Embry looked up and saw *King Nine* looming above him, nearly intact, but half-buried in the sand. The blackness was the bomber's shadow; the sigh, the desert wind; the twang, a loose portion of the fuselage that was flapping in the wayward breeze.

In a disjointed way, Embry could recall the difficulties of the return flight: How the wing tank had been hit, how the ship had been losing fuel all the way over, how they had fallen behind and gone off course. Embry was sure that they had bellied in, but suddenly he realized that he was basing that on what he saw. It certainly didn't explain how he had made a belly landing of his own, a few hundred feet clear of the bomber.

Odd, how deep the sand was around *King Nine*. No sandstorm could have piled it there or it would have buried Embry completely. Rather, it seemed the result of long accumulation, over weeks or more, but that was equally implausible. The logical answer was that *King Nine* had dug in hard when making that forced landing. The crew could answer that; but where were they?

"Did I order them to bail out?" Embry asked the question aloud, as though expecting *King Nine* to answer. "No, I didn't. We all rode it in, all of us." He paused; then named the list he knew so well: "Me, Robert Embry, captain. Blake, co-pilot. Kransky, radio op. and waist gunner. Jiminez, navigator. Connors, tail gunner. Kline, upper turret gun. Let's see — who else?"

The words were caught and echoed by the hot desert breeze: "Who else — who else — who else —" until Embry realized feverishly that there was no one else. Worse, even those names he had called were not here to answer, except Embry himself. He was all alone in the great white stillness of the vast Libyan Desert, he and a crippled bomber named *King Nine*.

Perhaps the ship itself could answer the riddle! Prompted by that thought, Embry clambered to the upper turret door and dropped down through. He reached the seats that he and Blake had occupied. Both were empty, so Embry took his seat, studied the control panel, and fingered the instruments, hoping the touch would clear his daze. An officer's cap was hanging on the stick, but it wasn't Embry's. Inside it, he read: "Blake, Gerald S., 1st Lt., USAAF."

Embry turned to the tail of the plane and called "Blake!" The only answer was the whine of the wind through a shattered window, followed by the *clack-clack-clack* of a pair of earphones dangling at the radio operator's seat. Now Embry shouted, "Kransky!" but again there was no answer, so he started a slow walk through the length of the plane, calling for the others: "Jiminez! Connors! Kline!" All to no avail.

At least, Embry saw their parachutes hanging on hooks unused. That confirmed his belief that the plane had bellied in and that he had been thrown clear and probably had been knocked out for hours. But the crew hadn't jumped, they weren't dead in the plane, so they must have left it and started walking. If so, why hadn't they taken him along?

While Embry pondered over that, he thought he caught the faint sound of a distant radio signal. He sprang to the operator's seat, grabbed one earphone and listened, while he flicked the switches and finally snatched up a hand mike. Tensely, but efficiently, Embry announced:

"May Day, May Day, this is *King Nine* calling Firefly. . . . *King Nine* calling Firefly. . . . Pancaked in desert. . . . One hour, thirty minutes from last check point. . . .Bearing two ninety degrees. . . . Area flat and sandy. Low hills to the north. No other distinguishing landmarks. No sign of crew. . . . May Day, May Day. . . . *King Nine* to Firefly. . . . Come in, please."

No response. The radio was dead. Perhaps its feeble crackle had only been in his imagination. But he wasn't imagining his responsibility. He was still captain of this aircraft, and it was his job to see his crew through to safety, if he could only find them first.

Embry clambered from the plane and climbed a sand dune, shielding his eyes from the blinding sun as he surveyed the desolate but irregular horizon. Nobody, nothing was in sight, so Embry started back toward the plane, only to stumble on an object buried in the sand. He picked it up, shook it — a canteen with water inside. It was marked with the name of Sergeant Kline. Embry heard himself laughing aloud, but without a trace of mirth:

"Kline, you stupid idiot! You dropped your canteen here! You crazy Bronx cowboy! You're in the desert! You'll need water!"

The only thing now was to find Kline and the others, whichever way they had gone. Almost aimlessly, Embry started plodding across the dunes, carrying Kline's canteen and talking aloud, in a rambling tone:

"Some crew I've got. Some idiot crew. They run around dropping canteens full of water. So I've got to nursemaid them." As Embry moved along, he raised his voice to a shout: "Hey, crew! Where are you? I'm responsible for you guys — or wouldn't you know? You're giving me some bum action!"

Embry tramped along silently then, through the vast hush of the timeless desert. He wanted to drink from the canteen, but wouldn't. He was saving the water for Kline, who would need it more. That brought Embry's mind back to his immediate mission. Again, he shouted:

"King Nine crew! This is your captain, here! Come home to papa. I've got to look after you guys. Where did you all go? Please, fellows, where are you? No more hide and seek. I'm responsible —"

Embry cut off as a metallic clank sounded — different, louder than the flapping from the plane's fuselage, which was far, far behind him now. The sound was ahead, dead ahead, for Embry suddenly stumbled on the cause. It was a flak helmet, hanging on an upright strip of metal, clanking in the wind. On the improvised marker, Embry read the simple, painted wording:

TECH. SGT. WM. F. KLINE
R. I. P.

"Kline, I'm sorry," choked Embry. "You must be the one who didn't survive that crash. Only the crew could have buried you here. Rest in peace, kid."

There came a sound from above, sharper than the desert wind, higher, louder, until it filled the whole sky. Embry stared upward, bewildered by the sight of three streaking planes with swept-back wings, leaving long vapor trails behind them as they sped toward the horizon.

"What kind of planes are those?" Embry asked himself. "I've never seen planes like that before. I've never seen any jets —"

He cut off at the word "jets" and stared in new amazement.

"Jet aircraft!" he repeated. "How can I know about jet aircraft, here in Africa, in 1943? There's no such thing as jet aircraft, not yet. But I know about them, F-106's, F-105's, B-58's. But where are they from? What are they doing here in World War II?"

Embry lowered his gaze again and gasped in astonishment. He was no longer alone, he was surrounded by faces, here at Kline's grave. Faces of men he knew, his lost crew. He was calling their names in the order that he saw them as he turned his head:

"Kransky — Conners — Blake — Jiminez —"

All were studying Embry solemnly, anxiously, like figures from a dream. Then, beyond them, Embry saw another face floating against the background of white sand, a face with a bloody gash across the forehead. Embry screamed a final recognition:

"Kline!"

Embry was on his feet, clutching for the phantom figure. Solid hands grabbed him, and he saw faces around him but no longer recognized them as his crew. Then, suddenly, Embry collapsed, but not on soft sand. Instead, he hit solid planking. When his senses returned, he was delirious.

It was many hours later at the South Shore Hospital on Long Island. The switchboard operator rang the head psychiatrist's office and said: "We have your call from Washington, Dr. Grantland."

Dr. Grantland, an elderly, methodical man, was keenly interested in the detailed report that came direct from the Pentagon. He stepped to an outer office and spoke to a middle-aged man whose tanned face showed deep concern.

"You are Mr. Morton, the friend who brought Robert Embry here?"

"That's right, doctor." Don Morton nodded. "But I've only known Bob for a few months. We met on a fishing boat off Montauk, and we've made trips together ever since. Like most folks who fish, we don't talk much. Coming into shore, though, he always says, 'Blue sky and white sand' — as if it was on his mind."

"He said that today? When you came in on the boat?"

"Yes, but nobody paid any attention. The news was coming over the radio, about them finding a bombing plane in Africa that had been lost in the desert nearly twenty years ago. Then Embry was suddenly shouting, wild-like. We'd just got him quiet when some jets flew over, and that started him off again. He was yelling for friends of his, calling us by their names."

"Can you remember any of those names?"

"Yes. He called me Conners — another fellow was Blake —"

"And Jiminez — and Kransky — and Kline —"

"Yes, all of those. Kline was the last one. By then, Embry wasn't looking at us. He was pointing over the side, as if he saw a face in space."

"You've helped us greatly, Mr. Morton," Dr. Grantland said, "and you've helped your friend Embry even more. None of those names was mentioned in the radio report, but Embry was captain of that B-25, and they were his crew."

"But how could he have gone on that flight with them?"

"He didn't. He was taken down with a fever the night before. They were all lost on the desert, trying to get back, except one, whose grave was found there: Sergeant Kline."

The doctor went in to see Embry, leaving Don Morton outside. The patient had improved and was sitting up, but his voice carried a challenge:

"Don't tell me I wasn't there, doctor. I saw *King Nine*."

"I know that you saw your plane in the desert."

"And there was something else that I found there —"

"I know what you found. Kline's grave."

Embry looked up, his face pleased. He had found someone who would believe him. His strained expression faded as he confided:

"For years, doctor, I've believed I was on that flight — or made believe. I've wanted to think that I was there. Suddenly, I heard that they had found *King Nine*. Then I *was* there — as you say — except I never really did go on that flight. But today, I *did* go back there — I'm sure I did."

"Yes, you went back, in your mind. Now you know what happened and that you were in no way to blame. They did the best they could, just as if you had been in command. You're going to be all right, so get some sleep now."

Embry leaned back, closed his eyes, and spoke earnestly:

"I told the crew I'd take them fishing, some day. That's what I was doing, fishing, when the word came. Fishing and trying to forget that I hadn't been there. Then I *was* there, lying in all that sand, struggling through it, as they did, until I found Kline's grave. Then I saw the faces of the crew, and when Kline's face joined them, I knew they were all gone. I'd have taken it easier if those jets hadn't come over. There were no jets back then, so that snapped me out of it — took me away from the past — too soon —"

Embry's voice trailed dreamily. Dr. Grantland left the room and spoke to Don Morton, who was waiting in the corridor and had heard the conversation.

"Embry has been living a strange guilt for twenty years," the doctor declared, "all due to the uncertainty of what really happened. Now that is over. He will soon go fishing with you again."

A nurse came down the corridor, bringing Embry's fishing clothes, which had been left in the examination room. The doctor gestured to a bench.

"Put the clothes there, nurse," he ordered. "I don't want the patient disturbed. I'm going into his room shortly, to see if he is asleep, so I'll take them in then."

Embry's shoes were on top of the pile and overbalanced it as the nurse placed the clothes on the narrow bench. As she quickly caught the pile, sand trickled from every fold and pocket; and when the nurse tipped the shoes, more sand poured out, adding to the sizable white heap. Dr. Grantland turned to Morton:

"How did you get Embry across the beach? Did you drag him?"

"We didn't come in on the beach," replied Morton in an awed tone. "We went out from the pier and docked there when we came back. From there, we took Bob straight to my car. I wouldn't know where that sand came from."

"Nor would I," said Dr. Grantland. "Good-bye, Mr. Morton."

But from the warmth of their parting handshake and the whiteness of the sand itself, Don Morton somehow knew that both he and Dr. Grantland had one place in mind — the Libyan Desert. For where else could that sand have come from?

The House on the Square

As a team of ghost hunters, Bruce Barlow and Jeff Shelby were top flight. They had fun and profited from their part-time profession, which began while both were students in an eastern college. During a summer vacation, they visited the old Black Swan Tavern, once an overnight stop for stagecoaches between New York and Montreal.

A new owner had restored the tavern for the modern tourist trade, but no one would stay there, because strange groans were heard at night which were attributed to the ghost of an innkeeper who had been murdered in the place, many years before. But Bruce and Jeff slept there willingly, for a fee, in order to dehaunt the inn.

They finally traced the sounds to the attic, but found only some old boxes, storm windows, and an ancient sign saying: HIGBY'S INN, J. L. HIGBY, PROP., that being the name of the murdered innkeeper. So the ghost hunters pitched their cots, but took care not to disturb any boxes, or the old sign, which was attached to a pole propped against the slanted attic roof.

After a few hours, the groans awakened Bruce and Jeff. Both flicked their flashlights on the same spot and exclaimed: "J. L. Higby!" But they didn't mean the ghost of the murdered innkeeper; they meant the sign that bore his name. Its pole had once extended above the tavern door, so the sign was attached by hinges. These had weakened over the years, and the wind coming through the eaves swayed the sign, producing loud groans that had magnified more weirdly in rooms below than in the attic itself.

That settled the problem of the tavern ghost; and Bruce and Jeff were paid off handsomely for their job. They debunked some more haunts that summer, but they cracked a still bigger riddle the next season. That was when they investigated a decrepit mansion where a mysterious pool of blood appeared at intervals in a corner of the living room, where one man had shot another to death during an argument over a gambling debt.

The ghost hunters were shown the room by a caretaker, who pointed out the exact spot where the strange pool appeared. He had photographs to prove it was no illusion. The pool measured eighteen inches across, and it was always at least a foot away from the corner of the room.

"You never know when you will find it," declared the caretaker. "One bright morning, you walk in and there it is. Always in dry weather."

"What happens the night before?" asked Bruce. "Do people hear strange sounds?"

"Not to my knowledge," replied the caretaker. "All they saw was the blood and that was enough. They walked out real scared."

"We won't walk out," promised Bruce. "No ghost can fool us."

They watched the corner of the room steadily, for one week. It rained on the third and fourth nights, then cleared. The fifth night was uneventful, but on the sixth night, Bruce said to Jeff: "Look there!"

A slow trickle was emerging from beneath the baseboard of the wall, gradually forming a reddish pool. They watched it for the next few hours, taking photographs in progress. It finally lessened, leaving a one-foot space between the wall and the pool. Bruce, studying the track that the trickle had followed, discovered some damp, paper-thin flakes.

"These are fragments of dried leaves," he declared. "They must have blown in through some opening up near the roof and then worked down inside the wall."

"And the rain of a few days ago must have come down through, too," added Jeff, "but the leaves kept absorbing it until they became over-saturated. Then the water began to trickle down and out."

"Let's get a carpenter's level and check this floor," suggested Bruce. "I'll bet we find a depression there, too slight for the eye to detect."

Bruce was right. Tests with the level showed that the floor was a trifle out of true, enough for the pool to form just far enough away from the corner to leave no trace of its source. Also, the ghost hunters took samples of the supposed blood before the pool dried, something that no one had done before. A chemical analysis showed that the ruddy hue was due to decayed vegetable matter, specifically dried leaves.

Summer after summer, the two ghost hunters pursued their intriguing profession, with more and more triumphs to their credit. Some of these proved to be surprisingly simple; almost ludicrously so. There was the case of an old house in New York's Greenwich Village, where the basement and ground floor had been made into a duplex apartment with a huge living room. In it was an old-fashioned chandelier suspended by a long chain from the ceiling. On nights when dinner parties were held, the chandelier was seen to sway, while lighted candles flickered on the table just below.

One local historian linked the wavering lights to an old Dutch legend of more than two centuries before, involving witchcraft; but Bruce and Jeff came up with a more modern solution. They discovered that tremors were produced by trains on a subway line that ran a block away. When a northbound express attained a certain speed its vibration corresponded to the building's sway, and the ghostly manifestations resulted.

Equally intriguing were the weird lights that danced in the windows of an abandoned country schoolhouse in Vermont. They were attributed to the ghost of a man who had committed suicide there, after trying to set fire to the building. Ghostly manifestations had been reported over the years but had taken on an almost nightly frequency when Bruce and Jeff came to investigate.

The ghost hunters found that the weird flickers were reflections from cars that took a little-used turnoff from a new through highway. Only cars that were using their bright lights could produce them. Other cars went by unnoticed due to a high intervening embankment.

There was an element of danger in some of these investigations, particularly when the two friends were searching old quarries or roaming swamps and woodlands where snakes and wild animals might be encountered. Nor did Bruce and Jeff discount the chance of running up against human opposition, such as poachers, moonshiners, or even escaped convicts.

In addition to cameras, flashlights, compass, and other equipment, Bruce always carried a long, stout cane with a heavy, bulb-shaped head. The stick, which his uncle had brought back from the Orient, was known as a "Penang lawyer" because; in the settlement of Penang, the only way to win an argument was with the use of a heavy cudgel, preferably of that type. Jeff, who was a good pistol shot, always carried a .32 automatic for emergencies.

Bruce's stick came in handy when they investigated a summer cottage which squeamish renters had left because of odd sounds they had heard from a closed bunk room. On opening the door, Bruce and Jeff were swept back by a blackish shape that swooped out with all the force and fury of a tornado. But Bruce was ready for it, swinging the bulbous end of the "Panang lawyer" into the thing, which scattered all apart.

The monstrous form was a swarm of bats that had been hibernating in the bunk room and were responsible for the weird sounds. But for Bruce's timely work with the club end, which he used with mallet-like force, he and Jeff might have been badly clawed and bitten by the winged horde that they had released. Instead, they soon cleared the cottage of the pests and the ghostly rumors as well.

Jeff's turn came one season when they were ghost hunting in an old mill which a prospective buyer wanted to turn into a country tearoom. Along with ghostly groans and moans, slow footsteps were sometimes heard descending the old stairway in one corner of the building. Yet no one had ever seen the spectral figure that belonged with them, and the fact that it was invisible made it all the more uncanny.

It didn't take long to track down the more standard sounds. The groans were due to the creaky condition of the beams and timbers; the moans were echoes from the gushing millrace. But Bruce and Jeff were watching the stairs, which were outlined in the dim light, when the footsteps began descending them in slow, even fashion.

That steady, invisible approach was enough to scare off almost anyone, but Bruce was ready to surge in blindly and start lashing with his cane at the imaginary prowler, when Jeff suddenly ordered:

"Hold it! I'll handle this!"

Then, pressing the switch of his flashlight, Jeff spotted its beam some four steps lower, and blasted point blank with his gun at where the unseen figure's feet should have been. One more footstep came with a halting plop, and Jeff's light was focused upon a very dead ghost in the form of a huge rat.

That was the creature that had produced the inexplicable sounds. Night after night, the rat had come boldly down the stairs, thudding its full weight upon each succeeding step. The corner served as a sound box that magnified the emphatic thumps until they reached the proportions of a cautious human tread, which had been accepted as something ghostly. Jeff's keen sight, plus his still keener insight, had given him an inkling as to the actual cause.

The ghost hunters promptly recommended that a crew of workmen strengthen the building by day, to eliminate the creaks; and that some capable cats should patrol the premises by night, to handle any brother rats who might be taking over for the martyred rodent who had played ghost. The result was that all unexplainable manifestations immediately ceased, and the team of Bruce Barlow and Jeff Shelby was paid off handsomely for their ghost-breaking job.

A marked difference grew between Bruce and Jeff during the years they worked together. To a great degree, it accounted for their increased success. Bruce became constantly bolder and more contemptuous of "ghosts," while Jeff chose a scholarly and analytical approach. As a result, they pleased both types of customers, believers and skeptics. Oddly enough, the careers that Bruce and Jeff chose after graduation from college had much to do with this. Bruce became a physical director and athletic coach at a boys' school, while Jeff continued with postgraduate studies and took his doctor's degree in philosophy.

Each summer they teamed as usual and profitably debunked their regular quota of haunted houses, though they differed in their manner of approach. Bruce was more than ever eager to smash right into a case on a trial-and-error basis, while Jeff insisted on a preliminary survey of a scientific sort. To that, Bruce objected strenuously.

"If I waited for you to analyze all these cases," Bruce told Jeff, "we would never get around to the real explanations of the so-called ghosts. That may account for the few cases where we didn't find an answer."

"Perhaps," observed Jeff in a speculative tone, "some of those cases were not as simple as you suppose."

"You mean you're beginning to *believe* in ghosts?" demanded Bruce. "You're crazy! Anyway, let's not talk about our failures. What we want is more jobs like the one we just finished."

Bruce referred to a "haunted" glen outside of New York City, close to the famous Sleepy Hollow where a headless horseman had once supposedly ridden. A luminous, beckoning figure had been seen below a rustic bridge, and the owner of the glen had installed big automatic searchlights to trap the ghost. But always the apparition vanished at the first blaze of the lights, recording another triumph for superstition over science.

When Bruce and Jeff had taken over, they promptly dismantled the searchlights. Instead, they took their stance at the spot where the ghost usually appeared and at the first bluish flicker, they had photographed it close up with infra-red equipment. The developed prints had shown it to be marsh gas that added a lifelike shimmer to a stump of phosphorescent spunkwood.

The searchlights had defeated their own aim by drowning the trifling glow with an overpowering glare.

Bruce and Jeff had come into New York City and collected a full fee with bonus from the owner of the dehaunted glen. It was early September, and Bruce had a week to go before his vacation ended, so he proposed that they make it profitable.

"A lady up at Sleepy Hollow told me that if we wanted a house that was really haunted," declared Bruce, "we would find one in Redgate Square, right here in Manhattan. She lived in the neighborhood, so she should know."

"All right," agreed Jeff, "Let's go and have a look."

They finally located Redgate Square, set back from a dead-end street near the East River. The fourth house from the left, which bore the number 306, was a misfit in an otherwise well-kept row. Its whole front looked neglected, its brickwork colorless, the white window trimmings dull and grimy. Its front gate was canted at an angle on a wobbly iron picket fence that was badly rusted. A low balcony jutted from its second floor front, giving it a squatty appearance. On the gate was a sign:

FOR SALE OR RENT
A. J. WHITTAKER REAL ESTATE

They checked the address, and Bruce flagged a passing cab with a wave of his Penang lawyer. Ten minutes later, they were talking with Mr. A. J. Whittaker in his real estate office. He was a quiet, elderly man, who gave a dry-faced smile when they told him why they were interested in 306 Redgate Square.

"Ghost hunters, eh?" queried Whittaker. "Well, I'm willing to meet your usual terms, if you will stay a week in that house."

Whittaker dug a big envelope from a bottom drawer and whacked it to get rid of a long accumulation of dust, as he stated:

"A confidential file on Number 306. Often, I've wanted to get rid of it, but I knew some day all this data would be needed."

From the envelope, Whittaker brought out title deeds, leases, floor plans, photographs, letters, and other documents, as he continued:

"One of the early owners was named Howard Glendon, who lived there with his uncle and a very powerful serving man named Crandall. At times the uncle became erratic — I might say violent — and had to be confined in a barred room at the back of the fourth floor. At other times, he was seen glaring from windows, or heard howling about the house. Only Crandall could control him. Later, Glendon sold the house and took his uncle abroad, so he said. But no one actually saw the uncle leave the house."

Whittaker produced an old photograph that showed the second story balcony of 306 Redgate Square. There, a man was glaring from a window above the wrought-iron rail, apparently enraged at the photographer who had snapped that chance shot of him. The man's face showed a demoniac leer, and his lips were distorted in a ferocious snarl. While Bruce studied those demented features, etching their details in his mind, Whittaker stated:

"That is Glendon's uncle in one of his milder moods. Otherwise, they would have had him confined in the top floor back room."

Jeff was becoming restless, but Bruce was intensely interested, Bluntly he asked: "Do you think the uncle died there?"

"He might have," replied Whittaker, "because all the disturbances have originated in that room at the fourth floor back. A family named Rowland moved in after the Glendons left, but they were glad to move out a few months later. They had trouble keeping servants, who were essential in those days."

"And then who moved in?" inquired Bruce.

"Several families." Whittaker gestured to the files. "They are all listed here, and they all had servant problems. Some closed off the fourth floor, letting servants sleep on the third floor, but they kept hearing things being moved above them, which was as bad as living on the top floor.

"Finally, the Ashursts took over. They had five daughters and three servants who had been with the family for years, so were willing to accept the odd situation. One maid, Della, had the back room on the top floor and complained about feeling ill, but she decided to stay it out, because the eldest Ashurst daughter was about to be married. On the evening of the wedding rehearsal, Della came screaming down the stairs, stark mad. They rushed her to a hospital, where she shrieked at any mention of the room where it all happened. Two days later, she died. Nobody has dared to sleep there since."

"Jeff and I won't mind," declared Bruce nonchalantly. "Let's go over to the square right now. The sooner we begin this deal, the better."

Soon they arrived at the house in Redgate Square, ready to invade it, bag and baggage. But for once, Jeff Shelby felt himself a silent and unwilling partner in a ghost hunt entirely engineered by Bruce Barlow.

From the moment the rusty gate groaned on its hinges and the flagstones gave dull echoes underfoot, Jeff felt that he and Bruce were unwanted in these peculiarly gloomy preserves. The overhanging balcony seemed like the raised jaw of a monstrous creature, ready to gobble its hapless prey, for its overhang cut off all view of the neighboring balconies. When the rusted lock of the heavy, dark front door refused to yield to Whittaker's key, Jeff was tempted to turn and dash out through the gate. Only his regard for Bruce restrained him from that cowardly act.

The door finally opened, and they entered a long, low hallway with a gloomy, stiffly furnished reception room on the left. The hallway led into a dining room, finished in oak, which added to the morbid *motif*. Jeff noted a prevailing musty odor and commented:

"Damp in here, isn't it?"

"Damp?" echoed Whittaker. "Why, this house is the driest in the block. Not a trace of mildew on the walls; and these floors" — he stamped loudly along the hall — "why, they haven't a warped board anywhere. Look at the furniture, all in perfect condition."

"Still, it seems so moldy —"

"What does, Jeff?" broke in Bruce. "Your imagination?"

That quieted Jeff, but when they reached the kitchen, he glanced suspiciously at an old-fashioned elevator device in the corner, which had been used as a dumb-waiter to send food and drink upstairs. Bruce noted Jeff's look and flicked a flashlight up the shaft.

"No skeletons here," laughed Bruce, "but we can look in all the closets as we go along."

They went up to the second floor and into the front parlor, which was weird indeed, for the overstuffed chairs and couches were draped with white sheets that gave them a ghostly look despite the strong afternoon sunlight. Jeff stopped at the very window shown in the old photograph and stared out over the balcony rail just as Glendon's uncle once had. Momentarily, Jeff wondered if something in the house could have caused the man's wild look; for Jeff felt a sudden mistrust of everything behind him, including his long-time friend Bruce Barlow and the polite, obliging Mr. Whittaker. Jeff shook off a sudden chill as he wheeled about, only to find that neither of his companions was even looking in his direction.

Bruce had opened a suitcase and was spreading the ghost-hunting equipment on a table he had cleared for that purpose. There were cameras, films, and other photographic equipment; also metal measuring tapes, a ball of cord, and some lead fish weights.

"We measure walls for thickness," Bruce explained to Mr. Whittaker, "and use the cord and weights as a plumb line to see if air shafts, wells, and so on are truly vertical. And here's an old friend" — Bruce brought the carpenter's level from the bag — "that enables us to spot slanted floors." Bruce gave a side glance toward Jeff. "Remember the old house with the pool of blood, Jeff?"

Jeff nodded. Now Bruce was spreading out a nest of small, shallow bowls with a flask of mercury and two pairs of soft-soled shoes.

"We fill the bowls with mercury," Bruce told Whittaker, "and set them at key spots. If anything more solid than a ghost comes prowling by, the tremors of the mercury will indicate it. Then Jeff and I put on the soft-soled shoes and go sneaking up on it. The mercury is good at detecting vibrations, too. That's how we tracked a subway ghost in Greenwich Village. Remember that case, Jeff?"

Jeff remembered and gave a shiver, but it wasn't recollective. It had to do with the atmosphere here in the parlor of the house on the square.

"This place is cold," he complained. "Terribly cold. Can't we start a fire in the fireplace?"

"Certainly," agreed Whittaker, "but I haven't noticed any chill."

"Neither have I," declared Bruce, taking a thermometer from the bag, "and what's more, the temperature hasn't dropped a single degree since we came in here. I checked it downstairs, and it is still the same."

Jeff decided to defer the fire, and they continued their tour of the house. The second floor back was mostly bedrooms, and so was the entire third floor. To Bruce, the third floor seemed less chilly than the second; but the fourth floor proved truly ominous. It was reached by a stairway that went up to a landing in a rear corner of the house; then turned and brought them to the approximate center of the top floor.

At the front were two bedrooms with a lengthwise wall between, giving each a large front window. But the arrangement at the back was quite different. Due to the back stairs, the space for bedrooms was limited, so they were arranged in tandem form. First, there was a squarish room, with no window;

only a transom above the door to admit light and air from the hallway. In the back corner of that outer room was a door leading to the inner room, which was also squarish and had a small window above a rear court.

Each room was identically furnished with a cot, table, and chair, but the inner room, despite its window, was the more ominous, for this was where the ghostly manifestations had presumably driven the occupants to madness and death. Bruce studied the window, noted its heavy frames and some deep holes that went into the woodwork beneath a metal reinforcement.

"These were for the bars originally on the window?" he asked Whittaker.

"Right," returned Whittaker. "The bars were removed after the Glendons sold the house and left."

Bruce thrust his head and shoulders out of the window, which was just large enough to accommodate him. He drew back in and gestured for Jeff to do the same. Jeff did and saw that the wall went straight down to the court, with no chance of reaching any windows on the floors below, as they were off at other angles. Again, Jeff felt the sickening sensation of a menace close behind him; but here it was worse than in the parlor two floors below, because the threat of a fall was actual. Jeff shied back into the room quite suddenly.

Again, the others were too busy to notice Jeff's reaction. Bruce was mapping out the campaign that he and Jeff were to follow, while Whittaker was listening with commending nods.

"We'll start right here in this room at midnight," declared Bruce, "since that seems to be the zero hour. I'll sleep here and let Jeff have the cot in the outer room. I'll get the facts first hand, and Jeff can attest them."

Jeff wondered how good a witness he would be if his present jittery mood continued. But he maintained a discreet silence.

"What about the rest of the house?" asked Whittaker.

"We'll keep tabs on it until midnight," replied Bruce. "Give it what Jeff calls a preliminary survey. I don't think we will have to investigate it further, once we've made short work of the ghost business up here."

"There is no electricity in the house," reminded Whittaker, "and it may take a few days to have it turned on —"

"And by then we won't need it," interposed Bruce, with a confident smile. "Anyway, this ghost business started back in the gaslight era. So they didn't have electricity, either."

Whittaker left, stating that he would have dinner sent in for the ghost hunters from a neighborhood restaurant. Bruce and Jeff made their immediate headquarters in the second floor parlor where they had their equipment, and their first act was to start the fire that Jeff wanted. But even that cheery blaze failed to lessen Jeff's occasional chills. Jeff was glad when Bruce suggested that they make a survey of the house; first, by the fading daylight, later with their powerful flashlights.

When the dinner arrived, they ate it in the somber, oak-furnished dining room; then went up to the parlor again, where, by the firelight, they made notes of all that they had accomplished so far, which in the final analysis, was very little. When they listened for suspicious sounds, all they heard was the occasional spurt of a taxicab out in front of Redgate Square. Then, as midnight neared, Bruce picked up his Penang lawyer from beside the fireplace and said:

"It's nearing the zero hour, Jeff. Let's go."

"Yes, let's go," blurted Jeff, "but not upstairs. Let's go down and out the front door. We can come back for our stuff tomorrow."

Bruce's face clouded angrily in the flicker of the firelight.

"You mean you really want to quit, Jeff?"

"I do. This place has got me, Bruce. It isn't right. No creaks, no noises, none of the usual stuff. Instead, it's filled with some gripping force."

"I've heard you talk that way before, but you always changed your mind before we finished the job."

"Yes, I have sensed things elsewhere," conceded Jeff, "but the force, or whatever it was, seemed to dissipate itself. Here it gathers and becomes stronger. Look, Bruce, some of those places really were haunted to a degree. Otherwise, every house, every swamp, every odd place would be haunted. But you know and I know that it only applied in certain instances. The influence, or whatever it is, isn't strong enough to hurt you if you see it through, as we have. But this house is charged with it, Bruce, charged like a load of mental dynamite. They've made tests in psychic laboratories, proving that thoughts can accumulate like thunderclouds and strike with physical impact!"

"And do you know what I think of those tests?" demanded Bruce, his face showing a weird grin in the firelight. "They are bunk — and more bunk. Speaking of bunks, ours are waiting upstairs. So come on."

They went up to the fourth floor back, sidestepping some mercury bowls and an automatic camera that they had planted on the final stairway, just in case of prowlers. They entered the two back rooms and flashed their lights about them. Bruce closed the hallway door and turned the key from the inside, but he left the transom open.

"If anything comes creeping up here," declared Bruce, "you will be the first to hear it. So pass the word to me in the inner room."

"Nothing will come creeping up," returned Jeff. "The danger is in there, Bruce. Let's move my cot in with yours, so we can meet it together."

"Not a chance, Jeff. I'm sleeping in there alone with the door shut between us. We've got to meet the original conditions."

Bruce flicked his light into the inner room, entered and turned to close the door, only to find that Jeff had followed him.

"Suppose something happens in here?" asked Jeff. "What then?"

"Nothing will happen," retorted Bruce, "because it can't."

"Don't talk that way, Bruce. It doesn't take a ghost to make things happen. Suppose you should hear something, as we have in other places —"

"If I hear anything," put in Bruce, sitting down on the cot, "I'll let you know. With a tap on the wall, like this."

Bruce used the head of his heavy cane to rap the wall at the very spot where Jeff's cot was located on the other side.

"Suppose you should see something," persisted Jeff from the doorway. "How will you signal that?"

"With two taps, like this." Bruce rapped twice with the Penang lawyer. "Only I won't see anything. Let's turn in and get some sleep."

"What if something more happens?" questioned Jeff. "What if this —
this influence *is* real —"

"Okay, okay," interposed Bruce indulgently. "In that case, I'll give three
raps" — He tapped the wall accordingly — "so close the door and call it a
night. By morning, we'll be laughing at this nonsense. Our big worry will be
collecting our fee from Whittaker."

Oddly, Jeff felt a lot easier when he closed that connecting door and went
to his cot in the outer room. It was as if a tremendous pressure had been
lifted from him. But it made him worry more about Bruce, who was not
sensitive to psychic impressions. Even this outer room had an oppressive effect
upon Jeff, but he felt that he could cope with it.

Jeff placed his flashlight and his automatic on the chair beside his cot,
finding it a help to have them there, for he was willing to admit that his fears
might be more physical than mental. He listened intently for any stir from
the inner room; then he realized that the wall was too thick for him to hear
anything less than heavy raps from Bruce's big cane. Finally, in the utter
stillness and complete blackness of the outer room, Jeff managed to drop off
to sleep.

How many hours passed, Jeff could not tell, but he awakened very suddenly, wondering where he was and how he had gotten there. He was really
chilled now, for he was in an ice-cold sweat despite the stuffy warmth of the
outer room. As he gradually pieced the facts of the preceding day and recognized his pitch-black surroundings, he realized that he was waiting, waiting,
waiting for something he was sure would happen in that stillness.

It came, the sound that jarred him into stark reality:

Knock!

It was sharp, from the wall beside Jeff's head, the signal that Bruce had
promised. So Bruce had heard something! Now Jeff was listening for it himself while he lay there unable to move. Something more was due; of that he
was certain. Then it came:

Knock — Knock!

The double signal jolted Jeff upright in bed. So Bruce had seen something, there in the inner room! Yet out here, all was still black. Tensely, Jeff
swung from the bed, then halted, again sensing that more was due:

Knock! Knock!! Knock!!!

Even as the heavy cane strokes thudded, Jeff was grabbing up his flashlight and his automatic while he headed for the door to the inner room. He
found the knob, wrenched the door open and plunged through to the other
room where he stopped. He pressed the flashlight button and swept its beam
around while he loosened the automatic's safety catch with the thumb of his
other hand. Then Jeff gave a short, nervous laugh at his own folly.

There was Bruce, lying comfortably in bed, the Penang lawyer propped
against the wall where he had placed it. Already, faint daylight was coming
in through the little window high above the courtyard. Possibly Bruce had
noticed it and had delivered those knocks to awaken Jeff and tell him that
the night's vigil was over. Yet it wasn't like Bruce to have carried it that far.
One rap would have been enough, signifying that he had seen something;
namely, dawn. Maybe Bruce had only half-awakened, given the raps and

gone to sleep again. Anyway, there was nothing to fear. Jeff stepped to the cot and said:

"I guess you were right, Bruce. There was nothing to worry about —"

Jeff caught himself as he saw that Bruce was staring upward. But Bruce wasn't awake, even though his eyes were open. At the glint of those wide, fixed pupils and the white surrounding them, Jeff was horror-stricken, there in the light of early dawn. He pressed his hand to Bruce's forehead; tilted his ear to listen for a heartbeat. The forehead was cold; the heart was still.

Bruce Barlow was dead!

Madly, Jeff Shelby dashed from the inner room, found the key in the outer door and turned it. He raced downstairs, jarring the mercury bowls, snapping the automatic camera as he passed. He reached the front door, unbolted it; then rushed across the square and down the street to an all-night lunchroom, where he put in a frantic call to the nearest hospital.

The ambulance arrived, but to no avail. Brue Barlow was pronounced dead, the cause heart failure. Yet in all the years that Jeff Shelby had known his fellow ghost hunter, Bruce had never shown a single symptom of such a condition. To Jeff, there was only one explanation for Bruce's death. The creeping, haunting, crushing sensation that Jeff had experienced in that house and had managed gradually to shake off, must all have caught up with Bruce at once, with a deadly result.

Only Jeff, who had stout-heartedly gone through so many earlier adventures, could testify to the existence of an unseen terror that seemed to emanate from the very walls of this house of horror, as though they had absorbed some murderous force, only to pour it out on anyone who challenged it!

They closed the old house after the inquest. For years, it remained unoccupied, becoming more and more dilapidated. During those years, Jeff Shelby tried to forget the tragedy that had snuffed the life of his best friend, Bruce Barlow. But often he would awaken in the dead of night, reliving that horrible blackness, again hearing those frantic knocks.

Had Jeff Shelby really heard them? That was the question he asked not only himself but other persons versed in psychic matters. They came to these conclusions:

Possibly Bruce Barlow had heard some weird sound, then had seen a strange shape; and finally had found himself ensnared in an actual death struggle with some unknown force. Bruce had remembered the signals and had given them, but too late. By then, the power had fully materalized from the unreal into the real; following that, it had returned to the unreal, being absorbed into the surrounding walls.

That was a theory that bordered on the supernatural. In contrast, some persons who accepted only the supernormal were inclined to the opinion that Bruce, in his sleep, had experienced a heart attack. It had created illusions in his mind — auditory, visual, and finally a sensation of imminent doom. Desperately, he had flashed the mental impression of those promised knocks to his only contact with the world, his close friend, Jeff Shelby. Already keyed to a high mental pitch, Jeff had caught those telepathic flashes and had believed that the knocks were real; which, in a way, they were, to a sensitized mind like his.

A few years later, this case had another tragic aftermath. Two sailors on shore leave found their way into the neglected old brick house on Redgate Square and looked for a place to sleep. They naturally chose the spot where they thought they would be least likely to be found and rousted out, the remote inner room at the fourth floor back. There, they pulled one cot in with the other and went to sleep.

Next morning, one sailor was found dead in the courtyard, where he had plunged to his doom. The other was picked up on the street, in a complete delirium. Accused of having pitched his companion from the window, he denied the whole thing. Jeff Shelby was called to New York to testify in the accused sailor's behalf, which he did.

In one of his more lucid moments, the surviving sailor was able to tell what had happened to his unfortunate shipmate. Graphically, he said:

"I woke up — and there was something closing in on my matey. I don't know what it was, but he was screaming, 'I hear it — I see it — it's got me!' And then he was breaking away from something, diving for the window, grabbing like he saw bars there — only there weren't any bars — and then he was gone — out through. But there was blackness still there — turning to come at me — so I didn't wait. It got me in the doorway — but I yanked clear of whatever had me — then I ran down the stairs — then outside —"

Hearing that, Jeff Shelby realized that it might have been his own experience, if he, too, had slept in the inner room as he wanted. In Jeff's case, the thing that had snuffed the life of Bruce Barlow had found its human prey and gone its way into the unseen before another victim came along.

Death's Masquerade

Nearly everybody in New Orleans knew Miro's in the old, old days. It was a little shop where faces peered from a window beneath an overhanging balcony just off the Rue Royale. Faces, faces — and still more faces! — some of them changing every day, so that the window, which to many people looked exactly the same, actually was always different.

Every year, there came a time when those faces began to disappear from Miro's window until finally none was left. But they could still be seen — all of them! — in the brightly lighted streets and popular meeting places of New Orleans. There, Miro's faces would laugh at you, leer at you, or give you a solemn, cryptic look, according to their mood and that of their maker, Miro.

For Miro made all the masks that he displayed in the window of his little costume shop, where people came to buy or rent costumes for the biggest annual event in New Orleans, the famous Mardi Gras. Miro put in new masks as he made them and took out the old, which was why the window always changed. It became empty around carnival time when the masks kept going out, until on Mardi Gras Day, which marked the climax, there wasn't a face left. They were all being worn by merrymakers called Maskers, who thronged all New Orleans.

Miro knew his customers like any other merchant. He was like the news dealer, who sold people their copy of the *Daily Picayune,* or the laundryman, who saw them once a week, or the barber, who cut their hair once each month. But Miro's customers only came around once a year. That was why he knew them so much better than the other merchants did. He had more time to think about them, and they were never in a hurry when he saw them.

Of course, Miro did some odd business between times. He had his lesser clientele, to whom he sold lottery tickets, good luck charms, and even voodoo powders when there was a call for them. But he was indifferent to such trade, just as Broullard, the confectioner who supplied the great frosted cakes for many Mardi Gras functions, cared nothing for the ragamuffins who came into his store to buy penny buns.

Of course, there was one noteworthy exception in Miro's case. That

145

was Paul Garneau, who stopped at the mask shop nearly every day and always bought some trifle. Paul had studied law, then had given it up because it interfered with his social life. He liked to watch Miro make masks, because they reflected the old man's moods. More than that, when Mardi Gras approached, Paul liked to watch the customers try on their choices and pose for Miro's opinion.

Paul observed that after each customer had gone, the old mask maker made an entry in a little black book. After some coaxing, Miro finally showed the book to Paul, under an oath of strictest secrecy. In it, certain names were followed by a neatly shaped death's head, and in every case, the person had died within the following year. In short, Miro knew when an annual customer was not coming back; and he told Paul why.

"Most of my masks are gay," declared Miro, "because the Mardi Gras itself is gay, and I try to catch its mood. But if I am sad or angry or utterly despondent, that mood goes into the mask I am making. Yet some people seek out those masks."

"You mean people who are in a mood to die?"

"In a way, yes, but not always. It is not until the person puts the mask on that I really know. Then, behind that person, I see a skeleton figure, with bony hands, the Grim Reaper, ready to take toll, which he does. Here, take my black book. Compare it with the obituaries in the *Daily Picayune!*"

Paul did just that and found out that Miro was one hundred per cent right. After that, Paul frequented Miro's steadily when Mardi Gras approached. When Miro approved a costume with a nod that seemed a trifle sad, Paul knew that the wearer would be listed in the black book.

Paul Garneau had an idea. He would make good use of old Miro's strange gift. So Paul began convincing his girl friend, Carlotta Engard, that she had a psychic sense. When they were dining at Dizard's or sipping coffee in the old French Market, Paul would say in a hushed tone:

"That person over there — can't you see Death looming behind him, ready to clutch him with those skeleton hands? My word, that can't be our friend Mr. Tyson, who opened that new jewelry store on St. Charles Avenue. Yes, I believe it is, but don't breathe a word about that skeleton you saw."

Poor Carlotta soon began really seeing such things because she believed them; and the reason for her belief was the accuracy of Paul's predictions, which he so craftily identified as hers, though they were really Miro's. After three or four years of this, Paul Garneau was ready for his grand coup, the winning of the Louisiana Lottery.

The Louisiana Lottery had been outlawed years before; but it still operated under cover, though its $10,000 grand prize was a mere picayune compared to the old days. What was more, no one could win the lottery, because it was fixed. But many tickets were sold by little shopkeepers like Miro, so it didn't take Paul too long to learn that the man behind it was Noel Dizard, whose restaurant was among the best in town.

Of course, Dizard always bought his Mardi Gras costume at Miro's, so Paul was there when the portly, ever-smiling restaurant owner made his annual call. Dizard recognized Paul as one of his customers; in turn, Paul showed Dizard some of Miro's nicest costumes. Rather reluctantly, Dizard chose a stony-faced Aztec mask, and Miro just as hesitatingly put a death's head after it in his little black book.

"I saw Death standing there," Miro told Paul later, "because that was the mood of the mask. But I wasn't too sure that it fitted the face behind it."

"That is because Dizard's smiling face is a mask itself," Paul said. "But I hope you are wrong this time. I like Dizard."

The curious fact was that Paul Garneau did like Noel Dizard, whose restaurant served some very fine dishes. But Paul could not let sentiment interfere with business, so he talked Carlotta into seeing the figure of Death close behind Dizard, every time they dined at the restaurant. Meanwhile, Paul kept buying lottery tickets at Miro's along with good-luck charms that practically guaranteed a winning number.

That Mardi Gras, Paul wore a costume representing the Laughing Cavalier. As such, he dropped into Dizard's for a late snack on the very night when the lottery winner was to be announced. Paul knew the way to Dizard's private office, and when he saw that the way was clear, he strolled in. Dizard had just returned from a grand ball given by a Mardi Gras group, or Krewe, and he was still wearing his Aztec mask and costume. The Laughing Cavalier sat down at the desk and faced the Aztec King. Then, before Dizard could ask his visitor's purpose, Paul laid his cards on the table in the form of a hundred dollars' worth of lottery tickets.

"One of these tickets should win the grand prize," said Paul, his tone deep and hollow from within the mask. "So pay me and save us both trouble."

Dizard's response was a laugh that sounded like a bellow.

"What if everybody asked to be paid one hundred to one?"

"Nobody else will ask. They don't know the lottery is fixed. I'm only asking you to be honest, Dizard, and declare an actual winner. Besides, I see the figure of Death creeping up behind you. I can ward it off, Dizard, by giving you these voodoo powders" — he tossed some packets on the desk — "which were especially prepared by Miro."

Angrily, Dizard brushed away the tickets and the packets and bellowed: "Get out of here!"

"I see Death closing in" — from behind the mask, Paul's tone was ominously persuasive — "I see bony hands at your throat, Dizard —"

Instinctively, Dizard raised one hand to his throat, then reached for a desk drawer with the other. Paul launched himself across the desk.

"Let me help you, Dizard! You are already in Death's clutch! Let me pull those bony hands away —"

A consummate actor, Paul Garneau was pretending that he was fighting off a pair of deadly, clutching hands. But Dizard, also grabbing for the hands that gripped his throat found only Paul's there. Gradually, the struggle ended. Dizard slumped dead.

"Too bad," Paul said in a solemn, musing tone. "I just did not have the strength to cope with Death himself."

In the desk drawer, Paul found the revolver that Dizard had tried to reach. Also, he found $30,000 in cash. Dizard's profit from the lottery. Paul, being honest, took only $10,000 for himself. Then he unlocked the back door of Dizard's office and hurried down a back stairs to a courtyard that led to the Rue Dauphine.

They found Dizard's body an hour later, along with the scattered lottery tickets and voodoo powders. Because of the money left in the desk, it didn't look like a robbery at first; but during the weeks that followed, Detective Henri Blanc, of the New Orleans police, finally eliminated all suspects except a man who had been wearing a Laughing Cavalier costume.

At Miro's, Blanc found that Paul Garneau had purchased such a costume and that he had also bought the lottery tickets and the voodoo powders. Also, Paul had been losing so much money in his favorite gambling houses that it seemed quite likely he had taken cash from Dizard's desk, as there was no other place where he could have gotten it. So, in due process, Paul was arrested, charged with the murder of Dizard, and brought to trial.

As a lawyer, Paul decided to take charge of his own defense. The odds, in local gambling circles, promptly rose to twenty to one against him, as the state was represented by Mark Zeeman, the most capable prosecutor in Louisiana. Using evidence supplied by Detective Blanc, the prosecutor traced every move of the Laughing Cavalier from the time he left Miro's shop until he entered Dizard's office.

Zeeman was a big man, with a broad, heavy, firm-set face which always maintained the same glowering expression, while he boomed away in a domineering tone. He was at his best when he called Paul as a witness and demanded:

"Can you, Paul Garneau, possibly deny that you were the last person to enter that office while Noel Dizard was still alive?"

Paul didn't deny it. Instead, he admitted it, which brought a gasp from the courtroom. Then, calmly, Paul related:

"There was someone already in there with Dizard, when I entered — a weird, grotesque figure of Death, clutching Dizard's throat from behind. I thought the attacker was some crazed Masker, and I tried to wrench him away. Then, suddenly, he was gone and there was Dizard, slumped on the desk. I decided that the killer must have fled by the back door, which was open, so I followed. But by the time I reached the Rue Dauphine, he had vanished. I knew then that Death himself had taken my good friend Dizard, so it was no use to go back."

"A highly imaginative story," sneered Zeeman. "It is just too bad that you cannot furnish witnesses to support such fanciful testimony."

"But I can," Paul assured him. "First, I shall call on Carlotta Engard."

Carlotta took the stand and sincerely avowed that she had often seen a figure of Death hovering over Dizard, as she had with certain other persons who had died quite suddenly. Scoffingly, Zeeman declared that her unsupported testimony would not do. So Paul called his next witness, old Miro. Blandly, the mask maker told how he, too, had seen the Grim Reaper looming above Dizard, as well as other persons. Under cross-examination, Miro produced his little black book. When names were read from it, an awed hush fell over the jury until Zeeman turned to them and stormed:

"All trumped-up evidence! All hearsay — all a trick! That book could have been faked to fit the case. Let's put this to a real test!" He turned to Miro, who was seated placidly in the witness box. "Since you are so good at seeing Death, look around this court and tell us where his figure is hovering now!"

That was an old trick which Paul had expected Zeeman to spring. Paul hoped Miro would respond in a way that would impress the jury, but he only shook his head.

"I judge masks," Miro declared, "because their features are fixed. I cannot judge people, because their features are mobile. Of course, there are a few people whose faces can be termed masks, due to their fixed expressions."

"And do you see any such faces in this courtroom, now?"

"A few, but they are not good examples, except for *your* face."

The judge silenced a ripple of nervous laughter from the courtroom. Paul Garneau leaned forward intently as Mark Zeeman suddenly demanded: "Then tell us, Miro, do you see a figure of Death behind me?"

Miro studied Zeeman as Paul had often seen him study customers in the costume shop. Then Miro began to nod slowly.

"Since you ask me," he said, "I do. It is coming closer — closer —" Miro turned to Carlotta, who was riveted in her chair. "You see it, too, don't you?" Then, as Carlotta hesitated, almost on the point of nodding, Miro stared at Zeeman and added: "Its fingers are clutching, now!"

Contemptuously, Zeeman turned to the jury, gave them his fixed glower, and raised his hands to his throat. In stentorian tones, he boomed:

"So these witnesses see me in Death's clutch, as Garneau claims he saw Dizard. They want us to believe that Dizard raised his hands like this and struggled against bony fingers that were otherwise invisible. Do you see any hands but mine, gentlemen of the jury? Can you see the bony fingers of Death?"

Zeeman reeled momentarily as he spoke. A gargling cry sounded in his throat. His body came up to its full height, bending back as though drawn by invisible hands. Then the unseen grip apparently relaxed, for Zeeman toppled forward, hitting the front of the jury box and sprawling across it, inert, while the jurors shied away and court attendants came rushing over.

The judge pounded with his gavel and called a recess. It proved to be a long one. Mark Zeeman was dead. And he had gone in the very manner that he had scoffed at as something impossible. He was gone, with Death's invisible clutch upon his throat.

The doctors pronounced it heart failure, and the trial was resumed with one of Zeeman's assistants as prosecutor. But the jury wasn't taking any chances; not after seeing what the figure of Death could do, even though visible only to a psychic few. They acquitted Paul Garneau on the first ballot.

Paul made out nicely because he had bet his bottom dollar that he would be acquitted. He went about with a pose of injured innocence, gambling more extravagantly than ever. Old Miro neglected his trade and began working on a special mask and costume which he said were to be his masterpiece. Then, realizing he was falling behind, he bundled it away and said nothing more. Paul knew about it, for he was keeping close watch on Miro. In his turn, Detective Blanc was keeping watch on Paul. As Blanc put it to his superiors:

"I still think that this man Garneau killed Dizard because he needed money. If he gets in financial straits again, he may try another murder."

But Paul, though he lost much through reckless play, did not run out of money. During his brief prosperity, he had met a new friend, Steve Lucas, who mistook him for a man of substance and lent him cash when he needed it. Now, a year had passed and the Mardi Gras again was due. So were some $10,000 worth of notes that Paul had given Steve.

What made it bad was that Paul had been winning lately and now had the money, or most of it. But to pay off Steve, he would leave himself broke, and Paul couldn't do that. Instead, he became clever indeed. First, he began telling Carlotta that he saw a Death figure hovering over Steve, and soon Carlotta began to believe that she saw it, too, as she had with Dizard. Even though Carlotta wasn't totally convinced, Paul did not worry. This time, things were well set.

At Miro's, Paul found that the old man was still seeing his vision of the Grim Reaper as before, but was not keeping such exact records. That, too, was helpful. This year, Paul bought a very special costume representing a Pirate Chief, but he did not put it on at Miro's. Paul just took it along and told Carlotta and others about it, so everyone knew that, come Mardi Gras, Paul Garneau would be swaggering about as a Pirate Chief, as he had previously swashbuckled as the Laughing Cavalier. Word of this reached Detective Blanc.

Then, toward Mardi Gras Day, when Miro's shop was all but empty, Paul stopped in one evening and confided in the old mask maker.

"I have a friend who wants a special costume," said Paul. "I know you have one put away back there in the shop, and I'm sure he would pay a good price for it. How about accommodating him, Miro?"

Finally Miro agreed and named a price. Paul paid the money.

"My friend is outside," Paul told Miro, "so I'll collect from him and send him in. He doesn't want to be known, so don't give him much attention. And don't mention this to anyone, ever. You understand?"

Miro understood. Paul went out, and his friend came in, a stooped, shambling man whose face was muffled in his upturned coat collar. He went to the darkened back corner of the shop. There he straightened up and became Paul Garneau. He found the special costume and put it on. When he was ready, he reverted to the shambling gait and stopped to ask in a disguised voice that he knew could not be recognized from within the muffling mask:

"How do I look, Mr. Miro?"

Miro gave an appraising glance, then tilted back his head and began a titter that became a cackle, then a laugh. He continued to laugh and laugh, as Paul had never heard him laugh before. That, of course, was the best of omens, for Miro was always saddened when he saw the figure of Death in the offing.

Paul left the shop. A block from Miro's, he phoned Carlotta and told her:

"Steve Lucas is expecting us at his apartment, because I said we would take him to dinner with us. Poor chap, we ought to see that he has a good time before Death takes him. So meet me over there, right away."

This being Carnival time, Steve Lucas was holding open house. As Carlotta walked in, Steve, a smallish man, was standing in the living room, wearing a sad-faced clown costume. He was just greeting Carlotta when a pair of French windows opened from a balcony behind him and the skeleton figure of Death launched into the room.

Never in her wildest fancies had Carlotta seen the Grim Reaper more vividly, nor had he ever shown his power so forcefully. With skeleton hands, the Death figure grabbed Steve by the neck and shook him as a terrier would a rat. Steve's clown mask came off and Carlotta saw his eyes go goggly while his face began to turn blue. Realizing how deadly that clutch of Death could really be, Carlotta turned and raced out the front way, screaming for help. On the threshold she ran into a man in the costume of a Pirate Chief, and she gasped in happy recognition.

"Quickly, Paul!" panted Carlotta. "Steve is in there — but Death is choking him — it may be too late to save him —"

It wasn't quite too late. Steve was still gasping when the Pirate Chief reached the living room and pulled an old-fashioned pistol from his sash. He aimed it at the figure of Death, and to Carlotta's amazement, the Grim Reaper, who should have feared no weapons, did an odd thing. He flung Steve aside and instead of vanishing, drove for the Pirate Chief, trying to wrest the pistol from him.

In the struggle, the gun went off. It was Death who took the bullet, for he sprawled to the floor. In the full light, Carlotta saw that he was not actually a skeleton figure, but that his costume consisted of bright white streaks painted on black velvet to represent ribs and other bones. His skull was a paint job, too, for it came off like a loosened helmet and rolled away, revealing the face beneath.

The man who had masqueraded as Death was Paul Garneau!

Amazed, Carlotta turned to the Pirate Chief, who should have been Paul. He unmasked and revealed himself as Detective Henri Blanc.

The situation really unraveled itself when Steve Lucas recovered sufficiently to talk. He brought out a wallet containing the notes for the cash that Paul Garneau had owed him.

"Paul said to have these ready," Steve related, "so he could pay them off. Instead, he tried to kill me so he could steal them back, and nobody would have been the wiser!"

"And he wore that Death costume," Carlotta exclaimed, "so that this time I would be positive I saw the Grim Reaper take his toll!"

"I knew Garneau was planning something," declared Detective Blanc. "So I kept watching his apartment. I heard him phone Mr. Lucas and arrange to come over. Instead, when I trailed him, he went to Miro's. I figured he planned to pick up a different costume, so I doubled back to his apartment and put on the Pirate Chief outfit, not just to surprise him here, but because he might want it as an alibi if he ducked back to his place. But I never expected to see him in a Death outfit!"

Later Detective Blanc talked to Miro and learned that the old mask maker had designed the Death costume, hoping it would clear his mind of those visions of the Grim Reaper. It hadn't helped, so he had packed the special outfit away. But Paul Garneau had been smart enough to find it; too smart, as it turned out.

"A very odd thing happened," explained Miro. "I half-guessed that the 'friend' Paul sent in for the costume was Paul himself. When he asked me how he looked in his costume, he was wondering if I saw Death in back of him. And I *did* see Death, so close that it could lay its hands on him.

"Ordinarily, that would have put me in a sad mood, and I'd have shown it. Paul knew that and was waiting for my warning nod. But when I saw Death — heh-heh! — I saw Death laying his hands on Death — heh-heh-heh! — a phantom Death gripping the man who was masquerading as Death" — Miro gave a high-pitched cackle — "it was so funny that I laughed — and laughed — Ha-ha-ha-ha-ha-ha-ha-ha-ha —"

The Riddle of the Crypt

The cabin cruiser *Rover* had just rounded Porpoise Point when Irene Morrow gained her first view of Cliff Island. Her brother Roy pointed it out as it loomed in sight, and Irene exclaimed, "How beautiful! How very, very beautiful!"

It was indeed a splendid sight, a mass of steep gray bluffs rising like the walls and towers of an enchanted palace floating on a clear blue sea. As the cruiser swung eastward of the island, the setting sun gave a scintillating touch to the granite heights, producing a scene straight from the pages of a fairy book.

As the boat sped closer, the island seemed to spread in size, creating another surprising illusion. Then, suddenly, a frowning headland cut off the sunlight and darkened the water with a sullen gloom, broken only by the tufted white of waves that crashed on the cold gray stones below. In a trice, all the sparkle was gone, and the face of the island became rugged and forbidding.

The transition struck Irene as she was repeating the enthusiastic words, forcing her to modify them:

"How very, very beautiful — and yet so weird and ghostly!"

In a sense, the change was fearful. The *Rover* seemed due to crash on the rocks. But Jerry Lane, the youthful skipper, deftly swung to port, almost skirting the spray of the treacherous breakers. Dead ahead, Irene saw a cleft in the rocky wall. It widened, and sunlight streamed through the jagged gap, transforming the moody black cliffs back to their glittering gray.

"We are coming into Middle Harbor," shouted Roy, above the tumult of the waves. "Don't let Jerry scare you. He really knows this channel."

The channel followed a fold between the high crags, and after a medley of sunlight and shadows, the cruiser hummed into a cozy cove where a few dozen speedboats and cruisers were moored alongside some trim sailboats and a motley lot of weather-beaten fishing craft.

From a short pier, a gangplank ran down to a float where arriving craft could pull alongside regardless of the tide, which was heavy along this part of the New England coast. Soon Roy and Irene were ashore with their luggage, which was handled by a lanky man in overalls, whose face was as rugged as the island's cliffs. He carried the bags to a car old enough to mark its owner as one of the early settlers. It bore the crude legend:

J. CUPPY — TAXI

The settlement about the pier was a combination of a fishing and tourist haven, with a post office, some stores, sea food restaurants, and fishing shacks. But the slopes that funneled up from the harbor were studded with cottages of early twentieth century vintage. They were reached by zigzag roadways and paths with rock-hewn steps that served as shortcuts. Then Roy drew Irene back to the outer end of the pier and pointed to a ledge set back beyond the very top of the slope. On that dominant height, Irene could make out the front of a brand-new ranch house, ruddy in the sunlight's glow.

"That, I will have you know," said Roy, "is our humble abode. The most modern habitation on all Cliff Island with the best outlook."

Irene's round, enthusiastic face beamed an appreciative smile. She was starting to say that the place looked wonderful, even from a distance, when Mr. Cuppy put the last bag in the taxi. So they hurried to the ancient car and climbed in while Cuppy took the wheel and asked:

"Where to, Mr. Morrow?"

"To Castle Rock," returned Roy. "We're living in the new ranch house there."

Mr. Cuppy sat as if frozen behind the wheel. Then he slowly turned his thin red neck and gave his two passengers a long, beady look, turkey fashion. Next, he made a move as if to get out and remove the bags. Then, without a word, he looked ahead again, wheezed the old motor into action and headed the car up the hill.

The view was increasingly beautiful all the way up the long zigzag road. Middle Harbor was an ever-changing scene, with occasional glimpses of the ocean through the rocky walls of the channel. Then, at the top, the island became a saucer-shaped plateau, and Irene could see the ocean all around, with an island-studded bay toward the west. There, the sun, going down beyond the mainland, blended crimson, gold and purple in one magnificent splash.

The taxi gained new life down a slight, winding slope. It passed a stretch of barren, rocky ground, veered away from a thick clump of pine trees, and groaned up a slight, curving quarter-mile grade that brought it in back of the ranch house. Instead of using the driveway, Mr. Cuppy stopped on the road, unloaded the bags while his passengers alighted, and said:

"That'll be one dollar."

As Roy handed Cuppy a bill, the taxi man clambered back into the car, saying, "Got to get down to the dock right quick. The *Countess* is coming in." With that he swung the car about and rattled away, as Irene asked:

"And who is the Countess?"

"A boat," replied Roy. "The steamer from the mainland. But she isn't due until nine o'clock tonight. I can't understand what's wrong with Cuppy."

"I can," came a cheery voice behind them. Irene turned and saw a smiling young man with a shock of light hair. "I've been watching from our ivory tower, expecting to see this happen."

"This is Alan Blount," introduced Roy, "who is helping me in my study of marine fossils. Go on, Alan. Why wouldn't Cuppy carry the bags?"

"Because no person living on Cliff Island will set foot on the blighted ground surrounding Castle Rock. That road is the dividing line. You'll see people walk by on the far side, looking at us as if we were saying, 'Shinny on your own side, this side is taboo.' A crazy superstition, that's all."

Irene smiled, recalling many places she had been where odd customs and strange superstitions were common; but they had never worried her. Besides, she didn't want to be bothered by visitors on Cliff Island. She was here on assignment for her company, International Metallurgics Associated. She had traveled through South America for I. M. A., and they had given her the job of translating and condensing all subsidiary reports from Spanish and Portuguese into English, a two-month job at least.

Roy, a professor of biology at a state university, had heard of the wonderful ranch house on Cliff Island and had rented it while making his fossil survey. So Irene had decided to come and do her work there. She liked the place as they entered the back door through a modern kitchen where Roy gestured to two bedrooms on the right and said:

"Those are bachelors' quarters for Alan and myself. You have the left wing, sis. It was planned as a garage, but nobody keeps a car on Cliff Island, or the taxi business would die. So they turned it into a studio with a glass window in place of a front door. Come and see it!"

It instantly became Irene's dream room. From the picture window, she could see the whole harbor, with the limitless ocean beyond, while a casement window at the side gave a view of the pine woods and the stretch of rocks beyond the curving road.

Each morning, Roy and Alan left early, and Irene went to work on her translations, pausing at intervals to look from the front window at a scene as varied as it was beautiful, for the moods of the clouds and the ocean were many. But at times, Irene found herself drifting into a dreamy state, in which the present faded and everything seemed as distant as the boundless sea. Always, she was jolted from such reveries by the sensation of watching eyes and a figure creeping behind her.

Then Irene would snap from the clutch of the unknown, often with an involuntary scream. All about, she would see floating blobs of blackness that would gradually dissolve. After such shocks, Irene felt an urge for human company. The fact that the Islanders regarded this ledge as taboo struck home with numbing force. Irene would rush out to the back road. There she felt safe, though no one was ever around.

Sometimes Irene regained her calm by walking down the road to the pine woods, which was beautifully shaped and exquisitely green, compared to the otherwise drab landscape of the plateau. In bright sunlight, the evergreens were restful. On cloudy days, or under the colorful tints of an early sunset, the grove took on a deeper green that absorbed Irene's worries with it.

The rocks beyond the grove were typical of the island's ruggedness. A hundred feet to the right of the evergreens, several hundred heavy stones were tumbled in a pile at least thirty feet across and half that high. The pile interested Irene, because it was man-made. She passed it late in the afternoons when she cut across to a path that led down among the cottages to the harbor. There she met Roy and Alan when they came in on the *Rover*. Often she stopped at an employment office to try to hire a woman to help with the housework. But when she said "Castle Rock" none was ever available.

Sometimes Irene had a fish or lobster dinner with Roy and Alan at one of the seafood places. Other times, she prepared dinner at the ranch house. Almost always, they went up the hill in Cuppy's taxi — until one afternoon when the whole ocean became a mass of white billows formed by a low-clinging fog that kept creeping up the island's craggy walls. By the time Irene reached the dock, she could just make out the bulk of a coast guard craft that was moored there. From it, a loudspeaker called off names, giving information about boats that were overdue. One announcement came:

"Miss Morrow — Miss Irene Morrow — message from the *Rover*. Fog-bound at Port Clarion — will return to Middle Harbor tomorrow."

Irene ate alone at the pier restaurant and stayed late, hoping that the fog would clear, but it lessened only slightly. She found Cuppy asleep in his cab, wakened him, and they started up the hill, with Cuppy working his way slowly in low gear. Irene decided that this was a good time to get first-hand evidence on the Castle Rock taboo.

"I won't ask you to drive me to my door," she said, "but I would like to know why nobody on Cliff Island will come to Castle Rock."

"Well, the Rock has a curse on it," returned Cuppy. "Some sort of spell that has never worn off from long ago. People have seen strange critters up toward the Rock, the kind that change to giant bats."

"If you mean vampires," retorted Irene, "they are bunk. I have seen vampire bats in South America, but they prey on cattle, that's all."

Just then, a huge, swooping shape came into the glare of the car's bright headlights. Its wings were like mammoth arms as it loomed from the fog. Irene's nerves, which had been getting worse daily, were so raw that she started to scream, but rather than show weakness, she reduced it to an "Eeeek!" An answering "Eeeek!" came from the flitting shape, which was gone instantly, leaving only the whitish swirl of the fog. Irene decided it was an ordinary bat, magnified by the fog to gigantic proportions. As they neared Castle Rock, Cuppy suggested:

"Look, Miss Morrow. I'll back my car so the lights will guide you into the house, so nothing can come at you in the dark —"

"You mean a vampire?" broke in Irene. "Like the one we just saw?"

"I'm not sure what we did see," returned Cuppy. "The worst thing is the yellow eyes that people see up here. They come from that pine woods" — he gestured to an ominous bulk of blackness on his right — "but lookee, lady. If you get in the house and keep all the windows tight shut, nothing can sneak in with you, not even none of the fog. That's all I've got to say."

Cuppy used his bright lights as a path to the house, and Irene followed it. Once she was inside, Cuppy cut his headlights to dim, probably finding they reflected less glare from the fog. He started back down the road, and Irene went into her studio-garage, where she looked toward the pine grove, wondering if she would see those yellow eyes.

Then, suddenly, she did. Tiny, yellow beads, they squinted from the swirl of the fog and hovered as though coming closer. Irene wondered if Cuppy saw them from his creeping car. Then, just as her nerves reached the shrieking point, Irene gave a laugh that was hysterical but glad.

Those yellow eyes were the taillights of Cuppy's car. Their red lenses had gone to pieces years ago, leaving only little bright bulbs, like yellow, beady eyes. Irene realized that when Cuppy swung past the grove, because then, for the first time, his dim headlights showed and the taillights veered at a new angle.

Irene wished that this harrowing night was over; instead, it had just begun. When she opened the front door for air, fog billowed in. When it vanished after she slammed the door, it seemed all the more like a living thing. There was a magnetic force here, that created living phantasms, for when Irene looked from the window, she could see fog-faces form there, then dissipate in ghoulish swirls. She ran about clamping windows and bolting doors, until overwhelmed by mental and physical exhaustion, she collapsed in a big chair in the living room. All the lights were on, but she was still fearful until she fell into a sleep so deep that when she was finally roused from it, she started up, trembling.

All the lights were still on, but their glare was lost in the dazzle of broad daylight. There were no longer fog-faces peering at Irene, but real faces, those of her brother Roy and his assistant, Alan Blount. It was morning, the fog had lifted, and they had come back in the *Ranger*. When Irene told them what had happened, they nodded.

Their own work was so exacting, so limited on board the *Rover,* that Irene's talk of dazed moods and the floating blackness struck them as the result of her daytime intensity and isolation. One night alone had touched off Irene's accumulation of nervous tension. Roy and Alan stayed home that day. At night, they strolled beneath the stars with Irene and pointed out the constellations, which made earthly worries seem small.

The next day, Roy had another idea. He told Irene:

"We've been talking this over, Alan and I. We want you to come with us to Port Clarion, and while we're studying starfish instead of stars, you can go to the library and dig into the history of Cliff Island. There may be something behind this nonsense about Castle Rock, so let's get to the bottom of it."

Port Clarion was much like Middle Harbor but on a larger scale.

There, Irene saw the tubby *Countess,* a little steamer with its two decks sprouting tourists, as she came in from her morning tour of the islands -of Fisherman's Bay, which included Cliff Island as the outermost. At the library Irene said that she was visiting Cliff Island — carefully avoiding any mention of which part — and that she was intensely interested in its history. When she joined Roy and Alan for dinner at one of the big pier restaurants, Irene was well briefed on her subject. But she waited until the *Rover* was speeding through the moonlit bay back to Cliff Island, with Jerry Lane at the helm. Then she sat in the cockpit with Roy and Alan while she went into her story.

"Apparently, Cliff Island was settled by the French in the early 1600's," stated Irene, "and they kept it clear up to the year 1715."

"That's not surprising," put in Roy. "The French had many outposts that they managed to keep from the British."

"In this case, they really held them off," Irene informed him. "The cliffs were like a fortress, and French peasants raised crops and cattle on the plateau, but occasionally their fishing was curtailed when the British occupied Middle Harbor. So about the year 1700, a French sea rover was appointed to take charge. He was called the Commandant Lesang, and he sailed into Middle Harbor on a ship called the *Aventure*.

"The first thing that Lesang and his crew did was build a citadel on the high rim of the plateau, right where we are living now. That is why it is called Castle Rock. He used to light beacons on a high point called *Cap Bec,* or Cape Beak, but which is now known as Signal Head."

"I know Signal Head," said Roy. "We'll show it to you when we get there. But go on with the story, sis."

"The arrival of the *Aventure* caused great joy," continued Irene, "but all changed to gloom when Lesang ruled the island like a tyrant. He and his evil crew committed murder, tortured helpless prisoners, and brought terror to the island. Finally, the British attacked, bombarded his citadel, and took over the island. The inhabitants were shipped away, and it was years before the island was settled again."

"And what happened to Commandant Lesang?" asked Roy.

"He disappeared," replied Irene. "Some say he escaped in a boat from one of the other harbors. Another account says that he was killed during the attack on the castle. It is even claimed that he was killed earlier but that his ghost returned and was still in command when the castle was demolished."

"That could be the groundwork for the vampire talk," agreed Roy. "Did you run across any of that stuff in the old archives?"

"Yes. Weird yellow eyes have been seen gleaming through the fog. People have been attacked by a gruesome monster that slashes their throats. Some persons have disappeared like Lesang himself."

"Disappeared completely? Without a trace?"

"In some instances, yes. But bodies have been found floating far out to sea and others have been discovered in the deep pit over which the old castle was built."

"Which is now our cellar," commented Roy grimly. "No wonder the place gives you the shakes. I can't blame people for not wanting to come near it."

"I'm sure I can stick it out now." Irene's tone was determined. "I should have laughed it all off when the yellow eyes turned out to be nothing but a taxi's taillights. However, keep a good grip on yourself while I tell you the most fearful legend of the lot. When the full of the moon arrives, the *Aventure* is sometimes seen sailing into Middle Harbor. Then things really cut loose."

"You mean all those things you've just mentioned?"

"And more. Once the ghost ship has been sighted, Lesang's own ghost is sure to appear. That's one legend that just won't die."

"It's a funny thing," put in Alan. "We've talked with a lot of characters around Middle Harbor, but they've never handed us any of this."

"Because that's the last place where they ever will talk about it," rejoined Irene. "The librarian, Miss Lacey, says that the Islanders are so afraid of its hurting the tourist trade that they've even suppressed all picture postcards dealing with it. Those used to be popular some twenty years ago, and Miss Lacey told me of a shop that was still bootlegging them. So I bought some."

Triumphantly, Irene produced a batch of picture postcards which Roy and Alan studied eagerly in the light of the cockpit. One card showed Castle Rock in its barren state; another, with an artist's conception of Lesang's citadel towering upon it. One card showed the pine woods, which was appropriately termed "The Haunted Grove," while another had the stone pile labeled "Old Norse Ruins." Another card depicted Signal Head, with its ancient beacon in full flare, and there was a closeup of a high ledge titled "Bat Roosts on Cliff Island" with bats hanging there.

"According to a book in the library," stated Irene, "those roosts were cleaned out long ago. Now the Islanders pretend they never heard of them."

"There would, of course, be some specimens remaining," declared Roy in his professorial style. "You saw one the other night, but Cuppy wouldn't admit it."

They were passing the *Countess* now, waddling in from her evening rounds, and ahead lay Cliff Island, more ghostly than ever, though Irene was ready to face its eerie heights with new confidence. Roy pointed out Signal Head, and Irene realized that the old beacon point was quite close to Castle Rock but off at a different angle than the road, which was why she had never noticed it. Then Irene remembered a postcard that she had been saving for the last. She brought it out and said:

"Here is the old *Aventure* herself, sailing into Middle Harbor. They've pasted her over a photo of the island, trying to make it look real ghostly."

They showed the picture of the *Aventure* to Jerry Lane. From her three tall square-rigged masts and high stern, he identified her as a French ship of the early 1700's. But the young skipper added that it looked like a stock picture from some old book and that it certainly was not a ghostly craft coming into the Cliff Island Channel, which was incorrectly shown in the composite photo.

When they finally arrived in Middle Harbor and docked at the float, Jerry ducked down into the cabin, then poked his head up and grinned at Irene.

"I hear you've been needing company up at the house, and I thought maybe I could help out," he said. With that, he brought a brown-and-white spotted cat into sight and handed it, purring, to Irene. "Her name is Ginger, and she came on board in Port Clarion. Maybe she'll be happier at Castle Rock than sailing in the *Rover*."

Irene thanked Jerry profusely and carried the contented cat to Cuppy's cab. Cuppy noticed Ginger, and while they were driving up the cliff road, he remarked:

"You may be needing that cat at your place. She looks like a good ratter."

"This cat," returned Irene, "still has all her nine lives, which is the same number as a baseball team. So she isn't a ratter; she is a batter. I may let her go after some of those bats that are still hanging around their old roosts under the cliffs. Like the one you and I saw in the fog, Mr. Cuppy."

That quip silenced Cuppy. For the next few days, everything was peaceful. Then, one mild evening, while Irene was doing translations in her study, and Roy was playing pinochle with Alan in the living room, a new scare struck. Irene had let Ginger out, and as the cat hadn't returned, Irene picked up a long five-cell flashlight and went out the back door to look for her new pet.

With the powerful beam, Irene spotted Ginger frisking halfway down to the haunted grove. Irene called and turned off the light as the cat came bounding toward her. Ginger's light color made her quite conspicuous in the moonlight that filtered through a film of wispy clouds. Irene was looking straight toward the blackish contour of the pine woods; and something she saw there made her laugh lightly. Then suddenly her throat closed up and she froze all over.

Coming straight from the woods were those yellow eyes! Irene's laugh, inspired by her recollection of Cuppy's taillights, faded as she realized his taxi wasn't anywhere around. The eyes grew larger as Irene stooped to snatch up Ginger. Then they were full upon her, and she was swinging the long flashlight wildly to ward off a clawing, jabbing fury that attacked her savagely from the dark. Half smothered by the monstrous thing, Irene kept clubbing with the flashlight as she raced to the house, screaming for Roy and Alan. They came out the back door just as Irene made a last valiant sweep with her improvised cudgel and stumbled into her brother's arms, still clutching Ginger. Roy and Alan identified the thing from the woods as it soared off.

It was a huge owl, the biggest that either had ever seen.

In the living room, Irene put salve on her scratched neck and wrists while Ginger stalked about gratefully. Then, with a forced laugh, Irene said, "Well, we have taken another chunk out of that vampire legend."

"And it's lucky the owl didn't take a chunk out of Ginger," declared Roy. "Considering that owls fly off with chipmunks, a cat isn't too big for them."

During the rest of that week, Irene found a new formula that helped her work and kept her cheerful. She broke those introspective spells by talking to Ginger. For variety, she took brisk walks across the fields. Soon she had found the perfect goal, Signal Head, which offered the best view of the island. There was a strange fascination about that jutting point. Often, as she approached it, Irene heard voices calling, "Irene — Irene —" and she smiled as she identified them as the cries of seagulls off the point. By then, she could hear an echoing "Irene! Irene!" and she would look almost straight down to the booming breakers, hundreds of feet below. By craning a bit more, she could see the narrow strip of rocky beach where the reluctant surf shattered, foamed, and retreated after every crash.

As Irene became accustomed to the scene, it became more alluring, magnetically drawing her to the cliff edge that she no longer feared. Then, one day as she was staring downward, the whole world seemed to fade except for that captivating tumult far below. Eyes half closed, Irene felt herself swaying forward, forward, forward, until a voice spoke from behind her:

"You would be safer back here a little way."

Irene spun about with a frightened shriek. She almost lost her footing on the brink, but the man had anticipated that before he spoke. His quick hand caught Irene's arm in an iron grip and with a strong tug, he had her a dozen feet back from the treacherous rim before she gained a glance at his serious, yet kindly face. Irene was amazed to see that the man, despite his remarkable strength and youthful vigor, was really quite elderly. Vaguely, she recalled having seen him down at the dock.

"I am Dr. Felton," the elderly man said. "I am the island physician. This week, they gave me a nice new six-year-old station wagon, the only car on Cliff Island that isn't a taxi."

Irene saw the car as they left Signal Head and started walking back toward Castle Rock. It was parked near where Cuppy always stopped.

"I need a wagon as an ambulance," explained Dr. Felton, "but in your case, it wouldn't have helped. Those rocks are a long fall down."

"I know." Irene nodded. "I shouldn't have been so near the brink. But how did you realize that I was in danger?"

"I've been coming up here every day," returned the physician, "to see a sick farmer at the far end of the island. Each day I have returned at the same time, and I have seen you looking over the cliff. Always, you seemed to be getting closer to the edge. I knew it wouldn't do."

They reached the front door of the ranch house. "Won't you come in?" Irene asked, and when the doctor nodded, she exclaimed happily:

"Why, you're one person who isn't afraid to walk in here!"

"I'm not an Islander," Dr. Felton replied. "I retired a few years ago, and the township appointed me as resident physician here. But I've heard all about Castle Rock" — his gray eyes narrowed but remained as kindly as ever —"or perhaps I haven't heard all about it. You might be able to tell me more."

Irene sat down in a big chair and began to fondle Ginger, who nestled, purring, in her lap. Though willing to talk, she parried: "Like what?"

"Well, those scratches on your neck and wrists, for one thing," said Dr. Felton. "You certainly didn't get them from this amiable pet of yours."

"I got them from an owl," Irene informed him. "A big owl, while I was saving Ginger from it. I saw big yellow eyes, coming at me from the woods—"

"And you had heard of those eyes before. They must have frightened you."

"They did," returned Irene, grateful for the doctor's understanding. "I saw a bat one night, too. I've seen floating blackness by day, and I've watched the fog make faces by night. But I'm over all such things now —"

"Except cliff walking. Other people have felt that urge, too."

"You really mean there is — there is something uncanny here?"

"I mean, don't be frightened, whatever does happen. Have you ever seen a full-rigged ship come in by full moonlight? Like a ghost ship?"

"No, but I've heard of it," admitted Irene, "and I know what it signifies. Doctor, is there anything to this vampire talk involving a Frenchman named Lesang, who lived more than three hundred years ago — and yet —"

"And yet may still live today?" Dr. Felton shook his head slowly. "It's hard to tell where legend ends and fact begins. You're a sensible young lady, so I can tell you this: I have been in many parts of the world, and I have found the same taboos, the same superstitions, the same unexplainable ailments or accidents, so often attributed to the same strange causes, that it may be they have much in common. Here on Cliff Island there have been too many odd deaths."

"I know that," agreed Irene. "I was reading about some of those cases in an old book over at the Port Clarion Library."

"I'm not talking about what was in old books," rejoined Dr. Felton. "I'm talking about what was in the newspapers during recent years. One woman was found dead in the haunted pine grove, very badly clawed. From your own experience, an owl could have been responsible, though I think in her case, the wounds were worse than any owl could inflict.

"On three different occasions, people have walked off cliffs, one from the very brink where you were today. In every case, they were apparently drawn to their doom by some baleful, indefinable influence. People have seen mammoth bats; not just small ones that they imagined were large. Other persons have disappeared entirely from Cliff Island."

It was growing late in the afternoon, and the doctor noted that although Irene was by no means nervous, she was becoming restless. He asked the reason, and when she told him she would have to go to meet her brother and his assistant, Dr. Felton offered her a ride down to the harbor in his wagon. Irene accepted, and when the *Rover* came in, she introduced Roy and Alan to the physician. The result was that they all dined together in an outdoor corner of the pier restaurant, where spray from scudding speedboats occasionally flicked over the rail.

But their conversation, unlike the gay chitchat so common on the pier, concerned very serious matters. Much of the island's mystery, including the vampire angle, became more intriguing, but also more shuddery, the further they discussed it. When Dr. Felton learned that Irene had seen actual vampire bats in South America, he smiled slightly.

"So that was where you heard how vampires dissolve into black specks and fog," said Dr. Felton. "That means those experiences could have been your imagination. Still, I feel that a vampiric influence is at work and that after failing earlier, it resorted to methods unknown to you."

"You mean like luring me to Signal Head, to push me off?"

"Not to push you off. To hold you there, teetering between "Stop" and "Go," to put it in modern terms. The invisible creature — he could be the notorious Lesang — was waiting until dusk, when his powers grow to their full. Then he could materialize into a solid being and kill you, vampire fashion. After that, he would let you fall to the rocks below, as his alibi."

It was Roy who voiced a strenuous objection:

"Come now, doctor! Don't tell us that vampires need alibis!"

"Of course they do," rejoined Dr. Felton, more serious than ever. "How could a monster like Lesang go on living — I should say existing — except through ignorance on our part? In the Middle Ages, simple-minded peasants recognized such creatures for what they really were and proceeded to get rid of them. Today, we make foolish excuses. We blame these happenings on cliff bats, on broken taillights, on owls' eyes, on everything except what they really represent, the baleful influence of a vampire!"

Dr. Felton paused to let that unnerving statement strike home. Then, he turned to Irene and said calmly:

"Since you are already under the vampiric influence, it is waiting to claim you as its next victim. When it strikes, we must be ready."

"And that," said Irene, "means that I am just a guinea pig."

"You are a very wonderful guinea pig, who can lift the curse of three centuries and still remain unharmed, if we take due precautions. Believe me, Miss Morrow" — sincerity shone in Dr. Felton's gray eyes — "if I could make myself the bait for this experiment, I would do so gladly. You know how many lives have been lost already. I can assure you that as many more will be endangered, unless we stop this fiendish creature here and now. You understand?"

"I understand. If this influence is working on me as you say, I should be the one most interested in seeing it settled forever. But must I first see that ship come in?"

"It would be helpful," stated Dr. Felton, with a nod. "Real or imaginary, it would show that you are conditioned to become the vampire's prey."

Roy and Alan stayed close to Castle Rock from that evening on. During the day, one occasionally went out in the *Rover* with Jerry; but the other was always on hand. In the evenings, both were at the ranch house, helping Irene get dinner ready, for she had to stay right there to keep a lookout for the phantom ship that, in her mind, at least, was becoming very real.

At intervals each evening, Irene would stroll out in the brilliant moonlight, sometimes as far as Signal Head. She went alone, rather than risk breaking the spell. Roy and Alan would keep watching Irene from the picture window of her studio, ready to dash out if she ventured too close to the cliff edge, or if any other danger threatened. But always, Irene was duly cautious and soon returned to the house.

Then came the night when the rising moon was at the full. Irene's hopes — or were they fears? — had reached a high point when Jerry Lane arrived in Cuppy's taxi, with word for Roy and Alan.

"The fog warnings are out," informed Jerry. "Thought you ought to know in case you want anything in Port Clarion. The only way to get there is to head out tonight."

"Nobody's going to Port Clarion," rejoined Roy. "Send Cuppy's taxi down the hill and join us in a game of three-handed pinochle."

"Because you're going to stay all night, Jerry," Alan added. "Now that you're here, we'll need you to help watch for vampires. When it's foggy, they are most apt to be around."

Irene shuddered at that recollection. Then she realized that if the fog thickened, she would never see the phantom ship.

"I'm going out to take a last look at the moonlight," Irene told the three men. "Don't worry. I'll be back."

"You'd better be," returned Roy, "and anyway, we'll watch."

The full moon had risen high enough above the hazy horizon to show the harbor clearly and vividly, even to its tiniest boats, though off shore the mist was thickening, playing odd tricks while Irene watched. In the broad path of light that stretched from the moon across the dancing wavelets to the foot of Signal Head, Irene saw a billow of white that puffed like a balloon and floated onward. It was followed by another, then a third; and as those mighty masses moved shoreward they became the great white sails of a full-rigged ship!

It had to be a ship, because Irene could see a darkish line just beneath that rose at one end to a long prow; and at the other, to the high stern that marked it as the old *Aventure*. This could be no illusion, for Irene could make out every detail of the old-square rigger that Lesang and his cutthroat crew had sailed into Middle Harbor three centuries ago!

Irene wanted to rush back to the house and tell the others, but she couldn't take her eyes from the fantastic sight for fear of losing it. On quick inspiration, she walked slowly, steadily — but knowingly — toward the edge of the cliff. That brought Roy and Alan dashing to her rescue, as she knew it would. But before they arrived, the ship with the billowing sails had reached the channel and gone out of sight within its cleft.

"I've seen the *Aventure!*" exclaimed Irene as they drew her back. "Watch for it — you'll see it come from the channel into the harbor!"

But the ship was slow in coming through, and now thick fog, stirred by the wind that could not reach the cleft, was pouring in from the sea. Then, as Irene pointed out the prow and foresail of the *Aventure* nosing from the channel, the fog came with it, enveloping it so completely that only Irene really saw it.

"That was it," said Irene. "I saw enough of it to know."

"We saw enough to believe you, sis," declared Roy. 'Let's go back to the house."

"Ship or no ship," added Alan, "we'll keep close watch tonight."

Half an hour later, Dr. Felton drove up in his station wagon and stopped at the ranch house. He was enthusiastic when Irene told him that she was sure she had sighted the phantom ship; and he was pleased because there were now three men on watch in the house.

"I'm going on over to see my patient," stated the doctor, as he was leaving. "I won't need to stop on the way back. You have everything under control."

After another hour, Irene went to the studio and tried to rest. She kept awakening fitfully, and each time, a glance at the big picture window showed that the moonlight was still clear, though fog was slowly working up over the edges of the cliff. For the dozenth time, she studied the side window and saw that its metal casements were firmly latched. Except for just a touch of fog, everything was as clearly defined as if by daylight, except that the scene was colorless.

The pine boughs were one massive black blot, though Irene could make out the tree trunks beneath them, as straight as penciled lines. To the right the rocky ground was tinted a splendid silver by the moonlight. That applied particularly to the pile of stones forming the misshapen mound, which one legend claimed was the remains of a tower built by roving Vikings on early visits to America.

Either the wisps of fog were causing the effect of motion among the silvered rocks, or Irene was seeing black spots again, for she saw something gliding, snakelike, from the rock pile toward the grove. Then she was studying the blackened trees again and under the moonlight's bewitchment, the world about Irene seemed to fade as she was fascinated by the sight of gleaming yellow eyes, emerging from that darkness.

They were growing, those eyes, moving upward, hovering above the level of the trees. Then Irene was horrified to see that the eyes belonged to a mammoth creature with outspread arms, batlike in its shape, but human in its action. For instead of flying, it was approaching in a series of long bounds, until it was at the window, filling it.

Then Irene's hands were on the sill and she was staring through the panes, not only eye to eye, but face to face with the monster from the dark. It was a man's face, tawny, shriveled like the shell of a dried coconut, with long, jagged yellow teeth showing from a lipless mouth beneath a snoutlike nose. Its hands were beside its face, scratching at the window panes with fingers that resembled claws, yet which, like the face, were of man-sized proportions.

Frozen by that leering visage, Irene could neither move nor even think. She was like a terrified bird transfixed by a serpent's gaze, for at this close range, the yellow, fiery eyes were more fearful than anything that Irene could have imagined in her worst and wildest dreams. The tightly clamped window was her one guarantee of safety; but as Irene watched, it began to yield.

Those clawish fingers were working like knife points between the sections of the metal frames. First, the long nails, then the thin fingertips, then the leathery hands gained a powerful grip. The lipless mouth leered more viciously as tinkles of breaking glass told that the panes were falling from the yielding metal, which was twisting like mere cardboard.

Now the window was gone, and the ghoulish creature was doubling up, edging its head, arms, and legs in through the gap. More overpowering than that sight was the moldy odor of decay that permeated the room with a stifling pungency, choking Irene as she tried voicelessly to scream. Then the thing was upon her, those claw hands at her neck, the fang-teeth wide, as though to deliver a ferocious bite.

At last, despite the suffocating effect, the touch of those fearful claws loosened Irene's vocal cords. Her scream echoed from the studio walls and was followed by the clatter of an opening door, which projected a shaft of light from the living room. Roy's face appeared there, then Alan's, with Jerry's behind them. They saw the studio bathed in the moonlight from the picture window, with Irene in its midst, struggling with an indefinable mass that identified itself when she tried to twist away.

That was when a gloating face looked up triumphantly, just long enough to deliver a hateful snarl. Savagely, the defiant creature flung Irene from its hideous embrace, squarely at her rescuers. As Roy and Alan caught the girl, the vampire reversed its course, sprang to the window and doubled itself through and outward.

Roy gestured to Jerry to take care of Irene. Then, with drawn revolver, Roy rushed out the front door, while Alan, also armed with a gun, took the back way. They saw the monster plop from the side window, spread its winglike arms, and take off with long zigzag bounds toward the woods. They blazed away and despite its crazy course, Roy must have clipped it in one flank, for it sprawled to one side, bobbed up again and bounded away at another angle.

But before it reached the grove, a small squad of men with shotguns surged out from beneath the trees. Seeing its course blocked, the bounding creature made for the broken rock pile ahead of the blasting shotguns. Roy and Alan closed in upon the monster there and were joined by the men from the woods, headed by Dr. Felton, who had evidently induced some farmers to set up an ambush for the vampire in the grove. But when they clambered about the rock pile, they could see no sign of the monstrous figure. The evil thing had completely disappeared.

Dr. Felton gave an anxious look, which Roy understood.

"The thing got Irene," he said, "but I am sure she is all right."

"That we had better find out."

Dr. Felton told his men to stand guard over the rock pile, while he went to the house with Roy and Alan. Irene was all right, but very faint, more from fright, however, than from loss of blood. Dr. Felton was pleased to find that her wounds were scratches only; none from the vampire's bite. He treated the wounds, and Irene soon felt well enough to go with the group to the rock pile.

On the way, Roy announced that he had shot the vampire, and Dr. Felton was highly pleased by the news.

"When these creatures take on human form," declared the physician, "they temporarily lose what might be termed their inhuman immunity. In short, in order to become solid and therefore formidable, they also become vulnerable. I am told that it takes some time for them to change from one state to another."

"Then where did Lesang go," demanded Roy, "if he didn't dematerialize?"

"He went down into that rock pile. That's where we saw him last."

"But why would he go into that old Norse ruin?"

"It isn't an old ruin," put in Alan, in answer to Roy's question. "I've talked to fishermen on other islands, and I find that some of their ancestors go way back to Lesang's time. They say it was the peasants on the island who tore the castle down and piled it stone by stone over Lesang's grave. Then they went their way of their own accord, even though the English wanted them to stay."

"So Lesang was buried here," Dr. Felton exclaimed. "You have seen snakes go into stone piles, and rats, too. We have just fought and trapped a creature that can squirm like any snake or rat. Look here!"

Dr. Felton took a long stick, thrust it down at various angles into the rocks and probed about, discovering gaps a foot or more in size.

"This rock pit," he announced, "is honeycombed with passages big enough for that monster to squirm through. We will find him under it."

No one doubted that now. They set a watch over the rock pile, day and night until the fog lifted and heavy highway construction equipment could be brought by ferry from the mainland. Then they began excavating the great stone pile. As the work proceeded, two points became apparent:

These actually were the stones from Lesang's old citadel on Castle Rock, for mortar was visible on many that were underneath. They also found a definite course of narrow but well-propped openings that twisted down through to form a tunneled route that only a rat or an inhuman vampire would have dared to follow. At last the heap was cleared, and they came across a broad, flat stone inscribed with the name, Lavignac. That rang a bell with Alan.

"The fishermen told me about the Lavignacs," he exclaimed. "They were the original family who owned the island over several generations. Lesang claimed that they had given him their title. So he was buried with them."

Beneath the slab, they found the old Lavignac family crypt, with a central burial chamber arched to form a low vault. There they identified the Lavignac family coffins, all broken apart and scattered about, their remains reduced to skeletons. That must have been the work of the usurper, for in the one unbroken coffin of the lot, lay the leathery thing with long sharp teeth and yellow eyes, that could only be Lesang the vampire, its batlike arms folded and claws clenched like fists.

From its glassy stare, Dr. Felton decided that the thing had been caught in the midst of one of its transmutations, unable to leave the near-human form that it had temporarily taken. He found the wound that Alan's bullet had inflicted and the physician pronounced the creature dead. Whether the next full of the moon would revive the vampire, Dr. Felton did not wait to learn.

Late that afternoon, the Morrows were leaving Cliff Island in the *Rover*, bound on a cruise which they hoped would help them forget the recent harrowing events. Alan Blount, who was with them, spoke quietly to Roy Morrow, who turned to Irene and said:

"Look back, sis, at Signal Head."

There, on the Head, smoke was rising. Puzzled, Irene exclaimed, "Why, somebody must have started the old beacon, the one that —"

"That once marked Lesang's arrival," completed Roy, when Irene hesitated. "But in this case, it is marking his departure."

"What do you mean by that, Roy?"

"Only that Dr. Felton, as health officer, has just decided to burn a lot of rubbish and with it, that thing we found in the old crypt."

The smoke billowed high against the afternoon sky, forming a thick black cloud that spread oddly into a weird, batlike form. A higher tuft of smoke was caught by a slight breeze and thinned sufficiently for the bright glare of the golden sun to shine through two momentary openings, giving them the semblance of a huge pair of yellow eyes.

Then the illusion faded, as did the dying smoke itself. All that remained of Lesang, the vampire from the Cliff Island crypt, was a smoldering beacon on Signal Head.

Dead Man's Chest

If Lew Barton hadn't dreamed of some day owning a castle on the Hudson, he would never have seen the giant skull that was destined to bring him strange adventure.

Lew was working on the tanker *Eastern States* that made steady, plodding trips up the river from New York City to Albany. It was hot on the long, open deck of the Blister Wagon, as the crew appropriately nicknamed the tanker, so they preferred to go below and play cards; all except Lew Barton. He preferred to stay up at the bow and watch the ever-changing panorama from the Palisades on up through the Highlands and beyond.

What intrigued Lew most were the homes and mansions far up on the heights, some of them resembling European castles transplanted to America. Occasionally, Lew would look at some barren knob or towering crag and picture the kind of home that he would like to build there. But the giant skull was no such daydream, though it was partly an illusion dependent on one of the river's moods.

It was a hot Indian summer afternoon when the tanker swung around a bend into the blackness of low, glowering clouds, where a sudden breeze chopped the water into whitecaps. Instantly, the mountains were transformed to brownish monsters that loomed twice their normal size. Then, suddenly, the clouds opened and a great stream of sunlight came through the rift, striking a towering dome and turning it into a vast replica of a human skull!

Every detail was etched in light gray and deep black before Lew's riveted gaze. Foaming waves lapped the skull's jutting jaw. Above that were jagged teeth, a wide grinning row. Two matching blots formed the nose; higher, larger and much wider apart were the black hollows of the eyes. Above that, a great white bulge of rock became a forehead, which was lopped off squarely at the top, giving a flattish effect to what should have been a fully rounded crown.

Then the river squall hit with all its fury, and Lew was racing back along the tanker's deck, swept along by sheets of torrential rain. He arrived below drenched as a water rat, to the amusement of the card-playing crew. But the image of the giant skull was fixed in Lew's mind. He felt as though his sight had pierced a forbidden veil and made him a victim of the Storm King's wrath.

Often, Lew looked for the giant skull again, without result. Going up the Hudson, he seldom saw the same place at the same time and under similar conditions. Changes of season made a great difference. In the summer, the mountains were green, and many lost their rugged look. In the winter, when they were white, the river was often ice-bound, and Lew made no trips at all.

After Lew gave up his job with Eastern Tankers and switched to Wilton Barges, his trips became slower, but that didn't help. As they neared a point which Lew thought might be the one, a squall hit too soon. After they had thrashed through it and the visibility improved, Lew saw rugged cliffs and towering summits, but none of skullish formation or proportions.

Later, Lew began taking cabin cruisers up and down the Hudson and through the Barge Canal that ran across New York State to Lake Erie. In the winter, he took such craft down to Florida and soon decided that he no longer wanted a castle on the Hudson, but would settle for a cabin cruiser instead. But he needed money for overhead, upkeep, taxes, and other items.

Lew still remembered the great white skull, however, and kept on looking for it, but without any luck. By now he knew almost all the landmarks along the Hudson and had inquired into their histories, but nobody had ever heard of a huge death's head that leered downstream just when a storm was about to strike.

One autumn, Lew Barton heard from Craig Gentry, an affable young man with just enough means to loll about continuously in a good used cabin cruiser called the *Willy Nilly,* that went north and south with the birds, often with Craig as skipper and Lew as crew. So Lew stopped at his friend's tiny Manhattan apartment and found it overflowing with stacks of papers that came from half a dozen boxes of assorted sizes. Indicating the mess with a wave, Craig said:

"We're going treasure hunting, Lew. I'll pay expenses and we'll go fifty-fifty on whatever we find over that. It may take us a few years —"

"And whose treasure are we going after?"

"Captain Kidd's. I've gathered data on his entire career. He buried treasure in New England, Long Island, the Bahamas, up the Hudson —"

"Count that out, Craig. I've checked rumors about Kidd hiding treasure up the Hudson. They're either phony or all worked out. So count me out, too."

"I'll count the Hudson out, but not you. I'll tell you why."

Craig proceeded with an exhaustive and scholarly dissertation on the ways and wiles of the notorious Captain William Kidd, referring to documented accounts and even a few exhibits as he proceeded.

"Many pirates liked to kill an unsuspecting follower and bury him with their loot," declared Craig, "so that his ghost would scare off treasure hunters. But Kidd went them all one better, in a really gruesome way. He would kill a man by bashing him on the head with a bucket, a shovel or a cutlass, whichever was handiest. He would then bury the body, but bring back the head."

"The records show that?" asked Lew. "What was the idea?"

"Because ghosts, far from scaring people away, have been known to guide them to scenes of crime. Kidd was quoted as saying, 'It is the head that knows, because it contained the brain that knew.' So he kept the skulls of his victims, on the theory that the body would attract nothing more than a disturbed, unthinking ghost that could furnish no guidance whatever."

"Kidd really was kidding himself with that crackpot notion!"

"On the contrary, Kidd was far ahead of his time," argued Craig. "I have made a deep study of psychic phenomena, particularly poltergeist disturbances, where strange sounds are heard, objects are thrown about and unexplainable violence may bring injury or death to investigators. I find that they are often due to the presence of some elemental, as blundering, earthbound entities are called."

"And how can that help our treasure hunt?"

"Very effectively. The last headless victim that Kidd buried with his treasure was Jed Brock, a boatswain's mate from Kidd's ship, the *Quedagh Merchant*. And here" — triumphantly, Craig opened a square, brass-bound box measuring about a foot in each dimension and brought out an object from within it — "here is the skull of Jed Brock himself. It was brought to Kidd's trial in London, but was not produced as evidence, though it has been preserved ever since."

Lew Barton was staring at the skull as through a fog. He took it, held it at arm's length and studied it through half-closed eyes; then asked:

"You're sure this skull belonged to one of Kidd's men?"

"Absolutely," returned Craig. "See how the top of the head has been lopped off, squaring it behind the forehead? That was from a stroke of Kidd's cutlass."

"I have seen this skull before," affirmed Lew. "We are not ruling out the Hudson Highlands. Instead, we are going there first. I'll tell you why."

In detail, Lew described how he had sighted the giant skull and how ever since, he had tried to identify it with some headland, yet had failed. His account was quite as fanciful as all that Craig had related about Captain Kidd and Jed Brock, the bosun's mate. But Craig not only accepted it; he enthused over it.

"It fits Kidd to the dot!" exclaimed Craig. "His maps were false, his codes faked. He even buried some treasure openly, the part that he was willing for his backers to find as their share and think that it was all he had. Instead of a treasure map, Kidd fixed this skull to look exactly like one that he saw staring down the Hudson. You were lucky enough to spot the same giant skull, Lew."

"Then you think that's where Kidd buried the rest of his loot?"

"Certainly. Right in back of that flat spot that you noted on the cliff top. We'll take Jed's skull with us and look for the treasure in your skull."

"Don't call it my skull," rejoined Lew grimly, "until we find it."

They started on their quest in Craig's cabin cruiser. Lew was able to limit the stretch of river where he had seen the giant skull to a matter of about a dozen miles; but each time they covered it, they were disappointed. The season was right, but none of the hills fitted Lew's description.

"I've been over this a dozen times," declared Lew, "always wishing I could be my own skipper and try it again. Now I have that chance, but no luck!"

"We'll keep right on trying," assured Craig. "The harder it is to find, the smarter it shows Kidd was, making it all the more likely that he buried his treasure there. Lots of his logbooks start with comments on the weather, so that fits with the fact that the skull can only be seen under certain conditions."

For three days, they toiled up and down that stretch of river, trying new angles when rounding different points, until suddenly, during one late afternoon try, Lew pointed over a high ridge that flanked the Hudson and exclaimed:

"Storm clouds! Speed up, Craig!"

Craig gave it full speed ahead. They cut close past the point and shot straight out into the channel just as the high clouds opened above a low, approaching squall, as Lew had seen it once and only once before. Gleaming in the sunlight was the giant skull, its grinning teeth, hollow nose, and blackened eye-sockets forming the face of a thousand-foot bluff, its flattish top spoiling the contour of its otherwise rounded dome. Detail for detail, the mammoth death's head was a replica of the human skull that Craig snatched from its box and held at arm's length for comparison — the skull of Jed Brock, the bosun's mate!

Then the squall blotted out the cliff, and the cruiser was tossed like a cork on huge, churning waves that seemed to gush up from the riverbed itself. Never, even on ocean trips, had the *Willy Nilly* met with such a test. But Craig managed to weather it and dock the craft in the shelter of a little cove, where he and Lew danced in glee after the storm had passd.

Next, they brought out a topographical map and found the towering cliff that had so briefly disclosed its skullish secret. It was called Round Hill, and though it was skirted by a highway halfway up, its overhanging brow was too steep to scale. The best way to reach the top was to go around by a back road called Spruce Lane that led up from White Brook Hollow, then take an old trail that led past some circular pits called the Granite Bowls, and on up beside the brook to High Ridge, directly in back of Round Hill.

They had brought along hiking clothes, so they put them on and went ashore, carrying bags and equipment with them. They walked to an old river tavern midway between a little-used landing with its weather-beaten pier and the railroad tracks that were higher up on the Hudson's bank. They had dinner at the inn and then stayed overnight to make it appear that they were actually hikers, interested only in tramping the local trails.

The next morning was foggy, so there was no chance of going out on the river for another look at the giant skull. Anyway, they were eager to get to their new goal, so they started on their hike, loaded with their equipment, which included the square box containing the precious skull. It took longer than they thought, for it was mid-afternoon when they finally clambered past a little spring that marked the source of White Brook and came to High Ridge. Over that final hump, they continued to the flat ledge that so resembled the lopped-off skull of poor Jed Brock.

The ledge was perfectly smooth and level, forming practically a solid stone foundation. It offered a fine view down the Hudson, but they were too far back now from the brow of the cliff to notice any of the skull formation below But those, in Craig's opinion, did not matter. He was more interested in studying the ridge behind them. But all they found there was rough ground, small jutting rocks and scraggly bushes, a dull ending for a treasure hunt.

With dark, they pitched a pup tent at the rear of the flat ledge and tried to go to sleep, with the box containing Jed's skull between them. Distant lightning flashes and muffled rolls of thunder were ominous in the offing.

"I don't like it here," declared Lew. "We're up where thunderheads gather, right in the Storm King's lap. This may be a rough night before we're through."

"Rougher maybe than you think," added Craig. Then, cryptically: "When you deal with elementals, you are apt to rouse the elements."

"You mean having Jed's skull along might kick up a storm?"

"It did down on the river, didn't it? That squall nearly sunk us."

"Well, yes — but it had to be stormy when we saw the giant skull."

"That's it, Lew. The two are interlocked. You can't get around it."

Lew didn't agree with Craig's notions, which he was beginning to think were quite as crackpot as any ever held by the notorious Captain Kidd. But rather than carry the argument further, Lew compromised by saying:

"Anyway, Craig, we'll stick it out tonight, so we can hunt treasure tomorrow!"

They stuck it out, almost until dawn, when the Storm King struck with wild rage. The lashing wind swept away the pup tent and next, Lew and Craig were clinging to the rocks, wrapped in their blankets and their ponchos, while lightning flashed and split·trees within a hundred yards of them and the thunder roared above the fury of the gale. They managed to gain partial shelter from bushes where they propped up the tattered pup tent amid a tremendous downpour.

Then, when their hopes were at their lowest ebb and it seemed that no terror could be worse than the tempest raging about them, the climax came, in the form of a sight that buoyed their hopes, yet imbued them with new fear. From the ridge behind the fringe of the ledge where they were squatted, they saw a clumsy figure crawling upward as though emerging from the ground itself. Craig mistook it for a bear until Lew gasped, "It's human — yet it isn't human!"

Human in shape, yes, for a vivid lightning flash showed it to be a bulky figure clad in the clothes of an old sailor. It was inhuman, though, because in the brilliance of the lightning's flare, they could see right through the hulking figure to the background of the trees beyond the ridge!

Seldom had a ghost revealed itself under such singular circumstances. A ghost in broad daylight would have been startling enough; but in this pitch-black, rain-deluged darkness, the recurring appearance of the thing amid the blinding lightning streaks was beyond all sane belief. With each flicker, it loomed closer from the hump. After each blackout, instead of appearing in luminous form, it was gone, only to be back when the lightning blazed again.

Then, the fateful form reared to its full height, its arms raised in a menacing gesture, as though ready to hurl itself upon the staring men, while the terrific thunder reverberated like a peal of doom. In the glare that streaked the entire sky, the two men saw the most startling, horrifying thing of all.

The ghost of the mountain ridge had no head!

That sight could have caused the most stout-hearted viewer to turn and run, regardless of consequences, which in this case would have meant going over the front edge of the flat-topped ledge and down the bulging bluff to certain doom beside the river below. In fact, both Lew and Craig were coming to their feet, ready to flee, when they saw that macabre, terrifying touch of the missing head. To them, it had the opposite effect of what Captain Kidd had anticipated. Sight of a headless ghost stirred their numbed senses, bringing home the realization that this was the moment they had wanted.

"It's Jed Brock!" shouted Craig. "He's not after us — he is coming for his head!"

"Then let him have it!" Frantically, Lew was tugging at the box clamps. The lid came open and Lew gave the box a tilt. "Here it is!"

Craig caught the skull as it rolled out, held it poised for a breathless moment as the thunder finished a tremendous roll and the lightning flared again, showing the headless horror ready for its final lunge. Then Craig flung the skull with all his might, straight at the weird shape that had now materialized to completely solid form.

What happened then was strangest of all. The skull stopped in mid-air as it hit the grotesque figure; then dropped straight down. At the same instant, the materialized form vanished. The effect was elusive, for the lightning flickered at that moment, but when it flared again, there was no sign of the ghost or the skull. Both were gone, like the sudden, earsplitting thunderclap that came like a monstrous note of their departure!

Lew and Craig stayed huddled while the lightning lessened and the thunder rolled in dwindling fashion down the Hudson. The rain reduced to a drizzle and the entire storm abated, as though its work was done. In the light of the distant flares, they saw no further sign of the vanished ghost. Then dawn was streaking the sky and daylight brought the surety that the two treasure seekers had felt the night before.

Ghost or no ghost, the skull that Craig had flung in sheer, stark desperation could not have gone far. The slope behind the hump was studded with too many bushes, roots, and rocks for the thing to roll on down the path that followed the course of White Brook. Yet when Lew and Craig reached the exact spot where the skull had fallen as though striking something solid, there was no sign at all of the grisly object.

Could Jed's ghost have grabbed it and fled with it? If so, there was no reason why it should have gone far. Thinking in such terms, Lew, looking toward the beginning of the slope, suddenly pointed and exclaimed:

"Look!"

Little rivulets still were trickling from the heavy rain. Some were joining, others were forming pools. But one tiny stream was pouring down beneath a low rock, into a hole from which it did not emerge.

"The skull!" exclaimed Craig. "It rolled down in there!"

Together, Lew and Craig shoved away the rock and found a larger cavity. With a pickaxe and spade that they had brought, they worked frantically, digging through loose earth, prying out imbedded stones. Finally, the pickaxe struck metal, the rusted lid of an iron chest! As they dug around the coffer to release it from the roots that had gripped it over many years, they came across the bones of a human skeleton, all except the skull.

But when they finally managed to haul the heavy chest up from the hole, a loose object dislodged itself from between two stones that had trapped it, and tumbled down into the pit to join the skeleton remains. That rolling object, which for the moment was very like a living thing, was the missing skull of Jed Brock, reunited at last with the body to which it belonged.

For the coffer, when Lew and Craig opened it, proved definitely to be the dead man's chest. The name of Jed Brock, boatswain's mate of the *Quedagh Merchant,* was inscribed within its its lid. Captain Kidd, penurious to the last degree, had used his victim's own chest as a treasure coffer, possibly believing that it would further encourage Jed's headless ghost to haunt the spot. In the chest, Lew and Craig found Spanish dubloons, British sovereigns, French louis d'or and other currency which at the present value of gold were worth thousands of dollars, with added value as rare coins. There were jewels, too, that Kidd had looted from ships in the Indian Ocean; in all, a haul sufficient to guarantee each treasure finder a few new cabin cruisers and perhaps even a castle on the Hudson.

But it was after they had dragged their find down from the mountain and stowed the chest, treasure and all, aboard the *Willy Nilly,* that Lew and Craig began to realize how really lucky they had been. As Craig headed the cruiser out into the river and swung slightly upstream to clear the cove, he gestured toward the towering bulge of Round Hill and asserted:

"I sure called the turn. Kidd saw the mountain that looked like a skull, so he buried his treasure on top after making Jed help him lug it up there."

"If Kidd figured it looked like a skull," retorted Lew, who was studying the mountain, "he really had a wild, fantastic imagination."

"No wilder than yours. You saw the grinning mouth, the nose, the eyes, even the flattened top of the head. You pointed them out to me."

"Yes. But they weren't here when Kidd came up the river. Look."

As Craig looked, Lew continued:

"I know now why I couldn't see the skull except in just the right light and at the proper distance. As it gets close, it loses its effect. There's the mouth — see what it is?"

"Why — why" — Craig was stammering in amazement — "it's the posts of the old pier from riverboat days and the windows of the tavern and the old buildings spreading out from it. They haven't been here more than a hundred and fifty years — and that was long after Kidd's time!"

"Right, and the nose above came later than that," chuckled Lew. "It's formed by the twin tunnels where the railroad tracks go through the hill."

Utterly confounded, Craig looked higher and exclaimed:

"And those eyes — why they are part of the highway that curves around the mountain! They are the parking spaces that were built as overlooks, so tourists can stop and see the river view!"

"And away up above," added Lew, "is that flat place we mistook for a natural ledge. It is ground they leveled off and put in a concrete foundation for a new airplane beacon. That was several years ago, and here is a new map that has it marked as Signal Tower B, but it hasn't been built yet."

"Steamboats — railroads — automobiles — airplanes" — Craig listed them in order — "none of them were ever dreamed of, when Captain Kidd sailed up here with his treasure. What an imagination he had!"

"Maybe he just dreamed of the future," speculated Lew, "as we dreamed of the past. Anyway, Kidd's treasure is our treasure now."

"Thanks to Jed Brock," reminded Craig Gentry. "We started on this hunt with a dead man's skull, remember?"

"Yes," agreed Lew Barton, "and we're coming back with the dead man's chest."

The Thirteenth Story

Dolban and Chadley, Importers, were located in the Longview Building, one of those quickie skyscrapers that sprouted up during the Roaring Twenties and managed to survive even after modern glass, chrome, and plastic construction began to dominate the Manhattan skyline. Twenty-odd stories high, the Longview Building stood on a plot of ground the size of a postage stamp in comparison. It was tall, but so thin that each story had only space enough for an office in the front, a display room in the middle and a storage room in back, plus the single shaft of an elevator, which after many years, was converted to the automatic type.

The building was particularly suited to firms like Dolban and Chadley, because it gave them a whole story to themselves, without too high a rental. Homer Dolban, the senior partner, was a little wizened old man, who never smiled nor said much. Luke Chadley, the junior partner, was much younger and not only a glib, forceful talker, but a human dynamo. Like almost everybody else in the Longview Building, they seemed to know their business.

The only problem that Howard Crayle, the owner of the building, ever had with Dolban and Chadley was when they signed their lease. Dolban looked over the fine print and was willing to accept it, but Chadley, in booming, loud-voiced style, took exception to the very first clause, as he exclaimed:

"You've given us the fourteenth story! What about the numbering in this building?" he demanded sharply. "Does it have a thirteenth story?"

"Why, no," admitted Crayle. "It has long been a regular custom to leave out thirteen, when numbering the stories in a building."

"I'm not talking about custom," stormed Chadley. "I'm talking as a customer. This building is twenty stories high, so it must have a thirteenth story."

"Well," conceded Crayle, "technically it does have. But —"

"That's all I want to know," snapped Chadley. "Then this fourteenth story that you are forcing on us is actually the thirteenth story."

"No, no. It really is the fourteenth —"

"Don't tell me! I can count. I don't like the number thirteen whether it is real or disguised." Chadley turned to Dolban. "We won't sign, will we?"

The senior partner agreed that they wouldn't.

"The only other vacant story is the twelfth," declared the building owner, "but you may not want that either, because you see —"

"We'll see if we like it," put in Chadley, "and if we do we'll take it. But don't try to tell me that thirteen isn't an unlucky number. If it wasn't, there wouldn't be so many buildings without a thirteenth story. But one from fourteen still leaves thirteen; that's why we won't take the fourteenth story."

That settled it. Dolban and Chadley looked at the twelfth story, found it the same as the rest, and took it. But Howard Crayle couldn't help wondering why a man as keen-mannered as Luke Chadley should be so superstitious.

There was a very deep and totally unsuspected reason behind it Secretly Chadley was plotting a very dastardly but very clever long-range crime. He intended to do away with his aged partner when the right time came; and Chadley didn't want to worry about any silly jinx that might cause him to make a slip at the crucial moment. Having gotten the notion of the thirteenth story out of his system, he promptly dismissed it from his mind and concentrated on the project that lay ahead: murder.

The way Dolban and Chadley operated was this: Homer Dolban, through long years as an importer, had connections all over the world and made excellent deals. One month, the storeroom would be stocked with Swiss watches; the next month with Australian kangaroo leather, and so on. Chadley, making the rounds of the wholesalers, would often have the goods sold at a fancy profit as soon as the shipments arrived, for Dolban had an uncanny way of importing only the type of merchandise that was both needed and wanted by the trade.

With their profits, Dolban and Chadley bought other merchandise and finally accumulated a million dollars' worth of one very special item — diamonds. Old Dolban kept them in a wall safe in the office. And now, with the lease running out after a few years, he decided that this was the time to sell them and turn the profits into a whole lot more. Dolban preferred to go to California and make sales to jewelers there, while Chadley favored Europe. However, in this case, Dolban, as senior partner, had the entire say; not only that, their private agreement stipulated that only twenty-five percent of the total proceeds were to go to Chadley, as junior partner.

So Dolban, who alone knew the combination of the wall safe, decided to stay until about nine o'clock and then leave the office in time to catch his ten o'clock plane for Los Angeles. Chadley, without breathing a word to his partner, booked passage on a nine o'clock airliner to Europe for the same evening and reserved vacation accommodations at a resort hotel in the Swiss Alps.

Never had Chadley shown any dissatisfaction regarding his arrangement with Dolban. He had let Pop, as he called his partner, have full control. But they had kept their business so closely to themselves that if something happened to one, the other could walk out with all the assets and nobody would be wiser.

Something was to happen to Dolban tonight. To make sure it did, Chadley went up to the office with Pop after they finished a pleasant dinner together at a neighborhood restaurant. They entered the Longview Building and pressed the button for the elevator. It came down dark, as Lubin, the janitor, usually turned off its lights at night and Chadley often did the same. Dolban entered, turned on the light switch and pressed button Number 12.

When they reached their floor, Dolban stepped out first. Chadley, following, did two things. He pressed the top button to send the car up above the twentieth floor. Then he planted a gummed block of hard rubber against the end of the heavy door to the elevator shaft. When it closed, it did not go quite all the way shut.

After they chatted awhile in the office, Chadley said to Dolban:

"Look, Pop. I want to see some friends on Long Island, so why don't I take you in a cab to the airport, right now? We can talk out there until your plane time."

Dolban agreed. He opened the safe, took out the diamonds and put them in a very special brief case. He went out to the elevator, carrying the brief case. Chadley followed. About to press the button for the car, he asked:

"Your ticket, Pop. Are you sure you have it?"

Dolban set the brief case against the wall, found his ticket in his pocket, and nodded. He wasn't watching Chadley, who now pressed the door edge with his fingers, drew the door to the elevator shaft open, and at the same time reclaimed the hard rubber block. He picked up the brief case with his other hand and said:

"Here is the elevator, Pop, and here is your brief case. Somebody must have turned off the light, so step right in and turn it on again."

Dolban reached for the brief case and stepped squarely into the yawning blackness of the shaft. As he suddenly realized that the car wasn't there, the old man wheeled about and grabbed for Chadley, who expected it and knew that if Dolban's fingers gained a grip, it would be a death clutch. But Chadley was prepared for that. He swung the brief case hard against Dolban's face, literally sweeping him back into the shaft, like a figure of straw. That brutal blow was calculated to break any death grip, and with it, Chadley swung full about. He had planned that, too, for all in the same action, he grabbed the big door and gave it a tug that sent it clanging shut.

For one grim, prolonged moment, Chadley shut his eyes to black out not only the scene but all memory of what had happened. He was leaning against the closed door, as he had so often pictured he would be. In closing, it had cut off any sound of Dolban's last scream, as well as any crash from below. So now, to Chadley, it was just something that hadn't happened; at least, not yet. It was time for Chadley to be leaving for his plane to Europe; not for another hour or more would Dolban have been on his way to the airport. Later, people would think that the accident happened at that time.

Coolly, Chadley pressed the button that brought the elevator car down to the twelfth floor. It arrived there, lighted, and Chadley waved back to the office, calling, "Good-bye, Pop!" as though Dolban were still there. Then he went down in the elevator, turned off its light, and went out by the street door as he always did. Next, he was in a cab, telling the driver to take him out to Idlewild and to hurry.

Only the driver didn't hurry. They moved along at a steady, constant pace, while the cabby kept soothing Chadley in a monotone:

"Listen, friend, you never get nowhere, thinking ahead. Don't worry about places before you get there, or you'll be back where you started. Like with me, the time I went through a dead end and plunged into the river. I was in a hurry to get back to town, and do you know what? That's where I thought I was! All that evening I was at a party; then I was home and getting up the next morning to take a shower — and *splash!* I was in the river and it was the night before! That jarred me back to sense and I got the door open and came up. But that could have been the end of me and I'd never have known it until that last moment!"

The driver went on and on, but so did the cab. And suddenly, they were at the airport, with plenty of time for Chadley to make his plane. Then he was clutching Dolban's precious brief case — Chadley's own brief case, now! — while he was letting his other luggage be weighed. From there, Chadley next found himself at the gate, waiting for it to open, while he heard two army fliers talking nearby. One was telling of a harrowing experience.

"Believe me," the flier said, "when that chute wouldn't open, there was just one moment when I wished hard that something would save me. I must have blacked out, for I thought for sure the thing did open. There I was, floating down to the ground; then I was in the truck, going back to base; next I was getting my discharge, which isn't due for a year from now. Then I was in a bathing suit, roaring along in a speedboat — and *bang!* We hit a snag or something. There was a jolt and I was looking up at that chute just as it opened like a big balloon, putting me right back where I was when all that crazy chain of thought began. If I had hit the ground instead, with no chute, it would have been the same sort of shock, only it would have been the end of me!"

The two fliers drifted away, and now Chadley was on the airliner, dozing comfortably as they spanned the Atlantic. Next, he was going through customs in the same way, letting bowing officials see that the brief case contained nothing but papers, because all the diamonds were in a very clever double lining where Dolban had carefully placed them while Chadley had watched him.

Finally, Chadley was checking in at the Swiss resort hotel, where he was given Suite 3B, which he had reserved. Each day, he went out on the veranda, lolling around, having an attendant bring him the New York newspaper as soon as it came in. Always, he was looking at a distant, snow-clad mountain with rocky ledges. One day, two men paused near Chadley's deck chair. One had a limp and leaned heavily on a cane, as he pointed to the distant summit.

"That's where I went off," he said. "From that high ledge. We were on the way down when the rope broke. Just as I went over the brink, I seemed to catch myself. Then everything was all right and we came down the mountain, laughing at my near-accident. We were here in the hotel, I was at the dance that night and a big banquet a week later. Then, all of a sudden, I was overwhelmed by a huge avalanche —"

"That must have been when you hit the snowbank!" exclaimed the other.

"Exactly," the first man said. "You can see it there, a thousand feet below the ledge. I took it at a slant, and that's what saved me. But if I'd hit those rocks instead, my crazy dream would have ended as it did, but permanently!"

The two mountain climbers were gone and the attendant was stopping beside Chadley, saying, "Your New York newspaper, sir!" and Chadley glanced at the front page as he always did. His gaze was riveted by two photos, side by side, Dolban's and his own. With them was the caption:

PARTNERS IN LIFE — PARTNERS IN DEATH

Something seemed to crash Luke Chadley head on. His whole dream sequence ended, in an utter and absolute blackout.

A minute or so later, the attendant came back, found the newspaper flapping in an empty deck chair. He picked it up, carried it into the lobby and handed it to the clerk, who read English and liked American newspapers. The clerk saw the name, Luke Chadley, and exclaimed:

"My word, that's the name of the man who reserved Suite 3B beginning a week ago. No wonder he never came to take it."

"He looks a lot like the man out in the deck chair," commented the attendant, studying Chadley's photo. "What happened to this fellow?"

"He fell down an elevator shaft in New York," replied the clerk, "trying to save the older man you see here. They were partners and when the bodies were found, they were clinging tightly together, each with a hold upon a brief case that contained their whole fortune, a million dollars' worth of very fine diamonds. My, how unlucky they were!"

Those were the very words that Howard Crayle was saying in New York when he discussed the sad fate of two of the best tenants who had ever rented space in the Longview Building. Crayle was talking to Lubin, the janitor, as they studied the elevator and tried to figure why it hadn't been at the twelfth story when Dolban and Chadley thought they were stepping into it.

"My, how unlucky they were!" Crayle exclaimed. "But Chadley had a hunch that something of the sort might happen. He wouldn't take the fourteenth story, because he thought it was the thirteenth."

Lubin's face went puzzled.

"But isn't the fourteenth really the thirteenth story?"

"Not in this building." Crayle pointed to the button panel in the elevator. "See that letter M? It stands for Main Floor, which is really the first story. So count the rest going up: one will be two; two will be three; and so on. Stop when you get to thirteen."

Lubin counted and stopped on the number 12 as he announced:

"Thirteen! Say, but that's only the twelfth — and that was where Dolban and Chadley had their office!"

"You are right," responded Crayle sadly. "Theirs was really the thirteenth story."

Two Live Ghosts

Ever since the Civil War ended, Jeff Tupper and Hank Marchand had been working their way in and out of Indian country, disappearing for months at a time, only to return to civilization with new adventures to brag about. During the ten years, Jeff and Hank had switched from trapping to hunting, trading, or prospecting, whichever suited them at the time. They had learned a lot about Indians, and right now, they figured this was a good time to avoid them.

Jeff and Hank were a rugged pair, with their rough clothes and big boots. Each wore a heavy beard, Jeff's as ruddy as the gold they had been seeking on this excursion; Hank's as black as the gloomy, forested hills where they had found it and staked a claim. From beneath their slouch hats, they peered with eyes as sharp as the bowie knives they carried in their belts; and they had their rifles ready, while they led their pack mules along the mountain trail.

All during that hot June day, Hank and Jeff had been avoiding hunting parties composed of Sioux and Cheyenne Indians. Now, late in the afternoon, they decided to climb the ridge and see if there was an Indian village on the other side. If there was, they would have to work their way around it. So they anchored their mules with big loose stones and clambered up to a rocky lookout spot.

They were right, there was a village in the valley below. But there were not just dozens of wigwams, nor even just hundreds. Literally thousands of the conical tents studded the floor of the vast, winding valley. Interspersed with thatched shelters known as wickiups, they stretched for miles until they blended with the blue haze of the Black Hills beyond.

The fading sunlight tinged Jeff's beard with a coppery glow, and his teeth gleamed in a grim smile as he told Hank:

"No wonder those Sioux and Cheyenne hunters were too busy to notice us. They've got a lot to do, in order to supply food to all these tribes."

"There must be twelve to fifteen thousand of them," Hank calculated. "That's a lot of Indians to be off the reservation all at once. If the army scouts spot them, you can bet the boys in blue will show up in full force."

"The Indians probably have sent out their scouts, too," Jeff reminded him, "and it will be all up with us if they spot us. Let's get back to the mules and move along our side of the ridge."

Darkness was settling, but the rising moon provided enough light for the two men to continue on their way, mules and all. During their trek, they discussed further plans.

"We'll have to keep on to the far end of the ridge," Hank decided, "and then work over to the hills on the other side. From there, we can beat our way to the Powder River and follow it down to the Yellowstone. There, we'll find a river steamer and load these on board."

'By "these," Hank referred to the beaver pelts that hung from the flanks of the pack mules. In his turn, Jeff brought two small but heavy bags from his pocket and dangled them in the moonlight.

"And we can pay for our passage with these," he said, "provided the Indians don't catch us, or believe us when we say we were only trapping beaver. They don't like people who take gold from their sacred hills, where they think the Manitou dwells."

"Only those hills won't be theirs much longer," Hank asserted, "now that they've been fools enough to go on the warpath. That's all that was needed for the U.S. Army to mop them up for keeps. Those hills will be anybody's from now on — which means we will be able to go back there and work our claim."

They plodded along steadily, until clouds began to dull the moonlight. Then they worked their way down their side of the ridge and found a camping spot in some cottonwood trees beside a sluggish stream. As they lay awake, smoking their pipes, Jeff spoke in a reminiscent tone:

"A funny thing about those Black Hills, Hank. All the while we were prospecting there, I felt as if somebody was watching us."

"So did I," Hank acknowledged. "But I knew it couldn't be Indians. They won't go near those hills because they think the Great Manitou owns them. So that made it safe for us."

"Only I didn't feel safe," Jeff said. "Maybe the Indians have it right; maybe the Manitou was watching us. From the time we left those hills, I've felt that something was drawing us back."

"So it is," chuckled Hank. "Our mining claim, remember? This time we've struck it rich, boy! So let's get some shut-eye and hope that no Indians will be watching us when we hit the trail tomorrow."

They slept until noon, and even then they were cautious as they resumed their march. The trail followed gullies and folds in the hills as it continued upward, but it was rough and progress was slow. Again, it was late in the afternoon when they neared another lookout spot and Hank decided to make a new observation from the ridge and see how far they had come.

"We can't be much farther than the middle of that village," Hank commented, "considering there were thousands of tepees, as near as we could guess."

"Maybe the heat was getting us," Jeff laughed, "and all we saw was a mirage. It's worth another look to make sure."

Again, the bearded pair gained a full view of the vast valley, but this time from a new angle and with a totally unexpected result. Of the thousands of wigwams, not one remained. They had vanished as though swallowed by the earth itself, leaving Jeff and Hank gaping in amazed disbelief, wondering if it *had* been their imagination after all. Indeed, they might have been gazing into a totally different valley, except for one thing.

Though the thousands of wigwams were gone, odd clusters of wickiups still stood at widely separated intervals of a few miles or more. As a rule, Indians abandoned those crude shelters when they left a campsite and fashioned new ones when they reached their destination. So, unquestionably, there had been Indians camping in the valley, which in turn indicated that the vanished wigwams must have been real.

"What do you make of it?" Jeff asked, running his hand through his ruddy beard, as he always did when he was puzzled. "Why do you suppose those tribes cleared out all of a sudden?"

"So the army scouts wouldn't find them," Hank rejoined. "I reckon the Indians don't want anybody to guess there were so many of them all here together at one time."

"But they left a lot of wickiups —"

"That was the smart part. Remember how they were set up yesterday, kind of hit-or-miss among the tepees, all through the valley? Now they're all set wide apart."

"You're right, Hank. They must have cleared out the wickiups in between, so the rest would look like small campsites, instead of one big one."

"Either that, Jeff, or they want it to look as if they had moved from one campsite to another. They would look pretty far apart to anybody riding up through the valley."

Hank rose and started back toward the mules, with Jeff following, still a bit puzzled. Then Hank announced:

"We're taking on a new job. We're going to be army scouts."

"Army scouts!" echoed Jeff. "You mean, work cheap and spend your time riding from here to nowhere and back?"

"Not us. We've already done half our scouting. We'll ask a good price for telling what we know. The army will be right interested to hear that fifteen thousand Indians are on the move."

"And what if they ask us where they've gone?"

"That's what we're going to find out, Jeff, so we can supply a full report. We'll head on up to the end of the valley, spot the Indians again, and double back along our trail until we meet the U. S. Cavalry and get them to pay for what we know."

"What with beaver pelts and gold dust, we're doing all right on our own," Jeff said. "But I'll go along with you, Hank. I always have."

They reached the head of the valley the next day and began probing valleys beyond. From wisps of smoke that rose beyond a low ridge, Hank was sure they had located at least one new campsite. But he wanted to learn more, so late one afternoon, the two bearded men brought their mules through a narrow canyon into a small, grassy-sloped valley, where they stopped in amazement.

There, as though designed for some special purpose, stood a single tepee, one of the most elaborate that Jeff or Hank had ever seen. It was close to the side of the valley, but not another tent was in sight. This one was much larger than most wigwams, and it was decorated with crude drawings.

Though the fanciful tent seemed temporarily deserted, Hank didn't take it for granted. He beckoned Jeff back in the direction of the canyon and found a short, rocky gully where they tethered the mules.

"If we crawl along the slope through the thick grass," Hank said, "we can work our way down behind that tent, without giving anybody a chance to see us. With only two or three rods of open ground to cross, we can slide inside in a jiffy."

"And if we find any Indians there," Jeff added, adjusting his rifle sling across his shoulder, "we can settle them pronto."

"But not with rifles," objected Hank. "Leave those with the mule packs. No need to wake up the whole valley with a lot of shooting when all we need is these."

Hank tapped his bowie knife, and Jeff nodded approval. Soon they had squirmed down through the long, dry grass and were continuing their snakish course across the open patch, with the circular base of the tent amply hiding them from the valley beyond. Two odd things impressed them as they approached. Midway between the grassy slope and the tepee was a ring of stones surrounding the ashes of a council fire; and the closed flap that marked the entrance to the tent was toward the hillside, not facing the valley as the stealthy invaders had expected.

That, however, made the surprise attack all the easier. Hank nudged Jeff, and they sprang up and across the crude fireplace, reaching the tepee in a single bound. There, they whipped the flap wide and launched themselves inside with drawn knives. But all they found amid the gloom were stacks of buffalo hides, a large yellow bearskin, smaller skins of white wolves, large turtle shells, and several crude drums of medium size.

There were masks painted to resemble demons; others in the form of buffalo heads. Fire sticks, peace pipes, war clubs, and feathered headgear were also on display. The tent itself was nearly thirty feet high, and from near the top long strips of heavy leather dangled, firmly fixed in the stout, slanted poles that formed the framework of the tepee.

Hank Marchand summed up the scene when he exclaimed:

"A medicine lodge!"

The same idea was striking home to Jeff Tupper. He and Hank, in trading with friendly Indians, often had noted special tepees set apart for rituals conducted by the medicine men, or wizards, who really ruled the tribe. Jeff and Hank had witnessed sun dances, snake dances, and corn dances; they knew that the medicine lodge was a headquarters for such ceremonies and that all the necessary items were kept there.

But this was the first time that the bearded adventurers had been inside such a tepee, and the effect was weird. The fading daylight from the entrance and an open space at the very tent top gave only a vague view of part of the interior. The rest was obscured in darkness that seemed almost alive, for each gust of wind brought slight groans from the tent poles or flapping sounds from the overlapping hides that formed the walls, much like the beat of bats' wings.

"Those dangling straps," mused Jeff, stroking his ruddy beard. "I've seen them used to string up young Indian warriors as part of their initiation. You'd think, though, that they would have a place for a council fire, here in the tent."

"They probably use the one outside," returned Hank, thumbing his big hand toward the tent flap. "Like as not, only the medicine man himself is allowed inside here. There's something special about this lodge, being all by itself —"

Hank broke off, puzzled, as Jeff knelt suddenly at the center of the tent and placed his ear to the ground. Then, springing up, Jeff urged Hank out through the opening in the tent, exclaiming as he did:

"Hoofbeats! Coming this way! Back to the grass and quick about it."

Often, while hunting and trapping, Jeff had shown an uncanny sense of approaching danger, so Hank was quick to follow his advice. Hardly had they burrowed into the grass before a dozen Indian riders appeared from the gathering dusk. They dismounted, tied their horses, and began to build a council fire in front of the tepee. Jeff and Hank watched silently from the fringe of tall grass just behind them.

As the crackling flames threw a lurid light upon the painted faces and feathered headdresses of the assembled chieftains, Jeff gripped Hank's arm and pointed at an angle toward a hillock that showed against the fading sunset.

"Look there, Hank!"

A tall figure with folded arms was striding down the hill. About his waist, he wore a panther skin. His headdress was shaped like a raven's wings. His body, like his legs, arms, and face, was painted in vivid color that gave him the effect of a living rainbow as he stepped from the twilight into the glow of the council fire.

"I come as Numokmukana," the newcomer announced, "the first and

only man. I come from Wakonschecha to drive away Wakontonka. I come
to summon those who have died in battle, so that they may go to the happy
hills where Wakonschecha awaits them."

The Indian had spoken in a Sioux dialect that both Jeff and Hank understood. This man who posed as Numokmukana was obviously an important
medicine man. By Wakonschecha, he meant the great good spirit, or Manitou,
while Wakontonka was the spirit of evil. The happy hills, of course, were
the Black Hills where Jeff and Hank had staked their claim and to which
they intended to return.

Now began a most singular ritual. The medicine man swung his bare
arms wide, then brought his wrists together behind his back, where two of
the chieftains promptly bound them with rawhide thongs. From their grassy
hiding place, Jeff and Hank could study the medicine man's face, but if he
made a grimace, they did not see it. Possibly he was accustomed to the
cruel torture of the tightened thongs; or it might simply be that the paint
was dabbed on too thickly for his face to betray signs of pain.

Next, the chieftains were binding the medicine man's ankles in the same
thorough style, the thongs cutting deep into his flesh as he raised his voice in
a high-pitched babble, reciting the same theme over and over. Jeff and Hank,
still deep in the grass, kept translating it in undertones, and between them,
they managed to grasp all that was said.

As representative of the good spirit, Wakonschecha, the medicine man
was challenging the chieftains to do their utmost in behalf of the bad spirit,
Wakontonka. The medicine man wanted them to bind him so that he
would be utterly helpless when they placed him in the tepee; yet, he said, the
mighty power of Wakonschecha would prevail.

Finally, the tying was done. The chieftains thrust the medicine man into
the tepee, where he landed on his knees and sprawled forward on his face.
He was writhing helplessly in his bonds when they dropped the tent flap and
returned to the dying council fire. But the medicine man's muffled voice
kept on. In whispers, Jeff and Hank translated what they heard:

"The spirits of the warriors are coming from afar —
With all the power of the mightiest of winds —"

As if in confirmation, the walls of the tent began to quiver. While Jeff
and Hank stared unbelieving, the entire structure shook as though a wind
had caught it. Next, it swayed, as if impelled by fierce gusts that bent it almost
to the ground, first one way, then another. Though the whole tent heaved
violently, it never came completely from its moorings. At any moment, Jeff
and Hank expected to hear the tent poles crack, but the only sounds that
came from the tent were the sobs and sighs of the imaginary tempest. For
all about, the landscape itself was still, even the blades of grass as motionless
as though frozen by the moonlight.

The chieftains looked frozen, too, as they heard a new babble from the
helpless medicine man, bidding them call upon their departed friends. One
chief responded with the plea:

"Speak to me, O Matochega! Tell me how you died and where. Show yourself to us, here beside the council fire, where you were one of us, during the last moon!"

The tent ceased swaying as suddenly as it had begun. There was a momentary silence, then from near the very top of the thirty-foot tepee issued a stern but hollow tone:

"I am Matochega. I died when I was thrown from my horse, but not because of my fall. I was trampled by the horses of the enemy. I fired one— two—shots. With each shot, an enemy fell. I, Matochega, have told all."

An excited buzz came from the listening chieftains, proving that they recognized the voice of Matochega and that its statement was correct. The Indians were crouched in a semicircle, watching the entrance of the medicine lodge, when Hank whispered to Jeff:

"Matochega — that means Little Bear. But why are they all looking at the tent flap?"

"They probably expect the ghost to show himself," replied Jeff, "And maybe he will, if he can get down from that perch. Let's watch—"

Just then, the tepee quivered an interruption, ending in a convulsive shudder as the flap swung wide. There, against the blackened background, loomed a yellowish figure that danced about in clumsy fashion. One of the chieftains tossed a pine cone on the fire, and the sudden flare clearly outlined the dancing form as that of a huge bear. Jeff almost forgot himself as he rose from the grass for a better view, only to have Hank drag him down; but the chieftains were too concentrated on the tepee to notice the stir behind them.

Suddenly, the figure of the bear was gone, and as the tent flap fell, the muffled voice of the medicine man called anew:

"Summon your friends — those who died in battle — those who heard me promise they would return —"

There were calls from the council fire: "Neheowotis! Tahiska!" Then, as the brief flare subsided, voices spoke again, seemingly from the top of the tent. One was a long wail, "I am Neheowotis," and the other came in a booming tone, "I am Tahiska." While the two voices were telling how they had died in battle, Jeff whispered to Hank:

"Neheowotis sounds like Cheyenne for Wolf on the Hill, but Tahiska is a new one on me."

"It should be," chuckled Hank. "It means White Buffalo. The Sioux idea of something nobody would ever see — like a Purple Cow."

Right then, Hank and Jeff were seeing a white wolf, for the tent flap had opened again and a figure representing the spirit of Neheowotis was doing a dance. It dropped away and to Hank's amazement, the white buffalo came next, thrusting its horned head from the blackness and repeating in a hollow tone, "I am Tahiska!" Then, as the chieftains dumped more pine cones on the fire, the huge head bobbed away from the sudden glare, letting the tent flap drop again.

Considering the hides and costumes they had seen in the tepee, Jeff and Hank were sure the medicine man had gotten loose and was staging a masquerade. Evidently the Indian chiefs were skeptical, too, for with one accord, they rushed the tepee, whipped wide the flap, and revealed the whole interior in the glow of the firelight. Awed, they fell back in amazement, and from their vantage point, Jeff and Hank saw the reason why.

The medicine man who called himself Numokmukana was lying face down, completely exhausted from his struggle with the thongs and as tightly bound as ever. All the costumes and other implements were stacked in their proper places, exactly as Jeff and Hank had seen them. Apparently the chiefs knew all about them, for they made the rounds and came from the tepee shaking their heads as though really puzzled.

As soon as the tent flap dropped, more manifestations began. First came the excited voice of the medicine man, babbling in new frenzy: "Your friends, the departed warriors, are still here, even though you cannot see them! Matochega—Neheowotis—Tahiska—and many more — all here. You cannot see them, but you can hear them. Listen!"

From within the tepee came the beat of drums, the clack of turtle shells, the thud of stones against the leathery walls, followed by a chorus of blood-curdling war whoops that froze Jeff and Hank where they crouched. But such sounds were familiar to the assembled chieftains; they took them as a token of welcome. Again, they sprang into the haunted tepee, flinging its curtained front wide.

They were met with flying drums, shells, and stones that showered from above. Some of the chieftains actually reeled, as though meeting invisible attackers, but through it all, the medicine man lay bound and helpless as before. Again, the Indians emerged, dropping the tent flap. Then, as a parting manifestation, strange voices mingled near the tent top, followed by fiery sparks that issued from the opening like a miniature volcano. Again, the tepee was shaken violently and the figure of the bound medicine man was flung from within, carrying the curtained tent front with him as he landed, bewildered, beside the council fire.

In response to the medicine man's moans, the chieftains cut him loose and he came to his feet, weakly at first. Then, his full strength suddenly returning, he gestured to the empty tent, waved his hand toward the top and pointed off beyond the low hills that showed plainly in the moonlight.

"You saw them," he announced, "you heard them, and now they have gone, those warriors who returned from battle, as I promised. Now I, Numokmukana, shall follow them to the happy hills. But soon you, too, will be going into battle.

"To all of you who see me standing here and watch me lift my hands" — the medicine man stretched both arms high as he spoke — "to everyone who hears my voice and marks my words, I promise this. After the next battle, all of you will return here. Some of you will be living, to serve as witnesses to the presence of the others, who will come back as ghosts of the dead.

"I, Numokmukana, have spoken. Now I shall go. But I shall be here when you again assemble, ready to summon the missing warriors and send them on their way, as I have done tonight. Again, you may bind me, yet you will see the impossible happen, through the power of Wakonschecha, who conquers Wakontonka."

With that, the painted medicine man turned and strode away in the direction he had pointed, following the unseen spirits to the land where they had gone. There was nothing ghostly in his parting. He simply crossed the little hillock and dipped from sight in the uncertain moonlight. But he left a solemn group of chieftains beside the dwindling council fire.

They waited silently, as though expecting more to happen. Then, with one accord, they went to their horses, mounted and galloped off.

After the hoofbeats faded, Jeff and Hank sneaked forward to the tepee. They skirted the dying fire so their figures could not be seen, and on the way, Hank picked up a few pine cones. From near the tepee, he muttered, "Wait!" and as Jeff complied, Hank tossed the cones into the embers. As the flare came, the bearded partners converged upon the open tent front and drove in with drawn knives, flinging aside hides and masks, stabbing all about and even upward, in case any lurkers might try to spring upon them.

But their blades found only nothingness. They were alone except for their own shadows, which were as black as Hank's beard; shadows cast by a firelight that Jeff's beard matched in ruddiness. Hank's disappointed snarl ended in a short laugh.

"Guess there was nobody in here nohow," Hank decided. "Leastwise, nobody except the medicine man." Hank stalked out, stooped by the fire and picked up the cut thongs that still lay there. "A smart geezer, that medicine man. Smart enough to slip in and out of these rawhide strips and go cavorting all around the tent. Smart to have those dumb chiefs *cut* him loose later, so they wouldn't find the slack."

Hank handed the thongs to Jeff, who matched the cut ends in an effort to gauge the size of the loops.

"Maybe he could have slipped them," conceded Jeff, "but how could he have managed to do all those things all alone and all at once?"

"What do you mean, all at once?" demanded Hank. "First, he was dancing around in a bearskin, playing he was Matochega. Then later, he was that hill wolf, whatever the Cheyennes call it. He used a wolf skin for that —"

"And all of a sudden," put in Jeff, "he was Tahiska, the White Buffalo. How do you explain that?"

"Easy. He threw off the wolf skin this way" — Hank swept his arms wide —"grabbed up a buffalo head" — stooping, he brought his hands together — "and pulled it down over his own head, so his voice sounded like this."

Hank came erect as his hands moved downward to his shoulders and his voice took on a hollow tone, which brought a smile from Jeff.

"A good imitation," he approved, "except that the only buffalo heads in the tepee are all black. Go and look."

Hank went and looked. When he returned, he was stroking his beard in puzzled fashion, the way Jeff usually did. It was Jeff who inquired, "See any white buffalo heads?"

"No white ones." Hank stooped suddenly beside the fire and brought up a handful of gray ashes like a soft powder, which he trickled from one hand to the other. "Maybe the medicine man used some stuff like this. White ashes, sprinkled over a black mask to make it look white. He could have shaken it when he took it off" — Hank went through the motion — "and the stuff would all be gone."

"If he used ashes, some of it would have been left."

"It wouldn't have to be ashes. Maybe it was some special stuff, Jeff. Those medicine men know a lot of tricks."

"Like climbing to the top of a tepee and talking from there, while you still hear him moaning down below?"

"That's what they call ventriloquism —"

"Wait, now, Hank. I've seen ventriloquists. They talk without moving their lips, while you watch a wooden dummy open and close its mouth, so it looks like it was doing the talking. But this medicine man wasn't using any dummy."

"So what? He just threw his voice up to the tent top."

"But I've just explained that ventriloquists can't throw their voices. The act won't work without a dummy."

Hank shook his head at that. "You've seen the wrong ventriloquists, Jeff," he said. "When I was in Washington, driving wagons during the war, a fellow named Wyman the Wizard came there, soon after one of those Bull Run battles, I don't remember just which one. Anyway, this Wyman could throw his voice into a trunk, or up to the top of the theater, or even down under the stage. Maybe you just imagined it, but he did it, like this medicine man in this here tepee."

Hank gestured to the tepee, which was fully dark again, for the fire had subsided and clouds were obscuring the moonlight. Jeff went over and tried to shake the tepee, without result.

"You may be right about those things, Hank," Jeff conceded. "Loose thongs, bearskin, buffalo mask, white powder and ventriloquism. But what made this tepee shake?"

Hank shoved his weight against the other side but the tepee did not budge. The wind was rising and even the tall grass was waving. The tent poles groaned, and the leathery sides flapped, as before. Yet the tepee did not quiver, let alone rock.

"Another trick," grunted Hank. "The tent was moored tight when we first came in, so the medicine man must have found a way to loosen it. Then he fixed it tight again at the finish."

"Right smart of him," decided Jeff, "to do so much in so little time and leave us baffled like we are now."

"If I had time," Hank declared, "I could figure out this contraption.

But from the way it's clouding up, we'd better be getting back to the canyon. Let's go."

It was pitch black when they reached the canyon, and they would have lost their way if the mules hadn't heard them and brayed a welcome. There was no use trying to go on, so they camped there for the night. With morning, the sky cleared again and they continued on their way.

"First, we'll locate that village," Hank decided. "Then we can find the army and tell them where it is. Later on, we can go back and look for that medicine lodge and find out what makes it tick."

They worked their way through rolling country, pausing at intervals while one man would stay with the mules and the other would creep to the summit of a grassy knoll to look for the Indian village. It was well along in the afternoon when Hank came back from such a trip and gave Jeff the grim facts.

"The village is down in the next valley," Hank reported, "and it's a big one, running for miles along a river. We'd better spread the word right quick."

Hank's decision came too late. By the time he and Jeff were skirting the end of a high ridge, they heard a distant bugle call and looked up to see a troop of cavalrymen dismounting from their horses and opening fire at an enemy somewhere beyond. Then, looking the other way, Hank and Jeff saw a band of Indians riding up from a deep ravine, as though to flank the ridge.

Being directly in the path, the bearded prospectors hurried up the slope, practically dragging the mules along. Halfway there, they were met by a dozen troopers who came galloping down from the ridge and dismounted as they arrived. The soldiers were commanded by a sergeant, who included Hank and Jeff in his sharply barked orders:

"Get those mules back behind the rise, with the horses. Then up to the firing line, everybody!"

The troopers were shooting with their carbines when Hank and Jeff joined them. The two rifles proved helpful in stemming the attacking Indians, who spilled from their saddles and disappeared in the long grass at every volley. Soon, dozens of riderless horses were racing down into the ravine, but new squads of Indians came surging up to replace the fallen braves. Between volleys, Hank shouted to the sergeant, close by:

"You'd better be getting your men up to the brow of the hill. They can't take this much longer."

"They won't have to," the sergeant called back. "All we need to do is hold our ground. The general himself is in command, and he's handled plenty of hostiles in his time —"

There was an interruption while guns crackled at another surge of foolhardy Indians. Another half dozen tumbled into the grass, while the horses scattered wildly. Following that, the sergeant picked up from where he had left off:

"By now, the general is busting up their main force, chopping it into bits, the way he always does. Next, he'll be fanning out his command and they'll be coming this way to support us. You wait and see."

"But there are still more Indians down below," urged Hank. "Look how they are outflanking us."

"You think so? Suppose I told you that we have another whole troop coming over from the next ridge to outflank them. What would you say to that?"

"I'd say that they'd better come right quick." Hank turned to Jeff. "What would you say, partner?"

"I'd say let's start shooting again right now," snapped Jeff. "Here they come, the biggest batch yet."

Carbines and rifles blazed point-blank at some fifty Indian horsemen, who divided rapidly to get out of range, the riders swinging from sight on the far side of their mounts. Like the soldiers, Jeff and Hank followed the diverging horsemen with their guns, hoping to pick off a few. While they were thus diverted, Indians suddenly sprang up from the tall grass just in front of them and came whooping forward, another fifty of them, some with rifles, the rest brandishing knives and tomahawks!

These were the braves who had fallen earlier. Some actually had been hit, but they were comparatively few. The rest had purposely dived ahead of the rifle fire, knowing that the grass was high enough to hide them. All this while, they had been snaking forward, ready for the signal to attack. The moment had come; now the lurking Indians were about to overwhelm their foe.

Jeff and Hank weren't the sort to give up easily. They intended to hold out until the promised reserves arrived. Jeff shot down two attackers, used his empty rifle to club a third, then looked to see how Hank was faring. The man with the black beard was slashing at two Indians with his bowie knife, but a third was aiming at him with a rifle. As Jeff shouted a warning, Hank himself gave a frantic wave and pointed past his red-bearded friend. Jeff swung about and warded with his rifle just as an Indian swung a tomahawk straight for his skull.

There was time to divert the stroke, even though Jeff couldn't stop it. The hatchet turned in the Indian's hand, and the side, not the blade, crashed hard against Jeff's head. His slouch hat took some of the blow, but not enough. His whole head seemed to absorb one tremendous jolt that ended in a burst of stars and a mass of utter blackness.

Blackness still persisted when Jeff again opened his eyes, only now it was distant and velvety. The stars had returned, but they were not the bursting kind. Instead, they sprinkled the black canopy overhead and furnished a twinkling glow. Lying on the grassy ridge, Jeff was staring up at the night sky, slowly recalling how he had come to be here.

Once he had pieced the past, Jeff came to his feet without great effort and rubbed his head as he looked about. Except for a slight throb, he felt no aftereffects from the blow that had felled him. But the others had not fared so well. The army sergeant and the soldiers of his squad were sprawled in grotesque positions, all slain in that final onslaught.

Jeff's thoughts flashed back to Hank, but before he could call his partner's name, a figure arose slowly from among the dead. Face to face, the two prospectors grinned silently at each other through their beards, offering sober congratulations over their mutual escape. Jeff spoke first:

"Lucky for me that you pointed when you did, Hank. I just had time to slow that tomahawk. I guess the Sioux that swung it must have thought he killed me and kept on going after somebody else. Anyway, I'm still here."

"So am I," returned Hank, "thanks to you, Jeff. You pointed, too, remember? I turned and saw a rifle muzzle coming square at me. I grabbed it and the brave missed when he fired. But he managed to clout me with it" — Hank rubbed his forehead ruefully — "and that was the last I remember. I guess one of the soldiers plugged the Indian, or he'd have done me in for sure."

A night fog was creeping slowly up the ridge, and the moon, rising just above the brow, gave the whole scene a weird effect. In the swirling mist, the figures of the fallen soldiers seemed to stir, as though ready to rise up as living ghosts.

"We'd better mosey along," Hank decided. He glanced over the slight rise and added, "Horses gone — mules gone — packs gone. Guess the Indians must have taken them, which is why they didn't come back to bother us."

"And by now the main force of cavalry has caught up with them," Jeff said. "That's the end of those Indians."

"Yeah, but there's more on the warpath. We'd better find that cavalry brigade and tell them. Whoever the general is, we'll report to him in person."

"Good enough, Hank. We can take a look at the Indian village on the way and tell him about that, too."

Without the mules, the bearded partners found hiking easy, despite the long grass. They reached a knoll where the mist had lessened and saw the village spread distant in the moonlight. Many clusters of wigwams were clearly etched in the glow of huge council fires, where Indians were dancing about, waving tomahawks and war clubs.

"The army must have driven them right back to their wigwams," chuckled Hank. "Now they're getting all fired up to go out and get licked again tomorrow — unless the army attacks them sooner."

"There's too many for the army to attack at once," argued Jeff. "That gives me an idea, Hank. Let's us go back to that medicine lodge and be there when the chiefs show up again."

"And then what?"

"Then we can steer the cavalry there. Even a small detachment like the sergeant had would be enough to chase those chiefs and capture them. Without their leaders, the tribes will be as good as licked."

"You've hit it square, Jeff! Let's go."

By dawn, they were back in the canyon, and all that day they watched for the approach of army scouts or cavalry detachments, but none appeared. They also kept an occasional eye on the lone tepee in the hidden valley, and along toward dusk, Jeff came up with a new suggestion:

"Let's get into that tepee before those chiefs show up. If the army isn't here to chase them, maybe we can do it ourselves. We'll start yelling and tossing things around before the medicine man can even begin to work himself loose. With two of us, we can do it a whole lot better than he ever could."

"And suppose," objected Hank, "the chiefs start to search the tepee beforehand? What if they find us there?"

"They didn't search it the last time, not until after the commotion started. Then they were too scared to know what to look for. This time, they'll be even more scared."

"Maybe. But what about the medicine man?"

"He'll be the most scared of the lot, with things happening all around him before he can fake a ghost act of his own. When he gets loose, he will run like blazes and the rest will follow!"

"You're right, Jeff. Anyway, I intended to have another look inside that tepee, and this may be just the time to do it."

Soon they were in the tepee, picking out what they wanted. Along with the bearskin and the buffalo heads, they also found a pair of grotesque devil masks. While Jeff was trying on the masks, Hank began shoving at one of the slanted tent poles and suddenly exclaimed:

"Lookit, Jeff! The whole thing gives, and you can rock the tent with it. Try that pole on your side."

Jeff tried it and found that Hank was right.

"What a couple of dumbheads we were!" Jeff laughed. "When we tried to rock the tent from the outside, we couldn't, because the poles were tilted inward and we were pushing downward and throwing ourselves off balance. But from the inside, heaving outward, you can bring the other side right up!"

"So now we know," agreed Hank, "and once we start the tent rocking, we can grab some of those hanging straps and go up with them. Now, let's dig around and see what else we can find."

They dug among the buffalo hides and came up with a fair-sized powder keg that proved to be nearly full. That brought a chuckle from Hank.

"Remember those sparks that shot up from the tent top that night?" he said. "This is the stuff that makes them. Find me some chunks of paper, Jeff, and I'll rig some fireworks like they'll be showing at the big 1876 Centennial Exposition in Philadelphia, this summer!"

Jeff found some paper, along with a flint and steel, which he used to ignite some short candles, for by now, darkness was thick inside the tepee. By the time Hank was through preparing his pyrotechnics, Jeff's keen ear caught the faint thud of approaching hoofbeats. The bearded pair snuffed out the candles and had burrowed deep in the buffalo hides by the time the chieftains arrived and began to build their council fire.

Soon the babble of voices announced the approach of the medicine man, who began his speech in the tone of Numokmukana, but this time with a note of triumph.

"Tonight, you have all returned among the living, so there are none whom I must summon as I did before. None like Matochega, Neheowotis, and Tahiska, those who have already gone to the happy hills. But again you may bind me, so that you may witness the power of Wakonschecha, which will drive away Wakontonka, by *choncheha* and *wagamoo.*"

"*Choncheha* and *wagamoo*," Jeff translated in an undertone. "That means drum and rattle. Get ready with the tom-tom and the turtle shells."

"They're all set," Hank assured him, "but first we rock the tent, like the other night. Then the drum and rattle —"

"And after that, we'll put on those gruesome masks we found —"

"And finish with the fireworks. But hold it — here they come. Lie low!"

The chieftains had finished binding the medicine man. As before, they carried him into the tepee, dumped him there, and returned to the council fire. The moment the flap fell, Jeff and Hank sprang from hiding and made for opposite tent poles. In moments, they had the tepee quivering; then they began to jounce it.

Excited shouts of "Wakonschecha! Wakonschecha!" came from the council fire, for never before had the haunted tepee shown such immediate action. Now it was rocking at double speed, with Jeff tilting it one way and Hank the other. Next, Jeff sprang up the pole and clambered hand over hand toward the top, which doubled over and would have fallen, but for Hank's restraining action.

As the huge tent rebounded, Jeff grabbed for a leather strap that dangled from the top. Swinging like a living pendulum, he shouted a high-pitched jargon of Indian and English that issued from the open tent top. Awed howls responded from the council fire, where the witnesses were sure that Jeff's cries could only be of ghostly origin.

Hank was ready with drums and shells when Jeff dropped lightly beside him, and together they beat an outrageous din as they pranced about the huddled figure of the medicine man, who suddenly began to shout, "*Shesha! Shesha! Shesha!*" Hank recognized the dialect and panted to Jeff:

"He's calling, 'Come here!' to the crowd outside —"

"And here they come," put in Jeff. "Get ready for them!"

Jeff shoved Hank in one direction and sprang the other way, as the tent flap was flung aside and two chieftains came driving through, hoping to find the source of the disturbance. They were met with flying drums and turtle shells that Jeff and Hank flung from the darkness. Then, as the Indians tried to dodge away, the bearded men overtook them and half-thrust, half-kicked them into the arms of the others, who scattered as the tent flap fell. Immediately, Jeff panted:

"Quick, Hank! Give me a devil mask! That will hold them until you start the fireworks!"

Hank snatched up a mask, Jeff put it on and drew back the tent flap just enough to show the weird, grinning visage. It had the effect that he intended. The chieftains, ready to invade the tepee again, halted suddenly, crying, "Wakontonka! Wakontonka!" Clearly, they supposed that the spirit of evil, Wakontonka, had taken charge instead of the good spirit, Wakonschecha, whom the medicine man had promised to summon.

But now there was anger in their cry of "Wakontonka!" They felt that the medicine man had tricked them, or that he might be putting them to a test, to see if they were bold enough to defy Wakontonka's wrath. How long they would restrain themselves was a question. It didn't have to be very long.

Hank had snapped his flintlock and had lighted a candlewick. Now he was using the flame to ignite a paper tube, containing powder, which he had twisted at both ends. He tossed it up through the opening in the tent top, where it exploded with a burst of flame.

The group fell back as Hank flipped more explosives through the opening. A few of the tubes fizzled and spurted down to the dry grass around the tepee. The grass caught fire, and soon the flames were licking at the tent itself. At Jeff's call, Hank grabbed up the other devil mask and joined him, just as the front flap went up in a huge blaze.

The amazed chiefs saw the medicine man struggling with his bonds in the midst of an inferno, flanked by a pair of dancing demons. Suddenly, the two demons grabbed the medicine man and pitched him through the surrounding flames. He squirmed from his bonds and dashed for the horses, which were whinnying in fright at the flames. The medicine man's flight was enough for his followers. They rushed for their horses, too.

Hank and Jeff flung their demon masks aside and darted from the blazing tepee across the narrow clearing to the tall grass of the hillside. When they looked back from that vantage spot, the tepee had become a tremendous beacon, its flames illuminating the sky.

"If there are any soldiers within five miles," asserted Jeff, "just seeing that will bring them here."

"That's right," agreed Hank, "and what they'll be hearing in a couple of minutes will fetch them all the quicker."

Again, Hank was right. As the Indians stood beside their horses, still scanning the flames in search of the missing fire demons, the entire holocaust burst with one gigantic roar, rocketing the blazing fragments skyward and showering them about the landscape. The fire had reached the powder keg, which Hank had left half filled.

The Indians sprang to their horses just in time. As Hank had predicted, the blast sped the arrival of some soldiers who had sighted the beacon earlier. A troop of cavalry came galloping in from the canyon and opened fire on the chieftains as they raced down the valley, with the medicine man accompanying them on a spare horse.

Pursuit was brief, for the troopers were unwilling to ride into what might be a trap. A few of them dismounted to inspect the subsiding flames that had consumed the medicine lodge. One trooper spoke to the others. "I wonder why those braves set fire to their tepee," he said. "Anybody have any ideas about it?"

"We can tell them," Jeff whispered, as he rose from the tall grass. "Come on, Hank. Let's give them our report."

"Wait now," warned Hank. "Let's hear what those troopers have to say. You're likely to get shot if you walk up to them all of a sudden. They're quick on the trigger."

From the way the troopers held their hands on their gun butts, Hank was probably right. Jeff eased down to listen.

"No use taking chances chasing Indians," declared one trooper grimly. "Not after what happened on that ridge over by the Little Bighorn."

"The Little Bighorn," Hank said to Jeff in a whisper, "that's the river where we saw the Indian camp."

"It must have been right bad," put in another trooper. "I've heard that most of General Custer's command was wiped out."

"Custer!" Hank gasped. "He's the best Indian fighter in the army. He must be the general the sergeant talked about."

"Not just some of them," the first trooper was continuing, "but *all* of them. We found bodies all along the ridge, but most of them were near the top, and General Custer was lying dead among them. That's where he made his last stand."

There was a pause, punctuated by the occasional crackles of the lessening fire.

"The Indians outflanked the regiment," the trooper went on then. "They came up from the far end of the ridge, where there was only a sergeant with a small detachment to meet them. The Indians rolled right over them."

Another trooper queried, "How big was the detachment?"

"Not more than a dozen or so," the first trooper stated. "I was there when they counted the bodies. A few more than a dozen, I reckon, if you include a couple of guys who looked like trappers, or maybe prospectors."

"How could you tell that they were prospectors?"

"Well, they hadn't shaved in months. One had a big black beard, the other was kind of reddish. Instead of carbines, they had rifles. They were carrying big knives, too, bowie knives, that we found lying near their bodies—"

Hank and Jeff looked at each other. Their hands went to their belts, and for the first time since their return from the ridge, they realized that their knives were gone.

"They must have put up a good fight, that pair," the trooper told his comrades. "One had his head hacked with a tomahawk, the other looked like he'd been clubbed to death with a rifle butt." He paused, shrugged, and added, "Well, there's no need staying here. Let's mount and get on our way."

The troopers were turning to their horses, when Jeff, forgetting Hank's advice, sprang up and approached them, calling excitedly, "Wait! Wait!" One of the mounting troopers was gazing Jeff's way, but his eyes showed no change of expression, not even the slightest interest. Another trooper, too, was facing in the same direction, as they swung their horses about. Hank's whisper came to Jeff's ear:

"They stared right through us, Jeff!"

The troopers were riding off to the canyon. Beside the embers of the burned-out medicine lodge, Jeff heard Hank whisper again:

"You know what the medicine man said, the other night —"

"I know." Jeff's tone, too, was a voiceless whisper. "He said that all who saw him standing there, all who heard his voice, all would come back after the battle —"

"Come back after the battle." Hank's whisper seemed like Jeff's own echo, "either as living witnesses or as ghosts of the dead."

"We heard what he said," declared Jeff. "We saw him, too, although he didn't see us. But he meant us."

"Yes, he meant us because we were there. We came back here, Jeff, just as he said we would. We surprised him, but we didn't scare him, until he began thinking maybe Wakontonka sent us. Only we came here on our own."

"And we went to all that trouble, rigging up the ghost tent —"

"We just imagined that part, Jeff," Hank said slowly. "We didn't have to rig it, being as we were ghosts already."

"And where are we going now, Hank?"

"Where they all go after the medicine man calls them back. To the happy hills he talked about. We've got a claim staked there, remember?"

They were walking side by side, past the ruined tepee toward the grassy hillock beyond, two figures that were strangely elusive in the moonlight. Now, even their whispers seemed to mingle with the sigh of the night breeze. Nor were they looking at each other any longer, for each seemed to feel that if he did, he might find the other gone.

A cloud dulled the moonlight, the wind lashed the waving grass. The ghostly figures were gone, like pebbles in a pool that leave only ripples in their wake. With them went the secret of the shaking tent, the cherished mystery of the Indian medicine man!

The Edge of Doom

"Geordie! Geordie!"

The boy's frantic call went unheard as dusk settled over the windswept cliff. Slowly, he worked one hand upward and pressed his numbed fingers against the rock, to find it smooth, without the slightest crack. He drew his hand down again to the crevice it had left and made a try with his other hand.

Again, no luck. Now, with both hands clutching the crevice, he sought new toeholds, hoping to work his way down, if not up. But in extending his foot he forced his body back. One look over his shoulder showed the jagged gray rocks, waiting like hungry teeth in the darkness at the base of the Giant's Pillar, hundreds of feet below.

Having climbed this far, there was no other way to go but up. To make it all the more hopeless, the very brow of the towering cliff was no more than three feet above the boy's reach, if only he could have found one higher hold to work from! Now, clutching tightly to the only hold he could retain, the boy called again:

"Geooordieee . . ."

It was a hopeless cry, lost in the wail of the rising wind. Twilight was creeping down upon the cliff and the boy's only hope was to hang on until dawn. But if he could retain his agonized grip another half hour, he would not only be doing well, he would be doing better than he really believed was possible.

There were others, too, who had their doubts as to what might be possible.

More than a mile away from the great winding cleft where the Giant's Pillar loomed so formidably, oil lanterns were bobbing like tiny fireflies at the wooden marker where the trails diverged, one leading down into the deep ravine, the other following a slope up the back of the cliff.

It was Geordie Buchanan, a bluff-faced, rugged Scotsman, who had suddenly called a halt. A man in his mid-sixties, Geordie was still remarkably agile.

"What's up, Geordie?" the others were saying. "Which way do we look now?"

"Did you hear it?" Geordie asked tensely. "The bairn's voice calling for me, calling, 'Geordie—Geordie—' just as clear as I'm saying it now?" His eyes lost their faraway stare as he turned eagerly to a solemn man of about thirty. "Did you hear it, Lord Archie?"

"You heard that call before, Buchanan," Lord Archie reminded him, "but none of the rest of us heard it — or did we?" He turned to the others, who shook their heads.

"This time," one man spoke up, "all we heard was the howl of the wind. It's coming right strongly through the gap."

"Then that's where we'll find the bairn, climbing the Giant's Pillar, all on his own."

"You really believe that, Buchanan?"

Lord Archie's anxious query brought a solemn nod from Geordie, whose eyes, half-closed, seemed to be visualizing a distant scene. Lord Archie swung his lantern toward the lower path.

"Come along, men. Let's hope that we find him still alive and not too badly hurt, there at the bottom of the cliff."

The others followed, all but Geordie, who turned in the direction of the upper path. Lord Archie called after him:

"It's no use, Buchanan, he never could have climbed to the clifftop, a lad of only twelve years."

"But young Lord Francis is a Douglas," Geordie called back. "Like yourself, Lord Archie. Once his sight is set, he will see it through, so far as he is able."

"So far as he is able."

Lord Archie repeated those ominous words as he and his men continued down into the ravine, fearing for the worst where his young cousin Francis was concerned.

Alone, Buchanan scaled the slope to the very edge of the cleft, where he groped along, sometimes lowering the lantern over a void that threatened to swallow him if he took one false step. Echoing in his mind was the cry, "Geordie!" so real that Buchanan almost failed to hear the feeble gasp that actually came from only a yard below.

There, Geordie saw the chalk-white face of young Lord Francis, looking up from between two widespread hands, their fingers dug deep into the cracks of the cliff. Geordie placed the lantern on rocky ground behind him, squirmed to the brink and worked his body and one knee into a hollow. Extending his hands down over the brink, he ordered:

"Steady, now! When I take your wrist, let go with your hand. That's right. Now grip my wrist above. Keep it locked."

Geordie's other hand slid wide and gained a similar hold on the boy's opposite wrist. Calm as ever, he continued:

"I'm going to swing you to my shoulders, lad, as I did when you were a wee bairn. Let your feet loose, so your body dangles, but start those feet climbing when I haul you up!"

There was a slight jerk as the boy's feet went free. Then Geordie was swinging him pendulum fashion, one way, then the other. One wide swing took the boy far out along the cliff side, where he hung for a perpetual moment above the deadly void. Then Geordie's powerful arms brought him the other way in a still greater sweep. As it neared its limit, with the boy's legs pointed at a wide angle, Geordie's anchored knee gave a powerful upward drive. Recoiling as from a piston stroke, Geordie rolled completely over, in the opposite direction.

The light form of Lord Francis was snapped upward, almost to the brink. The boy was using his feet to clamber, as Geordie had told him, and his knees met the rock edge with bruising force. He was still short of the rim, but there was nothing that he could grab while his hands and wrists were locked with Geordie's. However, no grab was needed. Geordie's brawny forearms gave a timely tug in just the right direction. Boy and man finished their roll safely on the cliff top, in the glow of the lantern perched only a few feet away.

Soon Geordie was swinging that same lantern on the end of a long stick as a signal to those below. Shouts could be heard in the rising wind, but they were not needed. Lord Archie and his crew knew that Geordie must have found Lord Francis and that the boy was safe. But they did not learn the full details of the remarkable rescue until later.

Even then, and during the months that followed, people were more impressed by the events leading up to the rescue, rather than in the deed itself. That young Lord Francis had climbed to the top of a cliff no one ever before had scaled alone was almost unbelievable; but for Geordie to have sensed the situation, and to have found the exact spot where the boy clung, seemed still more wonderful. Then, too, there was that distant call, unheard by anyone except Geordie, for whom it was intended.

Gradually, the opinion spread that "Auld Geordie" was a "taisher" or a person "gifted" with the power of "second sight," which enabled him to vision events from afar and announce the approach of the unexpected. This was a common belief in the Scottish Highlands in the late 1850's, the period when Lord Francis had his boyhood adventure. But Geordie Buchanan was quite different from the usual Highland seer.

Never did Geordie display his strange ability by predicting local events, foreseeing funerals, or glimpsing weird lights known as corpse candles, which were regarded as spectral tokens of death or disaster.

Geordie's uncanny reputation hinged entirely on the affinity between himself and Lord Francis, who was young enough to be his grandson. From the day when Geordie Buchanan, the trusted famliy retainer, had first carried the wee bairn on his shoulder, he had come to know the child's slightest whim. Indeed, Geordie's tales of the Highlands could very well have shaped the boy's love of the fells and crags that studded his native land.

The fact that Geordie knew where young Francis might have gone, and why, could have accounted for the "inner voice" that had drawn the old retainer to the brink of the cliff. If it had stopped there, it might have been forgotten. As it was, from then on the affinity increased. There were times when Geordie probably furthered it and even may have laid the groundwork for events to come. Such was true the day when Geordie asked Lord Francis:

"Why, lad, did you climb the Giant's Pillar alone?"

"Because I wanted to be the first to do it."

"A fine thought, lad, but you can always share that glory with another. 'Twould have been better having someone start with you at the bottom, rather than having to call on me to help you at the top."

"That is true, Geordie, but I almost made it."

"And *almost* can be the same as *never*."

Thinking back, young Francis agreed that Geordie was right. Solemnly, he promised:

"All right, Geordie, I'll never climb alone again."

"Now, don't cut it that thin, lad," Geordie warned. "At times you can venture alone, but take the right precautions. When you climbed the Pillar, you might at least have carried a rope and looped it over some friendly rock."

"But how would that have helped me up?"

"It wouldn't have, lad. But it would have helped you *down*. Didn't you think of that?"

"No, Geordie, I didn't. All I wanted was to get to the top. That's how I managed to go that far."

"Aye, but it was not far enough. If you had gone down the cliff, lad, you could have tried going up again. 'If at first you don't succeed' — remember the old saying, lad?"

"I remember."

Lord Francis remembered Geordie's words a few years later, when he and a friend named Malcolm Hay had climbed through a snow-filled ravine to the 3,500-foot summit of Corrag Bhuide. From there, they had simply to follow a narrow ridge of barren rock to a twin peak. The danger seemed negligible.

Along the ridge were flat patches like solid steppingstones. To Lord Francis, now a lanky, agile youth in his early teens, they formed an inviting path that he could take in hop, skip, and jump. But he remembered that he had brought along the two things that old Geordie always advised — a companion and a rope. So he hitched one end of the rope around his waist and gave the other end to Malcolm, who smiled at the unnecessary precaution.

Then Lord Francis was on his way. The first stone wobbled and as he sprang to the second, it skidded sideways, so that he lost his footing as he reached the third. Sprawling, he grabbed for the next mound of rock while a whole surge of recollections swept through his mind, Geordie's warning face among them. Then he gave a frantic shout as he felt the last rock yield. Just above the steepest portion of the ridge, the youth could remember only how Geordie had once rolled him to safety on a brink like this. So he tried the same process on his own.

With that roll, Lord Francis reached the end of his rope, and instead of dooming him, it saved him. Malcolm, on the other end, was nearly hauled off his feet, but managed to cling to a solid rock beside him. The rope went taut, enabling Lord Francis to ease his grip on the loose stone. Instead of toppling, it settled back in place and he gradually drew himself up to it. From then on, it was just a case of being more careful when traversing those stones.

Malcolm's account added some startling highlights. In relating it to friends, he said:

"One stone was slipping, then another, and when Lord Francis called to me, 'Look out, Malcolm!' I braced myself. Then the last stone was toppling and I heard him call, 'Aye, Geordie, I'll hang on' — and hang on he did, though how, I shall never know."

Those who heard the story recalled that on the same day, Geordie Buchanan, ill with a fever, had kept asking about Lord Francis but had finally muttered happily, 'The bairn is safe. I see it.' With that, Geordie had gone to sleep, and it was not until the next day that anyone learned of the near-disaster on the summit of Corrag Bhuidhe.

Still more remarkable was the time when Lord Francis and two companions went on a rock-climbing expedition to the Isle of Arran, intending to scale the half-mile precipices of a ridge called the Great Comb. A dangerous mist set in, and at the end of three days, a party was sent to search the steeps and saddles that towered from the sea.

But this time, old Geordie had a different presentiment. His mind no longer pictured tors and crags. Instead he visioned a strange, hollow darkness, its hush disturbed only by the occasional shrieks of birds above the beat of surf, except for those intervals when he heard the prolonged call, "Geordie!"

So when the searchers disembarked on the fog-bound island and started up the Witch's Step to Cir Mhor, otherwise the Great Comb, old Geordie stayed aboard the steam launch and induced the pilot to cruise about the sea inlets and rocky promontories. There, they came to a sea cave that the tides had furrowed in the cliff, where human figures waved from among the rocks.

The group consisted of Lord Francis and his two friends. Their dory had been wrecked on the rocks before they had reached the landing near the mountains. For three days, they had been awaiting rescue, and often Lord Francis had gone to the mouth of the cave and called, "Geooordieee!" when the surf had lulled. For he was confident that when rescuers came, Geordie would be with them.

During the next few years, instances of this curious affinity dwindled, if any occurred at all. That only served to increase the interest in the old cases which were often exaggerated by those who recounted them. But the reach of mind to mind, the *rapport* between Geordie Buchanan and Lord Francis Douglas, was merely latent rather than extinct. There were unquestionably times when one gained some fleeting impression of the other, but apparently these were never checked.

There were two reasons, however, for this lapse. For one, Lord Francis had all but deserted his native heath and was traveling abroad each summer, so that his contacts with old Geordie were few. For another, he had learned his boyhood lessons so well that he no longer felt the pinch of distress that made him call mentally for Geordie's aid.

Both the lure and lore of mountain climbing attracted Lord Francis to Switzerland, where he became a welcome addition to parties of daring men who scrambled high among the summits of the mighty Alps. His ability at rock climbing made up for his comparative inexperience at traversing glacial ice. Each expedition included proficient climbers and capable guides, to whom every stage of the ascent and the return represented a calculated risk, which was handled accordingly.

Whatever the dangers, they never resulted in a foolhardy situation, such as Lord Francis had encountered in his boyhood. All due precautions were considered in advance, and ticklish assignments were given to the persons best qualified to handle them. Each group of climbers thus became a team of specialists, with any newcomers hand-picked to complete the party.

That was how Lord Francis Douglas happened to be in the mile-high village of Zermatt on Wednesday, July 12th, 1865. Outside the Monte Rosa Hotel, he was with a group who were studying the surrounding mountain peaks, a fantastic panorama that included the mighty Matterhorn, which rose like a massive sentinel of granite to an altitude of nearly three miles.

The summit of that formidable pinnacle seemed literally to overhang the snow and glacial ice that formed a vast apron beneath. Its forbidding appearance warned off anyone who might even think of scaling the towering crag. Yet the spokesman of the little group outside the Zermatt inn was planning the conquest of the Matterhorn, something never before achieved.

The spokesman was Edward Whymper, a twenty-five-year-old London artist who had come to Switzerland to make sketches of the mountains and had been forced to climb them to obtain the views he wanted. In four years, he had scaled many almost inaccessible peaks, including some of the highest in the Mont Blanc group. Whymper was writing a book to be titled *Scrambles Amongst the Alps,* in which he intended to relate not only his past but his future adventures — if he lived to tell them.

With Whymper were two other Englishmen, the Reverend Charles Hudson, who had spent many vacations in the Alps and had become as good a climber as any guide; and Robert Hadow, comparatively new to the sport, but a cool and calculating type that denoted the true Alpine scrambler.

Lord Francis was the fourth member of the group and the youngest, for he was not quite twenty. That particularly pleased Whymper, who had begun his mountain climbing at about the same age. Right now, Lord Francis showed all the youthful vigor and enthusiasm that Whymper had felt during his first Alpine scrambles, but he was far better qualified. Where much of Whymper's original climbing had been confined to three steep flights of stairs leading up to an art studio in a London garret, Lord Francis had been at home amid the Scottish crags, some of which resembled the Matterhorn in miniature.

That was why Whymper had welcomed Lord Francis on this expedition, which was to start from Zermatt the next morning. Whymper liked the cool, appraising way in which Lord Francis studied the massive monolith that was sharply etched against the sky. Often, the Matterhorn was shrouded by mist or lost in banks of clouds, but clear weather had been predicted for the next few days. That was one reason why Whymper was eager to get started on the climb. The other reason was that another party was getting ready to attempt the ascent from the Italian side, early in the coming week.

It was Whymper's ambition to be with the first group that scaled the Matterhorn, and even the hint that others were planning such an attempt invariably forced him to immediate action. So the spirit of rivalry was often in the air when Whymper arranged an expedition. But he never stinted in his preparations; always, he had the best available men on call. This occasion was no exception to his ironclad rules.

"I've hired Michel Croz," announced Whymper. "He is the best guide in Zermatt. We are also taking Peter Taugwalder, a guide of long experience, and his two sons, so that there will be a guide for each of us. All of them have tried to reach the summit of the Matterhorn, but have failed — as I have."

"And how many times," asked Lord Francis, "have you tried?"

"Eight," replied Whymper, with a smile. "Having risked eight lives, I am willing to take a chance with my ninth, like a cat. Yes, very much like a cat, because only a cat could climb the Matterhorn from this side, something that nobody so far has attempted."

"You can't be serious, Whymper!" Hadow exclaimed. "Look at the way that great brow juts over the snow below—"

"You started all your other climbs from the Italian side, so you are familiar with the back slope already—" Hudson began.

"Everybody is familiar with the back slope," interposed Whymper, "and each time, they encounter a new and impassable obstacle. I prefer to tackle it the hard way for once. Straight up the face of the cliff, which may not be so steep and forbidding as it looks. To find out, we must try it."

Whymper looked to Lord Francis for approval and received a nod of agreement. Eyes half-closed, Lord Francis was thinking back to some of his boyhood climbs. Formidable though the Matterhorn was, it might be easier to scale than the Giant's Pillar. There would be many more hazards, of that Lord Francis was sure, but he was thinking in terms of degree. The number of hazards did not matter, provided that none was insurmountable.

Whymper swung to the others and asked briskly:

"How about it, gentlemen? Are we all agreed?"

Hudson and Hadow exchanged glances, then nodded.

Despite themselves, these older men were swayed by the youthful enthusiasm of Whymper and Lord Francis. Preposterous though this new route seemed, the old one so far had proven hopeless. Almost anything was worth a try, with the Matterhorn as a prize.

They went into the hotel, where Lord Francis found a letter waiting for him. It was from his cousin Archie in Scotland, and it dealt with business matters up to the final paragraph, which read:

> *I told Buchanan that I was writing to you and he said, "Tell the lad to take good care of himself wherever he may be, for 'twould be hard for me to help him now, though tell him I would surely try." That is indeed true, for old Buchanan can scarcely get about without his stick but when he sits wool-gathering before the fire, he mutters about the past and seems eager to be on the go, much like those times when he went to look for you.*

As Lord Francis pocketed the letter and turned toward the fireside, here in the Swiss inn, a huge St. Bernard dog arose to greet him, reminding him of faithful old Geordie, there by the fire in the Scottish manor house. Just as the St. Bernards would go to the aid of travelers in mountain passes, so would Geordie still try to answer a call from Lord Francis.

That timely letter brought back other recollections as well. Lord Francis could almost picture Geordie beside him; he fancied he heard the old retainer's voice, offering canny advice regarding the coming climb. He knew well what Geordie would say: "Rest well tonight, lad, and take care on the morrow!" This was one climb during which old Geordie's rules would be followed to the letter.

Early the next morning, the party started off. Everyone was in a jovial mood except Hadow, who was somewhat superstitious. That became apparent when Hudson remarked, "Not a cloud in the sky. A perfect day for a climb."

"Except," reminded Hadow, "that today happens to be the thirteenth."

"But we'll be making camp tonight," Hudson asserted, "so we won't be tackling the summit of the Matterhorn until tomorrow."

"And tomorrow," declared Hadow glumly, "is Friday, which is another unlucky day."

The others laughed off such talk, and the march continued until noon, when the party had reached an altitude of eleven thousand feet, which meant a climb of only four thousand feet more. But that stretch would be the hardest, if it could be made at all. So they rested that afternoon, close by the towering upper reaches of the Matterhorn. Whymper made sketches, the others basked in the sun, and with nightfall, they pitched a large tent and crawled into sleeping bags.

Friday, the climbers were again up early, and a short trek took them over a slight ridge, bringing the whole massive face of the Matterhorn in view. To

Lord Francis, the sight was grand indeed, for this one gigantic cliff alone was greater in height than most mountains of the British Isles. But most intriguing to his practiced eye, the vast bulk reminded him of just one cliff piled upon another, going up, up, up, in repeated succession, each waiting to be taken in turn, with resting spots between, offering no great obstacles until the uppermost stages.

Whymper sized it up much the same way, and he decided to let one of the young Taugwalders go back to Zermatt. Whymper and Hudson took turns as leaders, choosing the best pathways in what was virtually a rocky ladder. Lord Francis and Hadow followed with the three guides, Croz, old Taugwalder, and his son. At times they used ropes, but often they did without them. Always, however, one climber was ready with a helping hand for another, and they kept close track of their course, so that there would be no problem when they made the descent.

After a climb of eighteen hundred feet, they rested on a convenient ledge for half an hour, then continued on their way. The next twelve hundred feet proved stiffer, but still they managed to avoid all obstacles. Every bulge of rock or wall of sheer cliff merely forced a change of course, for always there was some way around it. When the group halted again, they were at the fourteen thousand-foot level, with only about eight hundred feet more to go.

Below, a magnificent sea of Alpine summits billowed like tremendous ocean waves, their snowy tops resembling whitecaps. Looking down, the slanted cliff resembled huge steps, which could easily be followed down to the great glacier, nearly a mile beneath. But to these skilled climbers, that sight was not appalling. What interested them more was the climb to come.

The party was at the foot of the huge brow which Whymper had discussed in Zermatt. When viewed from a lower ridge, it seemed to overhang almost to the toppling point. But as Whymper had supposed and Lord Francis had agreed, that was largely an illusion. Some parts of the brow were precipitous; others offered enough backward slope for a safe climb.

After an hour's rest, they started up. At times, it was necessary to turn sharp corners in the rocky wall to find new steps. Again, the climbers came to spaces filled with snow, where they cut steps with their axes. There was ice on some of the rocks, another serious hazard, but one that could be countered with due care.

All during this climb, the members of the party were roped together, so that if one slipped, those above could draw him up. They came to a steep stretch of snow, where they hacked more steps and gripped the jutting rocks. There was no chance of any climber finding himself in a spot where he could neither go up nor down. No matter how precarious the perch, each man had another constantly at his elbow, ready with a helping hand. So it continued as they worked upward the final ledge and doubled back along it.

One jutting rock offered a bad obstacle, but they wormed around it. Then they were above the brow and on an easier slope, with the summit just ahead. Detaching their ropes, they raced to the peak of the Matterhorn!

The mighty mountain had been conquered!

There they planted an improvised flag and pole. For the next hour or more, Whymper made sketches while Lord Francis and the others admired the stupendous view from the very point of the pinnacle and fancied themselves at the top of the world. Then, about midafternoon, they began the descent.

As before, special preparations were in order. During the ascent, these climbers had encountered unusual obstacles, had shown continual initiative, and had exchanged so many ideas that they had become a working team. Each was willing to admit any weakness of his own, as well as admire another's worth. They took all such factors into full account.

Five were roped together, with sure-footed Croz first, to lead the way down. Hadow was second, so he could follow Croz exactly and at the same time be steadied by Hudson, who was third. Lord Francis was fourth, so that he could be guided by Hudson, with old Peter Taugwalder fifth, his long experience making him an ideal anchor man.

Whymper was finishing his sketches, so young Taugwalder stayed with him. Then, roped together, they started down and overtook the party at the icy steps near the brow. There, Croz was using the utmost care. He would move down a few steps, set himself firmly, then turn and bring Hadow's feet down, planting them in the snowy niches, one by one.

Hudson, Lord Francis, and old Peter could then follow in turn. The process was slow but sure, except for one factor. Lord Francis, whose gift for sensing imminent danger had become almost uncanny, saw the weakness and called to Whymper:

"You had better tie on to old Peter. If a slip should come, he might not be able to hold his ground alone."

"Quite true," agreed Whymper. "I'll tie on and let young Peter be the final man."

That was done, and they had a perfect arrangement. Like Croz, old Peter was the sort who would never slip. But with three men in between, a bad slip on their part might put two to three times the weight on old Peter, enough to pull him from his moorings. But with Whymper and young Peter as reserves, the chance was eliminated.

Hudson looked up as he awaited his turn to descend and gave a crisp congratulation: "Good thinking, Lord Francis. We may need that extra anchorage."

Good thinking it was, for Lord Francis had recalled his boyhood mistakes of only a few years ago and at the same time had remembered the wise comments of old Geordie. Here, among the highest of the Alps, he was applying the lessons learned among the Scottish hills. Yet with it, he felt a strange, vague premonition that some coming event had swayed his demand for greater anchorage, rather than a mere sense of precaution.

At that moment, the event came.

Croz had just planted Hadow's feet in new steps and was turning to pick up his axe and go down a few more. Hudson was turning downward, ready to brace Hadow, in case Croz should slip, though it was practically a certainty that Croz wouldn't, for he never did. Whether Hadow shifted or simply became dizzy from the altitude, he, the most firmly fixed at that moment, was the one who slipped. Somehow, he lost his balance, his feet shot from under him, and even as he gave a warning cry, he struck Croz full force, as the guide was taking his downward step.

For all his skill and experience, Croz hadn't a chance to sidestep or gain a solid footing. He was bowled over by Hadow and their double weight yanked Hudson from his steps before he was able to brace as he had planned. Croz, too, had given a shout, but there wasn't time for Lord Francis to plant himself among the rocks, with Hudson going out so suddenly. But even as Lord Francis lost his footing, his premonition or precaution — whichever it was — proved its worth.

That added moment enabled old Peter to throw his weight back and pull the rope taut. Whymper followed the very suggestion that Lord Francis had just made, adding immediate anchorage so that he and old Peter took the strain together. Fate hung momentarily on the ability of two men to restrain the weight of four. If they could, young Peter, bracing farther up, would provide the added strength to halt the slide long enough for the men below to regain their footing.

The pair held. For one fleeting instant, Lord Francis thought that his hunch had prevailed. But it was not the strength of the men that counted; it was that of the rope that linked them. The rope snapped at the point of its greatest strain, between Lord Francis and old Peter. Sliding, twisting, clawing, four of the party slithered downward, still roped together by a bond that now meant their doom, for if one had managed to gain a grip upon a passing rock or crevice, the weight of the others would have dragged him along.

Whymper, like the two Taugwalders, stood transfixed by the horror of those cruelly prolonged moments during which their four companions reached the brow and plopped over, one by one: Croz — Hadow — Hudson — finally Lord Francis — cascading into a series of mighty bounds from the jutting ledges of the Matterhorn to the great glacial expanses, nearly a mile below.

The last to go over the brink, Lord Francis managed to cling momentarily to a patch of rock and look upward to see the three men rooted in their tracks above him. There was a snap of the rope below and with it, he was yanked straight downward and his last, hopeless grip was gone. He was over the edge and his voice was unheard as he called to the shapeless rock and snow:

"Geordie — Geordie —"

In Zermatt, a boy was looking at the distant summit of the Matterhorn, when he thought he saw an avalanche descending from its very peak. The boy rushed into the hotel and told about it, but nobody believed him. Avalanches were not apt to start from that high up. Actually, the boy had seen a human avalanche, four tiny figures that looked like bits of sliding rock. But no sound could have carried over the intervening miles to Zermatt, least of all the trailing cry of "Geooordieee . . ."

In Scotland, hundreds of miles still farther away, an elderly man sat dozing by a fireplace, for even on this summer afternoon, there was a chill in the misty air. The man's eyes opened suddenly. Startled, he looked about. Realizing where he was, he reached for a heavy walking stick, arose, and hobbled across the great gloomy hall to the doorway of a lighted room.

Bowed above his stick, the old man studied a younger man, who was writing at a desk. Respectfully, he asked:

"You called me, sir?"

The man at the desk looked up. "Why, no. I did not call."

"But there are only the two of us here, Lord Archie —"

"Yes, that I know."

"And I was sure that I heard someone call, 'Geordie — Geordie —' just that plain."

The man at the desk smiled.

"Then it wasn't I who called you, Buchanan," he asserted. "It is only my cousin Francis who calls you Geordie. To me, you have always been Buchanan. Remember?"

"I remember."

The faraway look that came to Geordie Buchanan's eyes was something that Lord Archie, too, remembered, going back to years before. But he had never seen it so vividly as now. Lord Archie rose from the desk and clapped his hand on the old retainer's shoulder.

"You've been dreaming, Buchanan," he said in a kindly tone. "Dreaming of the old days, for which I do not blame you. I dream of them sometimes, too."

Lord Archie piloted old Geordie back across the hall, eased him to his seat, and smiled sympathetically as the old man laid aside his stick and resumed his doze. Then, of a sudden, Geordie was on his feet again, gripping Lord Archie's arm. No longer bowed, he had reared to his full height, seemingly shaking the years from him, for he strode forward without his stick. His eyes had a glint that even the fire could not match.

"I heard it again!" he exclaimed. "Someone calling my name, like that night we went to find the bairn, as you well remember, Lord Archie. It came twice — then again — a last, long cry; but it was falling — falling — falling—"

Geordie's own voice trailed, and his hands weakened as though to slip away. But as he swayed, he supplied a bony clutch as firm as in the old days. His eyes blazed anew as he demanded:

"Where is the bairn now, Lord Archie?"

"In Switzerland, Buchanan."

"How far away would that be from here?"

"Hundreds of miles. The last letter that he wrote took a week to get here."

"I have heard of Switzerland. They have mountains there."

"Right, Buchanan. Great mountains called the Alps."

"And Lord Francis would be climbing them."

"He is always climbing mountains. You know that, Geordie."

For the first time, Lord Archie had called Buchanan by his given name of Geordie. But old Geordie did not realize it. He was still thinking of that distant call.

"He would be climbing the highest of them," declared Geordie, the lids closing over his staring eyes. "I can see it, rising like a mighty stone above him."

"The Matterhorn. That was the mountain he planned to climb, according to his last letter."

"It will be his headstone. They will never find his body."

With that prophecy, old Geordie returned to his place by the fire and sat there, sorrowing and silent. Lord Archie, hopeful that Geordie's strange vision had been imagination rather than second sight, sent a telegram to Zermatt, addressed to Lord Francis. A reply came from officials there, telling of his young cousin's fate. For by then, Whymper and the Taugwalders had completed their perilous descent from the Matterhorn, and had made their way back to Zermatt, bringing the full story of how their four companions had plummeted to sudden death.

Search parties found three bodies on the great Matterhorn glacier, those of Croz, Hadow, and Hudson, all as close together in death as they had been in those last moments of their lives. But the body of Lord Francis was not with them. In that instant when he had poised upon the brink, sending that mental flash to Geordie, the rope must have snapped beneath him. The others had broken loose and Lord Francis had fallen after them, alone, to land upon some hidden ledge or in some deep crevice that might be anywhere on the mile-high face of the sheer precipice.

Days became weeks, weeks became months. Always the reports of searchers were the same: No sign of the body. During that period, old Geordie nodded more and more, as he sat beside the fire in the Scottish manor, becoming ever more feeble. When new reports arrived from Zermatt, Lord Archie would lay a hand upon the old retainer's shoulder and say:

"They have not found him yet, Geordie."

"Nay," Geordie would croak. "Nor will they ever."

So it went until Geordie's dying day, late that autumn. One misty evening, Geordie did not respond to the kindly touch. His features wore a fixed smile, as though his closed eyes had gained a distant glimpse of a familiar face; as though his lips, now sealed in death, alone could tell where Lord Francis' body might be found. For Geordie's expression was exactly as it had been those other times, years before, when he had gone to rescue the lost bairn. Wherever Lord Francis might be, old Geordie would be there, too.

Through the years that followed, searchers still failed to find the body. The little churchyard in Zermatt contains three tombstones, bearing the names of Charles Hudson, Robert Hadow, and Michel Croz. But the monument to Lord Francis Douglas is the Matterhorn itself, towering above his mortal remains.

The annals of pyschic science tell how travelers in remote mountain passes have occasionally encountered phantom figures, recognizable as those of climbers who were lost in those very reaches. There are cases on record where bodies supposedly have been recovered through the guidance of their own ghosts. But a somewhat different legend has grown around the mighty Matterhorn.

At times when the grim, gray shaft is draped with darkish clouds, climbers, feeling their way amid that dangerous pall, have glimpsed a beckoning figure, high upon some inaccessible shelf. But it is not the figure of young Lord Francis Douglas, gone a century ago, yet unforgotten still.

According to the fanciful reports of the few who have seen the specter closely, it is the wraith of an old, kilted Scotsman, an incongruous sight indeed, amid this Alpine setting. They say, too, that the apparition swirls into nothingness as elusively as the mist itself.

But as it fades the figure has been seen to gesture downward, below the rocky wall, while the wind, dissipating the phantom shape, has been heard to sigh, as though calling up from those depths:

"Geooordieee . . ."

The Fiery Spell

From the outside, Folsom's Rural Mart looked like any other old-time general store at a forgotten crossroads. Though only an hour's drive from New York, it had been bypassed by parkways, turnpikes, and expressways, so that the greater the traffic, the fewer the number of cars that went by Folsom's Corners.

As for local trade, it had been lured away by shopping centers, super-markets, and trading stamps. Other places gave much more for the money and carried a bigger stock than Folsom's Rural Mart. Nobody bought any-thing there except newspapers or cigarettes if they happened to be out of them.

That all pleased old Abner Folsom, who had acquired the corner store as a hand-me-down from his grandfather. When business fell off, Folsom let his niece Matilda tend store, while he roved the fields and woodlands, bringing back assortments of roots, herbs, and barks. These he boiled and distilled in a back room that had once been a cowshed, to concoct remedies that his grandfather had written down but had never made because he was too busy tending store.

Folsom soon found that these concoctions could not compete with the products of modern drugstores, so he delved into occult books for stronger ingredients. There he found such items as owl wings, toad brains, rabbit feet, wolf eyes, frog toes, adder forks, lizard legs, and bat's blood all recommended for various purposes. Folsom talked the boys of the countryside into bringing in such items and trading them for the candy and soda pop that he never managed to sell.

From his back-room brews, Folsom compounded potions, powders, philtres, and perfumes that he sold to city peddlers who guaranteed that they would bring luck, prosperity, and love to all who bought them. To increase their potency, Folsom also made up seals, charms, and talismans, engrossing them in gold ink on special parchment. He added skull rings, snake rings, and elephant rings to his line along with magic mirrors and crystal balls in which viewers hoped to envision the future.

The old country store formed a perfect front for this clandestine activity. Anyone who entered there found Matilda drowsing behind an ancient counter with high showcases fronted by curved glass and topped with antique candy jars. Old oil lamps hung above racks of post cards with cartoons that people once thought were funny. There were gum boots, straw hats, bicycle bells, and other leftovers that nobody ever bought. And over by the wall, where a tall clock kept the wrong time, was a cracker barrel with a checkerboard for customers who wanted to while away the day.

Occasionally, customers from the city would stop in and ask to see "Old Doc," as they called Abner Folsom. Matilda always waved them in to Uncle Ab's back room, and old timers at the checkerboard invariably chuckled over the fact that such slickers were being "tooken" by Abner. Anybody who bought the stuff that Folsom made up would have to be very stupid, but since city folk were very stupid anyway, one point just proved the other.

Rick Hendry, who was anything but stupid, usually was very cagey when he stopped at Folsom's Corners. His trick was to arrive just after the Rural Mart had closed, so he could pound at the door and claim that his car was out of gas. Then Folsom would come out and work the lone gas pump in the driveway. After that, Rick would go into the store with him to settle up. Always, Rick would leave with a package of Old Doc's back-room products, but from the bland look on his blunt-featured face, Rick might have been carrying a few cartons of cigarettes or some boxes of stale candy.

However, on this late autumn afternoon, Rick didn't have time to waste. He had three men in the car with him, and he told one to wait there, while the other two followed him inside. Matilda was behind the counter, and she gave a lazy nod when Rick asked if he could see Old Doc. A customer with shaggy hair and a white beard was sitting by the cracker barrel, and Rick turned to his two companions and said:

"Sit down, Ozzie, and play a game of checkers with this character. You think you're good, but I'll lay you even money that he takes you two out of three. And you, Mort, take a look at those post cards. Some of them are howlers. I won't be long."

With that, Rick went through to the back room and knocked on the door. He was admitted by Abner Folsom, whose long, thin, withered features had an anxious look until he recognized Rick Hendry. Then his straight lips cracked into the happy smile that he reserved for his best customers.

"I have just what you want," declared Folsom, reaching for a box of what appeared to be small hard candies. "Fast Luck Drops. Swallow one before a horse race and you're sure to pick a winner. They're better than the Gambler's

Luck Powder that you have to burn beforehand, because that's likely to wear off."

"Not now," rejoined Rick. "I'm after something else."

"Like Easy Life Powder? Or Lucky Number Oil?"

"No, no, Doc. I only peddle those to chumps. You know and I know that those things don't work enough to matter. I want something for myself. Something that's sure."

"Like a bat's heart tied to your right arm with a red silk string, so you can win any card game you play?"

"No, no, Doc. Stronger medicine than that."

"You mean an amulet to protect you against gunfire?"

"Those things sound good, Doc, but I've never known them to work. I want something better."

"Then you want a charm to ward off witchcraft," decided Folsom. "I have the very thing right here."

Folsom produced a small square of parchment, which bore cabalistic signs in gold and a square of Latin words in the very center:

SATOR
AREPO
TENET
OPERA
ROTAS

Rick studied the curious formula a bit skeptically. He had more respect for Folsom's powders and oils than for written incantations. Yet he knew that old Doc's ways were many and devious, which meant that this could be a mere prelude to something more important.

So Rick decided to listen further.

"Carry that," declared Folsom, "and nobody can bewitch you. Why, if you just write those words on a piece of paper and feed it to horses or to cattle, nobody can bewitch them, either."

"The next time I bet heavy on a trotter," Rick decided, "I'll slide one of those slips in his feed bag before the race."

Rick was smiling as he spoke, but his deep-set eyes had narrowed on Folsom, whose own face was very serious. Casually, Rick asked, "What's so extra special about those Latin words?"

"You can read them backwards or forwards," replied Folsom, "and read them down or up. Always, they'll be the same."

"And what do they mean?"

"Something about a workman holding back on the job, yet still having things keep rolling right along. There's power in those words that can be used for good or evil."

An eager gleam came to Rick's cold eyes, but he was quick to hide it.

"You know, Doc," he said smoothly, "with all this need for protection, there must be a lot of witchcraft going on. You'd think the only way to beat it would be to get the jump on it, with some witchcraft of your own."

"But that would mean calling upon demons," objected Folsom, "and using other things. Bad things."

"Worse things than an owl's wing or bat's blood?"

"Much worse, if you intend to hold people spellbound."

"So what?" demanded Rick. "You've a right to spellbind them before they can spellbind you. Or haven't you?"

"I suppose you have," replied Folsom slowly, his dry old face strained. He gave a worried blink. "That's all you're thinking of?" he questioned. "Your own protection?"

"What else?" Rick retorted. "That's why I've been buying all the stuff you've offered me. But look, Doc, I need more action. If somebody's trying to put the hex on me, I've got to flag them down before they can. That makes sense, doesn't it?"

"It does." Folsom stroked his smooth chin warily. "Would you pay five hundred dollars for a rare possession that would enable you to spellbind all your enemies and hold them utterly helpless?"

"I would." Rick brought a roll of bills from his pocket and counted out the amount in fifties and twenties. "Provided you can prove it works — and without fail."

Folsom didn't even reach for the money. Instead, he put a further question:

"And it will be for your protection only?"

"For my protection only."

Dusk was gathering outside, but since the windows of the back room were heavily shuttered, it was already dark except for the glow of a few oil lamps. Old Folsom turned the lamps down as he stepped to a stout cabinet and unlocked a heavy drawer from which he took a small oblong box, which was also locked. Opening it with a special key, he lifted out a gruesome trophy which brought a nervous stare even from the hard eyes of Rick Hendry.

The object was a scrawny human hand, its fingers long and bony, like a mummy's. In the dim light, its hue was yellow and it glistened strangely. That was explained by Folsom's next words, uttered in a hollow tone:

"The hand of a murderer who paid for his crime upon the gallows. It has been carefully preserved and dipped in a special wax, prepared from a secret formula, enabling it to be twisted into tiny wicks, like this."

Deftly, neatly, he narrowed the wax to little points at the tip of the thumb and each finger. That done, he stood the hand upright on the table, the thumb and fingers forming slender candles. Folsom lighted a match, and as he held it close to his face, his gaunt features took on a demoniac expression.

"Watch everything I do," Folsom said, "and listen very carefully, while I perform the ritual and recite the incantation."

Starting with the thumb, the old man applied the flame to the tiny wick; then continued finger by finger, pausing with each step to pronounce a word from the cabalistic charm that appeared upon the scroll: "Sator—Arepo—Tenet —Opera—Rotas."

Folsom shook out the match, leaving the hand alone illuminated, with each of its five wicks showing a weird, bluish flame. Then, in a hushed monotone, he declared:

"I command that all who dwell within this house and all living creatures beneath this roof shall be spellbound and shall remain so until the mystic flames have been extinguished."

The blue lights flickered slightly but continued to burn, casting ghostly shadows about the hushed room, giving its shelves and cabinets the appearance of living things. Then, suddenly, Folsom raised his voice to a tone of triumph:

"Behold, the Hand of Glory!"

Again, the flames wavered but continued to burn, as though responding to their master's call. Folsom stepped to the door, turned, and waved for Rick to join him, saying:

"Come and see how fully the spell has worked."

They went out to the front room of the store, where it was still daylight, and there Rick halted in complete amazement. Over by the clock, Ozzie and the man with the white beard were frozen in the midst of a checker game. Ozzie had lifted a checker to make a jump and was looking up at his opponent, caught in the pose like a waxwork figure.

Mort, equally rigid, was holding a post card, and his face was showing a half-smile as he read the gagline under the picture. Matilda was poised with the top of a candy jar lifted for the benefit of a new customer, a boy who had entered the store while Rick and Folsom were in the back room.

The boy was also standing stock-still, his hand pointing to the candy that he wanted. Beside the window, a black-and-white cat was stiffened with one paw forward, about to jump to the floor.

Rick watched while Folsom stalked about the store snapping his fingers in front of everyone's eyes, including the cat's and chuckling happily when they failed to respond. Finished with his rounds, Folsom cackled, "Are you satisfied?" and as Rick nodded, Folsom plucked the five hundred dollars from his hand and beckoned for him to return to the back room.

There, as Folsom was counting the money, Rick asked pointedly, "What if those flames should be blown out? Wouldn't everybody wake up before you wanted them to?"

"Try to blow them out," suggested Folsom.

Rick tried and failed. Each flame danced about but kept on burning. Folsom gestured to a fire extinguisher that was hanging in a corner. "Try that." Rick aimed the extinguisher at the blazing Hand of Glory and let forth a blast. A cloud of white vapor enveloped the lighted thumb and fingers. When it cleared, the blue flames had been reduced to tiny dots, but they popped back to full size instantly.

"There is only one thing that can put them out," declared Folsom, as he pocketed the money, "and that is milk. Just watch from the doorway and as soon as I extinguish them, take a quick look into the store and see what happens there."

Folsom poured some milk into a saucer and used his fingers to flick the liquid on to the candle flames. They were extinguished in quick succession, and Rick turned to the front room in time to see the human tableau come to life as though they had been playing a game of statues.

Ozzie finished his checker jump and grinned at his opponent, who began stroking his white beard. Mort completed a half-choked laugh and put the post card back in the rack. Matilda finished her sale and took a dime from the boy, who walked out the door eating his candy, followed by the cat, which by then had landed on the floor and stretched itself.

Nobody seemed to realize that anything unusual had happened, least of all Ozzie and Mort. When Ozzie saw Rick, he said, "Let's go, boss. Blimp will be tired of waiting." Mort grinned and announced, "You owe me money, boss. I just took two out of three games from my friend here."

"Okay," Rick told them. "Go on out to the car, and I'll be right with you after I say good-by to Old Doc."

The back room had a slightly acrid odor as a result of the blue flames, but by then Folsom had packed the hypnotic hand back in the box, along with a copy of the incantation.

"If you ever need more wax," Folsom told Rick, "I can make it up for you. But always have milk ready when you use the hand."

"Tell me, Doc, what do you suppose makes it work?"

"The evil influence," Folsom assured him, "that stems from a murderer's undying hatred toward the world. Persons who witness the ritual—as you and I did—are not affected. They simply relay its hypnotic force to overpower others —animals as well as people—but only under the same roof, at the time when the hand is first lighted."

"Then if the kid had come in for the candy after everybody else had gone into a trance, it wouldn't have worked on him at all?"

"Not at all." Folsom gave a chuckle. "Seeing people standing like so many dummies would have scared him so bad that he would be running yet. But he wouldn't have gone into a stupor."

"Now I know just as much as I didn't know before," declared Rick, in parting, "except that the thing works, because I've seen it. That's all I need to know. So long, Doc."

"But remember your promise—to use the Hand of Glory only for your personal protection."

"Of course, Doc. I wouldn't think of doing anything else."

Old Doc Folsom failed to catch the sarcasm in Rick's tone. He didn't know that the word "protection" in Rick's vocabulary meant the same as a license for committing crime. That became apparent elsewhere.

After Rick joined the others in the car, they drove halfway across the county. Blimp, a heavily built man, who formed the fourth member of the party, did most of the talking as they rode along. "It's going to be tough, Rick," insisted Blimp, "cracking that safe up at the Randall place, with all the family there and three or four servants, besides. We ought to wait until most of them are away."

"Except that when the old lady goes away," Rick reminded him, "she takes her jewels with her or else puts them in her safe deposit box."

"There's other jewelry in the safe, too," remarked Ozzie. "The stuff Randall is giving his daughter for a wedding present. That will be gone after she gets married next Monday."

"And all those paintings Randall bought in Europe," added Mort. "He's supposed to be going to give them to a big art museum. When he does, our chance of grabbing them is gone."

"So we stick our necks into a trap," argued Blimp, "and get ourselves caught. If just one person in that house wakes up and hears us, we'll be goners. The rest of them will be on us in two mniutes."

"But nobody is going to wake up," declared Rick. "I didn't stop at Folsom's Corners for nothing. I figured Old Doc would have the answer to our problem. He had it. Now I have it."

When Rick Hendry spoke with such confidence, nobody demanded further details. Conversation switched to other subjects, and soon the group stopped at a country night club called the Red Feather, where they had dinner and stayed to watch the floor show.

Between times, Rick looked over a floor plan of the Randall mansion, which Blimp had prepared while working with a crew of house painters who had redecorated the place in preparation for the wedding.

"The safe is behind a big mirror on the dining room wall," explained Blimp, "but the art gallery is on the second floor. Old man Randall's room is right next to it, and they say he sleeps like a cat, ready to wake up at anything."

"Tonight," Rick promised, "nothing will wake him."

"It better hadn't, because he's a big game hunter and has a whole collection of guns, all loaded. His three sons are sportsmen, too, and both the chauffeur and the horse trainer look like guys who would be tough to handle."

"About the chauffeur," asked Rick. "Does he sleep in the house or the garage?"

"In the house. There aren't any living quarters in the garage."

"And the horse trainer? Does he sleep in the stable?"

"No, only the grooms sleep there, but there's none of them around right now, because most of the horses have been taken South."

Rick's face showed a satisfied gleam but then became a trifle anxious as he queried, "What about the dogs? Are they kept in kennels, or in the house?"

"In the kennels, except for one that sleeps in the house."

"Tell me, Blimp, how late do the people stay up in the house?" Rick went on.

"Until about midnight. That's when Randall's son Bob will be getting home. He comes out on the train from New York, picks up his car at the station, and drives out to the house."

"We'll wait until one o'clock, then."

Rick's decision pleased Ozzie and Mort, as it meant that they could see the midnight show. But Blimp still fretted.

"People are apt to notice that big fancy car of yours, Rick," he declared. "If somebody reports it to the state cops, they won't have much trouble tracing it."

"And that," chuckled Rick, "will take them to the garage we stole it from this afternoon, where it won't be missed until tomorrow. By then, we will have ditched it."

Blimp subsided after that, but when they left the Red Feather at one A.M., he proposed a new precaution.

"On the road we're taking," stated Blimp, "there's a turnout where an old bridge used to be. We'd better pull in there and wait, in case a patrol is tailing us, the way they do with strange cars."

Rick accepted Blimp's advice. When they reached the turnout, he pulled in and parked beyond a clump of evergreens, where he turned off the motor and the lights. A few minutes later, a police car passed by and continued on the non-existent trail. Rick laughed as he turned on the ignition and used the backup lights to return to the road.

"Nice guessing, Blimp," he complimented. "Now, how do we get to Randall's?"

"Next left," directed Blimp, "and up Laurel Hill."

They took an obscure turn, made the climb and came to a huge gateway that marked the entrance to the Randall estate. The car continued along a driveway through a woods until Blimp supplied another warning:

"Slower now — and douse those lights!"

Rick complied, and they emerged beside a rolling lawn where a vast gray stone mansion sprawled like a monster in the moonlight. At Blimp's suggestion, Rick swung the car beneath the drooping shelter of some weeping willow trees. There the group stepped from the car and waited until drifting clouds dimmed the moonlight. Then, catlike, they crept across the lawn to a side door of the great dark house.

Blimp unlocked the door with the duplicate of a key that he had secretly stolen and returned. Rick gestured for Blimp to lead the way. Then Rick spoke in an undertone to Ozzie and Mort.

"Wait here and let me know if any lights show from upstairs. In a few minutes it won't matter. Then I'll call you."

Inside, Blimp led the way to the darkened dining room, where Rick noted a metal casement window with a broad ledge that showed plainly in the moonlight. He opened the box that he carried beneath his arm, brought out the grisly hand, and set it upright on the ledge. While Blimp watched in amazement, Rick lighted the waxen tapers one by one, muttering the cabalistic words:

"Sator—Arepo—Tenet—Opera—Rotas."

By the flickering blue flames, Rick then read the incantation exactly as Folsom had. Blimp, his fat face utterly agape, was duly impressed by the "command" for "all beneath this roof" to remain "spellbound" while the flames persisted. But he was really alarmed when Rick added loudly:

"Behold, the Hand of Glory!"

"Easy, boss, easy!" gasped Blimp. "You'll have the whole house awake!"

"Not a chance, Blimp." Rick went to the side door and called, "Come in, you guys! I've got something to show you."

Ozzie and Mort rushed in, their faces more startled than Blimp's. They had drawn their revolvers, as though expecting to shoot it out with the household. When Rick gestured to the grotesque hand with its flaming thumb and fingers, Ozzie and Mort halted, sensing that they were on the threshold of the uncanny. They had seen enough of Folsom's talismans to recognize that this must be one, and a very special one, at that.

They were impressed, too, by the strange hush that pervaded the mansion. Rick stressed it when he told them:

"Go upstairs and look around. Then let me know what you find there. Turn on lights as you go. They won't matter now."

Ozzie and Mort started out through a hallway, then up a broad staircase, gingerly at first, but becoming bolder as they proceeded. Meanwhile, Rick turned on the dining room lights, removed the mirror from the wall, and set it beside a heavy buffet table which was stocked with plates, dishes, and bottles of various types. Behind the mirror was the safe that Blimp had mentioned. Rick, who was an expert safecracker, promptly went to work on the combination, hoping that his trained fingertips could sense it from the fall of the tumblers inside.

All the while, the Hand of Glory cast its lurid, flickering glow on the scene, thickening the eerie silence. As minutes passed, the hush deepened, until finally Ozzie and Mort returned, more awed than when they had left. They watched Rick finger the safe dial and when at last he paused, Ozzie exclaimed:

"Walking away with those paintings will be a cinch! You could throw a hootenanny up there without waking anybody. Why, everybody upstairs is dead to the world, Rick. You never saw anything like it!"

"Except that I did," Rick returned coolly. "Only this afternoon, over at Folsom's Corners. Doc and I tested this gimmick and found that it worked."

Rick gestured to the flaming hand, and his companions stared, dumfounded. It was Mort who asked incredulously:

"You mean — on us?"

"That's right."

Rick followed with a play-by-play description of the scene at the Rural Mart, detailing the poses of the persons in the tableau. Hearing it, recognition stirred his listeners.

"I did get kind of hung up when I made that winning jump," Ozzie recalled.

"It was funny, the way the old timer kept staring at me, across the checkerboard."

"And that post card I was looking at," declared Mort. "The one with a picture of a fellow cranking a crazy-looking old car and saying, 'You auto go, but you don't' — it seemed like I read it over a couple of times."

"I saw the kid go in the store," stated Blimp, "and he stayed so long, I began to wonder what was going on inside. It seemed like the place had gone dead all of a sudden."

"Now you know why," declared Rick, with a laugh. "So let's get this safe job over with. If I don't get the combo pretty quick, we blow it. Nobody will hear it if we do."

The others watched while Rick resumed his manipulations, talking almost to himself, as he often did when working on the combination of a safe.

"Take a look in the refrigerator.... Maybe we'll want a snack before we leave.... And I'll be needing some milk.... Not now, but when we're ready to go.... So make sure there is some.... Milk is the only thing that will put out that blue fire...."

"So why," interrupted Mort, "should you put it out?"

"Yeah," agreed Ozzie. "The way everybody is asleep, why worry? There's even a big pooch upstairs, playing dead."

"He'd make trouble if he woke up," put in Mort, "and so would the people. So why let them wake up?"

"Because we want it to look like nothing happened!" snapped Rick, "so we can pull more jobs like this. Understand?"

Mort and Ozzie nodded that they understood.

"And we can use the Hand again," added Rick, "without going back to Doc Folsom for more wax, or refills, or charms, or whatever else he peddles. So shut up and let me get back to work."

With that, Rick turned again to the safe.

Moments of silence followed, while Rick concentrated on his job. Then he paused and tilted his head slightly. The others expected the safe to open, but Rick was no longer listening to the tumblers. Anxiously, he asked:

"Do you hear it? Something from outside —"

A faint hum reached the listeners. Ozzie dismissed it with the comment, "It's just a plane going over," but Blimp was more familiar with this area. His fat face showed worry as he exclaimed, "It's a car, coming in from the gate!"

"Turn out all the lights," ordered Rick. "Here in the dining room — any you left on in the hall — upstairs —"

The others hurried to obey, and by the time they were back, a pair of headlights had emerged from the trees and were following the curve of the driveway around toward the garage at the rear of the mansion. By then, the only light in the house was the blue flicker from the flaming hand in the dining room window, but the driver of the car could not have noticed it, for there was a slight rise of ground between.

"It must be Bob Randall," Blimp informed Rick. "I guess his train came in late or something."

Ozzie and Mort were prompt with suggestions.

"Let's get out back and head him off —"

"Or slide upstairs and lay for him —"

"Stay right here," snapped Rick, "and keep quiet. Give him time to turn in and go to sleep, like the rest. We'll have to be careful not to wake him, that's all."

Bob Randall had a key to the back door. He came in that way from the garage and went up the back stairs to the second floor. Bob was a nice-looking chap in his early twenties, but tonight he was fuming because he had found that the battery of his car was dead when he had tried to start it at the railroad station.

That had meant a half hour of phone calls before he could rouse the owner of a local service station, and another half hour before the man brought him another battery. It had taken more time to install it and on top of that, there had been the long drive home. So at the door of his own room, Bob paused to wonder if there was anyone awake who would like to hear about his troubles.

That pause told him that something was amiss. Never before had the house been so profoundly quiet. Nobody called to Bob, nor was there even the faintest sound of a familiar snore from any of the open doorways. Puzzled, Bob looked into one bedroom and saw his brother Fred facing straight up into the moonlight. In another room, Bob's father was equally sound asleep in a similar position.

Neither seemed at all relaxed, yet they did not stir. Really worried now, Bob knocked at his sister Pauline's door, because she was the lightest sleeper of all and was apt to be disturbed by the slightest sound. Indeed, Bob was already wondering why Pauline hadn't heard him prowling about the hallway. Ordinarily, she would have opened her door by now to find out who it was.

When there was no response to his light but repeated knock, Bob opened the door and saw Pauline half-reclining on the side of the bed. She had a dressing gown draped about her shoulders, and her hand was extended toward a bed lamp. She was posed exactly as if she had heard something and had started to turn on the light, only to be frozen through the intervention of some mysterious force.

Oddly, instead of facing toward the door, from which a sound logically would have come, Pauline was turned toward the far corner of the room. Bob's own eyes followed the same direction, and he saw Bolivar, their handsome Irish setter, that often slept in Pauline's room. The dog's reddish form was clearly visible in the moonlight, and his head was partly lifted from one paw, as though he had been half-awakened, yet his eyes were closed.

Pauline's eyes were closed, too, otherwise Bob would have supposed that both she and the dog were hypnotized. But if they had been, apparently they had gone back to sleep. As Bob analyzed it, something had awakened Pauline and she had called to Bolivar. The setter must have been responding when a new and sudden slumber overtook them both.

Bob stepped into the hallway, closed the door, and listened tensely, gripped by the unexplainable. He was fearful Fred and Pauline might be dead and that everyone else in the house had suffered the same fate. Yet, common sense told him that this couldn't be; that his strained imagination was influenced by the vague uncertainty of the tricky moonlight.

At the same time, an inward foreboding warned him not to turn on a light. It would do little good, he thought, to learn that a strange sleep rather than the grip of death held sway within this house, if he, too, fell victim to that weird, invisible force. He would have to trace the source of this incredible influence that seemed to paralyze its victims and hang them in delicate balance between sleep and death.

Bob moved toward the wide stairway, wondering whether some odorless gas had crept up from downstairs. He was thinking, too, that supersonic vibrations might be responsible. Whatever the case, the sheer prospect of some unknown horror retarded Bob's footsteps, giving him the urge to turn, rush out by the back stairs, and drive away before the unearthly dynamism trapped him, too.

Then, one step more showed Bob the faint glimmer of a wavery blue light below. Its very vacillation ended his own hesitancy. That flicker offered a tangible solution to the mystery that gripped this house. So Bob continued down the broad stairway, regardless of impending danger. Lured on by the bluish light, he finally reached the dining room and viewed the grisly object that flamed from the window ledge.

One glance at the macabre Hand of Glory told Bob Randall that this must somehow be responsible for the strange trance that had overwhelmed his family upstairs. But now he suspected that a human agency lay behind it. Instead of approaching the blazing hand, Bob turned to the big buffet table, pushed aside a jar of instant coffee and a bottle of ketchup, to reach for an object that suited him better, a heavy metal nutcracker.

Bob flung the nutcracker at the flaming hand, but it went wide. He pawed for another missile and came up with a silver sugar bowl. By now, figures were springing up from the darkness, and Bob found himself confronted by two men with revolvers, Ozzie and Mort. From the darkness came Rick's voice:

"No guns, you fools! Just grab him — that's all! He can't put out those flames, no matter what he throws!"

That gave Bob the moment that he needed to let fly with the sugar bowl, which only proved that Rick was right. The bowl struck the blazing hand squarely and toppled it back against the thick window panes, but the blue flames burned on uninterrupted. While Ozzie and Mort were pocketing their guns, Bob dodged away and grabbed the ketchup bottle next. He scored another hit, but when the bottle broke, the ketchup merely splashed the window, while the Hand of Glory blazed on.

Now Blimp hooked a burly forearm around Bob's neck, hauling him backward and half choking him, while Bob grabbed frantically for something else to throw and finally found an object. Ozzie called a warning:

"Look out, Blimp — he's grabbed the coffee jar. Don't let him konk you with it!"

"I"ll take it from him," put in Mort. "Just hang on, Blimp."

Instead of taking a swing at Blimp, Bob made a wild throw at the flaming hand. Blimp grabbed Bob's wrist as he threw and the rounded jar slid from Bob's fingers, scaling high and striking the window more than halfway up. It was the wildest, most hopeless throw of all, but as the jar smashed and showered its powdery contents down upon the Hand of Glory, it produced a singular result.

The blue flames quivered at the tips of the bony thumb and fingers. Their hue became purple, turned crimson, then faded, dwindled, and went out. With that last sputter, the room was plunged into total darkness. In the excitement Bob wrenched free and dashed out to the hall.

"Hang on to him!" Rick was shouting. "Hang on while I light the wicks. We've got to keep the hand burning!'

Rick Hendry was only partly right. He shouldn't have let the flames go out at all. Once extinguished, the Hand of Glory had lost its spell. As proof, shouts were coming from upstairs; electric switches were being pressed; lights were gleaming all over the house.

The Randall household was up and on the go. Bob's father and his two brothers were coming to his rescue with loaded shotguns. When Ozzie and Mort saw them, they forgot Bob and raced out the side door, through which Rick and Blimp already had fled. As the routed burglars sprinted across the lawn, the chauffeur and the horse trainer appeared at the back door and fired shots after them. But by then, Rick Hendry and his crew had reached their car and were speeding out through the woods. They continued on down Laurel Hill and drove off wildly into the night, hoping only that the state police would not catch up with them. All the while, Rick Hendry kept snarling:

"That crazy old fool, Doc Folsom! Telling me nothing would put out those flames except milk! So the guy throws a jar of instant coffee and it does the same job. Instant coffee is right; that's how fast it did it! I'd like to show Old Doc a jar of coffee and let him see how it works. Only I wouldn't crack it over the Hand of Glory, I'd crack it over Old Doc's head."

Though Rick Hendry didn't know it, he was being unfair to Abner Folsom. That was proven back at the Randall mansion where Lieutenant Tony Lambert, of the state police, was checking the scene of the crime that failed. Lambert was studying an odd trophy, a bony hand with wax wicks at the tips of its thumb and fingers.

"A crazy lot, crooks," declared Lambert. "They come up with all sorts of superstitions. They probably thought that by lighting this thing up, they would hypnotize everybody in the house. Actually, it was just coincidence that everybody stayed asleep."

Bob Randall didn't agree, but he said nothing.

Lieutenant Lambert turned to a state trooper, who was taking notes.

"Put this in the report," Lambert ordered. "The hand remained upright on the window ledge until its flames were extinguished by the contents of a jar of instant coffee —"

"One moment, Lieutenant," interrupted Pauline Randall, who was standing by the big buffet table. "There was only one jar of instant coffee on the buffet, and it's still here." She turned to her brother Bob and asked, "Are you sure you threw the coffee jar?"

"I thought I did," returned Bob. "At least, I was grabbing for it, but I might have got hold of something else instead."

"We'll settle that," decided Lieutenant Lambert. He went over to the window ledge, poked around and found the top of the broken jar. He held it to the light, read its printing, and said to Pauline, "You're right, Miss Randall. It wasn't the coffee jar."

The lieutenant turned to the state trooper and ordered, "Cross out the last line of the report. I'll give you a correction."

The trooper crossed out the line.

"Very well, sir. How would you like it to read?"

"The hand remained upright on the window ledge," the lieutenant dictated, "until its flames were extinguished by the contents of a jar of powdered milk."

Though he didn't know it, Lieutenant Lambert had solved the fantastic riddle of the fiery spell.

The Ghost of the Dixie Belle

When Silent John Moreland stood behind the big wheel of the steamboat *Dixie Belle* and studied the broad expanse of the Mississippi stretching off into the distance, his eyes took on a faraway expression that marked him as one of the greatest pilots on the river. That, indeed, was a high distinction, for this was during the heyday of the steamboat era.

Visitors in the pilothouse often watched Silent John "read the river," as they put it. The height of water at a landing, floating tree branches or stranded logs indicated whether the water was higher or lower upstream and told him whether he could "run a chute" or risk crossing a sandbar. Going downstream, he could always tell when or where the current was the best, or which course to take if it divided.

All these things paid off for John Moreland, as they did for other pilots. The difference was that he seldom talked about it, as the others did, which was why they called him "Silent John." But the difference went deeper than that. Where other pilots had their ways and whims, Silent John was as solid and as stolid as Old Man River himself.

When other pilots were in the money, they dressed in gaudy suits with ruffled shirt fronts, kid gloves, and high silk hats. When they had no berth, they would put on working clothes to make it look as though they were going to a job or coming from one. But Silent John always looked the same, with his long black coat, plain tie with wing-tip collar, and an old-style stovepipe hat. He wore the same garb in and out of the pilothouse, except for the hat, which he laid aside when he took the wheel.

As for expressing themselves, other pilots might hum hymns while navigating shoal water where their boat might run aground. They were known to whisper fervent prayers while making headway against a raging flood that threatened to twist the boat about and crash it into the canebrake along the riverbank. And when a timber raft or trading scow drifted across their bow or beneath a paddle wheel, they would let loose with all the profanity available in the vocabulary of the day.

Not so with Silent John. He either said nothing or spoke in language as pure as that of the religious tracts which well-meaning persons brought from New Orleans and St. Louis and handed out to loungers who watched the *Dixie Belle* dock at the river landings. Nothing, it seemed, could disturb a mind so dedicated to the river as that of Silent John Moreland.

There was one person who knew differently. That was Dave Shelby, the cub pilot who was learning the trade from John Moreland. For two years, he had been in the pilothouse with Silent John during nearly every watch, on other river packets as well as the *Dixie Belle*. Never once had Dave known his chief to depart from his usual form. But there were times when silent John let Dave Shelby take the wheel and gave him advice that no one else ever heard.

"Don't try to read the river just as you see it," Silent John instructed him. "Keep thinking of what it will be like in another hour or two, or some twenty to thirty miles farther along. The little things you see right now, floating logs and such, will slip into the corner of your mind and stay there, like part of the big picture."

"And suppose," asked Dave, "the picture isn't what you expect when you get there?"

"It always will be," returned Silent John. "At least, most always. There are times, though, when your thoughts can get out of hand. I might say, out of mind."

"Like when?"

"Like when you begin regretting things, thinking of what you might have done if you'd done different, or what you should have done if you could do it over. I'll talk about that some other time."

"Some other time" came a month or so later, when the *Dixie Belle* was plowing her way through a curtain of absolute blackness, beneath a clouded night sky, with Silent John handling her as nonchalantly as if it were broad daylight.

"This piece of river is just as I expected," declared Silent John. "I kind of daydreamed about it, earlier. But sometimes those daydreams carry you off somewhere — like into the past or into the future — or maybe just somewhere else. You understand?"

Dave didn't understand, but he nodded, and that encouraged Silent John to continue:

"I was about your age when I came downriver, with five hundred dollars to last me until I got a job. I took passage on the old *Queen City,* and I met a bunch of crooked gamblers who took me and my five hundred dollars.

"I landed flat broke in New Orleans, and I was ashamed to write the folks in Indiana for more money. So I wrote that I was shipping in and out of New Orleans on trading schooners, hoping to get a mate's berth. Instead, I was working on the docks as a roustabout, hoping some day I'd make enough money to go home."

"And how long did it take you?" asked Dave.

"It was a couple of years," returned Silent John, "before I could save enough to start learning the pilot trade and a couple more before I was really on my own. By then it was too late. There was a girl up in Newbury — that's the name of my home town — but she hadn't waited. She married someone else, so I never did go back, leastwise not in person."

They had turned the invisible point, and Silent John was clanging the bells for more speed as he added:

"On a black night like this, Dave, I'll sometimes see a light dead ahead. Then, of a sudden, it will burst and I'll find myself talking to the folks in Newbury —"

Silent John broke off as a bright light spurted from the void, streaked across the steamboat's bow, and burst with a brilliance that etched the pilot-house in every detail.

"Thought maybe it was some craft up ahead," commented the pilot, "but it was just a shooting star. A regular fireball."

Silent John was right, The sky was clearing beyond the point, revealing the twinkle of faint stars above the horizon. Evidently this wasn't the kind of light that Silent John meant, but somehow the strange coincidence left Dave Shelby awed.

The subject was dropped then, but a few weeks later, Silent John broached it anew. It was late afternoon and heavy clouds were deepening the river with a purple twilight as the *Dixie Belle* turned a bend to the westward. Silent John was at the wheel, when he confided in a hushed tone:

"It was like this the afternoon my mother died. I'd had no word that she was ill, nothing to forewarn me. Like now, it was after sundown, river time" — Silent John clicked open the case of his big watch, for Dave to see — "when the sunlight came through the clouds and flooded this very pilothouse."

In the dimness, Dave saw a strained, faraway stare on the pilot's face, as Silent John continued:

"Only it wasn't the pilothouse any longer. It was our home in Newbury, and I could see my mother's face and hear her voice calling, 'John — John — you are here in time.' My sister Esther was there, too, and my brother Hiram" — Silent John turned his gaze toward Dave — "and I saw them as plainly as I'm seeing you now. No, even more plainly, because as I said, everything was all bright and sharp, like daylight. They were both saying, 'Yes, John is here with us' — then, of a sudden, it was dark again."

Timed almost to those words, there came a blaze of sunlight from amid the overhanging clouds. Dave blinked, half expecting to see the pilothouse transformed into another place. Instead, the purple twilight returned, then deepened into sullen blackness as the *Dixie Belle* plodded on. But again, the strange coincidence of that returning sunlight seemed to verify John Moreland's story.

Afterward, Dave Shelby checked the exact hour and minute of the sunset with the "river time" used by the steamboats that plodded north and south along the Mississippi. He found out that Silent John was right; the sun actually had set before they had seen its burst from the cloud bank. Dave decided that it must have been a strange freak caused by the rain-laden atmosphere; but even allowing for that, the fact that it had happened just when Silent John mentioned it, made the coincidence border on the uncanny.

Again, on a night when a rising mist began to dim the moonlight that flicked the mighty river, Silent John reverted to his favorite theme when he and Dave were in the pilothouse together.

"A fog like this lifts me with it," John Moreland asserted. "Next, I've drifted home and I'm telling Esther things I know she hears, because she's my twin sister and we always knew what the other was thinking. Sometimes I get through to my brother Hiram, too.

"Maybe you're wondering why I'm certain of this" — Silent John looked warily at Dave to make sure he was interested — "so I'll tell you. Always, there have been letters come, confirming it. Hiram·and Esther both wrote me after Mother died, saying they knew I was there with them. Other times, they've written answers to questions I asked them."

Dave Shelby could well believe it, for the thickening fog had caught him in its grip, too. Then, as the swirl lessened, the floating sensation ended and they were thrumming along in the *Dixie Belle* with the steady pound of the big paddles echoing behind them.

Months passed and the *Dixie Belle* was bound downriver on a trip that was all-important to Dave Shelby, for he had served his time as an apprentice, and a pilot's license would be waiting for him when they reached New Orleans. They still had a two-day run ahead when Silent John Moreland announced:

"Dave, my boy, this is my last trip as a pilot on the *Dixie Belle*. I've arranged with Captain Hoskin for you to take over my berth."

Dave Shelby blinked in disbelief.

"You mean you're giving up the river, chief?"

"Not exactly," rejoined Silent John. "I'm going home, this time by water. I'm going to pilot an old stern-wheeler, the *Tecumseh,* that runs up the Wabash River to Terre Haute and lays over there weekends. So I can go to Newbury and stay with my folks."

There was no show of emotion in the veteran pilot's weather-beaten face, but Dave knew the sentiment that the words expressed. Right then, Dave Shelby felt happier for John Moreland than he did for himself.

"A right nice packet, the *Tecumseh,*" continued Silent John. "Her skipper won't allow gamblers on board, any more than Captain Hoskin would tolerate them here on the *Dixie Belle*. I made sure of that before I took the pilot's job."

Dave started to say something, then caught himself. He realized that Silent John was probing him with a keen, quick eye, so Dave hastily stammered his thanks for his new job and added congratulations. Next, he found an excuse to leave the pilothouse and go below.

Down in the steamboat's ornate main saloon, Dave entered the smoking room, studied a group of card players at a corner table, and spoke hastily to the steward in charge:

"If there are any professional gamblers in that crowd, better get them out; Silent John is on the warpath."

The steward blinked.

"But this is Moreland's watch," he reminded the young man. "How can he leave the pilothouse?"

"He could put anybody on the wheel," returned Dave. "We're going straight down a mile-wide channel with no shoal or reef in the next ten miles. I skipped out on purpose, but by now he could have called the engine room to send somebody up."

With a worried nod, the steward beckoned to one of the card players, a hard-faced man with a pointed mustache and goatee, who wore a plum-colored jacket and a gray velvet waistcoat with a huge gold chain across the front. The man laid his cards aside and came over to hear what the steward had to say. Mere mention of Silent John brought a disdainful smile to the gambler's lips. He strolled back to the group and told them:

"You'll have to excuse me until later, gentlemen. If you would like to play for some real high stakes this evening, you'll find me in the last cabin on the Texas deck. The name, just so you won't forget it, is Matt Kiley —"

"I won't forget it."

The sharp interruption came from the doorway of the smoking room. Kiley turned to see John Moreland standing there. For the first time in his long career, the veteran pilot was dropping his part of "Silent John" on this, his last trip.

"I remember you and other sharpers from a long way back," John Moreland said. "From the first day I piloted a packet, I've done my best to clear such scum from the river. Maybe I've been getting careless in the past few months, not looking over the passengers as I should.

"So you've been working in a cabin on the Texas deck, so I would think it was just a friendly game among the crew in their own quarters. You won't be running any game tonight, Matt, because you'll no longer be on board the *Dixie Belle*." Silent John swung to Dave Shelby and added, "We're stopping at Cedar Landing to pick up a passenger for New Orleans. That's where we'll put this thief ashore."

"You won't put me ashore!" Matt Kiley blustered. "I'm a paying passenger. I'll take this up with Captain Hoskin."

"Do that," urged Silent John. "Ask him which he'd rather keep on board, a crooked gambler or a reliable pilot. One of us is getting off at Cedar Landing. You or I, Matt."

With that, Silent John went back up to the pilothouse, beckoning Dave Shelby along. There, Silent John relieved one of the mates, who had been handling the wheel. Immediately Dave became apologetic.

"Chief, I didn't know Matt Kiley was on board," he said. "I'd never even heard of him before. I'd only heard talk about the captain getting lax where gamblers were concerned, probably because this was your last trip —"

"And you didn't want it spoiled for me," Silent John interposed in a kindly tone. "I understand, Dave." He brought his big watch from his pocket. "It's seven twenty now, and we're due at Cedar Landing in another fifteen minutes. I want you to make sure Matt Kiley gets off there. Then have some coffee and a piece of pie and be back up here at eight o'clock. Understand?"

Dave nodded and was turning to go, when Silent John said quietly, "Wait." Then, pointing down the river, he traced a grayish, ghostly outline that was barely discernible in the fading sunlight. Off beyond it, he indicated the blurred shape of the rising moon.

"Fog gathering ahead," Silent John declared. "We won't pull into the landing. I'll blow for them to bring out the yawl. You make sure that Matt goes ashore in it."

Dave went out and down past the Texas cabins, which were just below and behind the pilothouse. The last door was ajar and Dave could hear muttering that sounded like Matt as the gambler packed his carpetbag. Dave continued down to the galley, where he decided to have his coffee and pie before they reached Cedar Landing. But he had hardly ordered them, when he heard the clang of bells, calling for the stoppage of the engines.

Next the whistle throated a huge blast and as the *Dixie Belle* drifted with the current, Dave stepped out to the stern of the boiler deck, just as the bow of a yawl poked from the fog. A rower tossed the end of a rope up to the deck hands, who held it tight while the passenger came aboard. Captain Hoskin, who was standing by, expressed his admiration.

"Silent John has done it again, by cracky! I hope he's taught you to be half as good as he is, Dave my boy! Stopping right off the landing in a fog so thick a bobcat would have to claw his way through it. By cracky, we'll miss him after this trip!"

The yawl was getting ready to row away, but Captain Hoskin bawled to the deck hands, "Hold that rope, we're putting a man ashore!" Then, as the bells clanged for the engines to start, the captain demanded, "Where in tarnation is Matt Kiley?"

Paddle wheels were churning slowly, swinging the *Dixie Belle* into the current. The men in the yawl were getting fidgety, and within the next few minutes, Captain Hoskin became frantic.

"Get up to the pilothouse!" he exclaimed to Dave. "Tell Silent John to hold it. I don't want him raising hob because we still have Kiley on board!"

Dave started up to the next deck, only to meet Matt coming down, carrying his bag. Dave made way and a few moments later, Matt had reached the stern, where a pair of deck hands swung him over the rail into the yawl and tossed his bag in after him. The rope was released and the yawl was swallowed by the fog, the last impression being Matt's bearded face, glowering out of the swirl into the reflection of the deck lights, like some demon delivering its last defiance.

Now, the *Dixie Belle* was really making her way downriver, as though Silent John intended to get the most out of the packet, fog or no fog. Dave noticed it and grinned while he was having his pie and coffee in the galley.

"We're riding the current," he told the worried steward, "and since nobody will be bucking it, Silent John knows that the way is clear."

"But what if some pilot coming upstream has lost his way?"

"If he's that dumb," assured Dave, "he's the type that would tie up for the night somewhere."

The steward still wasn't convinced. He cocked his head and said anxiously, "Listen!"

From outside came the musical sound of a steam calliope playing the familiar strains of *Oh! Susanna*. Dave stepped to the door and saw a blur of lights so powerful that they managed to penetrate the fog somewhere on the shore.

"That's the showboat *Happy Days*." Dave identified it. "We must be passing Bondville, three miles below Cedar Landing. They've tied up at the Bondville wharf and are putting on a show there."

"But aren't we running close inshore?"

"Only because the current is," replied Dave, as the music faded off into the distance. "We'll be out in midstream soon."

Dave finished his pie and ordered another cup of coffee. He was taking his last swallow just as the galley clock reached two minutes of eight. This was one night when he must be punctual in getting back to the pilothouse, so he started up, only to pause on the companionway.

The *Dixie Belle* seemed to sidle as she sped along, as though only partly in the current. From dead ahead came the blast of a steamboat whistle, which Silent John should have answered, unless he happened to be trying to place it in the fog. Again, it blared, still dead ahead, and very close. Now — now it was too late for Silent John to answer!

Frantically, Dave made a dash for the pilothouse, though he knew that he would be too late, too. It was where he belonged and where he was needed— or had been needed. Regardless of that, the pilothouse was where he intended to be found, along with Silent John. Such was Dave's devotion both to his duty and to his chief.

Dave Shelby reached the Texas deck just as the crash came. Big though the *Dixie Belle* was, the other packet was bigger. Dave recognized her as the *Colossus,* a river giant that lived up to its name. The *Dixie Belle,* coming full steam downstream, might as well have struck solid rock. The bow of the *Dixie Belle* telescoped; her superstructure smashed as it met that of the *Colossus*. The twin smokestacks of the *Dixie Belle* tumbled backward like falling towers, one landing across the pilothouse, demolishing it.

Smoke was pouring everywhere, and shrieks were coming from cabins above the hiss of steam. Heedless of all that, Dave clambered to the roof of the Texas and peered into the ruin of the pilothouse. He saw Silent John stretched amid the debris between a broken three-legged stool and a pot-bellied stove that had overturned, spilling its live coals across the floor.

Dave squeezed through the window, grabbed up a poker that lay beside the pilot's hand, and used it to scrape the coals into a corner, where he crunched them beneath his foot to prevent a fire. But when he looked at Silent John, Dave saw that he was beyond help. The veteran pilot was either dying or already dead from a great gash in the side of his forehead, which had covered his face with a mass of blood.

The locked steamers were drifting downriver, but the lower deck of the *Dixie Belle* was already awash and her passengers were scrambling on board the *Colossus,* while deck hands were using axes to chop the boats apart. Grimly, Dave Shelby stayed in the pilothouse where he belonged, confident that the wreck of the *Dixie Belle* would go aground near shore.

Yet all the while, the thought was running through Dave's mind that if he had reached the pilothouse before the fatal hour of eight, he might have prevented this tragedy. For now, as the fog drifted about the sinking *Dixie Belle,* Dave was sure that Silent John must have let his thoughts wander far away, as he so often did on such nights.

So far away that Silent John had forgotten he was on the Mississippi and had failed to hear the warning whistle of the approaching *Colossus.*

There was another man who could have testified to that same singular fact. His name was Hiram Moreland, and he was dozing in front of the fire-place in the upstairs parlor of his home in Newbury, Indiana, when he heard the town hall clock strike the hour of eight. The notes echoed strangely in Hiram's mind as though time itself were standing still.

When Hiram opened his eyes, he felt that the night fog had entered the room, for it was chill despite the crackling log fire, and all about him was a grayish swirl. Hiram reached for his glasses but could not find them. Then, as he stared into the mysterious mist, his vision cleared and the swirl took on a human form that spoke the name: "Hiram."

Instantly, Hiram was wide awake and gazing into the face of his brother John, a face he had not seen in years, but which had appeared to him quite often in dreams. On this occasion, however, the appearance was too vivid, too fearful, to be a mere dream. John's solemn face, his gaunt form clad in its simple garb of black were real enough — in a way, too real.

His features were streaked with blood that shone crimson in the firelight, flowing from a gaping wound in his forehead. As Hiram watched, his broth-er's figure swayed, and his hands came forward appealingly, as he spoke again:

"Hiram — quickly — you must help — now! It may be too late — too late for me — but there are others — in danger. You must save them — save them — now —"

Those twitching hands had reached Hiram's arm; he could feel their sudden clamp. He was staring squarely into John's strained face, and he saw his brother's eyelids close like miniature hoods. The jaw drooped, the corners of the lips sagged, as Hiram clasped his own hand on his brother's. It was Hiram who spoke now:

"John — you've come to me for help. But John, you're hurt —"

"Hiram," the tone came like a knell, "I am dying."

"No, John — you can't be dying —"

"I am — dying. I am dying. Hiram, I am dead."

John's figure swayed, and Hiram tightened his grip to steady him, but too late. The fire crackled, a burning log fell forward and smoke gushed from the fireplace, clouding the wavering figure, which again took on a misty shape. Hiram, choking from the smoke, lowered his head as he was seized by a coughing spell. When he looked up, the smoke was gone and John's ghost had literally evaporated with it.

Hiram looked at his hand, thinking that it clamped his brother's. Instead, Hiram's grip was upon his own arm. Baffled, he sank back in his chair and closed his eyes. As he tried to reconstruct the scene, his mind went back to the start. Somehow, Hiram linked it to eight o'clock, and the echo of the strokes from the big town hall clock came to his memory like a dirge.

But had he really heard the clock strike eight? Or had that been an earlier dream with a time lapse following it? Hiram opened his eyes, almost expecting to see John again. He did sight the strange, grayish swirl, but now it was beyond the bay window. Hiram went to the window, opened it and stared out at an actual fog. It was coming from the Wabash and through it, the filtering light of the rising moon produced an effect that was truly uncanny.

More uncanny than Hiram realized. This scene on the Wabash resembled another, far down the mighty Mississippi, hundreds of miles away. Instead of Indiana, this could have been Louisiana. The bay window of this parlor above the family store that Morelands had tended for three generations was oddly like the pilothouse of a Mississippi steamboat. Nothing could be seen except the billowing fog, which gave Hiram the impression that he was drifting somewhere, perhaps down the river.

Then, like a tocsin, the town clock clanged.

Hiram Moreland waited, expecting seven more strokes to follow the first. Perhaps it was just now eight o'clock. For through Hiram's mind flashed the thought that he might have dreamed of something due to happen; that his real experience was about to occur right now. But only that one *dong* came from the town hall clock. The bell had struck the half hour.

Hiram turned up a kerosene lamp and looked at his own clock on the mantel. It said half past eight. His dream must have been intermittent, covering half an hour. All that time, perhaps, John had been trying to get his message through, and Hiram had either missed much or had been slow to comprehend.

From below, there came a sudden pounding at the door, verifying Hiram's thought that something still was due. Then an excited voice was calling:

"Uncle Hiram — Uncle Hiram — we need you! Please hurry — we need you right away!"

Hiram put on his hat and overcoat, went downstairs, opened the back door of the store, and found his nephew Terry Pendleton waiting there with a horse and buggy. Before Hiram could inquire what had happened, the youth told him.

"Mother's had another of her spells," Terry blurted out. "She's talking about Uncle John and calling for you. We thought you had better come out to the house. Dad said you would understand."

"I do understand."

They rode five miles out into the country to the large, pretentious farmhouse where Hiram's sister Esther lived with her husband, Roger Pendleton, and their two children. Roger was waiting on the front porch with his daughter Sue, and they were both glad to see Hiram.

"We were going to call the doctor," Roger told Hiram, "but maybe if Esther talks to you first, she will be all right. It's like those other times when she called for you, only now she thinks she's dying. She keeps looking far away and saying, 'I'm dying — I'm dying —' in a kind of gaspy voice."

"Let me talk to her."

They ushered Hiram into an upstairs bedroom where his sister was lying on the pillows. Esther looked up but said nothing until Hiram had waved the others from the room. Then:

"I've seen John again" — Esther paused — "as plainly as I'm seeing you right now, Hiram." Another pause. Then, her eyes becoming sharp and bright, she asked, "Have you seen him?"

Hiram nodded solemnly and Esther added:

"I've seen John — for the last time."

"I know."

"He was dying, Hiram. He said so. Did he say that to you, too?" Hiram nodded again. "I felt it here," continued Esther, pressing her hand to her heart, "and I called the words that I could hear from far away, 'I'm dying — I'm dying' — and I called so loud that the family heard me and came rushing in, thinking I meant that I was dying. But I meant John. That's why I sent for you, because you were the only one who would understand."

"I know, Esther. Tell me more about it."

"It was just before eight o'clock, because that's when Sue brought me my medicine, as she always does. It was just after Sue left. Sue! Isn't that odd!"

"It doesn't strike me as odd, Esther."

"It will when I get to that part. I had just taken the medicine and it had brightened me as it so often does, when I heard John's voice. It was right here in the room, and it was saying, 'Esther, I'm alone tonight, but soon I'll be coming home. You hear me, don't you?' I was answering. 'Yes, John,' when another voice interrupted."

"Was it close by, too?"

"Not at first. It seemed to be coming in from the hallway, saying, 'Now, listen to me, Moreland —' and John's voice was saying, 'I'll settle this matter right now.' Then there was a clatter all about me and I shut my eyes until it ended."

Esther closed her eyes and leaned back on the pillows. In a dreamy tone, she continued:

"Then I heard bells, Hiram. Steamboat bells."

"Like those other times?"

"Yes, when I opened my eyes, everything was misty. I seemed to be floating somewhere and all the while I was listening, hoping to hear John's voice again. But all I could hear was a steady, thrumming sound and occasionally, a moan."

Hiram pondered, taking all that Esther said as something very real.

"The thrumming could have been the steamboat engines," Hiram decided, "and what you thought was a moan might have been the creaking of the pilothouse."

"It was more like a human moan," Esther insisted, "but I couldn't make out any words. Then came the odd part that I mentioned. I heard music, loud and wheezy, like a showboat. Perhaps I dreamed it because Sue had brought my medicine."

"But what has Sue to do with it?"

"The music was playing *Oh! Susanna*. It became louder and then drifted away. Then I could hear the moans again. They were very real, Hiram, and gradually they grew into a voice."

"John's voice?"

"Yes. That's when I could hear him calling, 'I'm dying — I'm dying!' and I started screaming it myself..That's when the family came rushing in asking me what was the matter. But I couldn't tell them, because they wouldn't have believed me; and besides, I wanted to hear John's voice."

"And you did?"

"Yes. I was calling John's name — and yours — knowing you'd understand. Next thing, they were sending Terry to bring you and I was lying here, listening to John's voice say, 'You must help now — there are others in danger — you must save them.' John's voice kept repeating those words, Hiram."

"I know, Esther. I heard them too.."

"And then I heard him saying, 'I am dying — I am dying' — as he did before. And then —"

"And then you heard him say, 'I am dead.' Was that what you heard?"

"Yes. But that was not quite all. Just before John spoke, I heard a sound like a steamboat whistle. Then came his words, 'I am dead.' After that, the whistle came again, but closer. Everything seemed to crash about me and the room went black."

"And you heard nothing more?"

"Nothing more. When I opened my eyes, the fog was gone and they were bringing you in to see me. Did you hear from John, too?"

"Yes. We have both heard from him for the last time."

From Hiram's tone, Esther saw he was convinced that John was really dead. She nodded sadly as Hiram pressed her hands between his own. Hiram felt a sudden pang, for it reminded him of his recent vision, when he imagined that he had pressed John's hands in farewell. But Hiram did not mention that to Esther, because she was resting easily now, apparently willing to accept the inevitable.

Once back at the store, Hiram wrote down all that his sister had told him, for her account was much more detailed than his own. Also, Esther had experienced events in sequence, so that Hiram's detached impressions were merely pegs that helped verify the whole. But Hiram had sensed the physical presence and actual contact of his brother John; factors too substantial for mere dream stuff. The only course now was to wait for the news that would surely come.

Two days later, the morning mail train brought the newspapers up from Indianapolis. They were filled with headlines and detailed reports of the Mississippi steamboat disaster, when the *Dixie Belle* had run into the *Colossus* a few miles south of a town called Bondville. The accounts said that the collision was due to a thick fog and that John Moreland, pilot of the *Dixie Belle,* had died a hero, staying at his post.

The crash had occurred at approximately eight o'clock, and though the fires in the furnaces of the *Dixie Belle* had been stoked, she was racked by an explosion when the water reached them. That, however, was after she had grounded, an hour later. By then, the pilot's body had been removed and other fatalities were very few, though the *Dixie Belle* herself was a total loss.

Roger Pendleton was at the store soon after the newspapers were delivered, anxiously asking Hiram's advcie about breaking the news to Esther. Hiram took that duty upon himself. He went out to the farm, where he read the news to Esther as they sat alone together in her room. All Esther said was:

"I wish someone had been there to tell us more about how John died. Still, if he hadn't been alone, he wouldn't have called for us, when he saw that monstrous sight loom out of the fog."

Esther was quoting the report of an eyewitness aboard the *Dixie Belle* who had described to a reporter the sudden appearance of the *Colossus*. An artist, too, had done a pen-and-ink sketch of the crash, rendering it all the more vivid. Hiram nodded agreement to what Esther said, but he was wondering about other details. He did not broach those to his sister until after John's body had been brought back to Newbury.

Then, as they stood together beside the open grave in the Moreland family plot, Hiram said to Esther:

"If John only could have told us all that happened! There must have been more to this than either of us know, Esther."

"Much more, Hiram," Esther agreed. "John tried to tell us, though. Maybe some day we shall know."

A month after the funeral, Hiram Moreland was seated in his upstairs parlor on another foggy night. Again, the town hall clock struck eight, snapping

Hiram from his reverie. Then, as he dozed off again gradually, he awoke suddenly to see his brother John standing beside him.

This time, John was silent, but his gaze was reproachful and he made no effort to unfold his arms and extend a hand to Hiram. Nor was John's face all gory as it had been on that fatal night. He was the old John, whom Hiram remembered from former dreams. But the reproachful air was something new.

From then on, John's wraith appeared to Hiram at intervals of every few weeks, and at odd hours during the night, whenever Hiram happened to wake up. Hiram soon became conditioned to the apparition's accusing stare, but each morning, he woke up worried about what might happen the next time.

Why should there always be such silence? If John's ghost had a question, why didn't he ask it?

Hiram could only conclude that perhaps he was the one supposed to ask the question. But what could it be about?

Hiram never mentioned any of this to Esther, because he did not want to disturb her. But one evening, when she and Hiram were waiting on the porch for Terry to hitch the buggy and drive Hiram back to town, Esther suddenly exclaimed:

"Don't stand there, Hiram, with your arms folded and your face so solemn and reproachful. It seems as if instead of looking at you, I'm seeing John. I don't like it —" Esther broke off and added sadly, "I shouldn't have said that. Forgive me, Hiram. Or maybe I should ask John to forgive me when I see him again."

"You've seen him too, Esther?" Hiram asked anxiously. "Standing like this — saying nothing —?"

"I've seen him half a dozen times, Hiram," his sister replied. "John tried to get some message through to us that night he died, but he didn't manage it. We're still seeing him in our minds, Hiram, because we know there is unfinished business."

"To finish it," decided Hiram, "we must find out more about it. I think I'll take a vacation, Esther, and go along to New Orleans, to see that young pilot John used to mention in his letters. What was his name, do you remember?"

"Dave Shelby." Esther went inside and rummaged in a desk drawer. "Here is the letter he wrote us himself, after John died." She handed the letter to Hiram, who had followed her in. "Read it, Hiram."

It was for the most part a letter of heartfelt condolence, but it contained one statement that particularly impressed Hiram Moreland.

> *If only I had been with the chief before he died! He mentioned you often and I am sure he would have given me a message for you. When I was on my way up to the pilothouse, I felt that he needed me there, so I hurried, but the crash came first. He was either dying, or dead when I found him. He could not speak. I was too late.*

"Too late," repeated Hiram. "That's what John said to both of us. It was too late to save him." Hiram noted the letterhead, which bore the name of the Hotel Bontezan, in New Orleans. "I'll find young Shelby and talk to him."

A few weeks later, Dave Shelby came into New Orleans from a trip up-river and registered at the Hotel Bontezan. As Dave went into a little restaurant adjoining the hotel, the desk clerk nodded to a solemn-faced man who was reading a newspaper in the corner of the lobby.

The man got up, followed Dave into the café and sat down opposite him. There he put the quiet query:

"You are Dave Shelby?"

When Dave looked up, his eyes went wide for he believed he saw the face of Silent John Moreland gazing into his own.

"Chief!" Dave gulped. "You're back — you're alive — but you can't be —"

Even as he stared, Dave expected the figure to fade away. Instead, it stayed and the voice spoke again:

"I am Hiram Moreland."

Understanding dawned on Dave Shelby. He had always pictured Hiram as looking like his brother John, but he had never expected so close a resemblance. Silent John had become such a tradition of the Mississippi that he was regarded as unique. But Hiram was the image of his dead brother, even to his black coat, plain shirt-front and old-style stovepipe hat.

"Tell me," Hiram said earnestly, "about that night my brother died. My sister and I want to know every detail."

A deeper understanding dawned on Dave now.

"You heard — from Silent John — that night?"

"My sister and I both did," returned Hiram. "He called to us from the fog, as he had before."

"I know." Dave nodded. "He told me about those other times. I figured he might have tried to reach you again."

"He did. I heard a clock strike eight, the exact time of the collision. I dozed a few moments or maybe longer; then John was there and talking to me, saying that he was dying and needing help for others. I wouldn't know exactly when I saw him, because it was nearly half past eight before I was really awake."

Pausing, Hiram noted the eagerness on Dave's face. From his pocket, Hiram brought the detailed report that he had written from Esther's account of John's ghostly visitation.

"My sister's experience tallies with mine," Hiram said. "Or I might say, mine confirms hers. But she sensed things that were happening in the pilot-house and along the river, such as voices, music, steamboat whistles —"

Dave nodded a quick interruption as he started his finger down Hiram's list. But his forehead wrinkled in a puzzled frown as he stated, "You heard the clock strike eight, and your sister's dream began about that time. First she heard voices — then the sound of the music —"

"Yes. *Oh! Susanna,* coming from a showboat."

"That's the tune the calliope was playing, sure enough." Dave's puzzlement increased. "But it was at Bondville, ten minutes before the crash. The steamboat whistles were later — they came from the *Colossus* — but why did your sister hear them *after* eight o'clock?"

"Why not?" Hiram responded with a shrug. "It was after eight when I heard John say that he was dying."

"But he was already dead by eight o'clock," insisted Dave. "All these things your sister sensed were true enough, but they happened sooner. Wait, now! Eight o'clock. What time does your town go on?"

"Why, Indianapolis time."

"That's it." Dave's face showed grim satisfaction as he pulled a printed sheet from his pocket. "We're always getting mixed on time. Indianapolis time — let's see — it's seventeen minutes earlier than St. Louis time, which we use as river time, all the way down the Mississippi."

Now Hiram understood. These were the days before the nation had been divided into time zones. Such an arrangement had never been heard of, perhaps not even imagined. Each large city had its own time, calculated exactly by sunrise and sunset. This "sun time," as they called it, was absolutely correct.

Steamboats, railroads, even stagecoaches used the sun time of the city where they started, and this was accepted as standard by towns along the line. Hence the clocks in Newbury, which went by Indianapolis time, were just seventeen minutes ahead of those using Mississippi River time.

"Seventeen minutes to eight," Dave asserted. "That's just about when the *Dixie Belle* stopped at Cedar Landing, and we took on a passenger. That's when your sister heard voices" — Dave studied Hiram's list — "and then bells." Musingly, Dave thought back; then suddenly he exclaimed, "I have it!"

Checking Esther's account that Hiram had so carefully written down, Dave added data of his own to interpret it step by step.

"Silent John had ordered a gambler named Matt Kiley to be put ashore at Cedar Landing," Dave said. "Matt was up on the Texas deck, and he must have gone to the pilothouse while Silent John was sitting there, looking out into the fog and thinking of home. Your sister Esther was already sensing that impression when Matt barged into the pilothouse, to start an argument.

"It must have been Matt's voice your sister heard, saying, 'Now listen to me, Moreland.' Then she recognized the voice of Silent John, but he didn't say, 'I'll settle this matter right now,' as she thought. What Silent John must have said was, 'I'll settle this, Matt. Right now!' Do you follow?"

Hiram nodded.

"That's when the clatter started. Now I can picture just what happened." Dave pressed his hand to his eyes as he continued. "Matt must have grabbed that stool and hit the chief with it, because why should the stool have been broken, if he hadn't? Silent John maybe tried to ward him off with the poker — that's why it was lying by his hand — but he didn't have a chance. Matt slugged him down and left him dying. Then to cover his tracks, Matt rang the engine room and raced down through the Texas, grabbing his bag on the way."

"But in that case," objected Hiram, "the *Dixie Belle* would have been getting under way by the time Matt reached the stern deck."

"She was!" Dave exclaimed. "But they were taking it slow in the engine room. They generally do when there's a yawl alongside. There would have have been time for us to call in from the deck and have them stop the engines in an emergency. Anyway, Matt got off in a hurry, and now we know why.

"Silent John must have been lying in the pilothouse moaning while the *Dixie Belle* went by the showboat at Bondville. When he heard the whistle of the *Colossus* coming upriver, he must have gathered strength enough to cry for help, not for himself, but for all the rest of us aboard the *Dixie Belle*, seeing as she was steaming full speed for a head-on crash."

That anguished cry had been projected mentally far beyond the confines of the pilothouse of the *Dixie Belle* to the only persons who could have recognized it — John's brother Hiram and his sister Esther — but they had been too distant to help. Now, as Hiram Moreland weighed those facts, Dave Shelby felt himself amid a silence as deep as any he had ever experienced in the presence of Silent John. Finally, Hiram broke the spell with the calm query:

"Where can we find Matt Kiley?"

"Up in Natchez," replied Dave, "probably itching to get away, like most of the gamblers there. But they don't like to travel on cheap packets, and good ones won't take them as passengers."

"You're piloting a good packet now?"

"The *Lone Star*, one of the finest on the river."

"Couldn't word be gotten to Matt Kiley, saying he might slip on board the *Lone Star*, unrecognized or unnoticed?"

Hiram's tone was very solemn, very like his dead brother's. Dave felt as if it were an order from Silent John himself.

"I'll fix it through a deck hand on the *Diana*," he promised. "She pulls out today, but we don't leave until tomorrow."

When the *Lone Star* did pull out, Hiram Moreland was one of her passengers, but he kept close to his cabin, rather than have crew members note his resemblance to his brother John. The *Lone Star* reached the cliffs of Natchez the next afternoon and was promptly approached by a group of flashily dressed men from the section called Natchez-under-the-Hill, which lay below the bluffs and was notorious for its gambling hangouts.

None of these gentry was taken on board, but amid the turmoil, a man with the bearing of a Mississippi planter pushed his way up the gangplank and was bowed on board by a polite steward, who greeted him as "Colonel Bateson." Not a flicker of a smile showed on the pretended colonel's face; instead, he remained suave to the tips of his mustache and his pointed goatee.

Everything had been "fixed" very neatly. The deckhand from the *Diana* had visited Natchez-under-the-Hill and had singled out Matt Kiley from Dave's description. He had started a "chance" conversation with Matt and had confided that for a special fee, he could provide Matt with a password that would enable him to board the *Lone Star* and take passage up the river.

Fortunately, Matt happened to be in the money, and he had taken up the deal. The password was "Colonel Bateson" and by answering to that name, Matt was shown to a cabin on the *Lone Star,* where the steward waited long enough to be paid his share of the "fix" before the packet pulled away from the dock. In Matt's estimation, the price was picayune, compared to the opportunity of trimming the honest card players on board the *Lone Star,* which he could readily do in his false capacity of a Southern colonel.

Matt Kiley knew how to play such parts to perfection. He still wore his poker face when he entered the steamboat's gilded social hall, soon after dinner. There, he paused at a card table and was promptly invited to take a chair and join a friendly game. Matt did so, with just the proper show of reluctance. A few hands of stud poker were dealt, and Matt had won his first pot — a small one — when he began to take stock of his fellow players.

Then Matt's hard features froze. For the first time, he really noted the face of a player across the table, a man who until then had kept his chin deep in his hand while he surveyed his cards. Matt stared, incredulous. *Silent John Moreland!*

The fact that this was the poker table, which in life Silent John had shunned, made Matt all the more convinced that the pilot of the *Dixie Belle* had come back from the dead to haunt him. When the man looked up, Matt noted his plain shirt and black coat. Not only that, Matt felt the bore of eyes that seemed to stare right through him, as those of Silent John had stared.

For the first time in his gambling career, Matt wanted to quit a game in its early stages, but he couldn't. He was literally paralyzed, except for his hands, which were so used to shuffling and dealing cards that they went through the motions mechanically. But as hand after hand went by and the stakes became higher and higher, Matt found his luck deserting him in the very game that he had always regarded as his meat, stud poker.

Outside, a rising fog had enveloped the *Lone Star,* but Dave Shelby, in the pilothouse, was keeping steadily upstream, along the Louisiana shore, with the whistle blaring a repeated warning.

"It's along about here that the *Dixie Belle* cracked into the *Colossus* nigh onto a year ago," one of the poker players commented wryly. "That's why you hear those whistles."

"A lot of good they did the *Dixie Belle,*" put in another player, and added, "Some river folk say they've seen her coming downstream like a ghost ship on foggy nights like this."

Matt Kiley, staring straight across the table, looked for some change in expression on the face that so resembled Silent John's. None came; instead, the solemn man announced:

"It is your deal, Colonel."

Matt dealt. Already he had lost a few thousand dollars that he had taken from the other gamblers in Natchez-under-the-Hill. Now, he was betting his own funds heavily, card after card, until his hand showed two aces and two sevens, all face up, with his fifth card turned down as a hole card, as was customary in stud poker. Only one other player was still in the pot, the man who looked like Silent John. He had three nines showing, with a five as his other face-up card. Matt pushed his last thousand dollars to the center of the table and announced:

"I'll bet the limit on my two pair, aces up."

"They call that the Dead Man's Hand," came the solemn tone from across the table. "I'll raise it a thousand on my three nines."

"You'll have to call," said Matt. "That's all I have."

"I would be glad to accept your note, Colonel — if you should happen to lose."

Despite his tension, Matt started a smile which he quickly repressed.

"Thank you, sir, I'll call you, then," he declared. "My hole card is the ace of spades" — Matt turned it up — "and I win with a full house, three aces, two sevens."

"The ace of spades is called the card of death," came the solemn tone so like Silent John's. "In this case it is sudden death to your hopes, Colonel. I win with four nines.

With that, Hiram Moreland turned up his hole card to show the fourth nine. While Hiram was raking in the money, Matt Kiley called for pen and paper and asked, "How do you want me to write out my note?"

"Like this," replied Hiram. "Just say, 'I, Matt Kiley, hereby acknowledge that —'"

Hiram paused. Matt had fallen into the trap, writing down his own name instead of "Colonel Bateson." Hiram's voice continued:

"'That I assaulted and killed John Moreland, pilot of the *Dixie Belle,* and signalled for full speed —'"

"You can't pin that on me!" Matt snarled. "Nobody was there —"

"Nobody except you and John Moreland. First, you said '"Now listen to me, Moreland.' Then John Moreland answered, just as I am answering now, 'I'll settle this, Matt. Right now.'"

That was enough. If any man ever believed that he was faced by a living ghost, that man was Matt Kiley.

"So I killed you!" snarled Matt. "Now, get back where you belong — back on the wreck of the *Dixie Belle!"*

Matt was recoiling, betraying his fear of a vengeful ghost. But the other men at the table, none of whom had ever met Silent John, took a more practical view. They had recognized the name of Matt Kiley as that of a notorious gambler who now was admitting murder as another of his crimes.

"Grab him!" one man barked. "Don't let him get away."

Matt already was away, racing out through the main saloon until he reached the very bow of the boiler deck. There he wheeled, confronting his pursuers with an antique pepper-box pistol, a weapon with six barrels, clumsy to fire but deadly at close range.

"If anyone draws a gun," snapped Matt, "I'll shoot him. Get back, all of you, I'm looking for a ghost — to find out if he's real!"

The group scattered wildly, and Hiram, who had followed close behind them, was suddenly an open target. Matt's face gleamed in demoniac fury.

With that, Matt paused, his finger halted on the trigger. He was utterly puzzled by Hiram's reaction.

"I killed you once — now it will be twice —"

Despite the imminence of Matt's gun, Hiram's eyes were staring beyond him. So were the other men crouched along the deck. Their horror was so sudden, so real, that Matt, though he did not turn, could not resist a quick look over his shoulder.

Matt saw what they saw. Looming out of the fog was a steamboat the size of the *Lone Star,* about to meet the packet bow to bow. It was the same sort of crash that Matt had escaped when he had sent the *Dixie Belle* to her fate. Now, at the very bow of the *Lone Star,* he would be the first victim when the collision came.

Not Matt Kiley.

With a sideward spring, he cleared the rail of the *Lone Star* and hit the river, flinging away his gun as he tried to swim clear of the crash with mad, quick strokes. But in those same brief moments, the menace itself was gone. The bulking shape of an approaching steamboat dissolved in the mist like a phantom image. Fog, moonlight, the flares from the smokestacks of the *Lone Star* had produced a strange illusion that was no more solid than the mist itself.

That didn't help Matt Kiley. As the *Lone Star* plowed on, despite the clang of bells from the pilothouse, the curved side of the steamboat stretched toward the swimming gambler. Then the paddle box was upon him. With a shriek, Matt vanished under the sweep of a thirty-foot wheel that churned its way over him. Behind the *Lone Star* lay a bubbly wake, with no sign of Matt Kiley. That wasn't surprising. Those paddles had a way of mangling their victims and mingling them deep in the Mississippi mud.

They talked about it in the social hall after the steamboat tied up for the night amid the thickening fog. Dave Shelby, down from the pilothouse, introduced Hiram Moreland to members of the crew who had known Silent John.

Neither Dave nor Hiram talked about those ghostly visitations that had happened in Newbury. They said they had guessed that Matt Kiley was responsible for the wreck of the *Dixie Belle,* and that Hiram Moreland had played his brother's ghost to trick the gambler into a confession. That story satisfied all who heard it.

The money Hiram had won, he turned over to Dave for the river pilots' beneficial fund, to be donated in the name of John Moreland. With a sigh of relief, Hiram said:

"It worked as we had hoped, but we needed luck. I've heard of those fog reflections, but this is the first time I ever saw one. Looking up into the foggy moonlight, I would have sworn I saw the *Lone Star* coming at herself, like another ship." He turned to Dave Shelby. "Of course," Hiram added, "you couldn't have seen it that way, up in the pilothouse."

"No," conceded Dave, "I didn't. All I saw was the shape of another pilothouse, coming at me as if we were high up in the clouds of another world."

"Another pilothouse, with a wheel and a pilot behind it?"

"Yes, but it wasn't a reflection of the *Lone Star*. It was a pilothouse I had been in a lot more often and knew a lot better, with a pilot whom I had never expected to see again."

Dave said nothing further, for he knew that Hiram understood. There in the fog, Dave Shelby had gained one fleeting, evanescent glimpse of his old chief, Silent John Moreland, at the wheel of the *Dixie Belle*.

The Purple Testament

Captain Phil Riker watched the trucks rumble closer, one by one, each loaded with its quota of infantrymen back from combat. They had returned, all of them, to the Philippine Islands, in this year 1944, thinking that the war was won, only to find that there was still a lot of fighting to be done.

If you could return at all from that sort of fighting, you would be doing well. So all these boys were doing well, though none of them looked it. They looked bad, very bad. They were dirty, hollow-eyed, each face showing the shock that was the aftermath of violence, each creviced with lines of utter fatigue, and the backwash of sheer fear.

As company commander, Captain Riker wanted to know those faces individually, but they changed too often and too grimly. That was up to the platoon leaders, whose faces Riker knew perhaps too well. From their faces, Riker could tell, again perhaps too well, what was happening to the men under their command.

A truck stopped, and the driver came around to drop the tail gate. The men dropped down mechanically, one by one. A sergeant was helping a wounded man, and Riker moved closer.

"Evening, Captain," the sergeant greeted him. "Ain't it been a crummy night?"

Riker nodded. "Pretty rough, eh, Sergeant?"

The sergeant nodded in return and brought a bent cigarette from his pocket. While he was straightening it, Riker provided a light. The sergeant nodded his thanks.

"We got the bridge," he reported, "whatever they wanted it for. The Japs have naval guns stuck in the ground, and they're zeroed in on the town. That bridge gets it every three minutes."

"And how many did we lose?"

"Ten men wounded. Maybe twelve." The sergeant's face turned grim, as he added, "Four dead."

A tall, gaunt figure stalked forward. Captain Riker looked up and recognized Second Lieutenant Hugh Fitzgerald, who promptly added the names of the four: "Hibbard, Horton, Morgan, Levy."

With that, Lieutenant Fitzgerald swung to the sergeant. "Take care of the company, Sergeant. Make sure they get hot coffee and a meal. If they're not hungry, have them eat anyway. After that, bed them down."

The sergeant snapped to a salute. "Yes, sir."

He gave the order, and a straggly column of men followed him from the trucks toward the tents. The trucks pulled ahead, leaving the company commander and the lieutenant standing on the darkened road. Riker gestured toward a lighted tent and ordered, "Come on."

In the tent, a Coleman lantern shone brightly on a big wooden crate that served as desk for the company commander. There was a large map board set close to the desk, and an army cot in the corner beyond that. Riker sat down on the cot, reached beneath for a bottle and cup. He poured a drink into the cup, handed it to Fitzgerald and then drank from the bottle as he commented:

"Another rough day, Fitz?"

"Real rough." Fitz gave a nervous head-shake. "Twelve wounded, four dead. All in two and a half hours. Twelve wounded, four dead."

The note of finality in Fitz's tone brought a probing stare from Riker's gaunt, keen face.

"We've lost four men before," Riker reminded him. "We've lost eight and ten. You're taking this harder than usual, Fitz. Anything special about these four men?"

"They were all kids under twenty-two." Fitz's tone was tense. "Does it have to be more special than that?"

"No, it doesn't. But this has gotten to you, Fitz. I'd like to know why."

"Would you? All right, look at this."

From the pocket of his fatigue shirt, Fitz brought a crumpled sheet of paper, which he smoothed and handed to Riker. The company commander read the four names that he had heard before.

"Hibbard, Horton, Morgan, Levy." Riker looked up, studied Fitzgerald again, and added, "Four K.I.A.'s."

"That's what they are." Fitz nodded. "Killed in action, Philippines, June 13, 1944. I'll tell you what's gotten to me, Captain." Fitz hesitated, then announced bluntly, "I wrote those names down yesterday. I wrote them down before we went up, before I could even have begun to guess —"

Fitz broke off and Riker nodded encouragingly. "Why did you write their names down, Fitz? Go on, tell me."

"We were having a weapons check, yesterday morning," Fitz said. "I looked at forty-four faces, but when I got to those four, something came over them. It was almost like a light, that's the only way I can describe it. I knew that was to be their last day. I knew they'd get it.

"Then, driving up the highway this morning, I was in their truck. All four were sitting across from me, and I saw that same odd look again. They were completely set apart from the others, as if somebody had picked out those four faces with a searchlight, though it was broad daylight at the time. Again, I knew."

Riker pondered briefly; then he asked, "Did this ever happen before, Fitz?"

"In a way, yes," Fitz replied. "I guess it's been growing on me. I'd notice an odd look, a kind of glow on a soldier's face, and it would strike me as sort of funny, like. Only it wasn't funny when I didn't see that face again except maybe when it was dead."

"And did you make note of those?"

"No, I didn't. It just struck me as kind of a coincidence. You know, any guy might look odd, and any guy might get it. But when four of them stood out, just that plain, I knew what it meant. That's why I wrote those names down."

Riker studied the paper again.

"You're sure you wrote these names yesterday? You're sure it wasn't today? On the way back in the truck?"

"It was yesterday morning, Captain," Fitz insisted. "I swear that's when I wrote them down!"

"Take it easy then, Fitz. Get some sleep. You need it, real bad."

"I know that, because I haven't slept much, the way this thing has grown on me. If every time I stand in front of a platoon, ready to take them up, am I going to look down the line and tell which ones aren't coming back? We're not supposed to know such things. We shouldn't be able to tell —"

"I know that, Fitz. Let's forget it until tomorrow."

Fitzgerald's response was a sigh of relief. His problem was still on his mind. But at least Riker was now sharing part of the burden. That night, the lieutenant enjoyed some of the sleep he so badly needed. In the morning, he met Captain Riker, and the two of them went over to a dilapidated schoolhouse that the army had commandeered as a hospital. There Fitzgerald went upstairs to a ward to visit the wounded men from his platoon while Riker was making a routine report to Captain Roy Gunther, the medical officer in charge.

That report proved to be more than mere routine. Like Riker, Gunther knew Fitzgerald well. Riker gave the doctor a verbatim account of Fitzgerald's statements and showed him the paper with the four names. Gunther, a serious man in his mid-forties, weighed the matter carefully.

"It could be some mental aberration," he decided, "but it's hard to tell. His record is good. He's never been wounded, nor shown evidence of battle fatigue. Why should he get this weird idea all of a sudden? It's obviously illusory —"

"But Fitz believes it," Riker put in. "To hear him tell it, Doc, you'd almost believe it yourself. I'd appreciate your checking him over, when he gets through visiting the boys in his platoon. He's one of the best officers we've got, and I don't want to lose him. So perhaps —"

"Perhaps I shouldn't let Fitzgerald know you told me about this?" completed Gunther, with a wan smile. "I won't, Captain. I'll handle it as subtly as I can."

Fitzgerald, meanwhile, up in the ward, was chatting with a nineteen-year-old G. I. known as Smitty, whose right arm was in a suspended cast, and whose face was very pale. But Smitty's smile was cheerful as he kept his lips pressed on a dangling cigarette.

"You didn't come out so bad, Smitty," Fitz assured him. "When you get that arm patched up, you'll be heading home. That won't be hard to take, will it?"

"No, sir. It sure won't."

"Your cigarette has gone out." Fitz produced a pack of matches. "Steady, now, while I light it for you."

"No, thanks, Lieutenant." Smitty's tone was weary. "Could you just lay it there in the ashtray for me? I'll smoke it later."

Fitzgerald complied. "Take care, Smitty," he said in parting, and turned to leave, taking out a cigarette pack of his own. As he shook it, to joggle out a cigarette, the pack slipped from Fitz's hand and landed by the door. When he stooped to recover the pack, his gaze reverted to Smitty's cot.

That was when Lieutenant Fitzgerald froze, his mouth phrasing an unuttered "No!" That uncanny, unwanted power of Fitz's had returned, at a most unexpected moment. There, as clearly as he had described it to Riker, Fitz saw the same eerie glow that had highlighted the faces of yesterday's K.I.A.'s. Only this time it was shining on one face alone, that of the wounded boy, Smitty.

Now, as though hypnotized by that strange, ethereal light, Fitzgerald began to sway. He was struggling to find his voice and with it shake off the paralyzing sensation that seemed to clutch his throat. He swayed against the door frame, where his head thudded heavily. His senses were engulfed in a purplish haze that seemed to be swallowing him bodily. He collapsed on the floor, halfway through the door.

A passing orderly heard the clatter of Fitz's fall and dashed back from the stairway. He tried to help Fitz to his feet, asking, "Are you okay, Lieutenant? Are you okay?" His mind still shrouded in that purple pall, Fitz's imagery spread like the pages of an open book, which suddenly clamped tight shut and faded as his senses returned. Then, with the orderly's help, he reached his feet and rubbed his head.

"I'm all right," Fitz said. "I—I guess it was just a dizzy spell. Things went out—like a light—"

Fitz was looking toward the cot now, fearful that he would see the eerie glow again. He saw Smitty, but not plainly, for Fitz's vision was still blurred. But the orderly's eyes, following the direction of the lieutenant's gaze, suddenly opened wide. Forgetting that Fitz was just recovering from a faint, the orderly let go of him and sprang to the bed. Fitz, by now, had steadied sufficiently to follow, which he did, only to come up short.

The orderly was leaning over a lifeless body. His hands moved from Smitty's head to the side of his face, then his fingers went down to the free hand that lay motionless on the covers. The orderly felt the boy's pulse, then looked up.

"He's dead," he said in a hollow tone. "They go awful quick sometimes. Just like that. Awful quick."

The orderly released the buckle holding the wounded arm in traction and brought the arm down to the bed. He pulled the sheet up over Smitty's face, then turned and walked from the room, with Lieutenant Fitzgerald slowly following him. The orderly went along the corridor to summon a nurse, while Fitz continued downstairs, and ran squarely into Captain Riker, who was lighting a cigarette outside Gunther's office.

Momentarily, Riker's face betrayed an embarrassed grin, for he hadn't expected Fitz to come down from the ward so soon. Riker wanted to be gone before Gunther began sounding out Fitzgerald regarding his mental aberration; but since he was still here, he tried to think of some tactful way to bring up the subject. Fitz brought it up himself, when he said, "I was up seeing Smitty."

"I know." Riker nodded. "Doc says he's going to be okay now."

"He isn't. I took a look at his face." Fitz paused ominously. "Right away, I knew. Then a minute later—he was gone."

As Riker stared, his look of disbelief turned to awe and his tone became a low, tense whisper as he asked, "That same thing that you saw before?"

"The same thing. The odd look, the funny light, or whatever it is. But I knew, Captain. I knew."

"Fitz, I can't explain this, but—"

"I don't want you to explain it. How can anybody explain it? I want you to believe it, that's all."

Riker's slow nod showed that he was ready to believe it; then, as Gunther came from his office, Riker suddenly reserved decision. He was thinking now that perhaps the whole thing was imagination on Fitzgerald's part, since there had been no other report of Smitty's death. But while Riker hesitated, the orderly came down the stairs and reported to Gunther:

"Bed five, sir. Smith. He just died."

"Smith!" Gunther was startled. "I'll go up and look."

"For what?" Fitz demanded sharply. "There's nothing to look at except a body. I knew he was going to die. I read it on his face, as if somebody had painted it there."

"Go on back up," Gunther told the orderly, who stood staring at Fitz. Then, as the man obeyed mechanically, Gunther swung to Fitz. "So you knew it, Lieutenant?"

"You bet I knew it," returned Fitz. "I tabbed four men yesterday. I knew they were going to get it, too."

Gunther sidled a knowing look at Riker, then pressed the subject further;
"Odd, don't you think, Lieutenant?"

"It's not odd." Fitz forced a short laugh. "When you go thirty days on the
line and don't lose a man, that's odd. When you walk twenty miles and don't
get a blister, that's odd. This isn't odd; it's just sheer nightmare. I'm just a lousy,
dog-faced line officer who can see death on other people's faces. A lousy, dog-
faced line officer who would like to give back that power to wherever it came
from."

"Perhaps," observed Gunther calmly, "you're just a dog-faced line officer
who is cracking under the strain of having done too much and having felt too
much—"

"I'm five for five now, Doc." Fitz interrupted, with a broad but twisted grin.
"How many coincidences are needed to prove a fact? How many more faces
do I have to look into? Don't you realize that somewhere I picked up a talent
they don't teach at O. C. S.? I'm kind of a recording clerk for the Grim Reaper,
don't you know that?"

Fitzgerald's voice became hysterical as he demanded:

"Put tape over my eyes, won't you? Or can't you poke them out, or do
something so I won't be able to see? Anything, just so I won't have to look at
any more faces!"

Gunther turned and spoke quietly to Riker:

"Better take him along with you. Maybe he'll work out of his delusion.
If not, we'll pull him in and run some checks."

"Okay, Doc."

Nothing more was said on the subject by either Riker or Fitzgerald; at
least not then. Riker was willing to believe what Fitz had told him, and Fitz
knew it, so they were in close accord. That enabled Riker to keep his most
valuable lieutenant, for a time at least.

Then came the night when the G.I. trucks again were ready, with their tail
gates down and men packing gear by the light of lanterns in preparation for
a jump-off. In the company commander's tent, Captain Riker was in front of
a map board, talking to four lieutenants, among them Fitzgerald. All were in
fatigues, helmets, and side arms, ready for a move, as Riker told them:

"I'll give it to you just as I got it from Regiment. We spearhead the attack.
We go to this point on the Pasig River"—he indicated it on the map—"The
highway bridge is out, but over here to the east, the army is sticking across a
Bailey. It should be done by 0200. We'll move across as the point of the spearhead. Baker and Charlie company will follow us.

"Up here, some Filipino guerrillas will be crossing by boat unobserved—we
hope." Riker moved his finger up the river. "Their job will be to take any and
all guns the Japs have on the other side, so we should get across that bridge
against only small arms. Any questions?"

There were none. The four lieutenants simply stared at Riker, as though
expecting to hear more.

"That's it, then," Riker said. "We've got about twenty-two minutes before we load up on the trucks. Give each platoon a good briefing: Belts, five grenades apiece, six clips of ammo, no back packs. Good luck."

Three lieutenants filed from the tent. The fourth remained, still staring at Riker, who looked up and asked rather sharply, "What's the matter, Fitz?"

There was no reply. Riker ripped down the map, folded it up, and poked it inside the makeshift desk. Fitzgerald's stare remained fixed, but his eyes were going wider, and with good reason. From some unseen source, most certainly not the Coleman lantern, an odd light was bathing Riker's face in a weird glow, identical with the radiance that Fitz had seen on Smitty's face, and on the others before him.

Now Riker was meeting Fitzgerald's stare. Riker's next question was more pointed than the one before:

"Do you still think you're well enough to take the platoon, Fitz?"

Again there was no reply.

"I've been talking to Gunther," Riker continued. "He thinks you'd be better off with two weeks back at Division. This one tonight won't take more than a few hours, but it will be messy." Riker paused; now his eyes showed a widened stare. "What's the matter, Fitz?" Riker's tone rang with alarm. "What are you looking at? Fitz!"

Riker fairly shouted the name, and it snapped Fitzgerald from his daze. "Captain—you'd better not go!"

"Do you see something, Fitz?" queried Riker, running his fingers down his face. "Something — something odd — like with the others?"

"It's shining on your face," Fitzgerald replied in a hushed tone. "Captain, if you go — you won't be coming back."

"Get your platoon set, Fitz. You've only got about fifteen minutes."

"Then you're going, after what I saw?"

"Why not?" demanded Riker. "If I'm due to get it, that should be it, no matter how I try to duck it. But I won't get it, Fitz. You're going to find out that this illusion stuff of yours is just coincidence, which is what we should have labeled it in the first place. I'll see you at the trucks, Fitz."

Fitzgerald started to say something; then he set his lips grimly and left the tent. Riker looked at his watch, picked up his gunbelt, hooked it on, and reached for his helmet. He took his .45 from its holster, spun the cartridge chamber, then replaced it.

Again Riker glanced at his watch, wishing time would move faster. He took a wallet from his pocket, drew some pictures from it, studied them and put them on the improvised desk. As an afterthought, Riker took a signet ring from his finger and used it to weigh down the photos. Then he strode from the tent without looking back.

Lines of soldiers were already climbing into the trucks, ghostly figures even to the clanking sounds that might have been spectral chains but were actually the rattle and clash of fighting equipment. As Captain Riker eyed the scene, he saw Lieutenant Fitzgerald stride toward the trucks, where a squad of men awaited him.

One by one, Fitz studied their faces, and to Riker's amazement, they seemed to be inviting that test. Some tried to outstare Fitz, almost as Riker had. Others turned away uneasily. Now Riker had the answer to two things that had been bothering him: Fitzgerald's silence since Smitty's death; and a growing tension among the men of Riker's entire company.

The hospital orderly had heard enough to know about the power that Fitzgerald didn't want. The other patients in Smitty's ward had seen enough to verify it. Captain Gunther had also talked out of turn in his capacity of medical officer, even though he hadn't realized it. In merely discussing Fitz's aberration, Gunther had advertised the power that 'Lieutenant Fitzgerald honestly believed he possessed.

The thing was reaching a crux as Riker approached. Apparently, Fitzgerald hadn't seen a lighted face in a truckload of G.I.'s, but they weren't willing to let it go at that. Now that the secret was out, they thought that the gifted lieutenant was becoming reluctant to display his psychic ability. Actually, the case was just the opposite, as Captain Riker could personally testify. But that didn't help the present situation.

One young soldier, a youngster named Freeman, suddenly blurted out exactly what the rest wanted to say. Captain Riker arrived close enough just in time to hear him.

"What about it, Lieutenant?" Freeman's eyes were frantic as they met Fitzgerald's. "Everybody says you can tell. Everybody says you know who is going to get it and who isn't. How about it, Lieutenant? Give us a break. It ain't fair, you knowing and not telling us—"

Riker cut in on that, sharply and hard, with all the authority of a company commander.

"You, Freeman! Knock it off!"

The kid who had dared to demand an answer from a lieutenant wilted suddenly when challenged by a captain. No longer was Private Freeman the spokesman for a whole platoon, including corporals and sergeants, who would gladly have said their piece, once questions started to be answered. Captain Riker wasn't going to let it reach that stage.

If Captain Riker had given the command, "Eyes right!" he couldn't have accomplished more. His mere order, "Knock it off!" snapped practically the whole platoon to attention. They knew right then why Riker was the company commander and Fitzgerald a lieutenant. They forgot Fitzgerald's power of naming victims who were sure to die at his mere say-so, and who would wilt if they heard such a pronouncement.

Only two men did remember: Captain Riker and Lieutenant Fitzgerald. Only fifteen minutes before, Fitzgerald, who could see the light, had pronounced doom on Riker. But Riker hadn't wilted then, and he wasn't wilting now. Nor was Fitz expecting him to do so. Along with the eyes that turned toward Captain Riker, the company commander, were those of Lieutenant Fitzgerald, his subordinate.

"Hear this," declared Riker. "Somebody started a wild gag, and whoever did is going to get burned for it. Nobody in this company is a mind reader. That includes Lieutenant Fitzgerald." His eyes met Fitz's and he paused until all the rest had time to recognize that fact. "How about that, Lieutenant?"

Fitz held the gaze briefly, then let his eyes drop.

"That's right, sir."

"Okay, boys," Riker swung to the G.I.'s. "Let's hop."

Hop they did, into the trucks that lumbered away in procession, bound for a rendezvous on the Pasig River, from which some might never return.

Or from which one might never return. That one could be Captain Phil Riker. That one was Captain Phil Riker.

It happened on the Bailey bridge. The company moved forward to spearhead the attack, hoping that the guerrillas had fulfilled their part. Apparently they had, for there was no sign of opposition as the American troops approached the bridge, only to hesitate, until one man moved forward and waved the others on. That man was Captain Riker, and for the moment he was an open target for half a dozen guns triggered by enemy snipers.

Riker sprawled under the sudden volley. Instantly, the men of the lead platoon responded with rifle fire, then charged across the bridge, hurling grenades as they came. The miserable enemy resistance subsided as suddenly as it had flared up. Complete silence reigned along the riverbank, a silence in which, unfortunately, Captain Riker formed a part.

Lieutenant Fitzgerald took over, and the operation continued as Captain Riker had mapped it. Soon they were joining forces with the Filipino guerrillas, who had already completed their mop-up, except for the few die-hard Jap sharpshooters still stationed on the riverbank.

It was early morning when the trucks returned to the encampment, bringing back a smiling, laughing crowd of soldiers, who for once had experienced a comparatively easy time. There were moments, though, when faces went glum as they thought of the one man who had needlessly sacrificed himself in order to trigger the attack—Captain Phil Riker.

But had it been so needless?

The one man who might have answered that question was Lieutenant Hugh Fitzgerald. The lieutenant ordered a sergeant to take charge of the platoon. Then, in a numbed, mechanical way, Fitz entered the company commander's tent and stopped before the crate that served as desk.

From his pocket, Fitz brought out a chain with two dog tags and laid it alongside the ring and photographs. He sat down and stared at the desk with hollow, hopeless eyes. The tent flap opened and Colonel Lloyd Archer, commanding officer of the regiment, stepped in. As Fitzgerald started to rise, Archer waved him down.

"At ease, Fitz. I just came around to congratulate you boys on a job well done."

"The odds fell our way, sir. Those guerrillas knocked out the guns, and we should have walked right on across the bridge without losing a man. Instead, we lost the best man we had."

"I know." The colonel picked up the dog tags and the ring, then studied the photographs. "Too bad for Riker's wife and his two fine sons. But why did he leave these things here? Did he know, somehow, that he wasn't coming back?"

"Yes, Colonel, he knew." Fitz blurted out the words. "Riker knew because I told him; and I told him because I saw it!"

The tent flap opened again and Captain Gunther entered, to receive a nod from Colonel Archer.

"Some orders have come through on you, Fitz," said Gunther. "You're to go back to Division. They'd like to look you over. It will be a nice couple of weeks' rest. Better pack your gear."

From Gunther's anxious look, it was obvious that he was ready to call in a squad of men, in case Fitz offered objections. But he had none.

"It's better I should go," Fitz decided. "Better, after this." He gestured to the desk, as though to emphasize Riker's absence. "I may as well tell you that I saw it again—this time on Riker's face. You'd believe me now, Doc, if the captain could only be here to tell you the same. Only he can't be, because that would mean that I was wrong. That's how the whole thing defeats itself. Somehow I get a strange power—for what good?

"Only to tell somebody something that they shouldn't know. I saw that light on Riker's face, and suddenly he knew I saw it. If he'd only stayed here— well, I guess he knew it wouldn't be any use. They'd have bombed the camp, because he was sure to get it. I knew that from the light and when I shut my eyes, it was like closing a book—a purple book—like a book I heard mentioned somewhere, once"—he pressed his hand to his forehead—"odd how it comes to mind—a book called a purple testament."

Fitz swayed slightly as he stared from Captain Gunther to Colonel Archer, then back again. He steadied, snapped to attention:

"I'll go pack my gear."

Silence clung to the scene after Lieutenant Fitzgerald left. Musingly, Colonel Archer said:

"A purple testament. It sounds like a quotation from somewhere. But like that light Fitz talks about, it must be very real to him. Do you think he can get over this hallucination, Doctor?"

"Only when he gets some place where he won't be looking at people he thinks are due to die."

"Maybe it will be that way back at Division. Let's hope so."

In his own tent, Lieutenant Fitzgerald had finished shaving and was about to pack the last of his gear. He took one look into an old glass mirror, as he was lifting it from the nail where it hung. Suddenly, a glint came to his widening eyes, but it was slight compared to the glow that spread over his face. The light brightened to the intensity of a sunburst, playing on Fitz's features like a spotlight. It was then that the mirror dropped from his nerveless fingers and shattered completely.

When Fitz looked down at the fragments, they scintillated like diamonds and he could still visualize his own face, gazing up from amid that unquenchable iridescence. Fitz's eyes closed, and the light turned purple, shaping itself into a book that was closing, too. Suddenly a voice jarred Fitz from his reverie.

"Lieutenant Fitzgerald? Is this your bag, sir?"

The speaker was an ambulance driver standing by the open flap of the tent. Fitzgerald nodded.

"That's my bag. You can put it in the ambulance."

"Whenever you're ready to go, sir, we're all set."

Fitzgerald followed the driver to the ambulance, where Captain Gunther was ready with a parting handshake.

"It's for the best, Fitz," Gunther assured him. "Soon you'll be where you won't have to be looking at people and worrying about whether they are going to die."

"I know that, Doc. How well I know it!"

Fitzgerald's tone of solid conviction left Gunther a bit puzzled. He watched Fitz climb into the seat beside the driver, who was talking to a sergeant standing beyond the ambulance.

"You're going back to Division?" the sergeant was asking. "You're taking the Cavite Road?"

"I've got to, Sarge. The highway bridge is out."

"I know that. So I'm telling you, take care on the Cavite Road. The engineers think they spotted some mines a mile up the line. They haven't had time to dig them out, so stay close to the shoulders."

"Thanks, Sarge. I will." The driver turned to Fitzgerald with a friendly grin. "It's only a couple of hours drive to where we're going, Lieutenant. We'll be there before we know it."

"Yes,'" replied Fitz. "I know we will be. Sometimes a couple of hours seem only a couple of minutes."

Fitzgerald knew, because the driver's grin looked sickly. Not that it wasn't pleasant in itself. It was the odd light that had come over it, a flickering light that distorted the driver's features, giving them the pallor of death. But as it intensified, the glow broadened the smile, giving it a happy expression. He was in a hurry to get somewhere, this chap, and now the brilliance of his face was as vivid as Fitzgerald's own reflection at the time when he had dropped the mirror.

There was no use troubling the driver with talk of things that had happened, or other things that were sure to happen — and soon. A few minutes more or less would not matter. Fitz was wondering now if his own face had retained that effulgence that his eyes alone could see. He took advantage of the ambulance's hard, sudden swerve onto the highway to lean heavily the sergeant's way and take a quick look in the car mirror.

Fitz had guessed right. The radiance still shone from his features. Soon there would be another swerve, within a mile or so, when the driver would hit the shoulder as the sergeant had advised. That would give Fitz another glance at his own face and the driver's to see if they still had that growing, golden glow that seemed to emanate from another world than this.

Probably they would have, for Fitz had never known that strange radiance to vanish, once he had seen it; at least, not while life continued. So he shut his eyes, waiting for the swerve to come. He knew it would be a big one, but not big enough. Yet Fitz was satisfied, for this was the last time he would have to undergo the torment of viewing that fateful brilliance and knowing too well what it meant.

Those heavy eyelids, closing, were like the covers of a purple book, its hue due to a blending of that vivid light and the darkness that came when Fitz's eyes were closed. A mingling like the twilight between day and night, each prophetic in its own right, for together they told that day was ending and that night would soon begin.

Back by the tents, Captain Gunther was watching the ambulance as it dwindled beyond a curve a half a mile away and approached the sector where the engineers had so recently knocked off work. The medical officer was still pondering over those parting words, with Fitz's emphatic phrase: "How well I know it!"

Over by one of the tents, a boy with one arm in a sling was playing a harmonica with the aid of his other hand. The young soldier looked up as Gunther turned his way, and he gave the captain a smile, without missing a note on the harmonica. That was the way with all the boys in Fitzgerald's platoon. They were like Smitty and others who had gone before; they just wouldn't quit until their moment had come.

Maybe they figured that Fitz, too, thought that way. Whatever the case, his moment came right then. There was a distant sound like a heavy clap of thunder. The harmonica player cut off his tune and stared up at Captain Gunther, who had halted in his tracks. The boy's voice was strained. "Did you hear that, Doc?"

"I heard it," acknowledged Gunther. "Maybe it was just thunder. Storms come up quickly here. Go on with that tune. You are doing very well."

But Gunther knew it wasn't thunder. Soon everyone in the company knew it. They learned that Lieutenant Fitzgerald wouldn't be coming back to take over the command in place of Captain Riker. An enemy mine, planted too close to the shoulder of the road, had done it.

That night, Captain Gunther expressed his real thoughts to Colonel Archer, but only as a sidelight of his medical report.

"Fitz *must* have seen it coming to those others," Gunther said in a solemn tone, "for he saw it coming to himself. He told me as much, in just that many words."

"I know." Archer reached for a well-thumbed volume on his desk. "I've found that quotation of his. It's from Shakespeare's *Richard the Third*. It says, 'He has come to open the purple testament of bleeding war.' That's all."

That was all. For Lieutenant Hugh Fitzgerald, A Company, First Platoon, the purple testament was closed. Lieutenant Fitzgerald had found the Twilight Zone.

The Ghost Train

Pete Dunning swung from the Upstate Parkway and pulled in beside the Woodland Service station, where a neon sign said: CANTEEN. From behind the wheel, Pete gave Bert Carey a solid elbow in the ribs and told him, "Wake up! Coffee break!"

Bert opened his eyes, stared at a blanket of whiteness that loomed in front of him, and queried, "Where are we? Going up the Iron Mountain ski lift already?"

"That," Pete informed him, "is the windshield. The wiper needs a new pair of blades, because the snow is coming down in big beautiful blobs. So while the service man is fixing the windshield wiper, we'll go in the canteen and have coffee."

They went in the canteen, but only Pete had coffee from the coin machine. Bert settled for milk, saying it would help him go to sleep again and adding that this time he would take the back seat, so that Pete couldn't wake him up so easily.

Pete, meanwhile, asked the manager of the service station which was the shortest way to Iron Mountain.

"I'd stay on the parkway," the manager declared. "It's the long way but the sure way. But if you want a short cut, talk to old Smedley, when he finishes installing those wiper blades. He's lived around here before anybody ever heard of parkways."

Pete talked to old Smedley, whose face was as weather-beaten as the surrounding crags, and whose body was as gnarled as the trees that clung to them. Smedley grinned at the mention of a short cut.

"Turn right at the bridge across the reservoir," he said. "Keep looking for more bridges, and go over the second. Take the second road to the right, then one that goes left, but not sharp left. Keep going past the crossroads, where the old store used to be —"

Smedley continued with further directions, frequently correcting himself, until Pete decided that he had it well pegged. Then he and Bert drove off into the blinding storm, which pushed the new wiper blades to the limit. They were crossing the second bridge when Bert spoke from the back seat.

"There's a third bridge just beyond here," he said. "It looks as though a line of trucks is going over it. I see their lights."

In a glance, Pete noted a row of irregularly spaced lights, all moving at the same rate over the bridge that Bert had pointed out. Then Pete had driven across his own bridge and was trying to pick the route that Smedley had given him. All these roads were still packed with earlier snows, and as Pete swung along a series of sharp bends, he asked:

"Did Smedley say we would hit a crooked road like this?"

"I don't remember," replied Bert. "I guess I went to sleep while he was talking to you."

Bert's tone was drowsy even now, but before Pete could tell him exactly what he thought of him, a strange, distant wail sounded far off in the dark. Startled, Pete asked, "Did you hear that?"

"The wind, I guess," responded Bert sleepily. "It howls a lot down through these hills —"

"Wait!" interrupted Pete. "I hear something else. Maybe it's just the crackle of the snow, or it could be my ears cracking, because we're getting higher in the hills. But it does sound like bells. Do you hear them, Bert? Jingling bells?"

"Jingle bells, jingle bells" — Bert went into the old Christmas song — "jingle all the way. Oh-ho, what fun it is to ride in a one-horse open sleigh — hey-hey!"

"That's exactly what they are," Pete affirmed musingly as he applied the brakes gingerly. "Sleigh bells, up ahead. Going at just about the same speed we are." He pushed the foot button, bringing the bright lights into play. "I'd better slow up, or we'll ram into it."

Pete swung into a short, straight stretch as he spoke. Straining his eyes through the storm, he added, "That could be it, going up that short rise!" Then, suddenly, the jingle of the sleigh bells was drowned by a louder clangor. Bigger, heavier bells were sounding a mechanical warning, and red lights began flashing with them, revealing a sign that said RAILROAD CROSSING.

The station wagon slued about as Pete really jammed on the brakes. In one passing glimpse, Pete could have sworn he saw an open sleigh with human figures in it, outlined in the ruddy glare. Then that momentary image was obliterated by a great black bulk, bringing an even louder clamor, the *dong-dong* of the bell on an old-fashioned steam locomotive. The station wagon was stopped, canted at an angle to the right, as Pete saw the churn of big driving wheels and connecting rods carrying the metal monster across the road, a mere fifty feet ahead.

There was a brief flare from an open firebox, the blackness of the coal tender, then the *clack-clack-clack* of passenger cars. Some of their windows were lighted, but others were completely dark, indicating that those were sleeping cars whose occupants had retired to their berths. But as the dozen cars sped by, Pete Dunning stared in almost complete disbelief.

Though a steam locomotive was a decided novelty in the 1960's, passenger cars were commonplace items — but not passenger cars like these. All such cars that Pete had ever seen were painted in colors like black, red, or green. But this entire train, clear from its baggage car back to its old-fashioned observation platform, was painted an absolute white!

Gliding through the blizzard, its clatter almost completely muffled by the closed window of the station wagon and the enveloping snow, it was truly a ghost train, the like of which Pete Dunning had never before seen nor imagined!

Then the phantom streak of whiteness was gone, and Pete was wondering if he had even seen it. The only evidence remaining was the flashing red light and clanging bell of the warning sign at the crossing. Suddenly, both of those cut off, leaving only a blackened void. Pete backed the wagon and nosed it to the crossing, asking, "Did you see it, Bert? The ghost train?"

"I heard a noise like a train," Bert replied, "and I saw some lights like those trucks that were crossing the bridge."

"But it was all white."

"You mean the snow? Sure, the snow's all white. What would it be, green? Let me go to sleep."

Bert's tone faded drowsily as Pete reached the one-track crossing and felt the tires jolt over the rails. Then, as he passed the hump, he braked the wagon again. There, silhouetted in the bright lights, was the figure of a girl wearing a close-fitting bonnet and a flowing coat with full sleeves and a cape collar. Pete rolled down the window on his side and put his head out as the girl approached. Then he heard her plaintive tone:

"Please — please take me to my father's home, right away. He's ill, and I promised him I'd be back as soon as I left word at the doctor's —"

"Come around to the other side," said Pete. Then, as the girl complied, he reached over and opened the door. She was inside a moment later, and Pete added, "You really are in a hurry, aren't you? All right, which way do we go?"

"Straight ahead, to start." The girl was leaning forward, staring through the windshield, and Pete, with brief side glances, noted her straight little nose and rounded chin. "Here's where we turn off — to the left."

How the girl even guessed the road was there, Pete could not tell, for the snow was driving in with blizzard force. Blindly, Pete picked his way, ready to brake instantly, the moment the snow no longer crunched beneath his front wheels. But that moment did not come. Instead, the road actually opened up ahead, though it was narrow and at times so steep that Pete wondered if his brakes would hold on the slippery surface.

Pete darted glances toward the girl beside him, and always, she seemed to expect it, for she turned her eyes his way. They were gray eyes, the color of her coat and bonnet, and their gaze was searching, yet understanding. Pete's tone was strained, as he asked:

"How much farther do we have to go — and does it get much worse?"

"Only a little way now," the girl replied, "and the worst is over. For me, it was over — long ago."

"You mean you were worried because no one came along, until I finally did?"

"There were others who came along." The girl's tone was reminiscent, almost vague. Then: "Turn sharply here, across the covered bridge. Then sharply again, down the long hill."

She didn't specify "left" and "right," but Pete took those directions automatically, as though an invisible hand had swung the wheel. Another glance toward the girl, and this time, the dash light gave a hypnotic glint to her gray eyes. Yet, with it, he was swept with a surge of sympathy such as he had never experienced before.

"Don't worry about the hill," the girl was saying, "because we are almost there. I'm thankful, and you must be glad —"

"Glad that I could help," put in Pete, with another glance. Then, with a whimsical smile at the girl's old-fashioned costume, he added, "I feel as if I were seeing Nellie home. Your name wouldn't be Nellie, would it?"

"No, it's Ethel, and I'm not coming from Aunt Dinah's quilting party —"

"I was seeing Nellie ho-ho-home," boomed an off-key baritone from the back seat. "I was seeing Nellie hooooome! It was from Aunt Dinah's quilting party —"

"Don't mind Bert Carey," Pete interrupted. "He's just a newspaper photographer who was wished on me, cameras and all."

"And your name?" the girl inquired.

"Pete Dunning, sports writer for the *New York Classic*. On my way to cover the ski-jumping contest at Iron Mountain —"

"Turn here." The girl's hand pressed Pete's arm. Again, he swung the car the way she wanted, this time to the left, though he didn't know why. "There are the lights of the house. You can stop in front."

Pete pulled into a driveway that terminated in billowy shapes resembling snow-clad trees. The house was on the right, and he stopped beside an open space that appeared to be a walk. By the time he turned to look at Ethel, she had left the car, closing the door so softly that Pete didn't hear it, though he was sure he caught her murmured words of parting:

"Good night — and many thanks."

Waking to the fact that the girl was gone, Pete hurriedly backed the car so that the bright headlights shone along the path to the house, to guide Ethel there. But she must have reached the house by then, for Pete could not sight her in the thickening swirl of snow. All that he saw was the dim glow from the lights of the house, as he stopped the car abruptly, rather than back into a hidden ditch.

The jolt awakened Bert, who popped up from the back seat, staring wildly as he asked:

"Where are we? Off the road? Out in the middle of nowhere? I figured we would lose our way —"

"We haven't lost it yet," Pete interrupted, a bit testily. "Just watch how fast I pick it up from here."

He swung the car back to the road, giving a last glance through the snowy darkness, in time to see the lights of the house fade from view. Then he took the sharp turn through the covered bridge, which rattled behind him as he roared out the other end. Another swerve again brought Bert to life, with the query:

"What was that?"

"A covered bridge," returned Pete, "and this is the road we came from. Soon we'll hit the railroad crossing."

Only they didn't hit the crossing. Instead, the roads that Pete followed became increasingly unfamiliar. He took random turns, hoping they would lead to something better, but they didn't. Pete knew by then that he had really lost the way, but he didn't have to admit it, for Bert had gone back to sleep.

Pete simply kept on, hoping that the storm would lessen, which it finally did. He came to an obscure crossroad where a snow-capped sign pointed to the town of Lansford, which was a help, because the town was on Route 44. Pete knew this route led off from the Upstate Parkway. He followed the signs into Lansford, and there his problems ended.

At last, he was on Route 44, which led to Iron Mountain Lodge, although it was the long way round. After an hour's drive, during which the snowfall ended completely, Pete pulled up in front of the lodge, which was aglow with lights. There, Pete reached over to the back seat and gave Bert a solid punch, with the admonition:

"Wake up. We're there."

"Where?" Bert came out of his doze in a bewildered fashion. "You mean we're lost again?"

"We're at Iron Mountain Lodge," Pete informed him, "and right on the button."

Pete didn't add that his "short cut" had taken an hour more than the long way around by the parkway. The fact that he had reached his destination was enough. Bert, at least, was duly impressed, though he couldn't seem to remember any of the details of the long, worrisome, roundabout trip.

It was pleasant to be at the lodge, amid jolly company, seated in front of a huge fireplace. There was a dining room, a lounge, and modern guest rooms, which made the stormy weather and the difficult trip seem very remote. Besides, Pete and Bert were too busy meeting with other sports writers and photographers to think of anything but the ski-jumping contests scheduled for the next day.

It was nearly dawn when Pete turned in. When he looked out his window across the snowbound mountainside etched beneath the clouded moonlight, his mind went back to his meeting with the girl and the drive down through the covered bridge.

The only puzzling part was the jingle of those sleigh bells and the subsequent jangle which had ended when a ghostly train had slicked over the single-track crossing. But that, at least, would serve as a starting point from which he could find the snug little house down in the hollow. Pete decided to check the matter at his first opportunity.

That opportunity came late the next afternoon, following a gruelling day not only for ski jumpers but also for the sports writers who had to measure the jumps and the photographers who had to take pictures of them in mid-flight. Pete, Bert, and a dozen other worn-out representatives of the press were slouched about the lounge trying to recuperate, when Max Boswell, dean of the Manhattan sportswriters, sounded off in a style as scathing as his daily column.

"You softies should have covered the bobsled races back in the old days," Max declared. "No easy drive of a couple of hours up to a plush hotel like this, with every modern convenience including telephones, television, and picture postcards.

"No indeed. It was an overnight hop by sleeper, and at the finish you were at the other end of nowhere, living in a bunkroom where a moose was likely to poke his head in and honk you awake in the morning, except that the window was too small for his horns. They didn't have picture postcards, because the place was so remote, it would have cost a half-dollar postage to mail one home." Max finished his coffee with a deep, basso gurgle, and then inquired, "Did any of you inhuman products of the jet age ever take an overnight hop on a sleeping car? Did any of you ever experience a torture equalled only by a one-way passage on an Australian convict ship? Would any of you —"

"I would," Pete put in, before Max could finish. "I would have traded in my car for an upper berth on a sleeper just last night, when I stopped at a crossing to let a train go by. You see, I was lost, and the train wasn't. And those sleepers, at least they were headed somewhere, but I wasn't."

"What sleepers?" Max demanded. "Wait, now — they still run them on the main line to Chicago. So you stopped at a grade crossing on the main line — except it doesn't have any grade crossings. They got rid of them long ago —"

"And this wasn't the main line," Pete interrupted, "because it had only a single track. What was more, the train had an old steam locomotive —"

"And they got rid of them long ago, too," put in Max, "even on the branch lines. Am I right, boys?"

He turned to the other newspaper men, who chorused their agreement. That threw the burden on Pete. He had to tell his story to prove his case. So he told it.

Pete began with the jingling bells that turned to jangles, with the ghost train slithering through the lurid red lights of the crossing. He told of the girl, how he had taken her down through the covered bridge to her father's home. He described the return trip and for a clincher, he added:

"Bert Carey, here, will confirm all I've told you."

There was a momentary hush that reminded Pete Dunning of a vast vacuum. What a wonderful break Pete Dunning had given to Bert Carey! The moment that Bert nodded his agreement, he would be in, too, as a partner in a strange, almost fantastic adventure. But just then, Bert, instead of nodding, decided to speak his piece.

"It was a swell story, Pete," Bert declared. "So good that you should win the grand prize put up by the National Liars Association. Do you know, boys" — Bert swung to the group — "the way Pete told it, he almost had me believing it!"

"But Bert!" exclaimed Pete. "You should believe it. You were there with me. You saw and heard everything —"

"I heard you talk about things," Bert put in. "You said you heard bells jingling, so I started singing 'Jingle Bells' — remember? Then I heard a noise like a train —"

"That's right, Bert — and you saw it!"

"I saw some trucks, Pete, probably those that we both saw coming across the bridge, a little earlier."

"But you must remember the girl — and the house —"

"What girl, Pete? What house?"

"The girl who waved for us to stop, and asked me to take her home to her sick father, which I did."

"You mean when we began singing 'I was seeing Nellie home' — sure, I remember that part, Pete. But I don't remember any girl being with us. I thought we were just singing to cheer ourselves up."

"But I showed you the house, or at least its lights."

"You mean when you almost backed us into the ditch, Pete? I saw the reflection of our headlights from a snowbank, when you swung the car around, but that was all."

"Don't you remember coming through the covered bridge?"

"I remember hearing something rattle. But it could have been any of those fifty rickety bridges or broken-down culverts that we crossed, trying to find our way back to the right road."

Everybody laughed, and heartily, at Pete's expense, with one exception. That was Max Boswell, whose face showed a solemn, sympathetic expression. Pete put an appeal to Max:

"Believe me, I'd just like to go back there and prove it!"

"I believe you, boy." Max nodded. "But you would have to go a long way back to find steam engines roaming this country."

"But I *did* see one."

"Then you must have gone a long way back. Maybe to the nineteen thirties, or even the roaring twenties. Maybe even before that, when 'Jingle Bells' was the nation's number-one song hit."

"I'm sorry, Pete," Bert began. "Maybe I was just asleep or dopey. Anyway, I'm willing to believe you—"

"I'll bet!" snapped Pete. "I was dumb to bring the thing up, so skip it. But I'd like to drive back over those side roads in broad daylight, taking you along, Mr. Wise Guy, to show you all the things I talked about!"

Pete's chance came when the editor of the *Classic* called him by long distance the next evening.

"Send in your ski story and Bert's photos by messenger," the editor ordered. "I want you and Bert to spend the rest of the week driving around the reservoir section. Last summer we had the biggest drought since 1900, or whenever those valleys were dammed up. I want a picture story, showing how low the water really is."

"But there's been lots of snow up here, chief."

"I know that. But until it melts, the reservoirs won't get any of it. I want those pictures right now. Understand?"

"I sure do, chief."

Pete could have shouted for sheer triumph, but instead he calmed himself, looked up Bert and told him about the new assignment. The next day, they began their tour midway between Iron Mountain and New York City, where the reservoirs formed a sinuous chain, winding in and out of long-drowned valleys, with extensions spread out like a starfish, representing flooded creek beds and ravines.

There were many bridges, all of the steel cantilever type, crossing narrows where the reservoirs linked. There were also side roads that took the long way around the deeply indented shores and even crossed the big dams. These were connected by a maze of lesser roads, some winding deep down into valleys outside the reservoir district.

Pete took the side roads often, claiming they were short cuts, but he lost time when forced to inch the car down icy slopes alongside rickety fence rails, with deep gorges below. But in no case did he come to a sharp turn across a covered bridge, and down a hill to a dead-end lane with a cottage hidden amid the evergreens. That vista had vanished, and so had any semblance of a railroad crossing where the ghost train had slicked by. So Pete concentrated on the reservoirs, stopping at turnouts where Bert could take pictures, or letting Bert out of the car, so he could scramble over the double cable of a guard rail and wade through the snow to get closer to the shore.

The reservoirs were indeed desperately low. Where the water should have been lapping at the top of the embankments, there would be a huge, gaping basin, forty feet or more down to the water's edge. Stranded rowboats, used for fishing, indicated how the water had steadily receded. Along with those, Bert took shots of snow-clad meadows skirted by old stone walls, farm sites of a century ago. Those were level portions of rolling hillsides that had become shoals after the valleys had been inundated and turned into manmade lakes.

Bert took fine close shots of such scenes, including some with a telescopic lens, and he was sure that the camera's unflinching eye would bring out details that escaped human scrutiny. From a distant lookout, he pointed out a few to Pete, who noted them down for his story.

"See those two blocks of stone just poking out of the water?" Bert said. "They must be the abutments of an old bridge. You can see a gully leading down to it like a letter V in the snow. That's probably where the stream came from."

"But no road could have gone across there," argued Pete. "Look how steep the sides of the reservoir are."

"It must have swung up at an angle," Bert decided, "following along the line of that stone wall, up to the road that skirts the high ground above the rim of the reservoir."

"I guess you're right, Bert." Pete tried to trace the road down to an ice-covered stretch of water, only to note something else. "What do you make of that square enclosure, with stone walls all around it?"

"An old cemetery," Bert identified it. "They say the woods are full of them in these parts. Some of them date back to before the Revolution. Every family had its own graveyard."

That was just one sample of many observations and discussions during the daily rounds. Every night, they arrived back at Iron Mountain Lodge, where Bert Carey turned in, dog-tired from lugging his cameras through snowbanks. Every following morning, Pete Dunning took delight in waking Bert up with the announcement: "Three C's again today, my boy. Let's go!"

The "Three C's" referred to a daily weather bulletin posted on a special board, stating: CONTINUED COLD AND CLEAR. That was poison to Bert, for it meant another long and gruelling trip over the seemingly endless maze of roads, with Pete as a rigorous taskmaster. But Pete himself was showing signs of frustration. Toward the end of the week, when clouds began to gather in mid-afternoon, Pete halted the car at a turnout above a reservoir that looked like a collection of patchy, frozen pools.

"We've been over this before," he declared. "In fact, we've covered everything. Let's call it a day."

"Covered everything," Bert chuckled, "except maybe covered bridges and railroad crossings."

Pete gave him an annoyed glance that prompted Bert to continue:

"Not a single railroad line anywhere around here, except over toward Long Ridge, and the one that cuts across near Iron Mountain. They're both outside the reservoir district, or pretty near so."

"So what?" Pete demanded.

"You should ask, 'So where?'" replied Bert. "Because where are you going to find a railroad crossing that doesn't exist?"

Pete couldn't answer that, though he wished he could. But he found one question he could answer when they pulled into the lodge at Iron Mountain and read a new weather report. The "Three C's" had been crossed out and chalked in its place was the warning: BIG SNOW LATER.

"It won't be much later," Pete decided, noting heavy clouds above Iron Mountain. "Right after dinner, I'm going to drive into the city, taking your photos with me, so the *Classic* will be sure to get its precious reservoir story. You can cover the ski contests for me, Bert, and I'll borrow one of your cameras, in case I see a deer or something that would make a nice night shot to add to the reservoir pictures."

It was already snowing when Pete started to the city, and as he drove along, the flurries developed into a full-fledged storm. Pete's only worry was that it might change to rain, for it was getting late in the winter. Sleet would make the roads icy and driving dangerous, but that wasn't the worst part.

Gradually, Pete had come to the conclusion that there was something truly uncanny about the ghost train, and that the old road with the covered bridge and dead-end lane figured deeply in the mystery. Pete was sure he couldn't have been dreaming that other night, yet his reservoir assignment and the days of comparatively good driving had enabled him to double-check the entire area.

By a process of rational elimination, Pete had formed the theory that the hour, the season, and particularly the weather, might be factors that could lead to a duplication of the event. Fantastic, perhaps, where the ghost train was concerned, but after all, the ghost train was fantastic in itself. But that didn't apply to the sleigh bells, and to the girl named Ethel, who wanted a lift home.

There still could be some old-fashioned sleighs in use around these parts, but they wouldn't be out unless the roads were packed with snow, as they had been that night. Now, tonight, the snow was piling up again. Delay didn't matter; Pete had timed this trip to allow for that. The more snow, the more chance of hearing sleigh bells, was the way he reasoned it. Big drifts were forming across the road when Pete reached the town of Lansford, where house lights were barely visible in the swirl. Conditions seemed to be identical with those of the other night.

From Lansford, Pete tried to pick his old route in reverse. He'd been doing that all week, during his daylight excursions, but always he had missed out. Now, by avoiding all those mistaken turns, he hoped to find the elusive railroad crossing. But the snow was pouring into the windshield with blizzard force. Soon Pete was completely lost, his only consolation being that he had been lost like that the time before.

Still, a bad skid could pitch the station wagon into a gully or a gorge, and it might be all up with Pete Dunning. At times he thought he could hear the rush of water far below, and he was straining his ears as well as his eyes when he caught the distant jingle of the other night.

Sleigh bells! Pete would have laid it to his imagination, but they grew louder, which made sense, because he was traveling in the other direction tonight, and the sleigh—if following its same route—would be approaching him. Then the prospect of the railroad crossing suddenly struck Pete, and he jammed on the brakes just in time.

As the wagon swerved, Pete saw red lights flashing and a terrific jangle drowned the sleigh bells. While Pete was rolling the window down, a great hulk of blackness roared across the road, and as before, he saw the flaring firebox of an old steam locomotive. Pete grabbed the camera too late, but as the line of weird white cars clicked by, he managed to get a picture of their lighted windows. He tried for another of the observation platform, but the ghost train had gone by too soon.

The next act followed as Pete was straightening the car. Again, the girl with the flowing coat stepped out of the blizzard into the glare of the headlights. This time, she was on Pete's side of the crossing, and hardly had she given her plaintive call: "Please—please take me to my father's home!" before she was on the far side of the car and Pete was opening the door for her.

"Straight ahead," he said, with a nod. "Then a turnoff to the left."

"No," the girl objected. "You will have to turn around first. My father's house is in the other direction."

So it was, considering that Pete was coming the other way. He bumped across the tracks, found a place to turn, and went back over the crossing, where the lights were out by now and the bells were silent. Pete would have liked to have taken another picture right then, but he decided to wait until after he had taken the girl home.

From then on, the trip was strangely like that of the other night. The girl again told Pete that her father was ill, and that they only had a little way to go. Her words, "Turn sharply here, across the covered bridge, then sharply again, down the long hill," were springing into Pete's mind before the girl pronounced them. Then Pete asked the girl's name, and when she responded, "Ethel," he declared:

"Mine is Pete Dunning. That's my full name, And yours?"

"Ethel Barsden," the girl informed him. "Turn here. There are the lights of the house: You can stop in front."

Again, the girl's hand was pressing Pete's arm, as on that other night, but she gave no sign of recognizing him. This time, however, Pete didn't intend to let Ethel slip away as quickly as he had before. Even as Pete stopped the car, he peeled the glove from his right hand and pressed his hand upon hers, but the surprise that he received was far more startling than her elusive way of slipping from sight.

To describe that hand as icy cold would have been putting it in the mildest terms. The mere touch shot a paralyzing chill clear up Pete's arm, sending a convulsive shiver through his entire body. Pete was numbed, both physically and mentally, and the effect must have been more than momentary, for though his hand recoiled automatically, he found himself clenching and unclenching his fingers to learn if they were still capable of action; and during that interim, his thoughts underwent a total lapse.

By then, the girl was gone again, and Pete couldn't remember hearing her open and close the door, though through his mind were echoing her same parting words: "Good night—and many thanks."

This time, Pete didn't wait to back the car about. His hand was at least nimble enough to reach the far door and grab the window handle, which, cold though it was, seemed warm compared to the girl's icy touch. As he brought the window down with a few quick turns, Pete glimpsed Ethel's flowing coat and close-fitting bonnet as she started down the pathway to the house. He caught up the camera in one quick sweep, trained it from the window, and called, "Ethel! Wait!"

Pete was sure he saw the girl turn as he snapped the shot, for her face came vividly before his eyes as the bulb flashed. Pale almost as the snow, her features were etched against the dark background of her cape and bonnet. Then she was gone, and Pete hurriedly backed the car, so that its headlights again cut a swath along the pathway to the house.

All in the same action, Pete opened the door beside the wheel and sprang out to the driveway with the camera. He was working so quickly tonight that he again caught sight of Ethel as she reached the house, a small white cottage just within range of the headlights. By the time Pete got the camera into action and took the shot. Ethel must have gone inside, for she was no longer in sight when Pete looked again.

Back in the car, Pete swung about and headed up the road through the covered bridge. He was clocking the speedometer tonight, making mental notes of it. Somehow, he missed the railroad crossing, but soon he reached a bridge leading to the Upstate Parkway. There, Pete took an inbound lane, speaking to himself, half-aloud:

"Ethel Barsden. That's her full name, so it should be easy to trace her. When I do, I hope she won't be mad because I took those pictures. She might give me a stare as cold as those hands of hers!"

Pete stopped at the canteen for coffee and while he was drinking it, he looked about and asked, "Where's old Smedley?"

"He only fills in occasionally," replied the manager, "so he won't be around for another week or so. Anything special?"

"I want to find a family named Barsden, who live near here."

"I wouldn't know them. Smedley is the man to ask."

Pete managed to reach New York City before it was snowed under. He had his pictures developed along with Bert's, in the dark room at the newspaper office. Bert's came out fine, but Pete's didn't. The windows of the ghost train showed simply as streaks of light that might have been fireworks, or shooting stars. The flash that Pete had taken of the girl was a splotch of black on a muddy background, more like a bush than a human figure. When Pete studied the last picture, Buckley, the man in charge of the dark room, looked at it and asked:

"What's that supposed to be? A big snowbank?"

"It's a cottage," Pete explained. "A girl was walking along that path leading to it, but she went inside before I got the shot."

"If that's a path, what happened to her footprints?"

For the first time, Pete realized that there weren't any. As for the cottage, it was so far out of focus that it did look like a mere snowbank. As before, the less Pete talked about his adventure, the better, for those pictures were damaging rather than helpful. The lack of footprints meant that the girl couldn't have walked along the path. Again, Pete was forced to wait for another snowy night.

The current storm lasted only until late the next afternoon. The rest of the week, Pete was doing the reservoir story and covering odd sports events. Then came a spell of warm weather that started a sudden thaw, with predictions of heavy rains to follow, meaning there would be no more sleighing until next winter.

Pete found time to study old maps of the upstate area and look up names of families there, but the result was doubly disappointing. The maps were inadequate, and there were no Barsdens listed, either in old records or in modern directories. Pete was about to give the whole thing up, when a real break came. The predicted rain came through as a late, but heavy snow, and Pete was again sent to Iron Mountain to join Bert, who was up there waiting for the last of the winter sports, if there were any.

The snow was heavy on the parkway when Pete hit the Woodland Service Station and learned that old Smedley wouldn't be back for a few days more. The manager advised Pete to get on to Iron Mountain as soon as he could, claiming that the snow might turn to freezing rain at any time. But Pete still took the short cut, as well as he could remember it. The roads were deep with snow, but he could hear the roar of creeks far below, all swollen by the recent thaw. Then suddenly those sounds faded, and distant sleigh bells came through with their familiar jingle.

Out of the blinding snow flared the big red lights, accompanied by the louder jangle. Pete still had the borrowed camera, but he didn't try to use it as the ghost train rolled past, its big locomotive and line of white cars complete to the eerie glow from its observation platform. Then Pete crossed the single track and slowed expectantly, wondering what he would do if Ethel Barsden failed to appear again.

Suddenly, there she was, flowing cloak, bonnet and all. Next, she was in the car and was pointing the way down to the covered bridge, where the situation changed. Tonight, the tumult of a flooded creek was shaking the creaky old timbers. Pete stopped midway, wondering if it would be safe to go on over. Ethel smiled reassuringly.

"You wouldn't be stopping to make a wish, or would you?"

"You mean, should I wish that this bridge won't fall apart?"

"No silly. When you go through a covered bridge, you stop and wish for something nice to happen—and sometimes it does."

Pete leaned toward Ethel and kissed her. Though her lips were cold, they were not icy; nor did her hands give him marrow-chilling shivers when he pressed them tonight. There were shivers, though, from the bridge, as a gust of wind ripped loose boards from the superstructure and sent them clattering down to smack the creek below.

"We'd better go," Ethel decided. "This old bridge may collapse at any time. They haven't kept it repaired, because—"

"Because of what?"

"Why, you know what they plan to do." Even in the dim light from the dashboard, Ethel's eyes were probing. "They've talked about it so long. But I've got to get home"—her tone became anxious—"my father is ill and I promised I'd get back—as soon as I could—"

Pete nodded and gave the girl's hand an encouraging pat. Then he gripped the wheel again, easing the car on through the bridge, hoping its timbers would hold until he made it.

"Turn sharply again," Ethel said, "and down the long hill. But don't worry, we are almost there!"

As if Pete didn't know! He had heard this twice before, yet the girl again was treating him as a total stranger. Now she was saying, "Turn here," and Pete was on the point of introducing himself again, when he realized that he had to snap out of this strange, automatic mood that was like a record played over and over. He reached to the dash and turned on the car radio. A newscaster's voice broke in:

"Batten down the hatches for the big storm. Floods are already sweeping the Southern states, and our snow is turning to rain. Stay off the road and avoid fallen wires and washed-out bridges—"

Ethel gave the newscast no attention until the word "bridges" snapped her to sudden action. Her hands gripped Pete's arm, and there was a plea in the depths of her limpid eyes as she urged:

"You must come with me right now! You must talk to my father and tell him how serious things are. He won't believe me, though I've often tried to tell him. But he may believe you."

Pete jumped at the invitation. Tonight, this mystery girl wasn't going to slip from sight like the elusive ghost train. As Ethel opened the door on her side, Pete followed right after her, gripping her arm as they trudged knee deep through the snow along the path to the cottage. There Pete opened the door for Ethel, and they went through a little entry into a fair-sized room where a balding man of about forty was seated in an antique armchair by a crackling fire.

The place was more like an old-fashioned parlor than a modern living room. There were oil lamps on the tables, and the plain walls were adorned with embroidered samplers and lithographic prints. An oil stove that reminded Pete of an upright boiler provided extra heat in another corner. There was a high-backed sofa at one side of the room, with a straight-backed chair and a rocker directly opposite.

Ethel introduced the balding man as her father, Henry Barsden, and he promptly waved Pete to the straight-backed chair. Barsden's eyes were sharp and gray, like Ethel's, as they gave Pete a gimlet probe. Then, turning to his daughter, Barsden queried:

"Mr. Dunning isn't the young man you went with to the doctor's, is he?"

"No, father." Ethel's voice became a dull monotone. "That was Bob Trebor. He happened to be driving by, and I stopped him."

Barsden nodded. "Well, the doctor will be here soon, and he will tell me that I am going to be all right, if I ever can be all right again—after this."

Barsden was looking squarely at his daughter now, and to Pete, it seemed that both had that same hypnotic stare. Perhaps it was the strange monotone of their voices that furthered the impression. Pete could sense the impact of Ethel's words:

"Father, you must leave here. I mean it. Now."

"You've told me that before, Ethel, but I've stayed."

"But you can't go on living with things that are dead and gone. You can't."

"Why not? Memories are far better than hopes. You should know that, Ethel."

"I do know it. But you can take your memories with you."

Henry Barsden turned to Pete Dunning and asked:

"Did you come here to tell me this, too?"

"I can tell you that there's a big flood coming," returned Pete. "I heard the radio reports in my car. So I want to be on my way before that covered bridge goes out, which it soon will."

Pete turned toward the door, and Barsden arose from his chair to follow. On the way, Pete heard Barsden say to Ethel:

"You are right, daughter. You have tried time and again to convince me, but you have always come into the house alone. This time you have brought a young man who tells me practically the same thing. The past is dead, and I must live for the future. I shall go."

By then, Pete had opened the front door, and despite the driving sleet that had supplanted the swirling snow, Pete's car was plainly outlined at the end of the path, for he had left the door open, and the dome light had turned on automatically. Thanks also to that open door, the sound of the radio was coming full blast. A weathercaster was just repeating the storm warnings, and as he finished, the program switched to a blare of music.

As Pete glanced back over his shoulder, he saw Henry Barsden standing rigid, his eyes fixed in an unbelieving stare, his mouth wide open, as though trying to drink in the discordant sounds of jive that his ears already heard. Then Ethel, still wearing her coat and bonnet, motioned Barsden back.

"You'll catch cold here, father," she declared, "and if you do, you won't be able to leave soon, as you promised. You'd better go back by the fire, while I see Mr. Dunning on his way."

The door closed, and Pete was alone with Ethel, trudging through the snow again, his hand under her arm.

"I'll come back when the weather is better," Pete promised, "and if the bridge is gone, I'll find another route. It's nice knowing you, and I'm glad I met your dad. You're lucky to have him, Ethel. And I'd say that you're the one thing he is living for!"

They were close to the car, now, but somehow, Pete had lost his grip on Ethel's arm, and when he turned to say good-bye, the girl was gone. She couldn't have returned to the house that quickly and there was no sign of her along the path. Pete reached the car, and as he backed it, the headlights glimmered on a side path, leading off among the trees, but Ethel couldn't have gone that way, for the path ended in a stone wall that looked like part of a square enclosure.

Now the headlights were streaming down the pathway to the house itself, and Pete could clearly see two tracks through the snow. Figuring that one set was his, the other Ethel's, he tried to see where one trail veered off, only to realize that both tracks were his own. He had made one going to the house, the other coming back!

Yet all the way going, and at least part way coming back, the girl had been trudging along right beside him!

Pete sat transfixed by the glare of the headlights on that glistening path. Amid the mingled thoughts that were pounding through his brain came the increasing tumult of the creek, as though it called to him to be on his way. Grimly, Pete swung the wagon full about, sped up the slope and over the trembling covered bridge, all in one desperate spurt. Then he reached a maze of roads that were more confusing than ever, for tonight the sleet was freezing to the windshield, blurring the road ahead. Somehow, Pete made his way to Route 44 and from there, the road rose toward Iron Mountain, the air became colder, and the sleet soon turned to snow.

Pete was so tired when he reached the inn that he slept until noon the next day, to find the storm still raging. It all turned to rain during the next few days, and even after it cleared, radio and TV reports continued to tell of washed-out bridges and heavily flooded highways. When Pete finally drove back to the city, he managed to avoid the worst of it, but he was amazed by the changes that he saw along the countryside.

The vast expanses of snow had vanished, and spring was in the air. But streams were still on the rampage, flooding fields and sweeping along fallen trees and other debris. That changed when Pete reached the reservoir area, for there the brooks and creeks funneled into the reservoirs themselves, feeding them a huge, welcome runoff of surplus water.

Pete's editor had been smart indeed to order the picture story when he did, for now stone walls, meadows, and other relics of the past had vanished beneath the rising surface of every reservoir that Pete viewed. Even a few rowboats were afloat, and although the reservoirs were still comparatively low, they looked normal. Somehow, Pete's adventures on those snowy nights seemed almost forgotten, too, but he was determined to solve their riddle if he could.

With that in mind, Pete hauled into the Woodland Service Station, looking for the one man who might help. Today, old Smedley was on duty, but his wrinkled face went taut and his manner became noncommital when Pete asked if he'd ever heard of a family named Barsden.

"I might have," Smedley declared, "but maybe I mightn't. Why are you so interested, and what might your name be?"

"I'm interested because you sent me on a road where I saw a ghost train and where I met a girl who"—Pete paused—"oh, skip it! Nobody believes me. You asked my name; it's Pete Dunning—"

"Pete Dunning!" Smedley cackled excitedly as he pulled a folded newspaper from his pocket and spread it wide. "The fellow who wrote this piece about the reservoirs, with all these pictures showing how they looked when they were the lowest ever?"

Pete nodded. "I'm the man."

"Then I believe you." Smedley shoved his hand forward for a shake, as he looked around to see that no one else was near. "Trouble is, nobody believes me when I tell about things I've heard. Maybe they fit with what you've seen, Mr. Dunning. Suppose I slide out a few hours and go along with you, to show you—"

Pete interrupted by gesturing Smedley into the car. They took the short cut to the bridge that Smedley had originally mentioned. As they swung across it, Pete remembered something and pointed to another bridge a little way up the reservoir.

"That's where we saw a line of trucks come across."

You didn't see any trucks." Smedley shook his head. "That's an old railroad bridge they don't use no more. Take the road over toward it, and I'll show you."

Pete complied and found that Smedley was right. The bridge no longer had any approaches; they were grown over with thick brush. Pete had to get out of the wagon and mount a fence to see that the bridge had no roadway and that its track had been taken up. Getting back into the car, he remarked:

"People must drive past that bridge without noticing it!"

"That's right," agreed Smedley. "Now, if we go back and take the road you got onto by mistake, we'll come to where the old railroad line came through."

Within ten minutes they were there. But instead of a grade crossing with a flashing signal and a big bump over a single track, there was only a slight hump, from which they looked to left and right to trace what had once been the railroad's right of way. It was barely discernible, and Pete realized that with snowdrifts over it—as when he first came along—it wouldn't even be suspected.

"Bert and I must have seen that ghost train coming over the old bridge," mused Pete. "Then we got to this crossing just about when it did. But what has all this to do with sleigh bells—"

Pete broke off, studying old Smedley, whose eyes were narrowed in a faraway stare. In a reminiscent tone, Smedley began:

"It goes back to around 1900, before they'd added the last reservoirs to the chain. There was a girl named Ethel Barsden, who lived down in Pine Hollow with her father, Henry Barsden, or Hank, as his friends called him.

"He was took sick, Hank was, and one night when he was feeling worse, Ethel got a fellow named Bob Trebor to drive her to the doctor's in a sleigh. She told Hank she'd come back with the doctor, and if he was delayed, she'd get somebody else to drive her back. But when Ethel and Bob got to this crossing, they were in such a hurry, they didn't see the signal, or maybe it just wasn't working. Anyway, the night express came through and clipped them.

"It was during a big snowstorm, and from then on, whenever anyone came driving through on the same sort of night, they would hear sleigh bells ahead of the crossing signal, like a preliminary warning. And after the train went through, they'd see a girl right about up there"—Smedley pointed along the road and gestured for Pete to start the car—"waving for them to stop."

Pete's response came in an awed tone: "Ethel's ghost!"

"It must have been," Smedley assured him. "Over the next seven or eight years, there were dozens of persons swore they'd seen the same girl begging them to take her home to her sick father, which they all of them did. First it was guys in sleighs, but later, automobiles took over, you know, the kind they call tin lizzies. They all took the same route and with a few of them, it happened twice."

They were moving along that route now, and Smedley indicated a road that skirted the reservoir. They followed it to a point where Smedley said, "Turn left here." Pete hesitated, for the guard rail was there, but a moment later, he saw that it went off at an angle to form a turnout. Then he stopped on the very brink of the reservoir, with only the cables of the rail beween.

"That's where the old road went down into Pine Hollow," continued Smedley. "See it here, on this picture your photographer took?" He opened the paper and pointed to the picture that showed two stone abutments looming up on opposite sides of a V-shaped gully. "That's where the old covered bridge was. And if you follow down the other side"—Smedley was tracing it on the picture—"you come plumb to where Barsden's cottage stood under the pine trees."

Pete wished now that he had known all that when Bert shot the picture. For now the water had risen so high that it covered the abutments, though Pete fancied that he could make out one, just beneath the surface.

"So they damned the hollow and turned it into a reesrvoir," observed Pete, "and later they abandoned the railroad and pulled up the track. But why didn't that wind up the ghost stuff?"

"It did," returned old Smedley, "for maybe sixty years or so, until this winter, when the water got so low that everything was high and dry again, clear down past where the covered bridge used to be, to the place where Barsden's cottage was."

Pete was incredulous at first; then an idea dawned.

"So it all came back!" he exclaimed. "Like a living reflection from the past. First the ghost of a train—then the ghost of a girl—finally, even the ghost of her father, there in his cottage—"

"You've pegged it perfect, Mr. Dunning," complimented Smedley. "You see, I heard the other side of the story, too."

"The other side of the story? Whose?"

"Hank Barsden's. What do you suppose was happening with him, those snowy winter nights, during the next seven or eight years? Why do you suppose he was always wanting to stay in that cottage and never willing to leave?"

"I wouldn't know," admitted Pete. "It's beyond me."

"It was beyond me, too," Smedley chuckled, "until you brought in the final word today. You see, I knew Hank Barsden. Old Hank, we called him because he was pretty old when I was just a kid. I used to go fishing with him on Pine Hollow Reservoir down there, and he'd point down to where his cottage was and he'd tell me all about it.

"You see, there were winter nights when Hank would hear sleigh bells, too. They were outside the cottage and he'd listen until they drove away. Real sleigh bells, they were, meaning somebody had stopped out front to let a person out."

"You mean real people in real sleighs, bringing home Ethel's ghost—as I did!"

"Like you did, Mr. Dunning," Smedley nodded, "which is why I can believe

Hank's story now. But wait! There's more." He cackled in anticipation. Then: "Always, when those sleigh bells were fading away, Hank Barsden would look up and see his daughter Ethel, just as she looked the night she died. She would tell him that she had come back as she had promised and then she would beg him to leave and stop living with his memories, because soon the valley itself would be gone. But Hank just wouldn't listen."

"I can understand that." Eyes half shut, Pete could see Ethel's face floating above him, with that earnest expression in her gaze. "After all, if he kept seeing his daughter, he wouldn't want to lose her, ghost or no ghost."

"That's how Hank figured it," Smedley said. "Later on, instead of sleighs, he'd hear cars rattle up and chug away. Always, Ethel would come in and say the same thing, and Hank would argue the point, hoping to bring her back. He knew they wanted the hollow for a reservoir, but he was going to keep on fighting it, until one night, a strange thing happened."

"A strange thing!" echoed Pete. "As if the rest wasn't!"

"A couple of times," continued Smedley, "Ethel walked in without Hank even hearing a car drive up. Then one night, she walked in with a young fellow wearing clothes that struck Hank as funny, a hat with a feather in it, but hardly any brim, and an overcoat that looked like the bottom half had been cut off it."

Spontaneously, Pete's hands went to the pork-pie hat that he was wearing, then drifted down to the bottom edge of his short car coat.

"This young chap sided with Ethel," Smedley related. "He said the covered bridge was so shaky that it would soon be going out. Hank finally agreed that he would clear out soon. But he kept puzzling why he hadn't heard the car, so he went to the door and saw it, a crazier-looking thing than he ever could have imagined.

"Hank said it set low to the ground, like a sleigh, but that it was built like a truck, except that it had windows and seats, like a car. Hank could tell that, because the inside was lighted up. But what got him most was, there was music coming from it, like from a phonograph. But in those days, phonographs had to have great big horns, to be heard as loud as that, so big that you couldn't have put one in that car. Now, what do you think of that?"

Before Pete could respond, Smedley answered his own question, saying:

"I was just a kid when old Hank told me that, but now I'd say that Hank must have looked fifty or sixty years into the future and seen some fellow dressed about like you are, who had a station wagon just like this, and that the thing Hank thought was a phonograph was really a car radio turned on full. What would you say, Mr. Dunning?"

"I would say, Mr. Smedley, that you just about pegged it."

"Ethel never came back after that," Smedley added, "because Hank packed up and moved out as soon as he could. The old bridge lasted just long enough for sledges to haul his stuff over it."

"You say that Ethel never came back," queried Pete. "But where did she go between those times her father saw her?"

"To the place where she belonged." Solemnly, Smedley pointed to the newspaper photo, indicating the square, stone-walled enclosure. "That's where she was buried, in the family cemetery, off in the pinewoods. The trees were chopped down before the hollow was flooded, that's why they aren't in the picture. So that's about it."

Pete drove back to the Woodland Service Station and dropped Smedley off there, with due thanks. But all the way into the city, Pete found himself pondering more and more. Obviously, his mind could have gone back to the past, to see two ghosts, those of Ethel and her father, Henry Barsden. That made more sense than assuming that Ethel could have projected herself into the future, to see two living people, her father, and Pete Dunning.

Or did it?

What about Henry Barsden? He had been definitely alive the night he had seen two ghosts: one, a girl from the past, his daughter Ethel, who was dead; the other, a man from the future, Pete Dunning who hadn't even been born!

Still wondering whose story it really was, Pete decided it might be old Smedley's. Maybe many people thought they heard sleigh bells on snowy nights, or fancied they met girls like Ethel, who introduced them to her father. From such reports, Smedley could have concocted a fanciful story of his own to impress people like Pete. But at least, he hadn't explained the ghost train; not convincingly.

Just to be able to write that off as pure imagination, Pete stopped in to see George Larriman, the travel editor of the New York *Classic*, who arranged special excursions for railroad fans. In his most jocular tone, Pete remarked:

"Here's a good one, George, a real funny one. Did you ever hear of a ghost train?"

"Why, yes," replied George, "but there's nothing funny about it. Its real name was the New England Limited. Back around 1900 it made the overnight run on the Short Line Route, which has been abandoned since."

"And they called it the ghost train? Why?"

"Because all the cars were painted an absolute white, like no other train before or since. It looked real spooky gliding through the night. Pete!" George's tone gave way to alarm. "What's the matter? Why, you went so white, you looked like a ghost yourself!"

Pete was smiling by then, a forced smile, as he managed to thank George for the information and make a mechanical exit from the travel office. But once outside, he really had to brace himself, because he felt very weak indeed.

For all Pete Dunning knew, he was the ghost hero of his own weird adventure, who belonged in that strange lost limbo known as the Twilight Zone!

Beyond the Rim

Night after night, the scrawny horses had plodded westward, dragging the creaking, dust-coated covered wagons. Each morning they had halted only when the blazing sun had risen so high above the desert that its heat became unbearable. Yet, by midafternoon, Christopher Horn, the elected leader of the little band of pioneers, was up and about, rousing the men who were sleeping in the shade of the wagons, goading them to make ready for another start.

In this autumn of the year 1847, Christopher Horn was dedicated to the proposition of getting these worn-out men, horses, and wagons to California, even if they collapsed in the process. Horn felt that reducing the hazards of the road would shorten the time of the journey. He had sold the others on that idea; until now their patience had run short, but so far they had not expressed themselves on that point, for they knew that Horn's patience was still shorter — with one exception.

As Horn stalked among the sleeping men, chafing at their inactivity, he came to the back of his own wagon. There, the grim, hard-set lines of his face dropped like a discarded mask. Horn's tone was anxious, hushed, as he spoke to a woman who sat silently beside a crude cot, on which a child was moving restlessly.

"How is he, Martha?"

"The poor little thing is burning up with fever," the woman replied in a hopeless tone. "If I only had a damp cloth, Chris —"

Martha paused, staring beyond her husband's shoulder to a sheepskin water bag hanging at the rear of the wagon. Without a word, Horn brought a handkerchief from his pocket, poured enough water from the bag to dampen it, and handed the cloth to Martha. Gratefully, Martha bathed the boy's feverish forehead, knowing full well that Chris would cut his own water ration to allow for it. For if Horn drove others unsparingly, he spared himself even less. That explained how he had so far held the full confidence of this pioneer band.

But now that confidence had worn thin. As Horn turned from the wagon, he noticed that the other men had begun to stir. His face became a grim mask again, as he saw an opportunity for an early start.

"All right, men," Horn announced. "Let's be on the move."

The men looked at one another and began to shake their heads. One of them, a rangy chap named Charlie Crowell, stepped forward as their spokesman.

"We're ready to move, Chris," declared Charlie, "but not in the direction you want. We've been doing a lot of talking and a lot of thinking. We reckon we ought to turn back."

"Turn back!" Horn's eyes glared in furious disbelief. "There's no turning back, not after coming this far!"

"Look, Chris, you've been telling us that there's Apache country due south, that there's bad Indians down there —"

"That's right, which is why we're traveling due west, so as to avoid them."

"And meanwhile, we're running short on food and we're just about out of water."

"Those are the chances we have to take. There's been others over this trail ahead of us, so we know we'll come to water —"

"And what if the Apaches come up this way and find us first? They travel in big parties, Chris, and we've only got half a dozen rifles among us."

"That's another chance we have to take."

"We don't have to take it if we turn back. We figure we're about at the end of our rope. We're hungry and we're sick. If we don't turn back now, we'll die out here."

Horn's big fists tightened in a grip as hard as the lines of his face.

"You turn back and I'll guarantee you'll die!" he replied sternly. "Try to go back over fifteen hundred miles to St. Louis and you'll leave your bones bleached on the desert, or you'll have your scalps taken off, or you'll freeze to death in a mountain pass."

"Sorry, Chris," Charlie declared, "but there's no use going on. We're all dead tired —"

"And we were all dead tired a week ago!" Horn snapped. "And a month ago and a month before that. We were dodging Indian war parties back in Kansas, and we near froze to death in Colorado. We were out of our minds with thirst before we came to those last water holes. Now that it's all behind you, you want to go through that heat and cold and misery again. Does that make sense?"

The men had been moving away, ready to hitch up the horses, which could only mean that they were still intent upon starting the return trip. Now, something in Horn's tone caused them to hesitate. Charlie noted it and put a final argument.

"It's better we should go back, Chris, because at least we'll know what to expect —"

"That's just it!" Horn said. "Just the reason why you shouldn't go back. Maybe this time you won't be so lucky. But ahead of us, there's only four or five hundred miles to go. It's likely we'll strike water sooner than if we turned back. What's more, there's a war on with Mexico — remember? So the United States Army has been over this trail ahead of us, and you can bet they've made those Apaches skedaddle. The only Indians we'll meet will be the friendly kind. They'll trade us food for trinkets."

The men were really pausing now, and women were joining them from the wagons. Horn's throat was dry, his voice was husky, but his tone was convincing as he added:

"We can't stop now. If we do, we're dead. That's gospel truth. But give me one more week. I'll get us through. I promise you that."

The men looked to Charlie, who shook his head dubiously as he walked over to the nearest wagon and looked down into a barrel that was fixed on its side.

"This barrel is nearly out of water," he declared, "and the rest are most as bad. We could get back to a water hole within a week. I'd go along with you, Chris, if you could promise us water up ahead sooner than that."

"I'll get you water. I'll find it, Charlie—"

"How, Chris? With one of those forked sticks that you hold out ahead of you? The kind that dips down when it comes above a hidden stream?"

"A divining rod." Horn nodded. "I've done water-witching in my time. I could find it with a hazel stick."

"If there was any water to find."

"There may be," Horn said grimly. He turned and pointed up a slight slope, where the white sand of the desert formed the edge of a bowl against the deep blue of the sky. "Suppose I go up over that rim, there to the west. If I find water, or even signs of it" — his voice almost broke — "you'll believe me, won't you? You'll go on?"

That plea won the sympathy of the listeners. Not once had they doubted Horn's sincerity, otherwise he could never have forced them this far along the trail. Again, Charlie spoke for all:

"We'll go on if you really think there's water, Chris."

As Horn turned toward his own wagon, one of the women pressed a restraining hand upon his arm.

"We'll need more than water, Chris," she said. "We'll need food. And you'll need medicine, Chris, for your own sick child."

"I know," assured Chris. "We'll find all those things, if we just keep on."

Christopher Horn stopped by the wagon to bring out his loaded rifle. It was Martha's hand, now, that pressed his shoulder and he heard her whisper:

"Chris, I heard you say you were going over the rim. If you don't find anything else, you might look for a shady spot, a quiet spot, Chris, for a last resting place —"

Horn's face had softened, as before, but now it turned as hard as iron. His tone was sharp, determined:

"I won't talk about burying our son. Not while there's a breath of life in him." He turned, stepped away from the wagon, and called to the men:

"Stay close to the wagons. If you hear a shot, I may be picking off a rabbit or some other game. A couple of shots won't matter unless I fire them quick and close together. Then you will know it's Indians — and bad ones."

With that, Christopher Horn stalked off on his way over the rim, for a rendezvous — with what?

Hopefully, a water hole. Possibly, a few rabbits. Ominously, a tribe of Apaches. Perhaps, an enticing mirage. Almost certainly, just another patch of desert. Inconceivably, an adventure into a world that did not exist, at least not at that exact moment, yet which in its way — and in its time — was just as real and just as solid as the little world of Christopher Horn.

All during that westward plod, Horn's little world had been the wagon train, which had been following a steady course, but still had too far to go and too little time in which to make it. Yet, Horn, of all that party, was the man most dedicated to saving the wagon train.

And why?

Because his heart was there. His heart and that of his wife Martha, who had no more reason — and perhaps a great deal less — to be with the wagon train at all, except for their mutual interest, Christopher Horn, Jr.

That was why they were going West. To make a new life for their son. Everyone else in the party was getting away from the past. Only Christopher and Martha Horn were aiming for the future. So when Christopher Horn went over the rim, he was wishing that he could project himself miles ahead, all in a matter of moments, so he could bring back a true as well as encouraging report of a goal that the party soon could reach.

Unable to conquer the limitations of distance, Horn tried to shake off the shackles of time as he went beyond the rim. Through sheer intensity of mind, he visioned the future, in terms of the surrounding scene.

Across the vast expanse of desert stretched a wide, flat surface, running from one horizon to the other, a grayish strip amid a breadth of gleaming white. On one side, that singular belt was flanked by something even more remarkable, a row of stocky trees, all of the same height, with short cross branches of equal length, connected by long, taut ropes some twenty feet or so above the ground.

During the long trek west, Horn had seen forests of dead trees, some burned out, others blighted, a few drowned by flooded swamplands. Here, someone apparently had chopped down thousands of surrounding trees, leaving only one straight line, all equally spaced. The trees had then been trimmed to size and roped together so they would not fall.

But why all that bother over a row of dead trees? And what was the purpose of the wide, flat strip of smooth gray stone that ran beside them? As Horn stepped gingerly upon its surface, he felt a tremendous heat surge up. This stretch of stone, level as a billiard table, was no improvement over the desert trail. Horses and mules would wear out their shoes and lame their legs after a few miles of such going, if the heat didn't suffocate them before they had gotten that far.

From the distant horizon, where the gray stone pathway narrowed to a pinpoint, Horn saw a thing approaching that reminded him of a cross between a beetle and a centipede. He'd been warned against poisonous lizards called Gila monsters that were common in this territory, but he soon realized that this creature was something far more formidable. It emitted a huge roar as it increased in size, until Horn realized that it was bigger than an elephant and faster than a cyclone.

Frantically, but boldly, the amazed pioneer aimed his puny rifle at the roaring monster, hoping at least to divert it from its path, for it seemed intent upon swooping down on Horn as its prey. Then, when the thing was almost upon him, Horn dived for the sandy waste beside the stony pathway, feeling certain that the thing would pounce on him and perhaps devour him in a single gulp.

Horn's gun went off as he scrambled away; he felt a stinging sensation in his left forearm. The monstrous thing roared on past, creating a sudden concussion that turned the desert air into a furnace blast. Then the menace was gone, and Horn, dazed, was picking himself up from a ditch and looking at his arm, all bloody from a flesh wound. Methodically, he ripped off a portion of his sleeve and used it as a temporary bandage, congratulating himself that the bullet had missed the bone.

Now, half angry, half fearful, Horn tucked his rifle beneath his good arm and walked along beside the smooth, wide pathway toward the distant lair from which the murderous monster had emerged. He was ready either to fight or run, if another of the brutes should come roaring his way. Meanwhile, he glanced warily from left to right, expecting that something even worse might come stalking from the surrounding desert.

That was how Horn happened to see the painted sign that stated:

JOE'S AIRFLIGHT CAFE
GAS STATION
HALF MILE AHEAD

None of it made sense to Horn except the bottom line. That, at least, urged him on to what he decided must be some human habitation. He was wondering where he was, thinking that he must have come much farther than a few hundred yards beyond the rim. Actually, Horn had, but not in terms of space, for right now he was just about where he would have been, had he been plodding onward in the year 1847. But it happened that he was out of place in time and was traversing that same stretch in the year 1964.

The amazing pathway was a modern superhighway; the monster that had roared along it was a big truck, heading east. The driver, mistaking Horn for some crazed sniper — which in a sense he was — had simply barreled straight ahead, hoping that the man with the rifle would hit the desert dust, which he had.

Still grimy with that dust, Horn reached Joe's place without further incident and began to feel more at home. The Airflight Café was a simple clapboard structure with a lunchroom in front and a general store in back. There were two gasoline pumps out front, but since they weren't in operation at the moment, Horn took them to be decorations, nothing more. What interested Horn more was Joe Scarney, the proprietor, who was sitting in a wicker chair out front.

Scarney pushed back his cowboy hat and gave Horn an appraising survey which included the pioneer's rifle and wounded arm. Crazier freaks than Horn had wandered in from the highway, so Joe accepted this stranger with an affable greeting: "Howdy."

Horn nodded in return, then thumbed back toward the highway as he queried anxiously:

"Did you see it? That monster?"

"What monster?"

"That big animal-like thing that roared at me and almost hit me."

Joe rose from the chair to give Horn a closer survey and be ready for whatever happened next.

"I didn't see anything, mister," Joe said. "If there was anything, it never got to here."

"But it must have," Horn insisted, "because it came from this direction and it went by me, only a half mile back."

"You wouldn't mean the truck, would you?"

"The truck? What's a truck?"

Genuine puzzlement showed on Horn's face, enough for Joe to change the subject abruptly.

"Do you feel all right?" he asked. "I mean, how long have you been out on the desert?"

"A good part of a year. Leastwise, we've been traveling that long since we started from Ohio. I had six wagons to begin with. One of them was burned by Indians. Two of them turned back."

"Indians," mused Joe. "Wagons. Say, friend, why don't you come inside and rest up a bit?" His eyes shifted to Horn's bandage. "We'll have a look at that arm, too."

"I did that to myself," Horn admitted ruefully. "I jumped away from that monster so fast I landed on my face, and my gun went off. It's just a flesh wound, though."

"I'll have Mary Lou look at it," said Joe, beckoning Horn into the diner. "Mary Lou's my wife. She used to be a registered nurse when we were living over in Phoenix."

From Horn's blank look, Joe could see that his last statements had not registered. New wonderment showed on Horn's dryish features as he looked along the lunch counter and saw the coffee urn, the electric mixer, the napkin holder, and particularly the neon lights, which seemed to fascinate him. As Joe eased him to a counter stool, Horn licked his lips as though about to ask a question. That gave Joe an idea.

"Guess you're pretty thirsty, stranger," he said, stepping behind the counter. "How about a drink of water?"

Joe drew a glass of water from the soda fountain, while Horn watched, more fascinated than ever. Realizing it was for him, Horn forgot his injured arm and grabbed the glass with both hands. He gulped the water eagerly, until the glass was half empty. Then, with an effort, he restrained himself, taking the rest in short sips. Joe Scarney was impressed, for that was the way a man would drink if he had been rationing himself on water. Now, as Joe filled the glass again, Horn put an eager query:

"Where does all this water come from?"

"It's piped here," replied Joe, "from the reservoir over in Hidden Canyon."

Joe gestured toward a front window and Horn turned painfully to look in that direction.

"You mean off past that long row of trees?" he asked.

It was Joe's turn to be puzzled. "What trees?"

"The ones with the branches gone," Horn replied, "with the ropes between them, alongside where the monster came chasing after me."

"You must mean the telephone poles."

"Telephone poles?" Horn shook his head. "I reckon they are poles, alrighty, but I wouldn't know about the rest of it." He paused, then came back to the important subject. "You say there's water over that way?"

"Yes, just beyond those low hills. They're about five miles from here, on a beeline. The hills form a double ridge, and there's a creek runs in between, though you'd never think it, the ridge is so barren."

Horn nodded. "Only five miles away, you say?"

"That's right. In the old days, parties used to go on past it, never figuring there was water there. Steady now, mister!" Joe's tone showed alarm.

Horn's gaze had taken on a dedicated gleam, showing the almost fanatical intensity that had so often won the other members of the wagon train to his way of thinking. He was coming to his feet, reaching for his rifle, which he had laid against the lunch counter. His idea now was to follow that beeline Joe had mentioned until he reached Hidden Canyon. But the desert heat, his sheer exhaustion, and loss of blood were taking their toll. Joe's admonition, "Steady, now!" was warranted, for Horn swayed as he neared the door.

Hurriedly, Joe came from behind the counter and supported Horn on one side as Mary Lou made a timely arrival from the kitchen and caught him as he swayed the other way. Next, they settled Horn in a little booth at one end of the lunchroom and while Joe kept admonishing, "Take it easy, friend," Mary Lou brought a bowl of water and some bandages. Soon she was dressing Horn's wounded arm.

"He shot himself by accident," Joe told his wife, "with this." He held up the rifle, which Horn had willingly relinquished. Then, admiring the gun, Joe added "Say, this is a real oldtimer. Kind of an antique piece, isn't it?"

"I bought it brand new, just before we started out," Horn retorted indignantly. He shook his head. "But I've used it a lot, so I guess it does look old. We're running low on bullets. You wouldn't have any here, would you?"

"We don't carry any ammunition," Mary Lou declared. "This isn't a hunting area."

"No?" Horn was surprised. "What about Indians? It's Apache country south of here, isn't it?"

"Why, sure," began Mary Lou, "but they are not hostile Indians — at least not any more —"

She broke off and went quickly to a medicine chest beneath the counter, where she brought out a bottle of pills. Joe, meanwhile, was humoring Horn regarding the Indians.

"The Apaches are a long way south now," Joe said. "A long, long way —"

"Then it's safe to head for Hidden Canyon?" Horn asked. "I can take the wagons there? We can find water there?"

"Of course. All the water you need."

"And the water you need is right here," Mary Lou put in, in the pleasant but efficient manner she had used as a nurse. "A whole glassful, to help you take these penicillin tablets. They ought to keep any infection from your arm."

Horn took the two tablets that Mary Lou proffered. After he swallowed them, he glanced around again and it seemed to dawn on him that everything must be beneficial in a wonderful world like this. As he eyed the bottle in Mary Lou's hand, Horn asked:

"Could I buy those pills off you? I've got a real sick boy back in the wagon" — he glanced toward the window — "if I can ever find those wagons. You say these pills are good for sickness?"

"It depends on what the sickness is."

"Whatever it is, my boy has got it bad, nigh to death."

Joe was gesturing for Mary Lou to let Horn have the bottle of tablets. With a smile Mary Lou handed it over. "It's yours. Take it."

"No, no, I've got to pay for it," Horn insisted. He drew some coins from his pocket, counted them and placed them in Mary Lou's hand. Then, earnestly, he added: "I know fifteen cents is a lot for a bottle of pills, but they're worth that to me, Believe me, they are."

Horn turned away abruptly, to prevent Mary Lou from returning any of the money. It was Joe who started to smile now, until he saw that Mary Lou was staring in amazement at two tiny silver coins and five large ones made of copper.

"Look, Joe!" exclaimed Mary Lou. "You know how I've been going through the coins in the cash register, hoping maybe to find some Buffalo nickels, or Liberty quarters? These go back a hundred years before that! These little coins are silver half dimes and the others are big copper cents."

"They're worth a lot of money, Mary Lou?"

"Maybe a couple of dollars apiece, because they all are like new. I'll look them up in a coin book, and check their dates. But why should this man be handing them out? Where did he come from, Joe?"

"I wouldn't know. I'm beginning to wonder —"

Joe paused to watch Horn, who was studying the juke box at the end of the lunch counter, fascinated by its glittering chrome and the flickering colors of its neon lights. Horn's gaze went up to a calendar on the wall above, and his eyes showed new interest as he saw a large reproduction of an old lithograph, depicting a covered wagon and a group of pioneers.

"Say, that could be one of our wagons!" Horn exclaimed, "and the people in the picture look like our party, too. Where did you get it, mister?" Horn paused and noted the printed wording, reading it aloud: "Compliments of Pioneer-West Insurance Company, October 1964 —" Horn broke off and swung about, staring at the young couple in outright horror.

"Is this a joke?" he demanded hoarsely. "It's October all right, but it's October 1847, not October 1964." His eyes darted from the coffee urn, back to the calendar, then to the juke box, and finally out toward the gas pumps. "What's happening to me? Where are we? Who are you people? I've got to get back —"

Horn sprang to the door, snatched it open, repeating, "I've got to get back — get back to my own people!" Once outside, he was dashing toward the highway when an approaching roar attracted his attention, and he turned to see a red convertible streak by. As his eyes followed it, he saw a huge, silvery interstate bus looming from the other direction, and took it to be another incredible creature singling him out as its prey. Frantically, he raced back into the lunchroom, shouting, "More of those monsters — they're after me — help me, somebody, help me — tell me where I am — and why. Help me!"

Horn stumbled and sprawled against the counter, sinking to his knees as he turned his harrowed, piteous face toward Joe and Mary Lou. The lunchroom, despite its modern gadgets, had become his only refuge. That much Joe and Mary Lou could understand, though it seemed impossible that Horn could have hiked this far along the highway without having gained some familiarity with modern transportation. But Horn's distress won their sympathy. They helped him into the back room to a couch, where he sagged, moaning, with his eyes half closed.

"I'll stand by," Joe said softly to Mary Lou, "while you phone Doc Fletcher and tell him to get here pronto. Explain that it's a hitchhiker, took down with the heat."

Horn's moans subsided in the quiet of the back room, and he was half asleep when Dr. Fletcher, a stolid man in his mid-fifties, arrived about thirty minutes later. By then, two truckers had stopped for coffee and hamburgers, and Joe had asked them to stay until the doctor arrived, saying there was a sick man in the back room who might act up. Mary Lou had told Dr. Fletcher all he needed to know, and he went right in to see the patient.

There was one thing that had not changed too much during the course of a century; that was the bedside manner of the general medical practitioner. Dr. Fletcher must have reminded Christopher Horn of a country doctor of the horse and buggy era, for they chatted casually while the physican took Horn's pulse, and Dr. Fletcher soon learned essential facts as to the patient's condition as well as his past life.

When Dr. Fletcher came from the back room, he sat down at the counter, took a swallow from a cup of coffee that Mary Lou had poured for him, and met Joe's inquiring look with the statement:

"Malnutrition is the man's major problem. It could be responsible for his delusions, but he traces his imaginary life quite rationally. He thinks he's living in 1847, and he's anxious to go back over the rim, so he can lead the pioneers and their wagons to the creek over in Hidden Canyon."

"And did he tell you," asked Joe, "how he came to know about that creek?"

"Yes, he said you told him, and he asked me to thank you for it. He said he'd never have thought of heading that way himself."

"Did he say anything about his boy being sick?"

"Yes, and from the way he described the symptoms I'd call it pneumonia." Dr. Fletcher turned to Mary Lou. "He wants to thank you for the pills you gave him. Penicillin tablets, weren't they?"

Mary Lou nodded, but it was Joe who asked:

"What do we do about him, Doc?"

"I'll call the sheriff's office," Dr. Fletcher stepped to the telephone. "They'll find out where he really comes from. It's puzzling, though. Those clothes of his are real old-fashioned homespun, like they wore a hundred years ago. When I looked at his throat, I saw the fillings in his teeth. No modern dentist would have put those in."

"That gun he brought with him," exclaimed Joe. "It's a real antique, Doc, and he gave Mary Lou some old coins —"

Dr. Fletcher waved an interruption as his call was answered.

"Hello. . . . Dr. Fletcher speaking. Is Sheriff Valentine there? . . . Out on the highway? All the better. . . . Radio him to come to Joe's Café . . . We've got a man here who needs looking after. No, not violent . . ."

Hanging up, Dr. Fletcher turned to Joe and Mary Lou:

"At least he's as calm as any man would be if he suddenly thought that he'd waked up a hundred years past his time!"

At that moment, Christopher Horn was calm indeed. He was sitting up on the couch in the back room, staring at objects that were only slightly strange. The electric clock could have been mechanical; none of the floor lamps was lighted; the TV in the corner wasn't turned on. Other things gave him confidence, such as a strip of old-fashioned carpet, a rocking chair that had belonged to Mary Lou's grandaunt, and a large mirror in an old gilt frame.

There was a bookcase in the corner, with a row of books bound all alike. Horn thumbed through them, amazed by the pictures they contained, for he had never seen photographs before. He tried to pronounce the title, "Encyclopedia," and he came to a book that said, "VOL. XI. HAW - IVA." Horn drew it out, looked up what he wanted, and rushed out to the lunchroom.

Dr. Fletcher was examining Horn's rifle, by the juke box. He propped the gun against the counter and quickly asked, "How do you feel now, friend?" But Horn didn't answer. He wasn't interested in either the doctor or the gun.

"Look at this!" he exclaimed, planting the encyclopedia volume on the counter. "Hear what it says in this big book: 'Horn, Christopher Jr., M.D. Famous for his early work in childhood diseases, including'—here he stumbled over an unfamiliar word — 'including vac-cine research.' That's what it says." Horn looked up, a faraway gaze in his eyes, and his tone became awed as he added: "That's my son. That's Chris."

Now Horn was looking at the silent listeners, meeting their unbelieving stares.

"You want to know why I'm so sure of it?" he demanded. He laid his finger on the open page. "Because it says, right here, 'Born 1839' — and that's the year that Chris was born. But right after that" — his tone went hollow — "it says, 'Died 1914' — and that I can't understand."

He closed the book and added:

"I guess, well — I guess I'm either crazy — or the world has turned upside down. But I think I got put here for a reason—" He planked his big hand on the volume that he had just closed. "Yes, for a reason. Maybe to make sure that what the book says will come true. But I've got to go now. You've been kind to me and I appreciate it. But I've got to get back — back where I belong."

Horn glanced along the counter and saw his rifle propped there. In his limber way, he stepped over there and picked it up before either Joe or the doctor could stop him. But as Horn started for the door, Dr. Fletcher moved to intercept him.

"We want to help you, Mr. Horn," the physician stated. "You need rest and medical attention. Come back and sit down. I've phoned for the authorities."

"The authorities? Who might they be?" Horn's tone went puzzled. "And what was it you said you did about them? What was that word you used? Well, never mind. Just forget it. I've got no time to find out."

Joe now had moved ahead to block the door. Horn started to shove past him, and Joe made a grab for the rifle, arguing as he did:

"Horn, you've got to stay here. You've got to listen to the doctor."

All anybody heard was the roar of Horn's rifle as it blasted. Apparently, it had gone off accidentally, for nobody was hit. A big chunk of plaster fell from the ceiling above the lunch counter, but that was the only damage. Joe fell back, however, and Mary Lou screamed, while Dr. Fletcher made a lunge for Horn, too late. Profiting by the excitement, Horn had flung the door open and was now on his way.

The only way that Horn knew was the highway. Monsters or no monsters, he had to follow it back to the sign he had seen earlier and cut over to the rim from there. He was running fast at first, then as he looked back and saw Joe standing by the gas pumps, Horn reduced his gait to a dog trot. Still, he kept glancing back, if only because Joe was shouting, "Horn! Come back!"

It was then that the sheriff's car pulled into the service station. Horn saw this new monster in one glance, and in the next, he saw it swallow Joe. Then, for the first time, Horn realized that those animal-like things were actually modern conveyances. Before, he had thought that they were mammoth creatures trying to chase him; now he knew differently, but too late. This time one was really after him.

With that, Horn cut off from the highway, knowing that the car couldn't follow. He saw the rim of the slope, off at a different angle, and he headed for it, hoping he could dodge from sight, beyond some of the giant cactus that loomed amid the desert's growth. There was a shriek of brakes behind him; then Joe and Sheriff Valentine sprang from the car and took up the chase on foot.

Exhausted though he was, Horn felt that he still could outrace them to the rim, and that once there, he would be on familiar ground. The sheriff was shouting, "Stop! In the name of the law, stop!" but he wasn't drawing a revolver to back the order. During those brief moments in the car, Joe had told the sheriff that Horn had so far been comparatively harmless, despite his careless way of letting his gun go off.

After all, neither Joe nor the sheriff could guess the important part that the rim had played, once Horn had come beyond it. So they had no idea that some strange trick of time might work in reverse. But Horn was counting on it, so desperately that when he was almost at the rim, he stumbled. In catching his feet, he lost the rifle, stumbled along a few feet more and fell again.

Something fell from Horn's pocket with a slight clatter. He came to his feet, realized that he had lost the rifle, and looked back for it. He saw the gun, rushed back to pick it up, and froze in momentary despair. Rolling down the slope, past the rifle, and gathering speed as it went, was the bottle containing the precious penicillin tablets!

Without another moment's hesitation, Horn forgot his gun and sprang down the slope to scoop up the bottle. Hardly had he pocketed it, when Joe and the sheriff were upon him, but Horn wheeled about before they could grab him and sped up the last stretch of hard-packed sand like a coyote. Sheriff Valentine and Joe were caught breathless from their own sprint. By the time Horn reached the rim, he was a dozen yards ahead of them. Then Horn was over the rim and gone.

Horn's own sensation of those final seconds was drowned in a mottled whirl of gray, in which the dazzling whiteness of the desert sand alternated with the blackness of a fainting spell brought on through sheer exhaustion. This time, Horn sprawled and stayed awhile, closing his eyes to shut out that patchy gray impression, and trying to gather his numbed recollections.

Out of the whirl, he expected the sheriff's hand to clamp his shoulder, in a friendly way perhaps, yet one that would insist on hauling him off into a strange world where he didn't want to be. But no clamp came and Horn opened his eyes hopefully, to find himself in the world where he really belonged.

Below were the wagons, with some of the men starting to build a campfire, in a slow, half-hearted way, as though they intended to go nowhere. Horn looked for his rifle, and was puzzled to find he didn't have it. Vaguely, he recalled dropping it in his mad dash back up to the rim. Then he remembered accidentally firing it in Joe's Café. Maybe he'd really dropped it then, though the whole scene was too crazy to be real.

Then, his mind reverted back further, to the shot he'd fired when he dodged the monster that roared along a path as hard as rock, wide as a river, as smooth as a billiard table, and lined with dead trees strung together by miles of ropes. Maybe he'd dropped the rifle then, when he wounded himself in the arm.

Or had it happened at all? Horn looked at his arm now, and found that he was no longer wearing his improvised sling, nor was his shirt sleeve torn. In fact, the wound was only in his imagination. But he'd lost his rifle: that was certain.

Horn shook his head as he started down to the wagons. With every step, his whole adventure seemed crazier, so he decided not to talk about it. In fact, the less he thought about it, the better, except for two things that were literally branded in his mind.

One thing was something somebody had told him, about a creek in Hidden Canyon, only five miles across the desert, between a double row of hills that looked too barren for anyone to hope for water there.

There was something else that Horn remembered, as though he had read it somewhere. He was repeating it half-aloud: " 'Horn, Christopher Jr. . . . Born 1839. Died —' "

The words themselves died on Horn's parched lips. He was going to say, "Died in 1847," but he amended it, to fit with the fantastic fact that had somehow burrowed its way into his brain: "Born 1839, died 1914."

Now Horn was telling himself exactly what it all meant, speaking softly, as though rehearsing it:

"We're going to find water — in the hills — so we'll all live — to see California — including Chris —"

A harrowing thought gripped Horn, causing him to wonder if the thing he had read could be wrong. He'd forgotten something more important even than the rifle, which he now considered hopelessly lost. He thrust his hand into the pocket of his jacket, clutched the object that he found and brought it out, to stare at it with a happy smile. It was the bottle that someone had given him, still containing its precious pills that some doctor had practically prescribed for little Chris!

Horn passed the men by the half-made campfire and reached his own wagon. There Martha met him with the question:

"Did you forget something, Chris?"

"Why, no," he replied. "Except I most forgot where the wagons were. That's why I was so long getting back."

"But you haven't been long. You couldn't have gone any farther than just beyond the rim. That's why I asked if you forgot something and had to come back."

"No, I didn't forget anything," Horn returned. "I came back because I remembered something. These." He placed the bottle of pills in Martha's hand and while she studied them wonderingly, he added: "Give two of these to little Chris. We'll repeat the dose at intervals. I think it may save his life. In fact, I'm sure it will, Martha."

Martha nodded, though she didn't exactly understand; still, she didn't question her husband further. He had a way of picking up information about the trail, odd facts about Indians and weather, even remedies, such as these pills might be, and then forgetting them until the time came when they were needed. The fact that the pills were in an odd-looking bottle with a peculiar type of cap, only made Martha decide that they might come up to Horn's claims.

"I'll have to give the boy some water with the pills," she reminded him.

"Take all you need." Horn gestured to the sheepskin bag. "Bathe his forehead, too, and when the bag runs dry, get more water from the barrel. We're going where there's water. Plenty of it."

Horn stalked over to where the men were still building their campfire. Bluntly, he told them:

"Save yourselves the trouble, boys. We're hitting the trail at sundown."

The men began to grumble, and Charlie Crowell gruffly interpreted their sentiments.

"What trail?" he demanded. "And for how far? Don't you know that these men and horses are so weak, they can't keep going for more than a couple of hours?"

"And that's all the time we need," Horn retorted, "to get to where water is."

"Don't tell us you went and found water, Chris. Why, you weren't hardly gone beyond the rim before you came stumbling back, like you were the most tuckered-out hombre in the party."

"I didn't have to go farther. I saw where the water was."

"You mean you saw a mirage? Like a lake off there on the desert? That's no good, Chris." Charlie turned to the others. "We need a new man to run this outfit, instead of this guy who comes stumbling back like he's got the blind staggers, saying he's seen a lake out in the middle of the desert."

Under Horn's stern surface lay an ironical humor that he could use to advantage when needed. He proved that now.

"I said nothing about any lake." He gave a dry chuckle. "You were the one who brought that up, Charlie. Maybe you've been seeing mirages. I haven't."

"But you said you saw water —"

"Wrong again, Charlie. I said I saw where the water was. Right, boys?"

Horn turned to the men, who mumbled their agreement. "What I saw were hills. No mirage ever looked like hills."

"And why," asked Charlie, "should we find water there?"

"Because not long back, a fellow told me we'd find a creek in a hidden canyon past a ridge of hills, just like those I saw."

"Why didn't you tell us sooner, Chris?"

Horn shook his head. "I wanted to see them first, myself. I hoped I'd see them when I got beyond the rim, and sure enough, there they were. So let's hitch up and get started."

Horn's convincing words roused his listeners to new spirit. Even Charlie was won over, though to save face, he inquired with a pleasant laugh:

"Was there anything else to see beside hills, Chris?"

"There's a lot to be seen beyond that rim," replied Horn solemnly. "There's a whole new land, and people like us will be responsible for it. There will be big roads, huge machines like monsters, pipelines bringing water to the middle of the desert —"

He broke off, rather than carry his glowing speech too far. It wouldn't do to strain the imaginations of these listeners. Horn snapped from the fantasy of 1964 back to the realism of 1847. The horses were hitched, now, and he climbed to the front of his wagon, as he added:

"Of course, we won't live to see any of that. Even our children will only see the beginning of it." Horn looked back at Martha, who was helping little Chris sit up; then he flicked the reins. "Giddap, boys! We're stopping off at Hidden Canyon. Then on to California!"

The horses responded, the wagon wheels creaked, and Horn spoke as to himself, "And after we get there, I'll bet my son Chris will be remembered long after I'm forgotten!"

Two men hadn't forgotten Christopher Horn, Senior, though they were living in a far-off future. Dog-tired, Sheriff Valentine and Joe Scarney were giving up their hunt along the rim.

"The guy must have ducked behind some big cactus, right after he went over the rim," declared the sheriff. "It beats me."

"Me too," agreed Joe. "It's as if he vanished into nowhere."

"He just kept ducking farther, I guess. Pick up his gun and bring it along, Joe. And what did you say his name was?"

"Horn. Christopher Horn. It had to be, because his son's name was in the encyclopedia. It said Christopher Horn, Junior."

Sheriff Valentine dropped Joe Scarney at the gas pumps, and drove off in his car, half muttering to himself:

"Christopher Horn! I've heard that name — now I remember! He was the oldtimer who discovered Hidden Canyon, back in the 1840's. People had been going right by it, until he stumbled on it. But this fellow would be the great-grandson of that Christopher Horn!"

In the diner, Joe found Mary Lou alone. In answer to her puzzled gaze, he declared:

"The man plumb vanished, honey. But he dropped his rifle and I picked it up." Joe noted that Mary Lou was studying the gun, so he looked at it, too. "Why — why, it's changed. It's — it's just as if it had been lying in the desert for a hundred years!"

The gun most certainly had changed. Its metal barrel was dulled, its wooden stock dried out. Instead of a shiny specimen, it had become a worthless weapon. But it was the same type of gun that Horn had carried. Realizing that, Joe asked suddenly: "Those coins Horn gave you. Where did you put them?"

"Beside the cash register." Mary Lou turned in that direction. "I didn't want to get them mixed with the other change. But — but now they're gone! Maybe one of the truckers took them —"

"Unless Horn never gave them to you. Maybe he never was here. Maybe I just stumbled onto a gun that somebody dropped a hundred years ago. Unless he went back to a wagon train heading west to California in 1847."

"Back to that boy of his." Mary Lou looked at the encyclopedia, still lying on the counter. "Back to make sure that something would happen just as he read it to us, from this very book!"

That evening, during the brief desert twilight, Joe Scarney and his wife Mary Lou stood by the gas pumps, looking toward the ridge of low hills etched against the fading purple of the sky.

"You know, honey," said Joe, "sometimes, at night, I forget all the traffic that's going by." He paused as three cars shrieked past and a big truck supplied a certifying rumble. "And I sort of imagine that I can see wagon trains rolling west —"

"With one driven by Christopher Horn" put in Mary Lou, "on his way to find Hidden Canyon, that you told him about. I can see them too, Joe, though they should have been there long before this."

Odd, the spell of the desert at night! Christopher Horn was a man who pictured strange things too, that evening when his wagon train reached Hidden Canyon, to be welcomed by the roar of the gushing creek. While little Chris was sleeping quietly, Horn and his wife Martha had strolled up the hill to study the darkened desert.

"I thought I saw monsters there," Horn confided. "Manmade monsters, covering more ground in an hour than our wagons can in a week."

"Perhaps they really are out there," declared Martha, "roaring by like you said, Chris. But we can't see them in the dark."

"We should see them. They'd be sure to have big blazing lights, like those I saw on Joe's Café, so they could find their way."

"You're right, Chris! I see lights now, crossing the desert. Look!"

Horn looked, and for a fleeting moment, he thought he saw them, too. Then he and Martha laughed together — their first happy laugh in weeks — as the illusion faded. Those lights were the vivid twinkle of the stars, themselves the symbols of past and future, as timeless as the Twilight Zone through which Christopher Horn had detoured on his way West.

The 16-Millimeter Shrine

Always, when Danny Weiss strolled up the walk to the huge Hollywood mansion, he would shake his head and wonder at it. He was doing that again today, after more than thirty years of steady visits. Once it had been one of Hollywood's greatest showplaces, and for Danny's money it still deserved that distinction.

Of course, Danny was slightly prejudiced. This was the home of Barbara Jean Trenton, famous star of the early "talkie" days, and Danny had been her agent all through those years. But what amazed him was how the place, like Barbara Jean herself, had retained a lofty grandeur and had never really aged. Yet both had the same problem. They were outmoded, and in a way, that could be worse.

Danny entered through a large front door into a gigantic marble-floored hall, a product of the rococo architecture of the early 1920's, and reminiscent of the massive movie palaces that flourished during that period. At the rear was a huge grand staircase, leading to the scarcely used upper floors, for Barbara Jean Trenton now lived here practically alone except for a maid named Sally, who now answered the door in response to Danny's buzz.

The worry that showed on Sally's face brought an understanding glint in Danny's eyes. He nodded toward a pair of heavy walnut doors at one side of the hall and queried:

"Still there, in the projection room?"

"Yes, and it's getting worse, Mr. Weiss." Sally hesitated, then blurted out, "There's times when I've gone in there, and I could almost swear—well, like just now—"

"Go on, Sally, like what just now?"

"Well, I took a tray of lunch in to Miss Trenton, and there was the old picture running but I just couldn't see her anywhere. So I looked at the screen, and then all of a sudden, Miss Trenton was speaking to me, telling me to put down the tray. There she was, right beside me."

"Of course." Danny gave a nod. "It takes a few minutes for your eyes to get used to the darkness of the room. Watching the screen helped. That's why you saw her when you looked again."

"So that's how it is," breathed Sally. "I—I thought maybe something was getting me."

"It could be that, too," said Danny seriously. "I know that something is getting *her*"—he gestured toward the walnut doors—"and naturally, you'd sense it. Take it easy, Sally, while I try to straighten it all out."

Sally nodded and followed Danny eagerly to the projection room, to see what his reaction was. Danny knocked and entered, all in one action, but he was still too late to be deceived by any illusion from the screen. The picture was just going off, there was a fanfare of music, and the screened words THE END were followed by a white beam like a spotlight from the projection machine, which cut off automatically. The room lights came on, and there was Barbara Jean Trenton, in person, practically taking a bow for the benefit of her agent Danny Weiss, and her maid Sally.

Barbara Jean Trenton was anything but a faded beauty. Her face was attractive, her manner vibrant, and her figure striking, in black toreador pants trimmed with gold braid and a white blouse. Danny, in his turn, provided a really sweeping bow that the Three Musketeers would have envied.

"It's eleven o'clock in the morning," Danny announced, "and the sun is shining brightly. It's a beautiful day in Beverly Hills. The smog is conspicuous by its absence. The temperature is eighty-four degrees, and the atmosphere is balmy."

"And I," returned Barbara Jean, in a slightly metallic tone, "can do without your daily meteorological report."

"The big question," Danny returned, "is why don't you do something with them? You sit here in an air-conditioned cavern showing yourself one outdated picture after another—"

"Please, Danny," Barbara Jean interposed icily, "I'd rather skip that."

"Skip what?" Danny retorted, waving his hand around the projection room. "None of this is any good. No good, honey."

"I like your frank way, Danny. Let's go to the study."

They crossed the vast hallway to the study, which was actually jammed with the remnants of a career, in the form of movie stills, press photographs, souvenir programs, autographed portraits, and carefully pressed orchids.

"This is better," Danny decided, "because you can look it over and pick it all apart. What was the picture you were showing yourself back in there?"

"There were *two* pictures," Barbara Jean delivered the icy tone again. "One was *Farewell Without Tears*—"

"Produced in 1933, co-starring Jerry Herndon—"

"My leading man then," put in Barbara Jean, "and in a later feature, *A Night in Paris*—"

"Not much later. Only in 1934."

"Who do you think you are? Father Time in person?"

"Absolutely," Danny retorted. "Always, you are in that projection room trying to turn back the clock, twenty—twenty-five—thirty years. You keep turning your back on today, and that's real sick. Real sick, sick."

"And you, an agent, think you can tell me that?"

"Why not?" Danny clapped himself on the chest. "Why not, when I am here with an appointment all set up with International Films, who want you to star in a picture right now, today!"

Momentarily, the result reached Danny's expectations. Barbara Jean's eyes sparkled, her face brightened, and she whirled about the room excitedly.

"I hope it's a musical!" she exclaimed. "I'd love to dance again. Or to play romantic roles, Danny, with scenes like those I saw this morning."

She finished her pirouette underneath a large color portrait of a handsome man attired in the fashion of the early 1930's.

"Maybe I'll make love with Jerry Herndon again. I did three pictures with him. One was *A Night in Paris,* with Jerry playing a young American officer. I was Claudette, the little French girl." She began to caress the life-sized portrait, giving her words a foreign accent. "Ah, *mon capitaine,* tell me—"

"Cut!" snapped Danny. "That was thirty-odd years ago, *ma cherie!* That projection room across the hall is dark and cold and full of cobwebs. You're all tangled up in them, so get out in the sunshine and learn what it's like to live today. I'll meet you in Sall's office at three o'clock."

"Marty Sall! You mean he's still with International?"

"That's right. But he's mellowed with the years."

"I hope so. I never could get along with Marty Sall."

Barbara Jean Trenton still couldn't get along with Marty Sall, as was proven that same afternoon. Barbara Jean arrived at International overdressed, overly made up, and as coy as when she'd played those glamor roles of years before. Marty Sall, fat, paunch-faced, overlooked all that as he chewed an appropriately fat cigar, and studied a script. Then:

"We have a good part for you, Miss Trenton," Sall announced. "You play the part of a mother—"

"A mother!" Barbara Jean froze. "How old a mother?"

"Fortyish. But very vibrant, very much alive—"

"As compared to what? A corpse? Or a paunchy old relic like you? I don't play mothers. I never have—"

"And I suppose you never will. You're right, you won't. Not in any picture I have anything to do with, if you're going to get that particular."

Danny Weiss injected himself as a peacemaker.

"Look, Barby," he suggested, "we could at least take the script along with us, and read it—"

"You take it and read it!" broke in Barbara Jean, "and you play it. You'd make a good mother, Danny, the way you've been mothering me. As for this crude, tactless man"—she drew herself up haughtily and gave Sall a withering stare—"I didn't like him when I was under contract here, and I don't like him now."

"All right, Miss Prima Donna!" Sall was on his feet, waving his cigar angrily. "Why don't you try crawling back into some of your old films and see how far you get."

"Maybe I'll do just that!"

With those final words, Barbara Jean flounced from the room, while Danny shot a parting bolt at Sall.

"Don't think she won't, loud mouth. It took me weeks to haul her out of that projection room of hers, and now I've got to start all over!"

Danny Weiss was right. Barbara Jean said nothing until she was back on the familiar preserves of her own mansion. Then, as Danny was leaving, he remarked; "Don't worry about today, Barby, you're right, he is a mean guy—"

"You're talking about Marty Sall?" interrupted Barbara Jean. "Why, he doesn't exist! That studio doesn't exist. This is the world, Danny, right in here. From now on, I'm keeping the doors locked with drapes over the windows. I don't want any of the outside coming in!"

"But Barby! You can't just shut your eyes and say it doesn't exist because you can't see it."

"Oh, yes, I can. If I shut my eyes, it disappears, and if I wish hard enough, I can wish it away. As of this minute, this is the 1930's. This is a carefree world, with charm and romance."

"That's not true, Barby. It's nostalgic and nice, but it's phony."

"If I wish hard enough, it will be real. I'll give a party, Danny. Tell all my old friends, Paul Naider, Jerry Herndon, and Steve Black. Tell them I'll be waiting here—"

Danny interrupted again; this time with a shout, to overpower Barbara Jean's high, hysterical pitch. "Barby! Paul Naider has been dead five years. Jerry Herndon lives in Chicago. Steve Black hasn't been around since World War II. Barby, you're wishing for things that are gone. You're turning this mansion into a mausoleum!"

As Danny turned to go down the steps, Barbara Jean sprang to the front door, slammed it, and bolted it. Steadily, almost defiantly, she strode through the doorway of the projection room. Sally was in the hallway, and hurried after her, only to have Barbara Jean stop her with the firm pronouncement:

"Sally, I'm locking the door. I don't want to see anyone. Not anyone. You understand?"

"Yes, Miss Trenton."

The door closed, there was a click of a key in the lock. Soon the music from a movie sound-track filtered through the door. Sally gave a despairing shrug and went her way.

Two weeks passed. Every day, Danny Weiss showed up faithfully at the

Trenton mansion, only to be flagged by the equally faithful Sally. Each time, Sally looked more tired, and Danny looked more worried, until he finally arrived in a grim, determined mood. He gave the usual greeting: "Tell me, Sally, how is she?"

"I can't tell you, Mr. Weiss," replied Sally. "She's in that room all the time, day and night. She lets me come in and bring her something to eat, but only if I swear there's nobody else with me. But I can swear to you, Mr. Weiss, sometimes I see her—"

"Go see her now," interrupted Danny. "Tell her I want to talk to her, just to tell her something she will want to know. I won't try to make her decide what she wants to do. I just want her to hear me out. You understand?"

"Yes, Mr. Weiss, I'll tell her—if I see her."

Sally entered the projection room and halted as she closed the door behind her. Instead of a movie scene, or the beam of a white spotlight, the screen was diffused with a grayish flicker that filled the entire room with a peculiar twilight. Sally had entered a strange zone between the real and the unreal. Eyes still fascinated by the gray whirl, she moved slowly toward the screen, until she tripped over the electric cord and suddenly pulled it loose. The grayish twilight gave way to a white beam, and a voice spoke from beside the screen. "What is it, Sally?"

The maid clapped her hand to her heart.

"I didn't see you for a moment, Miss Trenton," she exclaimed. "Mr. Weiss is here, to tell you something special."

"I'll buy that. Danny is honest, and he smacks of the 1930's, though he won't admit it. Show him in."

Danny entered to find Barbara Jean still wearing her projection room costume of black toreador pants and flimsy white silk blouse. Noting his appraising glance, she demanded:

"What's the matter, Danny? Don't you care for the merchandise?"

"The merchandise is beautiful, but it looks as if it hadn't slept in a couple of weeks. It needs fresh air."

"It's quite satisfied, Danny. Hail and farewell. The door out is the same one you came in."

"Good. I'll tell that to an old friend of yours who is in town and wants to come and see you. Jerry Herndon."

The result fulfilled all of Danny's hopes. Barbara Jean ran her hands over her haggard face, then stared down at her disheveled costume.

"The way I look!" she exclaimed. "No makeup—and I need some time to dress! How soon will Jerry be here?"

"In a couple of hours. I'm picking him up at his hotel."

Danny smiled as he watched Barbara Jean dash up the grand staircase with all the vigor of thirty years ago. At last, the lost past of Barbara Jean Trenton was coming alive!

Two hours later, Sally was all smiles as she ushered Danny Weiss and Jerry Herndon into the study, which had been hastily rearranged for this visit. Along with Jerry's portrait, dozens of "stills" from his old movies had been given prominent display. The pictures showed him in the robes of a sheik, the uniform of an army officer, the football togs of a college star, and half a dozen other parts that he had played with Barbara Jean. In all, the accent was on youth, showing a slender, buoyant Jerry Herndon, who was very, very much alive.

"Boy, was that hot!" Jerry recalled, referring to the sheik costume. "Barby and I were on location in Death Valley when they took that shot. You'd never get me into an outfit like that today, not unless a portable air-conditioner was built in it."

"Remember, Jerry," Danny warned, "Barby's not well. Make a fuss over her and tell her how wonderful she looks. Play along with her whims. She needs your help. Here she comes now!"

Footsteps sounded as Barbara Jean came flying down the stairs, beautifully dressed, wonderfully vibrant, the absolute personification of her glamorous past. But she froze stock-still as she reached the doorway, staring first at Danny, then at Jerry, finally beyond them both as though looking for someone else.

"Hello, Barby," Jerry Herndon greeted. "It's been a long time, no see. Lots of water gone over the dam."

Barbara Jean recognized the voice and stared squarely at Jerry, her eyes widening, not in joyous recognition, but in stark disappointment. She, at least, looked to be the once famous Barbara Jean Trenton, but any resemblance of this man to the fabulous Jerry Herndon was purely coincidental.

Instead of a sleek, slender keen-eyed specimen of masculine vigor, Barbara Jean viewed a paunchy, balding, graying middle-aged man who wore glasses. Barbara Jean spoke slowly, sadly:

"It's odd the way we think of people as they were. I thought you would be here on a white horse in a sheik's costume, or an officer's uniform. I thought you'd be a young man, Jerry. I had a crazy idea that we'd do another picture together."

"No, no, Barby." Jerry laughed. "I gave up acting long ago. It went down the drain with my youth."

"You don't act any more? What do you do?"

"I run a chain of supermarkets outside of Chicago. There's a dream that really came through, Barby! Why, they hadn't even thought of supermarkets— they didn't know what the word meant—back when we were in pictures together. And now—"

"Dreams that come true!" Barbara Jean's eyes took on a distant stare that matched her strained tone. "I have dreams, too, and I can renew them. I can wish myself where I want to be and stay there, with people who are still alive." Her gaze was focused on Jerry now. "You are one of them. You are alive, the way you were. But as you are now, you are dead—like all the others." She turned to include Danny in her glance. "Go away—both of you!"

Jerry Herndon hesitated, then stepped forward and kissed Barbara Jean's cheek as she turned her face away. With a hopeless shrug, Jerry walked from the study, and Danny Weiss reluctantly followed. While Sally was showing the two visitors out, Barbara Jean strode rapidly and determinedly across the huge hall and into the projection room.

There, she flicked a switch. The room went dark. Soft, romantic music accompanied the color film that unfolded on the screen. The scene was a penthouse terrace. Barbara Jean Trenton appeared in an evening gown, a young Barbara Jean, but almost the image of the Barbara Jean Trenton who watched from a seat in the projection room.

Then, into the scene stepped a slim, sleek Jerry Herndon, attired in a form-fitting tuxedo. The contrast between this youthful Jerry and his portly counterpart who had just left the Trenton mansion was a thing that passed belief. Neither could have been identified as a reasonable facsimile of the other.

From the terrace, the girl studied the glow of Manhattan that never changed, even though the city's buildings might come and go. Perhaps that inspired the words that she spoke to the man beside her:

"You arranged all these lights just for me, Arnold?"

"Of course," the man replied, "and at twelve o'clock, they will all spell your name—Lillian."

"With two L's, I hope."

Coyly, Lillian drew away from Arnold's arms. Then:

"This is how New York should always be seen. From high above, not down in the streets where everyone scurries back and forth. Here it is like music— great music—"

"I shall give you music," replied Arnold. "Skyline—music—all for you, with love from me—"

Barbara Jean flicked off the film. Soon another reel was running, with the same people but a different scene. Or were they the same people? The scene was World War I., and the American girl in a nurse's uniform was truly Barbara Jean Trenton. But Jerry Herndon, as a young Italian officer, could never have been mistaken for the Jerry Herndon of today.

"So it is good-bye again," he was saying. "We should be used to good-byes. I used to think, when I was a little boy—"

"You used to think what, Tony?" the nurse interrupted. "I love to hear you talk about when you were a little boy. I'm jealous of those years, Tony—"

"Oh, Adele, my darling—"

They were lost in an embrace and in the wordless interim, the living Barbara Jean Trenton rose from her seat in the projection room and spoke for her filmed counterpart:

"There you are, Jerry! How well you look—how young—how wonderfully young! But there was a fat old man here, a while ago, who said he was you. Oh, Jerry—my real Jerry—I wish I could go where you are—I wish I could, Jerry—"

Rising music drowned her voice, but it drowned the voices of the screen figures, too. Barbara Jean Trenton was impressing her own self upon her screen self of Adele, just as the Tony of the picture was absorbing the last vestiges of Jerry Herndon. The projector kept on, while the film shuddered.

The door of the projection room opened. Sally entered with a tray that held a coffee pot and a plate of sandwiches. She looked about the room and spoke timidly:

"Miss Trenton, I brought you a little snack. Wouldn't you like some coffee —or some sandwiches?"

There was no response. Remembering what Danny had said about eyes becoming used to the darkness, Sally looked steadily at the screen. Her eyes went wide; she dropped the tray with a shriek. Dashing out of the projection room, Sally ran squarely into the arms of Danny Weiss.

"I came back, Sally," explained Danny, "to see how she was taking it. How is she, Sally?"

Speechless, Sally could only point to the projection room. Danny entered, with Sally close behind him. There, on the screen, Danny saw a scene that he knew well but had never viewed in movies before. It was the front door of this very mansion. Approaching it were actors of the 1930's headed by Jerry Herndon, as he had looked in those days. With him were others who had starred with Barbara Jean Trenton, back in that same period.

But what were they doing here, pouring into the ornate marble hallway, not just seeking admittance, but craving it? The camera now was centered on the marble staircase, and there, descending in majestic fashion, was Barbara Jean Trenton. Mere sight of her in that film brought a sharp cry from Danny:

"Barby! Please, Barby! Come back!"

There was a reason for those words. The Barby on the screen was the Barbara Jean Trenton of today, not the version of thirty years ago. She was wearing her black toreadors and white blouse, but she looked more glamorous than ever. They were crowding about her, those forgotten figures of a former era, acknowledging her as their queen.

Barbara Jean Trenton had gone back into pictures exactly as she wanted. She had wished the impossible into becoming true. She had turned her projection room into a sixteen-millimeter shrine, where she could welcome all those she remembered into the happy, fantastic realm of the Twilight Zone.

The Ghost of Jolly Roger

Hangman's Bay was named in honor of Governor Roger Crisp, who turned it from a pirate haven into a thriving colonial possession. Overlooking both bay and sea was Crisp's stronghold, Fort Defiance, which stood on a rocky promontory above a parade ground where Crisp publicly hanged his victims as an example to all seafaring folk who might yield to the lure of piracy.

The well-protected harbor had a settlement along its shore, while the waterfront was backed with green jungle slopes that rose to distant blue hills. Those were dominated by Mount Mogombo, a live volcano that frequently smoked by day and flared by night, but otherwise confined itself to ominous rumblings and the occasional scattering of ashes.

Here, in the late 1600's, Crisp himself had thrived as a pirate, usually taking sides with one or another of the big nations that were constantly at war. Crisp had gained the nickname of Jolly Roger, because his cadaverous countenance bore a striking resemblance to the skull and crossbones of the familiar pirate flag, particularly when he folded his long, bony arms across his chest beneath his chin. But when the various powers had finally combined their efforts to stamp out piracy, Crisp hauled down his banner and ran up a flag of truce instead.

"I'm against bloodshed," Crisp had announced, "and if you make me the governor of a colony, with a proper flag to fly from my masthead, I'll prove it. I'll talk my old comrades out of their wicked ways and if there are those who won't listen, I'll fight them and get rid of them. Without bloodshed, mind you, or at least very little."

A deal was made, whereby the reformed pirate became Governor Roger Crisp of the Colony of Cape Regal, a name which soon gave way to Hangman's Bay. For Governor Crisp had a very persuasive way of handling pirates without bloodshed. If they wouldn't reform, he went after them with so many ships that he overawed them and forced their surrender with promise of a fair trial. Such trials always resulted in the prisoners being hanged, so none of them lived to warn other pirates not to trust their former comrade, Roger Crisp. But from the way that captured corsairs vanished from circulation, it became certain that something was amiss, so those at large gradually shied away from Hangman's Bay and its new governor.

For years, the inhabitants of Hangman's Bay went along with Governor Crisp. Though no longer a pirate, he still was known as Jolly Roger because of the pleasure he took whenever a judge found a new crew guilty. Always, they appealed to the governor for amnesty and when Crisp announced, "Appeal denied," his thin lips spread in a skull-like grin that symbolized death.

At the executions, Crisp put on a show that really won the riffraff of Cape Regal. Poles were set up on the parade ground like the masts of ships, so the condemned men could be hoisted to the yardarms. Having met their doom, they were left to dangle until a new crop of culprits was brought in for trial.

Just before each multiple hanging, the crowd would look toward the sally port that opened onto the parade ground. There was a chance that a messenger might dash out bearing a reprieve, for the guardroom could be reached by a bell cord from the governor's apartment, three floors above. When no messenger appeared, all eyes rose to the governor's apartment three floors above, to see what Crisp himself might have to say.

Never did Governor Crisp fail them. Attired in a full and gorgeous uniform, he would appear at the window with folded arms, his sunken, leering face and bony hands a living representation of a skull and crossbones. A mere gesture from Jolly Roger would have stayed the executions, but it never came. Gloating, Crisp watched the hangings from a vantage point on a level with the struggling victims, his grin unchanged.

So it continued over the years until the brig *Falcon* sailed into Hangman's Bay, flying a pirate flag. Governor Crisp observed the ship from a watchtower and stalked back along the parapet to his own quarters, where he pulled the signal cord to the guardroom. Men rushed out to the parade ground and fell into immediate formation, while others dashed up three flights of zigzag stairs to receive the governor's personal instructions.

"Arrest them at the dock," Crisp ordered, "and tell them their case will be judged fairly. Learn all you can, for whatever they say will be used against them. But do not mention that fact."

The *Falcon's* crew were men who had been pressed into service by a notorious pirate named Tewkes. Once there were enough of them, they had overpowered Tewkes and killed him along with his few loyal followers. They had then put into Hangman's Bay. As their leader expressed it: "We'd rather be tried for mutiny than piracy."

After hearing the case, three judges decided that the crew was guilty of mutiny only, and justifiably so. That was when Governor Crisp arose in all his pomp.

"Mutiny is the same as piracy," he stormed, "and piracy is never justifiable. The verdict of this court is overruled. I declare these men guilty of piracy, their sentence to be death by hanging."

By execution day, however, the populace had turned against Governor Crisp. Their mutterings grew uglier and louder than the distant rumblings of Mt. Mogombo. If Jolly Roger could twist mutiny into piracy, he could twist mere insubordination into mutiny, making any trivial misdemeanor into a capital crime. Alarmed by the public attitude, Jed Hervey, the deputy governor, brought word to Jolly Roger that a riot might start on the parade ground.

"Order out the guard and have all other available men in reserve!" Crisp stormed. "But no bloodshed, mind you, if it can be avoided," he added with his most cadaverous smile, for treason also carried the death penalty, with a verdict in advance. He dismissed the deputy and poured himself a mug of bumbo, a fiery mixture of spiced rum with a sprinkling of flaked coconut. Crisp always insisted that it was brimstone straight from Mt. Mogombo, whose smoking peak was framed in the window overlooking the parade ground.

So Jed Hervey left Jolly Roger mumbling over his bumbo and went down to the guardroom, where he ordered out half of the hundred men he found there. They pushed back the crowd on the parade ground, and the prisoners were brought up from the dungeon. The crowd quieted to hear what the doomed men had to say.

"When we were pirates, we should have stayed so!" one shouted. "Jolly Roger hates bloodshed, and now I wish we'd shown him some by sticking his soldiers like so many pigs."

"That goes for Jolly Roger, too," another agreed. "He thinks we're going to die with our boots on. We'll make a liar of him here and now!"

With that, the man kicked off his boots and his dozen comrades did the same, while the crowd really roared approval and surged forward despite the soldiers. Hervey promptly settled that by calling out all the reserves, leaving the fort deserted except for Jolly Roger, in his apartment three floors up. The mob retreated, and the ropes were affixed about the necks of the prisoners. Again, there was a lull, and one of the prisoners shouted up at Crisp's window:

"You're a doomed man, Jolly Roger! You are afraid to show yourself, because you know your fate will be like ours. Death is catching up with you."

The crowd roared; even Mogombo seemed to rumble approval. Jed Hervey looked to the sally port, hoping that a messenger would appear there, but none did. At the last moment, Hervey stared up at Crisp's window, positive that the governor would show himself, if only in response to the crowd's defiance. Hervey was willing to take any gesture on Crisp's part as a signal of reprieve. But for once, there was no sign of Jolly Roger, with his skull-like grin and gaudy uniform.

The moment came, and the doomed crew were hauled struggling, strangling, to the yardarms, where their sightless eyes soon were staring at the empty window. The spell was broken, and the crowd, convinced that Jolly Roger had given way to fear, surged toward the entrance to the fort. Hervey managed to get inside with half a dozen men and clamp the sally port, leaving the rest of the soldiers to battle it out with the maddened populace.

First to reach the governor's apartment, Jed Hervey halted on the threshold. There he saw Jolly Roger slumped across the oak table, the mug of bumbo in one hand, the bell cord to the guardroom in the other. His face was staring upward, and never had its skull-like grin been more frozen. The shouts of the crowd had risen to a mighty tumult, but His Excellency Roger Crisp showed no concern. Jolly Roger was as dead as the dangling figures outside his window.

The situation was truly tragic. Apparently, the governor for once had decided to grant a reprieve and had tried to call the guardroom too late, for by then Hervey had summoned the reserves and the place was empty. Getting no response, Crisp had tried to rise and go to the window, but had succumbed from a heart attack through his own intensity over the excitement outside.

Word was passed along that Jolly Roger was dead, and the mob's antognistic mood changed to one of celebration. All that night they danced in the streets of Cape Regal by the lurid glare of Mogombo, which supplied a timely eruption as its contribution to the festivities. The bodies of the *Falcon*'s crew members had been lowered from the improvised yardarms; and now the rioters decided to hoist the corpse of Jolly Roger in their place. But before they could attack Fort Defiance, a series of earthquakes shook Cape Regal, demolishing half the town.

Parts of the fort were damaged, too, but Jed Hervey, now governor, put his men to work repairing the walls. Between quakes, he held a funeral for Jolly Roger and buried his coffin in a cemetery a few miles inland. Further tremors rocked the graveyard so that even the site of the crypt was lost; but there were persons who claimed that Hervey had simply buried an empty casket there to mislead the angry populace. By then, it was too late to matter. Fort Defiance was secure again, and the citizens of Cape Regal — or what was left of them — were crawling out from the rubble, ready to take orders from Jed Hervey, as successor to Roger Crisp.

The new regime did not last long, however. With Crisp gone, outside pressure caused Hervey to give up his authority. Cape Regal then became a simple colony that was occasionally swapped or seized by one big power or another. Fort Defiance was garrisoned in time of trouble, and during a century of social tranquillity it was practically abandoned.

Then, when big cruise ships began bringing tourists to Hangman's Bay, the old fort was restored as a museum. People were taken on guided tours between the hours of nine and five, while at night, the fort was locked up from the outside. Among its fanciful legends was one of a ghost that stalked its parapets, thought to be the restless shade of the notorious Governor Crisp. But since no one was allowed in the place, there was no way of finding out, as the ghost was never known to stroll about by day.

It took the progressive spirit of the atomic age to shake off the dust of decadent centuries. Nothing ever happened at Cape Regal, and the people were so contented that it became obvious something must be very wrong. So a vote was held throughout the surrounding region, and the former colony of Cape Regal overnight became the independent Republic of Mogombo.

That went off nicely, because the mother country accepted the verdict and bowed out quite prettily. The Mogombonians held another election, this time to choose their own president. There were three factions, and the vote was so close that all demanded a recount. When that was made, neither of the losers would accept it, and another election was scheduled. Meanwhile, members of each faction agreed among themselves that the only sure way to win would be to reduce the voting members of the opposing parties before election time.

They went at it with a vim that made the old days of piracy look tame. All types of weapons from poison darts to plastic bombs were called into action, while modern tanks went clanking into ancient jungle pits. But before the warring groups managed to converge on Cape Regal itself, the United Nations flew in an emergency force which took over Hangman's Bay as a supply base, under the command of Colonel Gandak, who headed a small, picked force from India.

Colonel Gandak promptly occupied Fort Defiance to prevent local factions from moving in there. More quotas arrived from other countries, and soon a very cosmopolitan group of officers and men were garrisoned in the ancient fort. There, Calvin Laxaman, the custodian, who also served as curator, showed the officers around the place and related its history. Entering by the sally port, the guardroom was on the right, and according to Laxaman, it had changed but little since the days of Governor Roger Crisp.

"If you measure the guardroom," declared Laxaman, in his precise tone, "you will find that it runs all the way to the west bastion, where new masonry was added to strengthen the wall."

Carefully, Laxaman paced off the distance; then stopped and eyed the wall through thick-lensed glasses, finally running his fingers over the masonry, as though to feel cracks in the mortar that his eyes could not detect. Colonel Gandak and the other officers who watched him agreed that a very fine job had been done.

"We think that this was done immediately after Jolly Roger died," asserted Laxaman, "because of earthquakes that called for immediate repairs. But maybe it was of later date. However, we have restored the guardroom as it was at the time of Governor Crisp, even including original bells found here."

Laxaman gestured to the doorway, where old-fashioned bells of various sizes were hanging in a row. Each bell was equipped with a clapper, and attached to the bells were strands of smooth, thin rope that ran up through holes in the guardroom ceiling.

"Special hemp," Laxaman pointed out. "Identical with the kind used three centuries ago, before manila hemp became famous. The same," he added pointedly, "as was used to hang the pirates. This rope runs down from the governor's apartment as in the old days."

In addition to its ancient benches, the guardroom now was furnished with army cots and folding chairs that the U.N. detachment had brought with them. Colonel Gandak was keeping a hundred men here, to be on immediate call if needed down in the town of Cape Regal, where most of the emergency force was stationed.

Across the corridor from the guardroom was the courtroom where the crew of the *Falcon* and other accused men had been tried. There the old benches had been restored, and Laxaman gave a description of the average trial procedure, making it graphic by constantly gesturing to a portrait of a broad-faced man with sunken features that glowered down upon the judges' seats.

"A very fine portrait of Governor Roger Crisp," declared Laxaman methodically. "Very lifelike, so they say, though we have such reports only through word of mouth over many years."

"But why," asked Colonel Gandak, "should the governor's picture have been hanging here?"

"To make the judges remember that he had the final say," stated Laxaman. "When his picture failed to do so, the governor would make his final say in person."

The U.N. officers exchanged knowing smiles at that. Apparently, Governor Crisp had run everything his own way, just as each warring faction in the Republic of Mogombo was trying to do right now.

Laxaman conducted the officers through a maze of narrow passages, low archways, and steep stairways that doubled back on themselves. These were hollowed in the masonry, and at various levels they opened into large rooms, many with narrow, slitted windows. One, which had served as an armory, was now filled with a display of antique weapons. Another as a museum, containing many old-time uniforms, including several of Crisp's own fanciful design.

There were several barrack rooms, where Colonel Gandak decided to station some of the U.N. troops, and a well-located room with several doorways, so nicely furnished in antique style that Gandak chose to use it as officers' quarters, a choice that Laxaman very solemnly approved.

"Deputy Governor Hervey used this room," he said, "but according to accounts, Jolly Roger was always coming in and out, telling Hervey what to do."

"It sounds as though his nibs was everywhere," put in Captain O'Shea, who was in charge of an Irish contingent. "Have you ever run into his ghost anywhere around the fort, Laxaman?"

Laxaman winced momentarily at the question.

"Sometimes I think I have," he admitted, "and almost everywhere. But maybe I do not see too well in the dark passages and stairways." He took off his thick-lensed glasses and wiped them with a handkerchief. "Shadows, doorways, almost anything can look like a person through these glasses."

That brought a comment from Lieutenant Alvarez, who commanded a platoon of Chilean troops.

"With so many passages," he observed, "perhaps you lose your way around here sometimes?"

"Lots of times," conceded Laxaman. "So I advise everyone to be careful! If lost, keep going, and you will always come out somewhere. Now, I will usher you to the governor's apartment" — he put on his glasses and delivered a dry smile — "if I have not forgotten the way there."

He led them up more stairs and through intricate passages until suddenly they emerged into blinding daylight upon the terreplein, or roof, of Fort Defiance. After their eyes became accustomed to the glare, the U.N. officers noted that there were several stairways opening onto the roof, along with one wide doorway leading to a ramp, so that cannon could be hauled up from within the fort.

Various antique cannon were already set in embrasures along the parapets of the roof, all pointed so that they commanded the open sea as well as Hangman's Bay. Sight of them brought smiles from the U.N. officers; for not only were the old guns obsolete, they came from different periods, representing a span of a few centuries. Evidently, they had been gathered hit-or-miss, simply to decorate the fortifications.

The watchtowers, though obviously reconstructed, looked quite authentic, and the same applied to Crisp's own apartment, where Laxaman now conducted the U.N. group. Up half a dozen steps, past a metal-sheathed door that groaned on ancient hinges, into a gloomy room with iron shutters; there, the officers paused until Laxaman reached the window and pulled the shutters wide.

Again sunlight dazzled them, this time with the view that Jolly Roger had so often studied from this very window. There was the parade ground with its modern replicas of old-time mastheads; beyond, the blue waters of Hangman's Bay, with the town of Cape Regal sprawled along the waterfront, its glistening white buildings giving an illusion of cleanliness that the place did not possess. Past that, the blue hills with a curl of grayish smoke rising from the cone of Mt. Mogombo into the cloudless sky above.

The scene was so timeless that it cast off the centuries and wrapped the viewers in a preternatural spell. When they turned to look at the room itself, now bathed in the sunlight from the window, they were even more impressed. Here, the past was visible in present form — the captain's chair in which Governor Roger Crisp had seated himself beside the huge oak table, with a silken bell cord hanging handy, and even a bottle of bumbo within easy reach, along with a half-filled glass.

"Exactly as on that last day," recited Laxaman, seating himself in the chair. "His Excellency was sitting here like this, drinking his bumbo" — Laxaman reached for the glass and paused — "when he heard shouts from the window and pulled the bell cord."

Laxaman gave a quick glance toward the window, then another and another, contorting his face as though expressing fear. Between glances, he kept tugging the bell cord, hard, harder, and still harder. Finally he slumped sideways and sprawled across the table letting his head lie there while he twitched his hands convulsively in imitation of Crisp's death throes.

"And this is how they found him," croaked Laxaman, cocking one eye at the group. "Lying dead, stone dead, when they rushed in."

Colonel Gandak, Captain O'Shea, and Lieutenant Alvarez repressed their smiles at Laxaman's crude dramatics, as did the other U.N. officers present. Then, suddenly, their amusement turned to alarm, as rushing footsteps clattered up into the apartment. They swung about, half expecting to meet a surge of old-time pirates. Instead, they were facing a squad of United Nations troops, headed by a sergeant named Dhazi, who hailed from Iraq.

"We heard the bells down in the guardroom, sir," reported Dhazi, saluting Colonel Gandak. "It sounded like an emergency call, so I brought a full squad up here."

"Quite rightly," approved Gandak, "but it was merely a test" — he glanced sharply at Laxaman—"or a mistake."

"A mistake," Laxaman apologized. "I should have remembered that the bells were recently connected as in the old days."

"You can leave them that way," decided Colonel Gandak, in a milder tone. "It's a good way to signal the guardroom."

That day, the U.N. peace-keeping force really took over Fort Defiance, and beginning with that night, the ghost started to walk. Not that Colonel Gandak and his hand-picked garrison realized it right away; far from it. The discovery was gradual because it took a week or more for enough persons to notice odd happenings and spread the word.

At that, the rumor might have been confined to different contingents, in which case they would have dwindled proportionately, except for the fact that the officers all shared the same quarters and talked one another's language. In their commodious room with half a dozen doorways and as many alcoves, the U.N. officers discussed all sorts of minor subjects, one of which — namely, ghosts — was due to grow to major proportions.

Lieutenant Alvarez triggered the subject with the query:

"Remember what Laxaman said about thinking he saw ghosts? Well, a couple of my men think they have seen them, or I should say, they think they have seen one ghost. It looked the same to both."

"Only one ghost?" put in Captain O'Shea, with a broad grin. "This old fort should be big enough for a flock of them."

"It is only one ghost," declared Lieutenant Hadrup, who commanded a Danish platoon. "Two of my men have said so."

"You mean they have seen the ghost, too?"

"Two. That is what I said. I mean two men, but only one ghost. Two men have seen one ghost."

"Interesting," chuckled Captain O'Shea. "Well, I've been too busy down in Cape Regal to check on things up here." He turned to Lieutenant Dolan, his subordinate. "Anything special to report, Lieutenant? Have our men been seeing ghosts, too?"

"Yes, sir. Not just two men, but three. All have seen the same ghost."

Now the subject suddenly became serious to Captain O'Shea. As senior officer among those present, he demanded details.

"What is it these enlisted men see?" he inquired.

Captain O'Shea wanted answers and he got them, all of a pattern. In each instance, a soldier — whatever his nationality — had been going up steps, along a passage or through an arch, when he had halted, startled by the sight of a skull-faced figure barring his path. Always, the follow-up had been the same. The soldier had done a double-take and the thing was gone. But each viewer had gained the same impression, that of a figure in a garish uniform, with plumed hat and a whitish cape trailing from its shoulders. Above all, the sunken countenance of Governor Crisp, alias Jolly Roger. That was enough for Captain O'Shea.

"These men," he asserted, "have been listening to crazy tales of old Jolly Roger."

"Sorry, sir," put in Lieutenant Dolan, "but I questioned them on that very point. They knew nothing at all about it."

"Then they've seen those uniforms up in the museum."

"Not my men, sir," declared Lieutenant Alvarez. "None of them have been there."

"Then they've been imagining things, as Laxaman said he did, when the daylight was feeble in the passages."

"But this ghost has been seen at night, sir," stated Lieutenant Hadrup. "All the men say the same."

"At night," declared O'Shea, with a shrug, "some of those stairs and passages must be really dark."

"No, they are very well lighted, sir," Dolan insisted, turning to the other lieutenants, who gave corroborative nods. "We have put cables up all those stairs and along the passages, with more than enough light sockets."

"So I have been wasting time among the bright lights down in Cape Regal. I should have been up here to enjoy the brighter lights of Fort Defiance. Those I must see. Show me."

They showed Captain O'Shea. They took him along corridors that were strung with electric light bulbs, through archways where there wasn't enough darkness to stir the slightest imagination. Yet they insisted, all three lieutenants — Alvarez, Hadrup and Dolan — that men under their separate commands had seen a plumed, caped ghost that could only be Jolly Roger. To that, Captain O'Shea made the straight-faced declaration:

"Convinced I should be — and will be — only if all of you should see this same ghost at the very same time. That would be droll indeed. Should it happen here in your own quarters, please tell me. Just send word to me down in Cape Regal."

With that, Captain O'Shea stalked out through one of the half dozen doorways from the officers' quarters and made his report to Colonel Gandak, who had taken a special room of his own. Naturally, Captain O'Shea said nothing about Jolly Roger's ghost. His report concerned conditions down in Cape Regal, where he promptly returned. Apparently, the captain had no more time to waste around Fort Defiance.

At least, so the lieutenants thought.

The next night, those same lieutenants and a few others were weighing those same rumors, plus a few new ones that had cropped up. They had interrogated their men thoroughly, and all had stuck to their individual stories. The consensus was that a ghost really was on the rove, and the group nodded solemnly when Lieutenant Alvarez declared:

"I should like to have Captain O'Shea here with us and have him see exactly what our men have told us, a ghostly figure of this so-called Jolly Roger—"

Alvarez cut short, staring toward a doorway, and the others followed the direction of his gaze. They froze at sight of the very figure they were talking about. There it was, clad in white uniform, plumed hat, cream-colored cape, swashbuckling boots of a light tan and a sash of the same color, from which dangled sword and scabbard. This full-fledged materialization of Governor Roger Crisp was clad in the exact replica of one of the uniforms in the museum room.

Eyes glued, the group tried to make out the face beneath the hat brim. It was whitish, skull-like, as they feared. These officers were unarmed, here in their quarters, but it hardly would have helped to draw a gun against a ghost. At least, so they thought, until Lieutenant Hadrup, crouching low for a better look up at the skull-like face, suddenly exclaimed:

"I know you! But until this moment, you had me badly scared, Captain O'Shea!"

At that, the "ghost" removed its plumed hat with a sweeping bow and revealed O'Shea's smiling features. The lieutenants, though taken in, laughed at the captain's prank.

"I went up to the museum," exclaimed O'Shea, "and borrowed this outfit to fool you. A pretty good job I did, too, but not quite good enough, was it, Hadrup?"

"No, sir," returned the Danish lieutenant. "Your face was white enough, but not as hollow as Jolly Roger's should be."

"My error," admitted O'Shea. "I used powdered chalk"—he rubbed his hand across his cheek and showed some that came off—"but I should have kept the hat brim lower, to cut off the light. I practiced it, but not enough."

O'Shea stepped toward a corner of the room, putting on the hat and pulling it down at a rakish angle.

"Let's see how it looks in the mirror," he said. "Why, it's perfect! A wonderful skull effect"—he leaned forward to study the face before him, then swung to the Danish lieutenant. "What would you say, Hadrup?"

"I would say, sir," Hadrup laughed, "that you were not looking into the mirror, because it is in the next alcove. You were looking into an empty doorway."

Captain O'Shea swung about, did a double-take of his own at sight of the empty doorway. Almost frantically, he whipped off the plumed hat and cream-colored cape and flung them on the table, following with the sash and sword.

"So help me," he exclaimed, "I thought I was looking into a mirror. I saw a figure like mine — its face a skull — "

"And now, Captain," interposed Lieutenant Alvarez, with a chuckle, "you are giving us that stuff you call blarney."

"But I am not. I saw myself — or so I thought! And when I looked again, just now, the figure was gone." O'Shea looked about appealingly. "Won't somebody believe me?"

"I believe you, sir." The new speaker was Lieutenant Ahmed, in charge of a small Egyptian detachment. "As you turned from the doorway, I saw a figure much like yours. But the plume was on the other side of the hat, the stock of the collar was higher, the sash was yellow, not tan. Then it was gone, in a flash."

Ahmed's calm manner, his facial expression as immobile as that of the Sphinx, made his words impressive.

"We've both seen Jolly Roger!" exclaimed O'Shea. Then, to the others, "Come on! What are we waiting for? It's up to us to track him down."

O'Shea led the charge through the doorway and up a fan-shaped staircase at the end of a short passage. At the top, the corridors diverged, but some officers took the one to the left; others followed the route to the right. So they continued, splitting a few more times, until suddenly they all emerged, like so many mice from their holes, arriving on the broad roof of the fort from different and well-separated outlets.

The sight of so many officers in varied uniforms rather startled the lone sentry who was pacing the roof. The moonlight was clear and the flaring summit of Mt. Mogombo added a lurid cast to the sky, so that faces were readily recognizable and the sentry had no need to challenge the excited officers. Instead, they pummeled him with questions, asking if he'd seen anyone in a uniform like the one that Captain O'Shea now wore.

The sentry insisted that he had seen no one at all, either in or out of uniform. After a futile search of the entire roof, the officers looked into Crisp's apartment and the various watchtowers. Those all proved empty, and the officers went back to their quarters, where O'Shea discarded the rest of the Jolly Roger uniform and disclosed his own beneath.

"I'll take these back where they belong," O'Shea stated, referring to the oversized pantaloons, doublet, boots, and other regalia. "I guess Lieutenant Ahmed and I were just imagining things. The sooner we forget it, the better."

It wasn't going to be that easy to forget.

Within a few days, a mysterious malady began to break out among the U.N. troops in Fort Defiance. It wasn't serious; it just seemed to affect those who were slated for sentry duty on the roof, during night hours. Once relieved of such duty, the patients immediately improved. The lieutenants quizzed their men and reported the findings to Captain O'Shea, who took it up with Colonel Gandak.

First, O'Shea frankly admitted that he had played a hoax on his fellow officers and described how it had developed into an actual ghost hunt. Then he came to the present problem.

"The men on sentry duty have been worried, sir," explained O'Shea, "whenever they've been detailed to the roof. They say that they always feel that someone is watching them, no matter which way they turn. It was getting on their nerves, though they didn't say so until the other night.

"Then, when we all came hopping up there looking for a ghost, the man on sentry go, Private Zuga, of the Iraq detail, became really worried. He told others what had happened, and now they expect a ghost to come up behind them, tap them on the shoulder, and maybe pitch them off the parapet. It's that bad, Colonel."

"And what would you propose to do about it?"

"Why not remove all sentries from the roof? The fort is in no danger while the Mongombonians are fighting one another."

"I have a better idea," Gandak decided. "We'll double the sentries, putting two men to a shift. As they keep pacing back and forth, each will be facing the direction the other is coming from. If there is any danger — ghostly or human — one will be sure to see it."

The colonel's plan was put into immediate effect and it worked to perfection until a night when Mt. Mogombo was rumbling ominously and spouting flames lavishly. Down in the guardroom Sergeant Dhazi was in charge of thirty men, who were playing cards and writing letters home, when a sudden jangle sounded above the guardroom door.

As Dhazi looked up, it came again, more forcefully. Someone was tugging the cord in Crisp's apartment and ringing the bells in the guardroom, just as Laxaman had. But since no one was allowed in Crisp's apartment, Dhazi decided that he was being hoaxed. As the bells rang louder and more violently, he shouted to his men, "Let's go!"

On the roof, Private Zuga of Iraq was on sentry duty with a companion, Private Mirza, of India. As Zuga turned, he saw Mirza halted, staring at the steps from Crisp's apartment. The glare from the volcano showed a strange, hypnotic glitter in Mirza's eyes, as though they were following a moving form across the roof. Then the spell was broken.

Dhazi's full contingent poured from the doorways and stormed Crisp's apartment, while Dhazi shouted at Zuga and Mirza, demanding to know who was in there. Both sentries insisted it was empty, and after a futile inspection, Dhazi and his men went back down to the guardroom.

But who — or what — had rung those bells? Both Zuga and Mirza swore that they had seen no person enter or leave the closed apartment. But when Zuga told about Mirza's odd behavior, Mirza changed his story during an interview with Colonel Gandak.

"I saw no person enter, sir," declared Mirza, "and I saw no person leave. But I did see something come from the closed door."

"And what," asked Gandak, "was that something?"

"A ghost," Mirza declared, "all in white, with a hat as big as a turban, and wearing a flowing robe. It must have been a ghost, for it came through the closed door. So I knew it was no person."

"And where did it go from there, Mirza?"

"Toward the watchtower, when Sergeant Dhazi arrived with all his men and — puff — the ghost vanished."

"That will be all, Mirza."

But it was not all. Talk of the ghost was now so common at Fort Defiance that the soldiers were becoming restless. It was obvious that they would have to be switched to and from Cape Regal to keep the situation in hand. Soon the fort would become simply a reception center for new troops before they were sent on peace-keeping expeditions or to round up insurgents in the mountains. That wasn't to Colonel Gandak's liking, as the U.N. Security Council had ordered him to create a permanent garrison that could be maintained after other troops had been withdrawn. So Colonel Gandak sent for Captain O'Shea.

"You started all this, Captain," Gandak reminded him in a tone of more than slight reproof. "If it hadn't been for that prank of yours, things would not be so bad. Can you suggest a remedy?"

"I made the ghost walk once," returned O'Shea, stroking his chin reflectively. "Maybe I should do the same thing again."

"But that would only make matters worse."

"I don't think so, Colonel. The officers saw through my masquerade, though we did chase an imaginary ghost later." O'Shea gave a short laugh, as though dismissing that recollection. "Suppose I stage another prank for Mirza's benefit, to let him see how he was fooled. That would impress the other sentries as well."

"You have my approval." Gandak nodded. "I'm quite sure that Mirza was halfway in a dream state when he thought he saw that ghost. It would be good to snap him out of such notions."

Captain O'Shea and a few fellow officers rigged the ghost. They ran a wire from the steps outside Crisp's closed door, over toward the watchtower. They doubled the wire around an intervening bastion, back to the cannon ramp. To it, they hooked a light dummy draped in sheets and crowned with a plumed hat. They hung this down over the parapet, with a line attached, so that it could be drawn up through an embrasure.

To do all this, they dismissed a pair of sentries late one afternoon, shortly before Mirza and Zuga came on duty. Once the thing was rigged, they let the wire lie slack. Then they went down to the officers' quarters to wait until the next change of sentries, in order to have more witnesses. In addition, Captain O'Shea told Sergeant Dhazi to have a few picked men ready as onlookers.

When the right time came, Captain O'Shea and Lieutenant Ahmed came up through the cannon ramp, with Sergeant Dhazi and a few men close behind.

Other officers and men were in different doorways, a few to each. A corporal was on the roof, with two new sentries to replace Mirza and Zuga. None of these men knew about the rigged ghost.

First, O'Shea drew the wire taut. Then he reeled in the line, bringing the dummy up through the embrasure and dragging it over to the steps of the governor's apartment. Mt. Mogombo was furnishing just the right amount of intermittent glow to outline the human figures on the roof. To reveal the ghost, Captain O'Shea gave the line a well-timed tug.

Private Mirza, staring toward the governor's apartment, froze in his tracks as the whitish form loomed upward and forward so suddenly that it seemed to have come through the closed door. Then its motion became a steady, ghostly glide; down the steps, as O'Shea slackened the wire slightly; then across the roof as he pulled it taut again and reeled in the line at a set rate. Coming into the glare of Mt. Mogombo, the ghost took on a ruddy tinge that heightened its weird, soul-chilling effect.

The corporal and the other sentries, noting Mirza, now saw what he was watching, and they froze as well. O'Shea spoke in an undertone to Ahmed.

"A better ghost than I was. It looks real, doesn't it?"

"Very real, Captain," replied Ahmed. "Almost as real as the real ghost we both saw later."

"Forget about that, Ahmed. Just watch this ghost — and particularly watch Mirza. He's taking it to be real, and when we show it to be a fake, his whole story will fall apart."

Shakily, Mirza was raising his gun, as though to fire at the gliding white shape. Then, losing his nerve, he sagged back. The rifle dropped from his numbed hands, its clatter providing the only sound that broke that deep, uncanny hush, with Mogombo rumbling in the distant background. The other sentries, witnessing Mirza's terror, began to cower, too. Coolly, O'Shea handed the line to Ahmed.

"Keep reeling it in," the captain said, "while I go out and show up the fake. This will really knock out the ghost business —"

Captain O'Shea spoke too soon. At that moment, Private Mirza snapped out of his coma and dashed forward on the double. Before the astonished eyes of the other sentinels and the hidden watchers as well, Mirza reached the gliding figure, snatched it from the line with his bare hands, tore it apart, hat from drape, and threw the pieces on the roof. Laughing at the top of his voice, Mirza stamped on the remnants of the ghost and shouted:

"A trick! A silly trick! Somebody thought they could fool me, me, the man who knows a real ghost when he sees one!"

O'Shea grabbed the line from Ahmed, hauled it in, and dropped it. He waved Ahmed forward, and followed by Dhazi and the others, they joined the group that was now crowding about Mirza, who had become the hero of the occasion. O'Shea, having disposed of the proof that linked him to the hoax, asked casually:

"How did you know it was a fake, Mirza?"

"It was very simple, sir," Mirza replied. "It looked like real ghost I saw that other night, until it came in front of volcano. The time real ghost walked by, I could see the mountain — smoke, fire, and all — right through it. With this one, I could no longer see volcano when it came between." He picked up the torn sheet, spread it to obscure the distant summit of Mogombo. "No mountain, no ghost. I mean no real ghost."

O'Shea's scheme had backfired, as was proven the next day, when the entire garrison accepted the ghost of the original Jolly Roger as genuine. The men became more jittery than ever, and kept going about in pairs, afraid that they might glimpse old Jolly Roger at any turn.

Colonel Gandak might have stemmed the growing terror of the unexplainable, but now the row of bells in the guardroom began jangling almost every other night. They would start gently, then become violent, causing a rush of soldiers up to the roof. Always, they found the sentries going their usual rounds, and always the governor's apartment was empty. But no one saw the ghost of Jolly Roger stalking in and out. Maybe the spook was piqued by O'Shea's prank. Perhaps he was just trying a new technique by jangling the bells and nothing more.

Either way, something had to be done. Colonel Gandak put a huge padlock on the door of the governor's apartment and kept the only key himself. But the bells still continued to jangle violently, every few nights. Gandak then had the officers trace the bell ropes down to the guardroom, to find out if anyone was tampering with them along the way. They followed them through every floor, including a small opening in the masonry that had been plastered over the bastion after Crisp's death. Yet nowhere could they find a spot where the ropes could be touched. When Gandak asked the officers what they thought caused the repeated ringing, someone suggested, "Rats."

"Rats!" the colonel stormed. "How could rats get into those stone walls? What would they do, gnaw their way up and down the ropes?" Gandak pondered. "Maybe they could at that," he said more calmly, "and the way to prove it is to get rid of the ropes."

Get rid of the ropes they did, and with that, the ghostly manifestations ceased. Mt. Mogombo flared nightly, sentries patrolled regularly, troops lounged in the guardroom. But there was no longer a parading spook, no longer any ringing bells. With Crisp's apartment padlocked, the bell ropes gone, all seemed fine. But Colonel Gandak was far from satisfied.

"All this is like sitting on top of Mt. Mogombo," the colonel told his staff. "The quieter it gets, the more likely it is to break loose suddenly, and on a grand scale. We know there is a ghost around, and we must find out what he is cooking up, to learn whether it is for good or bad."

Any other group might have taken this with skepticism, but the members of this U.N. occupational peace force included men from so many different countries, steeped in such a variety of legends that a mere exchange of ideas could cause them to accept almost anything in the realm of the macabre. By now, too, the men still at Fort Defiance represented a hard core, who were determined to see this struggle with the unknown straight through to the finish. When Captain O'Shea suggested calling in Laxaman, the one man really informed on the Jolly Roger ghost lore, the other officers were enthused at the idea and Colonel Gandak approved it.

Laxaman was present at the next conference. With him, he had stacks of records and reports pertaining to Fort Defiance. Colonel Gandak opened with the query:

"What is behind all this, Laxaman? We are convinced that the ghost is real, though we want the men to think otherwise. But why should Jolly Roger haunt this fort?"

"Opinions vary as to that," Laxaman replied, blinking in owlish fashion through his thick glasses. "I have talked with members of psychic research societies and professors from great universities who came here to investigate. They agree on one thing."

"That there is no ghost?"

"No, no. Like you, they think there is a ghost. They agree that such a specter must have some purpose."

"And what kind of purpose would it be?"

"Several types are possible," asserted Laxaman, in a scholarly tone. "Some ghosts have been known to guard treasure; sometimes driving people away, other times leading them there. The same applies to places where a body is buried. In other cases, a ghost seeks to make amends for some past crime. Until they have done that, they continue to haunt."

"Would that apply to Governor Crisp?"

"I would say so, but I do not know. I only give opinions of noted professors who study parapsychology and psychic science. Even they do not agree."

Later, Colonel Gandak held a meeting with his officers in the very courtroom where the portrait of Governor Crisp glowered down upon the judgment seat. There they decided on ways and means to bait his ghostly counterpart.

"Crisp was a pirate in his day," declared Colonel Gandak, "but he reformed, so he could have dug up his treasure long before he died. I think we can rule out that possibility."

"The same applies to the way he hanged pirates," Lieutenant Hadrup asserted. "That was customary in those days, so Crisp wouldn't have felt regrets over taking their lives."

"Up to that last time," Lieutenant Alvarez corrected. "He was wrong in hanging the men from the *Falcon*. Apparently, he was trying to prevent their execution by ringing the guardroom, and his ghost has gone on trying ever since."

"In that case," Captain O'Shea suggested, "we should put the ropes back on the bells." He turned to Colonel Gandak. "What about it, sir? It would give our ghost a fighting chance."

"As an operational peace force of the United Nations," declared Gandak sternly, "our purpose is to see that no one has a fighting chance, because our job is to stop all fighting. That goes for ghosts as well as political factions. If you refuse to pamper them, they will no longer bother you. Once you have them under such control, you can report your mission as accomplished."

By discouraging the ghost, Gandak hoped to prevent its reappearance. But he posted men at key spots in the fort, to relay word of any new manifestations. All men on patrol were to converge on any spot where the ghost was reported, while a picked squad was to come from the guardroom and cut off its escape. The rest of the garrison was to go out to the parade ground and watch for pranksters on the parapets.

Under these rigid regulations nothing happened at Fort Defiance until the night the operational force was ready to pack up and leave. Gandak read a report to O'Shea and asked what he thought of it.

"It's fine, sir," said O'Shea, "but all your emphasis is on the battling political factions, with no word about our ghost."

"This report is for the U. N. security council," retorted Gandak, "so they can open negotiations with the factions mentioned. Can you tell me how they could negotiate with a ghost?"

O'Shea couldn't answer that. But when he made a final inspection tour, he became very reflective when he reached the roof.

"Things are too quiet," Captain O'Shea told Lieutenant Alvarez, who had accompanied him. He gestured off toward the darkened hills. "Why, even the volcano has quit acting up. If Private Mirza was on sentry duty, he couldn't tell a real ghost from a fake tonight."

They passed sentries on the way down to the guardroom. Most of the sixty men there had already packed their dunnage for tomorrow's departure. But Sergeant Dhazi was maintaining full discipline.

"This is our last night to catch old Jolly Roger," said Dhazi, smiling from beneath his tilted beret. "My men would like that."

"All of your men, Sergeant?" O'Shea asked.

"All the inside guard," Dhazi amended. "They volunteered for that duty. The rest are assigned to the outside. If you want me to show you, sir—"

"No, no," broke in O'Shea. "The colonel might think it was another hoax. Tell me, Sergeant, how did you manage to build the men's morale up to its present state?"

"Because of the bells," Dhazi confided. "I mean, because they didn't ring. Before, the men worried about who had pulled the ropes, thinking it had to be a ghost. But when the colonel took the ropes away" — he shook his head and smiled — "they said it would take a real ghost and a good one, to ring those bells now. You see, sir?"

Captain O'Shea saw, though he hadn't before. He realized how cleverly Colonel Gandak had handled this group of varied nationalities, who believed in so many legends that it was easy for them to laugh at a ghost who couldn't ring bells.

"And what would happen if those bells rang right now?" O'Shea asked.

"I wouldn't want to say, sir." Dhazi paused and pondered. "Except the inside squad might become the outside squad —"

"And the outside squad?"

"Well, they would be on their way clear to Cape Regal, if nobody stopped them!" Dhazi looked up toward the disconnected bells. "If those bells began to ring right now, sir, I wouldn't be responsible for what might —"

Before Dhazi could add the word, "happen," it did. The bells began to ring! After a slight clank, they tinkled a trifle more. By then, the men were at attention, all looking up at the bells. So was Sergeant Dhazi. Tough though he was, he was the most impressed.

Captain O'Shea heard the bells and was quick to realize that it would not be smart to look at them. Rather than admit that they mattered, he turned to Lieutenant Alvarez, who was looking at Captain O'Shea with the same thought in mind.

"Dhazi is right," O'Shea muttered. "His men would be on the way out right now, if those bells were ringing hard."

"But why," asked Alvarez, "are they ringing at all?"

"I don't know. But if Dhazi doesn't act fast, I'll have to." O'Shea did some mental juggling, then suggested, "You ask him, Lieutenant."

"Muy bien," Alvarez agreed. "Very good." He stepped over, tapped Dhazi on the shoulder, and said, "It must be the ghost, Sergeant. Shouldn't you be giving orders?"

Dhazi turned with angry eyes and saw Captain O'Shea staring from beyond. O'Shea nodded, and Dhazi swung to his men.

"Inside detail, fall in!" The men snapped to attention at those words. "Follow me, on the double!"

It was timely, for by then the bells were ringing loudly, violently, despite the fact that they had no cords. Alvarez looked at O'Shea and confided, "You timed it perfectly, Captain."

"The credit is all yours, Lieutenant," O'Shea replied.

By then, the bells were setting up a terrific clangor. Dhazi's picked squad had fallen in, and he was simply waiting for word to be relayed by the sentinels, telling him just where the source of the trouble lay. But Captain O'Shea didn't need such information. O'Shea snapped to Alvarez:

"Take charge of the outside detail, Lieutenant. I'll handle this group." Then O'Shea barked to Dhazi, "Why are we waiting, Sergeant? We know where the trouble must be. Whoever is ringing these bells is up in the governor's apartment. Come along!"

As O'Shea started for the stone stairs, Dhazi yelled to his squad, "Follow me!" Dhazi's men followed on the double, and as they surged after O'Shea, they swept along astonished sentinels. Posted higher up, those watchers had heard the bells, but hadn't reported to the guardroom because it was from there that the terrific cacophony came.

Once Dhazi's twenty-man contingent was on its way up to the roof, Lieutenant Alvarez had no trouble marching the remaining forty soldiers out through the sally port, where he stationed them about the parade ground, to watch the ramparts and respond to any signals from the roof.

Meanwhile, Dhazi's squad was tearing past Gandak's office where the colonel was completing the report that completely debunked the rumors of Jolly Roger's ghost. Hearing the clatter, Gandak opened his door and caught the echo of the bells from far below. Realizing what must have happened, the colonel grabbed the key to the big padlock on Crisp's apartment, and joined the rush.

By now, the word had been relayed to all the scattered sentinels, who were converging in from their key posts and swelling the charging crew. In fact, the only men in complete ignorance of what was going on were the two sentries who were pacing the roof itself. They swung about, raising their rifles as the surge came from the ramp. Then, recognizing Captain O'Shea as the leader, they came to attention. O'Shea waved for his followers to fan out, which they did. Then Colonel Gandak arrived and handed him the big key, saying:

"Go on, Captain! See who the prankster is tonight, and find out how he's ringing those bells. Whoever he is, we'll discipline him, and properly!"

The scene, though very dark earlier, now was lighted by a sudden flare from Mt. Mogombo, as though the volcano, too, wanted to help expose the hoax. Hardly had that glare subsided before another came, still brighter. It was then that O'Shea halted, only a few dozen feet from the steps leading up to the governor's apartment.

In the sudden light, O'Shea could have sworn he saw a figure standing there, in the plumed hat and braided uniform of Governor Crisp, the lipless mouth grinning from beneath its hollow eyes. As the flare faded, the figure remained, a whitened after-image in the gloom. While O'Shea still doubted his eyes, one member of Dhazi's squad sprang up beside him, asking eagerly:

"Did you see it, Captain? Can you see it now?"

The questioner was Private Mirza. O'Shea nodded, for he, too, was convinced that this actually was a spectral figure.

"I can see it plainly, sir," continued Mirza, "and I can see right through it, as I did before. Look closely, sir —"

A rumble like distant thunder interrupted. The sound waves were arriving from Mt. Mogombo, as a result of that first volcanic flare. An echoing murmur came from the men who were fanning out from the ramp, now more than fifty in all, including the officers and the sentinels from the widely scattered posts. They were wondering why O'Shea didn't unlock the door to the governor's apartment, for none of them had caught more than a fleeting glimpse of the ghostly shape that loomed there.

"Go on, Captain!" stormed Gandak. Then, to Dhazi, who was standing by, he added, "Pick a few men, Sergeant, and go on in with Captain O'Shea. Tell him I said for him to give you the key if he doesn't intend to use it himself."

The sound from Mogombo's second flare was echoing as Gandak spoke, and before Dhazi could start forward, the volcano delivered its most vivid burst. The blast was so bright that it showed the roof and parapets of Fort Defiance as clearly as in dazzling sunlight. Colonel Gandak and those about him turned to see the whole great cone spread apart and crumble in a titanic explosion, in which a tremendous mass of flame disgorged a huge black cloud of ashes, dust, and brimstone that spread like a massive umbrella, a mile above the vanished summit.

In the sudden darkness that followed the terrific outburst, Captain O'Shea and Private Mirza, the only men still staring at the padlocked door, saw the figure of Jolly Roger fully materialized even to its skull-like leer, yet still transparent. But even more significant, Crisp's wraith had become a ghost with a purpose, for the phantom figure was raising its hands and sweeping them outward, in a gesture that could only be interpreted as a silent shout of "Back! Back! Back!"

O'Shea wheeled about and duplicated the gesture to the outspread men, starting toward them as he did. Mirza, too, was waving his arms frantically. Both were shouting, "Back! Back! Back!" Their words could not be heard because of the gigantic roar arriving from Mt. Mogombo, the result of the mightiest eruption in the volcano's history. But the U. N. officers and troops understood those gestures. They did more than just retreat; they scattered to the far parapets, and with good reason.

From Colonel Gandak down to the newest private in the corps, O'Shea's frenzied warning was certified by that of a fantastic figure they glimpsed beyond him, the uniformed ghost of Jolly Roger!

Moments later, the phantom was gone, as Fort Defiance gave a horrendous shudder. With it, the stone roof split from parapet to parapet, along a jagged angle that cut off the entire corner where the governor's apartment formed a lone tower above its bastion. Under the force of the most severe earthquake that ever rocked Cape Regal, the whole wall wavered outward and collapsed, toppling the crumbling structure that had been the governor's apartment down into the depths of Hangman's Bay! Massive ancient cannon, sliding from the embrasures of the caving parapets, added echoing splashes as they hit the seething waters, except for those that clattered down to the parade ground, crushing the paving there.

O'Shea and Mirza just managed to clear the widening crack before the corner tumbled. They reached the far parapets and clung there with the other members of the garrison, while the fort continued to shiver like a ship at sea. Mogombo's staccato bursts gradually subsided, and the tremors lessened accordingly. Soon the men on the roof were waving to their comrades on the parade ground below.

Though the fort still stood, except for its crumbled corner, inside passages and stairways were blocked by fallen masonry. If the officers and sentinels had remained there, they would have been crushed or trapped. As it was, scaling ladders were raised to the parapets, and they all descended to the parade ground. A roll-call revealed that not a single life had been lost.

"Give credit to the ghost of Jolly Roger," Gandak told O'Shea. "If he hadn't appeared on those steps and warned you back, there's no telling how many men would have been in that corner when it fell."

"That's why his ghost kept ringing the bells so often," O'Shea said thoughtfully. "He must have known what was coming, and he was trying to get us out of the fort. We didn't take the hint until tonight. It wasn't enough for a ghostly hand to pull those ropes and ring the bells. The ropes themselves had to be gone before we would believe it."

"Jolly Roger had a purpose," Gandak decided. "His ghost wanted to make amends for having hanged the crew of the *Falcon*. A dozen men died when Governor Crisp failed to ring the bells that day, but a hundred men are alive tonight, thanks to his ghostly hand. Imagine his haunting the fort for a couple of centuries, just to accomplish that!"

"I'm not so sure that was his only purpose," remarked O'Shea. "According to Laxaman, the ghost was around the castle when it was practically nothing but a museum, and nobody's life was in danger. Maybe Jolly Roger had a more personal reason, as well."

Captain O'Shea was still thinking in such terms when he and a volunteer search crew probed the interior of Fort Defiance the next morning. The guardroom was an utter shambles, for it was directly beneath the governor's apartment, and the caving of the west bastion had poured tons of masonry down through the intervening floors, bringing the floors themselves along.

Working through the rubble, the crew reclaimed the dunnage and other belongings from the guardroom and reached the bastion itself by late afternoon. There, Lieutenant Alvarez, busy with the diggers, saw something that caused him to shout for Captain O'Shea, who joined him at once.

Where the bastion had been strengthened following the death of Governor Crisp, chunks of loose stone and mortar showed that the reinforcement was nothing but a false wall, forming a shell with a hollow behind it. Along with the stone had tumbled an oblong box that looked like an upright coffin. When O'Shea and Alvarez removed the loose lid of the box, they stepped back in amazed horror.

There, in its improvised casket was a skeleton in full uniform. Oddly, the skull was recognizable by its shape, for its hollow eyes, fierce grin, and broad square jaw were much like Crisp's portrait, while they resembled his ghost as well. But the uniform that the skeleton wore was really the identifying factor. It was another of the garish, gold-braided creations of Governor Roger Crisp, clear from its plumed hat and doublet with gold medals, down to the pantaloons and swashbuckling boots.

"Old Jolly Roger himself!" exclaimed Captain O'Shea. "He gave us a double warning, that we knew; but he also had a double purpose, as I thought. Laxaman said something about a legend of an empty casket being buried in the graveyard, because Hervey, the deputy governor, was afraid the mob would dig it up. So Hervey hid Crisp's body in a wall, which he claimed he built to make the fort stronger. This is what Jolly Roger wanted us to find."

"Quite right," agreed Lieutenant Alvarez, "and I, for one, feel that we should bury this skeleton in the graveyard where it rightfully belongs. After all, we are lucky we are not buried here ourselves" — he gestured to the rubble that had once been the guardroom — "and we should show our appreciation by granting Jolly Roger his last wish."

A vote of the U.N. officers made it unanimous. With Laxaman's aid, they located the long-forgotten cemetery where Crisp's crypt had once stood with its empty coffin. There the skeleton remains were interred with due ceremony. Then the members of the garrison marched back to Cape Regal, where troopships were waiting to receive the U.N. operation force, while Mt. Mogombo rumbled a requiem from beyond the blue hills.

Colonel Gandak included all that had happened in his report to the U.N. Security Council, while Calvin Laxaman wrote a more detailed account to a psychic research committee in London. In it, Laxaman suggested that slight, imperceptible earth tremors, forerunners of the eruption of Mt. Mogombo, might have caused the bells to ring in the guardroom.

Laxaman added that suggestion because he felt that people generally were of the opinion that anyone who believed in ghosts would have to be crazy. But the U.N. officers and men who had garrisoned Fort Defiance did not agree with Laxaman.

In their opinion, anyone who *didn't* believe in ghosts would have to be crazy.

The House on the Island

The house on the island crouched like a prehistoric monster above the placid waters of the lagoon, its dimly lighted windows resembling a pair of watchful eyes, continually staring below. Surrounding it were the stark outlines of waving trees that formed fantastic figures against the night sky, while the lower ground, merging into marshland, seemed peopled with sylvan sprites, elusive elves, and even water goblins.

Such, at least, was the imaginative impression gained by Janice Coleridge as she drove her car across the narrow causeway to the island, that bleak November midnight. Janice was paying a surprise visit to her college chum, Marcia Woodruff, and her husband, Oscar, who had moved into the house during the previous summer. They'd told Janice to "drop in anytime" at the "spooky old place," as they styled their home, so here she was.

Or was she?

Janice lost sight of the house completely as the road from the causeway curved up through the trees. It was rocky, jouncy, and at times reduced itself to the status of a pair of ruts, which made Janice think it was leading nowhere. Then, suddenly, the headlights cut a swath across open ground, and Janice swung in beside the house, where someone was waving a flashlight to guide her to a parking spot.

The man with the flashlight approached as Janice was getting from the car. She heard a voice say "Hello, Janice," and she was looking at Oscar's round, smiling face beneath the shock of reddish hair that he seldom, if ever, brushed.

"Hello, Oscar," Janice rejoined. "How did you know I was coming?"

"I didn't", replied Oscar. "Marcia did. But don't ask me how. She just senses things—or I should say, hears them. Like your voice, saying, 'I'll be seeing you soon, Marcia—and after that she tells me, 'Go out with the flashlight, Oscar, I'm sure I hear the car'—and here you are!"

Janice laughed not just at the oddity of the thing, but because Oscar was so talkative, for ordinarily he was a strictly silent sort. She noticed, now, that the glowing "eyes" of the house were huge front windows on the ground floor and that the rest of the building bulked black above it, like the frowning forehead of some gigantic behemoth.

Oscar took Janice's bag, and they went through the front door into a huge, low-ceilinged living room, where logs blazed cheerily in a fireplace. Janice exclaimed, "How wonderful!" only to give a startled, half-frightened gasp as a whitish figure emerged from the deeper darkness into the flickering fringe.

Then Janice saw that it was Marcia, wearing a pale blue dressing gown that gave the spooky effect. But even more ghostly was the chalk whiteness of Marcia's face, which brought a really worried stare from Janice.

"Don't be concerned, Janice," said Marcia. "I'm not ill. I'm just dog-tired. What with Hallowe'en pranks, the servants all leaving, and now this business of a ghost hunt—"

"A ghost hunt!" exclaimed Janice.

"Let me tell it, Marcia," suggested Oscar. He turned to Janice. "What Marcia means is that we have poltergeists around the place. You know what poltergeists are, don't you?"

"Mischievous spirits," Janice defined. "Little unseen hands that toss things when you aren't looking, or make scratching sounds and raps. They inhabit a Twilight Zone between the natural and the supernatural." She stopped and her eyes widened, almost eagerly. "You have poltergeists? Here?"

"We thought it was the kids from town, around Hallowe'en," explained Oscar. "Then we thought it must be the servants, because we knew we weren't doing it. But when they up and left, and the sounds still kept on, that was it. Poltergeists."

"How thrilling!" exclaimed Janice. "Have you managed to track them down?"

"Not exactly," declared Marcia. "That's why I'm so worn out. Chasing poltergeists to make sure they don't set fire to something. They do that, too, you know."

"Anyway, we're cleared for action," Oscar chuckled, "so welcome aboard, Janice. I'll be sleeping here by the fire, so I can watch it. You and Marcia will be in the study over there."

Oscar pointed to a room lighted by oil lamps, for there was no electricity in the house.

"If you hear any snoring," Oscar went on, "blame me. If you hear prowling sounds, it won't be poltergeists. It will be Aunt Cathy, who came here to help Marcia keep house after the servants left. She's sleeping in the library"—he thumbed toward a closed door—"but she usually gets up around three o'clock and goes to the kitchen to make herself a cup of hot chocolate.

"And if you hear a real loud banging around dawn, that won't be poltergeists either. It will be Steve Hargis, the handyman, bringing in wood for the fireplaces. Anything else you hear will be poltergeists." Oscar yawned and stretched his arms. "I'm getting sleepy. So good night, all, and happy nightmares."

It was broad daylight when Janice awoke, to find that the others were already up. She joined Oscar and Marcia in a breakfast nook that led to a large, old-fashioned kitchen. Over bacon and eggs, Marcia remarked:

"Oscar and I have a few chores to do, Janice, so make yourself at home. Aunt Cathy has gone to town with Steve to bring back some groceries. She will be here in time for lunch."

"She had better be," Oscar declared, "or there won't be any lunch. She only shops for groceries once a week."

So Janice roamed about the grounds and studied the sprawling old house from the outside. She knew that the Woodruffs had bought it at a bargain, and since it was isolated, dilapidated, and haunted, Janice could understand why. In fact, when Janice went indoors, the gloom of the big living room depressed her, but she finally found an interesting book and a chair near enough to a window where she had sufficient light to read it.

After a half hour, Janice happened to look up. She smiled as she saw a newcomer who apparently had just entered the front door and then closed it. This could only be Aunt Cathy, for she was a middle-aged woman, dressed plainly in gray, and with a closely knit shawl of the same color draped over her head and shoulders. Janice was about to speak in greeting as the woman crossed the living room, but she suddenly decided it would be better not to startle Aunt Cathy, in this setting where poltergeists rambled.

The stairway to the second floor was at the far end of the living room, and the woman was almost there when she turned, so that Janice saw her face for the first time. It was a pale face, like Marcia's, indicating that Aunt Cathy had undergone a similar strain in these surroundings. Her eyes, though, were sharp and boring, whereas Marcia's gaze had been listless, even this morning. Yet, in staring at Janice, the woman seemed to look right through her. That only caused Janice's smile to widen at the thought that maybe Aunt Cathy acted that way with all strangers.

Then the gray-clad woman reached the top of the stairs, and Janice went back to her reading, only to be interrupted by Marcia.

"Well, Janice," she said, "I hope you like the place. Any questions?"

"Just one." Janice decided that a bit of wit might enliven Marcia. "Is Aunt Cathy your aunt, or is she Oscar's?"

"Why—why—" Marcia was puzzled, "she's Oscar's aunt."

"I thought so." Janice gave a nod. "She's the strictly silent type, the way Oscar used to be. I saw her walk in from the front door and she looked me over when she went upstairs, but she didn't say a word."

The effect was the opposite of what Janice had expected. Marcia's face turned more chalky than ever; her words came in broken gasps:

"You—saw—Aunt—Cathy—walk—across—this—room?"

"All the way across. Why, what's so odd, Marcia?"

"Only—only that—" Marcia caught her breath, "only that it couldn't have been Aunt Cathy. She isn't back from town yet."

"Well, I supposed it could only be Aunt Cathy. She was middle-aged, dressed in plain gray, with a gray shawl over—"

Marcia's interruption was a frantic call.

"Oscar! Come quickly! Janice has seen her—she has seen the woman in gray!"

Oscar arrived on the run, and after the excitement subsided, he sat down and spoke in his most serious tone:

"We'll give you the straight story, Janice. You've seen the ghost that haunts this house. There's no doubt about it. I've glimpsed her, so has Marcia, and so has Aunt Cathy. We're pretty sure the servants did, too. But you're the first of us to see her actually stalk through this room—like in the old days."

"Just what," asked Janice weakly, "do you mean by the 'old days'?"

"We've checked the history of this house," Oscar explained. "Back in the early days of river steamboats, it was an inn where passengers stayed overnight. This living room was the tavern and dining room of the inn; that's why it's so wide, but low."

"And that's why the kitchen is so big, too?"

"Exactly. Our breakfast nook was the old pantry. Anyway, some people who stayed in rooms up there—" Oscar gestured to the stairway "—were never seen again until their bodies began bobbing up in the lagoon because they hadn't been weighted heavily enough. So the law moved in on Nell Denby, the woman who owned the place—'Old Death Knell,' they called her later—and charged her with murder."

"You mean—she really killed—killed how many people?"

"As many as five. Her two sons tried to take the blame for it, but Old Death Knell was hanged along with them. Nell knew what was coming, because when the constables arrived to arrest her, she tried to set fire to the house, in order to destroy all evidence. Her ghost has been trying to do that ever since."

It was Janice's turn to speak in disjointed tones:

"I—saw—the—ghost—of—Old—Knell—"

"The woman in gray." Oscar nodded. "When someone tried to reopen the inn, her ghost was seen several times, and mysterious fires broke out, until finally the place was partly burned down. Ten years later, they started to rebuild it, and they'd gotten just so far when the same thing happened. Another fire, of ghostly origin."

"And it's gone on ever since," added Marcia. "Sometimes owners closed the place, but it would still catch on fire. They blamed it on tramps, but there are other old houses around here where nothing like that ever happened."

"That's right," Oscar acknowledged. "Whenever this house became unin-habitable, the ghost neglected it. But just let someone try to put it in shape, fires and everything else would start all over. It was just about falling apart when real estate values skyrocketed a few years ago, so the owners rebuilt it, and we bought it. Now the trouble has started again." Oscar shook his head, annoyed. "We've insured the place for what we put into it, but I don't want to be beaten by a ghost!"

"And that's what I call a real spirit!"

The interruption came from the front door, and Janice turned quickly to see the real Aunt Cathy. She was a complete contrast to the woman in gray, for she was cheery, energetic, and actually only a few years older than her nephew Oscar. Marcia introduced Janice to Aunt Cathy, and was starting to tell about Janice's ludicrous mistake, when Aunt Cathy spread her hands warningly.

"Just hold it," she pleaded, "until Steve has finished bringing in the groceries. If he hears a lot of this ghost talk, he'll take off the way the servants did."

During lunch, they resumed the ghost talk, and Aunt Cathy became enthused when she learned that Janice had seen the woman in gray.

"You are clairvoyant, Janice," Aunt Cathy declared, "and since Marcia is clairaudient, we should really lick this ghost business."

" I know what clairvoyant means," remarked Janice. "It's the ability to see things that some people can't, the way I saw the woman in gray. But what does clairaudient mean?"

"It means to hear things that others can't," explained Oscar. "Marcia has been picking up weird sounds all over the place. Last night, she thought she heard your car half an hour before you got here. That's why she sent me outside to watch for you."

Since Janice was now a fully inducted member of the ghost-hunting team, they took her over the sprawling old inn, upstairs and down, showing her where raps had been heard, where mystery fires had broken out, and even a few spots where the gray phantom had been glimpsed, though only fleetingly.

"I'll bet you're the first person to meet the ghost face to face in the last fifty years," Oscar told Janice, in an admiring tone. "If we can track down Old Death Knell, maybe we can put her through the wringer, and get rid of her once and for all!"

It was easy to joke by day, but as late afternoon shadows lengthened, and twilight settled over the house on the island, Janice began to have qualms. It was pleasant by the big living room fire, but disconcerting to look toward the dim corners beyond. Yet, Janice wasn't frightened; she was only tense, like Marcia, who was constantly straining to hear things while Janice sought to see them.

When dinner was over, Aunt Cathy washed the dishes and Janice dried them, so that Marcia could rest in the living room. That was when Oscar entered the kitchen and said cheerily:

"Don't bother with the cups and saucers, Auntie. I had Marcia use the old nicked set, so we can leave them for Knell's ghost to clean up."

Janice blinked, amazed. "What do you mean, Oscar?" she demanded.

"You'll see," Oscar promised. "One thing an earth-chained entity can't stand is bad housekeeping. Old Nell is no exception."

Aunt Cathy left the cups and saucers clustered on the side of the kitchen sink. They went into the living room, where Marcia, her eyes half-closed, soon spoke in a faraway tone:

"I hear footsteps—now a whisper—an angry, muttering whisper—it comes from the direction of the kitchen—"

"She's here," Oscar said in an undertone. "I'll go around the back way, Aunt Cathy, while you and Janice come through the breakfast nook."

Oscar started on his circuit, while Janice and Aunt Cathy made a cautious approach. Aunt Cathy was whispering, "Not too quickly, Janice. It never happens if you're close enough to watch for it." An oil lamp was hanging in the kitchen and they could just see it past the corner of the nook, when a click came from the direction of the sink, and Aunt Cathy exclaimed, "Now!"

They sprang forward as the cups and saucers came flying toward the center of the kitchen, where they smashed on the floor. By then, Oscar was dashing in from an opposite door, as another witness to the crash. Gripped by some indefinable impulse, Janice looked up toward the sink. There, beside it, she saw that some gray shape of a woman whose white face and boring eyes were partly hidden by a shawl. An instant later, the phantom was gone, but Janice thought she saw its arms recoil, as though its hands had flung the cups and saucers.

Back in the living room, all that came under discussion, and Janice found herself becoming an enthusiastic member of the ghost-hunting crew as Oscar mapped the coming campaign.

"We must learn where the ghost of Old Nell comes from," Oscar decided. "Between Janice, who can see her, and Marcia, who can hear her, we can do it, if we remain constantly alert."

Three strained days followed, during which Janice glimpsed the gray figure occasionally, and Marcia heard strange sounds, which she tried to follow to their source, but without success.

Each day, the incidents grew more striking and more startling or "more evidential," as Oscar termed it, when he heard the details from Janice and Marcia.

Toward noon on the second day, Janice happened to be out in a side garden that overlooked an arm of the lagoon. The garden was simply a hodge-podge of dried grass and scrubby bushes at this season, with a few broken rustic benches alongside an old flagstone walk. It had been long neglected, but the Woodruffs were planning to restore it, once they had put the mansion itself in shape.

At present, the old garden offered a vantage spot from which Janice could view the outside of the house and compare it with the interior. She was particularly impressed with one third-story window that opened out onto a little balcony with an old wrought iron rail, apparently a part of the original inn, that had survived fire, storm, and stress.

No matter where else she looked, toward gables, bay windows, or upstairs porches with wooden balustrades, Janice found her gaze reverting toward that single window, which curiously reminded her of a gulping mouth, its iron rail a row of jagged teeth jutting up from the outthrust jaw of the balcony.

It was as if some magnetic force controlled Janice's eyes, compelling them to focus there.

Even more forceful was the chilling thought that this was leading to some climax, that soon she would know just why that window fascinated her. So she gave a sigh of real relief as gathering snow clouds suddenly obscured the sun, transforming the noonday brightness into a sullen dusk. When Janice looked toward the window again, it had darkened, and the iron rail was scarcely visible, so it had lost its ominous touch.

Or had it?

As Janice was glancing away, she caught a flash of something from the corner of her eye. It was another of those momentary impressions, resembling a woman in gray. Eager to retain it if she could, Janice looked back at the grilled window automatically. There, her gaze froze.

That block of blackness was no longer blank. Etched in its framework was a life-sized figure in gray, the same one that Janice had watched as it crossed the living room, and which she had glimpsed at intervals since then. Now, it was in full view again, and Janice didn't intend to let it get away, or at least she was determined to watch where it went.

As darkness persisted, Janice was sure she could make out the phantom's whitish face, but the distance was too great to glimpse the sharp eyes that Janice had noted before. Now, however, she saw the figure raise one arm and make a sweeping gesture, as though beckoning to someone far away. But Janice wasn't letting herself be tricked by that.

Instead of turning to look that way, Janice watched the window steadily, not even blinking, for fear it might dispel the ghostly illusion. Then, oddly, the figure itself took action, swinging about as though attracted by something within the room. A moment later, it had literally whisked itself from sight, veering off somewhere to the right of the window.

Janice snapped from her half-trance and rushed into the house, calling to the others. Oscar responded from the second floor and relayed the word that the lady in gray had been sighted. A few minutes later, he and his Aunt Cathy had reached the living room and were listening to Janice's story. Her mention of the balconied window brought a knowing nod from Oscar.

"They call that the Lookout Room," Oscar recalled, "because it overlooks the lagoon. But I didn't know the name went back to the time of the old inn. It must have, though, or Old Nell wouldn't be haunting the Lookout Room."

Marcia arrived from upstairs just in time to catch Oscar's final words.

"That's where I heard footsteps!" Marcia exclaimed. "I thought they went past the Lookout Room, but when I didn't hear them any more, I started back. Then I heard them coming from the room, but I was too late to overtake them."

During lunch, Oscar balanced the two reports and came to one of his well-defined conclusions.

"So Marcia heard footsteps," he declared, "and Janice looked up from the garden at the same time. They each caught the ghost of Old Nell reenacting something that must have been a regular procedure."

Janice and Marcia asked in the same breath: "Like what?"

"Like signalling to someone down by the lagoon," replied Oscar. "That's where the boats came in from the river. Noon would have been a logical time to notify accomplices that they would be needed later, say around midnight, to lend a hand in murder or get rid of a body."

That brought a shiver from Janice, but fear wasn't exactly the cause. She had attributed her chill in the garden to the cold November air, more than the sight of a gray ghost at the Lookout Window. Now, it was Oscar's cold-blooded analysis of the situation that affected her. More than ever, Janice was anxious to track down the woman in gray and end this haunting.

So Janice was pleased when Oscar suggested to Marcia:

"Why don't you and Janice browse around the old attic and see if you can dig up some clues among the junk that's stored there?"

The attic was above a side wing of the house, and it had been boarded up for years, so it did seem worth while to look through trunks, boxes of letters, old clothes, tools and even toys that were stored there. Snow clouds had scattered and the afternoon was clear, so Janice and Marcia worked by a little window at the far end of the attic, bringing their "finds" into the light.

Very few of the items were really old, except for some candlesticks and lanterns. Marcia was examining a square-shaped lantern with crude glass sides, when suddenly she tilted her head and whispered:

"Listen! I hear footsteps—coming closer—"

Janice was looking about, from one corner of the long, dim attic to the other, while Marcia, still staring far away, added:

"Closer—closer—they've stopped now—"

At that moment Janice's sweeping gaze reached the head of the stairs at the far end of the attic. The footsteps had stopped; and so did Janice's glance, both for the same reason. Leaning over a low rail at the stair top was the woman in gray!

Again, the wraith of Old Nell had an ideal setting, for that end of the attic was very dark and shadowy. Just as the gray dress and shawl were conspicuous against that blackness, so did the whitened face and boring eyes stand out from their gray setting. Now, it was Janice who undertoned:

"Look toward the stairs, Marcia—not too quickly—"

While Marcia was turning her head slowly, Janice was easing herself forward, planning to approach the woman in gray and actually accost her, to learn whether the shape was wraith or real. Janice's nerves were tingling, but her mood was one of challenge, not dread. But at that tense moment, a sudden shriek from Marcia broke the spell.

Marcia, too, had seen the gray phantom. The lantern slipped from Marcia's nerveless hands, and as it crashed, the weird figure vanished. Janice was sure she saw it whisk down the stairs, and Marcia confirmed that with the added gasp, "I hear footsteps—going down!" But by the time Janice reached the steep stairs, there was no sign of the woman in gray.

Oscar came up with another plausible theory when he and Aunt Cathy heard Janice and Marcia relate their mutual adventure. He felt that the tangible evidence in this instance was the broken lantern.

"It dates back to Old Nell's time," Oscar said, as he studied the lantern. "She could have used it to signal, or carried it with her to light up some of her dark deeds. The mere fact that Marcia was meddling with it brought the ghost to the scene."

"I think you're right," agreed Janice. "From the expression in those eyes, the woman in grey seemed more hunted than a hunter."

"Or more haunted," Oscar smiled, "than a haunter."

The ghost hunt continued all the next morning, but somehow the edge had worn off. Either Old Nell had put in all her required appearances, or the hunters just weren't looking in the right places. It was difficult to tell, considering that even the ways of ghosts could seldom be defined.

Then, on the third afternoon, when Marcia was somewhere upstairs, Janice was alone in the living room when the fire gave a sudden crackle. Looking up, Janice saw the gray-clad figure of Old Nell between herself and the firelight!

Janice wanted to call, "Marcia! Marcia! Come quickly!" and in fact, those words kept beating through her mind. But she didn't utter them, knowing that they might break the ghostly spell. But when the figure reached the stairs and turned its cold eyes Janice's way, the spell itself was broken. Tingling with wild excitement, Janice dashed toward the stairs, shouting:

"Wait! You're not getting away, whatever you are!"

The gray shape glided up the stairs, with Janice in close pursuit. At the top, a figure met her practically head on. Janice made a grab for the ghost and found herself clutching Marcia.

"I was after Old Nell!" exclaimed Janice. "Did you see her?"

"No," replied Marcia, "but I heard her footsteps. They stopped right here."

There was a doorway at the head of the stairs, the only place where the ghost could have gone. It opened into a room just above the kitchen, furnished with an old-fashioned four-poster bed. There was a window in one wall, but it was latched. Yet there was no one in the room, other than the two girls themselves.

"This is the dead end where that ghost is concerned," declared Janice. "I am going to sleep in this room tonight!"

Sleep there, she did, while the others took turns keeping vigil in the downstairs living room. So the night passed until the faintest trickle of dawn came through Janice's window. That was when she awakened at the sound of a low chuckle.

There, at the foot of the bed, loomed the figure of the woman in gray! As Janice sat bolt upright, the weird form moved forward, its eyes burning now, taking on the glow of live coals. From the folds of the gray cloak came two long, enveloping arms that gathered Janice into their clutch. She could hear the crackle of a harsh voice:

"So, you thought you could outwit me! You thought you were smarter than those others. You knew they could not escape me when I was alive, but you felt it would be easy, now that I am dead! But I have come back from that realm of the dead to carry you there with me, my last victim!"

As those words drilled through Janice's mind, she tried to call out, "Marcia! Marcia! Come quickly!" But she was choking in the tightening grip of those gray arms and could not utter a word. She was slumping, almost completely stifled, as a gloating laugh sounded close to her ear, and the grayish swirl was all about her, smothering her. The blackness of death was overwhelming Janice Coleridge.

Downstairs, Oscar Woodruff sprang up suddenly from the couch beside the fireplace, as a hand touched his shoulder. Then he recognized his wife's voice:

"I heard a mental call from Janice, this afternoon," said Marcia. "She was calling, 'Marcia, come quickly!' and I did. Oscar, I seem to hear that call again!"

"So why are we waiting?" demanded Oscar. "Come on!"

They reached the room at the head of the stairs, and Oscar yanked the door open, to be met by a gigantic gray mass that completely enveloped him. The room was filled with smoke, through which Oscar fought his way, choking, until he reached the bed and wrenched Janice from it. He carried her downstairs, clear to the front door, where the outside air began to revive her.

Marcia, meanwhile, called Aunt Cathy. Soon both were at windows, shouting for Steve Hargis. But the handyman arrived too late. By then, the entire second floor was ablaze. Marcia and Cathy grabbed what they could, including clothes and blankets, and raced down the stairs to the safety of outdoors.

By the time the first firefighting equipment arrived from the nearest town, the house on the island had become a gigantic beacon. There was nothing to do but watch helplessly as the old mansion burned to ashes—a final tribute to the persevering ghost of old Nell Denby, the woman in gray!

As with all such cases, natural explanations were in order. It was obvious that the blaze must have started in a faulty chimney above the kitchen fireplace. That was how it had worked into the room where Janice was sleeping, preceded by a deluge of stifling, grayish smoke that had given her fantastic dreams before overcoming her as she was awakening. Fortunately, the other persons in the house had come to her rescue in time.

That story was good enough for the general public. But all those who had been in the house at the time, the Woodruffs — Oscar, Marcia, and Aunt Cathy — believed the story that Janice told to them alone. They had lived long enough with the ghost of Old Nell Denby to recognize the vengeful hand of the phantom woman in gray.

Oscar and Marcia made out all right financially, once the insurance was paid. But they were sorry to leave the house on the island, or rather, the few ruins that remained of it. Conspicuous among those was the chimney that had risen above the kitchen fireplace, and there, to their amazement, the Woodruffs saw the trademark of the person responsible.

Silhouetted against the whitened brick was the life-sized shape of a head and shoulders, exactly like the shawl-clad form of Old Nell Denby, the woman in gray!

The Man in the Bottle

Castle's Pawnshop was a beaten-down joint in a beaten-down neighborhood, patronized by beaten-down customers who tried to unload beaten-down goods on a pair of beaten-down proprietors. If it hadn't been, this story never would have begun nor ended.

The shop consisted of one badly cluttered, miserable little room, containing mostly junk, which included the showcases that displayed it. One in particular was an eyesore. It was broken — right where everybody could see it when they walked into the shop.

That showcase was just one bone of contention between the two proprietors, Arthur Castle and his wife Edna. Arthur was gaunt, worn, but still hopeful, though he looked ten years older than his age of thirty-six. Edna was practical, capable, and exacting, so she was wasting her time, though she didn't know it. That was why they argued about little things like the broken showcase.

Right now, they were arguing about a little thing like the gas and electric bill. Arthur was shouting his opinion from behind a counter at one side of the shop, and Edna was furnishing repartee from the depths of an old-fashioned rolltop desk across the way.

"That's one bill I can't pay," Arthur stormed. "I know it's a month overdue, but I just don't have the money."

"It's one you'd better pay," Edna snapped, "or you won't have any gas or electric — or any business either!"

Arthur Castle set his lips, then groaned to himself, "What business?"

It was a good question, and timely, for at that very moment the rickety door creaked open and provided the answer. An elderly woman entered, looking up with a timid yet familiar smile that finally rejected Edna and centered on Arthur. Despite his worry, Arthur Castle spruced up a bit, running his fingers through his thinning hair, and responding with a wan smile of his own. That smile was his undoing, along with his cordial tone:

"How are you, Mrs. Gumley?"

"Just fine, Mr. Castle." From under the shawl that she was wearing, the woman brought an odd-shaped blue bottle, about six inches high, with a stubby glass stopper that was sealed with a smudge of grimy wax.

"I've got something for you," the woman continued, setting the bottle on the counter. "An old family heirloom" — she gave an unhappy sniff and raised a torn handkerchief to her watery eyes — "but I'd let it go for a dollar, things are that bad."

"If I could spare a dollar," Arthur began, in an earnest tone, "I'd give it to you, Mrs. Gumley. But things have been bad here, too. I'm deep in debt myself" — he paused, noting the woman's quivering lips; then he reached to a battered cash register and banged the "No Sale" key — "oh, well, here is your dollar. I wish it could be more. I really do."

Mrs. Gumley put away the dollar bill, then on a sudden impulse, she grabbed one of Arthur's hands and kissed it.

"God bless you, Mr. Castle!" she exclaimed. "You're a wonderful man, a true saint, indeed you are."

She left the bottle on the counter, shambled to the door, and turned there, her hand on the knob.

"It's not an heirloom, Mr. Castle," she admitted. "It's just a dirty old glass bottle that I found in an ashcan."

"That's all right, Mrs. Gumley," Arthur assured her, in a soft, sympathetic tone. "Who knows? It might turn out to be a real heirloom."

"Only it won't, Mr. Castle. Oh, Heaven forgive me, for lying to a saint like you!"

Mrs. Gumley's sob was genuine as she closed the door behind her, but it brought an echoing croak from Edna's side of the shop.

"So, Arthur," came Edna's caustic comment, "you're a saint, now. Why don't you put two big gold letters, S and T, on the door? You know what they would stand for, don't you?"

Arthur gave an unhappy shrug. "Saint, I suppose."

"No, indeedy," snapped Edna. "They'd stand for 'Soft Touch,' and you're the type of Soft Touch that would stand for anything!"

"Poor Mrs. Gumley has to eat, Edna."

"And don't we?" Angrily, Edna came across toward the counter. "Arthur, we're on the edge of bankruptcy. We've got more creditors than we have cheap watches that nobody will buy. And you promised me, no more handouts!"

"Look, Edna! I can go on being a failure just so long!" Arthur's voice was rising, too, but it wasn't angry, it was frantic. "Now it's catching up with me. As long as I can help somebody I'm sorry for, like Mrs. Gumley, it isn't too bad. But I can't afford to be sorry for myself."

He paused, made a sweeping gesture about the shop, taking in its grotesque array of junk from stuffed birds, outmoded typewriters, old umbrellas, grimy crockery, and dented spyglasses to racks of secondhand clothing.

"Look at it," Arthur continued in a lowered tone. "My grandfather owned it, and it broke his heart. Then my father, and it killed him, too. The meanness of it, Edna. It isn't just a hock shop where you buy the pitiful remnants of people's better days. It's a shrine to failure, that's what it is.

"What's happened to us, Edna? We're not old people, and yet this place is making us old. There must be years ahead of us when we won't have to scrimp and count pennies and dodge bill collectors. Why can't we both snap out of it, instead of arguing over everything — even this worthless blue bottle —"

Arthur was swinging toward the counter, and his gesture carried too far. His hand hit the bottle, and it scaled to the floor, striking squarely on its glass stopper. The dried wax cracked, the stopper came loose, and a curl of thin, gray smoke emerged, wriggling at first, as the bottle wobbled on its side, then turning into a steadily rising column.

The Castles forgot their quibbling to watch the phenomenon with amazed eyes. As the smoke rose higher, it assumed a bulbous form, thickening as it spread wider. Its swirl seemed governed by some internal force, like a miniature cyclone in slow motion. Amazement became fear, as the bulbous mass increased and reached a height of seven feet, as though the column had become a tube, drawing more smoke from the inexhaustible bottle. Then, as Edna was gasping, "Maybe it's a bomb!" the shapeless, thickened mass shriveled into itself and dissipated.

In its place stood a man of medium age and medium height, mild in manner, impeccable in attire. He looked like a prosperous, conservative businessman, which baffled the Castles even more, for no person of that category had ever walked into their shop before. Then it dawned on both of them that this stranger couldn't have walked in at all, for the door was still shut. So they waited in wonderment, hoping that the mysterious visitor would declare himself, which he did in no uncertain terms.

"How do you do," he greeted, in a quiet, easy tone. "Rather than go into a lengthy generic explanation, suffice it to say I am a genie." He paused proudly; then noting the bewildered looks of his listeners, he added, "In simpler parlance, I am a mythological being" — again he was facing blank stares from the Castles — "what say we skip it, and come right to the point. As a genie, I can grant you four wishes with a guaranteed performance. What would you have in mind?"

"What—what—" The gasps came from Edna. "What have we in mind? Why—why, I haven't any mind right now." She sank into a rickety antique chair and looked hopelessly toward her husband. "Arthur—what—what's happening?"

"He's a hypnotist or something," Arthur gulped. "I think we'd better call the police."

"Why not just wish for them?" suggested the complacent stranger. "I can bring you the French Sûrété, the FBI, or Scotland Yard — which would you wish for?"

"None of them," returned Arthur. "Don't talk me into wishing for something I don't want. Listen, mister, I don't know what television program sent you here. We can't afford a TV set, and nobody ever hocks them here, so we don't know what's going on. But if you're really what you say, a guy that can make wishes come true, well, I wish you'd prove it to begin with."

"A good wish," the genie agreed. "But how?"

"Take that broken glass in the showcase," Arthur returned. "I wish you'd repair it"—he raised his hand above his shoulder and snapped his fingers—"just like that."

"You are serious, Mr. Castle?" queried the genie, with a cryptic smile. "Is that really your wish?"

Edna was grabbing at Arthur's arm, trying to restrain him, but he was too determined.

"Yes, that's my wish," Arthur blurted. "I want the glass in that display case to be repaired. That's official."

The genie gave a prompt imitation of Arthur's finger snap.

"Just like that!"

As the Castles turned their eyes on the showcase, its glass became one smooth, firm pane. The crack seemed to wipe itself away so smoothly, so rapidly that it left them gasping. Moments later, they were running their hands up and down the pane, only to prove by sense of touch what their sight already had told them. Edna sat down suddenly in a chair, while Arthur swung to the genie, who met his amazed stare with a bland smile, as he reminded:

"Well, Mr. Castle. You have three wishes left."

"Three wishes!" gasped Castle. "After what just happened, we can wish for anything we want, three times over!"

"And you've wasted one wish already," reproved Edna. "I tried to stop you, but you wouldn't listen."

"It wasn't wasted," argued Arthur. "If we hadn't seen it work the way it did, we wouldn't have believed it. Anyway, we only really need one wish, since we can get anything we want. Think, Edna, think! What do we want?"

"Arthur, I don't know. I'm frightened."

"How about a new shop, Edna? A real expensive shop on Fifth Avenue? We could have it, just for the asking."

"Arthur, it—it isn't right. There's something unholy about it. Such things— well, they just shouldn't happen."

"What's wrong about mending a broken showcase? Or going into business with a new shop at a better location? Maybe you want clothes, Edna, expensive clothes — or jewels — or a beautiful house. Or just no more worries—"

Up until that final phrase, Edna had been shaking her head at Arthur's suggestions. But now she paused, and the thought of no more worries brought an appreciative light to her eyes. She was starting to nod, when Arthur turned to the genie:

"That's it, mister. Something to end our worries. I know one sure cure for that. Money! That's what we want."

"The simplest of wishes," approved the genie, still wearing his fixed smile, "and the most practical. How much do you want?"

Arthur turned to Edna: "How much, Edna?"

"I—I don't know." Edna's tone was a gasp. "I—I've always dreamed, though, of having a million dollars."

"A million dollars," Arthur told the genie. "That's what we want. Let's have it in five-and ten-dollar bills, right here on this floor. That's our second wish."

The genie was lighting a cigarette as Arthur spoke. He flicked away the burnt match and in the same gesture, indicated the floor. As the Castles stared, they saw a mass of green sprout before their astonished eyes and spread itself like a growing cabbage patch. Then it was all around them, and the stuff was forming piles that were unmistakably money. Arthur and Edna were knee deep in the wealth that the second wish had brought them. They were stooping, scooping the bills and spreading them in the dull light of the shop to see if they were real.

Arthur was waving fistfuls of cash at Edna and shouting, "A million dollars, Edna, a million dollars!" and she was screaming hysterically, "A million dollars, Arthur, and it's all ours!" while the genie stood by with his placid smile.

In the midst of the excitement, the door of the shop opened, and Mrs. Gumley entered, stooping over a shabby purse from which she was counting some small change. Arthur and Edna suddenly quieted, and watched while the woman said:

"I've come to pay you back your dollar, Mr. Castle. I've got enough here to make it up, so you can throw away that no-good bottle—"

Mrs. Gumley's voice broke off as she looked up and froze at sight of the vast heaps of currency that were still accumulating in the middle of the shop. Then, Arthur, with his characteristic generosity, was counting bills into the woman's hands:

"Ten, twenty, thirty—no more picking bottles from trash cans, Mrs. Gumley! —one hundred, ten, twenty—put these bills in your purse, so you won't lose them —two hundred fifty, two sixty—come back for more when you need it!—three fifty, three sixty—"

By the time Arthur had reached five hundred, Mrs. Gumley was on the point of collapse, but Arthur kept on until he had stuffed a thousand dollars into the shabby purse. He steered Mrs. Gumley out the door, only to be crowded back by a man who wanted to shove a big bass drum into the pawn shop. It was Buggsy Jardine, a member of a musical group called "The Crickets," whose engagements were so far apart that Buggsy had to hock the big drum between times.

"Don't bring that thing in here!" Arthur rebuked. "We're so cramped for room that we're clearing stuff out."

"But Mr. Castle, I need money—"

"And that's what we're clearing out." Arthur waved to Edna. "Bring enough fives and tens to make room for a drum."

By the time Buggsy's drum was heaped with five thousand dollars, he, too, was glad to stagger away as Mrs. Gumley had, but not simply because he was overwhelmed. He was still staggering under the burden of the drum that Arthur didn't want. A small crowd gathered to witness that, so Arthur made the most of it.

"Step right in," he suggested. "Borrow now, pawn something later. If you can't find anything to pawn, forget it."

So they stepped right in. Among the customers were two sailors on shore leave who hadn't anything to pawn except the destroyer they came from.

"We can't hock our ship," one sailor said frankly, "because after all, it isn't ours. It's the government's."

"What about this money?" returned Arthur. "Whose name is on it? Mine? No, the government's. I say they should lend you a thousand each, with the S.S. *Finchley* as security"— he was studying the ribbons on their hats—"so what do *you* say?"

"I say, count it out, mate," replied one of the sailors, "and I only wish we'd come off a battleship, so we could make it a couple of thousand."

"Make it a couple of thousand." Arthur turned to Edna. "Count it out, while I talk to the other customers."

Talk to them, he did, or rather, his money did the talking as he handed it out freely. All he asked was, "Why do you want money?" and if anybody answered, "So I can spend it," Arthur said that was good enough for him. What was more, every time he handed out a thousand dollars, he insisted that the recipient take another sixty.

"That's the interest," explained Arthur, "on a six per cent basis. When a bank lends you money, they demand six per cent, because they know you can pay it. So I'm working on a six per cent basis, too, but since I know you can't pay it to me, I'm paying it to you."

That didn't quite make sense, even to the pitiful patrons of Castle's Pawnshop, but none of them refused the handouts that were given them. Many were old customers, and Arthur knew their wants as well as his own, so he provided accordingly. There was one man who always pawned something the day before the rent was due, yet never reclaimed anything he pledged. Arthur gave him enough money for a year's rent and told him to earmark it for that purpose.

There was a woman who ran a little variety store that was as dilapidated and downtrodden as the pawnshop. For two years, now, she'd been telling Edna that some day she would have the store painted and would put in new showcases; then business would be good. But that day had never come, at least not until today. Now, Edna was counting out the needed money and telling the astonished woman to take it and forget it.

Arthur was spicing his announcements with quips that pleased the patrons and brought smiles to hopeless faces. Flourishing two handfuls of bills, he declared:

"We've run out of trading stamps, folks, so we're giving these instead. Automatic redemption certificates that are good anywhere. Come and get them!"

They came and got them.

For a while, it seemed that the pawnshop would be swamped by eager customers, old and new, but gradually the situation changed. People like Mrs. Gumley and the rest were fanning out through the neighborhood, counting their money over and over, so stupefied by happiness that they were unable to tell anyone where or how they had gotten it. The crowd was following those lucky people, hoping to find out.

The result was a brief lull back at the pawnshop, and Edna, suddenly reverting to her practical self, took advantage of it to close and lock the door. Sagging into a broken-down chair, she told Arthur:

"Well, I've heard of castles in the air. We sure made them real for those people. Now it's time that we become Castles down-to-earth and take account of our stock, which right now seems to be money."

With that, Edna looked at the stacks about her, and gave a hopeless gasp:

"Oh dear! There seems to be more than when we started handing it out? How can that be?"

"Because it was still growing when we started sharing the wealth. I was only getting rid of the surplus."

"And how much would that be? Oh dear!" Edna was really bewildered. "There were at least thirty to forty people who came in here, and we gave some of them a thousand dollars, and others two thousand, and even more than that to a few!"

"I've kept count, Edna. Remember my talking about six per cent interest? That's what we've given away, sixty thousand dollars out of a million."

Edna gave a relieved sigh.

"Then we won't have to count all that's left to find out how much it is!" Edna stooped among the stacks of bills and picked up the overturned bottle. "And we owe it all to this. Oh, Arthur, until now, our lives were just a hope chest with a rusty lock and a lost set of keys. Now, we have everything we could ever wish for—"

"Not quite." The interruption came from the genie, who had been standing by while pandemonium had reigned and finally ended. "As owners of the bottle, you have two more wishes. Remember?"

Arthur had an answer for that:

"We'll give the bottle back to Mrs. Gumley and let her wish herself a million dollars."

"Sorry, Mr. Castle," objected the genie mildly. "You were the owner when the bottle was opened, so I can grant four wishes to you alone. I must then go back into the bottle for one hundred and one years, until a summons comes from a new owner—but only after that period has elapsed."

Arthur turned to Edna with a shrug.

"I suppose we may as well make a few silly wishes, so our friend Mr. Genie can go back into his bottle—"

"Unless he wants to stay out a while longer," put in Edna. "Maybe he would like to help us spend our million dollars."

"One moment, Mrs. Castle." This objection came from another corner of the shop. "We have a matter to discuss."

The cool, calculating tone brought both Edna and Arthur full about to view another stranger, who might have been the genie's twin, except that he was drably attired and showed no smile at all. To the Castles, he appeared to be a chance customer who had strayed in with the crowd and stayed.

Under his arm, this newcomer carried a zipper case, which he was opening as he stepped forward, carefully avoiding the piles of money as if they were so much dirt. By the time he laid his open case upon the counter, the Castles half expected to see another million dollars come teeming out of it. Instead, the man produced some printed forms, then opened a wallet to show an identity card.

Arthur did a double-take; then read it aloud:

"Internal Revenue Service."

"That's correct," the man replied methodically. "There is a matter of an income tax, Mr. Castle."

"Just send us the bill and we'll pay it," declared Arthur. "There's plenty here"—he gestured to the stacks of money, then kicked over a few piles to emphasize it. "But send the bill in a hurry, will you? My wife and I will be taking off for Europe very soon."

The revenue man took out pencil and paper. He began to jot down figures, then gave the Castles a dead-pan stare.

"Do you have any dependents, Mr. Castle?"

"Any dependents?" Nonchalantly, Arthur lighted a cigarette. "Sure, we've got dependents. The whole neighborhood. You saw us give money to thirty or more of them, and there's plenty more where they came from, just as we have plenty more of this"—he kicked some more stacks, hard enough to make the bills flutter—"to give them, when they ask for it. We'll keep the rest ourselves."

"They don't count," the revenue man declared. "No dependents."

He wrote down some figures, while Arthur stared across his shoulder. By the time the revenue man had added them up, the cigarette was drooping so low from Arthur's lips that it almost burned his chin.

"Wait a minute!" Arthur gasped. "That total—"

"Represents your income tax, Mr. Castle," the revenue man announced, "on the basis of a husband and wife return, using the standard deductions. You owe the government approximately nine hundred and seven thousand dollars—"

"No, no!" Edna gasped. "That can't be—"

"And for your information," the revenue man continued in his even monotone, "there is a state income tax in addition, which by rule of thumb would come to thirty-five thousand dollars. There will be a five per cent penalty if you fail to file within thirty days. Roughly, the total will come to nine hundred, forty-two thousand, six hundred and forty dollars. Fill out this form and send it to us with your check."

He handed the forms and figures to Arthur, then zipped his case, walked to the door, unlocked it, and went out, closing the door behind him. Edna hurried over and locked it again, only to have Arthur comment grimly:

"You did that too late, Edna." Then, staring at the heaps of money, he added, "We gave away sixty thousand dollars, more or less. Let's hope it was a little less, or we won't have enough left to pay the taxes."

"That," said Edna sorrowfully, "was quite a wish."

"You should have reflected longer," the genie told Arthur. "I tried to warn you to be careful, Mr. Castle."

"Warn me about what?"

"About such things as taxes—"

"Then why didn't you?"

"Because I wasn't familiar with the modern situation. The last time I was released from bondage was during the Middle Ages, when the robber barons simply took money from people by force. I realized when I emerged from my bottle today, that I was in a more enlightened era, but still—"

"But still you thought there was a catch to it," interrupted Arthur. "Well there was—and is—as you saw."

"How was I to know?" pleaded the genie. "I'm not all powerful, or I'd never have let myself be bottled up. I can grant wishes to people, under certain conditions, but that's all."

"I still have two more wishes coming!" exclaimed Arthur, suddenly brightening. "Suppose I ask for another million dollars, but specify that it's to be after taxes?"

He turned to Edna questioningly, and she replied in a hysterical tone:

"No, no, Arthur! No more money! There might be another catch! Wish for something else."

"A new store, maybe, with a complete stock."

"It might burn down an hour after we opened it, before we had time to insure it."

"A chain of stores, then—"

"They might burn down, one after another."

"I'll wish for success," decided Arthur. He swung to the genie. "How would that be?"

"It's no go, Mr. Castle." The genie shook his head. "Success is a matter of personal opinion or public acclaim, which makes it an intangible. I grant wishes for tangibles only."

"So there's a catch to that, too," declared Arthur glumly. "Here we stand in the middle of this miserable little hock shop, loaded with money that isn't ours, and the whole world waiting if we only wish for it the right way." He swung suddenly to Edna. "What's happening to us, anyway?"

While Edna remained silent, the genie replied:

"You are emotionally upset, Mr. Castle. I have seen the same thing happen with other persons in your situation. Whatever you wish for, you must be prepared to meet the consequences."

"That means something dead sure," Arthur decided. "Something really airtight. Money is no good, business is uncertain, success is out as such. I've got it!" He brightened again. "Power! To be a boss—a leader!"

"Like what?" asked Edna. "The president of a big corporation?"

"Sure," agreed Arthur. "That sounds good."

"But what if the company went bankrupt, as so many do?"

"That's a point, Edna. It would be better to be mayor of a city, or a governor of a state—"

"And get voted out of office? Where would you be then?"

"In hock, I guess," Arthur conceded glumly, "but without a hock shop. There must be some way to beat this thing." He brightened again, then exclaimed, "Of course! All I have to be is the ruler of a whole country, who can't be voted out of office." He swung to the genie. "How about that?"

"Quite simple," the genie assured him, "except it allows too much leeway, both in time and space. If you were more specific—"

"I'll give it to you this way," Arthur put in. "I want to be the head of a foreign country, who can't be voted out of office. Just keep it within the present century, so it's in my range of knowledge. Go back, say twenty or thirty years—or go ahead twenty or thirty. I'll leave that up to you, Mr. Genie. Right?"

"Right. Is that your exact wish?"

"That is my wish. Officially."

Before Arthur spoke the last word, the pawnshop began to tremble, then to whirl. Arthur Castle was undergoing the experiences of Aladdin, the hero of *Arabian Nights,* at the time when an obliging genie had transported his entire palace from China to Persia, with everybody on board. But in this case, the similarity applied only in the preliminary stages.

Within moments, Arthur was detached from his physical surroundings and was rocketing through time as well as space, leaving the pawnshop far behind, along with the months that were flicking past like solid seconds, adding up to years that were gone in scarcely more than an incredible half-minute.

Then the whirl stopped, but the haze was not quite gone, for Arthur found himself seated at a desk in a stuffy room, far more cramped than the familiar pawnshop. In front of him was an outspread map, which for some reason Arthur was able to understand, though its markings and lettering were peculiar. A man was speaking from across the desk in a language that also should have been unfamiliar, but somehow seemed to translate itself into English as its words drilled through Arthur's brain.

"My apologies, sir," the speaker was saying, "but the situation is just as I described it. The First Ukranian Army has cut us off from the south. They are in Berlin now. There is no sign of the reserve divisions that we ordered. According to latest report, there are no reserve divisions."

Arthur looked up from the map and studied the speaker, a burly, broad-faced man with a stubbly beard and haggard, nervous eyes. The man was wearing a disheveled gray uniform, with an army cap to match, and what impressed Arthur most—indeed, almost shocked him—was the emblem that appeared both on the officer's cap and armband.

That emblem was a Nazi swastika!

"We are doomed." The officer's strained voice was rising. "There is no hope for us now. No more hope, you understand? From now on, it is just mass suicide"—the officer's face was distorted and his final words became a frantic scream—"well, what about it, Mein Führer?"

That title "Führer" was a shocker that brought Arthur Castle bolt upright. While he waited for the Nazi officer to say more, he heard other sounds, more distant and muffled, but more graphic than words. Those were the sounds of dull explosions, from bursting bombs and heavy artillery shells. With those ominous overtones, Arthur could feel the cramped room quiver. Mechanically, he pushed himself up from the desk, came around it, pressed the officer aside and moved numbly toward a mirror on the wall.

"My third wish," Arthur muttered. "I wanted to be the head of a country— someone who couldn't be voted out of office. That's what I wanted to be—"

He looked into the mirror. Instead of his own smooth-shaven features and thinning, unkempt hair, he saw a face just as gaunt and hollowed, but one that wore a toothbrush mustache and was topped by slicked-down hair. Now Arthur's voice became a scream:

"That's what I wanted to be—and that's what I am! I'm Hitler—I'm in a bunker—it's the end of the war—and it's the end of me!"

Timed to that shrill pronouncement, the door of the bunker room opened and another Nazi officer entered. He stepped to Arthur's side, placed a glass vial in his hand and announced in a monotone:

"Here is what you asked for, Mein Führer. Very quick and very painless. We have given another vial to Fraülein Braun. The other arrangements have been made, as you ordered."

The officer stepped back, clicked his heels, and gave the Nazi salute. That was duplicated by the other officer, who was still standing by the table. The two of them went out through the door together, and Arthur heard them speak to someone else.

"It's almost the end. We've given them the poison. It's their only choice—"

"We'll come back after they've finished and take the bodies out to the courtyard. The gasoline is waiting there, to burn them—"

The only choice!

Arthur Castle heard the door of the bunker close. He looked down at the poison vial in his hand. He looked up to study the mirrored face that he knew was not his own. He heard a muffled explosion, more forceful than any before, because with it, the room quivered violently. So violently, in fact, that it reminded Arthur of the way the pawnshop had shuddered when the genie had launched him on his fatal trip back through time and space, to this rendezvous with doom. Now Arthur's eyes were again on the vial in his hand.

"What I'll do with this!" he screamed, "is what I should have done with that cheap blue bottle that Mrs. Gumley brought into my shop!" He turned, raised his hand, and flung the vial on the floor, shouting as he did, "I wish that I could be back where all this started—that I could be Arthur Castle again— just as I was!"

The room quivered under a heavier bomb burst, almost as though the

smashing of the vial had caused it. Again, everything began to whirl. Arthur
reeled around behind the desk, slumped there, propping his elbows on the map,
which faded, with all its mixed-up names and markings, until Arthur, to his
profound but happy amazement, found himself staring down at the counter in
his own pawnshop, which somehow had ceased its whirl and was back to normal.

Or not quite normal.

There on the floor beyond the corner in that space which not too long ago
had teemed with stacks of green; there, instead of that vanished wealth, lay
something that Arthur Castle was happier to see, the fragments of a broken blue
bottle.

"I'm here, a four-time loser." Arthur looked up to see Edna staring numbly.
"So you're here, too." Arthur looked around. "But where is he? You know who
I mean—or do you?"

Edna's solemn nod proved that she was thinking of the genie, too. Arthur
picked up a broom and dustpan and swept up the broken fragments of the
bottle. He was awkward with the broom, for as he poked the handle back over
his shoulder, he heard a sharp, crackling sound.

Arthur turned to see the showcase, broken as it had been when Mrs. Gumley
had walked in with the blue bottle. But now, as Arthur glanced again at the
dustpan, there lay the bottle, no longer broken but intact, even to the glass
stopper and dried wax seal!

Edna stepped forward, took the dustpan, and indicated the bottle with a
sweep of her hand as she announced:

"I'll put this back in the trash can where it belongs and can stay for the
next one hundred and one years!"

"Then you know?" gasped Arthur. "You know all that happened—and you
believe it?"

"I believe all I saw, and I'll take your word for the rest. You wished yourself
somewhere, and all of a sudden, you were gone. Then you must have wished
yourself back, for here you are, and I am very glad."

Arthur's face lighted with an appreciative smile.

"I think I'll stop wishing for a while, Edna. I can't afford a brand-new life.
I'll give the old one a new paint job."

"Arthur, I think that's a very good idea."

"For a while, Edna, I thought that this place was crawling with money.
But it's all gone, back where it belonged, with all the worries that came with it."

"I know, Arthur. Maybe we should worry along our own way, without a
lot of wishful thinking."

With that, Edna went out through the door to the street. But she was back
a few minutes later, triumphantly displaying an empty dustpan. Arthur's smile
widened.

Castle's Pawnshop was back in business, this time to stay, thanks to the
lessons its proprietors had learned from their brief trip into that mystic realm
known as the Twilight Zone.

The Mirror Image

The cold November rain was beating at the big front windows of the City
Bus Terminal, blurring the dim lights along the street and the driveway. It was
as if grim, black night had gathered the building in its all-enveloping folds,
turning the terminal into a small, detached world of its own.

On a night as bad for travel as this, the place was almost deserted. Ticket
office, baggage room, lunch counter, all were staying open only because they
usually did, until the last bus arrived. Tonight, however, prospective passengers
were very few. There was an elderly couple seated on a wooden bench at one
end of the terminal; and a girl in her early twenties at the other.

The girl's name was Millicent Barnes, and she was fidgety enough to make
up for a whole busload of passengers. She kept looking at her wrist watch and
comparing it with the big clock over the door. She looked at the ticket window,
where a complacent ticket agent was reading a magazine; then at the baggage
room, which was deserted, and finally to the lunch counter, where a patient,
middle-aged woman was putting things in order for the next day.

Millicent's own patience must have reached its limit, for suddenly she arose,
walked over to the ticket window and rapped its grating to rouse the agent's
attention. As he looked up, Millicent asked crisply:

"The bus to Cortland. It was due half an hour ago. When will it be in?"

"She'll be in when she'll be in." The agent laid his magazine aside and gave
the girl a fixed stare. "I told you that the last time you asked, and the time
before."

"Why, the only time I've asked is right now!" exclaimed Millicent. "All I
want is a civil answer from you—"

She broke off abruptly, staring into the baggage room, which connected with the ticket office. There by itself, was a bright blue suitcase, with brass trim, somewhat the worse for wear, as indicated by its taped handle. Millicent swung about, stared back at the bench that she had just left. There was her own bag, identical in every detail, even to the taped handle and a red baggage stub attached to it.

Millicent started toward the bench, then pressed her hand to her eyes, turned around and went back to the ticket window, where the agent said caustically:

"Well? Shall we run through it all again?"

"I want to know more about that suitcase," returned Millicent. "The one in the baggage room. It looks just like mine."

"And why shouldn't it? It is yours. You checked it just a little while ago."

"But it can't be my bag. That's mine, over there—"

Millicent turned, gesturing to the bench, only to break off again. There was no bag there!

Now the ticket agent was mingling sarcasm with a bit of sympathy:

"Why don't you go over there and sit down, miss? You're walking in your sleep, or you're seeing things, or something. Just rest quiet and let me read my magazine. When the Cortland bus comes in, you'll hear a big roar from the motor, and you'll see people walk in through that door. Then you'll know the bus is ready."

"But I—I can't remember checking my bag—"

Somewhat dazed, Millicent walked past the bench and went over to the lunch counter, where she sat down and stared vacantly, until the counter woman asked, "Are you all right, miss?"

"Why, yes." Millicent studied her reflection in a mirror behind the counter. "Don't I look well?"

"You look fine, honey," the woman replied. "But you sat down and stared the same way when you came over here before."

"Why, I wasn't here before!" Millicent exclaimed. "What is this? I checked my bag without knowing it, I'm told I asked questions before about the bus. Now, you tell me—"

Millicent's thoughts broke off in the light of stern reality. While staring in the mirror, she had let her gaze revert to the reflection of the bench, to make sure that her suitcase hadn't returned there. It hadn't, but she had!

There, seated where she had been a short time before, Millicent saw the mirrored image of a girl who was her identical twin. Either that, or Millicent had become someone else and was looking back at her old self of ten minutes before.

"What can I get you, honey?" The counter woman's voice was worried. "A glass of water—a cup of coffee—maybe a cold cloth—or an aspirin?"

Millicent shook her head as she clutched the counter to keep from falling off the stool. From that angle, she could only see her own face in the mirror, and it was very white. But the coldness of the counter revived her enough to wrench herself full about and stare at the actual bench.

Her double was gone, but the suitcase was there!

Unsteadily, Millicent walked to the bench, keeping her eyes on the suitcase all the way. As she sat down, she pressed her hand on the bag, to make sure it was really there. She gave a challenging look at the ticket window, and the agent looked up from his magazine to return a knowing smile. Millicent arose, took a few compulsive steps toward the window, then decided to avoid another argument there.

If the ticket agent had seen Millicent's double, he might try to confuse her more. What Millicent wanted now were some witnesses in her own behalf, so she turned her steps to the other end of the waiting room and approached the elderly couple seated there. The man was dozing, but the woman was awake.

"I was wondering," said Millicent, "if you saw someone sitting in my seat, only a few minutes ago."

"Why, I don't think so, miss," the woman replied. "Of course, I wasn't particularly looking in that direction."

The elderly man heard the voices and awoke with a sudden start. Querulously, he asked, "Has something happened? Is there any trouble?"

"No trouble." Millicent smoothed the situation hurriedly. "I thought I saw someone I knew. I'm sorry I disturbed you."

She went back past the ticket window, noting her own suitcase still by the bench. She was ready to have it out with the ticket agent, but first she threw a sharp glance at the baggage room, only to stop short with a double-take.

The room was empty, with no sign of the duplicate suitcase!

"What's happening to me?" Millicent breathed. "Am I having delusions? Am I running a temperature?" She pressed her hand to her forehead. "No, I'm not even warm. No fever."

Millicent stiffened, realizing that her present actions were making her more conspicuous and perhaps creating new suspicions in the minds of her watchers. She looked toward the door, tempted to rush out into the rain, if only to get a moment of relief from this growing feeling of madness. Right then, the door opened, and a tall man entered, shaking the rain from his hat brim and bringing an attaché case from the folds of his drenched topcoat.

As he walked forward, the man pushed back his hat to reveal a smiling, friendly face. He was about thirty years of age, and apparently had traveled extensively, for he appraised the bus terminal in one sweeping glance. He was starting toward the ticket window, to make an inquiry there, when he suddenly turned toward Millicent, who was already coming to her feet.

"Your handbag," the man said politely, stooping to pick it up. "You just dropped it."

Numbly, Millicent realized that dropping a bag containing all her money was worse than forgetting what she had done with a suitcase. But she managed to return the man's smile as she murmured her thanks, so he asked her for information.

"The bus is late—I hope?"

"Yes, over a half an hour late. You mean the Cortland bus, don't you?"

"That's the one. If it wasn't late, I would have missed it for sure. I shouldn't even be here—"

The young man paused, noting how Millicent's smile had faded, showing her face to be drawn and white.

"Pardon me, miss." The man's tone showed concern. "You aren't ill, are you? Is there something I can do?"

"It's just that odd things have been happening. I've been—well, I guess I've been seeing things."

"Seing things?" The man's smile broadened. "What sort of things?"

"Maybe I shouldn't tell you." Millicent gave a nervous laugh that seemed discordant to her own ears. "You might call the police or an ambulance or something."

"Tell me, and maybe I can help. My name is Grinstead. Paul Grinstead. I'm from Binghamton."

"I'm Millicent Barnes." Her tone still hollow, she looked around almost wildly. "At least I *was* Millicent Barnes. I'm a private secretary, and I've just taken a new job in Buffalo. That's where I'm going tonight. To Buffalo."

Millicent finished on an earnest note, as though hoping to convince this new listener that she was sound of mind as well as sincere. Paul promptly responded in a similar vein.

"I was supposed to be in Syracuse tonight, but the planes are all grounded. I took a cab from Binghamton, and we got stuck in a ditch, and I had to hike two miles to get here." He took off his soaked overcoat, shook it, and draped it over the bench. "I'm about four hours away from Binghamton and about five minutes away from pneumonia." He paused to deliver his friendly smile. "That's my story; now go on with yours."

"It's not quite that rough," Millicent began. Then, with a sudden frown, she amended, "Maybe it's rougher. All my trouble has been right here in this bus station. The ticket man says I've asked him about the bus three or four times, but I'm sure I only went to his window once. The woman at the lunch counter claims I was there before, but I'm sure I wasn't. And then, when I looked for my suitcase—"

Millicent broke off as she looked toward the end of the bench, then added with a suppressed scream, "It's gone again!"

With a smile, Paul reached beyond his draped coat and brought the suitcase into sight, saying, "Sorry. I didn't mean to hide it."

"I thought for a moment it was starting all over again," Millicent confessed. "The ticket agent said I checked my suitcase, and there was one that looked just like it in the baggage room. But when I came back from the lunch counter, my bag was here, and the one in the baggage room was gone."

Paul glanced toward the ticket window and studied the drab-mannered man behind it. With a shrug, he remarked, "That character doesn't look energetic enough to go playing tricks with suitcases. Who else could be doing it?"

"No one," replied Millicent. "No one, unless"—she paused warily—you'll listen if I go on, won't you?"

Paul Grinstead nodded. "Go on."

"When I looked in that mirror behind the lunch counter"—Millicent gestured in that direction—"I could see this bench where we are now, and I saw—I saw—"

"Just what did you see, Miss Barnes?"

"I saw *myself*, sitting on this very bench!"

In one brief moment, Millicent realized that she had raised the real issue too soon. With all his sympathy and understanding, Paul Grinstead couldn't quite accept that. Who could? Not even Millicent herself. With that, she decided to backtrack.

"You're thinking I had some kind of delusion," she declared frankly. "But I'm not really ill. I don't have a headache, I'm not running a fever. But it isn't just seeing things that don't exist. Why did the ticket man—why did the lunch counter woman—why did they both think they had seen me come there before?"

"I don't know," Paul replied. "It's tough to figure."

"It is tough," Millicent returned, confident that she was winning her point. "Because whoever it was—whatever it was, I saw the same thing. We all saw the same mirror image, which is about the best thing to call it. Maybe they're a couple of kooks"—Millicent's sweeping gesture included the ticket office and the lunch counter, with their present personnel—"but I'm not. Maybe they see crazy things regularly—I might, too, if I spent my life behind a ticket window or a lunch counter, but—but—"

"But they shouldn't unload those ideas on you," Paul said. "Is that it?" Then, as Millicent nodded, he questioned, "You've never had any mental problems, have you?" He waited for her headshake, then assured her, "Of course you haven't. That means there is an explanation somewhere."

"Right," Millicent agreed, "but like what?"

"Like somebody who looks like you—like somebody you know—maybe playing a joke on you—or something—"

Millicent's dander was really up by now.

"Look, Mr. Grinstead," she said firmly. "I know I'm shuffling off to Buffalo, and you're wading in from Binghamton or staggering on to Syracuse, whatever the case may be. What would you think if your double showed up here? Do you have any friends who would come this far for a gag?"

"I guess not." Paul spoke as though he had been fully convinced. "Why, they couldn't even get here to begin with."

"That's how I feel," agreed Millicent. "Maybe my problem was just frustration. From the moment I walked in here, I wanted to hear them call, 'All aboard the bus for Buffalo!' and my worries would have ended there. Wouldn't yours?"

"You're right, Millicent. The sooner we go somewhere—"

A great roar interrupted, punctuated by the stabs of a bus horn that was followed by the throbbing whimper of a diesel motor. The ticket agent laid his magazine aside and bawled out the announcement:

"Bus now arriving for Cortland—Syracuse—Buffalo—"

Paul Grinstead picked up Millicent's suitcase and said, "Let's go." He had his coat over his other arm, and he was carrying his attaché case too, but his broad smile showed that he didn't mind. The elderly couple arose from the far bench and also moved toward the bus platform. With a genuine laugh, Millicent confided to Paul:

"That ticket agent really does see things. He said a crowd would be coming from the bus. But there's nobody getting off."

"Right," Paul acknowledged, "but we're getting on."

The elderly couple were first. The bus driver punched their tickets, handed back the stubs, then looked up, startled, at Millicent Barnes, whose face had gone dead white as she tried and failed to stifle a scream.

There, framed in the bus window, was a lone passenger, who either had arrived on the bus and stayed there or had slipped aboard unseen, ahead of everyone else, from this very bus station. That passenger's face was one that Millicent knew too well.

It was her own!

Now, Millicent was backing away toward the swinging door leading into the bus station. Then, with the same mad impulse that she had resisted earlier, she turned about and made a dash for freedom, but not out into the open. She was going back into the very trap that she had been so eager to escape, and Paul was hurrying after her.

He overtook her by the bench where they had met. He folded his coat inside out and bunched it as a pillow. The woman from the lunch counter brought the damp cloth that she had recommended earlier. Millicent was lying there, eyes closed, moaning slightly as the bus driver arrived and spoke to Paul.

"We've got to be on our way. Very late now. Are you and the lady coming, or aren't you?"

Paul Grinstead shook his head.

"We'll wait for the next bus."

The ticket agent shambled over from the booth to put in his say:

"Next one ain't due until seven in the morning. You've got a long wait."

"We waited long enough for this one," returned Paul, "and we don't have to be anywhere until tomorrow, anyway."

The bus driver turned and went out to the platform, calling, "Okay, folks! We're on our way!" A mingling of roar and rumble followed, and the bus was off.

Silence resumed its sway at the City Bus Terminal, but it was a deeper silence than before. The ticket agent flicked off some of the lights, reciting, "When not in use, turn off the juice. That's my motto." In the gloom that followed, the lunch counter woman came over and spoke to Paul.

"I'm closing for the night and going home. I hope she gets to feel better." The woman gestured toward Millicent, who by now appeared to be asleep. "But, offhand, I'd say she needs medical help"—the woman tapped her forehead as she spoke—"if you know what I mean."

The counter woman practically had to feel her way out of the bus terminal, for it was almost dark now. Anyone coming in would be guided by a few dim lights, and the ticket booth, where the agent had resumed his reading, served as a final beacon. In fact, it was the light from that caged window that vaguely illuminated the bench where Millicent was lying, throwing a pattern of darkened cross-lines upon the girl's huddled form, while Paul watched from the shadows beyond.

For seemingly interminable minutes that tableau continued. It might have lasted until passengers began arriving for the early morning bus—as they would be doing, four or five hours from now—but suddenly Millicent stirred. She looked up, as though wondering whether to be soothed or frightened by the surrounding gloom. As she saw Paul's face leaning toward her in the criss-crossed light, she gave a smile of half-recognition.

"The bus?" she queried. "You didn't take it?"

"No," replied Paul. "I stayed to look after you. There will be another bus in a few hours. You're feeling better now?"

"A lot better." Millicent was staring up at the ceiling. "I once read something about parallel planes of existence, like twin worlds side by side. Each of us has a counterpart in the other plane, and sometimes the two worlds converge. The counterpart steps into our place and takes over. Maybe—maybe the woman I saw—maybe she was my counterpart—"

"Snap out of it, Millicent!" Paul interrupted. "There's got to be a more rational explanation. Anyway, we won't have to wait for that bus. I have a friend in Tully. I'll call him and have him bring his car down here and drive us to Syracuse. All right?"

Millicent nodded, then closed her eyes again. Paul walked over to the ticket window and asked for change to make a phone call. The ticket agent had heard all that was said, and now he expressed his opinions with a snort:

"Parallel planes! Twin worlds! No wonder she's off her rocker, believing that stuff. Are you going to call your friend in Tully? The one with the car?"

"I haven't any friend in Tully," Paul confided. "I just wanted to make it easier for her. She needs medical help, so I guess I'd better call the police. What do you think?"

"A good idea. She gives me the willies, and I'd just as soon she got out of here, somehow."

While Paul was making his phone call, Millicent arose unsteadily and approached the lunch counter, where she sat on a stool and studied her reflected image in the mirror.

"Are you somebody else?" she whispered. "If you are, then tell me—who am I?"

Approaching footsteps brought her about, startled; but she smiled wanly when she saw it was Paul. Casually, he suggested:

"Let's take a walk out by the bus platform. The rain is letting up, and the fresh air will do us good."

As they reached the platform, Millicent halted at sight of a police car. She gasped, threw an accusing look at Paul and tried to run, too late. Two officers grabbed her and pushed her into the rear seat. One got in with her, the other took the wheel and the police car pulled away. Glumly, Paul returned to the waiting room, picked up Millicent's suitcase and took it to the ticket window, where he told the ticket agent:

"I got her off all right. They're taking her to the hospital for observation. They'll pick up her suitcase later."

"I'll put it in the baggage room."

"By the way," added Paul, "awhile ago, she told me that you insisted she had already checked her suitcase."

"She said I said that?" The ticket agent shook his head, amazed. "Boy! She wasn't only seeing things—she was hearing things, too!" He gestured to the bench. "Better get yourself a snooze, mister. You've got four and a half hours to wait."

Paul laid his attaché case on the end of the bench and tried it as a pillow, but it was too uncomfortable. He became restless and began to walk about, as Millicent had. He reached the lunch counter, sat down on the same stool and stared in the mirror. His gaze took in the bench, and his eyes went wide and startled.

His attaché case was gone!

Excitedly, Paul Grinstead rushed to the ticket window and began to rattle the bars. The ticket agent looked up from his magazine, as Paul gestured toward the bench, exclaiming:

"My attaché case—it's gone! Who took it?"

"Who took it?" the agent echoed. "There's nobody here but you and me, mister, and I haven't been away from this window."

Paul's sweeping glance took in the doorway to the bus platform, and he was sure he saw a figure in its shadows. He raced there, shouting, "There he is!" only to halt abruptly.

Facing him, as though reflected in a mirror, Paul saw a human figure, the exact counterpart of himself. Then, as he blinked, that living image was gone. Madly, Paul dashed out to the platform, shouting, "Hey, there! Wait!"

Paul Grinstead found himself alone. He was staring one way, then the other, his hair disheveled, his face streaked with sweat, his eyes stricken with fear. He shouted louder:

"Who are you? Where are you? What are you doing here?"

Those repeated shouts reached the ticket agent, and he spoke into the telephone:

"Police? This is the bus terminal. Better get over and pick up the guy who called you about the girl. He's gone even battier than she did."

As he laid the phone down, the ticket agent added:

"Parallel planes! Twin worlds! Humph!"

Significant words for all persons planning an extended tour through the Twilight Zone. But don't expect to get your information from the window in your local bus terminal!

The Man Who Dropped By

Nearly everybody living in the old Abington Arms was glad whenever Wilfred Laraby dropped by. That wasn't surprising, for he was the one person in the apartment building who looked prosperous and gave the place class. Although the Abington Arms was conveniently located near the center of New York City, it was due for demolition within the next few years, so nothing was being done toward its upkeep. As a result, most of the more prosperous tenants had moved out. Mr. Laraby was the sole exception.

For one thing, Mr. Laraby lived in the penthouse, which perched on top of the six-story building, forming an abbreviated seventh floor, the rest being a water tower and an open roof where Mr. Laraby strolled about and even raised flowers on a low parapet that overlooked a rear alleyway between the Abington Arms and the solid wall of a big warehouse.

The apartment building was a story higher than the warehouse, so Mr. Laraby had a nice view. The automatic elevator took him clear up to the penthouse, when he pushed the button marked PH. Mr. Laraby didn't like crowded elevators and sometimes waited awhile in the lobby, before starting up.

Coming down, he never knew how many people would get on at intervening floors, so rather than be cramped in the car, Laraby always walked down from the penthouse. That was how he happened to drop by on people along the way and listen to their troubles.

Jerry Roscoe, who kept and sold macaws and parrots in his third-floor apartment was worried because there was a law about bringing such birds into the country. One day a man with a customs inspector's badge walked in and threatened to seize the birds and fine Roscoe five thousand dollars. Just then,

Wilfred Laraby happened to drop by. He vouched for Roscoe's integrity, so the customs man settled for fifteen hundred dollars, which he said would cover the duty. Roscoe was very grateful to Mr. Laraby and begged him to drop by any time.

Hugo Droz, who lived in the third floor back, worked as a strong man at a Broadway freak museum. One day an immigration officer came to pick up Hugo's passport, saying he'd overstayed the limit on his permit. Hugo was pleading brokenly when Mr. Laraby happened to drop by. In his quiet, convincing way, he insisted that it was a mere oversight on Hugo's part. As a result, the immigration man back-dated the permit and extended it to cover the rest of Hugo's engagement at the museum. It cost a thousand dollars, which Hugo paid gladly. Hugo overwhelmed Mr. Laraby with thanks, and he, too, pleaded with Mr. Laraby to drop by and see him often.

One day, Mrs. Agatha Tolliver was sobbing in her fourth-floor front apartment, when Wilfred Laraby dropped by. He learned that Mrs. Tolliver, who ran the ground-floor beauty shop, was being sued by an actress who had come in to have her hair bleached, for a part she was to play in a new show.

Through some mistake, her hair had turned green, and the actress wanted fifty thousand dollars, right at a time when Mrs. Tolliver had forgotten to renew her liability insurance. Between sobs, she handed Mr. Laraby a paper bearing the names of the actress, her agent, and her lawyer.

"Don't you worry, Mrs. Tolliver," declared Laraby, in his reassuring tone. "I'll drop by and see all these people. I'm sure they will listen to reason. People always do when I drop by."

So Mr. Laraby dropped by and saw them, and then dropped by the beauty shop, bringing forms for Mrs. Tolliver to sign, squaring the whole thing for a mere two thousand dollars, which Mrs. Tolliver gladly paid. She, too, was insistent that Mr. Laraby drop by again.

These were but a few of the helpful things that Laraby did for people when he dropped by. He was always willing to lend people small sums without interest, and they were prompt to pay him back, so they could borrow more when they needed it.

Often, people would wait outside their apartments, hoping to hear Laraby's footsteps coming from the stairs, so they could stay and greet him when he dropped by, which would give them an excuse for telling him their troubles. Those stairs also served as a fire tower and the steel steps gave out echoes when Laraby came down them.

But when he reached a hallway, his step was very light, indeed. He practically glided along his way, pausing only to glance in open doorways, or to knock occasionally at closed doors, where there were people that he promised to see. Of course, if anyone ran into Mr. Laraby and said, "Hello," he was glad to see them, too.

Though frail of build, Laraby was spry of step and probably was older than he looked. His cheerful voice, his perpetual smile, and his quick, birdlike eyes marked him as a man without worry.

Word soon spread that Wilfred Laraby had sold out a successful business and had retired early to enjoy life by making other people happy. That was all the more reason why everyone at the Abington Arms was glad when he dropped by.

That is, everybody except Milton Casper, who lived in a little apartment on the fifth floor back, just two stories beneath Laraby's penthouse. Casper was a stamp collector, who bought and sold rarities, but only by mail. His apartment door had a double lock to protect his precious stamps, but he seldom went out, except to the post office, or to the lunchroom across the street.

While working with his stamps, Casper kept the window closed rather than have a chance breeze blow them away. When he needed a little air, he opened the apartment door. Then he could be seen in his small front room, busy with albums, tweezers, magnifying glass, watermark detector, perforation gauge, and other accessories of the complete stamp collector.

The only person who made a point of dropping by was Wilfred Laraby. Sometimes, when Casper was completing a rare set or studying a watermark, he would hear a slight stir behind him. Then he would snap about nervously to see Laraby glancing over his shoulder with an appreciative smile.

"I'm glad I dropped by," Laraby would always say. "I once collected stamps myself. A fascinating hobby, philately, but business pressure forced me to abandon it. I'll drop by again."

There were times when Casper kept the door shut while he classified his stamps. Then Wilfred Laraby would knock when he dropped by. If Casper didn't respond, Laraby would repeat his quiet, methodical knock, and Casper, deep in his philatelic pursuits, would involuntarily call, "Come in!" Next, he would realize that somebody was right there behind him, and he would bob about nervously to see Wilfred Laraby, smiling in his disarming, kindly way, and saying, "Hello, Casper. I just decided to drop by."

Sometimes, Casper couldn't remember calling, "Come in!" so he began locking the door while working on his stamps, until the room became too stuffy. Meanwhile, if Laraby dropped by and kept up a repeated and persuasive knocking, Casper would finally let him in. But there were times when Casper wouldn't unlock the apartment door for anybody.

On those occasions, he would go to a tiny back room and close its door. Then he would open the lone window, to get some air. Next, he would run his hand along a shelf of old stamp albums until he came to one marked J-3, which was almost out of sight behind the molding of the bookcase.

Casper would squeeze the other albums closer, to pull out J-3 and place it on a table by the window. But when he opened J-3, it wasn't an album at all. It was a dummy box, containing a set of engraver's tools, two copper plates, a powerful eye lens, and two twenty-dollar bills mounted on a cardboard easel, so as to show both sides of the note.

In his secret life, Milton Casper bore the unenviable distinction of being the nation's number-one counterfeiter!

Here Casper was working under ideal conditions. The blank wall of the warehouse across the alley cut off any chance of observation, while Casper's floor, the fifth, was high enough to give him good sunlight for the few intensive hours that he devoted to this painstaking job. The room was fanned by occasional breezes from its lone but ample window; and on dull days, Casper devoted himself to stamp collecting as the perfect "front" to cover his clandestine activity.

This had been going on for months, with all of Casper's expenses being underwritten by an underworld syndicate that was eagerly awaiting delivery of the plates. Then Casper was to receive a cash sum—in genuine U.S. currency —that would enable him to be far away, living luxuriously in some foreign land, by the time New York was being flooded with fake bills printed from his plates.

Gradually, however, Casper had fallen behind schedule. That rather surprised him, because in this work, every detail was essential, so it was as difficult at the start as at the finish. By Casper's reasoning—as well as his past experience —his hand should have become more deft as he approached the final stages.

But now, with his task almost done, Casper couldn't work. A pigeon fluttering past the window, a breeze flapping the curtain, jarred his tense nerves. But he had a cure for that. He brought a small packet of paper from his pocket, opened it and poured its powdery contents into a glass of water which he swallowed. Soon, Casper's nerves began to calm.

The physician who had given Casper that prescription had warned him never to take more than one powder at a time. But Casper promptly proceeded to take another, and the effect was startling indeed.

To his mind, seconds began to lengthen into minutes; soon minutes would seem to be hours. Yet, despite the way the potion made time stretch, Casper remained alert, more capable of fine, delicate work than when in a normal state. His hand poised the engraving tool, much as the pigeons seemed to hover in the midst of their flutters outside the window.

Then came a series of slow, repeated knocks. It was Laraby, dropping by. But the time between the knocks was so great that it drove Casper to distraction. It seemed like hours before the knocks ended, proving that Laraby had gone his way. Worried, Casper put away his tools in dreamlike fashion and left the apartment. He took the elevator down to the lobby, and started out the door, only to meet Laraby coming in!

"So you were in your apartment when I dropped by," Laraby chided. "Why didn't you answer? I knocked three times."

"I know." Casper's tone was a lazy drawl. "I mean—you see—I didn't hear— didn't hear you. I—was asleep."

"You sound as if you were asleep now," said Laraby. "Better get yourself a cup of coffee. I'll drop by and see you tomorrow."

The next morning, Casper decided to get some work done before Laraby dropped by. He walked about, muttering over the details:

"Close the hallway door . . . Lock it . . . Lay out albums in the front room . . . Go into the back room . . . Open the window . . . Chase away the pigeons . . . Breathe some fresh air . . . Now, the duplicate albums . . . A–B–G–I–J-1–"

All this while, Casper had been suiting words to actions. His hand was about to move from J-1 to J-2, when something caused him to break off in his nervous way. Looking over his upraised arm, he saw the smiling face of Wilfred Laraby, here in this back room!

"I knocked," said Laraby blandly, "and you called 'Come in,' so I did." He looked at the shelf. "What have we here?"

"My duplicate stamp albums," Casper explained. "I was just taking down J-1, so I could check it with my master collection."

"I see that you have the window open. Aren't you afraid the wind will blow the duplicates away?"

"No, no. I always take them into the front room."

Casper motioned Laraby into the other room, and there Laraby watched Casper compare his duplicates with specimens in a master album. Soon Laraby left, and after a few minutes, Casper peered out into the hall. He could hear voices coming up the stairs, and he gathered that Wilfred Laraby had dropped by to see Mrs. Tolliver on the fourth floor.

Quickly, Casper turned the key in the double lock and hurried to the elevator. He reached the lobby ahead of Laraby and kept on to an outside phone booth, where he called a number and asked for a man named Griff Burlick. A hard-toned voice came on the line and Casper nervously announced:

"I've got to see you right away, Griff. Emergency."

"Okay. Meet me at the Three Trees, in the back booth."

The Three Trees was a bar and grill five blocks away. Soon Casper was in the booth at the back, and there he was joined by Griff Burlick, a stocky, powerful, square-jawed man with a face as tough as leather.

Griff was Casper's only contact with the syndicate backing the counterfeit plate project. In case of trouble, Casper had to call on Griff, much as the other residents of the Abington Arms called upon Wilfred Laraby.

That was a real switch, to call on an outsider like Griff, instead of a man like Laraby, who was ready to help anybody and everybody. Except for one thing: A man engraving counterfeit plates, like Casper, would rate as a nobody in the opinion of an honest man like Laraby. So Casper had to tell his troubles to Griff Burlick instead.

They waited until they were sure that no listeners were near the back booth of the Three Trees. Then Griff gave a nod which meant for Casper to talk.

"Things have gone bad, Griff," said Casper. "Real bad."

"What about the plates?" Even Griff's undertone was sharp. "You said they'd be finished by now. I don't like to be kept waiting."

"They'd be done by now, Griff," Casper said, "only I've been having trouble with that guy Laraby, who lives in the penthouse. He's practically begun to haunt me."

"You mean the do-gooder who is always dropping by to see people and help them out? The fellow you mentioned once?"

"That's right. Yesterday he knocked at the door just as I was starting work. It gave me the jitters and I had to quit. Today he walked in on me when I was reaching for the tools. I was just in time to stall him by taking down Album J-1."

"Wait now! You mean he walked clear into the back room?"

"I thought I'd locked the hallway door," explained Casper, "but I must have forgotten it, that's how nervous I've been getting. He claimed I called for him to come in, but I'm sure I didn't. Maybe"—Casper licked his lips again—"maybe Laraby is a T-man."

"Not a chance. Once those Treasury boys barge in, they take over. Now, listen close, Casper. Today I get a line on this Laraby character. Tomorrow you get to work and finish those plates, first thing!"

"I wish I could, Griff, but I get shaky—"

"Then shake off the shakes. Get back to work."

"And what about Laraby? What if he drops by?"

"He won't. I'll go up to his penthouse and sell him some bill of goods, which should be easy if he's as dumb as most honest guys. If he's smart"—Griff's leathery lips broadened their smile—"well, handling smart guys is my specialty. So don't worry."

The next morning Casper went out to breakfast, then stopped at a drugstore and had his usual prescription filled. On the way back, he poured a powder into his palm and licked it down, so he was feeling quite calm when he reached the Abington Arms.

Once in his apartment, Casper made sure the door was double-locked, then swallowed another powder. He seemed to float into the back room, where he opened the window and took down Album J-3. The slow-motion sensation sharpened his nerves for the task ahead. Poising his engraving tool above the portrait of Andrew Jackson, Casper gave a slow grin that seemingly took hours to complete, as he said:

"Got to get you right, Jackie boy! This should do it!"

That did it. Deliberately, painstakingly, Casper finished the finest set of counterfeit plates ever turned out by an engraver's skill. In dreamy fashion, he took a third powder to celebrate the triumph. He let the paper fall from his hand and instead of fluttering, it seemed to hang there in the air, moving almost imperceptibly toward the floor, so slow had Casper's impressions become.

Griff must have sold a real bill of goods to Laraby, for there had been no knock at the door, and now it wouldn't matter. All Casper had to do was sit tight in his happy stupor, and deliver the plates after he awakened.

Then a slight sound caused Casper to turn in that slow, year-long style, his eyes widening in total disbelief. There, looking over his shoulder as before, was Wilfred Laraby!

Instead of a benign smile, Laraby now wore a distorted leer, which Casper took to mean gleeful triumph. How Laraby had come here, Casper couldn't guess, but his hands seemed to be moving toward Casper's shoulders, and the forefinger of Laraby's spread right hand was pointing accusingly to those telltale plates.

Now Casper, in his own labored style, was trying to avoid Laraby's slow-motion clutch. Alert of mind despite the illusion of a dream state, he tilted his stool and went into a prolonged fall. His hands, inching toward the table, reached the plates and took them along. Laraby by then had begun a sidewise dive, but Casper's twist was carrying him away from it.

On the floor, Casper rolled over, came to his feet and then his knees, all in a fantastically labored way. In a chance glance, he saw Laraby making a futile slow-motion grab, several feet behind him. Then Casper loped, dream-fashion, through the front room to the hallway door. Instead of going for the elevator, Casper took to the stairs, and as he took prolonged leaps downward, he could hear footsteps pounding after him, like echoes from a far world.

In the lobby, Griff Burlick was emerging from the elevator as Casper arrived. Still in his dreamy haze, Casper thrust the plates into Griff's hands, as he gasped:

"Laraby—walked in again—he saw these. Take them—he's after me—"

"He can't be, you fool!" Griff hissed. "Get back where you belong. Sit tight. Forget you saw me—"

What followed still seemed slow to Casper, but it looked fast to observers in the lobby. Griff tried to shake off Casper as they reeled out to the street, each thrusting the plates on the other. There, two policemen grabbed them, and Griff pulled a gun, only to be overpowered before he could fire it.

Next, Casper was in the grip of the officers, who took him back through the lobby, where he looked toward the stairway, wondering hazily why Laraby hadn't arrived. One policeman said:

"We may as well go out the back way and see the body."

They took Casper with them through the alley, and there, staring up from the cement, he saw the dead face of Wilfred Laraby!

Hours later, they talked to Casper at police headquarters. The effect of the sense-slowing potion had worn off, but he was still hazy about what had happened. After admitting that the counterfeit plates were his handiwork, Casper said:

"I was worried about Laraby, who was always dropping by. Griff said he'd get a line on Laraby and go up to the penthouse and keep him busy, so he wouldn't drop by again."

A police inspector swung to Griff Burdick, who was standing by, heavily bandaged. "Hear that, Griff?"

"Sure, I got a line on Laraby, all right," Griff agreed. "The guy was a crook himself. He rang in phony inspectors to shake down Roscoe and Hugo. He had a fake actress threaten to sue Mrs. Tolliver. Each time, Laraby split the take with the people who worked with him. I told him I knew his game, and he put up an argument. That was all."

"And in that argument," added the inspector, "you found that he knew your game, too. So you shoved him over the parapet behind the penthouse, and he plunged to his death in the alley. You hurried down in the elevator hoping to get away before we arrived."

Griff clamped his lips tight shut, unwilling to admit the charge. The inspector turned to Casper, whose mouth was agape.

"But I saw Laraby," Casper began. "There, in the back room—"

"You saw him," put in the inspector, "but not in the room."

"But if he wasn't there, then how—where—"

"Laraby fell past the window where you were finishing up those plates. You looked around and saw him, and the way that stuff was slowing your impressions, he looked like he was hanging in mid-air."

"He did," Casper gasped. "I thought he was in the room with me, grabbing for the plates. When I ran downstairs, I was sure I heard him coming after me—"

"But all you heard was the echo of your own footsteps on the stairway. That shows how your imagination gripped you."

"It sure did," Casper admitted, "but seeing Laraby was what triggered it. Why, I was so startled I never thought of him being outside the window. I—well, I thought he was just dropping by."

"And for once, he really was," the inspector agreed, in a tone as solemn as a knell. "Just dropping by."